NOVA REFUGE

The Legend of Saber-Scorpion – Book 1

WARRIOR BORN

Written and illustrated by
Justin R. Stebbins

2015 Re-Print
First published in 2008

ISBN: 0-9727341-1-2
ISBN-13: 978-0-9727341-1-0

Cover design and all illustrations by Justin R. Stebbins

Visit us online at:
www.novarefuge.com – official Nova Refuge site
www.saber-scorpion.com – author's personal website

TABLE OF CONTENTS

To my mom, Mary Stebbins.
I owe her everything.

- PROLOGUE -
ARMAGEDDON

Against a canvas of black, there hovered an unfathomably immense ball of churning red heat. Coils of yellow, orange, and white, some thin and others thick, stretched in curling patterns over its surface. Still more coils wound their way completely off the main orb… long, white-hot strands, stretching in flaming arcs and loops. There were many of these… too many. It gave the impression of looking at a blazing hot ball of yarn, slowly unraveling.

But this was no ball of yarn; it was the Sun… and its unraveling would mean the end of everything Humanity had ever known. The Sun, a sphere larger than one million Earths, composed mostly of hydrogen and helium, depended on nuclear reactions to sustain its own life. Its very existence was an ordered chaos, a stable instability, which, tipped too far in one direction or another, would spell doom for the planets that depended on it. So far, it had always kept itself in order… but apparently, something had gone wrong. This image was proof.

This was the image that now presented itself before the eyes of the American scientist Doctor John Gaston. For months now, he had been working hard to refute what he was looking at… to deny that it was happening. But it was all too clear to him now, laid out for the naked eye to see. You didn't need to be a professional astronomer and physicist to understand these pictures. They were beautiful and terrifying all at once.

For the last year, communication on Earth had been growing steadily more difficult. Satellites had broken out of orbit, falling and burning up in Earth's atmosphere. Astronauts, exposed to waves of radiation like nothing ever before recorded, had been killed while working in space… and the already weakened atmosphere was taking a toll as well. Though they continued to deny it, deep in their guts, everyone knew that something was terribly, terribly wrong.

John looked down at the book beside him, a fairly new but already worn-out copy of the bluntly-titled *The Death of the Sun*, by an English scientist named Arthur Randolph. In this book, Randolph had professed his belief that the sun was dying at a very rapid rate. Not only was it dying, he said, but it was also becoming highly unstable in the process. Randolph had come to the conclusion that the sun was about to supernova. But this was, as every schoolchild knew, impossible.

Impossible...

Humans were always a smug and prideful species, Randolph claimed. Throughout history, every race of Humanity believed they were superior, that they were the chosen of some god or another. Claims changed over the decades, and as science came to the forefront, Humanity made other bold statements. They claimed they were the peak of evolution, the most perfect beings in existence, here on their almost perfect world. And their sun... their sun was also perfect. It was the most perfectly ordinary, healthy young star that anyone could ever desire. Everything was set up perfectly, whether by God or by random chance, to suit their needs.

Oh yes, our beloved Sun was ordinary. It was a perfect, medium yellow star, young and in the prime of life, with so many years ahead of it that the number was nearly beyond Human comprehension. When the event of the Sun's death finally got here, it would be slow. The star would grow larger and brighter and hotter, evaporating all of Earth's oceans and destroying all life. Then it would follow the other stages of the typical life cycle, living on as a giant, aging star for billions upon billions of years before it actually faded away.

And by the time Earth was destroyed, Human kind would already have left. We would have depleted our planet's resources and migrated to other worlds, prepared centuries in advance for the destruction of our original home. Of course, it was all in the unforeseeably distant future, so there was little need to worry over such things in the present. This was the dream that men still claimed with smug surety would be our destiny.

But according to Randolph, they were very, very wrong.

Four years ago, scientists had noted increased activity on the surface of the sun, in the form of solar flares... explosions equal to the force of tens of millions of nuclear warheads. These events were ordinary occurrences, but extremely powerful flares were happening now in great frequency. Randolph insisted that the sun was showing increased instability, and soon it would explode in a tremendous supernova, engulfing the entire solar system... and much more. In a bold move at which the scientific and political community deridingly scoffed, he called for an evacuation of everyone on Earth to the newly-discovered planet of Terra Nova.

Terra Nova had only been found a few decades ago. Humanity had but recently taken its first fledgling steps into interstellar travel with the help of a series of breathtaking discoveries in physics that utilized breaking portals into parallel dimensions in order to propel starships well beyond the speed of light, something considered impossible until only recently. At first, the plan was to send probes through this dimension at random. The probes would then exit beside distant stars and search for habitable planets, returning with the information they had gathered.

But this was quickly rendered unnecessary, for a pre-existing portal was discovered within Humanity's own solar system. This portal became known as the Breach, a name that was later popularly used for the very dimension into which it led. The first probes sent in either came back empty-handed or did not return at all, so a manned exploration ship known as the *Argo VII* quickly followed. What they found was Terra Nova, the first Human-habitable world ever discovered outside Earth itself.

Many scientists had already traveled there now, establishing research stations and small outposts on this new frontier. These outposts soon grew into colonies as entrepreneurs and brave pioneer settlers followed. So when Earth laughed at Randolph and refused to call for an evacuation of the planet, he left for Terra Nova with his entire family. This was expected to cause a stir, but instead only created a few murmurs, and most just shook their heads and went on lying to themselves.

And even now the world continued to scoff at Arthur Randolph. *The sun could not supernova!* Everyone *knew that!* But secretly they began to worry that something, perhaps, truly was wrong. So a team of bright young scientists from all over the world had been put together by TerraCom, the greatest of Earth's mega-corporations, to perform only one simple job: to monitor the sun and make sure everything was exactly as it should be. They were to make sure that Randolph's critics were right after all, and everything was okay. Gaston was the leader of this team, and what he saw now made one thing perfectly clear to him…

Everything was most emphatically *not* okay.

For days now he had been arguing with himself, lying to himself, trying to find a flaw in the pile of evidence that just kept growing larger. He had kept things from his own team, tried to hide facts until he could "disprove" them, as if "disproving" them made them simply go away. He was trying to do just what Randolph had accused them all of doing… lying to themselves and everyone else. *The sun wasn't going to supernova! That could never happen!* But it was.

And it was going to happen very soon.

Gathering his papers and stuffing his private datastick into his coat pocket, he made his way to the elevator and proceeded to the conference room downstairs. When he walked into the room, he saw his colleagues gathered around the table, talking excitedly. They began to grow quiet as he entered. Most of them were smiling in a friendly, carefree way. For all they knew, they were on the road to disproving Randolph's cataclysmic theories. It was something that Gaston had said was their main goal.

Now, when he sat down in his chair at the far end of the long, oval-shaped table and carefully laid his papers down before him, he looked at them all with a grave expression. Their smiles disappeared. He was sure his skin was as pale as a ghost.

"What's wrong, John?" the man closest to him asked.

John tried for several minutes to speak, to force the words to come out. He shook his head, shuffled his papers, anything to avoid speaking of it.

Finally, he quietly said: "We have to go, Karl."

Then he swallowed and looked down. The room fell very silent. Everyone stared blankly at him.

After a few seconds, Karl nudged him, chuckling nervously, hoping this was some kind of joke. "John? What are you talking about? Go where?"

John Gaston, feeling a sudden surge of determination, looked up and met his colleague's eyes.

"We have to get everyone off this planet."

FOUR YEARS LATER

"I never thought it would come to this," Charles said. "I don't think anyone did, really."

Jim Arkan didn't reply. He just gazed through the crystal-clean airport window at the runway outside. San Francisco Aerospace Port was huge; a vast plain of hot, shimmering asphalt stretching away into the distance. Where the runways terminated could not be seen; there was only a shivering reflection, like distant lakes mirroring the sky far away on the horizon. Behind those mirrors rose the mountains, almost as if they were floating in midair. But Jim Arkan had seen such sights before; it was the spacecraft that interested him the most.

The aerospace transports were astounding machines. They were larger even than the biggest commercial airliners, but their shape was astoundingly simple. They appeared to be nothing more than gigantic, flat, thick wings lined with narrow windows… like wide, sleek, flying buildings. These viewports were barely discernable black slits on the otherwise smooth surface. Jutting down from the gracefully curving belly of the craft were long, round tubes… elevator lifts that allowed the passengers a quick and easy way inside. No simple ladder would quite do the job for these monsters.

But the engines were the most amazing part: the entire back of the vehicle was covered in great, gaping thrusters. But they were not like the solid and liquid fuel engines of an old Space Shuttle; these were Starlight Drive engines, shaped like a stack of elongated, rectangular slots that stretched from one end of the ship to the other. They were fueled by a special gas that had been discovered decades ago in outer space; Jim could not remember its scientific name. Today most people just call it Starlight Gas. When these starships take off, the engines glow bright white, tinged with blue, and the ship makes a much quicker, easier escape from the atmosphere than any rocket had ever accomplished.

And then they would propel the ship to speeds faster than light once they entered the Breach.

Charles tried to awaken his friend Jim from his silence by continuing the conversation. "How much of Earth's population did they say they've evacuated to Terra Nova now? Thirty percent? Forty?"

"Close to forty, I think. But I heard that a few months ago. Could be more by now," Jim replied, still staring out the window, his expression blank.

It had all happened so quickly; it made his head spin just thinking about it. One day, without warning, a government official had announced that the world was going to be destroyed by the supernova of the sun. It was no joke; his voice was deadly serious. The video was shown all over the world, and other world leaders reiterated it again and again. Scientists came on day after day, explaining how they had discovered some sort of anomaly in the sun that was causing it to become rapidly unstable. Some... imperfection. At first no one seemed to believe it. No one talked about it. They tried to forget it, to deny it. They even laughed about it.

But then the reality slowly began to sink in. Humans were experts at denying the truth, at lying to themselves, but even they could not deny this forever. Before long, each country on Earth began preparing its spacecraft, cramming them full of evacuees, each ship headed to the only other habitable planet that anyone knew anything about, located in the distant galaxy...

"Nova Refuge..." Jim murmured.

It was ironic, really. The name had originally been chosen simply to mean "new refuge," but now it seemed almost prophetic, foretelling its current usage: as a refuge from the nova of the sun. Since Humanity's efforts at terraforming barren planets, moons, and asteroids had been less than successful so far, the planet Terra Nova in far-beyond-distant Nova Refuge was now their only hope... the last refuge of Human kind.

Naturally, the new sun around which the precious Earth-like planet orbited was unimaginatively named New Sol, and the planet itself was unimaginatively named Terra Nova, Latin for "New Earth." Ironically, the name also meant the same in Portuguese, the language of some of history's greatest colonists. It was fitting, since Humans once again were playing the colonists. The boats were bigger, the destination was bigger, and the sea they had to cross was much, much bigger... but the idea was basically the same.

Only this time, the Old World would be wiped out behind them, and they could never return.

"I always thought it was a lie," Charles said, squinting as the sun reflected off the hull of an aerospace cruiser that was taxiing down the runway outside. "Figured it was just them trying to get that new planet inhabited. No one wants to fly that far away from everything they've ever known. Heck, it still might be a lie. Every minute longer that I sit here, I wonder if I'm doing the right thing. What do you think, Jim?"

"We've talked about this before, Chuck," Jim responded in a sad monotone. "We're two bachelors too old for our own good. If we do ever get around to building families, better to do it there than here. Besides, would you rather stay here, on a planet that's being emptied of all Human life? Stay here with all the ones that get left behind, all these panic-stricken mobs tearing the place apart?"

The first few days after the story had spread, everyone was skeptical. Fear loomed over them like a dark cloud, a feeling deep in their gut and nothing more. On the outside, no one wanted to take it seriously. But a few weeks after that, everyone started to get scared. The hype built up more and more, and then people started to panic. Mobs tried to break their way into the aerospace ports, trying to get tickets before anyone else. That's why there were so many soldiers around now, in an attempt to keep the peace.

Ever since the announcement, people had been divided into three camps: those who believed the stories and were rich and influential enough to afford the move, those who did *not* believe and were trying to stop the whole Exodus, and those who *did* believe but were too poor to escape their doomed world. Benevolent governments tried to aid those in the third camp and help them get away, but members of the second camp fought them at every turn. So as the rich believers left, the only wealthy, influential people remaining in power on Earth were those who did *not* believe. And that made it much harder for members of the third camp to get a passport to the Refuge.

This was causing conflicts everywhere. Aerospace ports were torn apart, entire governments were overthrown, and some starships had even been stolen. Legends were born, such as the story of the Golden Ark, a huge starship being constructed by world religious leaders with the help of God, a ship that would be used to save all those of the Faithful who deserved Exodus. And wasn't there another story about a ship built by the Illuminati? Jim didn't care to remember. It was all just false hope anyway.

"I don't know if the sun's going to destroy Earth," Jim concluded, "but if it doesn't, the people will. Before long the planet will be in a state of anarchy. They've been talking about it on the news. I don't need to say it all over again for you."

Charles nodded and let out a long sigh. He knew it was true; why else would he be here?

At last, a calm female voice announced over the building's speaker system: "Flight 102 ready for departure. All passengers for Flight 102 please leave through exits 4 to 8."

The densely packed crowd around Jim and Charles began to shuffle a little, trying to make the lines move faster. Slowly, people began leaking their way out of the building, herded into tight lines by the soldiers guarding the place. Jim and his friend stood up and joined the crowd, making their way out into the sunlight. The sun was even brighter outside the windows. Jim reached up and flipped down his sunglasses.

"Single-file please," he heard one of the armed guards say. "No pushing."

Jim looked up. The aerospace cruiser appeared even bigger up close. It draped them in shadow as they stepped under the wing. Between the metal belly of the ship overhead and the runway below, the crowd suddenly felt like the fillings in a colossal sandwich. In the distance were the elevator tubes, which suddenly looked much larger as well. They could apparently hold about a dozen people at once, and there were several of them. As he ascended the hollow tube, Jim tried not to look out the windows at the people below. How high up in the air was the passenger cabin on this thing? He hated heights.

When he was inside, he felt a lot better. Charles followed him in, and they made their way down a very long hallway to the back of the ship. They were lucky enough to get cabins near the back with windows. There were two folding mechanical chairs that also served as beds, and there was a tiny, cramped lavatory. Now that he thought about it, there was no wonder they were called space-*ships* instead of space-*planes*. It was much more like an ocean-going vessel, like a cruise ship, than a mere airliner. After all, even when traveling through the alternate dimension popularly called "the Breach," it was still a long, long trip to Terra Nova.

Trying not to think about it, Jim sat down and buckled himself in as tightly as he could. It didn't matter though; the chair buckles tightened automatically a few seconds after he secured them. He felt the belts bite into his skin, and then relax a bit.

"These takeoffs can get bumpy, I guess," he said.

"Yeah, and I know how you are about heights. Don't look out the window, okay? We'll be climbing almost straight up at one point, it says here in the brochure. There's artificial gravity, but I don't know when they start the generators…"

"I'll be fine," Jim replied.

Suddenly there was a third man in the room… or at least his upper torso. It was a three-dimensional holographic projection of the ship's captain.

"Hello," he said in a friendly voice, "I'm Captain Walton, and I'd like to welcome you aboard my vessel. Everyone strapped in? Good. I doubt if any of you have ever been on a flight into space before now, so I'll go over everything I can. Now that you're all buckled, you can't unbuckle yourselves. This is for your own safety. Blasting our way through the Earth's atmosphere and breaking its gravitational pull is a smoother ride than it has ever been before, but things can still get a bit bumpy, and your harnesses will tighten automatically to adjust for this. Also note your viewport windows, made of four layers of solid transperium. They're designed to minimize the intensity of the light outside, automatically adjusting to changing light levels, while also blocking out the sun's harmful rays…"

Jim Arkan stopped listening at this point and lay his head back on the headrest. He tried to relax, which he was usually able to do in an aircraft… but he found it impossible. When the Captain quit speaking, he expected Chuck to begin talking excitedly, which was what usually happened, but there was only silence. It was far more uncomfortable.

"God, I'll be glad when we reach Terra Nova," he said at last, in a low whisper, as if he was afraid to break the silence.

Then the muffled scream of the Starlight engines broke it for him. The aerospace craft began to move, propelled down the huge runway by the Starlight Drive, sending it coasting along faster and faster. After just a couple of seconds, the nose lifted off, and then the rear of the plane followed. Chuck gazed out the window.

"We're making a pretty rapid ascent," he said.

Jim just groaned. He hated heights, so he quickly closed his eyes. Things got better when they flew into a cloud, its mist blotting out the view from the windows. Chuck told him it was over. At first Jim was glad. But then he suddenly had a pang of regret: why hadn't he looked? That could very well be the last he would ever see of Earth. He wished he could have looked out at its beautiful landscapes, even if all he could see was the barren California desert. Why hadn't he looked? He swallowed hard. *Get a hold of yourself…* he thought. *Stop being silly. You've seen Earth plenty of times before.*

But now Chuck was thinking the same thing. "You know... I... I wish I had seen more of it. Earth I mean. I always wanted to visit the Great Wall of China... or some natural wonder. Natural wonders are so rare these days. They... Which ones did you get to see, Jim? Ever go to the Grand Canyon?"

Jim stared at the solid whiteness outside the viewport. He suddenly thought of all the things one could only experience on Earth. All of the natural and man-made wonders that only existed on mankind's home planet. Why hadn't he done more with his life? His life on Earth? *When I get to Terra Nova,* he thought, *I'll see every major landmark they've discovered there; travel the planet. I'll make it my mission.*

Finally the mist outside gave way, and now he could see the land far, far below, with the clouds looming over it, casting their shadows down upon the vast city of San Francisco and the California desert landscape. He had always said he hated the desert, but now he could think of nothing more beautiful.

He was thinking of the desert and the mountains, but Chuck was thinking about the city. "How long do you think it took to build all that? Think about all the people that spent their lives building up that city. It was built by Human hands... worked on by millions of people, growing over time. Now it's abandoned, left in the dust."

Jim only nodded. Did he have to keep *talking* about it? Chuck just kept rambling, in a lost, hopeless voice. It made him feel better, Jim realized. Unfortunately, it only made Jim feel worse.

Chuck cleared his throat. "How many people have they evacuated again? Thirty percent?"

Jim just stared down at the rapidly-disappearing Earth. It looked exactly like on the maps, he thought. It almost looked fake, especially with the pristine white clouds swirling over land and sea. It looked just like in the pictures... Pictures; that's all he would ever see of Earth from now on.

"I wonder what mach we're at now," Charles said. "Or what warp. Mach is the speed of sound and warp is the speed of light, I think. So Warp Two is twice the speed of light... right?"

Jim blew out a sigh. "Chuck, I'm getting a headache."

The Captain reappeared on the wall. "Attention all passengers. You can unbuckle and move about now. It will be a while before we reach the jump point and enter the Breach. Feel free to explore some of the ship, but be prepared to return to your cabins on a moment's notice."

Chuck already had a map in his hand. He pointed. "Let's go to the viewroom. There's one at the end of the main hall in the middle of the ship. The window there is the biggest, a heck of a lot bigger than this thing."

Jim just wanted to relax, but he was feeling too tired to argue. So he followed his friend into the hall, where they joined a few more of the quickest passengers. There was indeed a viewroom in the far back. There were rows of chairs in here, all facing toward the rear, as if it were a movie theater. The whole far wall and part of the ceiling was composed of a huge, extremely thick window. The vastness of space lay spread out before them, with Earth looming in the distance, heedless and uncaring of the events that were taking place.

They sat there for a long time, staring out the back window as the room filled up with people. Everything seemed to move so slowly. He wondered how long it would be before they reached the jump point. But before he knew it, the moon was upon them. He was watching its pockmarked grey surface, covered in shadowy craters and mountain ranges, passing by below them. Suddenly the moon seemed more real than it had ever seemed before.

And so did the sun. He had been trying hard not to look at it, because it was bright even through the tinted glass... but now he realized how wrong it looked. It wasn't shaped right. It was all bulging, like it was covered in bubbles. He never thought the sun could look that way. Suddenly, the fear washed over him... the fear that had gathered up in the last few years, as he had read the unbelievable stories. Now he was actually seeing it. He closed his eyes and tried to forget the sight, but the blue-green afterimage remained burned in his vision, against the black of his eyelids. The strange, blobby shape waxed and waned as he blinked. There was no way the sun could look like that!

"Attention, everyone on board," they heard the Captain say over the ship's speakers. "You should start returning to your cabins now. We'll be making the jump soon."

Was it just him, Jim thought, or did the captain sound on edge... worried? It sounded like he was trying to cover it up with a commanding voice. That sickening feeling in his gut returned.

"Maybe we should go back to our cabin," Jim said.

Chuck didn't hear him. He was currently in an animated conversation with a female passenger. Jim sighed. At least people were talking now. It helped him to relax, hearing the people talk. He didn't like to talk himself, but the droning sound of all the hundreds of voices talking at once calmed his nerves. He was on a great survival vessel of Humanity, soaring through space. He was surrounded by his fellow Humans, all very much alive and talking. Talking, talking, talking...

Silence.

Jim looked up. Passengers were prodding each other, all of them turning to look out the rear viewport. There was no chattering now – only low, hushed whispers. Most had risen to a standing position to get a better view. Jim turned, his eyes passing over Chuck's face as he did so. He looked like a ghost. His skin had lost all of its color; it was nearly as white as his eyes, which were open wide. Then, as his gaze turned toward the rear viewport, Jim saw why, and he too jumped to his feet.

They had passed by the moon now, and its shadowy form dominated nearly half of the scene... But behind it, there was a terrible thing. A great wave of white light, growing larger and larger... a sphere of pure heat and illumination.

It was the sun. It was growing.

No, Jim realized... it was an explosion; an explosion of enormous size... and most unsettling of all, utterly silent.

The ball of white light reached the Earth. Jim could see the planet's round shadow against the wall of fire. The familiar circle of their world, always depicted against a canvas of black specked with white stars, was now a simple black circle against a background of pure white light. Then the circle grew rapidly smaller.

The explosion engulfed it, covering it completely in less than a second. In a blink, it was over… It was all over.

Some screamed, some fainted. Some prayed, some cursed. Some merely stood there, in silence and awe. But none who witnessed it would ever forget that terrible sight. None who now stood in the back of that last, lonely transport, would ever forget what they had witnessed: the supernova of the Sun and the destruction of Earth.

The beautiful planet that had nurtured Human kind for as long as it had existed… was gone.

And then, just before the wall of light could reach them, the silver starship engaged its Interstellar Drive, opening a swirling portal into the Breach, barely slipping away in time to escape the grasp of the explosion… and was gone.

- CHAPTER ONE -
MORE THAN MEN

In the vast expanse of stars that made up the galaxy known as Nova Refuge, there was one single yellow orb that was most important to mankind. Named New Sol in honor of the old sun, it was on a planet orbiting this star that Humanity had finally found another world capable of supporting their species. For millennia, such a thing had only been dreamed of, yet here it was. Terra Nova, the New Earth, was somewhat larger than the old one and capable of supporting a much larger population; a fact that itself was a blessing, for Humans knew the difficulties of overpopulation. As a result, the force of gravity was somewhat greater, and days and years somewhat longer, though the Earth-year or Terran Standard Cycle (TSC) still remained in use for basic interstellar time measurement by Humans.

On this frontier world, rich with untapped deposits of natural resources, mankind developed its first settlements before the supernova was more than a rumor. They started out as little more than scientific research outposts but soon grew into colonies. After the Great Exodus, as the evacuation of Earth came to be called, the arriving Humans began to settle around the four original colonies in great numbers. By the time Earth's government leaders arrived, they found themselves combating the already established leaders of their own colonies, which had grown increasingly independent over the years. Those governments who could not reach a compromise with the colonies simply failed to reestablish themselves and were lost to the annals of history.

Over time, the first four colonies grew into the most powerful nations of Terra Nova: the "Big Four." West of the Infinite Ocean, actually the smaller of Terra Nova's two largest seas, lay a large continent that was divided into the countries called Victory and Yavakaro. East of the same ocean lay a continent of roughly equal size. This was divided into the nations of Xarkon and Zygbar.

But all was not as easy as Humanity had hoped… for they were not alone. They found several species of aliens already inhabiting Terra Nova, each of them being the colonists of their own species that had been living in the Nova Refuge galaxy for millennia. Since the Humans themselves were the true "aliens" to the Refuge, these beings became known as the Natives. There were four main species of Natives: the proud and angelic Sarran, the fiery and warlike Mahlok, the aquatic and reclusive Achmer, and the monstrous and barbaric Slashrim.

In order to secure their foothold over this new world, the Humans began to take land from the Natives, at first using diplomacy and later switching to force. During what became known as the Xenocide War, all of the great nations of Terra Nova formed an alliance to push the Natives off the two main continents. The war raged for nearly a hundred years, growing more or less intense at intervals, and some say it continues even today. At its "official" end, the two largest alliances of Natives surrendered their colonies, and the Native colonists who refused to leave Terra Nova were exiled to the dark and mysterious continent of Womloc, which Humanity had long ago regarded as too inhospitable for extensive settlement.

So it was that the new world evolved in much the same way as had the old. Loyalties shifted, wars raged, and the great world-binding alliance known as CONON, the Council of Nations of Nova Refuge, was formed to replace the old United Nations of Earth. Despite the many failures of the old system, Humans began reverting right back to it. After three hundred years, a historian could look back on the short history of Terra Nova and call it a parallel to the recent history of Earth. Everything was different, yet nothing had changed.

However, at least one chapter of Earth's bloody history had been skipped, and it was possibly the worst one… There had never yet been a true "world war," at least not between the Human-settled nations of the world. There had been skirmishes and short battles, but never a worldwide conflict between all of the Big Four. With the advanced weapons of this modern age, and in a galaxy populated by warring Natives who would be eager to take advantage of any internal conflict, such a war between men was everyone's greatest fear…

But it was one man's greatest dream.

And in at least three different places, projects were now underway to bring war back to its founding point: the man… the soldier. So Xarkon, Victory, and Grimm's Mercenary Army laid their schemes to find, raise, and train the ultimate soldiers…

The warriors born.

Year: 318 PA
(Post-Armageddon)
Location: Xarkon

Silence.

A sound in the distance… a rumbling, muffled explosion. The clattering of raining debris on a rooftop above. A few distant screams, slowly dying away.

Silence.

A young man speaks: "Clear."

An older, deeper voice: "All of 'em?"

"Aye, sir. The target and every house nearby."

"Talk about cleaning up the neighborhood."

Silence... then a scream... the high-pitched crying of an infant, calling for something that had been stolen away... something very dear.

"Shut that kid up. Damn High Command. Put too much stock in this genes business."

"Colonel... We weren't supposed to let any of them get away, sir."

"I know that, Sergeant! I didn't see *you* shoot her."

"What'll come of 'em, you think?"

Silence reigned, broken only by the snuffling of the baby.

"Same thing that came of the other one, if High Command's got it right."

"I guess it's destiny."

A derisive snort. "Destiny, genes. Whatever. All I know is, these kids were born to fight... and this world won't ever let 'em forget it."

FOURTEEN YEARS LATER
YEAR: 332 PA
LOCATION: VICTORY

The soldier could see the whole scene spread out on his helmet's HUD (Heads Up Display). The mazes of hallways and rooms that made up the facility were outlined in green, and the soldiers in his team appeared as blue dots, sliding through the corridors and hugging the walls at corners. In truth, he didn't like the map. It made things too easy.

But that was how things were meant to be in some stages of training: too easy. He often felt that he was far ahead of his class, that the rest should be pushed to keep up with him...

Finally, the signal came, cutting his thoughts short. Time for his team to move. The soldier flipped up his HUD visor, and his men met his keen blue eyes. He was young, younger than many of the other trainees. But standing there in his heavy suit of Victorian nanoduranium armor, currently camouflaged to a dark metallic grey to match the walls around him... he hoped he looked old enough to command his soldiers' respect.

"Amazon," Orion said, "you take gold team and head up on the left. Blue team, fall in behind me. Let's move!"

LOCATION: THE GRIM ISLES

The girl looked down at the thing in her hands. When she'd first picked it up, the gun had seemed heavy and uncomfortable. It still felt that way, but she was learning to handle it. She squinted at the target. It seemed so far away, out there on the edge of the cliff, overlooking the sea. It was a big wooden dummy with a red dot between its eyes, over its heart, and in one other place that they had told her was almost just as good.

"Not so hard," said Douglas Boyle, watching her with his keen grey eyes that looked down over his scruffy mustache as he towered above her. "You look too long and everything goes hazy and wobbly. You gotta do it fast; use your reflexes. Be sure o' yerself."

The girl looked away, lowering the gun. Her ponytail whipped around over her shoulder. She closed her eyes, took a few deep breaths, and then swung around again. The dummy was waiting. The gun came up before her eyes. Once the sights matched up… she fired.

It took a few minutes before the dummy's head landed in the crashing waves far below with hardly a splash.

"Good shot, Jade."

Location: Xarkon

The junkyard extended almost as far as the eye could see. Row after row of scrapped tanks, troop transports, scout vehicles, and fighters stretched away to the horizon, seeming to go on and on for miles. The sky was overcast, sinking the scene into a deeper shade of grey. Then the rain began to fall, and all became noise. All around was a sea of metal, and now a downpour of heavy water droplets came slamming onto the surface of it, sending out a reverberating clatter that seemed to drown all other sound in the world.

This was the Iron Graveyard, the remnant of a war fought between Xarkon and Zygbar years ago, a war some said was still going on today, but more quietly. Xarkon usually made some attempt to recycle destroyed vehicles, but since Zygbar's vehicles were often junk anyway, they returned to the scrap from whence they came as soon as they ceased to function and could no longer be repaired. After the end of the much-celebrated Golden Skye Dynasty in Xarkon, during the Zygbari war for independence, there were many long battles on the Xarkon/Zygbar border. This resulted in the creation of the Iron Graveyard: a field of dead machines stretching out behind the cover of some desert mountains in far southern Xarkon. And it was into this field that two squads of Zygbari rebels now wound their way, in search of a single target.

The men could barely hear their commander over the deafening racket of the rain as he shouted, "Keep moving, men! And by God, if you see, hear, feel, or even smell anything, call out! Remember your training!"

The commander of Team Alpha, a grim and dark-eyed man named Haddam Bakar, looked back at his troops and shook his head. They lacked the discipline of the Highlander guerillas he used to work with. He would still be working with the Highlanders if Zygbar had not absorbed the mercenary group into the army proper. That was part of the reason he had joined up with this band of rebels. They were bent on overthrowing Zygbar's current ruling regime yet again, as countless factions had been doing since the earliest days of the country's chaotic history. One of the rebels' secret bases had been discovered by an infiltrator, and two squads had been sent out to track down and eliminate the spy. Bakar was in charge of Team Alpha.

In their primitive dust-colored uniforms and rusty metallic armor, the rebels blended almost perfectly with the muddy scrapyard. So far it had not done them much good. Their enemy was clothed in a strange, solid black outfit that made him look like some kind of ninja, yet they had entirely lost track of him. He, on the other hand, had managed to take down two of their number already.

"We are not going to lose anymore men!" Bakar barked. "Got it?"

"Yes, sir," their voices responded through his helmet's commlink.

They proceeded on their way, back to back, never letting one another out of sight. There were two dozen men in all, split into two separate groups, and the enemy was but a single man. He would not be easy to spot in this mess, and to think they could possibly hear him in this downpour was laughable. But he could not possibly engage them now that they were moving as one fully composed unit. Bakar looked around him at the heaps of rusted slag and loaded his rifle. *Too much cover*, he thought.

"Don't underestimate him," he said quietly. "He's only wearing that black suit, but it's probably reactive nanofiber or energy-absorbent mesh... or both. Hardens on impact, dissipates laser heat... maybe even has active camouflage. The kind of thing the wealthy and wasteful can afford. So eyes on the shadows, and report any movement!"

The largely desert nation of Zygbar was the poorest of the four great Human factions, with relatively few off-world possessions, and it was nearly always engulfed in chaos. The country seemed to thrive in it, as different factions warred for control. Whoever managed to win earned the hatred of all of the others, for there was no one Zygbar hated worse than the rich and powerful. And that described their nearby neighbor, Xarkon, perfectly. Bakar would have bet his blazer assault rifle that their assailant was Xarkonian.

"Blazer" rifles were the most popular modern small arms currently in use throughout the Refuge. The common name "blazer," derived from "bullet" and "laser," aptly described their functions. As the bullet traveled through the barrel, it was "charged" with a shield of hot energy, which wrapped itself around the surface of the special metal alloy. This hot energy coating could enable the projectile to burn through most anti-ballistic armor, and the cold metal bullet beneath could still do damage if the target was heat-resistant or wearing an energy-dissipating mesh. This meant that the bullet was at least moderately effective against all kinds of armor, making it the best all-around weapon available. Bladed weapons, like swords, daggers, and bayonets, were also commonly equipped with blazer shields, giving them the same properties. Bakar's rifle was equipped with a bayonet as well; blades were always more effective than bullets against advanced armor meshes, if you could only get close enough...

Someone shouted, "There!"

As one, they all turned to look, raising their rifles. And as they did, a shadow leapt from a ruined transport truck behind them. There was a muffled scream, and they all whirled back in the opposite direction... just in time to see the feet of one of their number sliding away between two of the wrecked vehicles, his boots dragging deep gorges in the soggy earth.

"Six to each side!" Bakar shouted.

Though the group was composed now of only eleven men, they automatically split into a group of five and a group of six, each taking the opposite route around the old transport. It was an ancient Zygbari vehicle, wheeled instead of hover tech, adapted from a civilian cargo truck only by the addition of a canvas covering on top and a desert camouflage paint job.

The rebels emerged on the other side of the wreck with their guns raised... and found only the body of their comrade. The commander spotted another pair of feet disappearing, but this time it was the feet of their target, disappearing under the canvas atop the ruined transport.

"Visual contact!" one of them shouted.

"Hold position!" shouted Bakar. "Fire on the canvas!"

The harsh staccato of gunfire split through the rain as brightly-flashing blazer bullets pierced the covering of the old vehicle of war, burning and ripping it to shreds. But as Bakar had expected, there was no sign that their target had been hit.

"Hold fire! Forget the truck! He's gone by now. Eyes on all sides!"

A crash erupted from somewhere nearby, but the commander did not turn to look, even as he watched his men do so. He instead kept his eyes on the other piles of slag around them, looming like the skeletons of forgotten warriors. Not a shadow moved in his sight, so when he heard another sound, he too turned to look.

"There!" shouted one of the soldiers, firing randomly into the debris.

"Hold fire, soldier!" the commander shouted back. "He's being noisy – trying to lure us!"

"So what do we do?"

Lieutenant Bakar hesitated for a second, looking around for some alternate route. Then he shouted in anger and frustration, "Oh, just follow him! But by God, stay alert! And don't jump at every little noise!"

He realized that he was both echoing and directly contradicting his previous orders, but his men understood his meaning. They resumed their previous tactic, moving as a group through the hallways of mud in the walls of broken metal, their motley assortment of rifles bristling in every direction.

"Beta One, this is Alpha One," Bakar said, trying to contact the other team. "Haven't you heard a single cursed thing that's going on over here? Where in hell's name are you?"

"Where in blazes are *you*?" came the response from Beta Leader. "I lost four of my men! Four! They got pinned down and next thing I know...!"

"I've already lost men too. Makes me wonder if there's more than one out here. Nevermind. Just close in on my position and we'll take him down together."

"Fine. We're on the move. *Squad! Form up!*"

Commander Bakar could see the other team commander marked as a blip on his helmet's HUD, quite a long way off. The signal was weak. Was there a problem with the machinery, he wondered, or was it all of this scrap metal and rain causing interference? Blasted salvaged gear...

"Visual contact!" shouted one of his men. "Up there!"

Bakar turned and gazed in the direction his soldier was indicating. There, far in the distance, stood the enormous, black metal shell of a dead giant. Looming over the Iron Graveyard like a silent guardian stood a towering humanoid walker.

Walkers were the most advanced military technology on Nova Refuge. For centuries the idea of a battle tank mounted upon a pair of mechanical legs remained firmly grounded in science fiction alone, but then technology originally developed for hi-tech crane arms made it distinctly possible. Legs capable of as much agility and strength as a Human's of equal size could be developed, making for the ultimate all-terrain vehicle. It was, as one military R&D engineer had put it, the natural evolution of the tank from crawling on all fours to standing on its own two feet. Walkers had been in use on Nova Refuge now since before the Xenocide War.

This ruined one that watched over the Iron Graveyard like a silent and terrible lord was an older model of the Xarkon Dingo, its dark hull covered in scorch marks, dents, and dust. And atop the beast was a smaller figure of matching proportions but miniscule size by comparison... a man clad in black, completely unarmed, staring coolly down at them. He did not move, even as the soldiers took aim. He simply stood there, looking down without fear, like a mortal standing tall and confident atop the shoulders of an ancient god. It was him...

"Saber-Scorpion..." Bakar muttered under his breath.

That was the name they had found repeated in their computer systems after the infiltration. Whoever this man was, he knew what he was doing, wanted everyone else to know what he was doing, and furthermore, *wanted* someone to follow him. He was begging to be hunted, urging them on. Well, he would get his wish.

"FIRE!"

Ten blazer rifles rang out into the storm, firing burst after burst of ammunition at their target. But by the time they had started firing, the dark figure atop the old walker had stepped aside, taking cover behind one of the machine's shoulder-mounted, empty missile racks. In the blink of an eye, he'd disappeared. Bakar could hardly believe it.

"RPGs!" he shouted quickly. "Fire the rockets!"

Six of the soldiers quickly swung the rocket-propelled grenade launchers from their backs and took aim.

"What are you waiting for, a fancy invitation? Fire, fire!"

The six RPGs burst forth, cutting through the rain, smoke trails hanging in the air behind them. They all struck the walker in different locations... one directly in its transperium cockpit windshield, which it failed to penetrate, another in the shoulder, and two more directly upon the missile rack behind which their target had disappeared. The combined force was enough to turn the huge old machine slightly to one side, and then the weight of its arm did the rest. Without its automatic balancing system, or the use of its legs at all, down it came, leaning backward slowly and then picking up speed.

On the opposite side of the walker, behind its back, the commander of Beta Team looked up at the shadow looming above them. He had not seen the figure atop it, nor had any of his men. He only heard the gunfire, the explosions of the RPGs… and now he saw the great beast falling straight toward them.

"Run! Run! Retreat!"

There above them, clutching tight to the maintenance rails on the walker's back, was Saber-Scorpion. As Beta Leader watched, the black figure climbed like a spider back over the walker's head, even as the great duranium monster continued to fall. Then came the crash. The ground shook, throwing him off his feet. He heard the screams of some of his men through his helmet as they were smashed beneath the fallen giant.

"You idiot!" Beta Leader shouted to Bakar through the commlink. "You just crushed my entire squad!"

On the other side of the com, Bakar paused. "Say again?"

"I said your trigger-happy…"

He stopped in mid-sentence as the shadow of a Human figure, unarmed, gradually unfolded over the ground before him. Turning cautiously, he looked up to behold Saber-Scorpion, standing on the hull of a crushed tank, staring down at him with that same calm, impassive gaze.

He was not extremely tall, standing just over six feet, nor was he bulging with superfluous musculature. He did not look vicious; he was not even armed. Indeed, there was nothing too terribly imposing about the young man. Yet his stance, the sureness he showed with his every movement, and the look of calm determination on his face, swayed the confidence of his enemy. Only his eyes were visible behind the mask he wore: a pair of keen, cold blue-grey orbs, narrowed to slits.

"It will take more than you…" panted the soldier, "to kill all of us."

The young man looked coolly down at him, and as soon as the soldier's gun came up, he pounced. There were two shots, then a scream.

From across the junkyard, Cmdr. Bakar shouted, "Beta? Come in! Anyone in Team Beta, respond!"

Haddam Bakar looked around desperately, searching for any blips on his HUD that would indicate the soldiers of the other team. But all he saw was the rain-drenched duranium and rusty metal of the Iron Graveyard. The rain was helping to quickly settle the cloud of dust that had arisen with the falling of the walker.

Around him, his men were panicking.

"Let's get the hell out of here!" one of them shouted.

Bakar pointed to him. "Don't move!"

"He just took out *all* of beta team!" cried another.

"I said don't move!"

"We've got to retreat!"

The lieutenant spat on the ground, "Fine. You lot just run off like headless chickens. That way he can pick you off one at a time, at his leisure!"

One of his men gave a laugh, shouting, "Not if he's after you!" as he disappeared into the junkpile.

Another followed him, and then another. Then two others ran off in the opposite direction. Only three men stayed with their commander, and as they heard the screams of one of their number on the commlink, they were glad of their decision.

Lt. Bakar looked at his remaining men. Even in his dark eyes, the eyes of a seasoned veteran, now flickered the glint of terror, mingled with rage… and humiliated indignation.

From the shadows, Saber-Scorpion watched, amused at the spectacle.

"Sometimes the only thing that keeps a man brave," he said in a low voice, "is his fear of running away."

Finally Bakar summoned the courage to give the order.

"Retreat!" he shouted. "Everyone retreat!"

Only four of them ever made it back. The rest joined the unsung skeletons of the Iron Graveyard. *If the sheep can't work as a herd*, Scorp thought, *they become prey for the wolves.*

Later, far away on the northern border of the scrapyard, Saber-Scorpion walked out into the desert canyon, wet with rain and filthy with a mixture of grime and blood. As he made his way along the rocky path at the foot of the Backbone Mountains, he slid off his mask and let the rain wash over his face. There was a wound in his left side, but none who saw him would have guessed it.

His hair was slightly over regulation length and dark brown in color, though the water made it appear black. His features were strong and handsome in a way that matched his Olympian physique, but also a bit rough around the edges, with thick eyebrows and an unshaven face covered in thick stubble. His eyes were a deep greyish blue, and conveyed the years of combat experience he had behind them. All in all, he certainly looked more mature than his nineteen years of age would imply. But that was the way it was with most of the chosen super-soldiers… the Xarkon Enomegs.

"You need a shave, Justin," said a stern voice.

Scorp had already noticed the camouflaged transport vehicle hidden among the rocks, and now the hatch opened and an older man in a black Xarkon army officer's uniform stepped out. Master Sergeant Brinkmann had been training Scorp for three years now… and Scorp had just passed his final test under him.

"Yes, sir," Scorp said, slightly irritated at his teacher's way of greeting. "When you're out wandering in the mountains for weeks in search of a hidden rebel stronghold, sir, shaving isn't exactly a top priority."

Sgt. Brinkmann frowned. "The way I see it, keeping yourself neat is a sign of self-discipline."

Scorp shrugged. "The way I see it, a beard is a sign of being a man, and fussing over your appearance every day is for girls. So pardon me for not shaving every morning."

Brinkmann shook his head. "Be glad some of the female trainees didn't hear you say that."

Scorp gave a short laugh. "I don't think Tanya would mind."

"Yes, she doesn't mind much of anything. But enough talk. I'm not here to argue with you, son. After all, you did a good job. I can't believe it, in a way. I mean, we always get the students to take on a real combat mission for their last test before ETAB transfer, but most of them just hunt down a fugitive, bust up a gang operation, something like that. But you, you got to take on an entire stronghold of Zygbari rebels. You found the place, hacked the computers, and got away with no followers."

Scorp nodded. "And without firing a shot."

"What?"

"I took out the last group that followed me from the shadows, one by one. Couldn't use a gun without giving away my position."

Sgt. Brinkmann laughed again and shook his head, staring off into the distance. "Well, that's very impressive, Corporal. So you just never bothered to arm yourself, eh?"

"No, sir."

"That was stupid," the sergeant said bluntly. "You're experienced enough to be past the stage where if you carry a gun you'll be tempted to use it when not necessary... and to know when it *is* necessary."

Scorp brushed off this comment. "Yes, sir."

"You don't have to call me 'sir' anymore, Justin. You're a Stage Six Enomeg Trainee... closest thing to a full-fledged Enomeg there is, short of Dark-Dragon himself. And according to these infernal new rules that put the Enomegs above us poor grunts in the army, you're now my superior... sir."

Scorp's features took on a slightly thoughtful expression for a moment, as he stared away into the desert. Then a corner of his mouth lifted in a smile. He nodded. The rainy world suddenly seemed a good deal brighter.

Brinkmann cleared his throat. "Well, time to be getting back to base then, I suppose? I await your order."

Scorp smiled. "Yes, sir."

"I just told you, you don't need to call me..."

"I know. But it's been an honor working with you, sir."

The older man frowned and leaned on the side of the transport truck. "Don't do that, son."

"What?"

"Don't be *nice*. Not anymore. Because it won't help you where you're going."

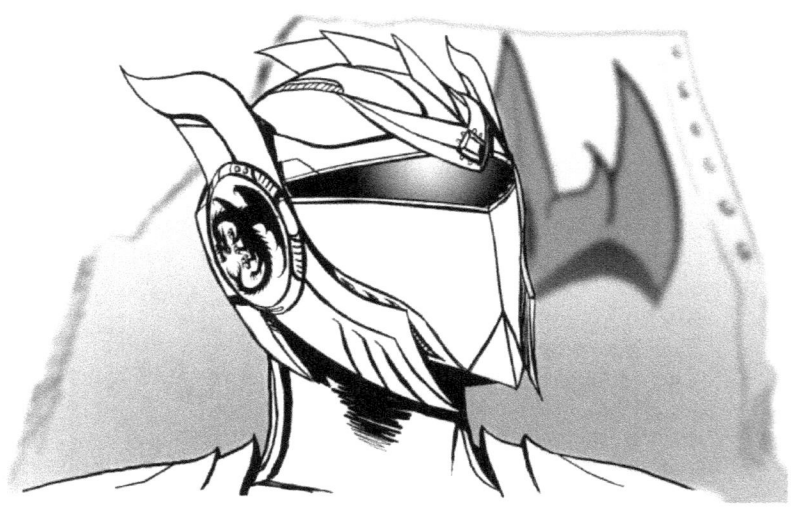

- CHAPTER TWO -
SOLDIERS ARE MADE

On the windswept savannah of central Xarkon, there moved an odd bulge in the field of golden grass. Its colors matched its surroundings, right down to the last flicker of shadow, and the only sure evidence of its passage was the bending of the blades beneath where it hovered. This mysterious shape was a Xarkon HT8 "Bergelmir" armored hover transport. Like all vehicles in the richest, most modern militaries, it was equipped with reactive armor plating, made of an alloy called duranium and enhanced with imbedded nanomachines that allowed it to both instantly harden at the point of impact and to shift hue in real-time, effectively granting it active camouflage. This same technology was used with infantry armor as well. It was not invisibility, but it was close enough.

Beneath this fancy hull, however, the Bergelmir was basically a hovering box, with a row of slits in either side for the passengers to stick their guns through… a primitive but effective tactic. The slits could be covered with a slide-down panel of armor when the vehicle was under particularly heavy fire, and it would still be under the protection of the single unmanned gun turret on top.

The Bergelmir was an old, reliable troop transport that had been in use for years now. Only recently, with High Commander Lucas Mars's insistence that all Xarkon military vehicles bear the shape of the Crown of Xarkon, had two large armor panels been added to the front to give it the vague shape of the nation's well-known emblem. The interior was as plain and bare as the exterior: a row of seats on either side, facing inward. There were lights, gun racks, and handrails. Everything was hard, dark metal. Xarkon soldiers typically referred to the Bergelmir as "the Berg."

Despite the feel of the seats, for which the word "uncomfortable" was an understatement, it was a smooth ride, as hovercraft rides usually were. The vehicle occasionally bobbed when it went over a sharp incline or drop, but otherwise just floated smoothly along. The eight soldiers seated in this particular vehicle, however, were as alert as if they were on a battlefield rocked by explosions and gunfire. For they were Stage Six Enomeg Trainees, and one of them was Saber-Scorpion.

Scorp looked around at his fellow soldiers. He had been training with many of them for years, and although he usually kept to himself, he knew a few of them well. There was Seth, who went by the odd codename of Electric-Eel due to his passion for electronics and skill at hacking. He had been one of Scorp's closest friends during much of his training. Indeed, nearly everyone liked Seth, besides those who were jealous of his abilities. The red-haired young man seemed to simply glide through his training naturally, without letting it – even beatings and lashings – affect his attitude. This left him with an optimistic, almost naïve demeanor that was most unusual among the Enomegs.

Beside him was Tanya, a young woman who had been Scorp's main rival a few years back, until they had settled things and grown to trust each other while out on a particularly dangerous mission together. Tanya was a military woman through and through, with severe features, short-cropped black hair, and narrow, cold blue eyes. Scorp knew that her hair was actually light blonde, but she dyed it black to keep her dark, intimidating appearance. Most of the Enomegs were peering out the slit windows, but Tanya was just staring straight ahead. When Scorp caught her eye, she simply gave him a nod and then recommenced staring. That was how she'd earned the codename Silent-Cobra.

But among these familiar faces were a few Scorp did not recognize… and one in particular. Scorp noticed him immediately: a young man with jet black hair and cool, pale grey eyes with only the faintest splash of blue. He had a somewhat large forehead, Scorp thought, but overall he was what most would have considered quite handsome, with fine-carved, aquiline features that gave him an air of nobility. The expression of contemplation and confidence that he wore as he looked around the room only served to amplify this. When the young man looked at Scorp, the two of them locked eyes and held them there. Instantly, Saber-Scorpion knew this man was an equal.

"You need a shave," said the mysterious trainee.

Scorp rubbed his chin. "That's what they tell me…"

"Headed to the ETAB too?" he asked.

Scorp nodded. They all knew the last stages of their training would be in the ETAB, the Enomeg Training Academy Base. It was almost legendary among the trainees, though to most others it was top secret, only spoken of in whispers.

"I guess we'll be training together," the trainee continued, "since we both survived the same hell. I'm Luke Blood-Raven."

Since the Enomegs had been given only first names by the government, they often used their codenames in the place of surnames.

"How did you earn a prefix like 'Blood'?" Scorp asked. "Kill a lot?"

"They say I'm the best," Raven said frankly, "a warrior by blood. Beyond that, I don't know. I didn't pick it."

Justin nodded. "Well, I did pick mine. I am Saber-Scorpion."

Raven grinned, and something about the way he did it immediately struck Scorp as obnoxious. "Well now… an Enomeg who made up his own name? Mighty brash of you. I'm surprised they let you keep it. So how'd you come up with something like Saber-Scorpion?"

Scorp didn't answer. He leaned backwards and peered through the slit window. Only one thing was now visible on the field of grass that stretched away to the horizon… a simple flat bunker, not unlike the one he had just come from, except a bit larger. The top was camouflaged by trees, and the sides bore the emblem of Xarkon's crown. Was this the fabled ETAB, the Enomeg Training Academy Base? Scorp found himself highly disappointed.

"Maybe I'll tell you when we get to base," he answered Luke at last.

He heard the driver of the Berg reply, "We're there now, sir."

Suddenly the vehicle stopped. Scorp peered through the slit again. There was the bunker, still far off in the distance. Why had they stopped? Then the vehicle began to drop, and Scorp saw the ground rise up to his window and then go past it. They were on a hidden lift, descending into the earth – the real ETAB was underground.

When the elevator slowed to a halt, the Enomeg trainees marched out the back of the Bergelmir. They found themselves in a huge, open room, like a hangar bay of some kind. But it was too crowded and messy to be a hangar. Catwalks and scaffolding crisscrossed the upper levels, covered in chaotic piles of crates and dangling crane cables. There were only a few vehicles to be seen – a couple of rows of hoverbikes, mostly sleek Xarkon Hornets, another Bergelmir, and a great Nidhogg air transport looming in the back. There, in a large clear area below the tangled mess all above, stood four rows of men and women, about sixty people in total. All were clothed in the usual sleeveless black training uniforms, with only light armor padding on the shoulders, shins, and lower arms.

Suddenly Scorp saw him. At the end of the four rows of students stood a single man, clad in intimidating pitch-black battle armor, highlighted with marks of deep, blood red… the fabled exoskeleton of the Enomeg super-soldier, advanced beyond anything that had ever before existed. A few years ago, an exoskeleton of that power would have been a bulky mass of metal like a small walker. Some of these exo-suits were still in use and were quite agile, but the advantages of a human-sized soldier as an infiltrator remained indispensible. Now, using nanotechnology, the Enomeg exoskeleton retained the strength and speed enhancing properties of its predecessors, but the small size and agility of the soldier remained.

Most modern armies had some "heavy" soldiers who wore this kind of suit or similar, but none were as form-fitting or highly advanced as the Enomeg exoskeleton, each of which cost a small fortune. Scorp had never seen a fully finished suit in person, even throughout his training – only prototypes. This was their commander for certain. Scorp had met him a few times before, years ago. This was Dark-Dragon, the first and last of the Phase One Enomegs.

The Enomeg Project had first begun when a small group of veteran soldiers and officers in the Xarkon military had proposed to High Command that they begin an all-new super-soldier program, based on genetic aptitude and long years of hard training. It was like the society of the ancient Spartans, selecting only the best children and training them to be the ultimate warriors. But now, they could select genetically, seeing beyond what the Spartans ever saw. And now they trained the mind as well as the body.

Dragon and his compatriots, unlike the current Enomeg trainees, were not children when they started the program, but merely young soldiers who met most of the genetic requirements and were eager to serve their country. Few know how many soldiers initially entered into Phase One, but only three made it all the way through... and the only one still standing today was the Dragon. Now he was passing his knowledge and expertise on to Phase Two. The hope was that, if they proved successful, the Enomeg project would eventually be expanded until there were hundreds or even thousands of such soldiers, able to beat any ground force the enemy could produce.

Dark-Dragon's gruff voice filled the room, filtered slightly by his helmet: "Finally, our latecomers are here. Welcome, potential Enomegs, to the Enomeg Training Academy Base. Take your places at the end of the lines. The ETAB will be your new home, all of you. You'll learn to hate it."

Scorp and the other trainees from his transport took their places at the end of the long lines of soldiers, and then they turned to watch the man in black armor as he paced between them, looking at each soldier so that they saw their reflection in his intimidating, angular facemask. Saber-Scorpion had heard much about Enomeg armor, but seeing it in person was more impressive than he had expected.

The duranium armor plating was sleek, smooth, and curved. The design appeared more artistic than it did functional, as many things in modern Xarkon did. Nevertheless, it was packed with nearly every feature a soldier could desire, in addition to its physical ability enhancements. Its intimidating design immediately struck the viewer with awe, even fear. A single curved, horn-like spike projected from the elbows and knees, apparently only for ornamentation though they could no doubt be quite deadly in battle as well.

But it was the helmet that was the suit's most striking feature. Two flat, metallic silver panels covered the wearer's mouth, while his eyes stared at onlookers through a narrow, triangular visor. Three fins protruded from the top of the helmet, curving backward and upward, and a lower pair of fins came down in the front, covering the gas-mask vents on either side of the faceplates like cheek-guards. Each helmet was unique, yet all of them bore these same basic features in some shape or form.

Each Enomeg exoskeleton contained features that suited its individual wearer. Metallic grey circles were located on either side of the Enomeg's legs, arms, and helmet that displayed the image of the animal that represented that Enomeg, the animal in the Enomeg's symbolic codename, chosen for them at Stage Five in their training. In Dark-Dragon's case, the animal was a fearsome dragon, with wings outspread, long neck curling in an arch, and toothed jaws open wide.

"Atten*tion!*" shouted the Enomeg commander.

The trainees snapped their heels together and saluted. The standard Xarkon military salute was known as the "Heartbeat," and surly boot camp instructors loved to point out that if they didn't see a heartbeat when they shouted "attention," that trainee would never have another heartbeat again. The salute was performed by slamming the right fist against the chest, roughly in the position of the heart. The room fairly shook with the deep thudding of so many heartbeats.

"Very good," said the Enomeg. "I'm sure there's little need for introduction. You know who I am… Long ago, I began testing the very limits of my Human form. Along with a group of like-minded men and women, I started a project to create the ultimate living soldiers. As the tests we inflicted upon ourselves and each other grew ever more strenuous and dangerous, we were stretched to our limits. Many of us died. A few others quit. When it was all over, I was one of only three men left standing. In the honor of Xarkon, by the will of the Emperor, for the glory of the Crown… I am Lieutenant-Colonel John Dark-Dragon, leader of the Enomegs."

After a pause, he went on: "And now, it is my duty to make sure that all of you follow in my footsteps. You all know how the Enomeg project works: When you were born, your genetic code was scanned in search of what we call the 'soldier genes.' According to our research, these are the genes that code for the aspects necessary to make a good soldier, the aspects described in Xarkon's motto: Honor, Loyalty, Bravery… *Supremacy*."

Saber-Scorpion had seen this speech coming. All throughout his training, every time he switched bases, his commanders always gave this speech to uplift the trainees' spirits before treating them like dirt later in the course. It was always the same… telling them how lucky they were, and then going on about the oft-repeated Xarkon slogan. He prepared himself to be standing a while longer.

"Some might argue that gene therapy or cloning would be a more practical way to breed the perfect soldier, but these methods often produce side-effects, flaws. For the Enomegs, we wish to preserve the purity of the natural Human form. So, shortly after your birth, as soon as it was found that you were born to be soldiers gifted to survive a life on the battlefield, you were whisked from your caretakers and pronounced officially dead. Your family mourned for you, but they would be proud if they knew what you have become. For in secret, you were then taken to a military facility to begin your true calling, your new life: a life as a soldier in the service of Xarkon. You were given new names, both a traditional name and a symbolic one. When my partners and I, the first Enomeg trainees, began our project, we did this to protect our identities. Now we do it to *give* you yours."

Long ago, Scorp had accepted the idea that he had been taken away from his family by the government. After all, the fact had never been hidden from him; it had been told and explained to him for as long as he could remember. As far as he was concerned, it seemed perfectly natural. It was merely a fact of his life. Every morning started at the crack of dawn or earlier, every day consisted of study, training, practice, and tests of the very limits of his skill and endurance. Every night saw him return to quarters, sore and aching from head to foot, if not grievously wounded. Then there was the short but deliciously sweet reprieve of sleep, before it started all over again. This was all he had ever known.

Dark-Dragon went on. "After training in facility after facility, under master after master, you have finally worked your way here, to the highest level. Your rank is above nearly every infantryman in the Xarkon military, as is your skill in combat. You are truly Xarkon's finest. You deserve the respect of every soldier in all of the Armed Forces."

At this point Dark-Dragon reached the end of the line again, so he turned about and looked long and hard at every face pointed in his direction. The odd bit of vehicular armor plating that rested against the wall behind him fittingly bore the Crown emblem, like the dented old veteran version of a battle standard.

"But do you have *my* respect?" he asked. "*No.* You will have to work still harder to earn that honor. You will be driven to the breaking point. You will face challenges that no mortal would dare take on willingly. You will survive hardships that would drive most men to suicide. You will shed sweat, blood, and tears… but you will emerge stronger than before. You will be true men, and yes, I say that even to the women here, for I am speaking in the figurative meaning of the word, not the base, physical one. When I say men, I mean individuals hardened to endure any obstacle and come out on top, individuals of the highest caliber in every conceivable way, individuals that represent the best to be found in Human kind… the Enomegs."

At this, Dark-Dragon let his arms fall to his sides and dropped into a more relaxed stance.

"And you've all heard this a thousand times before, haven't you?"

There was no response.

"No, go on and nod. I know you have."

Down the line, one soldier after another began to nod. Finally, Scorp nodded as well.

"Very well," said Dark-Dragon. "Enough of the pep talk. Now you can familiarize yourselves with the Enomeg Training Academy Base. This underground facility was originally constructed for secret scientific research, but soon that research became part of the Enomeg project, and its purpose changed. You will be given a map soon to show you most of its tunnels and rooms. Memorize it as best you can, because afterward you will be required to hand it back in, and it will be destroyed. There are no maps kept of the ETAB, and you are never to describe what you see here to anyone outside of this base. Are we clear? Yes, I know we are. See you soon."

As Dark-Dragon left the room, the Enomeg trainees did not move. When a few of the other instructors, clad in crisp Xarkon officer uniforms, came by and handed each one of them a slip of paper, they accepted them with a stiff nod. But still they didn't budge.

Then, finally, Seth ran a hand through his red hair and walked casually to one side of the room to seat himself on a crate. "He said relax, guys! Don't you people know how to follow orders?"

Scorp followed Seth and sat down nearby. He flipped open his pamphlet. Inside was a map of the base and an ID card. Scorp unfolded the map and started memorizing. After a few seconds, nearly every detail of it was burned into his mind. He would never have to look at it again.

The ETAB was almost all underground. There were only two aboveground structures… one squat bunker hidden in a small grove of trees that he had seen on arrival, and another bunker disguised as a rock. Both were little more than exits to the world above, and along with the elevator platform on which they had entered, they made up the only exits to the structure. Currently, all of the students were in the smaller of the two hangars located along the north side of the complex. Apparently this particular hangar had been partially converted into a training ground, which explained the mess. The southern half of the complex was mostly row after row of trainee quarters. Each soldier had his own room, a rare luxury in the Armed Forces of Xarkon.

The west side of the complex was mostly offices and classrooms, with the commander's office, which belonged to Dark-Dragon, being the farthest west, next to a long meeting room. Scorp had no difficulty imagining an equally long table inside of it, lined with holoprojectors. The east half of the ETAB was the most interesting. There were a dozen training rooms, several armories, and one large virtual reality room. Scorp wondered what that was like. He hoped it did not involve putting on a pair of VR goggles and matching suit. He had heard rumors about top-secret military experiments to solidify holographic projections, but so far they had gotten nowhere, or so he thought. Finally, there were also some rooms marked as off-limits. He had no doubt a terrible fate awaited whoever tried to enter an off-limits room in a place like the ETAB. But that might actually be the point; sometimes such rooms were created for the express purpose of testing the trainees further, including testing their discipline in restraining their curiosity.

Finally Scorp stuffed the ID card into a pocket on his belt and folded up the map. Looking around, he inspected his fellow trainees. There were many faces he did not recognize, since not all of the Enomegs had trained in the same bases at the same times. One girl in particular caught his eye. The fact that she was female was not a surprise; women apparently suited the genetic requirements nearly as often as men. Unfortunately, because of specific requirements regarding physical "supremacy," many of them also looked like men.

But not this one. Her physique was most definitely feminine, toned to perfection, and her face was not bad either. She had deep blue eyes and medium-length brown hair. Her movements were so careful, graceful, and silent that she seemed like a ghost not truly in this world: one that could be seen, yet not heard. Scorp had seen many Enomeg trainees who were experts at stealth, but with her it seemed to come naturally.

Raven, who was standing not far from Scorp, gave that obnoxious grin of his when he spotted her and waved. "Hey, here's one I haven't met before. I couldn't have forgotten those eyes. Or anything else, for that matter."

The woman gave him an intentionally uninterested-looking glance. "I'm Cathryn. This is Lee."

Scorp had not even noticed the trainee behind her, who stood shorter than most of the other men there. He had dark hair pulled up into a topknot that suited his clearly Asian features. A thin mustache was visible on his upper lip, and his features were as sharp as his eyes. But despite their keenness, the man's dark orbs gleamed with a friendly light as he smiled and gave a nod.

"Pleased to meet you," he said. "They call me Blade-Mantis, and Cathryn here goes by the very fitting codename of Shadow-Cat, so you can call her Cat either way. Convenient, yes?"

Cat smiled and rolled her eyes.

Raven was about to introduce himself, but Scorp beat him to it. "I'm Justin Saber-Scorpion. The kid here is Seth Electric-Eel."

"I prefer Seth," Seth clarified as he clumsily folded his map.

Though he was the same age as the rest of them, Scorp always thought of Seth as a kid because of his attitude. Everything seemed to come naturally to him, and though he was not quite the best in any particular field, he rarely completely failed, gliding from one exercise to the next. Because of this, he was less hardened by the life of training than most of the Enomegs, and he never seemed to take things as seriously as many thought he should.

Lee nodded toward Raven. "What about you, my friend?"

Luke looked at him briefly, and then looked back at Cat smiled. "I'm Luke Blood-Raven."

Cat's eyebrows rose. "How'd you earn a name like that? Bloodthirsty?"

"I suppose you could call it that. I see it more as doing my job. Some soldiers like to spare the enemy, so they get them to surrender. Others like to have their fun with them, give them a fair fight. I just kill them. It's more efficient."

Lee laughed. "Well, the way I got my name is pretty obvious. I'm good with a blade. I wager our friend Saber-Scorpion is too, yes?"

"Yes," Scorp replied, "although I actually chose the other half on my own, in a way. I was on a training mission in the jungle, and we had to make our own camo while waiting for a convoy we were supposed to ambush. I found this plant that squirted red ink – juice, whatever – and drew a scorpion onto my shirt. Scared the hell out of my team, at first; they thought it was my blood. After that, the name Scorpion just sort of stuck, so the instructors let me keep it at Stage Five. You can call me Scorp."

"Didn't like Justin?" Cat asked.

Seth gave Scorp a slap on the shoulder. "Nah, the instructors just kept telling him he was starting to make a name for himself, and he took it too literally, as usual. He can't even get jokes."

Lee joined in the laughter, but Raven shot him a disapproving glance. "I for one will use the name that Xarkon gives me, until She decides to grant me another."

This sobered them up a bit. *She*, Scorp thought. *She*. The way Raven said it, he could almost hear the capitalization, as if Xarkon were more of a holy power than a country. This, coupled with the way Raven was now looking at him, gave him a single distinct feeling: he and the Blood-Raven were not going to have an easy time getting along.

The meeting room in the Enomeg Training Academy Base was almost exactly like Saber-Scorpion had imagined it: a long, narrow room, containing a long, narrow table, lined with holoprojectors. There were seats enough for the entire Xarkon High Command council and then some, but currently there were only two occupants, and both of them were standing: Dark-Dragon... and Lucas Augustus Mars, High Commander of the Armed Forces of Xarkon.

Dark-Dragon was not an exceptionally tall man. Indeed, he would have been slightly shorter than Scorp had he not been wearing his armor. His face was covered in short stubble, as it usually was near the end of the day, and several scars were prominent on his rough skin. He had short, thick black hair that was turning grey in the back, and a pair of alert but almost tired-looking blue eyes. He certainly looked tough, but all in all, he was not like some might have imagined the only currently living, fully-trained Enomeg to be. He was rough and ready, not tall and glorious.

Mars, on the other hand, *was* tall and glorious. The High Commander of the Armed Forces of Xarkon stood over two meters tall and looked nearly half as wide across the shoulders. He wore a crisp black officer's uniform, with the shining red and gold High Commander rank emblem pinned on his breast. Mars was known for his exceptional discipline, and this could always be seen in his appearance: his glistening black boots and matching gloves, his massive clean-shaven jaw, and his dark black hair that was combed back from his receding hairline, forming a sharp V just above his forehead like the prow of an advancing battleship.

As always, the High Commander's heavy brow overshadowed his eyes, but Dark-Dragon could make out those keen, steel-grey orbs cutting into his soul. Indeed, steel-grey was the best way to describe Mars's eyes. They were almost entirely colorless, with hardly a hint of blue to be seen in his irises. They were also as keen and sharp as a metal blade, and nearly as threatening. It was his eyes that contributed quite a bit to his overall impression of cool, calculating intimidation. There were said to be only a tiny handful of people who truly knew the High Commander personally... and one of them was now standing in the room with him.

"War," said Lucas Mars. His voice was incredibly deep and powerful, and it gave his words an ominous, foreboding tone, as if they were some prophecy of doom. "Its fires are almost upon us now. It is a day I have long awaited. A day *we* have long awaited."

Dark-Dragon nodded. "They're all here. We're almost ready."

"I'm not here to give you a speech or tell you how to do your job," Mars said. "I know this project means as much to you as it does to Xarkon... perhaps more."

Dragon nodded. "They're my children. I've watched them all these past nineteen years. Indirectly, I've already shaped and molded them, even put them to death, even as each death killed a part of me. Now I'll make them hate me even as it makes me hate myself. But as long as it makes them ready, I will have succeeded. Maybe someday they'll thank me."

Had it truly been that long? The lifespan of the average Human was longer here in Terra Nova than it had ever been on Earth. Advances in medical technology, understanding of genetics, and nutrition were backed by natural advances in biology that resulted in most Humans living well past a hundred TSCs, or Earth-years. So even though many Humans seemed to mature earlier than ever before, even entering the military at fifteen or sixteen, the Enomegs were set to train until they were twenty.

Mars nodded. "One more year now, and you will find out."

"It hardly seems like enough. We've been preparing them their entire lives for the tests they'll face in the ETAB…"

Mars nodded again. "True. All their lives they've been taught exactly how to react in any given situation. That's what battlefield tactics consist of, basically: simply reacting to each situation as it arises. It's like programming, in a way…"

Dragon frowned. "I prefer not to think of it like that. I'm just sorry that they'll be out of here in only a year. I wonder how many will be left… a hundred? I doubt it. A dozen? Eight? Six?"

Mars pursed his lips thoughtfully. "The rest of High Command will no doubt be hoping for more than that."

Dragon turned a pair of tired eyes in the direction of his commander and friend. "And you?" he said.

Mars arched a thin eyebrow. "I would appreciate it if you aimed for at least a dozen."

"It's not up to me; it's up to the kids."

"They aren't kids anymore, John."

"*Exactly*," Dragon said vehemently.

Mars smiled slightly, a rare sight. "So you haven't picked any favorites?"

Dragon snorted. "You're not here to check up on him, are you? I doubt he'd appreciate it, if he knew."

"I'm always interested in the progress of our best trainees. If one of those just happens to be… of personal interest to me, all the better."

Dark-Dragon tapped a button on the nearest projector, and a hologram appeared, hovering in the air before them. It showed a cluster of ten three-dimensional Human heads, projected in glowing red. Their expressions were stern; the Enomegs certainly never smiled for *their* school portraits.

"These are the current top ten," Dark-Dragon said, moving his gloved and armored hand over the projection. "Luke Blood-Raven, Justin Saber-Scorpion, Lee Blade-Mantis, Tanya Silent-Cobra, Kade Gun-Barracuda, Vincent Magnum-Coyote, Cathryn Shadow-Cat, Seth Electric-Eel, Daniel Stone-Lizard, and Hans Thunder-Hawk. Luke and Justin, or Raven and Scorpion, are nearly tied in their scores. I think if Justin attended more recreational activities, team screamerball and the like, then his grades would improve… since we watch them even during the off-hours, of course. Games are sometimes just as indicative of ability as battle tests. Still, they are all doing better than even I could have expected. I just don't know how they'll fare in the four final trials…"

Mars's severe forehead wrinkled even more. "The Tenets of Xarkon: Honor, Bravery, Loyalty… Supremacy. When do they begin those?"

"They will begin the Supremacy trials almost immediately. The Test of Supremacy is somewhat like a tournament. Every Enomeg will face a series of increasingly hard battles in the holo-room against special forces soldiers and the like. The final fight is practically one man against a small army. If they make it past all of those battles, they officially pass the test, but then they move on to see who truly 'wins,' so to speak. The best of the best, on top of the ladder, will face each other in a final fight to help determine who will take my place as 'leader' of the Enomegs."

"It seems a misnomer to me, since they seldom work as a group."

"It is a misnomer," Dragon said flatly. "The Enomeg 'leaders' are something of a public face. We'll put them on a pedestal to exemplify the success of the program. In more than a year though, they'll rarely command their fellow Enomegs in the field. They'll rarely even *be* together in the field."

After a pause, Mars said, "I need them, John. I need them soon."

Dark-Dragon looked at the High Commander's face for some indication as to what he spoke of, but his features and his cold, grey eyes betrayed no emotion. Mars was an expert at hiding his feelings, as both of them were. They had come to trust each other mostly because they acted and thought alike, and had lived similar lives. Both of them were soldiers, and both of them believed in the ideals of war: man against man, a test of Human strength and will, the defense of one's country and its values.

"You'll start the war soon, then?" Dragon asked, not hesitating to pose a question that most in High Command would have planned for days before asking.

Mars nodded. "Yes. Xarkon needs to move, and it needs to move now. Victory is tightening its grip over Human space even as we speak. CONON may seem impotent from a military perspective, but the power of its politics is even worse. While they claim to promote peace and liberty, they continue to require all countries to follow their rules, to share their chosen form of government, as if it were the only way man can live. They are making every country a province of Victory not nominally, but practically.

"We must put a stop to this, but not as soon as I would have hoped… or in the *way* I would have hoped. Emperor Orrick and I are having… disputes. He has his own plans on how to deal with the thorns that remain in Xarkon's side. He wants to step up the timetable; we may have to delay the end of the Enomeg training at some point, put it off to send them on a mission. Do you think you can work that into your plans, John? Will you and your children be ready?"

Dragon stood taller and looked his commander in the eyes. "If Xarkon calls Her men to duty, the Enomegs will always be ready."

Her men. Mars smiled. He could almost hear the capitalization.

LOCATION: THE GRIM ISLES

Jade approached her den with the air of a warrior queen returning to her throne. The other young soldiers, most of whom were fighting in the dust, training themselves in hand-to-hand combat, respectfully stopped what they were doing as she passed. They were all only teenagers – sixteen at the most – but each looked rough and ready, and all were armed with an assortment of guns and knives, despite being in their home territory.

The soldiers of Grimm's Mercenary Army called them "the Devil's children." On the Grim Isles, many of the mercenaries had families, and though there were many ramshackle makeshift communities littering the isles, a family hardly lived up to the name when one or both parents spent most of their time on the battlefield, even off-world, fighting on some distant planet. Many children ended up as orphans before they could even speak.

The orphans of war led more than just a hard life – they led a life of battle from the moment they could walk. It was a battle for survival at first, and then a battle to be on top. Their environment only encouraged it, with the mercenary warlords rewarding the kids who trained the most and fought the best, preparing them to be soldiers of fortune. Grimm's Army was only a few decades old, so the project of training orphans of war was little more than an experiment at this stage, but Grimm expected it to pay off in the long run, and likewise so did his men.

Among those kids who had excelled in the mercenary army's training program, Jade was the queen. Each trainee was given a small personal home in one of the fortresses to upgrade with the rewards they earned when they excelled. Jade's was known as the Jade Palace for a reason. Grimm was said to pamper her with prizes, as every greedy merc on the island knew.

But today as Jade approached the door to her den, nestled away there between the high walls of one of Grimm's island fortresses, she paused. The outer walls were reinforced with armor panels painted in a dark green jungle camouflage pattern – now covered in dents. Yet nothing seemed to be out of place about her abode that an untrained eye would have noticed. Jade, however, knew the place like the back of her hand, and upon close inspection of the edges of the window, she could no longer doubt it: there had been a break-in.

The other children watched with keen interest as she entered her little fortress, as carefully and silently as a tigress hunting a predator that had just made the mistake of wandering into her territory. She knew the mercs stole, and she had done it herself from time to time. It was just part of survival. If she left something lying about the base, she fully expected it to be gone upon her return. But she drew the line at her own front door… and this thief had just crossed it.

"Better call one of the officers, Jacin," said a boy to his friend nearby. "Tell 'em someone's about to get killed."

The appointed messenger boy reluctantly ran off, and then there was a long moment of silence as the audience breathlessly watched and waited. Suddenly the stillness of the air was split by blazer machine gun fire, echoing from inside Jade's quarters. It seemed to last a full minute before stopping, and then there was another pause... followed by the loudest shot yet, like a Slashrim

Sovalok's screeching roar coupled with an explosion. A bright flash of light erupted from the windows of Jade's den, and a dark body came hurtling out of one of the windows, sliding across the street, kicking up a cloud of sand as it went.

When the dust had settled, there stood Jade in the broken window, holding a starfire rifle, the glow in its barrel still dimming after the release of the charged-up blast. The mercenary officer the boy had summoned arrived just in time to see this, looking between her and the dead body.

Jade's voice was surprisingly deep for a girl of her age, and no one laughed when she coolly said, "Tell Grimm I've got a room full of bulletholes that need fixing… and a dead rat outside."

LOCATION: VICTORY

Orion spoke into his commlink. "Amazon, do you read?"

A woman's voice replied, "Loud and clear, Orion."

"What's the situation?"

"Level one clear. All hostiles neutralized. Orders?"

"Hold position until I give the word."

"Aw, come on, Ryan. I was really looking forward to getting a *few* more kills."

"*Hold*, Amazon. Completing the mission comes first."

"Fine, fine. Holding position."

Orion checked his gear. He was armed with a laser pistol and laser knife. The pistol was built to match the size, shape, and weight of the standard Victorian sidearm. The knife was made to match the Victorian Bowie-II energy knife, which was standard equipment for all soldiers. However, both of these particular ones were fake. The pistol fired invisible lasers and the knife emitted a short-range, invisible beam. Both of them, when they met with the outfits the enemies were wearing, would cause the enemy's suit to automatically incapacitate its wearer. It was simulated violence, without resorting to the unreality of VR.

Swiftly and surely, he drew out both of these weapons. Holding the pistol out before him and steadying it with his knife-hand, he advanced.

There were four hostiles in the corridor. He'd counted them earlier and told his team to wait back. He didn't need help to handle just four men. The first one was completely unprepared for his assault. Orion came up from behind and grabbed him by the throat, holding his knife outward. The other three turned to face him as he ran toward them, rapidly pushing his hostage, giving him no time to fight back.

Once he was right next to the second man in the hallway, Orion slit his hostage's throat and shoved him forward. He fell onto the other soldier, who quickly shoved him off… but not quickly enough to prevent Orion from grabbing him and stabbing him in the gut. The remaining two fired, but their invisible blasts disappeared into their comrade's back. Tossing the limp man aside, Ryan then took them down with three quick pistol shots.

He cursed himself under his breath… It should only have taken two.

- CHAPTER THREE -
MOUNTAINS OF ANTHILLS

The life of an Enomeg trainee was not all combat training; there were also more traditional academic activities required. Enomegs were very well-educated by civilian standards, and even by the standards of most military officers. Like officers, the classes they took were mostly related to military tactics. In psychology, they first learned how the mind worked, and then they were taught how to use this knowledge against the enemy: how to evaluate their weaknesses, to make them believe that defeat was imminent even if they were actually winning, to make them become overconfident and make mistakes… or simply how to make them quake with fear.

They also learned a bit about troop morale, but as Enomegs it was not their job to lead armies and keep their spirits up. Each Enomeg was a lone soldier, a one-man army who would fight in an extremely small team of his peers at the most. He had to keep his own wits about him, not anyone else's.

Of course, even these regular classes were made into physical endurance tests as well. Throughout the entire session, all of the trainees were forced to stand, rigidly at first, until they were allowed to slacken up later. But if any showed so much weakness as to sit down or lean against the wall, the trainer would quite literally beat the exhaustion right out of them. Only during especially long sessions or exams were they allowed to sit.

Scorp was used to it. Today he was in Xarkon Government History class. It was a large, open room, with walls covered in posters showing various historical timelines and battlefield layouts. These posters were actually holographic projections that changed at the will of the instructor. The instructor himself, a man named Garfield, was currently pacing back and forth in front of the row of students. He was an older, balding man in a crisp black Xarkon officer uniform, and he was currently droning on about the legendary Age of the Golden Skye.

Scorp had heard about the reign of Empress Kristal Skye at least a thousand times during his schooling and seen hundreds of pictures of her. His instruction had practically begun with her, and now it was clearly going to end with her as well. It was under her reign that Xarkon was officially and finally converted into an empire, a one-man – or, at that time, one-woman – dictatorship, and it was she who designed the distinctive five-pronged crimson crown that now stood as Xarkon's symbol on just about everything, including its flag, currency, and military vehicles.

"During the Empress's reign," the instructor said, "she was extremely popular with all of her subjects. But there's *always* someone who will act against even the greatest of leaders: some rat who either wants to seize power for himself, is bought like a prostitute with enemy money, or simply 'catches democracy.' One man in her advisory council, whose name is not passed through history because of his actions, actually tried to *assassinate* the Empress. Before he could execute his plans, however, a close friend that he had confided in revealed his secret to the rest of the council."

At this point, Instructor Garfield turned to face the room and fix each student with a glare. "His friend – a man whose name, Patrick Ergoff, *is* passed through history – revealed the secret during a public ceremony, in the face of an audience of citizens. Quite frankly, the traitor started to shake like a hairless Yeti, revealing his obvious guilt. The people of Xarkon then rose up and tore the traitor down from his speaking podium. They threw him to the ground, and he was beaten to death there in the square by the angry loyalist mob. Now, I have a question for you, students, and I want you to answer this with all honesty: what is your opinion of the fate of the would-be assassin? Was it just, or was it wrong?"

Silence reigned over the assembly. The students stood still, a few of them going even more rigid, staring at the instructor. The room may as well have been full of statues. Finally one of them spoke up. It was Raven, who was standing in the foremost row. His eyes narrowed as he spoke, and he stiffened even more in his tight black uniform, if that were possible.

"It was no more than he deserved. He betrayed the leader he had sworn to serve, a leader who had done nothing but strengthen Xarkon, a leader that the people of his country loved. He was a coward and a traitor. So the people protected their Empress. They did what was right."

Garfield nodded, but said nothing. He continued looking around the room, indicating that someone else should speak up. As much as Scorp wanted to remain silent, as he usually did, he found himself strangely eager to compete with Luke, even in this. Raven was overconfident, and Scorp was sure of his ability to beat him in logic.

"I disagree," Scorp said. "His punishment was unfair. He was not justly accused, not proven guilty, and his punishment was decided by an angry mob. One of Xarkon's tenets is honor. There was no honor in the way this man was killed. This was unjust."

"Another of Xarkon's tenets is loyalty," Luke said, finally breaking his attentive stance to look back across the room at Scorp. "He was disloyal to his leader; the people were loyal to theirs. So they…"

"Wasn't *he* one of their leaders?" Scorp interrupted. "He was a member of the Council of Advisors."

"But he did not wear the Crown," Luke rebutted, "which is what the people are truly loyal to."

"Today, yes… now that the Council has all but ceased to exist. Back then, however, it was still a full Council, and still constituted nearly half the government."

"Because then the government was corrupt!"

Scorp gave a short laugh. "And the people were supposed to know that somehow? They were told by the laws to follow the government, just as we are today. The people are never told *today's* government is wrong, only yesterday's. They are never told that *our* government may be wrong, only the government of our enemies."

Scorp paused. Had he gone too far? Something he said had not sounded right. This was why he always preferred actions to words…

Luke smiled, realizing he had the upper hand. "You just said that the people were wrong, and now you're saying the government is wrong… So just who are you fighting for, 'Saber-Scorpion'?"

Scorp's eyes narrowed. It was then that the instructor took up his cue.

"You fight for Xarkon," Garfield said, standing up straighter. "You fight for its government, whatever it currently is… you fight for its people, whoever they currently are… but most of all you fight for the symbol, for the ideal. You fight for what Xarkon stands for… honor, bravery, loyalty, and supremacy. Today Xarkon continues to evolve, and it is closer to the purity of those ideals than ever. But it has always striven for them, so it has always been Xarkon."

The instructor turned to look at Scorp and said, "Nevertheless, you got it right, son. The traitor's punishment was unjust. The courts of Xarkon and the will of Empress Skye should have decided his fate. By punishing him themselves, the people of Xarkon were disobeying the law, killing one of their leaders on a mere impulse. In their own way, they were traitors as well. That is not to say that the traitor did not deserve his fate. If convicted, he'd either have swung or been shot, possibly lost his head… but those are still preferable to a mob beating. For if we let the whim of the people, of simple emotion, dictate our every action, then chaos will reign. Such is the difference between vengeance and justice, impulse and strategy, mob rule and government. And in your case, that's the difference between a simple fighter or warrior… and a true soldier. That's all for today, trainees. You're dismissed."

The room was clear in a couple of seconds as the Enomegs filed out like clockwork. Scorp, however, intentionally hung back to dodge Raven. As he did, Lee backed up and bumped into him in the hallway.

"Did you really mean all that?" he asked.

Scorp made no reply. He gave a slight shrug.

A broad smile spread across Mantis's face, and his dark eyes gleamed. "I mean, that was close to treason, my friend. For a moment, I wondered what kind of training centers you had been to before this one. Ha! But you were right in the end."

Scorp knew what Mantis meant. He had been raised in these military academies his whole life. Through all of his classes, they always filled his head with propaganda. They taught that it was wrong, that propaganda and censorship were used by enemy nations to make the people condone the evils of their government... but it was exactly what they were doing. Subtly, ever so subtly, even while sounding coldly and perfectly logical, they were actually teaching blind loyalty to Xarkon.

Of course, Scorp realized it was what every nation must do. When he had first started his schooling, he'd simply accepted the propaganda as truth. Later, he had rebelled against the contradictions it presented, only to be argued with and browbeaten into silence. Now they were appealing to his "logic" through arguments about government policy, and he was ready to either beat them at their own game or finally make them really *convince* him. He explained these thoughts in brief to Mantis.

"Still I am not sure," Mantis replied. "Such indecision can lead to similar unclear thoughts on the battlefield, where you should be fully focused. It is a weakness, in its own way."

Scorp gave a short laugh. "So thought is a weakness?"

Mantis shrugged and stood closer to the metal wall of the corridor to let more of the trainees slip past. "Vague, questioning thoughts, yes. Unfocused thoughts are like inaccurate weapons. Would you wield a gun that you can hardly control, or one that shoots straight ahead, never veering?"

"So now we're nothing more than guns?"

Without a moment's hesitation, Mantis nodded. "On the battlefield, my friend, we have to be."

Scorp laughed again. "Maybe *you're* the one who should be teaching these classes."

He had to admit, Lee was almost convincing him. The young man spoke with such pure conviction, such clarity of mind, that Scorp could not help but admire him. And strangely enough, despite his disciplined loyalty, Lee had a laid-back, smiling demeanor that was almost disarming. In fact, despite the debate they were currently having, Scorp found he couldn't help but like him. Just as he was about to continue the argument, Raven appeared and broke in on their conversation.

"You were right back there, in a way," Raven said, looking across at Scorp, for they were almost exactly the same height. "You did good. But don't think you can beat me out in the field."

Scorp shook his head. "Are you really trying to turn this into some kind of personal competition? You barely know me!"

Raven smiled that irritating smile of his, that confident smirk, and said, "Oh, but I do know you. I've studied all the best trainees, those with the highest marks... and do you know who the highest ones are?"

Scorp shrugged. "Me?"

Luke snorted derisively and squinted his cold grey eyes. "You and *me*. You don't get it, do you? We're not in school anymore. This place isn't an education center or a training ground... it's a test, the final test. Most of the ones taking this test will either fail and be sent away, or fail and *die*. When the test is through, only a handful will have passed. And out of these few, one will be appointed to replace Dark-Dragon as the leader of the Enomegs. And that leader is going to be *me*."

"Well, good luck with that," Scorp responded. He shoved past Luke and stalked off down the hall.

"What about you?" Luke shouted after him. "What's your goal... *Scorp?*"

Scorp paused and glanced back.

"To be the best," he said.

LOCATION: XARKON CENTRAL PLAINS

The sunlight nearly blinded Saber-Scorpion as he stepped out of the lift – the exit to the ETAB that was disguised as a standing rock. It was good to be out in the fresh air again. The wind was cool, and the coarse, dry grass of the savannah rippled in the breeze. He had come here early, and at first he thought he might be the first one out... at least until he noticed the fist flying toward his face and reflexively ducked.

He looked up at his assailant. It was another trainee, who stood a good three inches taller than Scorp. The padded black armor they wore served to enhance his shoulders, which looked almost half as broad as he was tall. His head was bald, and his elongated face featured a vertical scar running from above his eyebrow all the way down to his chin. Scorp did not know how he had gotten a mark like that, but he could guess it was from a blow that would have felled most mortal men.

The man said in a deep but clear voice, "I should beat you to within a centimeter of your life, traitor, for what you said in the classroom back there. If we were back at my old base right now, the boys and I would show you, you two-tongued little snake. You ain't fit to polish my boots."

This was a tradition at the ETAB bases. Most Enomeg students took their training... their job, their life... very seriously. And if anyone was seen dropping out of line, it was viewed by these zealots as bad for the whole group. Thus, they took it upon themselves to aid the instructors unofficially by knocking the wanderers back in line. It was known as "peer discipline" by the trainers, and they usually avoided siding either for or against the practice, letting it slide right under their noses.

Scorp gave a short laugh. "Well, I guess your 'boys' didn't make it to the ETAB then? That's too bad."

"Some did," answered the giant, "but you won't hear me bawlin' just 'cause someone didn't make the cut. That's nature. My name's Kade Gun-Barracuda, and you'll remember that name when I put you back in line, whelp. Your lack of honor weakens us all."

"Instructor Garfield didn't seem to agree."

Kade shook his head, the muscles on his neck bulging in the process. "The instructor was only tryin' to teach you on your own terms. But now I'll teach you on *mine*."

Suddenly a voice broke in from the door behind them. "Hey, why don't you pick on someone your own size, fish-boy? Someone like me."

Scorp turned to see another trainee approaching, a grin spread across his face. He had short, dark hair and a bright gleam to his fiery hazel eyes that gave his grin both a playful and somewhat menacing look. Despite his remark about size, he was a good foot shorter than Barracuda, and a bit shorter than Scorp as well. Yet he moved with ease and confidence, raising his fists.

Barracuda sneered. "*Coyote*. You know, seein' you and *'Brutus the honorable man'* here at the ETAB makes me really question the effectiveness of the Enomeg program."

"Yeah, it's not all it's cracked up to be, I guess," Coyote said with a shrug. "I just didn't want to say that, since, you know, it might be *treasonous*."

"Take one step closer," Barracuda said in a smooth, deep growl, "and we'll see how good you look with a gap in those teeth you're always flashin'."

The giant raised his fists. The bulging of his muscles gave Scorp the impression of rolling boulders... or the formation of a mountain range at the meeting of two tectonic plates. Most of the Enomegs had sleek, well-toned musculature, but clearly Barracuda was as much a body-builder as an athlete.

Coyote did not mind a bit. "Well, come on then. Take one good swing right here at my face. Put all your weight into it too; no fakin' it! Gimme your best shot!"

Barracuda did not hesitate. The huge arm unfurled and erupted forward. His fist connected with Coyote's jaw, and the shorter man's head was twisted abruptly sideways. He twirled into a heap on the ground. Staring down at the body in front of him, Barracuda blinked curiously. Then he looked sour. He knew he had failed to hit Coyote, because he never felt his knuckles touch, but somehow the act had looked so convincing that it had baffled him for a bit. Coyote jumped up and flashed another grin.

Scorp smiled and nodded. "Bravo."

"*Gogk*, that was stupid," Barracuda said, cursing in the Slashrim tongue. "I felt my fist graze your girly-smooth cheek. One more millisecond and you'd have been spittin' bloody teeth, maybe with a broken jaw."

Coyote laughed. "You kidding? I've been practicing that trick for *ages* just to pull it on you. You put too much stock in your muscles, Kade. It's your *weakness*."

"Yeah, great trick, Vinny. You'll make a great actor, since that's what it looks like you're training to be." Kade scowled with derision. "You two are an insult to the Enomegs, and you make me sick. I don't know how you've made it this far, but mark my words: the training here will either beat that crap right out of you, or it will kill you. I'd settle for either result."

With that, he turned and stalked off toward the edge of the clearing. Coyote just shook his head.

"Some people can't take a joke," he said.

"Well, he was right in a way," Scorp said, "You must be one crazy nut to try that on a guy like him. He could probably rip a tree right off its roots."

Coyote gave a dismissive wave of his hand. "Ah, I know how to deal with Barracuda. We've tangled before. Name's Vincent Magnum-Coyote. Best shot and fastest runner in the Enomegs."

Scorp shook the offered hand. "Justin Saber-Scorpion. Best swordsman and probably a lot more in the Enomegs. In fact, I'd like to test you on that 'best shot' theory…"

"Unfortunately we don't have time," said a filtered voice issuing from the bushes behind them.

Scorp turned. At first he saw only the waving grass, but then he noticed a dark shape rising out of them not too far away. It was Dark-Dragon, still clad in full exoskeleton, which now appeared to be a dull golden-brown color, striped with shadows. The suits carried the same automatic camouflage technology as the armor plating of the vehicles. They watched as Dragon reached up and removed his helmet, revealing his battle-scarred face. The active camo effect switched off, causing the color to slowly drain back out of the suit, leaving it black and deep crimson like before, the default colors for the Enomeg Commander. The bright gleam of the metal returned as well, reflecting the empty plains and clear sky that surrounded them.

"Not many Humans live out here," Dragon said. He did not have the deep, commanding voice of Lucas Mars, but it still had an effect of its own. He kept it low, plain, and serious, and it carried with it a clear message of battlefield wisdom. "There isn't a man for miles. There also isn't much water for miles. The plants out here live off the sun and the dirt, and it rarely rains. It's practically a desert – in this area anyway. See these plants? Ukrak, the Mahlok called them. They hate 'em. They're coarse, dry, tough… and the tops of them have seeds covered in tiny blades that bite into you like claws. That's why most of the animals out here have such thick hides and little fur. In the spring, these grasses bloom like you wouldn't believe. This whole bloody field turns bright, shining yellow, like the surface of the sun. Sometimes it's so bright it disrupts passing satellites, or so I've heard. But those are probably just tall tales."

By now the clearing in which they stood was full of trainees, and the last few latecomers were filing out of the exit. Scorp had known they were there, but had not paid much attention, for he was focused on Dragon's voice. Apparently it was having the same effect on everyone else. They were staring off in the direction their commander was now pointing. Scorp followed suit.

"You see that mesa?" said Dark-Dragon. "It's the liveliest place out here. A bunch of strange birds make their nests in caves all along the sides, which are steep and treacherous to climb. On the top, however, is a virtual paradise. Somehow, that flat rock is where all the greenest plants grow. But they aren't the only secret up there…"

At this point he abruptly stopped talking. The other students dared not interrupt the sudden silence. They simply stared at him as he looked out at the mesa. The wind blew gently, rustling the grasses, making a dry rattling sound.

"What else is up there?" Seth said at last.

"You'll find out," the Enomeg replied, "because you're going to climb it."

They all looked out at the mesa again with renewed interest. The sides of it were solid rock – a very bright red rock, unlike the soil of the plains. The top of the plateau was lush with green plants, mostly small bushes. Look as he might, Scorp could not make out any of the birds that Dragon said dwelt there. However, he did see the dark holes in the cliff face that must be the caves in which the creatures nested.

Terra Nova was an Earth-like planet in almost every sense of the word, with the primary difference being the longer days and nights and stronger force of gravity. Still, humanity had adjusted, and in some ways the fact that everything was now a bit heavier ensured that the population of Terra Nova remained fit. The planet's ecosystem was much the same as well, and the life that inhabited its surface, both plant and animal, had evolved along much the same patterns, resulting in a surprisingly familiar environment for its first Human settlers. There were blue skies, green trees, and creatures very similar to birds, reptiles, mammals, insects, and all the rest. Scorp could hear this wildlife now… the singing bugs and the calls of a bird far in the distance. Of course, there were some oddities on the planet that were unlike anything seen on Earth. Scorp wondered what kind of birds dwelled on that mesa…

"I'll go first," Dragon said, striding forward. "After about five minutes, I want you all to follow me. Just go as you see fit, whenever you deem yourself ready. But remember, this is a very important assignment, and if you give it anything but your best, you'll probably end up as a scout on the Mordark border when this is all over, not an Enomeg super-soldier. This is the Test of Honor, the first of four main tests you must undertake. All of the tests here are of the utmost importance if you ever wish to wear this armor," he said while performing the Heartbeat salute, "but these four will be the greatest. Do I make myself clear? Good. I won't say it again.

"Now… You have to use the equipment in your backpacks and whatever you find around you. Pick a few teammates if you want, but don't let them slow you down. The first few to make it to the top have to look for something… a bronze replica of the Crown of Xarkon. When you find it, I'll know. For now, enjoy the view. And remember, don't make a mountain out of an anthill."

All of the trainees simultaneously turned to look in the direction he indicated. The sun was glinting beautifully off the waving grasses. It looked like an ocean of gold, rippling gently in the wind. Besides the mesa, the base entrance rock, and a clump of trees far in the distance, there was nothing to be seen except a vast, empty sky above a vast, empty plain. When they looked back, Dark-Dragon was nowhere to be seen either. Scorp shook his head in amazement.

Then he realized something: Dark-Dragon mentioned backpacks – and he saw most of the other trainees wearing theirs – but he had never picked up such a pack. He looked around and noticed that Cobra was not wearing one either. Neither were Raven or several others. They were wearing only their black training garb, like him. Had they been talking when the order was given? That was highly unlikely; apparently this was something the instructors had planned. Scorp watched as Raven walked over to the door of the base and pressed a button on the controls, asking if they could be let back in to get their packs. The response was apparently negative, for Luke cursed and stormed back to stand beside Scorp.

"Out of curiosity, who were the best students on that list you said you saw?" Scorp asked him.

Raven scowled. "Look around... most of the top performers don't have a backpack. Apparently they're trying to slow us down. Although I'm surprised Mantis has one; he was near the top. I don't know what they're trying to prove here, but I'm not letting this stop me..."

Scorp nodded. "Want to team up? The two best students, even without packs..."

"I'm going in alone," Luke replied, interrupting him, "with or without a pack."

Scorp shook his head, although he had not expected any other response. He too preferred working alone. He'd settled a rivalry with Tanya Silent-Cobra a few years ago simply by working with her, but something told him Raven's attitude was different than hers, and besides, they had bickered for at least half the mission before getting on each other's good side. He certainly didn't need that kind of thing slowing him down today. Then he saw Cat and Mantis approaching.

"Hey, would you like a teammate?" Cat asked Raven as she fastened up her hair. "Most of the others seem to be going in teams of two."

"I just said, I'm going in alone," Raven replied, turning to leave.

"Without any gear?" Cat scoffed. "I wouldn't have taken you for a fool, but I guess it's hard to tell. When you change your mind, come find me."

Scorp felt a pang of emotion that he instantly recognized as jealousy, perhaps because Cat had asked Raven to be her partner first and not even approached him. Apparently Raven's desire to make this into a competition between the two of them was catching. Scorp tried to shake off the feeling. He didn't need that now; he only needed to win.

Raven seemed to have the same idea. "Good luck, Cat," he said as he walked away.

Cathryn stomped her foot in irritation.

Mantis gave her a slap on the back. "I guess you're stuck with me then, Cat... as usual. Let's go."

By then, Scorp had already set off through the grass alone. As he walked, Scorp could feel the seeds that Dark-Dragon had told them about. At first they could not get through his suit, but gradually they began to wear away at it, and he could feel his sides starting to bleed. Looking down, he saw the suit was now torn in several places. He wished he had his nanofiber mesh, but the instructors often stressed the point that they should not come to rely on technology. Deciding the only way to get past the seeds was to get below them, Scorp got down on all fours and began to crawl.

Soon he noticed that there seemed to be small pathways cut in the bottom of the grasses, perhaps by the passing of some kind of animal. By following these narrow passageways, he was able to move through the fields undetected, since he did not bend any blades as he passed. This must be how Dark-Dragon was able to move around so completely unseen, he thought. The Enomeg knew the area well.

Every now and then Saber-Scorpion pushed the grasses aside and stood up to survey the landscape and make sure he was headed in the right direction. One time that he did this, he saw another of the trainees standing a short distance off. Scorp recognized him from a previous training camp as someone named Daniel, though he could not remember his codename.

Suddenly Daniel fell face forward into the grass. He disappeared beneath the blades for a moment, and when he stood back up, his backpack was nowhere to be seen. He turned around, kicking at the grass and searching in all directions, but he could not seem to find it. After only a few seconds, his face and arms were cut horribly by the Ukrak seeds. Scorp instantly knew what had happened... and a few minutes later, his suspicions were confirmed as he saw Raven stand up farther off, strapping on a backpack.

"So much for honor," Scorp muttered to himself before sinking back down to continue his crawl.

Finally he reached a spot where the Ukrak blades grew shorter. He had passed into the shadow of the mesa. Scorp stood up and saw the tall rock formation looming above him, the sun behind it illuminating its edges in a halo of light. When he reached the side of the mesa, he put his hand on the rough red stone and looked straight up. The rock rose up almost as straight and featureless as a skyscraper before him. There were no discernable hand or footholds with which to climb.

He looked around and quickly spotted Seth, standing next to the mesa and strapping on a pair of climbing bracers from his backpack. Each one had a row of spikes along the side, and they sank right into the side of the mesa in only one or two strikes. The rock was apparently softer than it looked, which went contrary to what Scorp had heard about the formation of mesas. There was something quite different about this particular one, apparently.

So he needed something sharp to climb with. A quick scan of the area revealed nothing of use, so he crouched down and began digging in the sand at the foot of the mesa, looking for some long rocks... anything he could use. Finally he found something, but it was not a rock. He pulled it out and inspected it. It was a bone... probably the remnants of a meal eaten by the cliff-dwelling birds Dark-Dragon had mentioned. Still, it was quite long and sharp, and it felt strong enough as well. Taking it in one hand, point down, Scorp slammed it into the cliff. It took a few strikes, but he finally got it far enough in. Gripping it tightly, he pulled. It held his weight.

Without another moment's hesitation, he grabbed another bone and began scrambling up the cliff face as fast as he could, slamming the bones in rapidly, one after another, sticking his feet into every minor foothold that he could find. As he climbed, he kept his eyes straight up, staring over the shadowy face of the smooth red rock and the darkening sky above, never looking down to see how far he'd come. That was one trick of the trade that really worked; the other was to never stop climbing. Once you stopped, your body took the opportunity to tell you just how tired you really were.

He could make out several Enomegs around him, including Seth not far above, and Coyote and Cobra far off to his left. Scorp could not tell if he was catching up with any of them or who was nearest the top, but at least they were still in sight. He did not dare to look down and see if he was ahead of anyone. Keeping his thoughts thus occupied, he continued mercilessly on.

It was not long before his arms began to burn as if they were on fire. If only he could pause and regain his strength for a moment, he thought, then he could easily make it the rest of the way. But if he stopped now and simply hung there, he knew he'd never be able to summon up the strength to continue, and he'd be left hanging. That was when he remembered the bird nest caves. Looking around as much as he could, he saw what looked like one not far above. With all the effort he could muster, he started making his way toward it.

He also took note of the other trainees around him. Not too far off on his right, almost level with him, were Mantis and Cat, with Mantis in the lead. And just below them was Kade Gun-Barracuda. He had apparently taken a while to get to the foot of the mesa for some reason – maybe because he was too big to crawl under the grass – but now he was making amazingly rapid progress. He slammed his spikes into the cliff with only a single blow... one, two, one, two. It was so easy for him that he looked like a spider.

Scorp was about to look away, but Kade quickly caught his attention again when he suddenly reached up and grabbed Cat's leg by the ankle. Grinning viciously, he gave it a twist and a jerk. Cat was startled and cried out as one of her climbing bracers was wrenched from the wall. She struggled now to stay clinging to the cliff, while Kade tugged at her leg from below, sneering. Cat reached down with her free hand and tried to unclamp Kade's iron grip from her foot, but it was clearly no use.

Scorp, his fatigue forgotten for the moment, suddenly found himself fighting with the terrific urge to rush to her aid. He did not know what he could do, but he felt he had to do something. They were a good way up the side of the mesa now, and a fall like that could be fatal. He felt himself almost unconsciously making his way sideways, toward the struggling figures that were silhouetted against the sky. His arms burned with the effort.

But he was too slow – for suddenly, Cat fell. Scorp quickly knew something else was afoot, however. It looked more like a gymnastics move than a natural fall, the way she arced backwards off the cliff, still holding onto Kade's wrist with one hand, her other arm held out before her. Kade's arm was twisted backwards, and his grip was torn away from the rock. He made a few desperate grabs at the wall... and then fell with a scream. Cathryn's own extended wrist slammed back into the cliff below Kade, while he fell down past her. Exhausted though he was, Scorp heard himself laugh in amazement.

But Kade recovered quickly, slamming his arms into the cliff as he fell. They dragged long cuts into the red rock until his falling body jerked to a halt, and for a second he hung limply from his bracers. Cathryn proceeded upward as fast as she could, but she had twisted one of her wrists and was clearly straining to go on. Just when she felt she could use that arm no longer, she suddenly felt someone else's hand on hers.

"Lee…" she panted, "Thank God."

But looking up, she beheld Saber-Scorpion, his blue eyes squinted and his hair whipping in the wind. He smiled. Cat stared at him for a second, then returned his smile and allowed herself to be pulled up. When she slammed her free hand into the wall next to Scorp, she felt him put his arm around her torso.

"Hold onto me," he said.

She took a deep breath. "Can you… can you make it?"

Scorp grunted. "No, but I will anyway."

Cat threw her injured arm around his neck and held on as tightly as she could as Scorp pulled his bone free and slammed it in again. Then she drew her bracer spikes out and allowed herself to be pulled up again. In this way they continued, working as one, until they heard a voice above them.

It was Lee. "Hey, up here!"

Their eyes rose toward the darkening sky, and they saw a hand flailing about above them, extending directly out of the rock wall.

Suddenly a head appeared beside it. "I found a cave! One of the bird nests, I think! Come up, and I'll pull you in!"

They both tried not to let the relief get to them, for they knew that once they did, the pain of their weary muscles would become overwhelming. Luckily, he was not too far above them, for they were barely able to make it up. Mantis reached down and pulled them up one at a time, over the lip of the cave and inside. Then they sat there together, panting as if they had just run all the way from Xarkopolis.

Scorp slowly released his grip on the bone in his hands. As it fell to the cave floor, he noticed how the tip had been broken and worn away. It was almost no use anymore, and he marveled that he had been able to make it at all. His hands were feeling the stress too; his fingers would barely move from their gripping position… and his arms seemed to be burning with the heat of a dozen starfire engines. He felt like he'd never be able to move again.

"You've been climbing all the way up here with *that*?" Lee exclaimed incredulously. "Are you insane?"

"I didn't… didn't get any bracers…" Scorp said between breaths. "Lots of the trainees didn't… I think we were… supposed to work… to work as teams…"

"And you didn't," Lee said flatly. "You must be a complete idiot." Then he laughed. "And a spectacular one too!"

Scorp blew out a sigh. "Well, I guess… I'm with you guys now. If you're willing to help me… Otherwise I'll need to find some new bones in here…"

Lee laughed and clapped him on the shoulder.

"Of course we'll help you," Cat said, "you crazy nut."

Scorp looked at her. Some of her hair had come loose during the struggle and was now whipping in front of her face. The soft light that was leaking into the cave served to frame her silhouette with a golden glow and light up her eyes. To a civilian on the street, she might have appeared dirty and plain, but Scorp couldn't help but wonder what she would look like if she were really cleaned up and…

He caught himself and stopped. These adolescent tendencies were supposed to have been burned out of them years ago in their training. Though the instructors didn't exactly want to discourage reproduction or the keeping of such perfect genes as the Enomegs' out of the gene pool, they also didn't want frivolous flirtations distracting them from their training. So they taught them discipline, to keep their base emotions under control. And of course, they punished any deviation from this discipline harshly.

But Scorp had never been very good at denying his emotions completely. *I really don't need a distraction like this right now*, he thought. But it was too late. He'd put his foot in.

"Okay," Scorp said, having almost forgotten his pain. "Let's go."

- CHAPTER FOUR -
PEACE ON NEW EARTH

There was no sound. Somehow, Rick Radcliff, Victorian Grand General though he was, never got used to the lack of sound in space. He was a ground man, more used to battle in the atmosphere with real gravity, not just artificial. As he stood there staring out of the hangar doors of CONON space station – the headquarters of the Council of Nations of Nova Refuge – the approaching Xarkon aerospace craft made no audible sound at all. It was like the approach of a hungry lion that refused to growl or roar... just stalking.

The sleek but heavily-armored Xarkon XVT-17 VIP transport floated lazily toward the station, skimming past the uppermost wisps of the atmosphere of Terra Nova below. It was escorted by a pair of Xarkon Crown-shaped Vidofnir medium fighters made of shining black duranium, complete with large crimson highlights. The transport between them, however, was solid black, with only a few markings in deep maroon and a name written along the sides: *Harbinger V*.

That was the name given to the personal transport craft of the High Commander of the Armed Forces of Xarkon. As Rick watched, the escort fighters broke off and the royal starship dropped slowly lower, its forward Starlight thrusters glowing slightly to slow its steady approach. The pilot was an expert of his craft, for the ship floated lazily through the force field over the hangar entrance. Now under the influence of the station's artificial gravity, the ship's lower thrusters lit and four claw-like landing gear extended, bringing it to rest on the gleaming metal floor.

Out of the back, a long boarding ramp lowered like a tongue, and down strode High Commander Lucas Mars, followed by a contingent of Xarkon Royal "Bloodguard," dressed in their deep maroon and gold uniforms, fashioned to look like modern, stylized versions of ancient Greek or Roman armor. These were the expert soldiers who normally guarded the Emperor on his public outings, but even among these hardy and disciplined soldiers, Mars seemed far superior, standing tall and erect in his crisp black uniform, his keen grey eyes glinting beneath his heavy brow.

Rick Radcliff himself was significantly less intimidating. He was of average height where Mars was a giant, and he lacked Mars's tangible air of superiority. Rick usually tried to keep his demeanor at least somewhat friendly when at a diplomatic meeting such as this, which was something Mars never bothered with, as evidenced by his current stony expression. In stark contrast, Rick had relatively kindly features and light, sandy brown hair. Today he was dressed in the standard navy blue uniform of the highest-ranking Victorian soldiers. He wore a pair of stark white gloves, and on his chest were pinned many medals celebrating his acts of heroism and superb leadership in battle.

The most singular aspect of Grand General Radcliff's appearance was the mirror-like visor he always wore. It looked similar to a pair of reflective silvery sunglasses with no frames, formed entirely of a single curved piece. Long ago, Rick had been infected by a strange alien disease while on a mission in the Outlook system. It had left him nearly blind, and now only his protective glasses, with their array of vision-enhancing lenses and other technology, kept him from losing his eyesight completely. In addition, the glasses also served as a HUD visor, allowing him to keep track of the movement of his troops while commanding on the field. And at dull political meetings like the one today, they at least allowed him to catch a few winks unnoticed.

Staring through these strange spectacles, Rick now watched Lucas Mars approach. The Victorian General forced his face to remain cordial so that he did not appear as emotionless as the man to whom he was speaking, but this proved difficult... since Rick utterly hated him.

"Good morning, High Commander," Rick said with a nod.

Mars did not return the nod as he replied, "You may refer to me as Mars, General Radcliff. Or even Lucas if you prefer. I respect you enough to allow that, though I doubt you respect me as much as you let on."

Mars's voice was deep and stern, the voice of a true military commander. To hear him speak was to hear the timeless power of military authority harkening back to the days when vast empires were forged by the hand of a single leader, riding at the forefront of his armies on the back of a mighty steed. Rick had always wished that he possessed such a powerful voice. He had often been praised for his speaking abilities, but his voice was better suited to speaking to politicians or the civilians of Victory than to his soldiers. His voice conveyed a feeling of trust and goodwill, where Mars's evoked feelings of respect and loyalty. In some ways, he envied Mars for it.

"I respect you due to your rank and as an individual for your exceptional skills and abilities," Rick replied at last.

"But you feel that my personality is lacking?" Mars asked, raising one of his low, dark eyebrows, which caused his forehead to wrinkle severely.

Rick looked back at the *Harbinger*. "Perhaps. But more than that, I simply feel that it is strange for a nation's Emperor not to attend such important meetings as this himself. Politicians should handle politics first, not military officers. But I already expressed my concerns on that subject."

"Well, you need express them no longer," Mars replied, "for the Emperor has decided to quit his sickbed and attend this meeting after all."

Mars took a step back and turned to look in the direction of his transport. There, descending the narrow ramp of the vessel, assisted by a naval officer, was Emperor Marius Orrick. Even though modern medicine allowed some individuals to live well past one-hundred TSCs, Marius Orrick had always been known for his poor health. He had gained the Crown when he was fifty, and now, at eighty-eight, he looked even frailer and weaker than ever. Apparently Orrick was aware of this, for when he reached the bottom of the ramp he shooed away his assistant and began walking with only the assistance of his long, slick black staff.

The Emperor of Xarkon was dressed in richly embroidered red robes with shimmering silver and gold ornamentations. Rick wondered vaguely how the old man was strong enough to carry such a burden of clothing – previous emperors had cared little for such superficial pomp. His face was lean and haggard, his pallid skin hanging limply from his bones. When he looked about, his sunken eyes surveyed the landscape from beneath drooping lids, and his thick grey hair was most likely false. Nevertheless, the two rows of royal guards that had followed Mars out of the dropship stood with heads bowed in respect as the Emperor passed before them.

When Mars left to follow his liege, Rick Radcliff turned back to join his own group, the Victorians, who stood gathered on the landing pad in front of their own aerospace craft. In the center of a circle of silver-armored Victorian guardsmen stood John Exsyl, Ordinator of Victory. Unlike the Emperor of Xarkon, Exsyl's power was not supreme. Governmental power was divided between him and Victory's elected parliament. Although centuries ago, Victory had once been under the grip of its own military dictators, Exsyl was a good-natured man with no interest in conquest.

"He is here," Rick said as he approached.

John Exsyl frowned. "Who?"

"Orrick. The Emperor of Xarkon is here."

"Here in the flesh?" Exsyl's forehead wrinkled as his eyebrows went up. "Well, that should make this meeting more interesting."

John Exsyl was a tall, handsome man for his age. He had thick, silvery white hair and a well-trimmed white beard. In the customary dark blue, well-tailored suit of a Victorian Congressman, he appeared to be a much more modern politician than the Emperor of Xarkon. He was also much fitter and healthier, standing tall and erect and striding confidently at the head of his guard as he made his way to the CONON Great Hall.

The central room of CONON station – the Great Hall – was a spectacle one never forgot in a lifetime, a true marvel of engineering and architecture. Imagine a space station with a great oval-shaped hole the size of a stadium cut perfectly through the center, with both the top and bottom of the hole closed off by immense transperium viewports, making the central area airtight. Inside, one could look up and see the stars of Human Space and the rest of the Nova Refuge galaxy, plus all of the universe… and upon looking down, there would lie the surface of Terra Nova itself: clouds floating lazily over vast oceans and landscapes dotted with cities.

Around the perimeter of this great round room was a walkway, attached to which were the platforms on which the representatives of each Human nation stood, surrounded by the flags of their country. Some of the platforms were below the walkway, some high above, depending on that group's status. The representatives of each nation spoke into microphones so that their voice was amplified throughout the room. Armed guards patrolled the corridors and platforms, wearing blank grey and white armor as a show of neutrality toward all nations, though everyone knew they were mostly Victorians. The personal bodyguards of the representatives were not allowed to carry ranged weapons – only ceremonial swords and pikes – and everyone had to pass extensive screening processes to enter.

There were dozens of platforms representing the many independent planets, colonies, and small countries in Human Space, but looming over all of them stood the great towers of the four most powerful Human factions, those that dominated the geography of Nova Refuge and controlled more off-world possessions than any other Human power… the Big Four: Victory, Xarkon, Yavakaro, and Zygbar. Victory and Xarkon were the two wealthiest and most powerful, but Yavakaro and even Zygbar were quite influential as well.

Zygbar, which rested on the southern half of the same continent as Xarkon, had the golden-orange Sun Dragon as their national emblem. Their leader was Chancellor Roscoe O'Donnel, a rather bloated and pompous fellow with a large black mustache. The medals that decorated his brown greatcoat were merely for show, as the dictator never truly fought any battles himself. He used propaganda to sway the people to support him, even as they themselves remained poor. Still, he was an expert politician and one of the most persuasive negotiators on the planet, and during his twenty-three years of rule he had almost singlehandedly raised Zygbar from a patch of dirt riddled with warring rebel factions to a country worthy of a seat on CONON.

The country of Yavakaro rested on the same continent as Victory, occupying its southern half. The emblem of Yavakaro was a unique one, containing much symbolism. Their flag was white on the upper half and dark purple on the lower half, and it bore the symbol of an open eye, peering over a range of mountains. Atop the eye were six yellow "eyelashes" that resembled beams of light. These lashes represented the six members of Yavakaro's oligarchic ruling council, known simply as The Six. They watched over the mountains below, which represented the land of Yavakaro.

The Six kept their identities a secret, concealing them behind their deep purple robes with cowls and masks. Although their names and faces remained hidden, one of the men always stood out… because of the pair of large grey wings sprouting from his back. Referred to in conversation as the Angel Councilman, this mysterious individual was the only Sarran who occupied any government station in the Big Four. He apparently represented the relatively small Sarran minority of Yavakaro.

The third tower, which belonged to Victory, was very metallic and angular in shape, like a great silver and blue crystal suspended in the air. Victory's symbol had always been a simple three-dimensional V: the V for Victory. It was into the council room with the large viewport at the top of this tower that Rick – along with Ordinator John Exsyl, some representatives from Parliament, and several bodyguards – now marched.

And finally, in the fourth tower, adorned with the crimson Crown of Xarkon, sat Emperor Orrick in his high golden throne, flanked by High Commander Mars and the Xarkon royal guard. A few political and military advisors stood behind them, but they rarely made any input. The other governors of Xarkon were nothing before the Emperor, just as the other leaders of the military – the "High Five," as they were called, in charge of the army, navy, aerospace force, and walker division – were nothing before the High Commander.

"So he really is here," John Exsyl said softly, staring across the room at Emperor Orrick. "The last of the Orrick dynasty shows himself again."

"The last?" Rick asked.

"That's right," Exsyl replied in a grave voice, which he masked with his cordial smile. "Orrick's son died in a hovercar crash just this morning. I wonder if the Emperor has even heard."

"How did you find out?" Rick asked, looking across at the old man, who was staring blankly at the floor in the Xarkon box, his head shaking slightly, while Mars stood beside him like a statue.

"I was informed by the Victorian police earlier. The young man crashed in Nutopia, Victory, while on a diplomatic mission. They don't know how it happened yet, but the investigation is already underway."

"Do you think they'll blame us?"

The Ordinator shrugged. "The Emperor might. Mars probably wouldn't, although he would insinuate that it could have been caused by the scheming of dishonorable politicians… That's me, you know. Now you, you're a general. You he's okay with."

"I'd rather he wasn't," Rick replied bluntly.

For over two years now, Emperor Marius Orrick had disappeared more and more from public life. He was gravely ill, reports said, and probably did not have much longer to live. During all this time, High Commander Lucas Mars had been the face and voice for Xarkon, filling in for the Emperor in nearly every important meeting, making speeches for him and announcing his decisions. He was finding it easy to control the will of the Emperor, since the old man was too weak to enforce his own. But Mars was a man of honor; he would not attempt to claim the crown until Orrick was dead, or perhaps if the Emperor dishonored it somehow.

The Victorians, especially Rick Radcliff, who hated Mars, had been longing for the day that Orrick's young son would take the throne and thus usurp the power that Mars now held. But now there suddenly was no heir. Who would wear the Crown of Xarkon after Marius Orrick died? The answer was obvious, and it bode ill for Victory. Mars was, above all, an honorable man… and he would honorably go to war with the "honorable" excuse of avenging the young prince's death. Or would he go to war simply to claim the glory of overthrowing Victory? Rick wasn't sure. No one was. As far as Rick knew, only one man truly knew Lucas Mars, and that was the man himself.

"The old dictator should have had more children, in his position," Exsyl said with a mirthless chuckle. "I have six myself, and I'm not even a monarch. Back in the old days, when the colonists first arrived after the Exodus, a high birth rate was encouraged to help off-world colonization efforts and defend against the Natives. These days we've gotten more complacent again. I wonder where that will lead us…"

Rick had apparently not been listening, for all he said was, "Mars hates us. He wants to destroy us."

"I think you misunderstand Mars's motives," Exsyl answered, in a soft voice. "He does not hate us. In fact, I actually believe that he does not hate anyone in this room, not even you. But he does love power. Mars respects anyone who can compete with him for power. He won't raise a hand against the Emperor, of course, but once he's out of the way…"

"Anything goes," Rick concluded solemnly.

"Quiet," Exsyl cautioned. "Here comes Howard Cohen."

Rick looked up. On one side of the vast room was a particularly tall seating box that was branded with the symbol of CONON, a globe with a pair of feathered wings embracing it. Howard Cohen stood at the top of this box, behind a podium. Cohen was a short, plump man who always seemed quite jovial. He was the coordinator for the CONON meetings, and he ensured that everything went as smoothly and peacefully as possible. To make doubly sure that he remained true to his role, he was not from any of the Big Four nations, but instead from the Republic of Apollo, a small country beside Yavakaro. Apollo had no military whatsoever, and they cared little for the affairs of other countries. All they wanted was peace. Since that was the purpose of CONON, Cohen made an excellent overseer of the meetings.

Howard Cohen smiled at the assembly and spoke, his voice filling the great hall. "Welcome, representatives, to this meeting of the Council of Nations of Nova Refuge!"

The term "CONON" had originally stood for "Council of Nations of Novaterra," the name of the planet being forced to coincide with an easily pronounceable acronym. When its influence spread off-world, its meaning was changed to a galactic scale and became "Council of Nations of Nova Refuge," though the abbreviation of CONON remained. This new name offended many Natives, since CONON hardly governed all of Nova Refuge, with Human Space comprising only about a third of the galaxy.

"Everyone is accounted for," Cohen went on, "except for the nation of Mordark, which is most unfortunate since we have business to discuss involving them… In fact, that is the first item I wish us to discuss. There is a bit of an incident now taking place in the city of Shardasha, Xarkon. So far, this is the information we have:

"A group of terrorists, believed to be composed of vengeful Natives, are holding the city of Shardasha for ransom. They claim that they have some way to destroy the city, literally wiping it off the map, unless Xarkon hands over a portion of their nation to them, consisting of one of the upper 'arm' peninsulas. Until this happens, they are not allowing civilians to leave the city. They have taken control of its perimeter defense network and are shooting down any vehicles that attempt to flee. Some Xarkonian citizens and soldiers have joined the rebels in an attempt to separate from the Xarkon Emp-"

"Unconfirmed rumors," interrupted the wavering voice of Emperor Orrick, who was now fixing Howard Cohen with the cold stare of death. All eyes shifted to him, but the old man hardly seemed to notice.

Cohen cleared his throat. "The Coordinators ask that Xarkon please hold her objections until we have finished introducing the situation."

"I simply wanted that to be noted as we begin," said Orrick, clearly used to being in complete control. "You may continue."

Cohen cleared his throat again and shifted a bit behind his podium before going on. "As I was saying, some Xarkonians *may* have joined with the terrorists in an attempt to separate from the Xarkon Empire. This information, however, *is not confirmed.* What is also not confirmed is who is leading this dissent. Two groups that were visiting the city at the time of the infraction are now our prime suspects.

"The first group is the 'Blackwings,' as they are called... a group of Sarran who have used questionable methods in the past when fighting for the supposed rights of their people to this planet around which we are now orbiting. Since the end of the Xenocide War, it has been illegal for such a coordinated group of Natives to hold meetings here outside the continent of Womloc. The Blackwings continue to do so, without the consent or support of the main Sarran government in Nova Refuge, the High Council of Harmony. Sources indicate that these Blackwings were holding a meeting in Shardasha at the time of the incident, so they are likely to be involved."

Rick shook his head slowly. He found it hard to believe this was the work of any group of Sarran, terrorist or otherwise. The Sarran were a proud but reclusive species of Natives widely regarded as beautiful but ice-cold by Humanity. In appearance, they hardly differed from the idyllic image of an angel: they looked from a distance like little more than Humans with bird wings extending from their back. Their features were sheer and angular, their ears pointed, and their skin unusually pale, sometimes appearing almost blue. Their feathers, on the other hand, came in a wide variety of colors, both dull and bright. There was no superfluous hair on their body, and even the "hair" sprouting from their head was light and feathery. Exceptionally tall and strong, a Sarran warrior was a match for any Human. They were used to living in cold climates, which was fitting, because it suited their personality.

The Sarran were simply cold... at least toward Humans and other species. They were haughty and uncaring, usually staying out of the affairs of others, almost as if others were beneath them. After the Xenocide War, during which many Sarran people, cities, and ships had been destroyed, they retreated from Human-controlled space almost entirely, leaving Humans largely to their own devices. Only a few estranged Sarran still lived on Terra Nova, and they mostly kept to themselves on Womloc, almost entirely cut off from the High Council of Harmony, which ruled over Sarran and Achmer-controlled space. The Blackwings may have been involved in some underhanded methods of warfare around the time of the Xenocide War, but that had been almost two-hundred years ago. Rick doubted they would start it all up again now.

"The second group in the city at the time of the incident were representatives of the country of Mordark, which, as you know, borders Xarkon. Lord Zegaldorph, the Mahlok who has ruled Mordark since 313 PA, was on a business trip in Shardasha when the incident occurred. It is possible he may have had a hand in it, or it is possible that he is actually just another victim. In any case, we do know that he and his cohorts never left the city…"

Rick Radcliff shook his head again, more strongly this time, so that Ordinator Exsyl would take notice. The Mahlok were perhaps the most powerful species of Natives in Nova Refuge, in control of a vast empire that they called the Helexith Coalition. Mahlok were of Human build and size, but the similarities ended there. Utterly hairless and with thick, rubbery, translucent red skin, the Mahlok were known as the People of the Flame, because not only could they absorb heat, but also create it, shooting fire from their very skin. With no facial features at all except for a pair of glowing yellow eyes, and with the bizarre patterns of black lines like natural tattoos that wound their way over their reddish skin, a Mahlok was an intimidating, if not terrifying sight.

As the two most powerful and influential Native species, the Sarran and the Mahlok had always hated each other, so it was highly unlikely that they were now working as allies. It was also unlikely that the Natives were doing this on their own. Their numbers on the main continents of Terra Nova after the end of the Xenocide War remained extremely small, mostly concentrated on the dark continent of Womloc. Without the backing of their galactic factions, Helexith or Harmony, the Natives on Terra Nova knew they were no match for the far larger Human nations.

Still, it was possible, if only remotely. The enforcement of the treaty that had ended the Xenocide War weakened year after year. Not only were there more Natives on the main continents now than ever before, but there were also Natives in positions of power in Human nations, in clear violation of the treaty. The most prominent examples were the Sarran member of Yavakaro's Council of Six and Zegaldorph, the Mahlok lord of Mordark, a small peninsula jutting off the northern coast of Xarkon. Zegaldorph had always been widely regarded as perhaps the only Mahlok ever to betray his own species, so it was possible he might have allied himself with the Blackwings, who had a similar reputation among the Sarran…

But the small size of Zegaldorph's domain and its proximity to Xarkon were the primary reasons that Rick had trouble believing Zegaldorph was behind this incident. His country shared borders with Xarkon and Xarkon alone, and it actually rested within a bay formed by Xarkon's large, curved "arm" peninsulas.

At this point, Rick spoke his mind. "I highly doubt that Zegaldorph has anything to do with this. He knows that if he were to anger Xarkon, they could easily conquer Mordark. So why would he be initiating this rebellion?"

"Because he wants more breathing space," answered the powerful voice of High Commander Lucas Mars, who was staring coldly across the room at Rick Radcliff. "As Cohen just mentioned, the rebels are demanding that we surrender one of the Arms of Xarkon, our largest peninsulas... a good portion of our territory. If Zegaldorph were to gain control of one of the Arms, it would put Mordark in a much better position to be free of our influence."

Ordinator John Exsyl raised an eyebrow as he looked at Mars from across the vast stadium of CONON. "So you honestly believe that Lord Zegaldorph is trying to do this," he asked, "by taking a single city hostage?"

Mars shook his head slowly. "I am saying that we should not deny the possibility. At the moment, all that really concerns me is taking steps to regain control of Shardasha from these... terrorists."

"Rebels." Chancellor Roscoe O'Donnel of Zygbar broke in, rolling the R as was his habit, though his precise accent remained unidentifiable and possibly fake. "Terrorists is just a political term for rebels."

"It is a term," Mars rebuked sharply, "for cowards who refuse to fight wars directly, and instead..."

Rick interrupted, saying, "Do you think that any rebels would be stupid enough to fight with Xarkon directly?"

"No." Mars replied, and Rick thought he saw the High Commander flash a quick, smug half-smile as he said it. "No, they would not."

"That is the trouble with the modern world..." Roscoe mused aloud, leaning the bulk of his body back farther in his chair and staring up reflectively at the stars beyond the ceiling. "As the cohesion of Humanity increases and governments become more widespread and pervasive, more closely allied, the influence of the opposing minority grows smaller and less powerful by comparison. In order for the minority to battle those in power, they must do so unfairly, since they could never engage them in the open, lacking the influence, wealth, and technology to do so. And so, our own attempts at world peace, at world government, have created those we call 'terrorists.' We really have no one to blame for their existence but ourselves. We label them as terrorists merely because they fight using the only means that we leave available to them. Highly ironic, isn't it?"

Mars frowned. Rick could feel the tension between the two men. Roscoe was only defending his people's way of life; Zygbar was always in a state of chaos, with various groups constantly fighting for control or for "freedom." Most of the time, they were too small to gather sizeable armies, so they resorted to terrorism. It was this terrorism that had won Zygbar its independence twenty-eight years ago, when the Sun Dragon Rebellion successfully ended seven decades of Xarkonian rule. Roscoe now sat at the helm of what had once been that Sun Dragon Rebellion, so he had to show support for the methods of his people. Behind the cunning dictator, his generals and guards nodded in grave agreement.

Howard Cohen reflexively raised his arms into the air in an attempt to draw attention to himself. "Let us not take the debate off onto a tangent. At any rate, the dispute in question is whether or not Xarkon should be allowed to take military action against the rebels in Shardasha. As High Commander Mars said, they are technically terrorists, and taking action against terrorists within one's own nation is perfectly legal under the terms of the Pax Nova. However, there is more to consider. The terrorists are currently in complete control of Shardasha and its defensive turret grid. That city's population is very large. So large, in fact, that if Xarkon were to attack it directly, they would be violating rule one of the Pax Nova, unless they acted with permission given by a majority vote here in CONON."

The holographic viewscreens below the representative podiums now displayed the visage of Lucas Mars, his brow furrowed in thought. Rick studied his features, looking for some sign of derision or disgust. He knew Mars had no respect for the document known as the Pax Nova, which had been created and signed by the Big Four shortly after Xarkon joined CONON in 308 PA. The Pax Nova stated, simply put, that due to the danger of alien aggression and to sustain Humanity's place as a galactic power, no Human nation was ever again to attack another Human nation without the permission of the council, or all the member nations would unite against the aggressor. Rick saw it as a perfect goal to strive for. Mars saw it as a pipe dream.

"The question of whether or not the… rebels are truly in control of the city is also in doubt," said Lucas Mars. "Technically, they have not taken control of its actual *government*. They are not trying to rule the city; they are merely holding it and its people for ransom."

"So why not go ahead and attack them?" asked Rick Radcliff, speaking on a sudden impulse. "Why are you even requesting permission, when they are so clearly terrorists?"

Mars turned his head, slowly and coolly, to face General Rick Radcliff. "Because," he said, "we want to make sure that our intent does not provoke an adverse reaction from the other members of CONON."

Right, Rick thought. *You don't want to go to war yet, do you, Mars? Not until you're good and ready.*

"Which is what you should do!" shouted Howard Cohen, nodding rapidly. "So, if there are no further questions, I propose that nations' leaders begin the vote…"

"I have a question," said one of the members of Yavakaro's Council of Six, a young Asian woman obscured in violet robes. "What about the leader of this rebellion? Once it is discovered who is leading the terrorists, there should be another vote before Xarkon is allowed to take action against this leader. After all, if the leader *does* turn out to be Zegaldorph, then this would most definitely be an act of war and a breach of the Pax Nova."

At this comment, Roscoe O'Donnell gave a laugh. "An act of war? Zegaldorph is acting completely outside of Mordark. If he really is leading these terrorists, then he has forfeited his leadership of that nation quite completely. And there will always be others to take his place."

"Unless the other governors of Mordark are in on this," commented Yavakaro's Sarran councilman in an even voice, shaking his masked head.

The great grey wings on the councilman's back flexed in and out, as if to reiterate their presence. Clearly, he did not like the anti-Native direction that this meeting was taking. A thought that had been bothering him suddenly struck Rick Radcliff with renewed clarity: if Zegaldorph did turn out to be the leader of the terrorists, and the Xarkonians were to kill him, then that would leave Mordark open to conquest by Xarkon. The Grand General whispered this observation in the ear of Ordinator Exsyl beside him.

John Exsyl nodded. He then turned and spoke to the other representatives. "I agree with the councilman of Yavakaro. If this council agrees to let Xarkon take action against these rebels, then there must be a clause added to the agreement. If Xarkon discovers Zegaldorph is truly behind this incident, they must not take this as permission to begin a war with Mordark. This may be out of that nation's hands entirely. They are, after all, not represented in this council at present. And the tendency at meetings is, as they say, to blame whoever is not in the room."

At that moment, Rick noticed Lucas Mars glance in his direction. Though Mars's facial expression barely changed, Rick perceived a sudden and almost tangible hostility aimed in his direction. Mars must have seen him whisper to Ordinator Exsyl, Rick thought. Perhaps he had hit nearer the truth than he had first suspected.

Mars's nostrils flared visibly as he said, "Is the idea of war in response to an underhanded attack by a hostile nation really so –"

"Oh, enough," interrupted the listless voice of Emperor Orrick from where he sat below Mars. "We agree to these terms, Cohen. Xarkon will not attack Mordark."

Mars stiffened and stared straight ahead, across the room. Rick wondered vaguely if he were repressing anger at this interruption from his Emperor, or if this was his way of showing respect and obedience. Rick guessed it was the former. He highly doubted Mars respected anyone enough to show them true obedience.

The Emperor went on. "We do, however, request permission to eliminate Zegaldorph, if it turns out that he is acting alone and in charge of the terrorist rebels."

"Only," said Ordinator Exsyl, "if absolutely clear incriminating evidence is provided."

The Emperor waved his hand. "Of course."

Howard Cohen nodded. "Very well; the terms have been set forth. Now, if all nations would please discuss the situation among their own representatives, and then cast their vote."

The dull murmur of low voices immediately filled the room as the representatives began discussing the decision. Rick saw the Yavakarese Six huddled in a circle, talking rapidly. Roscoe was speaking in hushed tones to his most trusted war leader, General Azar Khan. Even the representatives from the other, smaller nations were debating the subject. Only the Emperor and the High Commander of Xarkon remained silent. Mars stared blankly across the room like a statue, while the Emperor had once again slumped back in his chair and was staring at the surface of Terra Nova through the great viewport below, apparently lost in thought. John Exsyl turned to the other occupants of the Victorian booth:

the small parliamentary council of which he was the head, who were seated on two long benches behind him and Rick.

The Ordinator addressed his fellow politicians. "I am prepared to cast the vote to allow Xarkon to take action. Do any here oppose?"

The parliament simply stared at him. Finally a senator near the front said, "We're all behind you, John."

"Thank you," Exsyl said, and then he nudged Radcliff. "So... what do you think, Rick?"

Rick turned to regard the Ordinator. Exsyl was always very frank and open with his allies, and in return they gave him their trust. So Rick answered him with equal frankness.

"I think we should vote against it. I have a sneaking suspicion that Mars is hiding something from us. In fact, I think he's even hiding it from his own Emperor. Did you see how he acted when Orrick interrupted him?"

Exsyl nodded, almost amusedly. "Yes, I suppose I did notice that. But I do not think that was what you interpret it to be. It merely startled him. It startled me as well. I did not expect the Emperor to interrupt his own High Commander, who had stood in his place for so long. No, Rick, I think you're interpreting all of Mars's actions according to your own personal feelings toward him. You should not let your feelings cloud your judgment."

"Sir," Rick answered somewhat stiffly, "feelings are a very important part of judgment."

Exsyl gave a chuckle and nodded. "Yes, in many ways they are, that's true. But my own feelings on this subject are equally strong. Victory cannot take a position that would be supporting terrorism, Rick. The Emperor agreed not to attack Mordark. If we voted against this action, we would be setting a bad precedent."

Rick blew out a sigh. He hated politics. Some people likened politics to a battlefield, but in Rick's mind, it was all nothing but a game show... a game show played by careful politicians, and things like these "precedents" were the rules. Even when a politician was confronted by hard facts and plain truth, he had to dance around them in order to play by the rules of his game.

"The Council of the Six of Yavakaro casts its vote in favor of this action," said a voice from across the room.

"You're right," Rick said to John Exsyl, reluctantly relenting. "I guess you're right."

John Exsyl rose to a standing position and spoke in his clearest voice: "The nation of Victory casts its vote in favor of this action."

Zygbar soon joined Yavakaro and Victory, followed by the other small nations. Once the Big Four led the charge, the others always followed. That was the way things worked in Human Space. From the planet swirling about below them to the stars wheeling overhead, those four towers decided the future of mankind. Or so they thought, at least.

"The action is passed," said Howard Cohen, smiling and bobbing up and down. "Now, on to the next order of business..."

Rick Radcliff looked across at Mars. The High Commander had finally taken a seat now, and he sat staring at the far wall, turned away from the meeting hall. Clearly, the only question of today's council that he was truly concerned about was the Shardasha incident. All of his thought was concentrated on it. And that was what had Rick worried.

But for the moment, he tried to shake such suspicions from his mind. After all, he still had the rest of a long and tiresome political meeting to sit through. He glanced at the agenda. Most of it was the same old garbage that politicians had been debating for decades... perhaps centuries.

"The more things change..." Rick muttered, settling back in his chair and closing his eyes, "the more they stay the same."

"And the next issue on the table..." Howard Cohen's amiable voice announced, "virtual reality simulations! Are they to blame for the outbreaks of violence in our planet's educational centers?"

- CHAPTER FIVE -
THE TEST OF HONOR

Like ants ascending the trunk of a tree, the Enomegs climbed with stunning rapidity up the side of the lonely mesa that watched over the Enomeg Training Academy Base in the Ukrak plains of Xarkon. But among all of these young men and women, one individual stood out as he climbed, hand over hand, foot over foot, with stunning grace, speed, and expert precision.

Luke Blood-Raven knew he was the best. It was partially this satisfaction that allowed him to remain so cool-headed in combat. The first rule of conflict, above all else, was to keep one's head, and Luke was an expert at that. It was only in more peaceful settings that he tended to let his anger get the best of him. When he knew he was not allowed to cut his enemy down with either bullets, swords, or a few well-placed strikes of the fist… then he had trouble holding his temper. His home was on the battlefield, and only there did he feel comfortable. Only there did he reign supreme.

At least, for now.

And for now, he wanted nothing more than to cut down Saber-Scorpion. Most of the Enomeg trainees were entirely concentrated on simply finishing their tests and assignments, in an attempt to survive the trials and become Enomeg soldiers. But Luke considered himself above that. He knew he could pass the trials… it was *everyone else* that he truly concentrated on passing, both in rank and skill. There were only two ranks among the Enomegs: the commander, and the others. So far, there had only ever been one commander, and the plan seemed to be to assign one commander per phase. He was determined to be the one.

And only one individual seemed able and willing to stop him: Justin Saber-Scorpion.

Raven was jarred from these thoughts when he finally reached the top of the mesa, pulled himself up into the light of the setting sun… and ran directly into Seth. The young man's red hair shone like fire, backlit as it was by the sunset. He scowled at Luke.

"I saw what you did to Daniel!" he shouted.

"Look, kid," Luke said, "I really don't want to fight you. It'd slow me down too much."

Seth's eyes burned as brightly as his fiery hair. "This is the test of *honor!* Where is the honor in what you did?"

"Honor," Raven said coolly, "is always awarded to the victor. But if you understood that, you would be running ahead instead of trying to fight me. So let's just settle this quick…"

Raven was actually on the verge of charging him when they heard a strange clattering sound coming from the bushes that grew atop the mesa. Staring into the shadows, which were growing deeper and deeper as New Sol sank down over the horizon, the Enomeg trainees spotted something glittering between the leaves and branches. It looked like eyes reflecting the deep red light of the setting sun… only there were far more than a pair of them. As the branches of the bushes swayed in the wind, they heard the clacking sound grow louder, like the movement of armored legs.

Seth shot a furtive glance toward Raven. "You don't think…"

"They'll be all around us soon…" Raven breathed, looking around for something to use as a weapon.

"They can't be – Dark-Dragon wouldn't lead us into a full-blown Skrakki hive, not alone like this. No infantry unit this small could infiltrate a coordinated hive. They've probably already cleaned this nest out and just left us to fight the stragglers… Right?"

"And maybe the stragglers rebuilt the swarm. And maybe a new colony spore landed here overnight. And maybe it doesn't matter at all since *we've got to survive it.*"

Seth turned and saw Raven sharpening a stick with the blades on his climbing bracers. The star student's brow was wrinkled with concentration, and his cool grey eyes did not even look up to meet Seth's inquisitive glance.

"That won't…" Seth started to protest, but Raven cut him short.

"I don't expect this twig to punch through a Skrakki exoskeleton, but I do expect it to at least make the bug keep its distance until I can hit it with these bracers or kick it. And if you just plan to stand there and watch then I'll do the same to you once I'm finished."

"Actually, my plan was more along the lines of hiding."

"Sounds about right," Raven said, finishing up his spear and twirling it hand over hand. "You just run along then."

Holding the primitive weapon out before him, the young man advanced toward the brush. Seth ran his hands through his hair and sighed nervously. He knew he could not just abandon a fellow Enomeg in a situation like this. In fact, he never really considered it. Apparently Raven did not expect him to either.

"You go around and jump on it from behind," Raven said, "if you want to help, that is."

"I'll do it, I'll do it. Moving…"

As quietly as he could, Seth bounded over the brush and through the shrubbery. Keeping his eye on the shining exoskeleton of the creature patiently waiting between him and Raven, hidden though it was in the shadow of the tall bushes, he made his way around to what he estimated must be its back. His own breathing sounded heavily in his ears as he lifted his climbing bracers, pointing their spikes outward, ready to pounce.

"Now!" he heard Raven shout.

Seth sprang out like a silent leopard uncoiling toward its prey. With precision and strength, he slammed his bracer spikes into the creature's back, putting all the weight of his flight into the blow in order to break the Skrakki's legendarily thick carapace. He was rewarded with the snap of chitin and the clatter of falling legs… but not with the feeling of striking flesh or spurting blood. Indeed, the creature simply fell out from under him like a pile of old bones. As Seth stood up from the mess and brushed himself off, he realized that was exactly what it was: a skeleton. It was a shed exoskeleton left behind by a growing Skrakki guard possibly months ago.

And Raven, of course, was nowhere to be seen.

It seemed to take hours, but finally Scorp, Cat, and Mantis made it to the top. Mantis was the first to pull himself up, and then he helped up his companions. Together, they collapsed on the grassy turf in exhaustion. After passing through the aptly-named blades of the Ukrak grasses on the plains below, the green foliage atop this mesa was like lying on a cloud. It had been a long, hard climb, especially with Scorp sharing climbing bracers with Cat.

Saber-Scorpion blew out a sigh and stared at the stars beginning to shine through above. The last rays of New Sol were now receding from view, and the galaxy of Nova Refuge lay sprawled out overhead. In one corner hung the beautiful and mysterious three-armed sister galaxy of the Refuge, called Nova Shelter. Some might say that its tentacles grasped at the night sky like those of a twisted sea star, sparkling with bits of sand. But Scorp thought it looked like an enormous bladed *shuriken*, or some nasty Slashrim weapon. Everything was a weapon to an Enomeg trainee.

But this was no time for stargazing. Scorp turned his head to see Cat resting, looking almost asleep. But where was Mantis?

Then he heard footsteps behind him, followed by Mantis's voice. "Scorpion… I scouted partway around the edge of the mesa. Most of the other students are already up here. We had better get moving if you want to find that prize, my friend."

Scorp and Cat got to their feet and looked around. The top of the mesa was completely flat, but it was covered in a growth of bushes and scrubby trees.

The other trainees must be wandering somewhere in all of that, he though, searching for the crown. They could be anywhere, nearly impossible to detect and certainly impossible to track.

"Someone's surely found it by now," Cat said. "We took forever getting up here."

"Possibly," Scorp replied, but he walked on anyway.

Now that he was no longer toiling up a mountainside, Scorp suddenly realized that he was angry... partially with himself, but mostly at his instructors. Why hadn't they given him a fair chance? How was he supposed to prove himself with no climbing equipment, without resorting to dishonorable methods as Raven had done?

The fact that they had sent him up the river without a paddle was no surprise; he'd been there plenty of times and gotten back, but the fact that everyone *else* had a paddle made him indignant. He would have expected such treatment as *punishment*, but this was no time to be punishing him, in what Dragon had called the Test of Honor...

"Could have just beaten me with a stick like in the old days..." he muttered aloud.

Cat was not sure what he was talking about, but apparently she was eager for conversation. "That's nothing," she said. "What about when they make you beat *yourself* with the stick? You want to save yourself some pain, so you try not to hit hard, but you know if you don't hit hard enough, *they'll* step in and help out. One time the mere thought of it made me nearly break my own leg with the damn club..."

Mantis nodded, with a knowing expression in his dark eyes. "I think that Scorpion here is already beating himself up as we speak."

Cat looked up. "What?"

"Come on, my friend," Mantis said, giving Scorp a friendly punch on the shoulder. "Even if you do not 'win' this assignment, you have still proven yourself more than sufficiently honorable. Perhaps that is the real test, yes?"

Scorp nodded, but now he was concentrating on the task at hand: searching. He could tell that there was a clearing ahead, so he slowed his movements, trying to stay silent. Using the standard Enomeg sign language code, he signaled to the others to be quiet as well. They understood completely, and almost disappeared from even his senses after he gave the signal. They were truly experts at stealth, he thought. The fact that they were still able to follow him showed that he was not quite at their level of expertise in that particular skill.

Finally, he reached the edge of the clearing. They were in the very center of the plateau now, he judged. Here in the middle was a large, circular clearing that had been cut away and trampled into dirt. There were tracks everywhere; small, claw-like scratches. As Scorp walked out farther into the circle, he noticed a large hole in the center, leading down into a dark cave. There were footprints in the soft earth near it... not the claw-marks of Native creatures, but Human boots. One of the other trainees had already gotten here.

"Probably Raven," Scorp said aloud.

"What?" Mantis asked, suddenly appearing from the brush to walk up behind him, followed closely by Cat.

"Luke… he's already been here," Scorp explained.

Lee looked down into the hole and whistled. "What do you suppose this place is? It's very dark down there. We are likely to be eaten by a Groo."

Cat gave him an incredulous look. "A what?"

"It's some kind of Slashrim superstitious nonsense," Scorp explained quickly. "Now come on, you two, and cut the chatter."

Scorp jumped down into the hole. Inside was an underground tunnel, perfectly round, lit by a soft glow coming from a row of mysterious round lights imbedded in the ceiling. There were markings on the walls, written in a language none of them could recognize, and strange sounds echoed faintly down the corridors. Then came a sound that was not so faint: a distant screeching, so high-pitched that it threatened to crack the listener's skull. *KEE-EEE-EEE…*

"What… was that?" Cat asked in a whisper.

"Skrakki," Scorp replied matter-of-factly.

"It couldn't be - they'd have been all over us by now!"

"Hm, yes…" Mantis put in. "I thought I saw the crushed exoskeleton of one outside… and the grove atop this mesa is typical of their gardens."

A smile crept over Scorp's face. "Well, if there are Skrakki here, then they're after the first intruder, Raven, not us. He's cleared us a path… Come on! Let's find that crown, fast!"

Without another word, the three of them set off at a run, especially when they heard the footsteps of another trainee approaching outside. As they continued, the tunnel began to break off into smaller corridors and alcoves, many of which were covered in a foamy green residue.

When they rounded another corner, they heard a faint clittering overhead and stopped in their tracks. Looking up, they beheld nothing more than a small, cat-sized, beetle-like worker Skrakki, apparently injecting some kind of bioluminescent liquid through its proboscis into the lights overhead. It paid not the slightest bit of attention to them as it continued about its work.

"We passed several hallways full of dead lights," Cat said, gingerly touching the small creature, which paused to run its antennae over her fingers. "I think the Skrakki abandoned this place a long time ago, or else it'd have better maintenance. All we see here are the stragglers."

"Let's just keep moving," Scorp commanded.

Cat pointedly paused to inspect the creature a while longer, as it ran its feelers over her arm and face. Impatient, Scorp signaled for Mantis to follow and ran on ahead. The two of them had barely gone twenty meters before they heard a chittering sound, followed by a long cry: *skrak-kak-kak-KEE-EEE-EEE…*

Not far ahead, the creature calmly stood, illuminated from above by the dim bioluminescent bulbs and by its own strangely glowing yellow-green flesh, visible in the cracks between its natural armor. Its sleek exoskeleton was covered in sharp black barbs and spines, and the head that hung low between its long, blade-like arms featured not two, but *five* sharp mandibles. As they watched, these claw-like mouthparts slowly opened, and an acidic green substance dripped out, sizzling on the floor.

"A guardian," Mantis said. "We should charge him together."

"Now!" Scorp shouted.

The two of them crouched low as they ran, successfully avoiding the acidic saliva that jetted overhead where they had just been standing. Once he was close enough, Mantis stood up and landed a downward-swinging kick right between the creature's multifaceted eyes. It did not cry out in pain, but continued to repeat its long call of *skrakakakaKEEEEEEE...* though no other Skrakki arrived to aid it. It took a scissor-like two-armed swipe at both of the Enomegs, who ducked and rolled back out of the way, though Scorp heard Mantis hiss in pain when the blades grazed his back.

Scorp dodged a stab from one of the razor-sharp arms, and then rolled in low and grabbed the inner joint of the appendage. The creature was not terribly strong. With relative ease, he was able to force the leg backward toward the creature's head. Its mouthparts began to open, so Scorp quickly sidestepped, jerking the arm with him. The acid this time landed directly on the beast's own limb, burning through the exoskeleton and allowing Scorp to break the leg free.

He may have been stabbed then by the Skrakki's other arm had not Mantis copied his earlier technique, rolling in and grabbing the blade before it could strike. Then Saber-Scorpion, wielding the broken leg like a spear, shoved the tip of it into the Skrakki's throat. Glowing yellow-green blood splattered onto the floor as the Skrakki's last cry echoed through the corridor... and its body curled up on the tunnel floor.

Mantis looked at the corpse thoughtfully. "They must make the call with their wings, since he was still able to sing after you... Hey, wait!"

Scorp was already on the move again. The tunnel ahead was completely dark; the lights on the ceiling apparently had not been cared for in some time. As he ran blindly along, Scorp's other senses took over. He felt the walls with his hands, smelled the dampness in the air, and heard the footsteps of Mantis catching up behind him, as well as Cat's voice faintly telling them to slow down. Then he suddenly heard a sound ahead of him, barely a meter away: *skrakkeeee...*

Scorp stopped dead in his tracks. "Great."

"Wait!" he heard Cat shout behind him.

As he slowly stepped backward, Scorp felt her brush past him. He tried to grab her arm and stop her, but she was too quick. Then a strange sound came that made all of them pause. It was the sound of the massive Skrakki, dead ahead, faintly buzzing in a low, contented way, almost as if it were purring. After a second, the creature simply shuffled off, and they heard it leave down another of the tunnels.

"What did you do, Cat?" Mantis asked.

"While you guys just rushed ahead without thinking, I got the little worker to climb onto my arm. Once the guard ran its feelers over him..."

"Great thinking, Cat," Scorp interrupted, "but you can give us the details later. Let's go!"

Cat blew out a sigh as she and Mantis fell into a jog behind their leader. A little light was beginning to filter in now, and Scorp could clearly see the footprints of an Enomeg trainee in the green residue on the floor ahead… right past the massive semi-unconscious form of Gun-Barracuda, whose head appeared to have been bashed into the wall several times. He was still groaning, so it must have been recent. Without stopping to check on him, Scorp broke into a run, making his way recklessly down the tunnel. Cat and Mantis rushed to keep up with him, their footsteps echoing through the hall.

Suddenly Scorp reached a large opening in the cave, and a flying elbow almost connected with his face. He drew back just in time, receiving only a slight blow to the forehead instead of a broken nose. He then backed up a step and rolled forward, right past Raven and into the main room. When he stood up, he saw a rune-covered pedestal at the far end of the cave, on which sat the bronze replica of the Crown of Xarkon. He started to run, but Raven lunged at him from behind and caught his foot, tripping him. Scorp fell to the ground, wrestling to get free while Luke wrestled to get ahead of him.

It was then that Cat and Mantis entered the room. Raven heard them and was sent into a panic. He clawed at Scorp's face, and then rose up quickly, shaking off Scorp's attempt to restrain him. Before any of them could stop him, he was there at the foot of the pedestal. The illumination from the single functioning light in the room surrounded him, projecting a halo around his silhouette. And then Luke turned… and set the Crown upon his head.

Scorp, who was still charging at him, stopped in his tracks and looked up. At first he felt only rage; rage at Raven for reaching the prize first, and more rage at him for having the audacity to place the crown on his own head. Then, however, a strange thought struck him, as he stared at Luke… The crown seemed to suit him. The Crown of Xarkon, despite the ugly, tarnished bronze color of the replica, added an undeniable air of regality to Luke's already princely features.

The desire to swing a hard right at his opponent's face gradually left Scorp's mind and was replaced by a slight feeling of respect, mingled with jealousy. He suddenly wished that he had followed Luke's example and run off alone. Either way, Luke had the crown now, and Scorp was not going to try to stop him. He had won. Cat and Mantis glanced at Scorp, who stood panting, wiping the blood off his face.

Cat's eyes narrowed. "We aren't going to let you get out of here with that."

"Yes," Mantis said, putting his hand up before her, "we are. He won. Dragon said whoever reached the Crown first was the winner. There is no more we can do."

Cat shot him a look that clearly said: *surely you must be joking?* Suddenly, the sound of clapping echoed through the small room. They turned to see a figure emerging from the shadows to their left. It was Dark-Dragon, still clad in his fearsome onyx and blood-red Enomeg armor.

"You did well," Dragon said.

Raven grinned. "Thank you, sir."

71

Dragon shook his head. "And yet, sadly, you have forfeited your success for failure…"

Raven's joy turned to confusion. "Wh-what?"

"Idiot! Did I not tell you this was the Test of *Honor?*" Dark-Dragon shouted.

His hand shot out like a whip and smacked the crown off Luke's head, sending it clattering across the room.

"What?!" Raven said again, angrily this time.

"First you beat up the other students like a common bully, trick them, leave comrades to die, and then you do *this?* You were told to *find* the crown, not *take* the crown! You have put the symbol of the Emperor upon your own head! You have taken, claimed to *be* that which you *serve!*"

"I…"

"This is treachery just as any other treachery," Dark-Dragon went on, walking around the trainee in a circle now. "In fact, worse. By betraying what you swore to serve, you have forfeited your victory in this competition."

"But you said nothing of such a rule!" Raven shouted back angrily.

"Silence!" Dragon roared. "You should *know* this rule, and I have not given you permission to speak!"

"You can't just –"

In a flash, Dragon was upon him. His fist connected solidly with Luke's stomach. The young man did not even have time to react. He doubled over and stumbled backwards, hitting the pedestal with the small of his back. With a growl, he stood up again. For a moment he looked as if he would return Dark-Dragon's attack. But, with an effort, he suppressed this urge and simply closed his eyes. His head sank.

"Do you understand what I just told you, soldier? Do you understand?!"

"Yes, sir…" Raven said under his breath.

"If you don't learn some simple respect and obedience, Luke, then you will forfeit far more than your victory in this contest. With an attitude like that, you will never become an Enomeg at all. Now, listen to me. I could beat you up some more, and you have *no idea* what a good job I could do… but I know it would do no good. The thing you have to understand is this: There are many aspects to these tests. I am not just testing your ability to carry out orders and successfully complete missions. I am testing your honor… and your loyalty as well. These tests weigh your skills and your personality; they reveal your true colors. Are they red, like the honorable blood of Xarkon? Or are they yellow as a coward, or green with envy and greed?"

After a pause, the Enomeg commander finished: "Now… put the Crown back on the pedestal."

Scorp hadn't realized it, but he had backed up several paces. Cat and Mantis had as well. Something deadly serious in Dragon's tone, as sharp and real as a steel blade, had intimidated them. They were not about to get involved in this dispute. They merely observed as the proudest of the Enomeg trainees, Luke Blood-Raven, humbly crouched in the corner and retrieved the bronze crown.

72

With the utmost reverence, he set the symbol back upon the stone altar. He looked up at his commander.

Dragon's voice was as cold as the mountains of Ecirron, the frozen homeworld of the Sarran people, as he commanded, "Bow to it."

For a second, Luke's expression changed to outrage. But one glance up at Dark-Dragon cowed him once more. With clenched fists, he dropped to one knee, and then lowered the other. He then proceeded to prostrate himself before the pedestal. Scorp shook his head in amazement. As he did so, he noticed something out of the corner of his eye... Mantis was also bowing. He was on his knees, his eyes locked on the Crown. Cat noticed too; she bit her lip and kneeled. Scorp stood for one second longer, watching as Dark-Dragon carefully placed the replica of the Crown into a black box. Then, before the commander could turn and see him still standing, Scorp too dropped to his knees. He felt all of his pride fall with him.

"Good," said Dark-Dragon, looking around the room.

Following his gaze, Scorp noticed that they had been joined by a few others: Seth was standing in a corner, and Coyote and Cobra were also there, supporting Kade Gun-Barracuda's semi-unconscious body between them. Dark-Dragon nodded to them, and then began pacing. He removed his helmet and ran a hand over his graying black hair. In the dark cave, the contrast of the lighting outlined the multiple scars on his face with shadow.

"You know what the creatures you fought today were, of course," he said. "The Slashrim call them 'Skrakki,' after the sound that they sometimes make when calling for help. They actually only do this in dire situations, since normally they can communicate nonverbally through the neural network they form with other members of the hive. The Skrakki are quite literally a hive-mind; when together, they think as one unit, with no need for a leader or a central brain. The more there are, the smarter they all become. Even the 'queens' as we call them are really just used for reproduction. They have none of the dictatorial power their name implies.

"The Skrakki are an insect-like species, uniquely able to spread colonies onto other planets using egg-pods launched into space from the largest hive-worlds. It was on one such planet, in a hive much like this one, but far, far larger, that my platoon and I were stuck for three weeks. We weren't expecting the Skrakki hives to be there when we dropped in; the main hive had been bombed from orbit months ago, so the most we expected to find were a few confused and stupid stragglers like the ones you encountered here. We were actually hunting a band of rebels that we suspected were using the caves there as a hideout.

"What we found was a brand new hive in the process of being built. The Skrakki weren't as coordinated without a central mind or queen, but they were still deadly. The flying ones they call Virasps shot down our dropship, preventing us from escaping, and then the digger-worms – I don't know what they're called – caved in the tunnels so we couldn't even get to the light of day. For weeks, we wandered the hive, avoiding and killing Skrakki as we went. It was dark, it was disgusting, and it was like nothing we had ever experienced before... like nothing any Human was *meant* to experience.

"A pair of Slashrim mates – slaves, of course – were supposed to guide us, since they had fought the Skrakki years ago... but when the male got killed, the female went into a berserk rage and left us behind. We later found her dead atop a heap of Skrakki she'd ripped to shreds with her bare claws. The Humans were already mostly dead by then. Some had been killed by Skrakki, others by terrain, since not all the tunnels were very stable, and still others from exhaustion or starvation before it was all over with.

"The worst ones, however, were the ones who just couldn't take the strain. They snapped, started raving, and many of them just ended it the quickest way they could. One of my best friends in the platoon, trying to save all of his ammo for us to use later, took his own life with a severed Skrakki claw he'd been carrying around his neck to take home as a souvenir. I still have it in my quarters. In the end, the only thing that got back out of there alive... was me.

"For days afterward, I argued with myself over what had caused all of my teammates to die while I carried on. Was it my fault for not doing all I could to save them? Had they not been trained well enough? Was it their equipment? Was it simple luck, or fate? Finally I struck upon the cold, hard truth of the matter: they just *didn't have what it takes*. Some of it may have been luck or training, but for most of them, especially the ones who just lost it... they died because they were not *meant* to be soldiers, not *born* with the will to survive in combat. And that is why I started the Enomeg project. You, all of you, *were* born to be soldiers. Now, enough talk. I have some climbing bracers here for those of you who did not get a set. It's up to you how you get out of here. Dismissed."

Scorp could not help but think that he had never heard a man give a speech of such emotion without once changing his expression or altering the inflection of his voice. And even now, he did not move, standing still as a statue. Without another word, the trainees filed out of the cave, as Dragon disappeared into the shadows again behind them. For a moment, they all stood silently, exchanging glances. Raven was the first to stalk off, followed by Barracuda once he found he could walk again.

Scorp blew out a sigh as he strapped on the bracers Dragon had given him. "Well, looks like we have to find our own way out of here. Up or down?"

"The climb or the promise of more Skrakki?" Coyote mused. "I think I'll take the climb."

"Aw," Cat said, as she stroked the beetle-like worker that was still clinging to her arm, "I don't think they're so bad..."

"Don't tell that to Dark-Dragon," said Silent-Cobra.

Eventually the group settled on going back the way they had come, since there was no way of knowing how deep the tunnels went or which one led outside. Exhausted as they were, all of the trainees were forced to climb back down the cliff once again. The descent was twice as hard as the ascent had been, but none dared to try their luck in the Skrakki nest.

When they finally reached the bottom, they made their tedious and painful way back through the Ukrak field and met in a circle just outside the secret ETAB entrance. Every muscle on Scorp's body was aching so badly that he vaguely hoped Raven would come up behind him in a fit of rage and knock him out cold. At least then he wouldn't have to feel this deep, throbbing pain all over.

It was completely dark by the time they reached the ETAB, but the two large moons of Terra Nova lit the field with a pale, bluish illumination. The students, some of them bloody and battered, all of them tired and worn, gathered there in a circle, in the center of which stood Dark-Dragon, as composed and imposing as ever. He looked at each one of them, and they all tried their best not to show their fatigue. They did a good job of it.

"So," Dragon said, "you all made it out alive. Good job. Congratulations to Seth Electric-Eel for being the first one to make it to the top of the mesa. Congratulations to Luke Blood-Raven for being the first one to enter the tunnels, fight his way past most of the Skrakki, and enter the room with the Crown. Unfortunately, Luke made a few mistakes along the way. He stole a set of climbing bracers from Daniel, he used Seth's loyalty to trick him, and he beat up Kade and left him in a vulnerable position for the Skrakki to find. Indeed, had it not been for Tanya and Vincent arriving in time to save him from a Skrakki scavenger, Kade may have been taken as food while he lay unconscious.

"However, all of this may have been excused were it not for Raven's biggest mistake: he placed the Crown of Xarkon upon his own head. This act of borderline treason has destroyed his chance for victory in the contest. Congratulations to Justin Saber-Scorpion for being the one to catch up with him next. Even when he saw Luke taking the Crown, he did not try to stop him. He saw that he had honorably lost the contest. For this, he is now the winner of this practice competition."

If Raven had not liked Scorp before, he veritably hated him now, and it was all the young trainee could do to keep his expression from showing his outrage. For his part, Scorp's mind was on his companions.

"Sir, what of my partners, Cat and Mantis?" he asked.

"Partners?" Dragon replied, giving a short laugh, "If they were your partners, then why did you attempt to abandon them?"

Scorp recalled running ahead several times in the tunnel. "I did not intend to abandon them, sir. I was just trying to make sure we didn't lose."

Dragon nodded. "I see. You were trying to make sure that *you* didn't lose. You were simply using them to get to your goal, because you did not have a backpack, isn't that right?"

Scorp didn't know how to respond to this accusation. He knew it was true, at least partially. All he could manage was, "I could not have made it without them."

Dark-Dragon simply nodded, smiling ever so slightly. "Exactly. There is no shame in what you did. Had I *ordered* you to work as teams, I might be admonishing you right now for running ahead. But no, I simply said that you *could* work as a team, if you wanted to. Using others to your own advantage is one way to win, Justin. If the others had truly been bent on winning, they would have run ahead instead of you."

"Sir," Mantis spoke up, from the other side of the circle. "Permission to speak."

"Granted."

"Scorp did work with us, sir. Cathryn only had two climbing bracers, so Scorp shared the pair with her and helped her climb up the mountainside. It was amazing how well they worked together, and that they were still able to reach the goal right behind Seth and Raven."

Dark-Dragon turned to regard Scorp with an upraised eyebrow. "Hm. I see. I was unable to watch your climb up the side in person, unfortunately. I only saw what took place after you reached the top of the mesa. So… you really did help them then? I'm surprised; this doesn't fit with what I've been told about you. I was told you almost never worked in a group."

Scorp nodded once. "I prefer to work alone, sir."

Dark-Dragon shook his head. "Then perhaps you should have done so this time. Had you simply gone on ahead, you could have made much better time and probably reached your goal before Luke, winning easily. Think about this next time. As an Enomeg, it will often be your job to work alone… as a one-man team. But enough talk. Class dismissed. I'm sure you all need some sleep."

The circle broke up as Dark-Dragon walked back to the hidden door and entered the code, then stood aside to let the students in. They looked like an army of the undead, with their limbs hanging limply at their sides and their eyelids half closed. A few of them were nursing injuries. The only thing on everyone's mind was how quickly they were going to fall asleep that night.

Except for Saber-Scorpion. He was scanning the crowd for someone… and it didn't take long for him to spot his target. Barracuda's bald head stuck up above the other, shorter trainees by a mile. Scorp saw Kade's face and remembered the cold sneer that had crossed his lips as he'd tried to pull Cat down off the cliff face. It would probably have killed her.

Scorp knew Barracuda was strong, possibly the strongest man here, and he'd had both of his climbing bracers. He could most likely have passed Cat, Mantis, *and* Scorp if he had simply ignored them. But no, some spark of malevolence had driven him to try to dislodge one of his opponents… for no real reason at all. Scorp suddenly realized how tightly he was clenching his fists and let go. His hands – still sore from the climb – ached from the effort. But still the rage burned inside him.

Without another second's hesitation, Scorp made his way through the crowd toward Gun-Barracuda. Grabbing him by the shoulders, he slammed his foot behind the larger man's knee, throwing him heavily to the ground.

"If you try something like that again, *Barracuda*," Scorp said, "I swear I will put an end to your training permanently."

By the time he finished talking, Barracuda had leapt to his feet and given him a hard shove on the shoulder, nearly knocking him over. "What are you talkin' about, you whiny little blowhard? If you want to try me, come on, 'cause I'm not really in the mood for more games right now."

"I'm not either, so stop pretending you don't know what I'm talking about. I'm talking about you trying to toss Cat to her death! It takes a real piece of scum to do something like that. Especially since you're apparently too dumb to realize that if you'd just kept going, you might have beaten us, instead of nearly falling on your ass like you deserved. Try something like that again and I'll make sure you *do* get what you deserve. You *get* me, Kade?"

Barracuda's face took on an incredulous expression, and he shook his head slowly. "What...? I don't have to take this from you. If you want me to finish what I tried to start earlier, then shut your rat-trap and let's do it! You're the treasonous little wretch here, not me. You're the one who needs a lesson!"

Scorp, his dark eyebrows arched almost to a V, took a step forward, ignoring the fact that the eyes of every student were trained on him now. "You're wrong there, Kade. See, I don't like overgrown school bullies like you trying to become Enomeg super-soldiers. Maybe *you're* the one playing games here. Maybe *you* should grow up a bit and actually try to win instead of taking time out to pick on girls and rough people up out of spite."

Barracuda interrupted him with a loud, roaring laugh. "Just where did you come from, you little squirt? I don't know how you've survived your training this far if you try to take on everyone who eliminates his competition. People *die* in this training, kid! That's what it's about... weeding out the weak from the strong! Haven't you learned anything?"

"Haven't *I* learned anything? This training isn't just about weeding out the weak; it's also about weeding out petty excuses for men – like you – to keep them from staining the honor of Xarkon. Haven't you learned the four tenets? You don't deserve to be declared a champion of the crown..."

Barracuda gave a growl that could have rivaled a Stage Four Slashrim. "That's it! Time to shut you up!"

A fist like a bulldozer came smashing through the air toward Scorp's face. Scorp dodged the blow, caught Barracuda's wrist, and attempted to trip him up and throw him to the ground. But the giant was as immovable as a mountainside. His other fist snapped around and slammed into Scorp's gut, doubling him up on the grass. Scorp rolled to his feet quickly, but his eyes met Barracuda's laughing face and the staring faces of a score more trainees. Finally, rage overcame his discipline. Giving a cry that was as primal as the emotion of anger itself, Saber-Scorpion charged...

... and ran into Dark-Dragon. The Enomeg turned him over and tossed him easily onto his back in the grass, knocking the wind out of him. He then casually did the same to Barracuda, who had also been charging. Scorp blinked and looked up, as Dark-Dragon grabbed them both by their collars and yanked them to their feet.

"What's the meaning of this foolishness?" the Enomeg shouted, looking back and forth between Scorp and Barracuda.

It was all Scorp could do to restrain himself from trying to rush past Dark-Dragon. "He nearly killed–!"

"*Silence!* This is Enomeg training! People are going to die. But in case you didn't notice, Justin, neither Cat nor Kade *did* die. This proves that they have what it takes. Cathryn doesn't need your protection, and Kade doesn't need your punishment. You may leave his punishment up to *me*. Fighting in the ranks is never permitted except when *I* say it is. Understood?"

Scorp took several deep breaths and then lowered his head, taking a step back. He gave a half-hearted Heartbeat salute and said, "Yes, sir."

Dragon wheeled to face Barracuda. "As for you, Kade, perhaps you didn't hear me during your briefing… This was the Test of *Honor!* Exactly what kind of training centers did you go to before this one? Scorp was right about one thing: Xarkon does not need your kind as its chosen super-soldiers, nor does it want them. If your attitude doesn't change, you will have no place here. You have failed the Test of Honor!"

There was another moment of silence as Dark-Dragon stood between the two trainees, looking back and forth at them. All of the black-clad super-soldiers in training had forgotten their weariness in light of this new event. They watched as the trio faced each other, illuminated in the blue light of the two moons. Dragon was shorter than either of the men he was confronting, but clearly, neither of them had any desire to fight him.

"Now…" Dragon said at last, dropping into a more relaxed position, "I feel some sort of punishment is in order. I was hoping I would not have to do this to ETAB students, since you should be too advanced for this sort of thing by now. But I can see that I was wrong in that regard. For your petty and childish antics here in the field today, both of you, Kade Gun-Barracuda and Justin Saber-Scorpion, will be spending the night outside in the Ukrak grasses. I hope you can find a comfortable place to sleep, not to mention some food, because you won't be let back in until we have reason to come outside and get you. You'll have to find your own breakfast. However, if you have the skills to find your way back into the base without inside help, you may do so. That is your call. The rest of you, stop gawking like morons and get inside, before I consider making half of you wait out here with them."

There was a shuffling in the ranks as every student moved toward the secret entrance door. Dragon himself slid back into the crowd and was soon nowhere to be seen. After a while, there were only about eight people left in the field. Cathryn had lagged behind intentionally, and now she approached Scorp with a worried look on her face. Saber-Scorpion tried not to look at her at first, but he saw there was no use in that course of action, so he turned to face her. Scorp's expression was determined. Cat just looked disappointed.

"I can hardly *believe* you, Saber-Scorpion," she said. "Are you crazy? I've fought off jerks like Kade my whole life and had no trouble at all; I don't need you to protect me – to *patronize* me! Surely you saw that!"

Scorp shook his head. "It wasn't about you, Cat. It was about him. He acted dishonorably…"

"*Pfft* – Right!" Cat laughed disdainfully. "I didn't see you off taunting Raven about stealing Daniel's gear!"

"I've taunted Raven plenty," Scorp replied. "I stole his victory, remember?"

"I know the truth," Cat went on. "You were trying to protect me because I'm a *girl*. I even heard you say it, in so many words. Well, get over it, Scorp! The 'girls' around here don't need your protection. Not only is your silly 'chivalry' act disgusting; it'll get you *killed* if you don't cut it out. I'm surprised you've lasted *this* long."

Scorp sat and endured her words. Whatever his thoughts were on the subject, he voiced none of them. Cat got the distinct impression that he had sat through very similar lectures before, and none of those had worked either. As she vented her indignation, he just stared at her with a respectful but almost sad expression, as if he knew he deserved the punishment but also knew it would ultimately do no good. Finally she blew out a long sigh and bit her lip. She wanted to punch him, but she knew he would just take it. He'd let her beat him into a pulp before raising a hand in his own defense. It was ludicrous.

"I'm sorry if my actions offended you," Scorp said at last, "but nothing can change the fact that it was something I had to do. He tried to *kill* you, Cat. I'd kill him *for* you if you asked me to."

She looked up at him with wide, startled eyes. She could tell by his expression that he meant what he said. There was nothing condescending about his tone, but somehow that only infuriated her all the more.

"I don't *believe* you…" she said, in a low voice. "You're… *Ooohhh*, forget it! This is your problem, not mine. I'm just trying to give you some good advice: cut it out."

Scorp nodded. "Thank you."

Shaking her head, Cat headed for the door and disappeared. Then the trainee that had been following her stepped up. It was Magnum-Coyote, who was grinning more than ever. He looked like watching Scorp's fight and the resulting drama had drained all of the exhaustion right out of him.

"Scorp, Scorp, Scorp…" he said, "I am really starting to like you. Seeing the look on Kade's face was priceless, and now I won't have to hate the fact that he succeeded when I failed."

"What did you do to fail?"

Coyote chuckled. "Dragon was just scolding me about it before he went to interrupt your fight with Kade. I guess I screwed up when I stole Hans Thunder-Hawk's cuffs to use them on my legs. Anyway, a while back, Kade beat the snot out of me. I'd have beat him back, but he took me by surprise and roughed me up pretty bad, see? Eventually I just hid up a tree to get away from him. When he tried to follow, one of the limbs broke, and he fell on his ass. It was great… Maybe you should try *that* next time."

Scorp shrugged. "I can handle Kade."

He grinned again. "That sounds familiar. Ha! You're probably right. Next time you're in the lounge, come see me and we'll have a drink; I've got some alien stuff imported from the Outlook system that really kicks. You should try it. I'll see you around."

With that he turned and ran off. Scorp blew out a sigh as he saw Mantis approaching. He was beginning to feel like some sort of carnival attraction.

"Fiery, isn't she? Cat I mean," Mantis said with a broad smile spread across his face.

Scorp shrugged. "Is she?"

"Don't worry," Mantis went on, "you merely embarrassed her. I actually think she *liked* your little display."

Scorp seemed to doubt it. "If you say so…"

Mantis shook his head in amazement. "My friend, I am sorry I ever doubted your loyalty to Xarkon. You truly have what it takes to become an Enomeg soldier. Your grasp of honor and loyalty amazes me. We could all learn from your example. I only wish Dragon hadn't stopped you from fighting with Barracuda. I know you could have taught him a lesson!"

Scorp gave him an amused half-smile. Actually, now that he thought about it, his little speech about honor and the tenets of Xarkon had surprised him as well. Where had all that come from?

"Thanks, but you had better be getting back inside now, before they decide to lock you out too. Most of the others are already gone."

"Would you like me to sneak out some rations for you in the morning? If there is anything substantial to eat in this desert of grass, my eyes have not yet seen it! And after today's events, I think we're all starved…"

"No, no," Scorp said, shaking his head, "don't risk it on my account. I can survive in the wilderness; you know that."

Mantis shrugged. "If you say so. See you tomorrow then."

Scorp rubbed his chin, which was getting rough again… Apparently he would have to hear more comments about his shaving habits the next day, after a night in the wilderness. As he found himself wondering if civilians took personal hygiene as seriously as did the military, he noticed Raven approaching, with eyes and teeth gleaming in the moonlight as he smiled tauntingly at his foe. Scorp merely rolled his eyes.

"Looks like you'll get some small victory," Scorp said, "after losing the larger one."

Raven sneered. "I beat you, Scorp. In the *real* contest, I beat you."

"The *real* contest?" Scorp began to argue, but Raven cut him off.

"For someone who claims to want to be the best, you sure don't seem to concentrate on it! You're too busy trying to catch Cat's attention. It looks like you're better at that."

Scorp raised an eyebrow. "Better than you, you mean?"

Raven's expression darkened. Scorp knew he'd touched a nerve. This was a man who hated to admit he was not the best at *anything*. And apparently he saw Scorp as his only real competition.

"I think Tanya's more my style," Raven said at last

Scorp gave a short laugh. He knew Tanya Silent-Cobra. She was determined, focused, and took her training *very* seriously. He knew her well enough to know that she had absolutely no interest in flirting around with Raven, or anyone for that matter. She was too concentrated on succeeding; she simply had no time for such games.

"*Luke*," Scorp said at last, "let's get this straight. I don't really care about competing with you…"

"Well, that's pretty clear," Raven said with a laugh. "But if you don't care, *Scorp*, then how about this: Just stay out of my way."

Scorp shook his head. "I can't stay out of your way, Raven, anymore than two big cats can share territory. And speaking of which, you'd better run along unless you want be sharing *this* territory with Kade and me all night."

Luke shrugged and walked off. Finally the clearing was deserted, and the tiny speck of blue light near the top of the rock went out as the door closed behind the last trainee, leaving Scorp and Barracuda blinking in the moonlight. Scorp blew a sigh of relief. He and Kade stared at each other in silence for quite a few minutes before either of them moved. Scorp was merely waiting for the big brute to pounce.

To his surprise, Barracuda merely said, "I'd still love to beat the ever-loving *klagk* right out of you, but I don't feel like givin' you the gratification. Good luck findin' a nice rock to sleep under, *Scorp*."

"See you in the morning then. Wake me if you change your mind. I'll be ready."

With that the two of them parted, disappearing into the darkness.

- CHAPTER SIX -
PREPARING THE PIECES

Orion would have tossed his pistol away in disgust, but he knew the sound of it clattering on the floor of the dimly-lit warehouse would have alerted the guards to his whereabouts, even in this maze of tall metal shipping crates. He had just expended the last of his ammunition on the previous group of soldiers he'd dispatched, and part of the mission parameters was that he had to use his own weapons, for his opponents' guns had safety features that prevented any individuals not part of their team from using them. Since he was working alone this time, without Amazon or any of his other teammates, that meant all he had left to fight with now were his knives.

Good thing he'd brought a spare. Lifting the second Bowie-II energy blade up to the first, he ignited them and crossed them in front of his face. The normally-bright shafts of blue light were so pale on these training weapons that they did not even cause his holographic HUD visor to darken. By adjusting a knob on the side of the device, Orion was able to lengthen the blade to about a foot from pommel to tip. That, he thought, should be enough.

Sneaking around a corner, he peered out and inspected the situation. The lights on the high ceiling of the warehouse were so distant and dim that they barely cast enough illumination to outline the hallways of crates. Even the dim light from Orion's blades lit up the area a bit, and the hallway flickered as he twirled the twin knives over in his fingers, bringing their blades point-up, into the dueling stance. He then switched them off to conceal his location, but kept them held at the ready as he crouched down and began slinking between the crates. He was supposed to be a super-soldier hunting these mercenaries like a hungry wolf amidst the fold...

but he felt more like he was a lost sheep in a pack of hungry wolves instead. But this sheep *did* have teeth.

The first one came upon him by surprise, rounding a corner right in front of him, and Orion acted completely out of instinct. It was the ultimate killing blow, a double-slice to the throat. Had his knives been using actual "hot" energy, they might have cut the man's head completely off. As it was, the soldier's eyes just rolled back in his head, and he went down like a stone. Orion caught him to prevent his armored body from hitting the floor, a sound that would surely draw attention to him. Then he slid the unconscious soldier into a space between two crates to keep him from being spotted.

With this accomplished, he continued through the maze, as silently and alertly as possible. He was surprised not to hear the guards' voices echoing through the warehouse now and then, but apparently they knew he was coming and had ceased any idle chatter, now communicating exclusively by heads-up display. After all, these were professional Victorian soldiers only posing as mercenaries.

Suddenly he heard a cough. Springing into the shadows, he tried to pinpoint from which direction it had come. Even with the echoing here in the warehouse, he managed to pick it out and follow it. He took a left at the next junction in the makeshift labyrinth.

Orion now found himself in the main hall... That is, the large open space in the middle of the warehouse, between two exceptionally tall stacks of shipping crates. He took a peek around the corner and saw nearly a dozen guards standing around or sitting on the smaller crates, all armed and watchful. Most of them wanted to win this little competition very badly. After all, the Immortal Soldier Project was quite controversial. Several political and military leaders in Victory were opposed to it, including Grand General Rick Radcliff himself. Most of the soldiers tended to agree with him, for they all looked up to him. He was a hero.

Orion's thoughts were interrupted as he suddenly spotted his target: the box. It was easily identifiable, with TOP SECRET written on the side in far-too-obvious lettering, visible even in this dim lighting. Still, it was his goal, and he had to do his best to get it. Thinking quickly, he turned and tossed his empty stun gun high toward the ceiling. As he'd expected, the guards jumped to look in the direction of the clang when it landed, and Ryan took the opportunity to make his move into the center hall, crouching quickly into the shadow of a small crate on the floor. There he waited for the commander to order some of his men to check out the disturbance.

It never happened. Apparently they had already decided not to move from this position, thus forcing Ryan to fight them all here at once. In that case, he would oblige them. Taking a deep breath, he struck so quickly that they never even saw him leave the shadows. One of the soldiers fell clattering to the floor, and another let out a scream as Orion held him up at knifepoint. He tried to use him as a shield but was forced to slit his throat quickly and duck for cover, as these soldiers seemed to have much less reluctance about firing on a comrade than the last bunch.

Orion rolled behind a crate and quickly gathered his bearings. Faint white tracers showered the stack of crates behind him as the soldiers fired their rifles. Taking a major risk, Orion put his weight against the box he was hiding behind and pushed. One of the soldiers had been advancing on his position, and the sliding crate slammed into his knees. There was a momentary halt in the firing as the injured soldier fell with a startled scream.

It was all Orion needed. In an instant, he was up. He stabbed the fallen man as he passed and, using him as another human shield, moved on to his nearest comrade. One of his knives suddenly went twirling through the air and bounced off an enemy's chest. The toss was true, and the blade's stun effect sent the armored man clattering to the floor.

Orion scooped the fallen blade back up as he rolled for cover once again. He heard the clatter of feet behind his crate and noticed a shadow pass over him. Someone was climbing on top of the crate. A quick jab to the heart did this one in, but it also brought Orion out from behind his cover, if only slightly, as he lunged upward. Heedless of their companion standing over him, the remaining soldiers opened fire on Orion. He felt a shock spread over him; his whole body seemed to shudder, all breath leaving his lungs. Then he fell to the ground, his vision full of dancing spots of shadow and light.

"Cease fire!" a voice rang out, echoing through the warehouse.

The soldiers lowered their rifles. Two officers immediately appeared from the shadow of the largest stack of crates, making their way briskly across the room. Both were clad in crisp dress uniforms, one stark white and the other deep blue. Each bore a good number of pins and medals, but the one in blue was lavishly decorated… and one glance at the man's face, half-covered by a chrome visor, revealed why. He was Rick Radcliff, Grand General of the Victorian Defense Forces.

The other man, who had sandy blond hair, a thin goatee, and a much thicker neck, turned and shouted at the nearest soldier. "I'm disappointed in you, you little spawn of a Skrakki brood-worm! Can't you keep your own soldiers in line?"

The squad leader of the pretend-mercenaries stiffened. "Sir! My soldiers fired on the enemy as ordered, sir. They –"

"Fired on an ally, that's what they did! If this had been a real combat situation, that man Orion stabbed would'a been riddled with blazer fire, probably while he was still alive. His dyin' thought would be: 'Damn, I shouldn't have put my life in the hands o' those good-for-nothin' Victorian fightin' men. They'd as soon shoot an ally in the back as look at 'im.' Is that the message you want to send to your men, Sergeant?"

"Sir, the men will be reprimanded for –"

"Sergeant, it is *your* job to reprimand your men, and it's *my* job to reprimand *you*. As far as I'm concerned, this is as much your problem as if your men had merely been your fingers as you pulled the trigger. Get your boys in line and follow your orders next time! Dismissed. Not another word, Sergeant! I said *dismissed*."

"Yes, sir!" The soldiers marched out of the room.

With that, the white-clad officer reached down and rudely jerked Orion to his feet, brushing off his shoulders. "You alright there, son?"

"Wasn't... fair," Orion muttered.

The colonel frowned. "Fair, eh? So you thought this would be fair? Well, son, I do have apologize for the performance o' those sorry sacks o' flesh tryin' to pass off as Victorian special forces. But they did no more than what some dirty rent-a-soldiers would do."

"Colonel Jenkins, sir," Ryan breathed, standing on his own somewhat groggily. "I know that, sir. That comment just slipped out before I was quite awake."

"Then it was a hell of a lot truer than what you're spewin' now, so I'm glad I heard it. Get that 'fair' thinkin' out o' your system, Orion. That's for civilians who think the world owes 'em somethin'. We fightin' men know different. Am I right, soldier?"

Ryan seemed reluctant to respond, since he had by this point noticed Grand General Radcliff. Colonel Jenkins guessed that the young soldier probably hadn't heard half of what he'd said, but he didn't press the issue.

"Thank you for that, Colonel," Rick said. "I'd like to have a word with Orion alone now, if you please."

"Right," Jenkins said. "See you later, Rick."

The colonel walked off, giving a good slap on the behind to a groggy soldier who had just woken up from being stunned. Once the room was cleared, Rick turned back to Orion, who had seated himself on a smaller crate and was massaging his forehead. He noticed the General was still there and tried to stand.

"At ease," Rick said, taking a seat. "Sit back down, Ryan, and take off that visor. I think you've had enough fun this evening."

Orion tore off his holographic visor and threw it angrily across the room. Looking up, he saw in Rick's silvery glasses the reflection of his own blue eyes, full of fire, and a twinge of fear. He ran his hands through his thick brown hair and blew out a deep sigh. He noticed that Rick had not used his codename. Was it because he was getting to know him better? No, he had always called him Orion before, even after Ryan had asked him not to. There must be some other reason.

"It's good to see you, Sir," Ryan forced himself to say.

Rick laughed. "No, it's not. Jenkins is right; you wouldn't have said that if you weren't fully awake. Then you might have admitted that you're worried about why I'm here. You did good in this exercise, Ryan... better than any one man is expected to do. That will help you in the future."

Ryan's heart sank. Now he knew something bad was coming.

"I just came back from another CONON meeting," Rick said, in a tone that clearly told how little he had enjoyed it, "and Ordinator Exsyl and I met with the Six afterward... the ruling council of Yavakaro. We started discussing the super-soldier projects, and the Six mentioned how threatened they felt without a program of their own to match Xarkon's mysterious Enomegs, and our own Immortal Soldier Project... not to mention what Zygbar is rumored to be doing now with its Highland Guerilla corps..."

"And you expressed your opinions clearly," Ryan said as he stood up and took off his simulation vest.

Rick also stood. "Yes, of course I did. We came to the agreement that we would end the already controversial Immortal Soldier Project as long as Yavakaro didn't start one of its own. These training processes are inhumane, Ryan. What they put you kids through in the academies... I can't believe you aren't relieved at it ending, and I'm sure most of the others will be."

Ryan tugged at his hair again, but said nothing.

"I know," Rick said for him, "you *did* want it to end, but end successfully, not like this."

Ryan looked at the Grand General, who was about the same height as he was. He got the feeling that, behind those glasses, Rick really *did* understand him. He was not used to explaining his feelings to other people, but he decided to give it a try anyway.

"I want to go to Xarkon," Ryan began.

"Yes, I know what you want, and I know why you want it. You want revenge because of what happened to you in your past, when your family was driven out of Xarkon. You want to right those wrongs; you want to make a difference. You want to change the government of your old home country, to make it more like Victory, the only home you've ever really known."

Ryan paused a moment, as if reluctant to proceed. "There are other reasons, sir."

"You can tell me, son," Rick said, giving that warm smile of his that always worked so well at the political meetings. "I want to know, to help you proceed as a soldier after the cancellation of the Immortal Soldier Project. Whatever your goals are, I can help you achieve them."

Ryan wasn't sure he believed all that, but he nodded anyway, and took a deep breath to steady his determination.

"I was only two years old when Mom... when my mother fled the country with me, but her hatred of Xarkon had started years earlier than that. She said that my father was a staunch Xarkon loyalist, a military man through and through. He was hardly ever around, never spoke much when he was... insisted it was all for a good cause and would be over someday. She always spoke of him a bit sadly..."

Ryan realized he was getting pretty personal now and cut his story short, turning back around to face Rick again. "Anyway, things came to a head when her next child – my little sister, Maegan – never left the hospital she was born in. They told us she was dead, but Mom had other suspicions, since they had said the same thing about her first son... my older brother. My father was furious when he found out that his own wife was taking advantage of his government connections to dig up information on the Enomeg project. She didn't find out much, but it was enough to know where they'd taken Maegan... and enough to wonder if her first son had also been taken for the same project."

"To make a long story short, in order to get Maegan back, she got involved with an underground group opposed to the Xarkon Empire, and they barely made it back home alive, with soldiers of the crown hot on their tail. A firefight broke out while Mom put me into a sub that the rebels had prepared for an escape route. She tried to go back and get Maegan, but the rebels were pulling out, and they forced her back into the sub and left. Later we heard that the entire block was destroyed in an explosion not long after we escaped. We never found out what happened to the rest of the family."

Ryan took a deep breath and looked at Rick. He seemed reluctant to continue. It was not often that he bared himself like this in front of anyone.

"Go on," Rick said encouragingly. "Speak freely."

Ryan took yet another deep breath. "There's not a lot more to tell. When I grew up and she told me the story, I figured… if my sister and my brother had the right genes, maybe I do too. Maybe I could fight for Victory that way and make a real difference. So I tried to transfer to a military academy at fourteen. Mom didn't want me to go, really, and I guess I can't blame her – I got a little too caught up in it. She almost convinced me to change my mind about it, but apparently she saw I never would. So then, when she was sure I was not going to change my mind, she said something that changed my goals entirely."

Rick looked surprised. "And what was that?" he asked.

Ryan unfastened his vest and reached inside, drawing out a small black booklet. Rick took it and held it open. Inside were only two pictures, both of infants. Rick could tell immediately that they were related to the young soldier.

"She showed me that," Ryan went on, "and she said… *Find them*. Find out what happened to them."

Rick stared at the photos for a long moment, trying to feel what Ryan must have felt. He was a family man himself, and often felt sorry that his military life kept him so far from his loved ones. That was one reason he'd convinced his son Harry to join the military, much to the displeasure of his wife Elizabeth. The only time anyone had ever threatened either of them, however, Rick had immediately dealt with it. As soon as his wife said Eric Grimm had assaulted her, he challenged his fellow Victorian officer to that fateful duel of honor…

"Anyway," Ryan said, breaking Rick's reverie, "I never even told Mom about my volunteering for the Immortal Soldier Project. If she knew half the things I've been put through, she probably would have campaigned twice as hard as you to stop the project. But apparently I'm good at keeping secrets. I've never told anyone else that story before…"

"Not even Evelyn?" Rick asked, raising one eyebrow.

Ryan allowed himself a bit of a grin, "You mean Amazon? No, not even her. You're the only person I've told about this, ever. You asked me about my goals, so there they are."

Ryan rarely explained himself like this, but he was hoping he could convince Rick to let the Immortal Soldier Project live on. But as he and Rick stood up, and Ryan looked across at what he could see of his commander's features, he knew he had not succeeded. The opinions and personal feelings of Rick Radcliff were as steadfast as he had been told.

But then the Grand General's expression changed. "Come with me, Ryan. I think there are some matters of mutual interest we need to discuss."

LOCATION: THE GRIM ISLES

The waves crashed with tremendous force onto the cold grey island cliffs, smashing away at the rocky coastline bit by bit, doing their best to erode the foundations that had stood there for millennia. And high above them was a fortress that could have been nearly half as old... an ancient and crumbling stone castle thought to have been built by the Slashrim, the species of lizard-like warrior Natives that had inhabited this area long before Humanity came in and claimed it as theirs. The series of towering island strongholds had long ago been almost completely destroyed, having served as hideouts for both the Natives during the Xenocide War and a gang of bloodthirsty pirates decades later.

But it was to those pirates that the ruins owed the fact that they were still standing, or at least to the mercenaries who had succeeded them. Grimm's Mercenary Army had rebuilt and reinforced the old forts with modern duranium plating and girding, creating a clashing blend of old and new, ancient and modern. Many said that it was a disgrace, a terrible use for historic landmarks that should have been preserved, not hideously clashed with modern warfare and turned into hives of scum and villainy.

But Grand High Warlord Eric Grimm I could not possibly disagree more. He was presently leaning on the crenellations at one of the few locations where the old stone part of the fortress reached to the very top of the wall. As he looked down over the raging sea and the rows of fortresses lining his islands... he knew that the grizzled old Slashrim warriors who built the place would be proud to know that their structures were still being used for their intended purpose: as strongholds of war.

Indeed, one such Slashrim stood behind the mercenary now, and Grimm looked back to regard him. The Slashrim were hulking, muscular, dinosaur-like humanoids, with thick, leathery skin that came in a variety of mostly dull colors. They had sharp teeth and were typically covered in spikes and horns in a variety of places. One of the peculiarities of the species was the vast amount of variety in their genetics, so that even family members sometimes looked extremely different.

The Slashrim life cycle was divided into several stages. They started out as small but vicious children, grew into mature adults with reasonably intelligent faculties, and then started growing dumber again as they aged... but never stopped growing bigger in size. Usually they were killed off by their own warlike society before reaching the later stages of life, but in these modern times many lived to be enormous, and their great muscular power was used as a source of cheap labor by plenty of species, even their own kin.

This particular Slashrim was a hulking, eight-foot-tall specimen with burnt-orange skin. Grimm did not know his real name, but everyone called him Hurk. Possibly as old as sixty TSCs, he was now entering the fourth stage of the Slashrim life cycle, commonly called "trolls" by Humans. Grimm had purchased him from a slaver in Zygbar and now used him as a bodyguard. He was as dumb as a rock, and since Grimm treated him well, his loyalty to the warlord was just as solid as one.

As for the warlord himself, Eric Grimm I was nearly as old as Hurk, but as a Human, he wasn't quite as tall – in fact, he stood under six feet. But as some often said, what he lacked in height he made up for in mean. All scars and muscles, he certainly looked the part of a mercenary warlord in his dented but high-quality black and green battle armor. Although his hair was mostly black, graying in only a few places, his rather lengthy eyebrows were stark white, and clashed violently with the black eyepatch that covered his missing right eye. Thick stubble covered his face at all times, and his yellowed teeth glared as he let out a great laugh.

Hurk gave him a confused look, wrinkling the brow over his eyes that were even more vibrant green than Grimm's own. "What so funny, boss?"

"That… that beard!" Grimm shouted, his laughter somehow just as gravelly as his voice. "It gets me every time!"

Hooded and cloaked, and standing nearly as tall as the Slashrim Hurk, Lucas Mars paid no attention to Grimm's mirth as, flanked by several of Grimm's green-armored elites, he strode out onto the wall. For several months now, to serve as a disguise, he had been exchanging a false beard with his chief general, Jacob Black. Since Black was about the same height and build as Mars, the façade worked perfectly from a distance, and it allowed Mars to slip away unnoticed, since the media – and hopefully Victorian spies – paid less attention to the movements of Mars's subordinate officer. He had used this method to meet with Grimm several times. The warlord always greeted him with laughter, and Mars always ignored it.

"So how are things on my little islands?" he asked.

"*Your* islands?" Grimm replied with a laugh. "You sold 'em to me fair an' square, Mars. Don't be backin' out now."

"I encouraged the Emperor to 'sell' them to you for a modest fee in the agreement that you would help keep the pirates and the rest of the underworld in check, and agree to give me a 'preferred customer discount' on your… services."

Grimm frowned and nodded. He knew the score. This had all started twenty years ago, when Victorian forces under the command of Rick Radcliff had been sent here to the Grim Isles to clean out a gang of pirates that had set up operations in the ruins. Grimm had been a colonel in the Victorian army at the time, and was under Rick's command during the attack. When it was all over, they returned home as heroes.

But it didn't last long. Grimm seldom talked about it, but only a few weeks after their return, Rick's wife accused him of assaulting her, and of stealing funds from Radcliff's vast fortune. Rick believed her and challenged Grimm to a duel of honor, which was legal under Victorian law if both parties accepted. Perhaps foolishly, Grimm did accept.

They fought with swords – solid blades, not energy or blazer ones. Grimm still carried scars from that fight, and no doubt so did Rick, but the legendary Victorian General proved to be the better swordsman, and Grimm ended up losing his right eye. Rick could have finished him there, but instead he spared his life. Perhaps this also was foolish.

After that, Grimm fled back to the islands with a few of his most loyal troops – including Nick Wolf – and rounded up the scattered pirates that were still there, along with any mercenaries or bounty hunters he could find… to create Grimm's Mercenary Army. In the two decades since then, he had turned the ruins of the Grim Isles into a line of fortresses that few would dare to assault, and forged what started as a ragtag gang of mercs and criminals into one of the most feared military forces in all of Human space… and beyond. With his own stolen and salvaged starships, Grimm even had a hand in interstellar affairs.

The warlord's reverie was broken by Mars's impatient voice. "You have something to *show* me, Grimm?"

Grimm nodded toward the inner edge of the fortress wall on which they stood. The High Commander approached the parapets there and looked down into the courtyard of Grimm's main base. There were several mercenaries milling about in the area of hard-packed dirt below, which usually served as a training course and a meeting place for Grimm's elites, his best and most trusted soldiers.

Today, however, it was filled with what looked to be regular mercs – identifiable by their motley assortment of clothing, consisting largely of trench coats, ponchos, and jackets, most likely bristling with concealed firearms. They were seated at a long, narrow table, on which had been laid a veritable feast of barely-cooked meats and barrels of unknown kinds of borderline-toxic alcoholic beverages. Even from high above, their coughing and swearing could be heard as they laughed and drank.

Mars raised a dubious eyebrow and looked sideways at Grimm. "You called me here for some kind of a party?"

Grimm, having no right eye, was forced to turn his head to look back at Mars as he answered scoffingly, "You know better than that, Mars. I ain't that stupid. See that bald-headed ass-clown down there in the red n' green Christmas armor? He's been tryin' to form a breakaway faction o' mercs for weeks now. See that pale fella and his big black buddy? They've been runnin' a smugglin' operation – shippin *my* guns *off* the isles to sell to a buncha' gangs in Mordark! All these clowns think they've been pullin' one over on ol' Grimm, and they think they ain't been caught yet. Well, I'm about to teach 'em a lesson… one they won't live long enough to appreciate. You'd better step back once it starts."

"Going to shoot them from the walls?" Mars asked in a bored tone.

"Just watch, Mars. You might wanna step back, like I said."

He cleared his throat, as if to make a speech. Mars did not budge, even as the Elites stepped forward, their advanced blazer rifles at the ready. Hurk too swung the immense light machine gun off his back and made sure it was prepared.

"Hey-hey, scumbags!" Grimm shouted with a grin, causing the mercenaries below to squint up at him in the bright sunlight. "I'm glad y'all could make it here on this great day. We've got quite a congregation here, don't we? A warlord and a few bosses, a couple elites, a few gun-runners and grease-monkeys, and even some genuine scum!"

Mars shook his head. "Warlords" were Grimm's chief officers, those in charge of entire legions and fortresses. Apparently the one in what Grimm had called "Christmas armor" was the warlord, for his chestplate bore the standard long-toothed, snake-like skull insignia that Grimm used as his battle standard – taken and modified from the pirates he had conquered. They called it the "Not-

So-Jolly Roger." "Bosses" was a general term that applied to a warlord's subordinate officers, the elites were Grimm's best soldiers and the only ones with standardized armor and weapons, gun-runners were smugglers, and grease-monkeys were mechanics.

As for the scum, they were the lowest of all Grimm's mercenaries. Instead of fighting for pay, they simply fought for food and board. They were usually criminals looking for sanctuary from one of the Big Four factions for atrocities they had committed there, or simply the desperately poor, willing to do anything for a secure livelihood. All of these types thrived in the strange, ordered lawlessness that could be found in all of Grimm's hideout, both here on Terra Nova and off-world. Most of them here in the Grim Isles lived in Merctown, the vast settlement of shacks, shanties, and bars that occupied one of Grimm's largest islands.

"As I said, I called y'all here for a celebration," Grimm went on. "A celebration of what? Why, of loyalty! Yeah, I know what you're thinkin' – we're mercs; the only thing we're loyal to is money! Well, that's true enough. I can't blame ya for that. If you see an opportunity, you take it! That's why I'm so good about lettin' contracted mercs go if they wanna explore other opportunities. All you gotta do is ask, an' we'll cut you your last check."

By now the mercs were beginning to understand what this was all about, and they began exchanging worried glances and muttering to each other. They glanced at the exits and noted that all were closed and barred. They were locked inside the courtyard, surrounded by ten-meter-high walls of metal and stone. Most of their firearms had been taken upon entry, apparently, but like any good *desperado*, they still had a few hidden about their person. They didn't dare to draw them out yet, but one thing was certain: no one was eating anymore. Grimm had their full attention.

Suddenly the Grand High Warlord's grin disappeared, and his voice took on a deadly serious edge. "But it's when you *don't* ask that I get a *little* annoyed. When you start cuttin' in on *my* profits, disruptin' *my* army, underminin' *my* authority. I can't have that! It just ain't good business! Now, in some cases I can be a pretty understandin' guy, but all you fellas have just gotten under my skin. It's time to set an example, and that example is *you*."

By this time, Mars had taken a cautious step back, for the mercenaries were growing bold enough to draw out their pistols, submachine guns, knives, and assorted other weapons of stranger descriptions. The High Commander noticed that they had been joined on the wall by Grimm's right-hand-men, Warlords Douglas Boyle and Nick Wolf. Boyle's steel gaze and matching grey mustache were as impassive as ever, but Nick's clear blue eyes looked almost worried, though his thick yellow beard hid most of his expression. Nick had started his career as a Victorian soldier, while Boyle had merely been a bounty hunter – though quite a legendary one. Perhaps Nick was worried about the implications of this incident in the army's discipline.

Finally Grimm completed his speech. "And you know what else you are? *Target practice!*"

The harsh staccato of gunfire erupted from the courtyard immediately, all of it directed at Grimm and his guards. Luckily, they were better equipped than most of his mercenaries, and thus had seen fit to activate their personal force fields before the shooting started. Every round of small arms fire directed at them was deflected either by their shielding, their duranium armor, or their nanomesh suits. Meanwhile, they stepped back out of range, never firing a shot.

Suddenly, bursts of flame erupted on all sides. It was coming from jetpacks – the jetpacks of soldiers that had been positioned around the rest of the perimeter wall. Instantly, these flying soldiers were everywhere, gleaming bright emerald green against the sun-lit blue sky above. Behind them trailed tails of white fire, and from strange cannons mounted on both of their arms spouted pulsating bursts of green-white energy. The shadows cast by the wall onto the courtyard below disappeared as the entire area was illuminated in flashing green light.

"Pulse rifles," Mars noted loudly, speaking over the din of battle that was suddenly all around them.

"*Starfire* pulse rifles!" Grimm shouted with a laugh. "Brand new tech; they call 'em Pulsars. Nothin' but the best for my new elites!"

Mars watched as the jetpack-mounted, pulse rifle-armed soldiers flew in an odd formation overhead, scissoring past each other two at a time, always landing on the opposite side of the perimeter wall again to wait and allow their weapons to cool. This ensured that the men below were constantly under a shower of energy fire and never knew how many enemies they were facing in all. Meanwhile, their own feeble attempts to fire their pistols and other small, concealable weapons at the enemy that flitted overhead in the glaring sunlight met with little if any success. The traitors were being utterly slaughtered.

Then the systematic destruction came to a pause, as one of the mercenaries' shots hit a more rewarding target. There was a barely-audible scream from the flying soldier as he plummeted out of the sky, his jetpack swerving out of control. Mars, Grimm, and Nick scurried to the parapets and peered over the edge, where they beheld the fallen flyboy. His suit was flecked on the side with white foam: the wound-sealant nanocrystals released automatically by the mesh when it was breached. Struggling to his feet, he drew a long combat knife and waved it menacingly at the approaching mercs. The victims of the execution were stalking forward with their own knives drawn, savoring what would perhaps be their only kill.

Mars heard a young female voice on Grimm's commlink say, "I just lost Jacin. Orders?"

Nick Wolf grabbed Grimm's arm. "Let's just finish this and pull the boy out. Order the elites to fire, boss!"

"Forget about it, Wolf," argued Boyle. "If he makes it, let this be a lesson to the boy."

Nick's eyes burned with indignant fire. "He's only *fifteen!*"

Mars listened to this argument silently as he looked down into the courtyard. If Nick had looked as well, he might have seen Jacin putting up quite a fight on his own. It was a rough, dirty scrap quite unlike the almost artistic sparring of the Enomegs. The fight was such a blur of flailing bodies and flashing blades that it was difficult for an onlooker to follow, but somehow the boy seemed to follow it, moving in and out of his uncoordinated foes and letting them become entangled with each other as much as with him.

Grimm silenced his warlords as he barked into his commlink, "Continue making your passes, Jade! Keep 'em off Jacin if you can."

"On it."

They immediately heard the jetpacks fire up again. At almost the same instant, Nick Wolf stood up, whipping out his bayoneted rifle and aiming down into the crowd. He noticed that Jade had landed now and pulled Jacin out of the fray. Now she was covering him by sweeping her arm-cannons in scissor-like motions while firing constantly, covering the area in bursts of starfire. Nick was about to help out, when a hand suddenly appeared from below and grabbed the end of his rifle, jerking him down.

Apparently one of the mercs had somehow managed to climb up the inside of the wall and attack the snipers on the parapets. Nick just managed to grasp the wrist of the mysterious arm as he fell, pulling the unknown assailant down with him. They both plummeted onto the drill field below, luckily landing on a sack of dried grasses that had been there to serve as a practice target. The bag burst open, releasing a cloud of dust so that the two mercenaries could barely see. Nick felt his attacker's fingers at his throat, and saw the glimmer of his red and green armor…

Meanwhile, back on top of the wall, Douglas Boyle stood up and drew his blazer revolver, a customized .45 caliber SAB2 "Rattler" that still used a chemical explosive-based firing mechanism with shelled ammunition, unlike the caseless firing mechanism that was now the modern standard. Boyle was legendary for his sharpshooting skills and his preference for revolvers.

The gunslinger first looked down to see if he could help Nick, but the dust prevented him from seeing that area, so he turned his attention to the other men in the courtyard. His eagle eyes scanned the field and quickly put a bullet into anyone who happened to still be moving. The gunslinger used up all six rounds in his revolver in only a few seconds, seemingly firing at random and without aim, yet each shot somehow scored a hit. Only one merc was left.

Then Nick emerged from the dust cloud, rolling along the ground, wrestling with the treacherous warlord. They were both struggling to gain control of Nick's rifle bayonet, but when they came to a halt, Nick was the one on top, preventing his allies from safely aiding him from above. At first it seemed to be an even fight, but then Nick, seemingly tiring of the game, simply headbutted his opponent's bald cranium. As the warlord reeled in pain, Nick wrenched free of his grasp, hefted his rifle, and planted the bayonet into his opponent's forehead. Then he threw back his head and let out a victory cry that echoed off the fortress walls, sounding more like a wild beast than a man.

High above, Mars looked down and nodded. "So that's why they call him the Werewolf."

"Yeah, somethin' like that," Grimm replied, and then he spoke into his commlink: "Okay, show's over. Nick, get a medic for Jacin. Jade, gather your troops and form up on the wall."

Jade ignited her pack and flew up toward them. She and her comrades controlled their flight with great precision using a pair of small thrusters on their legs, in addition to the rotating winglets and jets on their backs. Their armor was sharp and angular, and their primary weapons were the pair of highly advanced pulse rifles that were mounted to their very arms, completely covering their hands. As Mars watched, the young soldiers attached these cannons to their legs and slid their hands out. They then gave a simultaneous salute.

"Just five of them?" Mars asked.

Grimm blew out a sigh. He should have known not to expect Mars to give the slightest hint that he was impressed.

"Six, if you count Jacin down there in the courtyard. Jade's the best one. The others are Jacinth, Jargoon, Jet, Jasper..."

"Cute," Mars said coldly.

Grimm frowned. "They're orphans of war, all of 'em. Sometimes the father was the soldier, with a poor wife somewhere in Merctown or on some off-world base, who can't afford to support the kid without 'er husband. Other times, mommy and daddy were both mercs, blown up together in some starship with a kid back at base who barely knew 'em. And all too often they just abandon 'em, an' even we don't know who the parents are. No matter which way it happens, we take the kids an' put 'em through... the *program*. It ain't pretty. But neither is lettin' 'em grow up on their own. At least our way, they learn to defend themselves and get rewarded for fightin' good."

"It's not as sophisticated as the Enomeg project," Mars mused, "but it works, I suppose. A simple Darwinian mindset sometimes does."

Grimm cleared his throat. "You like what I've done with your Enomeg prototype designs? There's plenty of modifications, like the leg-jets for maneuvering in flight, and the arm-mounted Starfire rifles, capable of either burst or beam fire. They can even put the two guns together and make a Starfire cannon capable of bringin' down a walker leg."

"The similarities to the Enomegs are definitely noticeable, although I question your judgment in making all of these exoskeletons for teenagers."

Grimm laughed. "What, you think I specially-designed each suit for each soldier like you crazy Xarkonians who spend money like you breathe air? No way, Mars. The armor components are modeled to fit body parts of any size, and the nanofiber mesh'll mold itself to anybody. *You* could put on one o' these suits!"

"Doubtful."

Grimm blew out a sigh. "Alright, boys n' girls. Play-time's over. Dismissed!"

They watched as the green-armored young men and women marched off, disappearing into a door on one of the tall, cylindrical turrets that marked the corners of the perimeter. Boyle followed them, nodding once to Grimm as he left. Soon they were alone with the elites and Hurk once more. The bulky Slashrim was watching as the bodies below were being dragged away.

"Go help 'em clean up, Hurk," Grimm said offhandedly. "Just don't eat anyone."

Mars smirked. "You don't encourage the healthy use of resources?"

"Well, I guess it ain't exactly cannibalism since he ain't Human," the warlord conceded, "but it still ain't right."

Mars shrugged. "If you say so."

Grimm shot him a one-eyed, disapproving glance. "I may have ordered those men killed, Mars, but at one point or another they *were* my soldiers."

"I doubt they quite deserve a burial with full military honors."

"I'm gonna dump 'em at sea, now that you ask. But that ain't the point. I mean… come on, don't *any* of the so-called 'horrors of war' *ever* bother you? You're only Human."

A cold smile crept over Mars's false-bearded face. "*Exactly*. Humans love war, Grimm… almost as much as Slashrim, in their own way. Even if they won't admit it, the world out there is always looking forward to the next good war. Humanity thrives on adversity. Look at the media, at our entertainment, at our works of art and literature… all of our greatest works, our greatest acts, are born from strife and conflict."

"Not all of 'em…" Grimm began to argue, just for the sake of it.

Mars waved a dismissive hand. "Yes, they are. Even those works promoting peace are responses to war. Without war, they would not exist either. Conflict is the essence of nature, and humanity is part of nature. Who would we be without it?"

"It's only Human," Grimm replied, relinquishing the point with a disgruntled sigh. "So anyway, now you've seen my official status report. How are things on your end?"

Mars looked away at the sea. "The last CONON meeting was slightly less than satisfactory. The Emperor continues to fail at his job just as his pitiful dynasty has always done for the past half-century. But regardless of the inevitable failure of his foolish plans, *mine* are coming along perfectly."

"So the Enomegs are ready then?"

"Ah, Grimm. Always trying to get more information on the Enomegs… Suffice it to say that they will be ready in time. Just see that you are ready in time as well."

Grimm laughed. "Mars, like you just said, I'm always lookin' forward to another great war."

Mars fixed him with his iron stare. "Ah, but this is not merely a great war… it is the *ultimate* war. And it is not simply another war… it is *my* war."

- Chapter Seven -
The Virtue of the Vicious

Saber-Scorpion awoke to see the sun rising lazily above the misty horizon. The mid-Xarkon plains that seemed to stretch on forever during the day merely faded out into a grey haze in the early morning. This fog condensed on the shimmering blades of Ukrak, forming droplets that ran down toward the base of the plant. Many of these droplets were caught before they reached the earth by the same animals that had cut the pathways the Enomegs had used to pass through the waving sea of blades.

As the light of New Sol filled the atmosphere, Scorp stood up and did his morning routine of stretches. As he did so, he looked around for some sign of Gun-Barracuda, wondering where his companion in punishment had spent the night. He also looked around for some water – he knew there was a river around here someplace... But then Scorp's eyes landed on something else: the base entrance. The door was open!

"Huh," Scorp huffed.

He walked down the hill, away from the lone tree under which he had slept. As he approached, he noticed that the control panel beside the door had been torn completely off, the wires behind it hanging out in disarray. Although all Enomeg trainees were electronics experts by most standards, it was not Scorp's greatest skill. He knew enough about bypassing security devices to see that the controls had been hotwired, but he could hardly believe it was possible; the technology used at the ETAB was extremely advanced. It would take a true expert to break in.

"Huh," he said again. The sound seemed to fit the situation.

He was genuinely impressed. Clearly, there really were some brains behind Barracuda's thick, bald skull. Well, Dark-Dragon had said they could come back in if they found a way to do so without inside help. Apparently Barracuda did not have the patience to wait. As for Scorp, he had been enjoying the relaxation. But he had to admit he was rather hungry. So he made his way into the base and headed straight for the mess hall.

The mess was probably the loudest place in the ETAB, but even it would have seemed eerily silent compared to most. It was a long metal room full of tables and chairs, decorated only by a few long, dark flags of Xarkon hanging from the ceiling, their crimson Crown emblems watching ominously over all below. Still, it was a surprisingly small room, and only half of the tables were full. There were not nearly as many students here as there had been in Scorp's previous training centers. Only the best made it to the Enomeg Training Academy Base. And as the tests grew harder, even the best were starting to thin out.

After getting his portion of rations, which he did not even bother taking the time to identify since he knew it would be highly nutritional yet entirely tasteless as always, Scorp walked over and sat down on one end of an empty table. Out of nowhere, Blade-Mantis soon moved to sit opposite him. It seemed to be one of his many mysterious powers.

"Congratulations on making your way back in," he said.

Scorp shrugged. "Wasn't me. Did Barracuda tell you how he did it? He hotwired the door controls somehow."

Mantis looked impressed. "Just goes to show that, with an Enomeg soldier, there is always more than meets the eye. So... off this topic, what's the story behind you and Raven? The whole story, I mean."

Scorp looked up. "There is none. I met him in the Berg on the ride to the ETAB. I never saw him before that day."

"Well, one would think there was a history between you two. He seems to take a particular interest in beating you at everything you do."

"It's petty, childish rivalry..." Scorp said with a bit of contempt, "a simple feeling of jealousy that I do not share."

Mantis grinned and gave an expression that clearly said: *oh, really?* Scorp looked back down at his food and continued eating. Again there was a moment of silence.

This time it was Scorp who spoke first. "So, what's the history between you and Cathryn?"

Mantis shrugged. "We were friends in our previous place of training. Nothing more. We helped each other rise to the top and make it here, but I never let it become more than that. To do so would have been foolish."

He was looking pointedly at Scorp as he said this.

Scorp merely nodded. "Agreed."

Mantis frowned. "So would be going out of my way to protect her..."

"So if Barracuda had killed her..." Scorp said calmly, looking up at the flags above them, "if by some chance she had been caught by surprise or slipped... you would have done nothing."

97

He looked back down, expecting Mantis to show some sign of honorable indignation… a furrowed brow, pinched lips, nostrils flaring… but instead, Mantis was still smiling.

"It did not happen," he replied evenly.

"So you don't think it was possible? You're a fatalist, or something along those lines?"

Mantis shrugged. "I'm a realist. I've known Cat a long time, my friend. I know she can get out of her own scrapes. We have helped each other many times, but never have we *depended* on each other. That is the way of a regular soldier – a team player – not an Enomeg, meant to stand alone. She would not *want* me to help her. Nor would she want me to avenge her. If she had slipped, I would have reported Barracuda's dishonorable actions to Dark-Dragon and let him decide the proper punishment."

"I would have *killed* him," said Saber-Scorpion, "even if it had been someone else he jerked off that cliff… Seth, Cobra, possibly even Raven."

Mantis's eyebrows went up as he nodded thoughtfully. "Well, I suppose that is why you won the test of honor. You have a very strong sense of it. I am glad, at least, that you are not trying to compete with Raven or trying to seek the Cat's affections. I am glad of this because otherwise it might bother you that they've been over there flirting with each other during this entire break."

Scorp turned, more quickly than he had intended, to look in the direction Mantis indicated. Sure enough, sitting opposite each other at a table in the far corner of the room, were Cat and Raven. They seemed to be enjoying each other's company more than Scorp thought possible considering Raven's acerbic personality. But somehow they were talking animatedly, smiling and laughing. Scorp looked back down and finished his meal.

Mantis gave a short laugh. "As I said, he tries to beat you in everything."

"Well, he's not going to beat me in this little game," Scorp said as he stood up to leave. "Because I'm not playing."

"You think you aren't… but when the Cat wants to play, she usually gets her way."

"You know this from experience?"

"No, no, merely from observation. I'm not playing either. But Cat enjoys this game. She is very good at toying with people's emotions, pulling their strings… much like a cat playing with a ball of yarn."

Scorp got up to leave, and upon noticing that he was heading for the exit nearest Raven and Cat, Mantis hurried to follow him like an excited spectator. As they passed, Cat looked up at Scorp with an expression of surprise, but he looked away and matched gazes with Raven instead. All mirth immediately fled Raven's face, which again turned as cold as it always was when speaking with his opponents.

"I thought you said Cobra was more your style," Scorp commented.

Cat shot Raven a glance, which he ignored. He only grinned. "I thought that was what *you* said," he replied. It was all he could come up with.

Scorp shook his head. "Nah, Tanya and me… we keep things professional, unlike some of the trainees. See you around, Raven."

Having hopefully sewn the seeds of dispute into each of them, Scorp turned and walked off, forcing himself not to look back at them as he headed for his quarters. Maybe he'd still have time to shave that morning after all.

Location: Xendra Jungle, Xarkon
Six Weeks Later

The dim blue light of the Terra Nova moons at night blended with the dark green of the forest below to form a deep turquoise, one that shone on the leaves of the trees but could barely pierce the unfathomable blackness of the depths of the Xendra Jungle. The ocean of trees lay stretched out like a blanket over the feet of the Backbone Mountains in southern Xarkon, covering them in shadow.

Appearing almost tiny in comparison to the vast jungle below them, a pair of great onyx and crimson Nidhogg dropships rustled the leaves of the canopy as they passed along, low to the trees. The bright glow of their lower engines cast a blue-white light over the leaves as they passed, almost touching the highest branches. Birds and animals scattered in all directions as the monstrous war machines loomed overhead.

Inside these two vehicles sat no more than a few dozen men and women, yet together they made up enough manpower to take out at least a large military installation… or perhaps a small country. For they were the Enomeg trainees, making their way now to take the second of their four final tests… the Test of Loyalty.

"Which is greater," Dark-Dragon said as he paced back and forth inside the first dropship's cramped and dark interior, "honor or loyalty?"

The Enomegs, who sat facing each other in the two rows of seats on either side of the Nidhogg's hold, paused and reflected. A few of them shot glances to each other, but none would admit their confusion. They had never before been presented with the possibility that any of the four tenets of Xarkon could be greater than another.

"Let me ask a few of you in turn…" Dragon said. "Seth? David? Vincent?"

Seth's blue eyes roved the compartment thoughtfully. He bit his lip. Finally he said, "Honor is the most important."

"What he said," Coyote said with a nod.

David rubbed his shaved head. "I'd say Loyalty, sir."

Dark-Dragon nodded thoughtfully but not affirmatively as he moved to the next trainee. "Kade?"

Barracuda responded without hesitation, his voice so deep it seemed to vibrate the metal walls. "Loyalty."

Dragon repeated his thoughtful nod and walked on. "Cathryn?"

Cat bit her lip. "Supremacy is probably the most…"

"Forget the other two," Dragon interrupted quickly.

She shook her head. "Then… I don't know. Both of them equally?"

Dragon paused for a moment this time, but then shook his head. "What about you, Tanya?"

Cobra only shrugged. "Couldn't say."

Dragon seemed to accept this, but moved on. "Alright, speak up, the rest of you. Scorp? Luke? Lee?"

Scorp and Raven's voices mingled as, staring directly at each other, they both simultaneously answered with opposite replies.

Scorp said, "Honor."

Raven said, "Loyalty."

After a thoughtful pause, Mantis finally answered. "I cannot speak for others, sir, but to me, Honor and Loyalty are one and the same. Loyalty is honorable… One cannot have honor without loyalty."

This time, Dark-Dragon smiled. "Correct. That is exactly what I was looking for. Some of you here may think that honor is a personal code, one that denies such things as, say, killing unarmed civilians, for example. That is ethics or morality, not honor. A part of honor, yes, but not true honor. True honor goes above and beyond mere ethics, looking toward the greater good, toward history… future history. Loyalty to a greater cause is a fundamental part of true honor; to be disloyal to one's cause is to be *without* honor.

"Sometimes loyalty may cause you to break your own code of ethics. There are some 'unarmed civilians' that can do more harm to a country than a whole legion of well-equipped enemy soldiers. These 'civilians' may use your own sense of honor against you by refusing to draw a weapon, by playing on your emotions and your weaknesses… your ethics. In these cases, loyalty to the greater good must override your personal feelings. Only then will you be a soldier of honor."

He stood in silence then, allowing his words to sink into them. After a moment, he turned on his heel and strode toward the cockpit. "We're approaching the L-Z now," he said. "There may not be a clearing large enough to hold the Nidhogg, so get ready for a fast-rope descent. Now, Enomegs!"

As the vaguely Crown of Xarkon-shaped Nidhogg dropships slowed to a hovering halt over the jungle canopy, startled Mocco birds took off in all directions, their long, colorful tails flowing behind them. With all their lower engines burning on full to help the hoverpads maintain their altitude, the doors of the Nidhoggs slid open. Like uncoiling snakes, several ropes dropped from the belly of each craft, and down slid the shadowy figures of the Enomegs. Once they were all unloaded, the dropships' engines flared, and they rose away into the night.

Tonight the Enomegs were wearing their usual dark, padded armor… but around their wrists were thick bracers made of a dark metal. On top of each hand was strapped a metallic square wired into the bracer, along the forward side of which was a small slit… a slit that could emit a Starfire Blade, one of the deadliest melee weapons ever invented.

These devices were the Enomeg hand-blades, signature weapons of an Enomeg super-soldier. The Enomegs had trained with them endlessly, but were only allowed to use them in the field once or twice. They treasured every opportunity, and all eagerly awaited the day they could wear them permanently. They were known as the Star-Talons.

Stretching his arms as he looked about at the moonlit jungle, Saber-Scorpion resisted the urge to activate his own pair on the spot. The weapons operated just like Starfire rifles or cannons, by first forming an invisible force field "bubble" in order to give the blade its shape, and then filling this bubble with superheated Starlight Gas, the same as that burned by the engines of modern starships and aerospace craft. The resulting heat would have been enough to set the wielder on fire if not for the force field, which only parted when it encountered something solid.

When the force field was breached, the heat of the starfire blade was unleashed, cutting instantly through most known materials. The only thing capable of blocking the force field without breaching it was just that: another force field, which allowed for duels to be conducted between two foes both armed with the blades. The weapon's only real drawback was that it could deplete its small Starlight Gas canisters relatively quickly while burning through an object. So it was that Scorp simply let his hands fall to his sides and continued exploring the area.

He walked to the edge of the nearby cliff and gazed into the chasm below. A dense jungle lay spread out beneath him, climbing up the hills, growing thicker and darker in the lowest spots of the valley. Fog lingered on the edges of the gorge, glowing softly in the bright light of Terra Nova's two moons. The air was thick and heavy, and it echoed with the exotic calls of jungle wildlife. Scorp kept his eyes keen for movement, either for some unknown assailant that might be part of the test or for the monkey-like creatures that he knew lived in the trees here. He heard they traveled easily between branches in the crowded canopy and enjoyed pelting intruders with... projectiles of a rather unclean nature.

By this time, the Enomegs had gathered in a small clearing near where they had disembarked. Without a word, almost subconsciously, Dark-Dragon drew their attention back to him. He stood at the edge of the clearing, an armored silhouette against the blacker shadow of the jungle behind him.

"As I said before, today's mission will be the Test of Loyalty," Dark-Dragon said. "I've already introduced you to the concept of loyalty, so we will skip right to the instructions. A number of prisoners have been transferred to a detention facility here, hidden in the low-lying mountains. These prisoners will soon be released into the valley below us, and it will be your job to hunt them down... and execute them. Kill every last one of them. If any of them survive, we will know it. Each of you will be assigned one single prisoner to hunt and kill. That one prisoner will be your sole responsibility. Do not interfere with any of the other trainees or their targets."

At this point, Dragon began handing out small paper cards, no doubt containing information they would soon be required to destroy.

"These cards will tell you about your target. On each one is all of the information you should need to know... photo, age, height, weight, nationality, species, race, hair color, eye color, skin color... even an image of their footprint and fingerprint. This will be a test of your tracking and identification skills.

Remember, if you kill anyone besides your own target or let your own target escape, you have failed the test. And of course you have failed the test if you somehow manage to get killed, but I doubt there is anything out there that will be a danger to you. The criminals are unarmed, and you know which animals to avoid. There, that's everyone. Now, are there any questions?"

Scorp swallowed hard. He had guessed from Dragon's talk about the nature of honor on the ride over here that this would be a difficult trial, more on a psychological level than a physical one. Now he was facing the grim truth of it: they were here to hunt down and kill unarmed prisoners, men and women who had no hope of fighting back. He knew that it had to be just, that Xarkon would not have invoked this sort of death sentence on a convict who did not deserve it, but... he still could not bring himself to look at his card.

He tried to keep his voice entirely level as he said, "Sir... do they know? Do they know we are hunting them?"

Dragon shook his head. "No, they do not. This is their final punishment, to be hunted down like animals. It is nothing less than they deserve, nothing less than many of them have done to others. Some of these people are terrorist leaders, others homicidal madmen... They all deserve what is coming to them. They have been told that no transportation vehicles are allowed to stay at this maximum-security prison, so they have to make their own way through the jungle to the nearest town after their release. There is a small village on the other side of those mountains, along the right side of the valley. That is where they will be headed... but they will not arrive."

Scorp closed his eyes. He heard the voice of Daniel ask almost excitedly, "Sir, should we punish them? Prolong their death to make them *suffer* for what they've done?"

Dark-Dragon hesitated. "No. That is not your role. These prisoners have already received the suffering that was due to them in prison. Your role is that of executioner. You are here to end their suffering along with their life. Those are your orders. Follow them. When you are through, return to this clearing. That is all. Good luck to all of you."

With that, the Enomeg disappeared. Even now, as they neared the end of their training, none of them could detect him when he slipped away, or could tell where he went. Suddenly all was silent except for the forest animals. Scorp turned and quickly flipped open the card he had been given. He was shocked to see the face of a beautiful young woman in the photo. She had pale skin and long, slightly curly auburn hair. Her strangely golden eyes were narrowed to slits, in an expression of defiance. The deep blue moonlight almost seemed to make the photo come alive in Scorp's imagination. He could see her now, standing before him as a person, that same look on her face.

And he was supposed to kill her, cutting her down with his blades of red-white fire.

Scorp closed his eyes for a few seconds, trying to clear his doubtful thoughts, and then he continued reading. He was surprised to discover that she was actually not even Human; she was Sarran. Her wings matched the color of her hair, the card said, but they had been clipped so she would be unable to fly.

Scorp had never heard of that before, clipping a Sarran's wings. Something inside of him immediately cried out that it was revolting and cruel... like severing a Human's hamstrings or cutting off their thumbs. His training moved quickly to silence these misgivings.

Not quickly enough.

"*Damn*," Scorp swore under his breath.

"This guy should be easy to spot," said Shadow-Cat, standing beside Scorp. She held out her hand. "He's got a beard this long!"

"The beard actually might make things worse here in the jungle," Blade-Mantis commented with an amused grin. "They can make decent camouflage, you know, especially when *filthy*."

"Who did you get?" Cat asked.

Mantis waved his paper in the air. "Some fellow with bright red hair. That'll make him really easy to spot. It says he's a vicious one though. I'd better be careful, no?"

He gave an easygoing smile, his black eyes gleaming, eager for the hunt. Cat laughed. Magnum-Coyote was talking to Cobra, chuckling as he showed her his target. All of this triggered a deep, profound feeling of disgust in Saber-Scorpion. He hated everything about this; it all felt wrong. He had been loyal for all these years, for his entire life, and now they asked him to prove his loyalty with this execution... this *murder?* It was not *right*. Or perhaps *he* was wrong? It was not as if he was opposed to the idea of the death penalty for terrible crimes. Perhaps these people really deserved what was coming to them. He had to believe that... or somehow find out the truth.

Seth laughed. "This kid looks easy. Look at his cocky grin; who smiles like that for a prison mugshot, anyway?"

"You, probably," Coyote put in, provoking laughter all around.

Barracuda snorted. "Mine doesn't look much better. You can tell by the way his mouth and eyes sag that he's as dumb as a stone. I doubt there will even be much brains to spill when I cut his skull open."

"I'm going after a girl," said Raven, with a laugh. "She's pretty. Should be pretty easy then."

Saber-Scorpion tried not to listen to the conversations around him. He had killed before, of course, plenty of times. He remembered his first kill... One of his previous training bases had come under attack by a group of Zygbari rebels, probably looking to raid it for weapons, and the unit commander thought it would be a good idea to let the Enomeg trainees have some target practice. In that situation, he had gladly killed his enemies, shooting at them across the range as they fired back at him.

But this... something about this was different. He didn't like it. He asked himself, how is it different? These criminals were fighting against Xarkon too, much as the Zygbari terrorists with their khaki desert uniforms and second-rate blazer rifles had been. Did they not deserve death as well?

But this Sarran girl...

"Who did you get?" Cat asked him, interrupting his thoughts.

"Same as Raven," he answered, his voice surprising even him with its cold lack of emotion, "another pretty girl. Ironic, huh?"

Cat smirked, and one of her eyebrows went up. "You think she's still pretty after being in prison for that long?"

"Why shouldn't she be?" he asked. "Sarrans live a long time."

"She's a Sarran?"

This drew their interest. Cat and Mantis stepped closer and peered over Scorp's shoulder at the picture just before Coyote reached out and took it. He laughed and handed it around. Raven just rolled his eyes, stuck his own card in his pocket, and tightened his bracers. Finally Mantis snatched Scorp's card from Seth and glanced at it briefly before handing it back to its owner.

"She really is rather attractive," he admitted.

"I've never seen a Sarran," Cat said. "This should be good training for you though. We might end up fighting them someday."

"Might as well learn how to slaughter them now," Scorp concluded, his voice flat.

"Are you having second thoughts, my friend?" Mantis asked.

"Second thoughts about what? This woman is already dead."

He crumpled the paper up in his hand, squeezing it into a tight ball. Did he put a bit too much into this display? He looked up and saw Cat looking back at him thoughtfully. Once their eyes met, she looked away and slipped into the jungle foliage behind Raven. Scorp turned and nodded to Mantis. They separated and each disappeared into the forest as well. Soon the clearing was empty and silent, and the animals started to return.

Shadow-Cat found that she was able to sneak through the dense jungle foliage with ease. Only the most perceptive beasts of the forests – natives of this strange world, who were one with the land and observed its every slight change – could possibly have noticed her passing. She slid from shadow to shadow, like a snake between the leaves. Indeed, she was part of the blackness itself... she merged with it and traveled through it like a sister of the shadow. Meanwhile, she followed her target's trail.

The hunt was long and tedious. A less skilled tracker would have grown tired of it, lost patience, and given up. But Cat did not have that choice. For hours, she moved through the leaves, occasionally encountering signs of passage, but always the trails grew cold or ended with the wrong target. And throughout all of this, she managed to keep up her unrivaled level of stealth. Even though it had practically become second nature to her now, it still took concentration to keep it up for this long. But, she thought, this was no doubt part of the test.

Now the foliage began to grow less dense. She was approaching a clearing. Ahead, a shaft of moonlight shone down onto a platform of stone on which no trees grew. On that platform stood three men, all busy making primitive weapons. One had a long beard and large bags under his eyes. His hands shook as he tried to make his stick sharper with a rock. That was her target. He looked pitiful. He would give no resistance. Beside him was a strong, vicious looking young man with messy red hair. He was looking around with wild eyes, breathing heavily, and holding a pair of sharpened sticks. The third man in the group had dark hair and was holding a large branch like a club, a look of determination in his eyes.

"Maybe they won't find us," Cat heard the old man say in a hoarse whisper. "Maybe they won't come here at all."

"Like hell they won't," said the red-haired man between gritted teeth. "You saw that one that passed us by, the giant bald-headed bastard. Said we're *not his target*... But I'll bet my bottom Crown there's another out there lookin' for *us*."

"I say we dig a pit," said the dark-haired man.

"No time," answered the red.

In her mind, Shadow-Cat named them: Red, Brown, and Geezer. She wondered which one she should take out first, and then she remembered that she was to only kill her own target. This could be harder than she had first anticipated. At least, so she thought until she saw Blade-Mantis suddenly step from the shadow of the trees on the other side of the clearing. He activated one of his Star-Talons, which lit up the area in red light as it came online with a sharp hiss. The three convicts looked down at him in horror. They seemed to be staring at his Starfire blade more than anything else.

"W-what are we supposed to do against *that?*" cried Cat's target, the Geezer, as he crouched behind his companions and picked up a large stone.

"Don't move," said Brown, waving him back. "Let him come to us."

Red bit his lip and held his sticks at his side. Then one of his arms whipped up, and with a cry he threw his makeshift spear with surprising accuracy at Mantis's dark form. Despite the man's skilled aim, the Enomeg trainee dodged the missile effortlessly. Then he advanced. Mantis thought the man had no chance. No, he *knew* the man had no chance. He could look at his inexperienced stance and tell that this enemy was no challenge.

This was the full extent of the thoughts that passed through the Enomeg's mind. Then he felt his enemy's spear nick his arm. He grabbed it, twirled, dodged the first swing of the dark-haired man's club, and sliced open Red's chest. Then the club came back around, and this time it struck Mantis directly in the face. He tumbled onto his back in the grass.

Brown waved his club and laughed, standing over his unconscious foe. But he was surprised to see no blood on the Enomeg's face where he had been struck. Then Mantis's eyes burst open, and he winked. But before either of them could make a move, a rock sailed out of the foliage. It struck the back of Brown's head with a sharp crack, and down he fell like a stone.

Mantis stood up and deactivated his blade. "Thank you, Cat. I'll also have to thank Coyote for showing me that trick of his."

Then Mantis assumed a passive stance, watching now without much interest as the old man scrambled to his feet and turned to run. In a blink, Cat materialized directly in front of him. The fugitive screamed in fear and fell backwards onto the stone. There was a snap like cracking bone as he hit the rock, and he cried out into the night.

"N-no! NO!" he screamed. "P-please don't!"

Shadow-Cat stepped closer and looked down at the pitiful creature. His frail, thin body was wracked with pain, and his face was a mask of the purest terror. Cat's Starfire hand-blade screamed to life. The clearing glowed red in its light. She saw Lee watching, his dark eyes gleaming.

"Please... please don't..." the old man gasped. "I... I'm an old man, weak from years of prison life. I can do no more harm to Xarkon! P-please... just let me go..."

Cat hesitated. She looked at her own lean but strong arm, the hot blade of energy sizzling from the ebon bracer strapped to her wrist, and she compared it to that of the old man. It was like the arm of a skeleton. In fact, it actually looked like he had broken it in the fall. Cat noticed that her mouth was open, her hesitation evident. She looked at Mantis, who was watching her. His expression was cold and hard as stone.

"It's your duty," he said.

Cathryn swallowed hard. For a moment, she felt almost afraid of him... afraid of Mantis, standing there in the light of her energy blade, the dark jungle trees behind him, clad in his shadowy armor, his two black eyes gleaming like gemstones... Then, in a flash so quick that the old man did not even have time to scream, Cat killed him.

She looked away quickly and deactivated her blade, stumbling off toward Mantis. He put a hand on her arm and looked reassuringly into her eyes. His expression was completely different now, more like the Lee Blade-Mantis she knew. But still she could picture that stone-cold look in his eyes, that person she did not know looking down at her like a statue.

Hesitantly, she said, "Well... I guess that's 'mission complete.'"

Mantis looked at her sympathetically. "Cat, you got a tough one. Mine was young and ready to fight, but your target was actually harder... because he fought with your emotions. Remember what Dark-Dragon said? Just take comfort in the fact that it was your duty to kill this man, and you did it well. You can see that you ended him quickly, caused him no pain in death... except for fear, I suppose. You have granted him peace, ended his mortal punishment. Now, let us head back to the rendezvous point, eh?"

Mantis turned to leave and stepped past the body of the unconscious man with the dark hair. He laughed. "Well, someone will have it easy because of you, Cat."

Cat smiled, very slightly. Mantis turned and walked off into the shadow of the forest, and Cat followed. As she did so, she glanced at the body of her victim. His head was thrown back, his mouth and eyes wide, staring straight up at her. His body was limp, its arms thrown out straight, a black streak burned across his chest. At peace? Felt no pain? He looked almost like he had been pinned to the stone with nails, crucified there for some crime that he had committed years ago. She wondered vaguely what the crime was.

Then she heard the buzzing hiss of an energy blade behind her. When she turned, she saw Silent-Cobra draw her blade back out of the unconscious dark-haired man's chest. The woman nodded to Cat once, quickly. There in that hot jungle, Cat suddenly felt a chill. But she returned the nod.

Then the two of them again merged with the shadows and disappeared…

LOCATION: XENDRA JUNGLE, DEEPER VALLEY

The jungle air was hot, thick, and steamy. Saber-Scorpion wiped his sweaty palms on his shirt. The outfits they had been told to wear were not actually suitable for the terrain. Not only were they stiflingly hot, but a knife would probably go right through them. Scorp supposed this was done to give the prisoners a glimmer of a chance at fighting them… though even that was laughable. As the Enomeg walked, he kept an eye out for any signs of prisoner tracks. It was confusing work, since there were so many indigenous creatures here. He had to pick out the clear signs of Human passage.

Or rather, Sarran passage, he thought as he spotted his first good clue. A large, reddish-brown bird feather was stuck in a bush. Most would not have noticed it, hidden as it was amongst the leaves, but Scorp's eyes detected it immediately. He drew it out and examined it. It definitely had not come from any species of bird in this area. How could the Sarran woman have been so careless, to leave such an obvious clue? Again Scorp felt the unfairness of the situation. The Enomegs had been trained to hunt and kill any foe under any circumstances. These prisoners were just lost and confused, frightened and desperate.

His train of thought was broken as he spotted some tracks in the dark, mossy earth of the jungle floor. They were hard to identify, so he just began following them, still trying not to think about what he would do when he found what was leaving them. He knew that he was approaching a river, but it surprised him when he almost stepped directly into it. He was aware that some of the prisoners would probably be trying to travel through the water in order to avoid leaving a trail, so he leaned out and took a peek.

It was a shallow river, wide and not too fast. Tree branches arced inward on either side, almost meeting in the middle, casting spotty shadows down over the muddy water. But one of these shadows was moving on its own, not far off, and Scorp quickly identified it as two or more individuals wading along with the current. They were making their way down the river toward him. He paused, hid himself more securely, and looked out a second time. As he suspected, it was two of the prisoners: a man and a woman.

Scorp looked them over. The young woman was muddy and wet from slogging through the shallow river. She was still unarmed, and her long, black hair was matted to her body, which was barely covered by a thin grey prison outfit that clung to her slender form. She looked tired. Still, she was clearly no Sarran. Was this Blood-Raven's target?

The young man behind her looked even more helpless than she did. He was pale and skinny, with hollow cheeks and a protruding rib cage visible beneath his wet shirt. He seemed to be reluctantly following the woman, shooting furtive glances in every direction at intervals. Apparently they knew something suspicious was afoot, which was to be expected. Who would be foolish enough to think that Xarkon would simply set prisoners loose into the jungle for no reason? They knew that they were meant to die.

But the question was… *why?* Scorp had to know. He had to find out what they had done to deserve this fate.

Without further thought and certainly without fear, Saber-Scorpion stepped out into the stream right in front of them. The girl gasped and stumbled back, almost falling over as the current pushed her forward. Scorp caught and steadied her, since he knew the man behind her probably couldn't. She looked up at him, her dark eyes glinting green in the moonlight, showing surprise, fear… and curiosity. He was only holding her lightly, but apparently her male companion felt that the Enomeg was a danger, so he landed the strongest blow he could to Scorp's shoulder. Saber-Scorpion ignored him completely.

"What was your crime?" Scorp suddenly hissed, giving the girl a light shake. "What was your crime?!"

He detected a touch of Mordark accent in her voice as she said, "You… You're an Enomeg, aren't you? You're one of the… the chosen…"

The other prisoner dropped his arms and took several steps back, what color that remained in his skin quickly fled from sight. He made a few indications that he was about to run.

Scorp shook his head. "Listen to me. I'm not going to hurt you. There *is* someone out there looking to kill you, *both* of you… but it is not me. Just tell me: *what was your crime?*"

"I… I worked with a hitman," the girl stammered. "M-my father… He did it all! I just followed him, did what he said. He… He was hired to kill some Crownie brass. When we were digging up dirt on him, we… we found out some things. And then *they* found *us*. But he's already been executed! He knew more than me, I swear! He never told me anything *important!*"

Scorp closed his eyes. She had been forced to follow the orders of her father, a hitman, who had made the mistake of trying to take out an officer of the Xarkon Armed Forces, a "Crownie," as mercenaries and Victorians sometimes called them. He wondered if she had witnessed her father's execution before her eyes. It sounded like he deserved it, but why had they kept *her* in custody? Why were they hunting her now? Scorp dreaded the answer, but he asked the question anyway.

"What *things* did you find out?"

She spoke in a whisper as she replied, "The Enomegs, Xarkon's top-secret super-soldier project. We ran across some names…"

"Names?" Scorp prompted.

"The names of the chosen… the children they took for their warrior genes. But I only know a few!"

Keeping his voice low and soothing, trying not to make it sound like a command, he said, "Tell me."

She took a deep breath and steadied herself. "Like I *told* the interrogators, the list was in alphabetical order by first name, and I didn't look at it very long. I only remember the first two and the last one. They were Cathryn Carla Frey, Daniel Davis Hobson, and Vincent Nathan Marshall. That's all I know, I swear!"

Scorp felt a chill run through him. *Our names*, he thought. *They used our real names.* He now knew the girl must be telling the truth. There was no other way she could know those names. That meant they were here to kill her just because of what she knew. Just because she knew their *names*.

His grip on her shoulders loosening, Scorp looked directly into the girl's wide eyes… brown, tinged with green… and as she stared back into his deep blue-grey ones and saw the honesty there, the fear slowly began to leave her. He could feel her shoulders relax. In fact, she almost seemed to be leaning against him now. He wondered vaguely if she was using him, putting on an act of innocence. But it was too late to wonder about that now.

"You can't fight them," Scorp said. "Neither of you would stand a chance. And you can't escape them by walking down the middle of the river like this. They're sure to suspect that."

"What… what do we do?" she asked nervously.

Scorp looked around quickly. He soon noticed that the skinny young man was no longer anywhere to be seen. Well, it would only go the worse for him. Scorp had planned to help him, but he was not going to go hunting him down through the trees for that exact purpose.

"The trees," Scorp said. "The creatures here climb between them. Do you think you can do that? Move between trees? The tree branches are thick and wind around each other in a lot of places."

She nodded. "I'm a good climber."

Scorp took a step back, running his hands through his hair. "Okay. Now, listen. Take off your shoes, if you have any. They'll leave more marks. Find a tree you can climb into and start moving from tree to tree. Stay off the ground. Move as far as you can as fast as you can, and then find a good hiding spot – I mean one hell of an *invisible* hiding spot. Then stay there and *don't move*. Don't react to anything. If you move, they'll catch you. If you make a single sound, they'll catch you. If you leave one sign on the ground of your passing, they will catch you. And if they catch you, that's the end. Wait until nightfall. In fact, don't move until morning. By then we should all be gone."

She shivered and looked around anxiously. "Why are you telling me this?" she whispered.

He paused. Why *was* he telling her this? None of the others would have done this… would have jeopardized everything they had ever lived for, the goal of their lives, just for a few criminals with death sentences. But it did not matter what the others would have done. There was only him.

"Because I have to," he said at last. "Now go. Go quickly. If you can find the one who was with you earlier, or any other prisoners, tell them everything I said. But don't waste time! Hurry!"

She nodded quickly and ran off, sliding into the bushes on the opposite bank. Would she even do as instructed, he wondered? Suddenly he felt sick with himself, and his mind started making up excuses: Aiding this girl had eliminated some of his competition, at least… even though this wasn't supposed to be a competition at all.

He shook his head. There was no use trying to reason with his own conscience. He knew why he had done it… and there was no changing it. His actions were embedded in his personality. To deny them would be to deny who he was, to deny the honor that was supposedly ingrained into him by the very genes that had caused him to be chosen as an Enomeg in the first place. He looked at the deep blue night sky, filtering in through the few tiny cracks in the branches above. Then he looked behind him, at where he had come from… at the river he had crossed.

"If, after nineteen years of hard training, even Xarkon herself couldn't change me… then there's no way *I* can do it."

He felt better after that. Then, with renewed determination, he continued his hunt.

LOCATION: XENDRA JUNGLE, UPPER VALLEY

The rail-thin convict slithered between the close-set trees like a snake, moving as quickly as he could to put as much distance as possible between himself and that muscular soldier with the black ninja suit. He had spoken enough with the girl to know what the Enomegs were, and when she claimed to recognize their assailant as one of these mysterious warriors, he fled as quickly as he could. The super-soldier could have that girl, if he wanted her. The convict only hoped that she would prove enough of a distraction for him to make his escape.

Of course, if the soldier did follow him, it would be easy enough to take care of him… for this particular criminal was not as stupid as the others. He had managed to steal a gun from one of the prison guards on his way out. Armed with the pistol, he now felt secure, since he had seen no such weapon on the person of the soldier who had confronted them.

His heart nearly leapt out of his chest as he heard a twig snap to his right. The gun whirled and spat fire. Once, twice, thrice he fired into the bushes. The shots seemed so loud… He could hear their roar echoing off the distant cliffs, as animals of various shapes and sizes took off from the treetops all around, their calls ringing out through the jungle. Then the prisoner took a few steps forward, leaning in toward the bushes he had shot. He pushed the branches aside to find…

Nothing. Sweating profusely and breathing heavily, the fugitive massaged his arm where the kick of his weapon had injured it. It was a CP12 blazer pistol, the standard of most Xarkonian police, who, like most Xarkonians, preferred big guns. Of course, even a round only a few millimeters wide fired by the gauss technology that propelled most modern caseless ammunition could create considerable recoil. The convict simply had no experience with this advanced type of weapon.

Suddenly another sound startled him, this time from behind. He whirled, pointing the gun. He cursed. Still nothing.

Then a voice above him said, "Boo."

He looked up to see the flash of Magnum-Coyote's smile, just before the Enomeg's black-booted feet descended straight toward his face. It was the last thing he ever saw.

- CHAPTER EIGHT -
JUSTIN'S JUSTICE

"Can't go back. No, not to that place. No, no. But can't escape either. Still they follow. Still they watch. Can't escape!"

Saber-Scorpion paused, and dropped reflexively into the shadows. He had been following what seemed to be the Sarran woman's trail for a while now, when suddenly this rambling voice had reached his ears. The tone was low, more coughing and muttering to itself than crying out into the forest, but still Scorp could hear it, meaning the raving man had to be close. From the sound of it, the man was clearly beyond help, yet curiosity lured Scorp to stay and listen.

So he began heading toward the source of the noise. The man was not hard to pinpoint, for he never stopped rambling, and soon Scorp found him wandering aimlessly through the jungle. The prisoner was hunched over, constantly rubbing his hands together or massaging his arms or face, as if to keep warm or to remove some stain from his flesh. If the latter was his intention, then he was failing miserably. Scorp had expected his eyes to be wide and wild, but they were actually dull and drooping, hardly visible in the dim moonlight, as if his senses saw nothing of the outside world. He was trapped in a world of his own.

"Can't escape Xarkon. Always here, never alone. Never alone, though we roam. Quantum phone… makes me roam…"

Scorp realized this one was a lost cause and was about to leave the unfortunate man to his fate when finally one word made him pause.

The man's voice was a muttering, gasping hiss as he said, "*Xarkon.* I know their darkest secrets. The kidnappings, the thefts, the slaves. They want to *take* those secrets. They want to *kill* those secrets. Kill the man; kill the secrets. Kill the man; kill the knowledge. Kill the knowledge; no one knows. No one knows; it never happened. It never happened; they did no wrong. They did no wrong! Xarkon can do no wrong!"

After this moment of clarity, his words began to return to nonsense. He was also getting louder, even as he wandered into the darker shadows of the jungle. Suddenly, the shadows disappeared as the entire area was bathed in a bright red glow. Scorp slinked back behind the bush as Gun-Barracuda came marching through the trees, unstoppable as a tank. The madman gave him a curious look, showing no fear even as the Enomeg's blade slid into his chest and back out again. Whatever knowledge he had carried died with him.

"Forty-*two*," Kade said, as he watched the body fall.

Scorp had frozen completely still, partially to avoid being detected, but also because of the shocking suddenness with which the scene had unfolded. One minute no one was there, and then Barracuda appeared, killing the raving madman with hardly a thought. And now the only thought behind the trainee's scarred face was adding another number to his growing kill-count. Once Kade confirmed that the man was dead, he simply walked off, heedless of Saber-Scorpion's presence.

The prisoner's last words kept repeating in Scorp's mind: *It never happened, they did no wrong. Xarkon can do no wrong!*

Finally he decided he'd waited long enough, so he stood up and returned to his own trail to continue his hunt. But even concentrating on the task of tracking his prey could not silence the echoes of that voice. *Xarkon can do no wrong.* It could not be clearer why the Enomegs were here. They were being ordered to silence people who knew too much. But why them? Was it part of the test, to endure the words of their victims but carry out their duty anyway? Was Scorp being weak by giving in, by letting it get to him? But that last man had not been making excuses or concocting lies; he had been talking to no one but himself. He had to be telling the truth.

As he followed the tracks before him, Saber-Scorpion became distinctly aware that he was getting closer. It was more of a feeling than any solid evidence of his target's passage. There was light up ahead where the forest drew to an end near the cliff edge, and if there was one thing Scorp knew about Sarran, it was that they hated closed-in spaces. All of their starships featured luxuriously spacious interiors to give them room to stretch their wings a bit, and most Sarran still felt claustrophobic even then. So he felt positive that his target would be seeking refuge from the oppressive gloom of the jungle.

As he stepped out into the clearing, the brightness of the moonlight surprised him, and he paused to let his vision adjust. He saw that he had reached the border of the lower gorge. An even deeper part of the chasm lay spread out below him, no doubt with another river cutting through it as well. And standing there before it all was Scorp's target… the Sarran.

He could see her long auburn hair mingling with the matching feathery wings that sprouted from a hole torn roughly in the back of her shirt. Two smaller winglets on her ankles protruded from similar gaps on her pants legs. As he watched, he saw her approach the edge of the cliff and spread her wings wide. The sight almost took his breath away. The great wings were far larger than he had imagined they could be, now that they were fully extended, silhouetted against the double moons of Terra Nova. It was a magnificent sight. Scorp noticed painfully that the largest feathers were absent from the very tips of her wings, where they had been cut off... clipped. It made the scene before him at once both proud and tragic.

Well, he thought at last, there was certainly nowhere for her to go.

But then, to his astonishment, she leapt into the air. For a moment, she floated as if suspended, and then she began to fall. Scorp made a mad dash forward, acting on instinct, and pounced upon her as she sailed over the cliff edge. Down she soared, with Scorp hanging onto one of her legs. She could not fly, but apparently she could still glide. The Sarran looked back at him and began kicking at his hand with her free leg. Scorp's fingers began to ache; she was surprisingly strong. But Scorp was stronger, and as a result of his weight, she began to fall rapidly.

They hit the ground hard, smashing through the foliage, which luckily was not quite as thick in this lower valley as it had been on top. Scorp jumped to his feet, and the Sarran pushed herself up with her wings. They rose simultaneously, and their eyes met... the alien gold eyes of the Sarran stared with defiance into the blue-grey orbs of the Enomeg trainee. He expected her to make a break for it, but she only stood there, looking at him almost haughtily. She was, of course, quite beautiful.

Scorp cursed under his breath. *Why did they always have to be beautiful?*

"What do you want, Human?" she asked. Her voice had an air of nobility about it, with a strange but dignified accent. She tossed the hair back out of her face and straightened up. Definitely haughty, Scorp thought.

"Well," said the Enomeg trainee, wiping the blood away from his mouth where he had been scratched during the fall, "technically I'm supposed to kill you."

She took a step back, looking around quickly.

He put up his hands in a show of peace. "Listen. Around two dozen men are scouring the jungle right now, searching for you and the other prisoners. We were each assigned an individual target. You are mine."

Her eyes widened, then narrowed. "*Why?*"

Scorp breathed a sigh. "You were sentenced to be executed, and we are your executioners."

She shook her head slowly. "Then why not simply kill us? Why this trickery, this hunt?"

Scorp shrugged. "We are soldiers. Ours is not to reason why. Tell me, what's your name?"

"They didn't even give you that information?"

"No," he said.

She shook her head slowly. "I knew Xarkon could stoop low... but I had no idea how far they could go. You don't need to know my name, Human. Just go on with your dirty work!"

Scorp found himself feeling almost proud of her bravery. This was no helpless prisoner like the two he had met in the riverbank, no raving madman like the one he had witnessed Barracuda kill not long ago. This Sarran's spirit remained unbroken, her head bloodied but unbowed. She would probably even put up a decent fight, before the end. But Scorp didn't want it to come to that.

"Maybe I don't even mean to carry out my dirty work," Scorp said. "What then?"

She squinted, looking him up and down. "I see… Well, if you must know, Humans usually call me Aeriella. But what does that matter?"

Scorp took a deep breath and looked away to one side as he answered, "I just wanted to know the name of the person I'm giving up my life for."

She paused and squinted down at him – for though she was not taller than he was, she had that Sarran way of looking down at everyone, as if they stood beneath them. Of course, she was not so much squinting as simply looking like herself. Sarrans were well-known for their large, keen eyes, which usually appeared long and thin compared to a Human's. They were said to have exceptionally keen eyesight.

"Your life?" she said. "What do you mean?"

He inspected the black blade emitters bound to his wrists. "Everything I've lived for so far, anyway. What they *tell* me is my life."

Her features softened. Suddenly she looked even more beautiful, he thought. "I don't understand," the Sarran said.

"My whole life I've been training to complete four final tests, to become the soldier I was born to be, and now I am about to fail one… because I just can't bring myself to kill you."

Aeriella opened her mouth to speak, but suddenly they were interrupted by a dark figure crashing out of the woods. Scorp turned and activated his star-talons reflexively. The energy beams emerged at his fingertips, flashing online with a loud *KEAOW!* Aeriella gave a gasp when she saw them. Scorp ignored her. He was expecting to see one of the prisoners come stumbling out of the brush, but instead it turned out to be another student, whom Scorp quickly recognized from his close-shaven hair and the determined set to his jaw. It was Daniel.

"You need some help, Scorp?" he asked. "My target can wait."

Scorp recalled Daniel's comment earlier about making his target suffer. He shook his head. "Situation's under control here, Daniel. Thanks anyway."

The trainee looked suspiciously between Scorp and Aeriella. He narrowed his eyes. Scorp saw his fists clench and unclench.

"Scorp…" he said, "what are you doing?"

"I'm standing here, waiting for you to move along," Scorp answered evenly, with an ounce of impatience.

He kept his blades activated. The Sarran woman was looking worried now. Her eyes darted from one trainee to the other, watching for movement. She hesitated, then took a step back.

Scorp turned on her quickly and snapped, "Stay where you are!"

"You're planning to let her go…" Daniel said slowly.

"Move along!" Scorp shouted. "That's an order!"

"You're presuming to give me orders?"

"No, Dark-Dragon is," Scorp replied. "He assigned us each a target, and this woman is mine, not yours. What happens to her makes no difference to you. Now *move along.*"

"It is our duty to kill these criminals!"

"And we do not even know their crimes!" Scorp shouted back, and then he turned to the Sarran. "You! What was your crime? Why were you arrested and sentenced to execution?"

Aeriella straightened herself up proudly once again. "My '*crime*' was investigating the abuses suffered by my people at the hands of Xarkonian 'scientists' trying to 'study' what you call our 'psychic abilities.' I discovered the location of a facility used to detain and test Sarran prisoners, a secret underground complex located in the plains of central Xarkon. I attempted to go there and ascertain if any of my kind were still held prisoner there, and if they were, to free them…"

"See?" Daniel shouted, interrupting her. "She's a rebel, trying to break free Xarkon's prisoners! She's the enemy!"

Scorp's resolve suddenly faltered. He was unsure. Just what was the right thing to do? After all, he had to think about himself. Didn't he want to complete his training? He looked back at her, standing there proudly in the moonlight, as she extended and retracted her wings once again, stretching them reflexively. Again he was struck by her beauty and grace.

"I consider myself capable of many things beyond the abilities of ordinary men," Scorp said slowly, as much to himself as to those around him, "but one thing I am simply not capable of… is cutting down this creature here. I am a soldier; I am a warrior… but I'm no murderer."

Daniel activated his hand-blades. "Murderer…? You're a *traitor!*"

He dashed toward Scorp, who dropped into a defensive stance.

"Daniel Davis Hobson!" he shouted.

Daniel froze in mid-stride, his eyes suddenly wide. "What? What's this nonsense? Have you totally lost it?"

"It's your *name*. One of the other prisoners told it to me. She knew our *names!* Don't you get it? We're out here killing these people because they know too much about the Enomeg project! We're ending *their* lives to help cover up the very thing that took ours away!"

At this, Daniel's look of outrage only increased. "Xarkon *gave* you your life, you treasonous ingrate! And you *don't deserve it!*"

There was a flash of light as their starfire blades met, the forcefields around the weapons creating a flash of energy upon contact that illuminated the clearing like lightning. Aeriella watched this furious battle in amazement. The clashing blades pulsated in the night like flickering stars. She had always wondered at the short span of Human life. Compared to the life of a Sarran, everything moved quickly for them. This gave them a sort of heated intensity that the Sarran lacked, and this showed in battle as well, as she could now clearly see. Her people were extremely skilled with blades, yet she had never seen any warrior of her own kind fight like these men now fought. They were completely absorbed in the fight; she could have left unnoticed were it not for her doubts about abandoning this Human who was now risking his life and career to save her.

Daniel slashed; Scorp parried. His blade came around; it was quickly blocked. But it all happened so fast that it was impossible to follow. Each man's face was stoic and emotionless, as still as their bodies were active. Indeed, their faces were the only muscles that did not move, for their feet and arms were in constant motion. She tried to follow each blow and parry, dodge and strike, but it was impossible. Clearly they were highly trained, and every move was calculated, but to an observer they were merely a blur.

What kind of men *were* these warriors that had been sent to kill her?

Then, at last, an injury took place. Daniel cut Saber-Scorpion's leg. They both stepped back as if to survey the damage, but this seemed only to make Scorp all the more determined. Where before he had been pulling his strikes, trying only to injure Daniel, he now allowed his training to take over completely. Suddenly going on the offensive, he became impossible to follow. Daniel was forced back, step by step. Once he had an opening, Scorp put both his hands above his head, interlocked his fingers, and made a great downward blow at his enemy's head. The trainee crossed his sabers for a block, and as he did this, Saber-Scorpion snapped up a lightning-fast kick.

As Daniel reeled from the blow, Scorp performed a quick sideways slice, which his enemy tried unsuccessfully to dodge. The heat of the blade sliced through his black shirt and the flesh beneath, leaving an even blacker line. And then Scorp moved in and gave the body one more stab in the back even as it fell, ensuring his enemy's death.

Then he paused. He blinked. What had just happened? There lay Daniel, his body burned and unmoving, the only sound coming from his still-active star-talons. Scorp shivered. That last fatal stab had surprised even him. He had not meant to do it; it simply came, as if by instinct. It was as if – as Mantis had said – he was nothing more than a weapon, and once the trigger was pulled, there was no stopping that deadly shot. Once his training had taken over, the rest of the fight had been like clockwork, like programming installed into him that, once started, could not be stopped until it was sure that its target was dead. And as the program fizzled out, Scorp felt the weight of what he had just done sink over him. The night grew blacker still.

He looked down at his hands. The weapons strapped to his arms, still burning like fire, were merely extensions of the arms themselves. *He* was the weapon. With or without a weapon – gun or blade – he would have killed his target, once that deadly intention was triggered.

What *was* he? Was he even Human?

Then he remembered the Sarran woman who was standing behind him and turned to make sure she was still there.

"I have just bought your freedom with blood," he said, his voice dark and sullen.

Aeriella was still staring at the dead body with an expression of astonishment. Scorp suddenly felt angry. He was trying hard not to consider what he had just done, and she was only making matters worse. He pushed the thought from his mind.

"Can you fly?" he asked quickly.

She was finally able to pull her eyes away from the corpse, but still she did not look at Scorp. "My… my wings were… clipped."

"Will they heal?"

She nodded. "Eventually… More quickly if I return to my people for aid."

"Then go. I am letting you go. You are my target. The others will not attack you. Go back to your people."

She nodded. "I will find them."

She turned to leave, but looked back at him one last time. He braced himself. He knew what she was going to ask… the same thing the other girl had asked, back at the river. Why was he doing this? But he had no answer. He was doing it because it was the only thing he could do. He could bring himself to do nothing else. It seemed in his mind to be his only choice.

But all Aeriella said was, "Thank you."

Then she turned and walked away. There was a nobility in her stride that Scorp could not help but notice. He shook his head. He had not expected her to be so fearless; it was directly the opposite of the other woman he had helped. She flexed her wings once more, and then disappeared between the trees. Scorp leaned over and picked up Daniel's lifeless body, switching off his Star-Talons before they caused an accidental blaze.

How would he explain this? He would have to make it look like one of the other prisoners had killed him. But there was no way any of them could have killed him… especially not with Enomeg hand-blades. Then he had an idea. He found one of the thick, strong vines growing on the trees nearby and wrapped it around the dead trainee's neck, trying not to look at his face. Then he tossed the other end over a tree limb and hoisted the body up.

Suddenly he stopped. His hands slipped. He choked.

The emotion was finally taking hold; he felt the regret rack him to the core. He fell to his knees, letting the body of the boy he had killed fall beside him. This young man was one of Xarkon's finest, chosen to be a great protector of his country. For his entire life, he had worked hard, lived and served, sweating and bleeding… preparing for a day when he would fight for his country as he so longed to do. And just as he was reaching the goal of his life… Saber-Scorpion had cut it short.

It was as if he had killed his own brother. He had *murdered* him. He had not meant to, but he had. It was impossible for him to fight an Enomeg super-soldier intent on the kill without being intent to kill in return. He had tried at first, but then Daniel had gained the upper hand. If he had continued pulling his strikes, Daniel would have been the victor, and both Scorp and Aeriella would be dead. Both *traitors* would have died by the hand of Xarkon's loyal champion. But that had not happened. Instead, Xarkon's champion was dead, and Scorp was left to live with it. Forever.

The stars in the sky above were beginning to grow dimmer by the time Scorp summoned up the courage to finish his grizzly task. At last, he hoisted the corpse back up on the vine and tied it tight. Trying not to look up at the thing swinging there above him, he held his starfire blade against his victim's foot. The plant matter stuck to Daniel's boots immediately began to catch fire. Then the tongues of light crept upward, licking at Daniel's skin and coiling around his body like serpents, and Scorp looked away.

He felt some sort of eulogy was required. He stood thinking for what seemed hours, searching for the right words. Few came to him. Finally, he decided they would have to suffice.

His own voice sounded hoarse as he said, "He did his duty."

The sun was just starting to rise when Scorp made his lonely trek back through the jungle to the rendezvous point on the hill. One Nidhogg had apparently found a clearing large enough to land, and the Enomeg trainees were standing around it, looking grim and sullen and tired, only a few talking about their experiences. The Enomegs were never an overly jubilant lot. Most of them were washing off in the nearby stream, cupping their hands and splashing their faces and arms. Scorp joined them, leaning over and dunking his face directly into the creek, letting the water wash him… of everything.

When he looked up into the red-orange light of the sunrise, he was able to make out Cat walking up to him. He found himself half expecting her to look beautiful in the twilight, like before on the mesa, but she merely looked tired, and her light brown hair was a mess.

"You're late," she said in a low voice. "Did you find your mark?"

Scorp just shook his head. Did he detect a bit of emotion in her voice? A familiar feeling? Cat nodded and sat down under a tree. She looked thoughtful, almost sad. Yes, there was definitely an all-too-familiar sentiment there. He opened his mouth to say something to her, but stopped himself. There were too many others around. Cathryn seemed to have noticed this, so she gave him a helpless smile.

"It doesn't matter," she said. "Luke didn't get his either."

Scorp knew what that meant: the woman that he had instructed to hide in the trees really was Blood-Raven's target. Scorp's advice had worked; she had escaped. Scorp felt a bit of satisfaction at that.

But Raven was not pleased at all.

"I'll get her," he said, standing up and crushing a stick under his foot. "I'll get them to call in satellites, spy planes – track her down! I'll cut her *apart!* This isn't over…"

"She escaped," Scorp said loudly. "She beat you at your own game. Get over it."

Raven suddenly turned and glared at Scorp. The half-light of the sunrise made his scowl look even more menacing. The shadows accentuated his muscles as they tensed.

"And I bet you got your mark?" Raven said. "Cut her down like a dog? I bet you're *real* proud of yourself, just because you got an easier target than me."

"I didn't find mine either, but you won't hear me whining about it. They got away. They beat us. They *earned* their freedom."

Raven laughed. "Oh, right. So you think Xarkon's just going to let them go? They'll still be hunted down. And I'll be damned if I'm not going to be involved in it!"

"If they can hide from *us*," Scorp said evenly, "then there's no way anyone else in Xarkon can find them."

"Listen to you! You sound like you *wanted* them to get away!"

Scorp's eyes narrowed. He did not move. "I am no traitor," he said.

"That so?" Raven taunted. "Maybe you are. Maybe you'll be the one getting hunted down next time. And *I'll* be the one doing the hunting."

"Then I guess I don't have much to worry about, do I?"

Raven bared his teeth and ignited one of his starfire blades, brandishing it before Scorp's face. The shadows were lit by its flashing red light. Still Saber-Scorpion did not move.

"I'll show you what you have to worry about," Raven said through clenched teeth.

Suddenly, a dark figure stepped from the shadows of the trees and held out a gloved hand. "*Stop!*"

Dark-Dragon stepped into the clearing with the reflection of the rising sun burning red on his visor, the rest of his armor a shadowy, unreflective black. "I will tell you what you both have to worry about. You have to worry about the fact that you both failed your mission. It turns out that our two best students aren't necessarily our two best after all. Out of all of the trainees, you were two of but three who failed this test."

Scorp took a step back from Raven, who clenched his mouth shut firmly and straightened up. Barracuda, leaning against a tree behind him, gave a rumbling chuckle, enjoying the show.

"The third suffered an even worse fate. Daniel was found dead in the lower valley, just a burning skeleton hanging from a tree like a piece of cooked meat. And the man he was sent to kill is still at large."

All around the group, eyes widened. An Enomeg soldier, killed by a mere prisoner? Such a thing was impossible. They shot suspicious glances at one another covertly. Scorp stared straight forward, resisting the sudden urge to stiffen… or to hang his head in shame. Dark-Dragon was scanning the group as well, perhaps suspiciously. His eyes seemed to linger on Scorp and Raven. Neither of them moved a muscle.

"Apparently…" Dragon said, "one of the prisoners was very skilled. Perhaps he or she was an unfair target. We did not know that any of these criminals would be smart enough to escape being tracked. And we certainly didn't expect them to… *hang* any trainees. But never mind. Tonight you will rest here in the jungle. Do as you like. Tomorrow we will return to the base."

As he turned to leave, Scorp and Luke exchanged glances. Then Dragon suddenly turned back, arresting everyone's attention.

"One more thing," said the Enomeg commander. "Luke, you are an excellent student… one of my best. Do not fail me again. Because if you do fail, even once, you will never become an Enomeg. I can only allow so many failures on the final tests. If you fall short again, I'm sure you'll make an excellent Spec-Ops commander."

Scorp glanced at Raven, who was simply staring straight ahead, his face like stone. Only his eyes showed what he was feeling. Behind them burned the fire of pure determination. Luke Blood-Raven would not fail again.

"And now," Dark-Dragon said, in a tone that was somehow even more grim than before, "I have to do my part. The job rests with me… to hunt down the ones you missed."

- CHAPTER NINE -
THE THIRD PARTY

When Grand General Rick Radcliff joined Ordinator John Exsyl in the Victorian booth of the dimly-lit CONON Great Hall, he was followed by another guest. The young man was awestruck by the splendor of the great space station, with its vast windows looking up to the heavens and down toward the earth. The old Ordinator looked the boy up and down, amused at his amazement. The young man's eyes were alert and his muscles tense under his crisp dark blue Victorian uniform. Clearly, he was not at home in this political setting.

"So this is the one you've told me so much about, Rick," Exsyl said.

Ryan took the Ordinator's offered hand. "Specialist-Sergeant Ryan Arkanian, sir. It's a pleasure to finally meet you in person, Ordinator Exsyl."

"Specialist-Sergeant?" Exsyl said with a laugh. "Is that the best rank Rick here could give you? Bah, that's a throwaway rank we give to good grease monkeys!"

Rick frowned. "It's a distinguished NCO rank. It's the rank being given to all of the former Immortals until they've proven themselves on the field. I have no doubt Ryan will prove himself and ascend higher through the ranks in short order."

"Yes, yes, of course, I was just teasing you, Rick. You're as up-tight as your nervous new protégé here. Come, sit down, both of you, and try to relax. This is just politics – just a bunch of old men bickering and trying to look important, not a battlefield."

They took their seats at the very front of the box with the Ordinator, the rows of chairs reserved for the other Victorian representatives positioned behind them. Ryan looked out at the vast auditorium, at the great towers for the Big Four and the smaller platforms positioned below. As big as the room was, it was hard to believe that, even in a place this grand, decisions could be made that influenced nearly a third of the galaxy.

Rick's voice took on a serious tone as he said, "Ryan, if you have any observations about the meeting... anything to say at all, just tell me. I'll be sitting right here. Consider it a test of your perception."

Ryan nodded. "I'll try my best. I feel naked without a weapon of some kind..."

"You'll get used to it," Rick replied, with an understanding nod. "Of course, it gets better once you can carry an officer's sabre... That's part of the reason it always pays to learn the art of the sword."

Exsyl looked up. "Here come the others."

The Ordinator watched as Rick stared toward the Xarkon box directly across the hall from them. He knew the Grand General was watching Lucas Mars. The Xarkon High Commander marched into sight with his head held high and did not bother to take a seat. He was followed shortly by the Emperor, who was again present, along with his royal guards. Mars stood rigidly, staring straight ahead.

Exsyl looked at Rick's expression and then turned to Ryan, saying in a low voice, "Well, for your first test, Sgt. Arkanian, what do you make of High Commander Mars?"

Ryan looked back and forth between Mars, John Exsyl, and Rick Radcliff. Even with his eyes covered by the large, reflective visor he always wore, Rick's expression was not hard to discern.

"Well," Ryan said, "he certainly looks as experienced and intimidating as they say. I'm not sure what conclusion to make beyond that..."

The Ordinator laughed. "Come now, you clearly observe more than that. What do you make of him as compared to Rick here?"

"General Radcliff?" Ryan paused thoughtfully, and his blue eyes turned toward his commander. He clearly did not want to say anything inappropriate. But after a while he made up his mind and said, "They appear to be very similar at the moment. Both of them look like they're trying hard not to make eye contact. Do they have a history?"

"That's better!" laughed Exsyl. "Rick, you should listen to your new pupil and try not to look so hostile."

"Sir," Rick said slowly, as if he had been trying to ignore the conversation going on around him, "I am trying very deliberately to do just that. Looking hostile is the last thing I would want to do in this room, of all places."

Exsyl laughed. "Well perhaps you should stop trying so hard then. Nevermind – here comes Cohen."

They all turned and looked up as the chubby little Director of CONON shuffled out onto his tall balcony and spread his arms. He smiled to the audience below him. All in all, he gave Ryan the distinct impression of a circus ringleader preparing the audience for some fabulous performance that was about to occur. It seemed a strange attitude for the coordinator of such a serious convention.

"Today," Cohen said, gesturing to a booth in the back, "we are finally able to welcome back the representatives from the prodigal nation of Mordark! They have returned to us to take part in the negotiations concerning the status of their leader, Lord Zegaldorph, who is still missing concerning the Shardasha Incident."

Rick laughed and said under his breath, "'Missing concerning'? Trying a little too hard to be neutral, isn't he?"

Exsyl chuckled. Ryan looked down at the Mordark podium, dwarfed by the tower of Xarkon beside it. The booth contained four representatives; two Humans and a Mahlok. The Human in front was a tall, broad-shouldered, imposing man with dark skin; clearly no politician. It was hard for Ryan to believe that such a person could be found in the densely-populated, polluted, congested city-state of Mordark. He looked up at the congregation with a stern but calm and honest face.

"This is Captain Borad Jaleiko," Cohen announced. "He is in charge of Mordark's City Guard. As you probably know, citizens of Mordark are not allowed to carry weapons within the walls of the City Core... except for the Police and the City Guard, who patrol the walls and protect the Core."

"And all of Mordark, when necessary," said Jaleiko's deep voice, in a friendly tone. "There is much I have to tell you, councilors. First, it is true that our leader, Lord Zegaldorph, is missing. The Mahlok behind me is his bodyguard, Xernoc, who was on leave at the time of Zegaldorph's abduction. My Lord was attending a representative meeting at the Mordark embassy in Shardasha when the incident occurred. I realize this looks incriminating, but it may be that the terrorists behind this want it to appear that my Lord is in charge of the operation. Whatever the truth may be, I will be working closely with the Xarkon government on this investigation from now on."

"I protest," said Emperor Marius Orrick of Xarkon, who paused a moment to ensure he had everyone's attention before continuing. "There is still the possibility that all of Mordark may be involved in this incident. I do not wish for our investigation to be hindered."

Jaleiko stood taller and looked up at the high podium of Xarkon, one of the Big Four, which towered over Mordark's. "And with all due respect, there is also the possibility that some of *your* people are behind this, your Highness. There is no proof to the contrary in either statement!"

The Emperor of Xarkon coughed indignantly and said, "Dare you accuse *Xarkon* of stooping to this level?"

"I simply do not wish to see my Lord murdered, by *either* side, and then labeled as a casualty of this conflict!"

As this argument began, Ryan found his eyes wandering down toward the floor of the great room – the immense window looking down at the planet's surface. By sheer chance, they were above Xarkon's coastline now, looking down at the Bay of Shards, in which rested the city of Shardasha. It was as if this council was gazing down at the city through the eye of that great window, all of its focus intense upon it. It seemed such a small matter when one looked up through the above window, at the stars, many of which were also under the dominion of CONON. Yet small matters often had great and unpredictable consequences. Wars been sparked with far less provocation in the past. Would the council prevent that, or was it only making things worse?

"Friends!" interjected the voice of Howard Cohen. "This bickering will not help matters. We must cooperate. That is what this council is for."

"I have a suggestion," Rick Radcliff said into the microphone. "Perhaps all of CONON should be involved. In order to avoid conflict between Xarkon and Mordark, it would be best to have a third party watching the proceedings first-hand, at least."

To Rick's surprise, Mars merely nodded. "Yes, of course. We will need to keep an eye on each other."

"And we will need to *help* each other," Rick said.

Mars gave a forced smile. "Yes. We will indeed…"

Rick got that familiar feeling in his gut that Mars was not telling them everything he knew. And Ryan got the feeling that if Mars truly wanted a war, these efforts for peace might be playing right into his hands.

Below them, Jaleiko was nodding. "This sounds fair. But who will it be, this party? Who will be the third?"

LOCATION: BAY OF SHARDS, SHARDASHA, XARKON

"The Third," growled Lashnar the Slashrim, as he took a seat on the bed in the cramped quarters of the dingy fishing boat. "I was under the impression that your name was Grimm the *Third*."

Grimm III, who was staring into the mirror and inspecting his messy stubble of a beard, grunted. "I *am* Grimm the Third, but I'm only his *second* clone. You know, the first *clone* was the second *Grimm*, and I'm the second *clone* and so I'm the third *Grimm*, but only the second *clone*. Get it?"

Lashnar nodded. Most Slashrim were rather feeble-minded, especially when it came to numbers, but Lashnar was what the Mahlok called *hakgrin* – smart. That made him dangerous. This was why the powerfully-built, red-skinned third-stage Slashrim "lizardman" had escaped slavery twice. The second time, it was the mercenary Grimm III who had helped him. That was why they were now working as partners.

Grimm III, known to some simply as "Three," rubbed his stubble of a beard as he gazed into the mirror. It was getting longer. Considering what he had been through, he was glad his beard was still growing at all… though now he was starting to look like a real bum. But that was the look he was going for. He had done nothing to his oily black hair in nearly a week, and it showed. It was unkempt and filthy, pointing in every direction. Below it, the stark white of the man's bushy eyebrows contrasted with it sharply. Beneath the right eyebrow was a single, bright green eye… and beneath the left was tied a black metal eye patch. The mercenary reached up to straighten it. He gave a short laugh. Besides his hair and beard being thicker, he was the spitting image of the infamous mercenary leader, Grimm I.

The legendary mercenary warlord had long ago created a series of self-clones in an attempt to breed the ultimate soldier. The first attempt had ended in disaster. The clone, genetically engineered to age rapidly to a certain point and then resume normal growth… never stopped aging. He became an old man before their very eyes, and it took all the efforts of Grimm's chief scientist, Hal Flyphe, to stop the aging process again before the clone died. But by then, Grimm II was hideous and completely mad as a result of multiple defects. He escaped from the facility and was never heard from again.

Grimm III was far more successful. In fact, his problem was that he was too much like his "father," sharing even Grimm's love for independence and tendency toward treachery. So one day, Three took his leave from Grimm's Army just as Grimm had formerly taken leave from Victory. But on his way out, he did something unforgivable. He used Hal Flyphe's advanced cloning machine to create a clone of himself – a clone of a clone – who would age at a normal rate. Three later explained to Grimm I that the boy had died anyway, but Grimm did not listen, and he'd hunted Three from that day on.

Later clones had suffered a similar fate. Grimm V and VI were created together… and both of them escaped together. They were currently residing in Mordark, hiding from their creator. At the moment, the last and only clone still loyal to the Grim Army was Grimm VII, because his genetic code had been altered to code for loyalty. But with loyalty came a lack of ambition and cunning, and so Grimm VII was a disappointment.

Unfortunately, Three himself was not a perfect clone either. Soon after he'd escaped Grimm's Army, he discovered that he still retained a little of Grimm II's problem; he was aging more rapidly than normal. At first he'd been frantic to reverse the process any way possible, and he'd tried many desperate means. Some had been more successful than others, and he was always hard-pressed for cash in order to keep his body in good shape. It required constant maintenance. But a few of the more expensive operations he hoped would prove more permanent…

Grimm III's thoughts were interrupted by a loud shout from up on the deck of the boat, "Hey, Erik! We're approachin' Shardasha now! They're hailin' us, tellin' us to turn back!"

That was him. Grimm III had many names. Grimm and his mercenaries just called him 'Three.' Those who knew him by his own reputation called him 'Erik the Red,' the infamous lone wolf mercenary. His friends called him… well, he wasn't sure if he had any friends.

Now he just had to decide which of the many available insertion methods he would take.

"Decisions, decisions," Three muttered as he reached into his pocket.

His hand reemerged holding a large, translucent red gambling die. He rolled it across the table. It landed on three: his lucky number. That meant he got to take his favorite course of action: the most reckless one of all.

"Not the die again…" Lashnar muttered behind him.

"Damn straight," Three growled, shooting him a sharp glance as he returned the coveted object to one of his many hidden pockets. "Now grab your gear; we're goin' for a swim."

As Lashnar readied his vicious axe-headed assault rifle, Three loaded his shotgun and tossed the strap over his shoulder. It was a ZRG-6 "Scatterstar," produced by ZygbariTech in southern Zygbar. One of the most versatile weapons ever invented, the Scatterstar was a fully-automatic blazer shotgun that carried its ammo in a drum, though it could also be loaded with a variety of ammunition on the fly through a special port on the top. And Three always carried a variety of ammunition. On his multiple ammo belts, he had durashot shells, firecrackers, slugs, flachettes, dragon's breaths, whistlers, gas rounds, beanbags, mini-grenades…

He also carried a backup shotgun of the simpler sawed-off double-barrel variety in a sheath on his left side, and a Victorian Bowie-3C blazer combat knife on the other. Over all of this he wore a dirty and worn black trench coat with a hood. He heard they were a popular fashion item these days, and the sleeves allowed him to cover up the small revolver attached to a device on his wrist that snapped it quickly into his hand. All in all, he was a walking arsenal. Most men would have gotten tired under the weight of all that gear, but Grimm III was very different from most men.

As for Lashnar, he was clad in nothing more than a few pouch-laden belts and bandoliers of ammunition. The Slashrim shunned armor and even basic clothing unless absolutely necessary. When you stand seven feet tall, your hide is as tough as most anti-ballistic meshes, and most of your body is covered in horns and spikes, armor is not only largely unnecessary, but also rather hard to wear. So the great "lizard-man," as Humans often erroneously called his kind, simply narrowed his bright green eyes and gave his partner a nod. Three slipped on his hood and stepped up onto the deck of the boat.

Grimm III's employers had provided their means of transportation: a rusty little non-submersible fishing ship. Gas-powered and made of iron, the thing was about as primitive as one could get without resorting to wood and sails. The "captain" of the miserable vessel was called Wallace, a rather obese Human with a grey beard. The rest of his crew consisted only of his son, who had stayed up in the "bridge" driving the boat the whole time Three had been on board. Right now Wallace was on the ship's deck, squinting out into the fog. Three and Lashnar turned to look. They could only see perhaps twenty feet across the tumbling grey waves, but the lights that were visible in the fog beyond were menacing enough. There was a ship out there… a big ship. Big enough to swallow a dozen boats like this one.

"Xarkonian gunboat," Captain Wallace growled. "Been hailin' us. They got Shardasha blockaded off an' says they'll fire if we don't turn back."

Grimm III yawned and stretched… not because he needed to, but simply out of force of habit. He said in his gravelly voice, "Crownies… you gotta' hate 'em. Tell 'em you'll comply, and turn this heap around, Cap'n."

"But how're you gonna get to…"

Three glared at the man from beneath a silvery-white eyebrow. "I'll take care o' that, Cap. Just turn this heap around."

The fat man shrugged, which made his neck almost engulf the sides of his face. "Aye, aye then - we're turnin' about now. Danny, you heard that! Turn us about!"

He signaled to his son, who was looking through the glass window overhead. The boy spun the wheel, and the boat began to turn. Lashnar stepped up to the edge of the boat and looked down at the grey waves below.

"Looks like pretty calm seas tonight," he said. "I could swim this channel in a full Slashrim warlord's panoply. Ha!"

"Yeah, but they'll spot you unless you've got a distraction," Three said as he turned to Captain Wallace and handed him a roll of paper. "Here, cap. A few Guildars for the loss o' yer boat. You an' Danny-boy get the hell off this sloop and head back the way we came, you hear? The way I swim, they'll think you fired a torpedo at 'em. An' Crownies only answer hostility with the likewise."

The captain laughed. "Ah, shut yer blowhole... The thought o' you an' yer dinosaur friend here swimmin' into Shardasha is laughable enough, but why in the name o' Queen Skye's dimples would they think I was firin' a *torpedo* at 'em?"

"Just shut up an' do what I'm tellin' you. I'm gonna swim, and then those Xark-sharks are gonna return fire. If you want to live, you'd best get off this boat, fast. Lashnar, go ahead and dive. I'll catch up."

The Slashrim nodded and leaped over the edge with surprising grace. He soon resurfaced in the waves below, the spines along his black-striped back sticking up like a shark's fin, his tail waving back and forth like a crocodile's. He made amazingly good speed, cutting through the water like a knife. Three had heard that the Mahlok sometimes bred Slashrim sea-warriors with webbing between their toes to swim better, but from what he'd seen, Lashnar didn't need it.

Wallace laughed nervously. "You... you fellas is crazy!"

Three shrugged. "Pretty much. Now, I ain't got time for this. It's your funeral."

"Wait!"

But it was too late. Three put one foot on the edge of the boat and propelled himself over the side. Wallace saw the mercenary's slick black coat disappear into the cold grey sea. He stared for a moment, waiting for his head to come back up... but there was nothing. Just the slosh of the waves. Even Lashnar was already out of sight. Wallace stared out into the fog and saw only the lights of the Xarkon gunboat. As he looked at its intimidating, vaguely crown-shaped silhouette, Wallace felt a chill run up his spine. Which was surprising, since people were always telling him he didn't have one.

"Get down here, Danny!" he yelled, running up to the bridge. "We're abandonin' ship!"

Onboard the Xarkon gunboat, the Navy Captain scowled at the computer screen.

The crewman looked up. "He's still turning, sir."

The Captain snorted. "What in blazes is taking him so long?"

"Captain! They're firing! I don't know how, but they're firing at us!"

On the screen, the green shape that indicated the fishing boat was still slowly turning, but now a red dot was leaving its location... headed very rapidly toward the gunboat. The captain began yelling orders to activate the countermeasures, but by then the projectile was upon them... and it missed. He watched as it glided past the ship and off the screen.

"It passed beneath us, sir. Apparently unguided."

"They fired that thing right under us!" the officer scoffed. "The audacity! Blow them out of the water!"

When Grimm III's head emerged from the waves behind the Xarkon gunboat, he saw, even with the fog, the bright orange explosion blossoming into the night sky in the distance. He shook his head... It was a shame to waste the poor captain's boat, but it was necessary both to distract the Xarkonians from himself and Lashnar, and for another reason: If anyone had known of his and Lashnar's coming, they would hopefully now believe them dead. And dead men could do many things that the living would not dare.

The mercenary ducked back under the waves and continued his swim. It took him only a few minutes to reach the docks of Shardasha. Looking stealthily up from the water, he beheld a pier ahead. Standing atop it was the unmistakable silhouette of his Slashrim partner: hunched over, back lined with spines, legs jointed like an animal's, and slits for pupils in his bright green eyes, though the slits were currently as wide as possible here in this darkness. As he approached, the Slashrim spotted him and reached out a clawed hand to pull him up.

"I already made a sweep of the area," Lashnar growled under his breath as he helped Three onto the pier. "Not a sentry in sight. No sign of your contact either."

"She'll be here," Three replied, drawing a long brown cigar from a waterproof pouch on his side and lighting it.

"I've told you not to burn those accursed weeds around me," Lashnar snapped. "By Helexith, and you Humans call *us* stupid. Besides, those are illegal here..."

Three took a long drag on his cigar and swung the Scatterstar down off his shoulder. "So's killin' folks," he said, "and that ain't stopped me yet."

He and Lashnar were now walking down the gently swaying pier toward the city. The fact that there was no sign of their contact was probably an indication that all was well. The woman he was supposed to meet moved in as silently and mysteriously as the fog that now enshrouded the harbor around them and left just as little to mark her passing. Even though she could not be seen, Three decided to give the signal anyway.

He approached a tall stack of crates, took the cigar from his mouth, and said calmly into the night air, " *'The fog comes on little cat feet.'* "

There was the sound of an uncoiling cable over his head; he recognized it instantly. The shape of a Human female, turned completely upside down and clinging to a metal cord attached to a device on her belt, slowly came into view from the shadow of the roof above. The dim light of the moon, even concealed as it was that night, still shone on her skin-tight black outfit, causing it to shimmer strangely purple where the light struck. The woman removed the complex pair of goggles she had been wearing, revealing a pair of dark, almond-shaped eyes, while her mouth remained covered by a mask. Strapped to her body were a wide array of tools and devices, including a long, thin sword and a highly advanced crossbow, the weapon's arms folded into either side of the main body.

Three nodded to her, and she flipped down to her feet and left the cable dangling. Then she looked up at Grimm III and extended a gloved hand. Three knew she was handing him something, but he took her fingers and raised them to his lips.

"Spectra?" he said, with a sly smile, causing Lashnar behind him to snort derisively.

" *'It sits looking over harbor and city on silent haunches,'* " she replied, her voice like silk.

" *'And then moves on,'* " Three concluded, finishing the Old Earth poem by Carl Sandburg that was their code. "What a sad ending."

She arched her eyebrows at him curiously, and he thought he saw the cloth over her mouth fold in such a way as to indicate a smile. Then she dropped the items she had been holding into the mercenary's hand. He looked down. There lay a keycard, a folded piece of paper, and a computer datastick.

"We will meet again, Erik. We always seem to."

With that, Spectra sprang away into the shadows and reappeared atop a pile of shipping crates. She continued her run, jumping from crate to crate, until she was out of sight. Three shook his head. She always had to make such an exit.

"How did you ever meet her anyway?" he heard Lashnar growl behind him.

Three turned and replied with a mouth full of cigar, "She's from Yavakaro. I was on a mission there and it turned out to have more ah... how'd she put it... *political ram'fications* than I thought. She helped pull my boots outta' the fire, an' I sorta owed her one."

Lashnar gave a deep, gurgling laugh. "So now when she says 'sick 'em,' you take to the chase faster than a trained Korgon hellhound."

"Shut up, Lash. I'm tryin' to read this crap."

Three looked down at the scrap of paper Spectra had given him. It said, in very fine handwriting: "The terrorists have agents everywhere. Xarkon soldiers working with them. The building you want is the Mordark Embassy. I will be in the Lambda Inn & Suites. Contact me there."

Three committed the information to memory. Xarkon was working with the terrorists? That was surprising. The target was the embassy. Spectra would await contact in the Lambda hotel. Then he noticed the end of the note.

"Bring the followin' supplies…" he muttered aloud. "One pack size X power cells, one box conventional mechanic's tools…"

Lashnar laughed aloud like a reptilian hyena. "A shopping list!"

Three crumpled the paper in his hand and lifted it to his cigar to burn. "Women…"

Suddenly Lashnar sounded less like a hyena and more like an angry space dragon. "*I'm* female, you ignorant swine!"

Three rolled his eye. "Look, Lash, everyone calls you 'he;' it's pretty easy to get mixed up."

Lashnar sneered, revealing her sharp, gleaming teeth. "Merely because the young of my species can take care of themselves, and we were gifted with some natural *decency* and a lack of… *mammary* glands…"

"That about covers it."

The mercenary looked up at the skyline of the city above. As the first dim light of the morning began to filter through the fog, he could make out the windows of the skyscrapers. There he saw the flag of Mordark emblazoned on a particularly tall, thin tower, with many hovercraft landings jutting from the sides and an aircraft landing pad on the very top. It was one of the tallest buildings he could see.

Grimm III whistled. Nothing like a hard day's work. Actually, more like a hard week's work, at least. It would take him quite a bit of time to plan this whole mission before they actually began it. Although everything about his appearance declared him to be careless, Three was anything but. He had to figure out a way to get past the Xarkonians and the terrorists, break into the building, find his target, and get out alive. And his target, he knew, would be well guarded.

For his target was Zegaldorph, Lord of Mordark.

- CHAPTER TEN -
QUITE A MERCENARY

Dark-Dragon raised his burning Starfire blade high above his head. The spike of energy extending at his fingertips had just ended the life of the young woman who had been hiding in the treetops… and now he was standing before a majestic Sarran on the cliff-side. She looked up at him with defiance in her chiseled features. Behind her was a wall of rock… and before her was a Xarkonian super-soldier. She had nowhere to run, nowhere to hide – so she was not even going to try.

"For the Crown…" Dragon said softly, and his arm descended.

The blade flashed through the air… followed by the falling of a body. Strangely enough, the scream came afterward. But it was not Aeriella's… It was Saber-Scorpion's.

Scorp awoke in a cold sweat, breathing heavily. He blinked and gazed around the room… at the Xarkon recruiting posters and the models of Xarkon fighters and walkers he had collected, built, and researched over the years while the other students had played endless games of screamer ball. He breathed a sigh of relief and of pain.

So it had been a dream. Perhaps a true one, perhaps not. But why was his decision in the jungle still haunting him now, several days later? Why couldn't he let it go? Again he tried to convince himself of a lie, to make the lie real: he had never met the Sarran woman. She had escaped without his notice. The Enomeg trainee that had died that day had been hanged and burned by an escaped prisoner, Luke's quarry, who had been smart enough to hide in the trees. Not because he told her how. He had not been responsible for any of it; it was not his fault.

Finished with lying to himself, Scorp sat up on the bed and stretched. From what he'd heard, it was going to be a long day. Today they were to begin

131

training in actual Enomeg armor. These were not the exoskeletons they would be granted upon completion of their training, which were each designed specifically for the individual wearer, but merely prototypes. Nevertheless, they were close enough to the real thing, and one of these very prototype suits had been worn by Dark-Dragon years earlier when he had hunted down and killed the rogue cyborg, Arnold Beiderman.

Scorp stood up, dressed quickly, washed – and shaved – and then stepped into the cold metallic halls of the ETAB. Technically, there was no reason for him to be awake yet, but he knew it was futile trying to go back to sleep, so he merely wandered the halls aimlessly, lost in thought. Inevitably, his thoughts wandered back to that fateful night. *Xarkon can do no wrong.* What was it that the Sarran woman, Aeriella, had told him right before his battle with Daniel? Something she said had seemed to him very important at the time, but Scorp had been so emotionally distraught over the following events that he had neglected to return to it until just now.

Suddenly it came back to him with harsh clarity: A facility. She had found out about a top-secret facility where Xarkon was supposedly conducting research on Sarran prisoners. And it was hidden in the plains. There was at least one top-secret facility in the central plains of Xarkon that Scorp knew about very intimately… and he was standing in it. Could this – the very Enomeg Training Academy Base – be the place she had attempted to infiltrate? It seemed logical; all of the other prisoners they had been sent to kill seemed to know things about the Enomeg Project in particular.

Scorp suddenly realized he was making his way toward the instructors' offices. They were all abandoned at this time, but when he entered one room, he was surprised to find Shadow-Cat standing there in front of him. He stopped. She had apparently been about to leave. He stepped aside to let her pass, but she just stood there, looking at him with her deep blue eyes. Her hair was down for once, hanging around her long, slender neck, just reaching her shoulders. She was pretty with her hair down, Scorp thought. He remembered the way she had looked at him that night after the Test of Loyalty… tired and worn. Was she ready to talk about that?

But Cat seemed to sense what he was about to say, so she interrupted him. "Morning, Scorp. Ready to fight Seth in the Test of Supremacy trials today? I'm supposed to fight Mantis…"

"Yeah…" he said absentmindedly.

"You shouldn't sound so uninterested. Luke has been really preparing for his fight with you. As usual, Dark-Dragon's put you and Luke at opposite ends of the tree, so that you'll inevitably clash in the middle… at the very end."

Scorp looked at the ceiling. "*'Luke'* and I are going to inevitably clash at the end anyway."

"Don't say that," Cat scolded him. "You and Luke need to stop this petty rivalry. I just wish the trainers would stop encouraging it even more. Anyway, most everyone has already passed the Supremacy test proper, so I don't know why they have to keep making us fight…"

Suddenly Scorp heard himself say, "Cat… in the jungle…"

She shook her head. "There's no need to talk about it, Scorp. I already talked with Lee about it, and with Luke. We… we did the right thing."

"Then why are you wandering the base at this hour?"

"I'm not… Listen, Scorp, there was no shame in what we did."

"You mean what *you* did."

Cat looked up at him comfortingly. "You only failed because you felt unsure of yourself…"

Suddenly, before he had time to think about it, the words left his mouth: "Not exactly, Cat. I failed because I chose to."

She looked dumbfounded, her eyes wide. "What are you saying? You… let yours go?"

He nodded. "And I do not regret it."

Cathryn's newfound resolve was shaken, and she seemed almost scared. Scorp could tell that she had felt the same as him after the test. But afterward she thought she had resolved the issue, and now Scorp was laying this information on her. The fact that he had let his target escape without a single regret gave her more than a pause for thought.

"But…" she said slowly, "you should talk to Luke about it. He said…"

Scorp gave a laugh. "Luke *Blood-Raven*? *Talk* to him? He already suspects what I did, and he wants to kill me for it. He wants to kill me anyway. He's hated me from day one."

"It's not like that," Cat said, stepping closer. "You two should really stop all of this! It may be a contest right now, but after we graduate, we'll be on the same team, and then this conflict in the ranks could hurt the whole group! Have you thought about getting to know Raven better?"

"I know him well enough," Scorp said with absolute certainty. "I don't know what kind of lies he's been feeding you, but –"

"No! No, it's not like that. He's *right*, Scorp. Luke, Dragon, Lee… they're *all* right. Those prisoners deserved what they got. We did the right thing, for Xarkon. If they had been allowed to live, those convicts would have just hated Xarkon even more for imprisoning them in the first place. They would just try even harder to destroy it. What we did was for the protection of our country, for the protection of the innocent."

"So what I did was the wrong thing then," Scorp said, looking at the images of the Crown and of Empress Skye behind the Instructor's desk. "I have caused the death of innocents… aided in the downfall of Xarkon."

Cat blew out a sigh. "I'm sorry."

"Sorry for what you did or what I didn't do?"

"I'm not sure. Are *you* sorry for what you did, Scorp?"

He shook his head. "None of it. I'd do it all again, given the chance. I know that."

"I won't tell any of the others…" Cat began.

Scorp shrugged. "Will it make any difference if you do? Dragon probably knows already, and that's all that matters."

She shook her head again. "I'm just sorry."

With that, she quickly slipped out of the room. Scorp watched her go. He was alone, he thought. Raven was against him, Mantis was against him, and now Cat was against him. He knew the others would be too. Perhaps, he told himself, he truly *was* wrong. He even felt a slight hope deep inside him that Dark-Dragon had found and killed the two criminals he had helped escape. The ones he couldn't kill himself.

Then he saw her. He couldn't explain it, but the image flashed into his mind: the image of Aeriella standing on the cliff edge, her wings outspread. Only this time, her feathers were not clipped. Something was odd about the image, and he realized it had come to him while he was absentmindedly scanning the office in which he now stood. But, looking around, he saw nothing that would have evoked this singular vision. There was a desk, with the usual built-in computer station, featuring a pop-up monitor and a holographic projector. Behind it was the usual patriotic Xarkon imagery. There was a three-dimensional scanning machine on the other side of the room for creating holographic images of whatever was placed inside. And finally, there was a white board on the wall, probably a screen of some kind.

Scorp paused as a small detail suddenly came to light. There were no controls on the screen, no visible buttons or switches, not even anything that looked like a sensor pad. He touched the white surface, but it did not activate. He could not fathom that it could be a mere marker-board or something similarly primitive; such things simply did not exist in the wealthy, modern nation of Xarkon. Then he took a step back to get a broader image… and everything became clear. He could see it now: the image of the Sarran with outspread wings. It was visible on the screen, but only very faintly, as if it really were a marker board and a picture of a Sarran had been drawn there and erased over and over again a thousand times.

Or the image was *behind* the screen.

His adrenaline suddenly heightening his senses, Scorp thought he heard someone in the hall outside and ran to look. Peering down the long, cold metal tunnel in both directions, Scorp saw nothing. So he pressed the control to close the door, which then shut him inside the office with a hiss. Returning to the mysterious white screen, he ran his fingers along the edges. He was feeling for some way to open the panel to reveal the image behind, but suddenly the entire screen became loose, shifting slightly. He pressed harder until one corner was protruding, and then pulled the whole panel away.

Saber-Scorpion found himself face-to-face with evidence of his – and Aeriella's – darkest suspicions. It was an anatomical drawing of a Sarran, perfect to the smallest detail, apparently rendered by a computer. Over it were scrawled dozens of notes and details, apparently written by a wide variety of people, judging from the changes in handwriting. Scorp randomly chose a note pointing to the Sarran's head and began to read…

Brain size normal; comparable to Human. No growths or tumors present. Only slight anomaly similar to subject B7.

Brain has been transferred to cold storage room for further analysis.

Scorp felt the same sick feeling as when he had first been told the details about the Test of Loyalty on that accursed night, only now it was compounded tenfold. He found himself walking toward the desk as if to lean on it for support. Then he really *did* hear a sound in the hallway, and he rushed to reattach the white panel. As soon as the last corner was in tight, the door behind him opened.

"Oh hey, Scorp," he heard Seth say, slapping him on the shoulder. "You using the scanner?"

"Uh, no," Scorp replied, backing up. "I was just leaving."

He noticed Seth was carrying a large box, which he set on the ground in front of the scanning machine. He looked up at Scorp and winked as he pulled out a strange clay figure. Scorp shook his head. He knew Seth was up to some prank or other. Somehow, even through trials like the Test of Loyalty, Seth remained the same kid at heart.

"Is that... Kade?"

Seth grinned. "There's this really clay-like mud outside the base. You can make a funny face, stick your head in, and it takes quite a bit of effort to pull it back out. Once you're free, you've got this nice image of your head, same expression and everything."

"And Kade?" Scorp prompted.

"Oh, well he and Raven were sparring near the mud-hole... they're real good buddies now, for some reason, Barc and Raven..."

"Barc?"

"Yeah, that's what Vince – that is, Coyote – and I call him. You know, short for Barracuda? Also because he's just a big trained dog and his bark is worse than his bite. Anyway, Raven knocked him flat on his face in the mud, and it made this hilarious imprint of his face with the stupidest stunned expression you've ever seen. Coyote and I thought it should be immortalized for all time, you know? Maybe we could pull it up during one of the meetings just to see him make the same look on his face again. Ha!"

"You really have nothing to do, Seth."

"Ah, come on, Scorp, you need to stop looking so grim all the time. Maybe you should hang out more often instead of just sulking around by yourself..."

Scorp shook his head. It was amazing how Seth still treated his Enomeg training as if he were just a kid in school. When he was killing people or learning how to kill them, that was just work. Any free time was fun and games. Still, Magnum-Coyote seemed to have a similar attitude, and so did Mantis to some extent. Part of Scorp envied them. Another part of him found their attitudes disgusting. How could they take it all so lightly?

Unable to bear it any longer, Scorp said, "I've gotta go, Seth."

"Suit yourself. See you around."

As he made his way toward the door, Scorp gave one last glance over his shoulder. There was Seth, grinning as he placed his practical joke into the hologram scanner… and behind him was the panel behind which lay the diagram of a Sarran who had probably been tortured, killed, cut apart, and studied. Trying not to think about it any longer, Scorp fled the room.

LOCATION: XARKON COAST, NORTH OF SHARDASHA

The rocky beach looked like a mountain extending out of the sea, the waves crashing in around the grey stones seemingly unable to blunt its craggy edges. At the foot of this mountain was the dark shadow of a cave, enormous and long, extending inward for more than the length of two full battleships, end to end. Indeed, two such battleships now rested inside of it, along with several other seafaring vessels of war.

This was the Seadragon's Maw, a huge cave supported by steel reinforcements, the interior of which served to hide a large part of Xarkon's naval power. The base was supposedly connected by a series of tunnels to the mysterious XUH, or Xarkon Underground Headquarters, Xarkon's most top-secret military installation… and some said it might even connect to an entire network of tunnels that stretched all the way to the ETAB. But if these tunnels existed, only those in High Command knew how to access them.

Xarkon's navy, floating there in those dark waters, consisted of many dark black and crimson warships, all sleek and modern, appearing more like spacecraft – with a few odd, exposed decks visible here and there – than seafaring vessels. This was because all modern military sea ships had the ability not only to ride upon the surface of the water, but to submerge beneath it. The submarine had slowly grown in use to replace other types of vessels altogether. The only non-submersible ships in any major power's navy these days were aircraft carriers, and those were becoming increasingly rare due to long-range aerospace craft making use of starlight drive.

But outside of this port, resting on the waves, was a vessel even larger and more intimidating than anything within the cave. Its hull was solid black, with only a faint streak of green encircling the upper decks. Long, runny white skulls were painted on the hull in various places, and a pair of large, tattered flags extended outward from the sides, each bearing the same skull emblem. The ship was heavily armed with guns of varying types and sizes, now fully extended from their holes in a show of might.

This vessel's forward deck, cut away from the its long, cone-shaped nose, was teeming with armed mercenaries… a motley and nasty crew, dressed in all manner of armor, armed with all kinds of weapons. This was the *Queen Skye's Revenge*, the flagship of the navy of Grimm's Mercenary Army, also known as the Grim Armada. It was one of the most fearsome ships on the seas of Terra Nova.

Also present was a rather large force of Zygbari armored ground vehicles, positioned at the top of the cliff above the cave, physically on top of the entire complex, looking down over the sea below. Zygbar was known for its extremely tough and versatile military ground vehicles, and this was shown in those parked there above the Seadragon's Maw today. Many of them were camouflaged perfectly by means of primitive yet highly effective nets thrown over the top, covered in artificial foliage.

Most were small hovertanks, now sitting on the ground at rest, ready to escort the larger tanks and troop transports. But in the center of this group lay a huge vehicle like a rolling fortress, seated upon several hidden rows of treads. Two long arms of treads extended from the front of it, lined with claws that could latch into the ground to hold the vehicle in place while firing the array of massive cannons that protruded from its back. This great beast, a mobile command fortress and armory, was known as *Behemoth Bertha*, the lead lady of Zygbar's army.

From where he stood in the docking bay of the Maw, on one of the side platforms overlooking the vast cave all around, the walker pilot Harry "Viper" Dalton blew out a long whistle. The wind whistled through his unkempt black hair, which was well over regular military length, as he squinted his green eyes in the sunlight. He had strong features, including a large jaw and slightly cleft chin, but the body under his crimson pilot suit was hardly a match for them. Viper cared more about technology than physical strength when it came to warfare. And the display of military technology that now surrounded him practically made him giddy.

A shining star of the Walker Division, currently holding the rank of Beta-Wolf, Viper had actually been taken into the Enomeg program at birth but had dropped out after only twelve years. "Dropped out" was how he liked to put it; he had actually been kicked out due to his headstrong personality, chaotic behavior, lack of discipline, and desire to cause trouble. At times Viper wondered how his genes could possibly have read "honor, bravery, loyalty, supremacy," when he did not consider himself any of the above. Quite the opposite, in fact… unless one was referring to skills with technology and engineering as "supremacy."

"What a show," he said with a laugh. "It's a good thing Grimm's Army and Zygbar are on our side this time, or we'd be in for some serious trouble right now, even with all the ships we've got packed in here and the firepower in the XUH…"

The woman behind him nodded. "I suppose so. Let's hope they aren't in a position like this when they do finally turn on us."

Viper turned to regard her. Senior Omega Amy Archer was possibly the most beautiful woman in the Xarkon military… even the world, Viper couldn't help but think. She had long, slightly wavy blonde hair that rippled as the sea breeze caught it, and clear blue eyes that sparkled in the sunlight. Her eyes were most peculiar. Besides being large and crystalline blue, they had a keen wisdom about them that was almost unnerving. Those eyes seemed to pierce into you, Viper thought, as if she were reading you like a book. It was the rare combination of beauty and intelligence that the Sarran seemed to possess in abundance, only this time within the softer features of a Human. Perhaps, Viper thought, this was why her parents had chosen for her a Sarran-sounding name, Amyliarra. Then again, taking Sarran names was a popular fad at the time. At least her name was easily shortened to Amy.

Amy had only recently joined the most rebellious walker pack in all of Xarkon: Viper's squad, which he called the "Snake Legs," a joke on the fact that he, a pilot of a walker, had chosen for his codename an animal that lacked the walker's defining characteristic. Of course, at the time he had been a prospective Enomeg hoping for the name "Cyber-Viper" or similar, due to his skill with electronics. In any case, the nonsensical name seemed to fit his pack, since they were well known for their long hair and lack of regulations.

In most cases, High Command would have cracked down on them by now, but somehow they were allowed to get away with it. Viper, who had never had much loyalty to Xarkon, only felt any real loyalty to his pack. They were his brothers and sisters, and though Amy was a recent addition to the group, Viper already liked her. A lot. She was quite a fascinating woman... if only, he thought, she wouldn't keep herself so aloof.

"So you don't think the alliances with Grimm and Zygbar will last?" he said at length, hoping to keep a conversation with her going for once.

"Well..." Amy said slowly, leaning against the railing and gazing toward the horizon, "let's see. Grimm's a mercenary, so you know his loyalty can be bought..."

"But who can pay more than Xarkon?"

"...and Zygbar hates us. They always have, at least ever since we conquered them during the Age of the Golden Skye and forced them to win back their independence."

"But now O'Donnell's in charge. The guy's not even really a Zygbari; I heard his family's from Yavakaro! And he's really turning Zygbar around, with Mars's help. Besides, both he and Grimm know they couldn't take us down."

Amy nodded thoughtfully. "Not alone..."

Silence fell over the two of them. Amy often did this; suddenly dropping out of conversations. As she stared out at the sea, Viper only stared at her... up and down.

At length he attempted to resume the conversation. "Well, you're right, both of them certainly love money. Did you hear that Roscoe's bodyguards are among the richest people in Zygbar? It's because he pays them so well. He even tells them that if they're approached with an offer to assassinate him, all they have to do is let him know, and he'll pay them double the amount! He knows loyalty can only be bought. My kind of dictator, actually... He's here, you know. I saw him earlier. He and Grimm and Mars are probably in a secret meeting room somewhere right now..."

Amy hardly seemed to be listening. "Would you look at that battleship, marring the ocean's serenity with its rusted sides? I'm surprised Xarkon allowed Grimm to name such an ugly hunk of metal after the Empress, even if it is an allusion to some old pirate ship."

Viper chuckled. "Ah, so this is the part where you say 'the sea certainly is beautiful', and then I say 'I wasn't looking at the sea.'"

"Well, maybe you should *try* looking it sometime," she replied, rolling her eyes. "I mean *really* looking."

"Only your eyes could look so pretty even when you're rolling them like that," he said. "You know, maybe you should wear a smaller flight suit. You know, something... tighter. Whatcha think?"

She smirked at him. "I'd say try wearing something like that yourself, only I doubt they make any men's flight-suits smaller than yours."

With that, she turned and walked off. Viper frowned; he rolled up his sleeve and flexed what passed for his muscles.

"Ah, Hell."

Viper was even more correct than he knew about the secret meeting in the XUH that day. To be precise, it was taking place in a very small, dark meeting room deep in the underground complex. A council was scheduled there between Grand High Warlord Eric Grimm I of Grimm's Army, Chancellor Roscoe O'Donnell of Zygbar, and High Commander Lucas Mars of the Armed Forces of Xarkon. Currently, however, the cramped meeting room was occupied only by the first two. They sat at opposite sides of the small metal table, staring at each other. Roscoe was smiling. Grimm was not.

Roscoe straightened his brown greatcoat as he fitted the bulk of his body more comfortably into the cramped black chair. "Ah, Grand High Warlord Eric Grimm the First... what a title! A man after my own heart. It is a pleasure to finally meet you in person. Mars has told me much about you."

Grimm rolled his single green eye. "Hi, Roscoe."

"Oh, come now!" Roscoe said peevishly. "No need to be sooo... well, grim, I suppose. Ah-ha."

Grimm hated just about everything about Roscoe, but when he spoke, it was probably the accent that got on his nerves the most. He couldn't quite place what type it was, but every letter R that Roscoe said went rolling faster than the man himself might have done if pushed down a steep hill. It was most likely either fake or highly exaggerated, like everything else about the man.

Grimm glared at him. "If one of my mercs were to crack that joke at me, I'd crack his skull like a dried-up nutshell."

Roscoe loosened his collar. "Ah... right. At any rate, we are officials of state – well, of power at any rate – and should speak to each other as such. I trust, eh, that you know who I am?"

"Yeah... You're that fat fella that's got his picture hangin' around everywhere in Zygbar. You managed to kick the last Zygbari ruler out, and now you're in his place. You're the current winner in the game of musical chairs down there in that lawless desert. Good for you."

Roscoe smiled. "Yes, I am. But I always make sure that another chair is empty so that my enemies are fighting over *that* one instead of mine."

"Whatever. I ain't really interested in your little political games, O'Donnell."

"Ah, what a shame, for I am so *very* interested in yours. Although I do it nearly every day now, I always find it exciting speaking to a fellow leader of a galactic power, as your army is shaping up to be. One thing I am curious about... why did you become a mercenary? What caused you to make that career decision?"

Grimm snorted. "Well, when I was a kid, my old man asked me what I wanted to be when I grew up. I said, whatever makes the most money. He said most people make money by sellin' somethin', so what did I want to sell? I said, well, what's the most expensive thing in the world? He laughed and said the most expensive thing in the world is probably a war. So that's when I decided what I was gonna do."

Roscoe gave Grimm a skeptical look, to which Grimm responded with a shrug. Then Roscoe suddenly burst out laughing. He had such an amusing way of chuckling that even Grimm cracked a little bit of a grin, though it was mostly at the fat man's antics as he bounced in his chair and slapped his knee.

"Sell war!" the Chancellor wheezed out at intervals between the giggling.

Grimm shook his head sadly. It was hard to believe a man like this was a world leader. Then again, he thought, maybe it wasn't.

When he was finished catching his breath, Roscoe said, "Oh! Oh… that was great. Very, very entertaining. But honestly… it's not the truth, is it? I know you rose through the ranks of the Victorian military first…"

"Hell yeah, it's the truth! I knew I wanted to make money through war, but first I had to learn about it. So I lied and cheated my way through the Victorian military academy, learnin' about how to be an 'officer and a gentleman' an' all that, until I finally got to see some real solid action in that campaign with Rick *Rat*-cliff. At first I thought I might be able to make a livin' that way, but obviously it didn't work out, so… here I am."

Roscoe smiled, his white teeth contrasting with his dark mustache. "I see. Well, my own career was not quite so simple…"

Grimm rolled his eye. "As if I care…"

Roscoe shrugged. "I'm going to assume that you are interested, even if you don't know it or care to admit it. Well, my family was struggling to make ends meet in the competitive corporate world of Yavakaro, when I decided there was much more money to be made in the 'developing' nation of Zygbar. Looking to start my own business to escape the failing enterprise of my family, I set up shop in one of the bustling marketplaces of Zygbar's current capital city, Daggarech. So when you read the propaganda in Zygbar that says I started from nothing, it's true! But soon I was one of the wealthiest merchants in the city."

Grimm nodded and grinned a bit, his teeth appearing yellow in contrast with his stark white eyebrows. "See? Jus' like my daddy told me… sellin' somethin'. So what were you sellin'?"

Roscoe twirled one end of his mustache between two fingers. "Ahh, and that is where we have something in common, my unshaven friend. On the outside I appeared to be importing and selling quite simple things like produce… fruit and such. On the inside, I was also selling war, much like yourself. Or at least… the weapons necessary to fight one."

Grimm nodded, rubbing the grey stubble on his chin. "So you were a gun-runner? That ain't exactly what I call 'sellin' war,' but I'll let it slide. Who were you sellin' to? The rebels, I reckon?"

Roscoe nodded. "But of course! As my empire in the weapons and supplies businesses grew, I slowly gained control over everything the Sun Dragon Rebellion needed to wage war with Xarkon and the other opposing groups in Zygbar. As my own influence grew, I gradually exerted more and more power over them. Eventually I joined their group, advising the leader on political strategies, with the help of Azar Khan, his war advisor."

"And then you and this Azar con-artist guy staged a takeover? A 'coup' as you'd probably say?"

"Well said! Absolutely!" Roscoe leaned back and proudly puffed out his chest, somehow managing to make it even larger than his stomach. "I was able to persuade Azar Khan that I made a better political figurehead than he, and so when we kicked out the old boss, I took his throne. I fought the battlefield at home with propaganda campaigns and political meetings, while Khan fought the battles with the opposing factions, and of course Xarkon on occasion. It all ran very smoothly, and almost exactly according to plan."

Grimm again shook his head sadly. "So you fight the political battles while he fights the real ones…"

Roscoe's expression darkened. "Oh, they are both very real battles. I can assure you of that. I would think you would know that yourself."

"Not quite," Grimm grunted. "But I don't feel like bickerin' over it."

Roscoe grinned. "Then you have just surrendered a victory to me in this little war of words, have you not?"

"If this is a war of words, you're just shootin' arrows at a stone wall, O'Donnell."

"Every stone wall has its cracks. Send enough arrows out and some will make it through."

"So your tactics are based on sheer numbers? I wouldn't advise usin' that strategy with your infantry. You'll run outta men real fast."

"Zygbar has many men."

"Not many worthy of the name, from what I've seen."

"Perhaps you should ask a few of my female consorts for their opinion on that."

"I wouldn't want to meet anyone who'd 'consort' with you, Roscoe."

"Oh, that's hitting a bit below the belt, don't you think?"

"Nah, I don't want to go there any more than your women probably do."

Roscoe's smile almost enveloped his face. "You are better at this sort of war than you let on! You know, I'm afraid I'm starting to like you, Mister Grimm!"

Grimm's frown deepened, but he said nothing. Then the door slid open, and the gigantic silhouette of Lucas Mars appeared in the portal.

His cool grey eyes peered at them beneath his heavy, ever-furrowed brow. "Enjoying yourselves, I take it?"

"Your mercenary friend is quite an interesting individual," Roscoe said, nodding toward Grimm, who said nothing.

"Well, we have business to discuss now," Mars said, taking a seat at the table and tapping his gloved fingers together in anticipation.

"Your war?" Grimm prompted.

Mars nodded and leaned back in his chair. "Exactly. As Roscoe here can attest, things did not go perfectly at the CONON meeting recently. The Victorians forced the council to come to the agreement that a 'third party' should watch over our operations in Shardasha. This could ruin our plans…"

Grimm frowned. "You mean *your* plans."

Mars shook his head. "No. Most emphatically not *my* plans, Grimm… these are the plans of the Emperor of Xarkon. My own plans would be quite different. I've read every book named *The Art of War* from Sun Tzu's to Machiavelli's, to the one written by Victory's own military dictator during the Xenocide War, General Stryker. I've studied war on and off the battlefield all my life… But still I have to bow to the wishes of an Emperor whose education hardly includes Old Earth, and who has barely set foot outside his own palace. At least, for now."

Grimm cleared his throat. "So who's this 'third party' then?"

"The Grand General, Rick Radcliff. Who else?"

Grimm gave a laugh. "My old pal! Old four-eyed tight-pants hisself… ha-*ha!*"

"The very same. Grimm, I can't continue my operations as I have been and still keep the secret of Shardasha from Rick Radcliff. He is sure to discover it."

Roscoe shrugged. "So, step up the timetable! We can do that, certainly. Just start the war…"

Mars shook his head. "I can't do that while the Emperor is still alive. He does not know about my plans. He merely wants to make it look like he actually *accomplished* something during the reign of his pathetic dynasty and his own pitiful rule. And of course, he wants to use trickery to do it. This cowardly game he plays wears on my patience. But I cannot let it show… Grimm, I need you to move into Shardasha and wrap this up."

Grimm frowned. "I thought you intended for *them* to do that… your Enomegs… your loyal new super-soldiers."

"I did at first, but the door is closing too fast. The Enomegs' training will take too long to complete. Listen, Grimm… I am *ordering* you to move in with whatever forces you deem necessary and kill Lord Zegaldorph. Send in assassins; make it look like an accident…"

"No," Grimm said with deadly seriousness, and then he grinned and laughed. "Mars, you seem to be forgettin' somethin', so let me say it straight: I ain't one o' your soldiers. And I say no, 'cause it's not gonna be me who pulls the first trigger in this war. I do that, and then your Emperor'll decide I'm expendable, put the blame on me, and I'll end up just like the pirates that used to live on my island… an old weapon, a hidden switchblade of Xarkon, thrown away as soon as CONON finds out about it. No, no, Mars, not happenin' to me; I'm not gonna be the only one left without a chair when the music stops. Ain't that right, Roscoe?"

"Indubitably…" answered the Chancellor.

Mars gave a very slight smile. "That's exactly what I thought you would say. And it's fine with me; I don't want things done this way either. And I know Dark-Dragon doesn't."

Roscoe looked at a loss. "But… you said your Enomegs would…"

"Oh, they will do it," Mars said firmly. "The Enomegs are, above all else, loyal. I only hope I can convince Dragon to move early, unless he manages to finish on time."

Roscoe rolled his eyes. "Well, obviously our best course of action would be to kill the Emperor and get him out of the way so that you can…"

"No," Mars interrupted. "Let me make this clear: I am no murderer. I am a man of honor. I cannot say I truly fight for Xarkon's values if I murder its Emperor. And, though this is beside the point… what kind of precedent would that action set if I were to gain the position that way myself?"

Roscoe sighed, rubbing his balding head and looking away. "I knew you were going to say that…"

Mars nodded. "Good. Then we understand each other. Although so far this meeting has done nothing but confirm what we already knew."

The Chancellor of Zygbar frowned. "But you know, you still may have to do it eventually."

Mars nodded and looked away. "If worse comes to worse… but I will do it in the open, not in the darkness. And I will make sure everyone knows why it had to be done."

"And after you make your glorious speech explainin' all that," Grimm said, "make sure no Marc Antony comes up and makes another one right after you…"

Roscoe shot him a surprised glance.

Grimm sneered at him. "Yes, I've read Shakespeare. Try not to have a heart attack."

Mars blew out a sigh. "Would you two try to be *serious* about this?"

There was a moment of silence as they all sat staring at the table in thought. This meeting was intended to discuss the beginning of the war… and now it seemed that none of them knew just how to begin.

Finally Mars broke the silence. "Well, that leaves us no choices, so we will just have to stick with the original plan. I will try to speed up the Enomeg training process so that we can proceed with the Emperor's folly. I'll make sure that the trainees have their codenames and armor within days. We need them on the field *now*."

Grimm and Roscoe only nodded.

Mars looked up. "And I need you both at the ready. Grimm, I want you to stay docked here in the Maw. Roscoe, you and General Khan are to move to our outpost near Shardasha for a while. I may not be able to reveal my allegiance with Grimm yet, but I can surely reveal my allegiance with you. If I have to fight this battle with Mordark and Victory by my side, then Zygbar can be there as well."

Roscoe smiled. "Of course, High Commander. It will be an honor."

Grimm nodded. "Well, Mars, it's comin' to a head now. The whole world is watchin'. Every Human eye on Terra Nova is focused right on Shardasha. Make sure you know what you're doin'."

Mars was turned around now, staring at the door. "Oh, I know very well what *I* am doing," he said, "but the problem is... I think Rick Radcliff does as well."

LOCATION: ENOMEG TRAINING ACADEMY BASE

Dark-Dragon led the trainees, his children, down the hall leading to the armory. Each of them was wearing a skin-tight black body glove made of the finest nanofiber mesh in existence. This time, not a bit of their skin was showing below their heads. Their bodies were enshrouded in shadow.

"You should all be very proud of yourselves," said Dark-Dragon, "to have made it this far. You are almost there now. Your brothers and sisters who failed will become great soldiers of Xarkon in the special operations division, and those who died will be honored... but only you have a chance at becoming true Enomegs, and only you shall wear this armor."

He gave the Heartbeat salute as they passed through a doorway and into a long room. Benches were lined up in the center, and there was a row of round, clear tubes imbedded in each wall. Inside each tube was a suit of shining red armor... Enomeg exoskeletons, all matching prototypes. Scorp approached his tube and peered through the glass. He recalled how impressed he had been by Dragon's armor when he first saw it, but somehow it was even more impressive now, in the metallic red and crimson colors of the Armed Forces of Xarkon. For some strange reason, he got the feeling that he was looking in a mirror... that he was looking at himself, as he had always wanted to be... as he was destined to be. And then the glass slid aside.

"Notice the icons," Dark-Dragon said.

Scorp removed the helmet from the tube and turned it over in his hands. Depicted on the silver disks on either side of the helmet... was the image of a black scorpion, its claws outstretched, its tail curling outward. As Scorp ran his fingers around the edge of the disk and stared at it, he felt pride swell within him. All the indecisiveness he had felt about his loyalty to Xarkon, all of his thoughts about the Sarran he had allowed to escape during the earlier exercise... were gone. They were swept away in this moment, as he stared at what he had been waiting so long to see. Now he truly felt like an Enomeg soldier.

Scorp could tell from his tone that Dark-Dragon was now smiling as he spoke... a rare event indeed. "As impressive as these suits are, they are merely prototypes. For the final versions, each exoskeleton will be specially engineered to suit its owner's needs – as mine was specially designed for me – and will contain many more features. These suits feature only the basic abilities. Indeed, the most highly-advanced part of them is the nanomachine layer, which was already present in the mesh suits you're so familiar with.

Scorp already knew about nanofiber mesh. The nanomachines built into it were programmed to strengthen the suit at the point of impact in order to deflect ballistic weapons, and to rapidly dissipate heat in order to protect from energy weapons. The nanomachines also allowed for instant cloaking by changing the color of the light they reflect to match the suit's surroundings. But most importantly, the machines also worked to augment muscle movements, effectively increasing the wearer's strength and speed.

"You may now remove the armor and begin suiting up," Dark-Dragon instructed as he watched his students. "As I said, these suits do not have the full functionality of Enomeg armor, but they do have the basic built-in computer, heads-up display, hand-blades, and a few other features. Don't forget to make use of them, especially the personal forcefield shields and the starlight gas-powered flight packs. You have also been provided with your personal weapons, based on your preferences and the weapons you performed best with in training. You will find them in the back of your capsule."

Scorp opened a hatch behind the spot where his suit had been and lifted out three guns, one at a time. Two were smallish pistols and the other was a long rifle. He laid the weapons down on the table behind him and began sliding the ammunition into his suit's pouches.

Blade-Mantis laughed aloud. "What is *that* old thing?"

Scorp hefted the rifle and grinned. "This, *my friend*, is a real gun. Just the basics, nothing fancy. Straight sight down the top, no scope, no laser dot, just a barrel as straight as a runway attached to a good solid gun. It's called the Worchester RBR-42 'Ironslinger,' developed during the Xenocide War. This weapon packs bullets that can pierce Slashrim or Mahlok hide as easily as a Sarran crossbow bolt. The ammunition is shelled, so even though bullets might be hard to come by, there's no risk of fusion crystal decay or faulty electronics, because there are none."

The other trainees were a little surprised that Scorp had chosen a chemical firearm. Most guns now used caseless ammunition, which was fired from the weapon using a Gauss rifle-like "coilgun" technology that took advantage of breakthroughs in repulsion with the development of hoverpads. The bullet was propelled from the chamber by a series of tiny but powerful hoverpad rings that boosted it faster and faster as it passed, until it left the barrel at an extremely high velocity. Since there was no need for explosives or bulletshells, the weapon held more ammo, required less maintenance, was less prone to jamming, and did not expel hot casings that could injure the shooter and leave a trail. However, if the electronics failed or lost power, the weapon became useless. The best high-tech guns were powered by tiny fusion crystals, but the crystals slowly degraded with continued use. Scorp's pistols both used this HPG (HoverPad Gauss) technology, but he liked to have a backup as well.

"Primitive," Magnum-Coyote said dismissively. "Now *this* gun takes advantage of HPG technology by having bullets that actually explode and fragment on contact. This baby's an official Xarkon Arms Magnum Sidearm. They call it the Dirge. Same gun Mars carries. It comes in one color: black, and if a bullet from this hits an unarmored opponent, it leaves a wound the size of a football... *field.* They don't call me Magnum-Coyote for nothing."

Shadow-Cat gave a snort. "You call that the weapon of an Enomeg? It's got no elegance! Now *this* is a bit more like it: the Outlook Arms PQ-6. The rounds are low-caliber, but designed for maximum velocity even when traveling through the gun's integral silencer. It's so quiet that the first thing you'll hear when I kill you is Saint Peter welcoming you to the Pearly Gates... if you happen to be religious."

Mantis laughed. "That's a good one! But I prefer even *more* elegance. Besides my SMG here, I also have this." The sword came out with an almost silken sound as the razor-sharp edge grazed the side of the sheath. "It's a duranium, diamond-edged blazer katana, traditional yet advanced. The laser shielding can be activated to cut through metal armor or engage in a duel with an energy blade, but when the batteries run out, it still makes a useful weapon, unlike, say, our hand-blades... or your HPG guns."

"How medieval," Blood-Raven said.

"Perhaps so, but that is what I prefer," Mantis admitted. "A metal blade is more solid, more dependable, more *honest*. It has weight to it. Also, call me old-fashioned, but when I go into battle, I prefer to spill a little blood."

"Hell with all your elegance and subtlety," grunted Gun-Barracuda, hefting his massive weapon. "This here's a XM-62C 'Buzzsaw,' and you won't find a gun deadlier. The bullets'll punch through a Victorian *tank*, and there's enough of 'em in this box to last for weeks. She can be an ammo hose if you need it, but not if you're like me. I always know where I'm shooting, and I always hit what I shoot at. Forget your magnum, Coyote... They don't call me *Gun-Barracuda* for nothing."

Tanya said not a word as she checked her sniper rifle and SMG, making sure they were in good working order. Scorp thought: They didn't call her *Silent-Cobra* for nothing.

Cat looked across the room toward Raven. "What about you, Luke?"

He merely shrugged. "I have a pistol. Just the standard Xarkon sidearm, but with a slide-out stock, HUD-link scope, removable silencer, and a few other tweaks and customizations. Should serve just about any purpose in the event that I do require a ranged weapon."

"You can't use your blades for everything, of course." Mantis said, nodding. "I too carry a similar weapon. But our friend Saber-Scorpion seems to have *two*..."

Saber-Scorpion lifted his pistols. "These are XK-61 machine pistols, highly dependable blazer weapons manufactured in eastern Xarkon. Nicknamed the Skorpyn, but that's not why I chose them. They're small enough to be dual-wielded and made to suit either hand, but large enough to have a decent range, and with a collapsible handle and stock. Elegant design, easily silenced... *extremely* versatile. Best gun in the world."

Cat laughed. "Even better than the Ironslinger?"

Scorp nodded. "As long as you're not *too* far away, yes."

Dark-Dragon had been listening to this entire exchange with a great deal of amusement. He was clearly enjoying it, and he wanted to let his Enomegs savor this moment, so he waited for the excitement to die down before he finally spoke.

"Alright, people," he said at length. "That's enough of that. Listen closely now, because this next mission may surprise you. It's not one of the four tests that you know of, but a fifth one you may have heard me mention that is almost equally important: the Test of Leadership. As an Old Earth general named Sun Tzu once wrote: 'The victories of good soldiers are not noted for cleverness or bravery. The victories of good soldiers are won because they position themselves where they will surely win, prevailing over those who do not. All other victories are flukes.' When you're on the field, all you can do is follow the plan and react to situations as they arise. It's up to your leader to react and change the plan appropriately, if necessary. Good planning, good leadership... that is the key to victory.

"This next mission will take place off-world. You will be flown to the planet Midas here in the New Sol system. As you probably know, they've been working on terraforming the place for a number of years now. You'll find the planet as barren as they come, and with slightly lower gravity, but with enough of an atmosphere for you to breathe normally."

Dragon pointed down each side of the row of benches in the middle of the room. "Here's how this will work... Everyone on this side will follow the orders of Saber-Scorpion, the leader of Team Garnet. Everyone on this side will follow the orders of Blood-Raven, the leader of Team Ruby. You will work together, but separately, each team entering the base from opposite sides and competing to reach the same target first. Your ultimate goal is to take down the leader of a group of rebels who are trying to overthrow Xarkon's control of the mining facilities on Midas."

He pointed to the rotating hologram of a man that had appeared. "This is the leader, a man named Kleiner. We want him alive if possible, dead if necessary. We aren't playing games with these people; kill every hostile you encounter, but try to spare the miners if they don't put up a fight. We only want to lose so many good workers. Intel is not entirely clear on how much resistance you'll encounter, as the rebels have hired mercenaries... ones who seem to be quite good at counter-intelligence.

"There's more. The Enomegs do not officially exist, and very little information about them has been leaked to the public. We wish it to remain that way. Leave no bodies but those of your enemies, and whatever you do, do not lose any of your gear. If you are captured, Xarkon will disavow all knowledge of your existence. Is this understood?"

They all nodded. No loud shouting was necessary among the Enomegs. These were not regular soldiers; they were far, far more. To Dark-Dragon, they were his children... and he was about to send them into battle. A real battle this time, not merely training. Still, the coming fight would be next to nothing compared to what awaited them. Dragon could only hope, perhaps even pray, that they would be ready when the time came.

And that *he* would be ready.

But outwardly, the Enomeg commander betrayed no such misgivings, his bearing as disciplined as ever. "Good. Your ride is ready outside. Well, what are you waiting for? Get to it."

- CHAPTER ELEVEN -
THE GOLDEN TOUCH

Saber-Scorpion looked back at his team. The seating was far more comfortable in the Fafnir aerospace transport/gunship than inside the cramped Nidhogg dropships they usually rode. Each passenger had a seat all to himself, with a small table at the side where he could prepare his guns and other gear. The tables were magnetic due to the fact that the Fafnir had no artificial gravity – anything not nailed down somehow simply started floating in midair, as Scorp was now doing himself. Moving along the handholds at the top of the wall, he made his way to one of the viewports to look out.

The others were strapped into their seats. Magnum-Coyote was poring over his table now, busily checking his standard-issue Xarkon X-33 carbine, which he'd brought in addition to his signature Dirge magnum pistol. Blade-Mantis was pulling back and tying up his hair, and Silent-Cobra was simply seated in a relaxed position, looking thoughtful. And Seth seemed to be picking something out of his teeth.

He noticed Scorp looking at him and cleared his throat. "You know, I really don't get why they're only considering you two for this leadership job. I mean, you have failed most of the tests. Raven's failed *all* of them. So what's the big deal? I've got good grades, good scores... Hey, has anybody seen my X9? My pistol? I thought I set it here..."

"Seth," Cobra said, "be quiet."

Scorp blew out a sigh. *If Raven wants this leadership job*, he thought to himself, *he can have it.* He took a deep breath. There was something about being responsible for a group of people whose actions were not entirely under his control and who depended on his command to make their own decisions that worried him. This was why he hated working in a group, and most of all, leading one.

"Alright, everyone!" Scorp commanded. "Let's go over this one more time..."

Seth looked up and ran his fingers through his short reddish hair. "Uh, *sir…* we've already been over it."

"I *know* that, Seth," Scorp paused. "Or should I say Electric-Eel?"

Seth rolled his eyes. "Don't remind me."

Where did they come up with these names? "Right," he said, "Electric-Eel, we *have* been over it. That's why I said 'one more time.' And don't call me 'sir.' Scorp will do just fine."

Seth nodded. "Yes, sir. Scorp. Yes, Scorp."

Coyote did the Heartbeat. "Yes, Sir Scorp!"

Scorp ignored them. "Cut the chatter and listen up! We're approaching Midas now. The target is Shaft-Master Kleiner, who has taken control of Shaft C, one of the mining tunnels located on the surface of the planet. Our L-Z is about two minutes out from the shaft in order to avoid detection. We'll have to foot it the rest of the way –"

"And then we begin the descent into the shaft," Coyote interrupted, "sneak into the base, grab the boss, and scoot. We get it, Scorp. You can…"

"Quiet, Enomeg!" Blade-Mantis snapped in a manner that startled Scorp. "Let your commander speak! There is a time for games, and there is a time for getting the job done. You and Seth should know the difference."

Coyote started to make a retort, but something about Mantis's narrow eyes and stony expression made him think twice about it. So he just shrugged, muttering something about hair-triggers.

Scorp cleared his throat. "Upon reaching the edge of the mine shaft, we then proceed swiftly and silently downward and head for the Shaft Boss's headquarters, which is where Kleiner should be located. Raven's team will be coming in through another entrance in the cliff face of a nearby valley, so they will enter from the side. We have to make it to Kleiner before they do."

Mantis nodded. "But what about…"

He was cut off by a deep rumble that seemed to come from the core of the Fafnir itself. The Enomegs reflexively reached for handholds as the whole ship vibrated. Scorp, who was not strapped into a seat like the others, tried to keep himself from banging into the ceiling as the vessel lurched violently.

Seth looked around. "Something just hit us."

Coyote gawked at him. "No way! And here I thought the Fafnir was just getting *hungry*."

Why do I always get the jokers in my squad? Scorp thought.

Cobra's eyes narrowed. "Do you know if Kleiner has access to any defensive guns or fighters?"

"We're about to find out," Scorp replied.

He reached behind him and opened the hatch to the cockpit. Scorp saw the stars whirling past outside the canopy of the gunship as the pilot went into a loop. The canopy of the Fafnir was situated in what could be called an "upside-down" position, for the curve of the clear transperium arced underfoot as opposed to overhead, and the pilot and copilot sat in chairs that hung suspended over the void yawning beneath them. Besides the information provided by the ship's instruments, there was only a single small window on the ceiling that allowed for a view above.

As Scorp looked down, then, at the view below him, he saw two shafts of light, almost blindingly bright and tinged with yellow, split across the stars. They were gone as quickly as they came, leaving only an after-image when Scorp blinked. The beams had been completely soundless, making them seem like nothing more than a non-threatening light show. But Scorp knew that, in reality, those were capsules of starlight heat compressed into a thin forcefield that, if it had struck the ship, would have burst into a violent explosion and caused significant damage to the Fafnir's force shields. There could be no doubt; they were under attack.

"Triple-A from the surface?" Scorp asked over the commlink.

The copilot looked back at the Enomeg from behind his large black visor and shook his head. "Enemy fighters."

"Looks like you were right, Cobra." Scorp turned back to the copilot. "Can you evade them or shoot them down?"

"We're on it," the man answered. "Shouldn't be a problem."

The pilot glanced at him quickly. "Divert power from engines to shields!"

"Done," the copilot said.

He reached up and flipped a switch over his head, staring at the row of colored bars beside it. Nothing moved. He flipped it again. Then he cursed. Scorp saw the surface of Midas whirl by, and then one of the enemy fighters buzzed past.

"Cloudbreakers," Mantis commented behind him.

Meanwhile, the copilot exclaimed, "It won't switch! I'll have to reroute manually."

He reached up and removed the entire control panel, then stuck his fingers inside.

"He's doing that wrong!" Seth protested from over Scorp's shoulder.

The pilot glanced up. "I'll do it, Carl. You take control."

For a split second, both the pilot and copilot had their fingers in the control box. It turned out to be the wrong split second. A bright flash lit the cockpit and Scorp saw electricity arcing over both men's arms. It took less than a second, and then both of them slumped over. Coyote actually laughed at the sight. Scorp shot him a hostile glance that immediately shut him up.

Not wasting any time, Seth shoved past Scorp and wrenched the pilot from his seat. Scorp ran to help him, dislodging the unconscious copilot. Then the two of them quickly sat down and strapped themselves in. Behind them, they heard the other Enomegs getting up to look. It was bad timing, for just then another blast struck the Fafnir's shields, sending the ship spinning. As soon as Seth took the stick and corrected it, Mantis's head appeared over Scorp's shoulder.

"I hope you got full marks in flight training, my friends," he said.

All Enomegs were trained in piloting a wide variety of vehicles. Scorp knew the Fafnir gunship inside and out. It was a large aerospace transport-gunship, armed with a wide array of starfire cannons and HPG ballistic guns, as well as bombs and missiles. Most of these cannons were situated on the bottom of the craft to allow for surface bombardment, the ship's specialty as it cleared a path for the troops and vehicles stored in its hold to land. This was why the cockpit canopy was positioned so oddly.

A proximity alarm blared and Scorp swung the ship hard to port just in time to avoid another fighter that was flying completely out of control. Black holes were burned in its hull, and it was trailing smoke. It spiraled out of sight, headed for the surface of Midas far below.

"I guess Raven's boys shot it down," Seth said. "Let's not let them have all the fun…"

Scorp cursed under his breath. "Coyote, Cobra, how about you make yourselves useful and man the gunner controls?"

He wished his soldiers would start acting like Enomegs and think for themselves. Did he have to give them permission to do everything?

The Fafnir's shields were still not operating at full power, but Seth didn't intend to use them. He simply watched the enemy fighters as they swung around for another pass, and then he engaged the main thrusters, heading straight toward them.

"What are you doing?" Mantis exclaimed.

Electric-Eel shook his head. "Are you with me, Scorp?"

"I think so. Belly-up?"

"Right. Coyote, Cobra, get ready to fire."

At that exact second, the Cloudbreakers launched their missiles. But with most of the Fafnir's power still on the engines instead of the shields, Seth was able to maneuver faster than they expected. Blue-white lines of burning Starlight gas erupted along the bottom of the Fafnir's right wing and the top of its left – the maneuvering thrusters lighting at full burn – and the vehicle was sent into a fast roll, which Scorp quickly stopped with the opposite thrusters. The enemy missiles streaked toward them and exploded violently as they were shot down by the Fafnir's automatic defensive cannons.

And now the enemy fighters were positioned perfectly in line with the ship's belly, which was bristling with guns.

Scorp looked up – or rather, down – through the viewport under his feet, as Coyote and Cobra locked onto their targets. The array of gun turrets on the Fafnir's underside looked like the heads of some subterranean insects protruding from the Earth, with bizarre eyestalks maneuvering to better see their assailant. Then the eyestalks spat fire. The Cloudbreakers never stood a chance. They got caught in a storm of light and blazer fire, blasting right through their meager shields. Soon both were spiraling toward the surface of Midas, and one exploded before it even entered the atmosphere.

Seth brought the ship back level with the planet below and engaged the shields for atmospheric entrance.

"Good flying…" Scorp said, "Eel."

Seth blew out a sigh. "I swear, I've got to put in a request for a different codename…"

LOCATION: SOUTH OF SHAFT C
XARKONIAN MINING COLONY
PLANET MIDAS, NEW SOL

Blood-Raven stepped out onto the surface of Midas with an air of cool confidence. Behind him, his men unloaded in single file, stern and disciplined. Raven couldn't help but smile. He was glad people like Seth and Coyote were not here to cut up and joke around. He liked things to go smoothly according to plan... according to *his* plan.

He looked over his group. Directly behind him were Shadow-Cat and Gun-Barracuda. His other two teammates were known as Luis Swift-Stallion and Hans Thunder-Hawk. Of the two, Hawk was the more formidable, but neither he nor Stallion had attracted much of Raven's attention, since they were not even close to the level of perfection shown by students like Saber-Scorpion and Blade-Mantis. Both had been soundly defeated in the ongoing duels of the Test of Supremacy.

I got stuck with the rookies, he thought, *but I can handle them. I can guide them, lead them. I can make them into something more.*

Raven flipped his helmet over in his hands and slid it onto his head. "Alright, soldiers, just follow my lead and stick to the plan. Cat, Stallion, you take point. The rest of you, follow me. Let's move!"

Raven looked up at the sky above them, which was hazy and slightly green, with a few stars visible even though the sun was out. Clearly, the terraforming project was not quite complete – the atmosphere was still not quite up to Earth standards.

The Enomegs were currently on a low area of terrain, inside a crater that had been on the planet's surface long before Humanity had given this world a protective atmosphere. Shaft C was located on the surface far over their heads, above the tall edge of the crater that now cast its shadow down upon them. The terrain in the bottom of the pit was littered with large, dislodged stones that made perfect cover for the team.

"Clear," Cat said, hefting her rifle as she headed for the next stone.

"Clear here," she heard Stallion report.

She slid behind the stone and peeked her head out to see around it. That was when she heard the deep mechanical groaning, followed by a low thump. She quickly ducked down lower and checked for movement, using her helmet's built-in optical amplification to zoom into the distance. This enabled her to see a swarm of insects in the air, which surprised her, considering how recently the planet had been made inhabitable. The sight distracted her for a second before she finally caught sight of the true source of the disturbance...

"A walker," she reported. "They have a walker."

LOCATION: NORTH OF SHAFT C

Saber-Scorpion stepped out onto the Fafnir's boarding ramp, flipped his helmet over in his hands, and slid it onto his head. The planet before him was composed entirely of dull, rust-colored stone, with a dim, greenish sky that made the entire scene all the more alien. They had landed on the opposite side of the mine shaft from Raven's team, on the surface instead of in the crater. Scorp could see both the shaft and the crater in the distance, one small pit and one very large one.

"Seth, Coyote, Cobra, Mantis… what do you guys think?"

Cobra gave him a quizzical look. "I think… that you're supposed to be our leader."

Scorp turned to regard her. "And I think that we're supposed to be Enomegs, not just grunts in the Xarkon army. We can think for ourselves."

No one here is a rookie, he thought. *No one here* needs *my leadership. Dependence upon it would only decrease their individual potential. It would make each of them something less.*

Cobra shrugged and looked around. "Not much cover. Better use active camo."

Scorp nodded and touched a control on his wrist. The others did the same. Slowly, their armor faded in color from bright red to a dull, ruddy brown, and their nanofiber mesh suits also shifted hue to match. Scorp slid his Ironslinger out of its sheath and cocked its antiquated lever-action handle, bringing the first bullet into the chamber. It was quite a satisfying action.

"Let's move," he said.

They kept down as low as possible, using what few scattered stones and low dips there were in the terrain as cover. While sprinting from one such hole to the next, Scorp spotted a patrolling sentry in the distance. He took in the whole scene at a glance and then ducked into the next pit beside Coyote.

"Everyone hold," Scorp said into the comm. "There's a sentry ahead, right next to the edge of the shaft. Can't shoot him or he'll fall in and give us away, and there's too much level ground between here and there to run for it without getting spotted and alerting them. Any ideas?"

Coyote peeked over the edge of the pit. "I can take this guy," he said.

Scorp took a long, hard look at his comrade. He would have liked to make eye contact, but it was impossible behind that triangular black Enomeg visor. Still, he sounded sure enough.

"How confident are you?" Scorp asked.

"Hey, I may joke around a lot, 'Sir Scorp,' but never in the field. And I'm telling you, I *can* take this guy."

Scorp nodded. "As I said before, we're all Enomegs. You know what you're capable of. If you can take him down without raising an alarm… then he's all yours."

"I'll get him," Coyote said, rising slightly into a hunched position and setting his legs to launch himself into the air, "Just, you know… cover me if I turn out to be wrong."

Before Scorp could protest, Coyote was gone. He quickly sat up to watch. Scorp could hardly believe his eyes; was Coyote simply going to *run* toward the sentry? It was quite a distance; surely he'd be seen… What was his plan? But apparently Scorp had already guessed it; Coyote simply set into a run, with his chest out and his legs moving in a blur, kicking up dust as he covered the distance in hardly two blinks. The sentry heard him approaching and turned to look… just as Coyote reached out, grabbed him, threw him to the ground, and gave him a single quick slice with both his star-talons.

"All clear," said Magnum-Coyote.

LOCATION: SOUTH OF SHAFT C

"Cat, repeat that last transmission…"

"I said, they have a walker."

Blood-Raven shook his head in disbelief, but Gun-Barracuda, perked up. "A walker, eh? What model?"

"How should I know?" Cat said with a snort. "I don't build toys of the things like you boys do."

"Looks like an older model Xarkon medium build," Stallion reported.

"Bloodhound?" Barracuda asked.

"Probably."

Raven continued moving forward, staying behind the rocks, heading for Cat's position. "Any way we can sneak past?"

"Out here?" Cat said. "No. From his height, he'd be sure to see at least one of us moving around. Well, except for me. I could do it, but you guys would stand out like sore thumbs. Especially skinhead."

"Shut up," Barracuda grunted.

"Cut the chatter!" Raven snapped. "We'll have to take the thing down. We've all run the simulations. Walkers are tough, but they're not invincible. Barracuda, give me some of your explosives, and then move up with Cat. You four take cover and prepare an ambush. I'll run ahead and distract the walker."

Barracuda handed his commander a packet of plastic explosives and asked, "How are you gonna do that?"

"I'll worry about that," Raven replied. "Just follow my orders."

He then slipped into the shadows of the rocks nearby and disappeared. It didn't take long for the walker to arrive. Those inexperienced with walkers often expected them to be huge, slow, clumsy beasts, lumbering along, shaking the earth as they walked. But the reality of a modern walker was quite different. They moved with such grace and precision, such perfect balance, that the thudding of their feet was quieter than the groaning of the machinery that powered them.

With the meticulousness of a striding waterbird, the Bloodhound picked its way between the rocks, its head swiveling slightly now and then as the pilot scanned the terrain below. The machine looked for all the world like a huge, armored animal, even with the boxy shapes of the old Bloodhound. Sleek, modern Xarkon walkers like the Fox looked even more organic.

But even this old walker bore enough weapons to take out an entire unit of hovertanks… and certainly enough to take down a few bloody footsoldiers. Barracuda's hand instinctively moved toward the rocket launcher on his backpack, which was attached to a sort of hinge just over his shoulder. He could swing it up and fire at a moment's notice, if necessary.

"I'm moving in," they heard Raven say over the commlink.

Cat peeked out past the rock behind which she and Barracuda were hiding. "Where is he?"

Barracuda merely grunted and shrugged. He stuck his head out again and started scanning the rocks in all directions, looking for their commander. Behind him, Cat followed his example, only poking her eyes up as much as necessary.

"Barracuda," she said slowly, "I know you tried to kill me one time, but just to show I have no hard feelings: *duck!*"

She quickly threw herself to the ground on one side as the walker's guns fired, splitting the rock they had been hiding behind into a thousand tiny fragments. She'd luckily had the foresight to activate her armor's force field just in time, so the shards of flying stone merely ricocheted off harmlessly.

All of the Enomeg suits were equipped with these shields, which emitted a "bubble" of "cool" energy that encased the wearer's body, "attaching" to the material of the suit. It was able to deflect both physical and energy blows. Although nearly all modern military devices were fusion-powered, the reactions were contained within Energite crystals that gradually degenerated as they were used. Rapid fluctuations in the amount of power being drawn, such as those caused by the shield systems, tended to degrade them even faster. For this reason, the Enomegs left their force-shield systems switched off until the threat level called for them.

Once the clattering of falling debris died down a bit, Shadow-Cat scrambled to her feet and dashed behind another rock, not bothering to look back into the cloud of dust behind her for Barracuda. He could take care of himself. She kept running until she reached the position of Swift-Stallion and Thunder-Hawk, joining them behind their cover.

"The walker spotted us," she said.

"Then just keep your head down!" Hawk exclaimed.

"Hang on! I'm trying to spot Raven!"

She stuck her head out again to look back where she'd come, but there was no sign of either Raven or Barracuda. All she could see was the walker, still strutting among the stones, its head looking this way and that, occasionally spouting small arms fire seemingly at random. He was clearly an unprofessional pilot, she thought. Had he even been trained at all?

That was when Raven struck. The walker had just foolishly placed its foot on top of a large, flat stone, when the rock suddenly exploded, sending it off-balance. It tried to right itself in midair, but failed, falling over sideways. Walkers, especially the newest ones, were not at all clumsy. They had automatic balance programming and safety features such as hoverpads to keep them from falling completely, giving them enough time to right themselves. In the hands of an unskilled pilot, however, they could still occasionally be caught off-balance.

Nevertheless, they were also quite adept at righting themselves once they were down. As Cat watched, the Bloodhound brought its massive feet up under it in an attempt to push itself back up. That was when Raven appeared and simply climbed on top of it. When the walker stood back up, the Enomeg was crouched atop its head, holding on tight to any handholds he could find.

"Barracuda," they heard Raven's voice calmly say, "I see you. Prepare to fire your rocket on my mark."

"Aye, sir."

All of the Enomegs were watching now, despite the danger of revealing themselves, as their commander executed his daring plan. He suddenly rocketed away from the lumbering machine, his jetpack spouting white heat. The walker moved its head up to fire at him, but at that very second, Raven gave the order to Barracuda, and the Enomeg's rocket streaked through the air, slamming into the machine's head. It recovered quickly, its armor damaged but hardly crippled, and swiveled to face this second foe... just as Raven activated the charge he'd planted above the cockpit's transperium canopy.

It was a daring move... so daring, in fact, that no other squad of soldiers would have even considered it. Of course, Raven hadn't even given his squad a chance to consider it; he had simply made the decision. But it worked – the explosion rocked the already weakened machine to its core, and the entire cockpit erupted in a ball of flame. The legs beneath the burnt frame stiffened in mid-stride, and the Bloodhound toppled into the stones, sending up a cloud of dust that blocked out the stars overhead. The Enomegs had pulled it off; a squad of mere footsoldiers against a towering duranium walker, a giant of the battlefield.

"One," Barracuda said.

"It counts as mine," replied Blood-Raven.

LOCATION: SHAFT C, NORTH SIDE

Saber-Scorpion carefully peered over the edge of the mining shaft. The huge, perfectly round hole extended deep into the surface of the planet, as if bored there by a single enormous drill. And indeed, perhaps it had been. The edges of the pit were lined with metal platforms like scaffolding, and some long, metal bridges crisscrossed the interior. About halfway down was a closed-in metal edifice built into the side of the wall; that was no doubt the main base of operations, where the mine boss would be located.

"A lot of mercs down there," said Electric-Eel, "close to a hundred, I'd say, from what I can see. Some are Slashrim, probably hired for cheap labor. Damn lizards."

"Don't underestimate the Slashrim, Seth," replied Saber-Scorpion, "They are much more than lizards."

Indeed, the Slashrim were not even reptiles, if one had to use the terms of the animal kingdom of Earth. Their body-build was distinctly reptilian, with bird-like dinosaur legs, bent and clawed, and hunched backs to match. But they did not have scales, being instead covered in a thick layer of leathery skin, and they were not cold-blooded – at least in the biological sense. They also had long, sharply pointed ears.

"Mostly Stage Two, as far as I can see," Cobra said.

"Orcs..." muttered Coyote.

As Slashrim aged, they passed through a variety of growth "stages." When first born, they were already strong and vicious, but only stood about a meter high. As they grew older and more intelligent, they rose to about the same size and build as a Human. This was Stage Two, the most favored stage for cheap labor, because they could wear Human clothes and do Human jobs, but were still stupid enough to keep under control.

At Stage Three they grew more cunning, and in the stages beyond that… enormous. They were certainly the most fearsome and barbaric creatures native to this galaxy that Humanity was now forced to call home. Humans, especially the military, often referred to them by monster names for short: goblins, orcs, lizardmen (or just lizards), trolls, ogres, and the oldest and biggest ones… the pseudodragons.

"All right," Scorp said, "Cobra, you're with me. We're Team Quickstrike. Mantis, you take Coyote and Eel. You're team Longshot. You head around the scaffolding to the right, and we'll go left. That way we can cover each other and prevent being taken by surprise. Now let's move!"

Instead of looking for a gentler method of descent, the Enomegs simply leaped over the edge, their automatic camouflage shifting to the darker hue of the mine as they fell. They hit the uppermost platform that encircled the perimeter of the pit with hardly a sound. Then they split up, with Scorp and Cobra taking one path as Mantis, Coyote, and Seth took the other. They ran doubled-over, almost at a crouch, and any sentries who might have heard their arrival and glanced their way noticed nothing amiss.

Unfortunately, Scorp ran into the first guard just as he was turning about, causing the Slashrim to start as he noticed the Enomegs approaching. Just as he was about to utter a cry of alarm, Scorp slid out his silenced XK-61 and put a burst of three bullets in the Slashrim's neck. The guard gurgled and raised his weapon, but another round sent him to the floor.

"Any sign of detection?" Scorp asked before his foe even hit the dirt.

"None," Cobra said as she peered over the edge of the walkway, noting that none of the Slashrim below had their pointed ears raised.

Mantis's team was lucky enough to find that the first guard they encountered was looking the other way. Mantis signaled to his partners to hold position as he darted quickly toward the Slashrim's back. The Enomeg's katana hissed out of its sheath and took the back entrance into its target's heart. With some degree of satisfaction, Mantis slid the blade back out and turned…

But he did not hear the Slashrim fall. Upon looking back, he received a clawed fist in the face, sending him sprawling. Coyote was quick to make up for his mistake, however, shooting the guard with his Dirge as soon as Mantis fell. From where they stood, the report of the magnum seemed to echo through the complex like an explosion, and once they were sure the guard was dead, all of the Enomegs rushed to the edge of the platform, sure that they had just given away their position.

"Well, that was foolish of me," Mantis was muttering as he stood up behind Coyote and Seth. "I knew Slashrim had multiple redundant organs…"

"Don't sweat it," Coyote said. "Just get ready. They'll know where we are now."

On the opposite side of the room, Scorp looked down through the metal grating of the platform on which he was standing. With cold efficiency, he chose a corner for each of his men to cover, picking one they could see well from their position. Upon pressing a button on the side of his helmet, it emitted a laser visible only through their HUD visors, with which he marked the position for everyone in his unit.

"I'm painting your targets, people," he said. "Just clear out the aggressors, not – wait, hold fire. They're falling back. Maybe Raven screwed up – it looks like they're all headed to his position."

The Slashrim and Human miners below rushed for weapons and headed for the southern side of the lower complex.

Seth shook his head. "Surely they heard Coyote's gun. You'd think *one* of them would be smart enough to think –"

"That's just it," Scorp interrupted, "not *one* of them is thinking. Only the Skrakki get smarter as their numbers increase, because of their hive mind. For most other species, it works the other way around. Every individual in the group ceases to think for themselves, and the result is mass stupidity. That's why they have leaders, and apparently none of those are here."

That's why we as Enomegs need to remember to think for ourselves, Scorp thought. Dark-Dragon often stressed that. Why, then, was this Test of Leadership necessary? But Scorp had already found out the answer: even the Enomegs had started looking to him for orders once he was appointed the leader of the group. They had been trained for Loyalty as well, creating a contradiction in training and purpose, because if they questioned *too* much, they might question the very foundations of the country.

They might question that Xarkon can do no wrong.

LOCATION: SHAFT C, SOUTH SIDE

"Form up, you worthless *kragduk!* Eyes to the south! That walker didn't blow up itself! Report anything that moves!"

From high above, Blood-Raven and his team watched as the enormous Slashrim warlord rallied his troops, directing them to guard the southern entrance to the mine. Forming a primitive line, they readied their weapons and pointed them toward the field of stones where Raven and his team had toppled the Bloodhound walker.

"Looks like they're all thoroughly distracted," Cat said as she crawled easily along the metal support beams lining the tunnel ceiling.

Behind her, Barracuda snorted. "I'm sure Team Garnet'll thank us."

"Have you spotted the target?" Raven asked in frustration, climbing farther out and closely inspecting the crowd assembled below through his helmet's optical zoom.

"Negative," Barracuda replied. "Just the Slashrim up front and some Human miners in back, lookin' scared and useless. No authority figures."

"I see three possible exits he could have taken," Cat put in. "There's an elevator shaft to the west, a small tunnel to the east, and main shaft to the north. If they took that route, Team Garnet will get him for sure."

"Don't count on that," said Hans Thunder-Hawk. "I've just made visual contact with Team Garnet now. They're on the opposite side of the roof, up on the rafters like us."

Raven immediately tensed up. "Fall in, people! Let's move!"

Crawling along the metal struts above the open cave, they made quick time to the other side, without attracting any notice from the soldiers on the floor below. When they reached Team Garnet, they saw Seth Electric-Eel closely inspecting a small metal grate on the wall for security measures. He looked back at Scorp and shook his head. Scorp was just about to kick the grate in when Raven grabbed him roughly by the shoulder.

"Is Kleiner in there?" Raven demanded.

Scorp shook his head. "Actually, I just smelled some fresher air coming out of this vent. Turns out this is an elevator shaft leading to the landing platform on the surface. Always follow your nose."

Coyote chuckled.

Raven shoved Scorp to one side. "Out of the way. I'm the one who distracted the guards for you."

Scorp grabbed Raven and shoved him back, almost pushing him off the narrow walkway. Raven grabbed his arm, and the two of them entered into a wrestling match, as their teammates watched in amazement.

Barracuda swore violently. "Idiots! Outta the way before I throw you both down!"

"You see what I was saying?" Seth said to Coyote. "*These* are our chosen leaders?"

The scrap was interrupted by a loud roar rushing past, coupled with a gust of air and burst of light from the small grate beside them. Scorp and Raven stopped in mid-punch, turned, activated their star-talons, and immediately began to cut away at either side of the grating. Scorp was the quicker to act. He kicked the grating in and leapt right after it, activating his flight pack as he went. A pair of blade-like stabilizer fins emerged from the sides of the pack as the blue-white starfire propelled him up the shaft with amazing speed.

Raven followed closely behind, rocketing his pack at full power, screaming in rage, "Scooorpiooooon!"

As Scorp slowed down to avoid ramming into the bottom of the elevator above, Raven caught up with him. Neck and neck, the two adversaries turned to look at each other… and Raven lashed out with a twirling kick, sending Scorp spinning off-course and slamming into the wall. Raven took the time to jeer at his opponent before gunning his engines, and during that time Scorp managed to lash out and grab him by the leg just as he ascended. In midair, the two of them wrestled, Scorp climbing up Raven's legs while Raven tried to kick him off.

Finally Scorp pushed away, and they began flying almost side-by-side again… just as the elevator above them stopped. With lightning reflexes, they swung their legs upward and crouched upside-down against the bottom of the lift, their magnetic boots holding them in place as each activated one of their energy blades and began to slice through the floor. As they cut, Shadow-Cat arrived and crouched beside Raven. At that moment, the two pieces of metal fell free, and the Enomegs slipped inside. Cat quickly followed, as all the other Enomegs flew to catch up, avoiding blazer fire from the guards at the bottom of the shaft who had finally caught on to their position.

Barracuda pulled out two grenades, activated them, and dropped them both. "Oops."

The explosion echoed up behind them just as Scorp and Raven emerged onto a large landing pad on the surface of Midas, where they saw a dropship resting idly, its lower booster engines already charged. Mine Boss Kleiner was standing at the bottom of the boarding ramp, glaring at them. He then turned and bolted inside, and the ramp started to close. Scorp and Raven burst into the fastest run they could achieve as they raced toward it, kicking a cloud of dust behind. The vehicle moved forward, dropping slightly out of sight as it clumsily flew over the cliff edge. It was at that moment that Scorp, Raven, and Cat, all nearly neck-and-neck, simultaneously jumped. They landed on the back of the dropship with a clang, each grabbing the first thing they could hold onto.

As their magnetic boots activated and took hold, the three of them climbed atop the huge vessel and looked around. Up ahead, near the nose of the ship, was an upper boarding hatch, probably leading straight into the cockpit. Slowly and carefully, Scorp began to half-walk, half-crawl his way toward it. With a growl, Raven followed.

"Come on, Cat," Raven shouted, "let's take him!"

Shadow-Cat dashed forward against the wind of Midas's meager atmosphere and grabbed Raven by the arm. "We can't *kill* him!"

Raven shook her off. "Watch me!"

Cat was about to grab him again when she heard the sound of another engine below them. It was not the low, dull roar of the dropship engines… but a high-pitched scream, like a fighter. Or perhaps two of them.

Raven, who had one star-talon activated and was about to advance on Scorp, stopped and shouted, "What's that?!"

Scorp also turned to look, just as a pair of Cloudbreakers floated up behind them and opened fire with their guns. Streaks of yellow-white laser cut through the air in flashes, blazing right over the Enomegs' heads. In a few places, the bullets even ricocheted off the dropship's armor.

"They're crazy!" Shadow-Cat screamed. "Don't they know they'll hit their own ship?!"

When there was a pause in the firing, the Enomegs stood up again and dashed forward, toward the dropship hatch. But before they had even gone one foot, the guns erupted again, this time from the second fighter as it made its pass. Scorp and Raven dropped flat immediately, but Cat was not as quick. As they watched, one of the streaks of light sliced past her leg, and she let out a cry of pain. Her leg slipped, and she fell backward a few feet before grabbing hold again. She tried to take another step forward, but the pain in her leg was too much, and she curled up again. Meanwhile, the first fighter was coming back around for its second pass.

Scorp and Raven, who were at an equal distance from the forward dropship hatch, exchanged glances. They could not see one another's expressions behind their helmet visors, but they knew well enough that their expressions would most likely match… and each of them was scowling with near absolute hatred for the other. Mentally and silently, they battled over who would claim Kleiner… and who would have to save Cat. They did not have long to think about it.

Scorp was the first to move. He suddenly deactivated his magnetic boots and slid backward several feet toward the rear of the ship before activating them again and grabbing hold. Then he began moving diagonally toward Cat… even as the bolts of white-hot energy whizzed past them once again. Raven did not stick around to watch, but instead took another few steps forward and sank his Starfire blade into the surface of the boarding hatch.

Meanwhile, Scorp put an arm around Shadow-Cat, just under her shoulders, and began helping her forward. But now the first fighter was right behind them, flying directly forward and taking careful aim at these two limping targets. Scorp quickly unclipped a grenade from his belt, activated it, and let go. There was a massive explosion directly behind them, its shockwave knocking them onto their faces, and they heard the fighter fall away beneath the dropship. Scorp doubted his fragmentation grenade had breached the fighter's shields, but at least he'd given them something to think about. He then stood up and moved as quickly as possible toward the now open front hatch, dragging Shadow-Cat along with him.

When he reached the hatch, Scorp lowered Cat inside, then dropped in after her, just as the guns from the remaining fighter scorched the air over his head. Once his feet hit the ground, Scorp turned, activated his blades, and looked around. What he saw was about five or six dead mercenaries, all cut apart by energy blades… and Raven, standing at the back of the dropship, with a body strapped to his chest: the body, no doubt, of Mine Boss Kleiner. Behind him, the boarding hatch was just beginning to open.

As Scorp watched, Raven laughed and pulled the cord on a parachute he had strapped on. A great black canvas erupted from his back and slid out into the open air… taking Raven and his prisoner along with it. As he disappeared from sight, Raven lifted his free hand and waved.

For a moment, Saber-Scorpion considered leaping out after his opponent, depending on his jetpack for flight, but he knew that was too risky. Besides, that would leave Cathryn here on this crashing dropship… and Raven had already won anyway. So Scorp simply turned away. Cat was standing there before him, leaning up against the copilot's seat. She looked at him for a moment, and then her head dropped. Scorp placed a hand on her shoulder as he walked past and took a seat in the pilot's chair.

"Strap in," he said, "and let's make sure this thing gets back to the ground without crashing."

Cat slid into the copilot seat and strapped in, but she still kept her face averted as she flipped the control to close the rear hatch.

"Coyote, Cobra," Scorp said into his commlink, "do you copy?"

"I copy," came Coyote's response.

"We're piloting the dropship now and headed back to your position. There's a Cloudbreaker or two on our tail. Think you can take care of them?"

"Good thing we brought the rockets…"

LOCATION: SHAFT C LANDING PAD
5 MINUTES LATER

After the success of the main mission objective, the cleanup was easy. The rest of the mercenaries had already flown, and when Scorp's dropship reached the main base tower again, a volley of Stinger-VII surface-to-air missiles launched by Coyote and even Barracuda, who could never miss out on the chance to blow something up, knocked the single pursuing fighter down in one swift stroke. But by the time Scorp landed, Raven had already brought in his prize. Scorp could not spot him, but he could imagine him down there in the crater below, dragging the unconscious or dead Mine Boss Kleiner back toward Team Ruby's extraction point.

All of the Enomegs on Team Garnet were watching Saber-Scorpion expectantly as he walked down out of the dropship's boarding hatch, with Shadow-Cat limping behind him. He removed his helmet and gave them a look that spoke volumes. Electric-Eel and Cobra looked away. Magnum-Coyote even jerked off his helmet and was about to throw it to the ground in a rage when he stopped himself from damaging such an expensive piece of equipment. Mantis stepped forward and put a hand on Scorp's shoulder, giving it a shake.

"You did excellent, my friend," he said. "None of us could have done better. Don't let this defeat get you down. All it means is that Raven may be the leader when the Enomegs fight as one, which will seldom happen anyway. But we still all passed the test… for we survived."

Scorp nodded. So there was not a single loss on his side. That was good to hear. He turned to regard Shadow-Cat and took a look at her wounded leg. It was not bad; she probably could not have climbed up to the hatch atop the moving dropship without his help, but she could certainly walk back out of the base alone.

"You've got to hand it to Raven," Coyote said, "he's good. When it comes to warfare, he's really got the golden touch."

"But not when it comes to helping his own team," Scorp said. "If anything, my losing for helping Cat should earn *me* the leadership position…"

Cat shook her head in amazement at him. "I wasn't even *on* your team! Don't act like what happened was my fault!"

"I'm not."

"You didn't have to come back and help me!"

"Yes, I did."

"I *didn't* ask for your help!"

162

Scorp turned to face her again, his expression tinged with disappointment, but with only kindness in his eyes.

"And you never will need to," he said.

She paused, staring at him. "You really are a piece of work, Saber-Scorpion."

With that, she turned and limped away toward the elevator, with Barracuda moving to follow her. When all of Team Ruby was gone, Scorp looked around at his own squad. Most of them were staring at the ground. Only Mantis was looking away into the distance. Scorp looked around to see what he was staring at, but all he saw was the barren and rocky wasteland of Midas, the deep crater that yawned below etched in contrasting shadows as the sun set on the horizon, highlighting the sky in red.

"An amazing view from up here, isn't it?" Mantis said.

"Yeah," Scorp replied, as he turned and marched back toward the elevator door. "Come on, Enomegs… Let's go home. You certainly don't have to wait for my orders anymore."

It was a fact that felt much worse than he had expected it to.

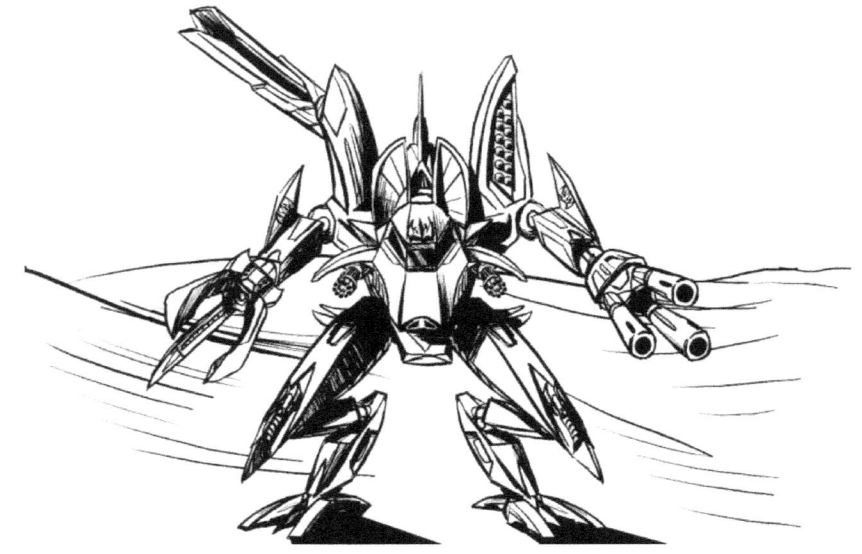

- CHAPTER TWELVE -
SETTING THE BOARD

Saber-Scorpion lay awake on his bed in his quarters, staring at the ceiling. It was something he seemed to do a lot. A few nights had passed since the Test of Leadership, his latest loss to his nemesis, Blood-Raven. Looking back, he realized that Raven had truly beaten him in every test – he had reached the Crown first in the Test of Honor, and he would no doubt have slaughtered his mark in the Test of Loyalty had Scorp not been lucky enough to encounter her first.

Thus, Scorp had been concentrating all of his effort lately on the Test of Supremacy. The duels had been going on for quite a while now, with students rising and falling through the twisted tree of victories and defeats. So far, only three trainees had never lost a match: Scorp, Raven, and Mantis. Although most of the students had already completed enough fights to "pass" the test, it was up to these final three to decide who the true victor would be.

If he could at least win the tournament, he would prove himself to be the best. Yet somehow even that goal, one he had thought about all his life up to this point, was beginning to seem hollow, distant… insignificant.

Breathing a sigh, Scorp went to his thankfully private shower – something he had never experienced before the ETAB – and massaged a few of the injuries as the cool water washed over him. As he stood there, he found himself wondering vaguely about civilian lives. He usually tried to stop himself from doing this, as the thoughts were sometimes painful. It was strange for him to imagine life outside all this, a life without the constant training and fighting. Was it as ideal as his imagination sometimes made it seem? He doubted it. But part of him longed to find out.

After his shower, he threw himself down on the bed again for another session of staring at the ceiling, though he could not see it in the utter blackness of the room, and tried to sleep. Gradually his thoughts began to wander… life and memory became hazy, and the dim half-life of sleep began to take over. Then, Saber-Scorpion began once again to dream.

He heard a soft voice at his bedside, whispering his names, both of them, in velvet tones. He thought he could see a shape of absolute darkness moving through the room, forming the curves of a lithe female body. He wondered vaguely if he was dreaming about Aeriella again… for he dreaded such a dream. He reached out as if to push her out of his mind's eye as he tried so hard to push her out of his memory.

And he felt her touch him.

Scorp started awake. "Who–?"

"Justin…" said the whispering voice, which he now recognized. "It's me, Cat."

Scorp reached out and felt her shoulders. "Cat?"

"I wanted to come and talk to you, one on one. I'm not sure how to put this… To be honest, I don't know whether to say I'm sorry or beat you like a stupid puppy that won't learn a lesson. I just can't let you keep losing these tests because of your perverted sense of chivalry toward *me*."

"Cat, I can't change who I am–"

He felt Cat's hands grip him on either side of the head as she said, "But who *are* you, Saber-Scorpion? Who *do* you want to be?"

"I am a soldier–" he began, but she interrupted him once again.

"Then be one! Scorp, you're destroying your career! Not to mention it's just insulting; have you ever thought of that? I took care of Barracuda by myself, and Lee could have helped me up the cliff. And I probably could have taken care of myself on the ship too if you'd just *let* me."

He could feel her caressing the sides of his cheeks with her thumbs. He remembered what Mantis had said about her toying with people's emotions, like a cat playing with a ball of yarn. He squeezed her hands.

"Cat, I–"

Still without letting him speak, she said, "Scorp, shut up and listen. We're set to fight each other next in the Test of Supremacy. You are going to duel me. And you are going to win. Do you understand me? I'm not going to let up in the fight, but I came here to make sure that you wouldn't do that either. Give me the same fight that you gave Tanya, Seth, and the others. I came here to make sure that you don't lose another test just for me."

She thinks it's all about her, Scorp thought. *She thinks I'm doing all of this just for her.*

"Don't apologize, Cat," he said. "If it hadn't been you, it might very well have been someone else… someone else I helped on that cliff, someone else I helped on that dropship. It's not you… it's *me*. If these trials were meant to test our character, and I lose because of who I am… then so be it. I see no shame in that."

There, he had said it. It seemed to come out so easily, and he sounded so sure of himself that even he almost believed it. But he felt sick deep in his guts at the mere thought of failing to become an Enomeg.

Her voice was more emotional as she replied, "You are amazing, Saber-Scorpion. In all my years as an Enomeg trainee, I think I've gotten pretty skilled in the art of manipulating people, but you're one of the few that I just can't seem to budge... except by accident. Perhaps it's just thickheaded stubbornness, but... I think you inspire me more than anyone else. More than Mantis, even more than Luke..."

At the mention of this name, the room seemed to grow even darker. "Do we have to talk about *him*?"

"No we don't..." she whispered, and he could tell she was smiling now. "Sorry, Scorp."

"Call me Justin."

"Justin... you feel nice when you're clean; did you know that?"

"So do you."

She curled her fingers under his and brought his hands down to her sides. "You've hardly even felt me yet."

He could feel her breath as she leaned in closer, and then her lips touched his.

LOCATION: RED CLIFF, VICTORY

The scream of engines split the air as the Victorian fighters soared overhead, entering into a trick loop worthy of the galaxy's best stunt pilots. Ryan looked up at the sun glinting off the fighters' silvery hulls, and when his eyes caught sight of the vessel on the landing pad beneath them, Ryan's jaw dropped. He had heard of this ship and seen pictures of it, but never before had he witnessed it in person. It was the *Silver Scepter*, the personal command ship of the Grand General. Its silver duranium armor shone almost blindingly in the sunlight, with bright blue highlights splitting along its angular edges. The almost crystalline shape of the hull was ideal for deflecting ballistic ammunition, while the reflectiveness aided against energy blasts.

The *Scepter* was a gunship, a transport vessel, and a mobile command base all in one – quite literally a flying fortress. It could carry a reasonably large platoon of troops, as well as small vehicles like hover tanks, and was armed with an array of weapons designed to fight foes both on the ground and in the sky. Gun turrets protruded from it in every angle, even some on the surface of its huge, downward-sloping wings. Since no propulsion technology had yet been invented that was powerful enough to allow a capital-size starship to travel within a planet's atmosphere safely, the *Silver Scepter* was probably the most powerful aerospace vessel in existence.

On top of the *Scepter* was one transperium viewport for the pilots and main gunners, and on the bottom were the viewports for the soldiers in the hold, beneath the vast wings that cast a shadow over the area where Ryan now stood. Near the center of the craft, just behind the nose, was the control room – Rick

Radcliff's main place of residence in the vessel. From that room, he could watch over everything on the battlefield. It was a flying observation post from which he was able to monitor and control the movements of his soldiers.

"Do you like it?" Rick said from behind him as they walked along the sun-soaked landing pad together. "That fighter leading the squadron above is the matching experimental one-man craft called the *Silver Dagger*. My son is the one flying it."

Ryan nodded. "I was just watching him. He's as good a stuntman as a fighter pilot."

"He's a showoff," Rick said with a disapproving glance at the squadron, which was now landing for refueling. "That's one reason he loves the *Silver Scepter* so much. I'm not really as proud of the ship as he is. It's too royal for my tastes – really stands out in a crowd, you know? I'd rather just be in a regular Crusader as my command ship, but my predecessors seemed to think something more was necessary for the Grand General. Ordinator Exsyl seems to think it's a great way to show off Victory's aerospace superiority. He talks softly, and *this* is his big stick. Come on; I'll show you inside."

The *Scepter* had several methods of entrance. There were ports on either side of the bridge at the top, a loading ramp on the back for the vehicles to ride up, and a pair of large, armored doors just behind the control room where soldiers could board. It was through these doors that they now entered, finding themselves in the ship's vast hold. Ryan was amazed at how spacious it was, but Rick ignored the view and quickly stepped up to the door that led into the vessel's nose and punched in a code to open it. Ryan followed him carefully, with the feeling that he was treading on hallowed ground.

Most soldiers only heard about the control room of the Grand General, the throne of war from which all the most important battle strategies were planned, at least in legend. But now Ryan was here, actually seeing it. It was a lot smaller than he had expected, with only enough room to fit about a dozen people. He had also expected far more control panels and display monitors, but instead everything appeared to be holographic. In its current powered-down state, it looked like little more than a lot of blank metal panels.

"I have to say, this part is impressive," Rick said, "When the control room here lights up, it's like the Christmas tree of a field commander. And it's also like the present he's always wanted. It really makes you feel omniscient, like... like..."

"A god of war?" Ryan prompted.

Rick frowned. Judging by the look on his commander's features, Ryan could tell he had chosen the wrong words. The young super-soldier ran his hand through his short but thick brown hair.

"Sorry," he said, "I wasn't thinking about Mars."

"Don't," Rick said with contempt. "Mars isn't any god of war, despite what he thinks. He's no more a god than any mortal man."

Ryan looked at his reflection in one of the blank silver control panels thoughtfully. "You a religious man, sir?" Of course, everyone in Victory knew that, but Ryan was trying to make conversation... one of the few skills in which he often found himself lacking.

Rick nodded. "Christian, through and through, just like the rest of my family. My ancestors might as well have come here on the Golden Ark. Who knows – maybe they did. I've heard rumors... So what about you?"

"Religion? Haven't had much time to think about it."

"That's not good. You should always set aside time to think about matters of the soul. Otherwise when you're on the field in a losing battle, you won't even know how to pray. You know what they say: there's no such thing as an atheist in a foxhole."

"I've heard. So where will we be going in this Silver Ark of yours?"

Rick sat down in one of the commander's chairs, which were padded with dark blue cushioning. "Xarkon. I'm not about to send subordinates to watch over the Shardasha incident. It's the biggest thing going on in the world right now, and I want to be there in person to take part in it."

Ryan nodded. "So do I."

At that moment, two more Victorian officers entered the room: an army and a navy man. Ryan recognized the army commander as Lieutenant-Colonel Joshua Jenkins, whom he had trained under previously. He had sandy blond hair and a goatee. Rick liked to surround himself with bright young minds in the military, as opposed to weary old men who were ready for retirement. He was pushing his son, Harry "Harrier" Radcliff, through the ranks of the aerospace forces faster than anyone had ever risen... and Jenkins, though not nearly as young as Harry, was one of the youngest colonels in the army. And, Ryan suddenly realized, there was also himself. Rick had been dragging him everywhere lately, telling him everything, almost like he was the Grand General's apprentice. Clearly, he too had been chosen.

As he sat down, Jenkins said, "Good to see you again, Orion. I've been hearin' a lot of talk about you lately. So, what's it feel like, goin' back to the motherland?"

Jenkins' grin was a well-meaning one, but Ryan felt a little annoyed at the question. "Just peachy, sir. I've actually been looking forward to it, although it'll take some willpower not to shoot every Crown symbol I run across. I like to use them for targets at the range."

"Way to foster the peace, son," Jenkins replied with a laugh. "I'm sure I don't have to tell you to keep your trigger finger in check, but I'm sure everyone in this room agrees with the sentiment."

Rick nodded solemnly. Their conversation was interrupted when suddenly the whole vehicle came to life. Glowing blue symbols appeared on the buttons all around them, and yellow holographic screens flashed to life, some emanating three-dimensional projections that hovered in midair.

"Takeoff in five," said a voice over the speakers, "four... three... two... one."

The vessel lurched, and they heard the lower takeoff boosters fire. These thrusters, combined with the power of the anti-grav hoverpads on the belly, provided just enough boost to give the immense *Silver Scepter* the VTOL capabilities that were so standard in today's aerospace vessels.

"We have liftoff."

Outside the *Scepter*, a lance of fighters rose from the landing pad behind them… Cavaliers and Paladins, led by Harry "Harrier" Radcliff in the *Silver Dagger*. A prototype fighter design, the Dagger was far narrower and sleeker than the angular and heavily-armored Victorian aerospace craft surrounding it. Entirely silver, only two thin blue stripes adorned it, and most of the weapons were tucked out of sight somewhere in the hull. It was definitely built for speed, and Harrier used this to his full advantage.

Ryan could see Rick smile as they heard Harry's voice say over the speakers, "This is Harrier. We're in formation. I've got your six, General."

"Good," Rick said. "Thank you, son. Now, set course for Shardasha. We're going to visit our old 'friends' in Xarkon."

LOCATION: CAMP RAGNAR, SHARDASHA OUTSKIRTS, XARKON

High General Black clapped his gloved hands together as he shouted, "Get moving, men! If you're not standin' at attention to greet the High Commander when he arrives, then you'll be guardin' a latrine on some backwater moon within a week, I swear to God!"

Of course, these threats were unnecessary, as the highly-trained Xarkonian infantry operated like clockwork. Every man in the row upon row of soldiers before him was standing in exactly the same position, unmoving, with exactly the same face, their true features obscured by their intimidating black-visored helmets. Their nanoduranium armor was currently set to ceremonial coloration mode, making each of them bright crimson and black.

Behind the rows of troops lay Camp Ragnar, the Xarkon war camp near Shardasha, positioned just behind some hills and out of sight of the main city. The camp itself consisted of tents thrown up for the infantry, a few armored command vehicles, and a great circle of tanks, both treaded and hover types, prepared to defend the base at all costs.

Once all were situated, General Black stroked his dark beard, the disguise he and Mars exchanged, as he turned about to face in the same direction as his men. All of them could only stare in awe at the silhouette now striding in from the east, the sun slowly rising behind its back. The ground vibrated underfoot as the gargantuan walker advanced, its lofty, curved missile rack and rail gun attachment rising against the sky like the towers of a walking castle.

The tiny slits of a red viewport on the walker's long, angular head looked like a set of thin, glowing eyes. This, combined with the ear-like appearance of the two curved radar dishes behind, created the effect of a wolf's head, though this wolf's head also featured a pair of enormous rotary Vulcan cannons on either side. From behind the hunched-over head of the monster stretched two long arms, one tipped with a huge, claw-like Starfire cannon, the other with three ballistic cannons in the same claw-like formation. All in all, the solid ebony walking fortress was almost indisputably the single most intimidating machine of war ever created.

"Men," General Black said into his commlink, knowing that all the soldiers behind him would hear, "meet *Manegarm*, Xarkon's greatest terrestrial weapon of war, and the new command vehicle of Lucas Augustus Mars, High Commander of the Armed Forces of the Crown."

As they watched, the behemoth came to a halt and began to lower itself onto its haunches. Its legs were shaped like those of a Slashrim, fashioned into a sort of crooked Z, with the blade-like knees hanging forward until they almost touched the ground. Thanks to this design, the legs could fold up beneath the walker until it was almost lying down, giving it enough traction to fire its enormous, long-range rail gun... or to allow the pilot to descend out of his cockpit. Lucas Mars was about to do this, removing his helmet and unstrapping himself, when Colonel Black contacted him.

"Commander, I'm sure you noticed the hoverbikes... The Grim Riders. They've been contacting us, requesting to be allowed into the camp. What should we do with 'em?"

"Let them pass," Mars replied, and then he finished dismounting from his war machine.

Finally the High Commander's shining black boots touched the earth, and he stood up to his full height, though even he was dwarfed by the vehicle he had just exited. He looked over the hundreds of soldiers who were now saluting him, and merely nodded to General Black, who dismissed them. The two commanders then approached and shook hands before looking away for the approaching hoverbikes. In a few minutes, the first of the mercenaries arrived. It was like a cavalry charge in some medieval epic, a horde of horsemen rushing headlong down a distant rise... only in this case, all were mounted upon hoverbikes instead.

Each bike was clearly different. The ones in the lead bore the long-toothed skull insignia of Grimm's Army proudly on the front, while the others varied in size and armor, some carrying unique personal insignia or painted odd colors that stood out in the crowd. All of the bikes were heavily customized, and all of their riders were heavily armed and armored. As they swooped in closer, it became apparent that most of them actually bore two riders, and some were nearly large enough to be called hovercars, though none featured a full canopy. The number of vehicles was impossible to count, but it may easily have approached a hundred.

Definitely enough to draw attention, Mars thought as he strode boldly forward to meet with the lead bikers. The skull-headed bikes stopped first, with the others coming to a halt behind. Mars quickly recognized the first to dismount as Nick Wolf and Jade. Nick's white teeth shone through his yellow beard as he approached the High Commander with extended hand. Mars noted his bare upper arms, showing off his impressive musculature, and the decorative horns that adorned his dented Zygbari battle helmet. Clearly his look was geared for maximum intimidation. Mars gave him a single black-gloved handshake, then drew back and crossed his arms.

"What are you doing here?" he asked bluntly.

Nick shrugged. "I would'a thought introductions were in order, even if we've already unofficially met. I'm Warlord Nick Wolf. Nice to meet ye, High Commander sair."

"My name is not Sair."

"Sir," Nick corrected. "I come from Northern Vict'ry ye know. We're a bit set in our old ways o' talkin' up there. But anyway, I'm guessin' neither of us 'ave much time… Oh, and I'm sure you remember Jade."

Jade snapped her heels together and gave a brisk salute. Mars looked down at her and actually gave a tight smile. It was slightly amusing to see such military discipline in this young girl with her long ponytail… but there was also something almost frightening about it. It reminded Mars distinctly of the times he interviewed the Enomegs as children, the coldly mature look in their young eyes. Mars looked about for some of her comrades… Jacinth, Jet, Jasper… but none arrived.

"I thought they called you Viking," Mars commented to Nick. "That doesn't strike me as a traditional Scandinavian accent."

Nick shrugged. "It's Terra Nova. Things get a wee bit mixed up when ye toss 'em all together so. Let's just say I hung out on the south-side o' town and ganged up with a different crowd than most o' the lads. Anyway, the boys usually just call me Werewolf these days. By the by, is that the name o' yer big, fancy walker there? If it isn't, it shoulda' been."

General Black gave a short laugh. "Some of the men call it the 'Big Bad Wolf,' actually."

Mars silenced him with a glance. "Its name is *Manegarm*. Now listen to me, mercenary. We should not be talking like this at all. We should certainly not be meeting here in Camp Ragnar, of all places."

"No one in Shardasha could see us where we rode," Nick replied.

"I'm not talking about the 'terrorists,' Warlord Wolf. This entire area is under intricately close scrutiny from observational satellites owned by all the major nations of Terra Nova. Perhaps even some Native ones. So you and your little band of riders had better be on your way before things look suspicious. Your bikes bear the Grimm's Army insignia proudly, and I cannot risk open association between us."

Throughout this short speech, Nick had been looking at his handheld computer instead of Mars, an act of clear disrespect that would have angered the High Commander had he not taught himself to accept such treatment from Grimm's men. Now the mercenary turned around again and held the computer out in front of Mars's face. It showed a map of the area with moving red dots.

"There's not a single satellite watchin' us right now, Commander," he said. "All yer big nations may have satellites fer watchin' the ground, but Grimm's got 'is own satellites, and they're nay pointed at the dirt… They're watchin' the other satellites!"

Mars nodded. "Very good. For a moment I thought I was about to be gravely disappointed in my expectations of your commander's intelligence. But you still haven't explained why you're here."

"'Cause even if Grimm won't kick the war off for ye, we still want in. Grimm wants to keep an eye on the mess ye got goin' on 'round 'ere. An' 'e wants Jade to learn a bit about real warfare."

"I can't possibly harbor…"

"We're not *all* gonna stay, man. Jus' me an' Jade 'ere, plus a few o' the elites there. Notice they're wearin' salvaged Xarkon armor, so they'll blend right in with yer troops, no problem. I'll be wearin' some too. As fer Jade, well, she can keep a low profile…"

"Fine," Mars said, stiffening. "Make it quick, before those satellites return. Move your rabble out and make sure all of the remaining bikes are well hidden. *Stay out of sight.* For all I know, Captain Jaleiko or even General Radcliff could be arriving here at any time."

With that, the High Commander turned directly around and marched off, headed for the largest command vehicle. Nick admired the way Mars strode away, in thought yet alert, towering over his armored soldiers while he himself wore only a black officer's uniform, armed with only a pistol sidearm and his personal long, straight-bladed officer's sword.

"Amazin'…" Nick said, shaking his head. Then he looked down at Jade, who was gazing up at him with large blue-green eyes. "So whaddaya think o' the place, Jade?"

The girl pointed to the simple canvas tents that had been erected at the western side of the camp, with only a few light armored vehicles standing guard. "Shouldn't those be near the back instead of toward the city? If the terrorists were to assault the camp, the armored vehicles could withstand the assault better than those tents."

Nick nodded. "Good observation. But no, those tents're there for a reason. It's because Mars an' the other High Commanders'll be meetin' back *here*. An' it's all about protectin' the leaders."

Jade made a face that clearly showed her disapproval of this policy. Nick laughed as he led her away toward one of the command vehicles. Meanwhile, his mercenaries, dressed in their Xarkonian battle armor, followed him. And behind them, the Grim Riders moved out once again. As the swarm of buzzing hoverbike engines faded out of earshot, Nick inspected his computer again. The satellites were moving back into place now. And what was more, they would soon have visitors.

At first, Nick doubted what he was seeing on the satellite feed, so he zoomed into the image. There was no denying it… no denying the squadron of power that now moved toward Shardasha. And in the very center of it… the Victorian command gunship known as the *Silver Scepter*.

"Bloody 'ell," Nick said. "Well, Jade, looks like you'll be gettin' to see more than one world military leader today."

LOCATION: THE ETAB HOLOROOM

Just about the last thing anyone would expect to find in the Enomeg Training Academy would be a treehouse. Yet that was what was now being

172

erected. Today was the fight between Blood-Raven and Blade-Mantis, one of the final duels in the Test of Supremacy. As the two Enomeg trainees entered the large, cylindrical metal room, they heard a loud hissing come from all directions. Long metal ramps extended from slots positioned randomly all around them. Five solid metal columns extended upward from the floor to the roof, each over a meter thick. Then, suddenly, the shining duranium surfaces all changed. Without flash or fanfare, but merely with a low, barely audible hum, the room transformed into a forest clearing. The columns became trees, and the long ramps became thick wooden planks like those of a treehouse.

The ETAB holoroom was a marvel of engineering, perhaps more advanced than any other in the world, but even it could not render solid objects holographically. Instead, the room used metal or other materials to produce solid surfaces and then disguised them using the hologram. The room had been specifically engineered to create a wide variety of environments. In every duel so far in the Test of Supremacy, the participating students had been asked to choose one of these environments for their duel. Then, under Dark-Dragon's orders, the instructors had disregarded their choices and instead picked something as far from their preferences as possible. Raven had asked to fight in a junkyard, and Mantis had asked for a rocky, icy mountain peak. So the trainers had taken their harsh, cold environments and turned them into a lush, inviting forest, complete with shrubbery, insects, and birds.

But the tranquil atmosphere was broken when the air began to thrum with the sound of spinning energy blades, as the two Enomeg trainees activated and brandished their star-talons. Raven paced in a circle, his movements mirrored by Mantis opposite him. Both were clad only in their usual training outfits, with the familiar black padded armor. Raven's face was a mask of determination and concentration, his keen grey-blue eyes narrowed to slits. Mantis, on the other hand, was smiling from ear to ear.

"Ah, the great Blood-Raven," he said, giving a bow. "It is an honor to finally face you in battle."

Raven did not reply. He only smiled, nodded, and then attacked. There was a flurry of flashes as Raven pushed Mantis back several meters in a wild rage. Mantis deflected every blow quite easily, still smiling at intervals even as he concentrated to take on Raven's calculated attacks. Finally, he leaped backwards up onto a platform at the base of one of the trees, and stood there panting. He blew out a deep breath as Raven paced back and forth in the holographic leaves below him, looking for an opening.

"Quite a workout," Mantis said. "Shall we dance on the catwalks?"

Raven's eyes narrowed. "I'd rather you get down here and let us finish this on level ground."

Mantis laughed. "So it's just 'Let's hurry up and get it over with?' I'm disappointed, Raven!"

Raven took a few steps backward. "If that's what you want…"

He dropped into a run and leaped up, swinging his blade in midair. Mantis backed up to avoid his slash, and Raven landed on his feet on the platform next to him. His attack was immediately blocked by Mantis's defense, but he did manage to force him backward. Soon Mantis was backed up to the edge of the platform, and again he leapt to another nearby catwalk. He tried at first to use the height to his advantage, but it was little advantage over Raven's expert swordsmanship. Raven was still able to deflect Mantis's blades and lash out with his own. Mantis took a few steps back to avoid having his feet cut off, and Raven leaped up after him.

Now they were positioned on a narrow wooden walkway extending between two of the trees. Still Mantis was losing ground to Raven, as they fought their way along the ramp. Raven moved like a whirlwind, and it was all Mantis could do to dodge his blows. The high-pitched buzz of flying starfire blades drowned out the sounds of the forest around them.

Then, Raven slipped. Mantis bounced the wooden board on which they were standing, which immediately rebounded, wobbling awkwardly. Raven was caught off balance, and one of his feet slid off the edge. It took only a second for him to recover, but it was long enough. Now the tables were turned. Mantis pushed Raven backward, step by step, pressing his advantage. He even managed to nick him on the shoulder, a small yet surprising victory in a fight with the Blood-Raven.

"You'll pay for that," Raven said between gritted teeth, even as the air sung with swinging and striking laser blades.

Mantis laughed. "Oh, so *now* you want to talk?"

"*No.*"

Raven made a hard right swing at Mantis, which Mantis ducked while deflecting Raven's other blade almost simultaneously. Then Mantis lashed out not with a blade, but with his foot. It struck Raven on the left side of his back and knocked him right off the plank. Mantis laughed as his opponent fell, but Raven caught on quickly – to the edge of the catwalk. He flipped beneath it, grabbed the opposite side with his free hand and let go with the other even as Mantis took a swing at it. Then Raven himself shook the plank. To the surprise of both Enomegs, instead of simply shaking… it gave way and broke completely off, taking both men with it. Apparently the simulation was more realistic than they thought – the platforms were not made of metal after all.

They landed in the hard dirt below and rolled off to either side. Raven was first to his feet. Now he rushed at Mantis with redoubled determination. As the off-balance Mantis tried to deflect the torrent of slashes that Raven now rained upon him, he staggered back, and then there was a particularly bright flash, and the light in the room dropped a notch. Mantis almost gasped as he noticed the smoke rising from the ruined blade emitter atop his hand. Even with the lessened power settings, the contact with Raven's energy blade shorted out the simple unarmored training emitter atop Mantis's glove.

Both of the Enomegs knew that it was over then, and so did the instructors and the other trainees watching from the hidden viewports and cameras around the room. And they were right. Mantis held up for an admirable six seconds before a quick slice straight across the chest sent him down. From speakers hidden somewhere in the room's walls, the sound of a horn blared out, and a voice announced: "The fight is over! Luke Blood-Raven is the victor over Lee Blade-Mantis."

Mantis massaged the slight burning sensation that he now felt diagonally across his torso. "I guess I should have used my solid blade after all, but I didn't think it would be able to keep up with you." Then his grimace turned into a smile, and he gave a slight bow in front of Raven. "Congratulations, sir. You really are as good as they say."

This time, Raven smiled as well, though only slightly. But his was a smile of self-satisfaction, a smug smile of victory. Still, he did return Mantis's bow, and then the two super-soldiers left the room.

There was now only one man standing between Blood-Raven and total victory, and soon he too would be eliminated.

- CHAPTER THIRTEEN -
THE BEST OF THE BEST

The next duel took place one day after Raven's victory over Blade-Mantis. Both contestants arrived at exactly the same time, each coming from opposite directions. Saber-Scorpion advanced down one side of the metallic hallway, and Blood-Raven down the other. They met in the very center, standing directly in front of the door that was their destination... the door to the virtual reality simulation room, the holoroom. The door to the final battle of the Test of Supremacy.

In this trial, the most important one in the eyes of many of the Enomegs, the instructors had made sure that each trainee faced every other. None were left out. However, they had also carefully ensured that Blood-Raven and Saber-Scorpion remained at opposite ends of the ladder, set to face each other last if they succeeded in beating out the rest of their peers. Secretly, the trainers had thought it impossible that they could achieve this goal. Any moment, a single mistake in combat with another skilled foe could leave one or the other defeated. But despite a few close calls, they had won every fight so far. The only trainee who could compete was Blade-Mantis, and both had now narrowly beaten him. The only question now was... who would come out on the very top?

As they stood there glaring at each other, waiting for the instructors to unlock the door beside them and thus mark the beginning of the duel, they were unaware of how much they looked alike. They were the same height and build, and both wore matching facial expressions of stern determination. Their eyes were also similar: a cold blue-grey. And both preferred the dual star-talon blades to any other weapon. Only their faces differed slightly. Scorp's hair was lighter, his jaw and brow a bit heavier. Raven's features, on the other hand, were sleek and angular, his hair jet black.

"Today is the day," Raven said with a smile.

Scorp nodded and flexed his fingers. "Do your worst."

176

Raven shook his head. "No. I'll do my *best*... and it doesn't get better than that."

"Quit taunting and let's find out," Scorp said, as the doors beside them opened.

Together they turned and strode into the room. Through cameras and hidden view windows, the instructors watched them with absolute scrutiny. Dark-Dragon was also present, along with nearly all of the Enomeg trainees. He had invited them to watch, for he knew every one of them wanted to witness this. The fight had not even started yet, but already the tension in the room was almost tangible. The two Enomegs moved in perfect unison, as if one of them was the shadow, the mirror, of the other. With equal confidence and matching stride, they paced into the very center of the room. Then both turned away and marched a few paces apart, finally whirling again to face each other.

Slowly, the room around them began to change.

The Enomegs did not know it, but they had both voted for exactly the same combat location: a simple vehicle hangar, crisscrossed with catwalks and machinery. The instructors knew why they had chosen it; they wanted to fight in a familiar arena, and the hangar they described was exactly like the one in the ETAB, where they had trained countless times. Both were quite used to those surroundings and knew that if there was any place where they could fight their best, it was there.

But as always, the trainers disobeyed, searching instead for something quite the opposite of what the students had requested. So they chose something as remote, bizarre, unreal, and unfamiliar to the Enomegs as possible. It had actually been programmed into the holoroom as an early experiment, never before used for any previous training session. It was the secret arena, and had been reserved especially for the star pupils.

From his box seat, Dark-Dragon said, "The storm approaches."

Suddenly, the floor beneath the two Enomegs started to rise. Not the whole floor, but parts of it. Rounded partitions – one under Raven's feet, another under Scorp's, and many more throughout the room – separated from the ground and began to hover through the air. The once empty room was now full of flying metal plates of varying shapes and sizes. Each featured one to three long, uneven spikes extending from the bottom, rough and covered in cracks, like stone. They were very well-balanced, and Scorp and Raven did not need to maneuver to compensate... but their constant movement had a dizzying effect nonetheless.

Then things began to get even stranger. The air about them grew dark and foggy, and hazy purple shapes formed in the mist. This fog gave way to a dim radiance, and then a flash. A white bolt of lightning split the air directly between the combatants, its afterglow lingering in their vision even after it disappeared. The resounding blast of thunder seemed to shake the whole room. Scorp knew the lightning was only a hologram, but he could almost swear that he had felt its heat. Perhaps they had set up some kind of electrical apparatus, like a glorified set of Tesla coils, to increase the tension.

As if it needed increasing. As the image became clearer, they could see the stars through a hole in the dark clouds overhead. The platforms on which they stood became floating masses of rock with flat tops and pointed stalactites dangling beneath. They were hovering in a strange clearing in the sky, surrounding by dark, churning clouds of black, grey, and purple, with lightning flickering blue and white in the distance. Far, far below, they could see the planet's surface... the dark ocean, barely lit by the moon filtering through the clouds and the lights of cities on the shore. They both caught themselves wondering how high up they were.

"Quite the illusion they have set up for our little battleground!" Raven shouted to Scorp, throwing out his arms and activating his twin Starfire blades, even as he threw back his head and looked up at the two moons above. "Haha! This *will* be a glorious victory."

Scorp shook his head in amazement at the hologram. "I had no idea the illusionists were this good! This is like a work of art!"

"Don't spend too much time gawking at the scenery! I'm hoping you'll at least put up a *little* bit of a fight before I take you down! Or would you rather just take off your blades now and surrender?"

Scorp smiled, activated his blades, and brandished them before his face in a fabulous laser show of twirling light. "Come and get them!"

Raven nodded, and then he advanced. Scorp stood at the ready and watched as Raven leaped from platform to platform... some lower, some higher than others. They seemed to move in a pattern, but it was difficult to discern at best. Scorp tried to learn it, but he had to keep an eye on Raven at the same time. He was moving toward Scorp's rock, which was one of the biggest... a sort of double-platform with two stalactites beneath it.

Finally he arrived, dropping down from above with both blades swinging. Scorp dodged his blow and tried to slice at Raven's feet as he fell past, but Raven was faster. One of those feet lashed out, connecting solidly with Scorp's face, sending him staggering back even as Raven rolled forward and quickly stood up. Raven expected to find Scorp off-guard when he swung around for another attack, but he was wrong. Saber-Scorpion showed no sign that he had even felt Raven's earlier blow. And suddenly Raven found himself retreating backward, closer and closer to the edge of the platform, as Scorp relentlessly rained blow after blow down upon his defenses.

But before reaching the edge, Raven was able to move outward to one side, and now the two Enomegs began to circle each other. This pause in the fighting was accompanied by another flash of lightning, temporarily blinding them both. And during the flash, Raven let out a cry of pain and rage as he felt one of Scorp's blades nick him on the arm. Had he not had the reflexes to dodge most of the blow, it could possibly have counted as a fatal one. Once the thunder had subsided, Blood-Raven spoke.

"You, Coyote, Mantis... you're all are so full of tricks. But it will take more than one little cut to stop me."

But this time, Raven did not advance recklessly. So far, he had gone into every duel with high confidence, but Scorp had quickly proven himself to be a worthy adversary, even more than Mantis had been. So it was with newfound respect that Raven cautiously circled his opponent, waiting for an opening. On the other hand, Scorp's confidence had been boosted, so this time, he was the first to strike.

The lightning could not possibly compete with the array of flashes that followed. Blade struck blade in a display of evenly-matched dual-sword fighting. The two of them began to sweat profusely, their bodies, arms, and faces glistening in the light of the flashing blades. Each opponent invented many of their techniques on the spot, attempting to catch the other off-guard with unexpected moves. And eventually, Scorp succeeded. He managed to get both of Raven's blades out to the sides, leaving his chest wide open. Exactly how it had happened, neither of them could afterward remember. But it was the perfect opportunity for a killing stab to the torso, and Scorp took it. Raven was cornered; there was nothing he could do to block this.

So he did not even try. He simply leapt backwards, right off the edge of the platform. Down he fell, into the churning mists below. Scorp quickly ran forward and looked down, but only distant city lights and sparkling water met his eyes. He cursed. In this environment, the instructors would no doubt count a fall to the bottom of the ring as a loss, but the hologram stayed in place, and no horns blared out. So Raven was still there, somewhere… and there was only one place he could be.

Scorp swung around, his eyes running along the circumference of the platform again and again, looking for some sign of Raven's fingers appearing to climb back up. But they did not come. He had to be on another platform! As soon as Scorp spotted another rock moving just below his, he leaped down onto it. Then he twirled again… and saw Raven waiting for him, hanging from the stalactites of the previous one. He only dangled there for a sliver of a second, and then he was in the air.

This time, Scorp was caught off guard, and Raven's kick did connect solidly with his face. He hit the ground hard and slid backward, just as Raven landed on his back on the ground next to him. Both of them expected the other to scramble to his feet, so both of them tried to catch the other with a surprise move. Without standing, they rolled toward each other, blades thrashing. When they met in the center, they did catch each other by surprise, but not as hoped. Still, they responded quickly. Each tried to stab the other in the face, and each grabbed the other's fist. Grappling for freedom and the killing blow, they rolled over and over… and right off the edge of the platform again.

The lightning split the air dramatically at the precise instant that they left solid ground. Scorp fell first, and he quickly grabbed one of the long, thin stalactites on the bottom as Raven had done. The rough stone was uneven enough for him to get a good grip, but he still slid down for what seemed an eternity until his momentum stopped. Once he had a good hold, he secured himself and looked up. Raven was gripping the edge of the platform above, but he was clambering sideways, hand over hand. Then he swung his feet forward and let go, grabbing onto the platform's second stalactite in mid-fall. Once he was latched on firmly, he turned to face Scorp.

Now each of them was hanging from his own stone spike… and each wanted nothing more than for the other to fall. So out came the blades, and they began a midair duel, each using one hand to fight and the other to grip. Blades struck blades and stone, as they tried to cut one another's arm or leg, to loosen their hold. They continued like this for quite some time, neither quite able to gain an advantage over the other. Slowly, ever so slowly, it started to look like they were tiring. Then, suddenly, Raven disappeared.

He had dropped onto another platform, one that had rotated around behind him. And as it floated on past Scorp, Raven lashed out, slicing his opponent right across the leg. Scorp let out a cry of pain and dropped down beside Raven, who did not let up. Now on one knee, Scorp deflected blow after blow as the torrent of heavy strokes fell. Then he rolled backward and leapt to his feet, though he faltered a bit in pain as he did so.

"A blow… for a blow!" Raven shouted between breaths. "Now… we're even again."

Scorp nodded. "For now."

The storm clouds could only envy the display of light that followed. Had there been any actual observers in the city far below the storm, the duel might well have been visible to them, like an unstable star or a small, angry, seething bolt of lightning, flickering to itself and building up energy before connecting with the earth. But neither of the Enomegs, despite how close they got to the edge of the stone slab at intervals, had any intention of plummeting down there.

The lightning flashed again, as if in an effort to compete. But the battling Enomegs, at the very height of their combat… moving now as sheer combinations of discipline and rage, speed and accuracy, training, natural talent, and instinct… paid the simulated display of nature's power no attention at all.

LOCATION: SHARDASHA, XARKON

"*Klagk.*"

Grimm the Third spat the Slashrim curse between clenched teeth as he attempted to pick the lock on the door before him. The city government building in Shardasha was made to look like an antique, as many of the buildings in the oldest section of the city were. It had a mostly marble exterior built to look like a Roman temple, with wooden doors and ornate brass decorations and knobs. But most antique-looking buildings were merely a coat of old style over an interior of modern technology, so Grimm had expected the same to be true of the doors…

No such luck. Any kind of modern device – a computerized lock, key-code, card swiper, data-stick port, or even some biometric security measure – he could handle… but an old-style keyhole, tumblers and all? He'd never imagined anyone still used them, especially the government. He had seen Spectra practicing breaking one with a pair of bent metal sticks, and he was trying to copy her methods now, but with no luck. Finally he spat out another vulgar curse and cast his makeshift picks to the sidewalk. He had not wanted to resort to physical damage, which would leave obvious traces of his presence, but clearly he had no choice.

"To Hell with it," he spat.

Grimm III dropped down on one knee and looked directly at the edge of the door… not with his good eye, but with his eyepatch, which was made of metal and appeared to have strange knobs on the corners. He then lifted a hand to the edge of this device, and a beam of red light shot out. He moved the laser up and down along the crack at the edge of the door until he heard the small, almost imperceptible clink of the metal bolt falling loose as it was cut in half. Then Three reached up to the knob and carefully pulled open the door.

Inside, all was dark. Three quickly lifted his square "eyepatch" device and slid it around over his good eye. Then he activated his night-vision, illuminating the room in an eerie green glow. To his relief, the space was full of modern-day technology and computers. There were huge mainframes built into the walls, and terminals in long rows on desks in the middle of the room. Three moved between them cautiously, looking for some sign of a guard or worker lurking about.

He found one: there was a man in Xarkon army fatigues lying asleep on a small couch in the far corner. Three stood for a moment and listened to his breathing. When he was satisfied that the man was asleep, the mercenary pulled a cord out of his pocket, sticking one end in his headset and the other in the computer terminal before him. Then he switched on the terminal's projector at the same time that he slid his eyepatch back to its normal position. A holographic image lit up the room in its soft lavender glow.

Three's single eye widened. The image was of Spectra; it was even her favorite color. Her mask was gone now, and she puckered her lips and blew him a kiss. Three grunted.

"Hello, Infrared," said her silky voice in his ear.

"Ultraviolet," he said, trying not to show his surprise. "Wasn't expectin' to see you here… sort of."

"We just happen to be in the same place at the same time," Spectra said. "I think perhaps we should coordinate our efforts a little better. I was hacking remotely into the same building you were breaking into directly."

Three wheezed out a little laugh. "You never cease to impress, Ultraviolet. I've never met anyone who can do so much while doin' so little."

"That's a bit self-contradictory."

Three shrugged. "Call it Zen, or whatever."

Spectra laughed. "Come now, you know I'm no mysticist. And anyway, I'm doing the same thing you are… except in cyber-space instead of real-space. It's sort of like an alternate dimension if you want to look at it that way… with its own landscape, its own weather…"

The mercenary yawned. "I thought you just said you weren't into mysticism…"

Again Spectra laughed. "Well…"

"Look, I've got a guard asleep in the room here. If you make me wake 'im up, I'll have to kill the poor chap. Now help me find what we're lookin' for."

"I've been trying to, but I can't get access. During the day it's too dangerous to log on since someone might spot me, and at night, like right now, there doesn't seem to be anything useful in the files…"

"But you said there were some encrypted signals comin' to an' from this old ruin…"

"Yes, and I'm sure they keep record of the transmissions, but they might keep them someplace that I can't hack into. Where are you right now?"

"Hey, I just got here… I'm in a side room, with Lashnar standin' guard just outside."

"Then the room they keep the data in must be farther into the building. Try digging deeper. I'll keep in touch on your headset and make sure you don't run into any electronic surveillance devices unaware."

Three nodded and switched off the computer viewscreen. Once again, the room was dark. The sleeping soldier did not make a sound. Three slid his patch back over his good eye and reactivated the night-vision. There were two doors here leading farther back into the building. Three took the right one, as he always did. Though he was loath to admit it, Three was a sucker for superstition.

The handle of a broom fell out and almost struck his head, but he grabbed it and forced it back into place. It was a closet.

The mercenary snorted and turned back to take the left door. He found himself in a long hallway, and he could easily hear the footsteps of the soldiers patrolling it even before he saw them with his night-vision. Quickly sliding out into the hall and silently shutting the door behind him, Three dropped into a small alcove and pressed his back against the wall. It was hard to make out the details of the room, but the corridor looked to be made of wood, with ornate gold designs lining the top of the walls. The government of Xarkon spared no expense.

Finally he saw the guard walk by… another Xarkon soldier, looking bored. He didn't spot Three though, so once he was out of sight, the mercenary continued sneaking down the corridor. He read the signs above each door as he passed them. Luckily, they were all clearly marked.

"They've got their own private armory in here…" Grimm III whispered, "and here are the restrooms, in case you wanted to know… and the elevator to the second floor. I've reached the end of the hall now. Any ideas? I don't suppose you know the layout of the Shardasha capitol building?"

"No, just the first floor," replied Spectra's voice, "and I can tell you there's nothing useful there, if that room you already came from was empty. So try the second floor."

"No way I'm takin' the elevator."

"Do you see the stairs?"

"No."

"Turn around."

Three blinked. Then he slowly turned to look, and sure enough, directly behind him were the doors to the staircase. There was no sign warning of an emergency exit alarm, so the mercenary gingerly pushed the handle. With a slight hiss, the door slid open. Now *this* was a bit more like the technology he was used to.

Without bothering to even draw a weapon, Grimm III began his nonchalant ascent of the staircase. He made his way up to the second floor without interruption. He pushed on the door handle, but it didn't move.

"Second floor's locked."

"Just a moment."

Three paused to listen. After a few seconds, he heard a soft series of clicks, and then a hiss as the metal door slid aside.

The mercenary groaned slightly. "You're makin' this too easy for me. Don't tell me you're takin' care of the cameras too?"

"Yes, I'm taking care of the cameras. Don't worry about that; just keep your thoughts on the guards. I'm just keeping an eye on you. I'm only a few blocks away."

Shaking his head, Three stepped out into the hallway, which appeared to be empty. "Nice. I'll have to stop by."

"I'd rather we not be seen together for long. Just stick to dropoff points and clandestine meetings."

"Oh, nobody'll see us. We can keep it real dark... in your room. I'll bring a bottle o' wine."

"Be still, my heart," Spectra said sarcastically. "How about this? If you manage to get what we came for, I'll let you in. We'll need to have a meeting anyway."

Grimm growled under his breath, which made Spectra laugh. But then he saw something that made him stop. There were two guards at the end of the hall, standing on either side of a door, assault rifles at the ready. They clearly weren't playing around at all. Anyone who would stand rigidly in front of a door like that for hours without moving, holding a rifle in both hands at all times, never played around. They looked like statues.

"Ultraviolet, I've just run into two armed guards. Crownie bloodguards with bearded AR's."

Spectra quickly translated this jargon into its true meaning: Xarkon royal guards, often called "bloodguards" since they guarded the royal blood, with assault rifles bearing axe-shaped blazer bayonets for melee combat, often called "beards."

"Sounds like you've stumbled across something important. We should definitely check out that room."

"Insertion?"

"No easy one. That's up to you, I'm afraid."

"Wait, there's a stalker comin'."

A patrolling guard had just exited from a door at the far end of the hall and was now marching his way toward Grimm III. The mercenary pressed his back against the wall as tightly as he could and hoped this guard would overlook him as easily as the last one had. Unfortunately, this hallway was slightly better lit, and the guard was slightly more attentive. As he passed by, his helmeted head quickly turned in the direction of Three. But he did not have time to react, because as soon as Three saw the light glint off his visor, he sank a knife into the soldier's neck. With a scream that was part gurgle, he fell to the floor, and Three saw the other two guards raise their rifles.

"*Klagk*," he said.

LOCATION: ENOMEG TRAINING ACADEMY BASE

Lightning flashed… one, two, three bolts in rapid succession. The storm was raging now, swirling about the two dueling Enomeg trainees as if they were in the eye of a hurricane, threatening to engulf them should their battle take any longer. And it suddenly seemed that it would not.

Scorp stared at the broken blade emitter on top of his hand in astonishment. He knew Raven was the best, but he had clearly underestimated the true meaning of that word. During their long fight, they had leapt from platform to platform, neither gaining any true advantage over the other, and now suddenly… it was over. It happened during a single blink of the eye; somehow, Raven had managed to cut the top of Scorp's energy blade emitter with his sword just as he had done with Mantis's, and now it was gone. Scorp now had only one weapon.

The onslaught continued, with renewed vigor. Scorp looked into the face of his opponent as he desperately dodged and deflected Raven's twirling blades. He saw there a smile… a smile of victory, of triumph. And suddenly, with the sight of that expression, Scorp's sense of defeat turned into rage. He could feel the anger surge through him, channeling itself into his muscles. And with a sudden barbaric war cry that mingled with the rumble of thunder around them, Scorp went on the offensive.

Raven had never expected this sudden shift. He found himself staggering backwards as Scorp's single blade, combined with occasional hand and foot attacks, moved with accuracy and speed that was almost impossible to follow, even for him. In their box seats, the Enomegs and their trainers, including Dark-Dragon, simultaneously rose to their feet. It was the best show of swordsmanship they had ever seen. And before he let his enemy have time to get his bearings, Scorp lashed out with a punch to the stomach.

Raven had seen it coming just in time to dodge the majority of the blow, but the knock to his side still caused him to become ever so slightly disoriented… just enough, and just long enough, for Scorp to take a strong slash at Raven's face. When Raven tried to block, he was not fast enough, and Scorp's blade connected with the top of his hand… and disabled the blade emitter there. The instructors high above exchanged glances. Never had they expected the fight to take such a turn. It seemed impossible.

Suddenly, somehow, both Enomegs had only one blade. Raven blocked a few more blows from Scorp and then leapt back to get his bearings. He was as astonished as all the others; even Scorp was surprised, though he did not let it show. Again he and Blood-Raven found themselves circling around each other, evenly matched.

"I guess that's my problem…" Scorp taunted between breaths. "I just don't know when to quit."

Raven snarled. His face was a mask of pure rage now; he hardly even looked like the same person. In fact, the way he now had his brow furrowed, with the lines creasing his face, he actually bore an uncanny resemblance to High

Commander Lucas Mars. This absolute seething fury was so pure that Scorp had never seen anything like it.

Saber-Scorpion brandished his blade. "Face it, Raven! I'm your equal, and I always will be!"

Suddenly Raven's face turned stony. Where once had been anger was now sheer determination. And somehow… this served to even amplify the effect of the previous expression. He now looked almost like the spitting image of the High Commander.

And Raven said, "Nevermore."

In a flash, they were together. Blade met blade, somehow in an even faster flurry than before when they had each been armed with two. And now, more martial arts became involved: kicks and punches, grabs and throws. Scorp was able to grab Raven's arm with his free hand and toss him to the ground. But Raven rolled right back to his feet and continued the attack with a jab to the gut. This Scorp dodged, but he was not able to dodge the elbow that followed, and it connected solidly with his face.

Scorp staggered back as blood streamed down from his nose into his mouth. He desperately continued to block Raven's attacks, but he was losing ground now, and there was not much of the platform left behind him. Finally he managed to grab Raven's blade arm again, but as he swung around for the killing strike, Raven grabbed his as well. They were locked in a wrestling match now, each one pushing the other around toward the edge of the platform. Unfortunately, Scorp was already the closest, and now he felt his heel slide slightly over the edge. Raven tried to knee him in the stomach, so Scorp brought his leg up to block.

This was exactly what Raven had expected. Now only standing on one leg, Scorp quickly lost balance and fell. However, he was able to alter the course of his fall to the side, and he rolled over onto the platform, then forward, and leapt back to his feet. Raven quickly twirled to face him, even as Scorp let out another war cry and began slashing furiously at Raven's face. As the instructors in the observation room above leaned forward, watching every detail of the fight, their vision was suddenly obscured by an intense flash of light. Thunder echoed through the small room.

And then Scorp felt it. It came so quickly, so unexpectedly, that it was almost impossible to tell how it had happened. Somehow, in an instant, the blink of an eye, Raven managed to slip in through Scorp's seemingly perfect defenses… and stab him right in the chest. The training blade was too weak to actually burn him, of course, but it did cause pain, and a direct stab was the worst. Scorp felt the strange electrical heat course through him, and he let go of Raven's wrist and staggered backward.

The horn blared out through the room, and the clouds quickly faded. The bizarre vista was suddenly replaced by cold metal, the storm clearing far more quickly than it had come. But Raven's rage did not. Even as the speakers blared out "Luke Blood-Raven is the victor over Justin Saber-Scorpion," Raven's blade continued its assault on his now helpless foe. Grabbing Scorp's single sword arm, Raven battered away at his side again and again.

In the observation box high above, Shadow-Cat turned to Dark-Dragon and shouted, "Stop him! Someone make him stop!"

Dark-Dragon signaled to Blade-Mantis, and the two of them hurriedly fled the room, followed by the others, who were too overcome by emotions the duel had evoked to stay put and follow orders. They ran down the curving staircase behind the observation room until they emerged from a secret door into the arena. Meanwhile, Raven had not stopped.

Scorp felt the pain course through his body as the training blade struck again and again, its heat intensifying, and gradually his black mesh outfit began to give way under the endless barrage. It sizzled into smoke, and his bare skin was blackened as the blade continued to burn. Done with this humiliation, Raven then threw Scorp to the ground and delivered kick after furious kick to his gut. Scorp saw spots before his eyes as he twisted and writhed in pain.

Raven had barely noticed that the platforms had all returned to their positions in the floor now, and only when Dragon and Mantis arrived, grabbed him by the arms, and pulled him physically away from his enemy did he even acknowledge their presence. His face was still a mask of fury as he was dragged out of the room. He saw Cat and Seth supporting Saber-Scorpion now, checking out his wounds. Cobra and Coyote could only stare in stunned silence. Only Barracuda was wearing an amused expression. Scorp's half-shut eyes turned in Raven's direction for a second, but his expression did not change... and then the door shut between them.

- CHAPTER FOURTEEN -
INTERESTING TIMES

"Major… Sir!"

The Xarkonian officer stirred in his sleep. Then, abruptly, he sat bolt upright in bed. The soldier took a step back as the half-dressed officer jumped to his feet and glowered at him.

"Alright, Sergeant, I'm up now. Perhaps you can tell me *why*. Out with it!"

The soldier was about to respond when they were interrupted by a series of explosions from the hall outside. The guard quickly crouched and leveled his weapon at the door, but the officer was not so easily dissuaded. Moving stiffly, he opened the door, which was the traditional hinged type, just enough to peek out with one eye. What he saw was both of his guards flying straight at him, their chest armor – and the chest behind it – blown apart by multiple explosive shotgun pellets. The officer was then forced to duck inside as a portion of the wall exploded. The two men inside took cover, the soldier crouching and the officer throwing himself to the ground with his hands over his head.

"What the devil?" he shouted.

The officer looked up to see a tall man in a black trench coat and an eye patch, holding in one hand an ancient-looking double-barreled shotgun with sawed-off barrels and no stock, and in the other a highly modern, fully-automatic, drum-loaded variation of the same weapon. While pointing the former at the officer, he nonchalantly turned the latter in the direction of his guard, without even looking. The guard immediately opened fire with his carbine, landing at least two blazer rounds into their assailant's leg. The attacker promptly ignored the wounds and blasted the unfortunate soldier with a burst of flame from his dragon's breath ammunition, still without turning to look. Seeing the charred remains of his guard's face, the officer wished he hadn't been looking either.

"All this for a damn computer," said Grimm III.

Before the officer could react, Three slung the strap of his automatic shotgun back over his arm, grabbed the officer by the throat, and lifted him right off his feet. He slammed the man's back roughly into the wall, which cracked slightly.

"W-why are you here?" the officer gasped. "The city is under lockdown by terrorists! We're trying to help! Are you-"

"Communication records," Grimm III growled. His voice reminded the officer of a snarling dog. "Where are they? Now!"

"We… don't…"

"Keep any, yeah, yeah. So where do you *don't* keep 'em, then? I know *you* have some, Major, unless you're one helluva lot dumber than I thought."

Three dropped the officer to his feet again. The Xarkonian choked and coughed. "They aren't… here…"

Three calmly grabbed the officer's shoulder, jerked him back up, and kicked him in the shin. There was a crack, and the officer doubled up screaming.

"My computer!" he said between screams. "It's… it's in my desk! Please, take it!"

Three turned his head slightly and rummaged through the contents of the officer's desk drawer. When he found the palm computer, he immediately shoved it under the officer's nose, right in front of the sawed-off shotgun, which still had not wavered.

"Codes," the mercenary grunted.

The officer's face turned to stone. "I… I can't give you those codes. You can break every bone in my body, but if I gave you the information in that computer, I would never again be welcomed back into my mother country. I am many things, but I am no traitor. Do your worst."

Three simply rolled his single green eye. It was the last thing the officer ever saw… though he might have registered the flash of the shotgun blast just before his face was blown off.

LOCATION: STREETS OF SHARDASHA, XARKON

"Just what we need…" Spectra muttered.

She had just arrived at the capitol building, inside which Grimm III was no doubt causing plenty of trouble. Luckily, the guards outside were well distracted… by the horde of rioters that had just arrived. Many of the men and women gathering up at the foot of the building appeared to be affluent, influential individuals, mixed right in with the common folk like dock workers and small business owners. This showed clearly how desperate they all were, when even the rich could not pull enough strings to avoid getting down and dirty with the common people on the street. This didn't stop them, however, from being at the front of the crowd and shouting out "Do you know who I am?" to the Xarkon guards who were holding down the building's entrances. A few people even had guns, Spectra noticed, and they probably knew how to use them, since the only civilians allowed to own firearms in Xarkon were former members of the military. Things could very well get messy.

Spectra, currently wearing a long, expensive white coat over her usual infiltration outfit, was able to blend into the mob so well that the rioters did not give her a second glance. They probably figured her for another of the wealthier citizens, since she gave off an air of sophistication, her hair tied up in a businesslike bun that was skewered through the middle with an ink pen for the final touch. For a moment, she listened to the shouts of "Xarkon has to put a stop to this!" and "Are there even any terrorists at all? Why aren't you fighting them?" Then she reached up and pressed a button on the thin headset she had clipped to one ear.

"Darkness, this is Ultraviolet. Do you read? I just lost Infrared – it sounds like he was under fire."

Lashnar's snarling voice sounded even gruffer with the static caused by the scrambled signal. "Rrraaargh! Yes, Red's in a fight. I'm on the first floor, headed to back him up."

"Belay that order, Lash. I'm getting into a truck now. Get back outside and clear a path for me. I'll tell Red to jump."

"Copy, Violet. They won't know what hit them."

"Keep your fire to a minimum - don't kill any civilians if you can help it!"

"Ah, do you have to take all the fun out of it?"

The wooden door that Grimm III had previously sliced his way into with the laser suddenly burst into splinters as a giant, blood-red Slashrim Zrillak came roaring through it, waving a heavy machine gun. The first Xarkonian soldier Lashnar saw stood no chance as she swung her weapon's heavy, axe-like bayonet in a chopping motion, slicing open his back. For a second, the stampeding of the panicked rioters was enough to keep the other soldiers from coordinating properly as Lashnar continued to cut them down, paying little heed to the few bullets that ended up lodged in her thick flesh.

When the captain finally ordered his men to turn about and point their weapons at the Slashrim, she opened her tooth-lined jaws and gave a blood-curdling roar that seemed to echo through all of Shardasha, causing the terrified civilians to flee the scene all the faster and the soldiers to pause in shock. This gave her enough time to level her own machine gun and open fire indiscriminately, showering them in blazer bullets fit to stop a small tank. Then came Spectra's stolen flatbed cargo truck, ramming at full speed into the guards who were still standing. Lashnar immediately leapt up onto the back, ignoring the droplets of dark green blood dripping from her wounds.

There was a crash high above them, followed by a shower of broken glass as a screaming Grimm III smashed through one of the capitol building's upper windows. Down he fell, landing with a tremendous thud on the back of the truck, causing the hover vehicle to bob so low that it scraped the pavement. Above them, the Xarkon soldiers who had been chasing Three now pointed their rifles down… at the spot where the truck had once been. They looked up just in time to see it speeding off around a corner.

The Xarkonian squad leader fired a parting shot, then turned to face the others. "So, who's gonna tell him?"

"Not me!" shouted the nearest corporal.

"Brave man," said the sergeant, shoving a palm computer into the corporal's hands. "Mars is on line two."

LOCATION: ENOMEG TRAINING ACADEMY BASE

Saber-Scorpion woke up feeling like he should have been dead. His left side burned like hellfire, he was terribly exhausted, and he had what was surely the worst headache he had ever experienced. But he was in his own bed, not the medical wing of the base, so that was a good sign. Slowly the memories began to come back. He saw images of Mars, like recruiting posters, and then Raven's matching face, scowling with rage. Blades flashed, lightning split the air, and it felt like it had struck him. His side burned…

Scorp sat up, ignoring the increase in pain as he did so. He crawled to his feet and tried to determine what to do. But he always knew what to do… Nearly every hour of every day of his life in the base was entirely scheduled. He looked at the clock. It was far later than he had expected. Apparently he had been out for a while after his fight with Raven. He noticed a note on the table beside his bed and picked it up to read.

"Justin, you fought well," he muttered aloud to himself as he read, "but Luke defeated you. I apologize on his behalf for his actions after your defeat. He was taken by the emotions of the moment, and I will see that he is reprimanded appropriately for it. However, the instructors and I have ruled in favor of Luke Blood-Raven being declared the successful victor of the match. I sincerely hope that you will bear him no ill will, for you two will now have to work together. And we need both of you, because you are clearly the best of the Enomegs… bla, bla, bla – Dark-Dragon."

Scorp tossed the paper aside and lay back on the bed, losing himself in thought. While he was trying to find more pleasant things to think about, he recalled the unexpected visit from Cathryn a few nights ago. Lying there wounded and aching, he found himself wishing she would pay him another one. Of course, she was unable to, since all the doors were locked. But hadn't they been locked the other night as well? How, exactly, had she done it? Only the instructors had clearance to enter locked rooms. Had she broken in? It seemed unlikely, unless she had gotten Seth to help her hack it… or perhaps Barracuda to hotwire it. But Scorp doubted either scenario would be the case.

Scorp had looked over his entire room multiple times for possible escape routes, but he'd never found any. Just to be sure, he walked over to the vent at the top of his wall and pulled it off. No, the ventilation shaft was much too small for anyone to fit through. Somehow Scorp found that very reassuring, though he was not quite sure why.

190

As Scorp speculated on other possible entry methods, he wandered into the lavatory and looked at the drain on the tiled floor there. He had always thought it looked rather large, but never really considered the matter beyond that. Apparently, Shadow-Cat had. Now that he looked, he found that the tile in which the drain was made had been recently removed. After searching for a tool with which to pry it open, Scorp soon slid it off again.

A tunnel as straight and dark as the mining shaft on Midas, only much smaller, threatened to swallow him whole as he peered down inside. This was no ordinary drainpipe, for the round metal walls were just barely large enough for a man to fit through, and there were ladder rungs running down one side. A damp smell wafted up from the pit, and when Scorp whistled, it echoed far down below. Without another thought, his pain all but forgotten, he plunged in.

When his foot touched the floor, Scorp dropped down off the ladder. Looking up, he tried to estimate how far he had descended... not as far as he'd thought. Now there was only one place left to go, and that was through a narrow crawlspace at the bottom of the tunnel. He crouched down and crept inside, following the tunnel until he emerged into a larger, open room.

Even though the tunnels had been made of artificial materials, this room was made of natural stone, like a cave. The only thing metal in it was the floor, which mostly consisted of a round grate about four meters wide, under which lay four large fans. There were more tunnels opening out of the cave in every direction, probably leading up into other rooms of the base.

Scorp immediately ascertained the purpose of this room, for there was a strange smell in the cool, damp cave air that made a chill run up his spine. Something, he knew, lay under that grate, and those fans were designed to blow it up into the students' quarters. He could see a sheet of metal behind the fans, and he assumed there were controls somewhere that could open it. There was a hatch in the center of the grating like a manhole, but Scorp did not dare to open it up for fear of what might lie trapped beneath.

Was it some kind of poison? Perhaps this was a contingency; if Xarkon wanted to suddenly destroy the Enomeg project, they could just waft poison gas into the Enomegs' quarters while they slept. But why would Xarkon want to do that? How could they possibly do that to their best, most loyal soldiers? Then he remembered Aeriella's discovery, and the drawing of the Sarran he had found. This was not intended for use on the Enomegs; it had probably been put here to deal with the Sarran. Perhaps it was some kind of an experiment?

He spent a few more minutes trying to find out which tunnel Cat had crawled through – which one led to her room – but he could not figure it out. They all seemed to be equally used. Perhaps Cat had sneaked into everyone's room, he thought. He chuckled. It was possible.

Done with his inspection, Scorp turned back to the tunnel leading to his own quarters. He would have to come back here later... and perhaps make use of it then.

LOCATION: CAMP RAGNAR, XARKON
INSIDE *BEHEMOTH BERTHA*

The world lay at his fingertips. He looked down and saw the grassy rolling hills, gradually ascending higher and higher into the forests and then the mountains. The coastline stretched away, its gently-curving border fringed with pearl-white sand, arcing in a great, gentle C shape around the Bay of Shards. In the middle of it all lay Shardasha, its tall, gleaming skyscrapers reflected in the glittering water. And on this water rested some two dozen warships, each shaped like the imposing silhouette of the Crown of Xarkon, which lay mirrored beneath them in the waves as well.

In the corner of this scene was a large clearing surrounded by hills, in which idly sat a wide array of military vehicles, like sleeping lions on the savannah. Their shapes, even though their colors were camouflaged, clearly indicated that they came from all parts of the world, with a wolf-headed black giant, *Manegarm*, watching over all.

All that he saw lay at his command.

But Lucas Mars was unimpressed, for he knew that everything he saw was merely a hologram, a copy of reality, not reality itself. It was a projection of Shardasha and the events taking place there, nothing more. Mars was never impressed by that which was not real. He had plenty of imagination, which was clear from his amazing ability to invent unprecedented military strategies on the spot, but this imagination was confined to the real and the possible. To spend time thinking about anything else, Mars saw as an utter waste of time.

He looked up, and his deep voice resonated through the room. "I am Lucas Augustus Mars, High Commander of the Armed Forces of Xarkon. With me are Jacob Black, High General of the Xarkon Army; Sergeant Hans Thunder-Hawk of the Special Operations corps, and Beta-Wolf Harry Dalton, commander of Walker Pack 212. Please introduce yourselves so that this strategy meeting can begin."

Behind him, Harry "Viper" Dalton cleared his throat as if to speak.

Without turning, Mars interrupted him. "You have already been introduced, Beta-Wolf. I was referring to the others."

Roscoe puffed out his chest. "I am Roscoe O'Donnel, Chancellor of Zygbar, and this is my military advisor, General Azar Khan." He indicated the man behind him, who had bronze skin, stern features and a neatly-trimmed, pointed black beard. "We would like to welcome everyone present to *Behemoth Bertha*!"

Roscoe gestured to the briefing room in which they stood, in a manner very reminiscent of Howard Cohen at CONON. Whereas one would surely find a bare, Spartan interior in most great military vehicles of the Big Four, the *Bertha* was more luxurious than the finest palace, featuring intricate carpets, finely-wrought gold furnishings, and plush cushioning throughout.

In the center of the room, the hologram of the city was being projected from a great, shining table that looked as if it were made of dark mahogany, but was no doubt some disguised artificial material. Similar tables shaped like curved computer desks, at which the military planners usually sat when controlling a battlefield from *Bertha*'s central cortex, sat in the corners. Mars hated entering the vehicle, since such a show of pomp disgusted him, but he had to admire Roscoe's audacity at so displaying his wealth to the military types now present. He wondered vaguely if Roscoe forced his subordinate officers to wear Napoleonic uniforms when on the field as well.

After everyone had examined the room with polite nods of satisfaction, the introductions continued. "I am Rick Radcliff, Grand General of the Victorian Defense Forces, and this is Sergeant Ryan Arkanian of the Victorian Army. He is my… pupil, you might say."

Ryan swallowed. So now he was Rick Radcliff's personal apprentice in the ways of war, and the Grand General had announced it himself in front of all these world military leaders, along with what sounded like a sudden promotion from Specialist-Sergeant to full-blown Sergeant on the spot.

It was the opportunity of a lifetime, but he felt more anxious than proud… though he was not sure why. It was due to these considerations that he did not note the startled look that had passed for a split second over General Black's face at the mention of his true name. The bearded man quickly turned to clear his throat.

Mars raised one great eyebrow dubiously. "Your pupil? I think I saw him at the last CONON meeting, yes. So why is he here instead of one of your higher-ranking officers?"

Rick paused before replying. "I'll brief them later."

Mars gave a thin smile. Oddly enough, it seemed to be a smile of sincere understanding. Ryan almost got the feeling that Mars felt empathy toward Rick, who was apparently trying to leave his subordinates out of the loop and make all of the decisions himself. This was an action Mars could clearly appreciate, for he did the same thing all the time. Whenever the commanders of Xarkon's four army divisions – the other four members of the "High Five" as they were jokingly called – accompanied Mars, they moved alongside him, silent and unnoticed, like his shadow. Just as High General Black was doing now.

The loud clearing of a throat sounded in the room. The commanders turned to see the last remaining person present, the broad-shouldered and bald-headed Captain of the Mordark Guard.

"I'm here too, if you recall," he said, showing his obvious irritation at having been almost completely ignored for the last few minutes. "I am Borad Jaleiko, Captain of the Mordark Guard. However, the Council has now granted me complete control of Mordark's military in this time of crisis."

Mars nodded. "Very well. Let's be seated and the meeting commence. This map shows Shardasha and the area around it, from Camp Ragnar to Sharpe's Point at the far end of the Bay of Shards. The yellow dots now appearing indicate the locations of all of Shardasha's defensive turrets. All Heimdalls, Xarkon's best defensive turret class."

"Although they do have plenty of weaknesses," Viper broke in. "They're slow at changing alignment and almost useless at close range."

Mars fixed the walker pilot with a harsh glare, but did not reprimand him for the interruption. "Yes, Beta Dalton here has done a grand job at keeping our walkers out of their clutches and avoiding detection. Quite a feat, since Shardasha was turned into a veritable fortress-city during the Xenocide War, and it has been mostly kept that way ever since. And now these terrorists have somehow taken control of the entire defense grid. They can shoot down anything that tries to leave or enter. They claim that they will use these weapons to destroy the city itself unless their demands are met... Demands Xarkon *cannot* meet."

Jaleiko nodded. "So what's the plan?"

Mars punched a command on the control panel, and a wide circle of uneven red dots appeared on the map, all well away from the city in the center. Some of them were moving as they watched. A large one over their war camp in the corner was flashing.

"These are my walkers, ships, and armor units patrolling the borders of the city," Mars said. "The ones in the bay there are Jormund Battleships and Kraken Frigates. The other indicators you see moving about the city border are all scouts. The larger ones are walkers, mostly Foxes and Jackals, and the smaller ones are scouting teams on Hornet hoverbikes. And finally, this is our war camp, Camp Ragnar. We haven't brought in any aerospace forces because they would be at the mercy of the terrorists' defenses. Just as the terrorists have ensured that none of our men enter or leave the city, *we* have ensured that none of *theirs* do either."

Jaleiko nodded again, impatiently. "Yes, yes. But what is the *plan*?"

Mars placed both hands on the table and locked his fingers together, leaning over and giving Jaleiko a piercing stare. "The *plan*, Captain, or Commander if that's what you're called now, is what we are here to discuss. My proposal is simple: we should send in elite infantry forces to infiltrate the city. They will stop the terrorists and recover the hostages as quickly and quietly as possible."

Now it was Rick's turn to raise a dubious eyebrow. "And Xarkon has both a way in and an infantry force capable of pulling off this feat?"

Behind Mars, the tall, blond-haired man he had introduced as Hans Thunder-Hawk nodded. "My Special Operations team is perfectly suited to handle such a job. We can drop onto the hull of a capital starship, crawl inside, disable the engines, and take the command crew hostage without being detected even once. This city should be an easy run for us."

Rick frowned. So Mars was still denying the existence of the super-soldiers. Or were they even real at all? Ryan, however, had different thoughts. He looked at the keen eyes and confident demeanor of the Spec-Ops commander, Thunder-Hawk, and wondered if he were not a super-soldier himself. Every word he had spoken, though they sounded like bragging, had been said in a tone of absolute, brutal honesty.

Ryan had no idea how close his thoughts were to the truth, of course. Hans Thunder-Hawk may have been denied his rank of Enomeg due to failing too many tests, but he was still eager to prove himself as a Spec-Ops commander, in the hope that he might one day be given his Enomeg exoskeleton regardless.

"The plan sounds like it's all we have to work with," said General Radcliff at length, "but Victory will have to send in some of *her* soldiers as well. Sergeant Arkanian here is the perfect man for the job. He and a handful of other elite Victorians will accompany your Special Operations team."

Captain Jaleiko nodded. "Mordark has also brought in some soldiers for this job. I have a dozen of our Lord's bodyguards with me."

Roscoe, who had said nothing until now, gave a slight smile. "The men in the red capes, you mean?"

Jaleiko did not return his smile. "They are highly-trained warriors who fight with fierce discipline. They will be entering the city in disguise, of course, not in their ceremonial outfits, Chancellor O'Donnell. What about you? Will you be sending in any troops? Any of Zygbar's fabled Highlander mercenaries?"

Roscoe made a disapproving clicking sound and shook his head. "No, no, no, not *mercenaries*. The High Desert Division is now an official part of our army, good Captain. But no, I will not be sending any of them in. For now, Zygbar will only watch. The soldiers will, however, be ready if you need them. I have several of them here in the transports surrounding *Bertha*."

"Very well then," Mars said, "I think that's everything. Are we in agreement, gentlemen?"

Jaleiko shook his head. "No. I want to see a copy of the mission outline, the briefing – the orders you're giving your soldiers. I want to make sure the safety of the hostages is the *top* priority. If our soldiers attempt to accomplish another objective first and make even *one* mistake, then the terrorists may start executing hostages. Make sure the orders are simple: Lord Zegaldorph must survive."

"Well," Roscoe put in, "there is no way we can be sure that he is even alive as it is, much less if…"

"I don't care," Jaleiko said sternly. "I want the orders to include that line: Lord Zegaldorph *must* survive. That is the lone objective for the first mission. If he dies, the mission has failed."

Ryan glanced at Rick, who was staring away in thought, his features tense. Ryan could guess easily enough what the Grand General was thinking. Rick was an ethical man, and Jaleiko's priorities were not ethical. He would place an entire city in danger just to save a single life, the life of his master. So why was Rick not protesting? Ryan could only guess that he simply did not want to show any support for Xarkon's side in this argument.

For good or ill, they were all surprised when Xarkon's side of the argument suddenly changed. Mars gave a slight smile and said, "Very well, Captain Jaleiko. I can certainly understand your concern. In fact, I appreciate it. It's good to see such loyalty in another individual. I would like to think that my subordinates would show such devotion to me were I in Zegaldorph's situation. I agree then, that Zegaldorph's rescue should be made the first priority. General Radcliff, what do you say?"

Rick nodded tersely. "Yes… Yes, I agree."

Roscoe grinned. "Then we are unanimous."

Mars nodded and rose from his seat. "In that case, let's waste no more time. Assemble your squads in the field outside my encampment. My scouts will look for the best opening into the city. We will prepare to move out in the next few days."

And, Mars thought as he left the room, *the Enomegs had better be ready to move in before then.*

LOCATION: PLAINS OF CENTRAL XARKON

It was at the crack of dawn that they gathered, with rain pouring from the sky in broad, sweeping sheets. The rain was always heavy on the Ukrak plains when it finally came, and today the Enomeg trainees' feet splashed into at least an inch of mud with every step. The place they were ordered to meet was imperceptible when viewed from the base. Where from a distance only level grasses could be seen, there actually lay a steep dropoff of many meters.

Dark-Dragon was waiting for them at the foot of this cliff, standing in front of a dark, yawning cave. Around the mouth of the cavern was a gateway of ancient stonework, covered in strange runes and images. As the Enomegs approached, Dark-Dragon moved to the cave entrance and ran his gloved fingers along the carvings.

"Can you read these?" he asked.

Seth quickly replied, "It's written in ancient Mahlo-Slashrim. It says: 'Cursed Cave of the god Sessith – Guarded by Spirits of the Dishonored Dead – Only by faith in Helexith may one enter unharmed.'"

Dragon nodded. "This is the Cave of Fear... the location for our last test, the Test of Bravery. But it's not faith in some alien god that will lead you through this hole alive. It's pure guts... pure courage."

The Enomeg trainees stared at the yawning mouth of the cave, as the rain battered down upon them. Somehow, after the large-scale battle that had taken place in the last test, this crack in a rock seemed rather anticlimactic, even with the storm. Dark-Dragon seemed able to sense their feelings.

"Don't worry," he said. "You will find the challenges in this cave more than worthy of your abilities. This is a test of your emotions, Enomegs. Emotions are part of our natural instincts; their purpose is to help us and our species to survive. Love encourages us to defend those who are close to us, anger encourages us to seek justice for wrongdoings... and fear tells us when a challenge is too much for us to face. These emotions all serve a good purpose, but we must learn how to control them, instead of letting *them* control *us*. We must control our love, so that we are loyal to those who deserve it, and not simply every fickle friend or pretty face that comes along. We must control our anger, so that we seek out true justice, not simply revenge. And we must also control our fear, to ensure that we do not run out on a mission that we truly can complete... because we must always think of the mission and our greater goals before our own survival.

"First, let us consider the nature of fear. Fear comes in two basic forms: fear of the known, and fear of the unknown. We experience the former kind when we have previously experienced a traumatic event, and we know what to expect when we see it coming again. This kind is the easier of the two to control, and as Enomegs, you have no doubt mastered the art of doing so. But fear of the *unknown* is much harder to suppress. The most petrifying terror that exists is the fear of something we do not understand. The reason mankind has always feared the dark is because we cannot see what it might be hiding. If our species could see in the dark, it would be as comfortable as daylight.

"In this cave, you will learn to master that fear of the unknown. There is something special about this chasm… there is a certain strange gas that seeps up through the ground. The Native Slashrim who lived here had no idea what it was, and they were too afraid to try and find out. And when I say afraid, I mean *literally* afraid. The gas causes hallucinations – it amplifies fear. When you think to yourself that there might be something lurking in the dark, you *see* it. The dark itself starts to move; it attacks you. It sprouts tentacles, and they encircle you, grasping at your very heart. You can feel them… and they feel cold as death. What you really feel is *fear*… fear itself. For that is what truly attacks you: not tentacles or death, but pure fear."

Dragon backed away from the entrance and pointed at Saber-Scorpion. "You will go first. Be warned, you will find worse dangers than merely a few shadows jumping out at you. We've set up plenty of real attackers in the cave, so be prepared. Simply make your way through the cave, for there is only one way to go. Keep going until you reach the end, and then exit. Don't die, and don't even think about turning back. That's all there is to it. Good luck, soldier."

Scorp took a few steps forward and peered into the deep, murky darkness. The entrance was squared off by the Slashrim that had enshrined it, but the tunnel grew wider and more natural as it continued. It was hard to see, for it was not only dark, but also enshrouded in mist. He guessed this was an effect of the gas seeping up out of the floor. As he continued slowly inside, taking in his surroundings, he listened closely for the ghostly whistling created by the wind that one always expected to hear when entering a cave like this. But no sound ever came. There was only stillness and silence, with the occasional drip of water echoing from far, far in the distance.

Scorp was wearing the same suit of incomplete Enomeg armor that he had worn in the Test of Leadership. The only thing missing was the facemask from the helmet, so that meant there was no gas mask filter to keep out the fear that lurked in the atmosphere here. As Scorp activated the suit's automatic camouflage, the color of his armor adjusted from shining crimson to dull, unreflective grey, like the mist. *He became the mist. He* was *the mist.*

That was often how he had fought his fears in the past, as a child. One of his first missions had been to hunt animals in the wilderness, for nowhere else were one's natural warrior instincts awakened so clearly. He had been terrified at first, until he finally convinced himself that he was not an intruder in the wilds, but *part* of them. He was a part of the natural world, an animal in the jungle just like the ones he was hunting. And now he used that same method, looking down at his dark grey armor and saying in his mind: you are a ghost, a creature of the mists. The gas of fear does not affect you because it is part of you. You are one with it.

And then he felt the first chill touch of the fear.

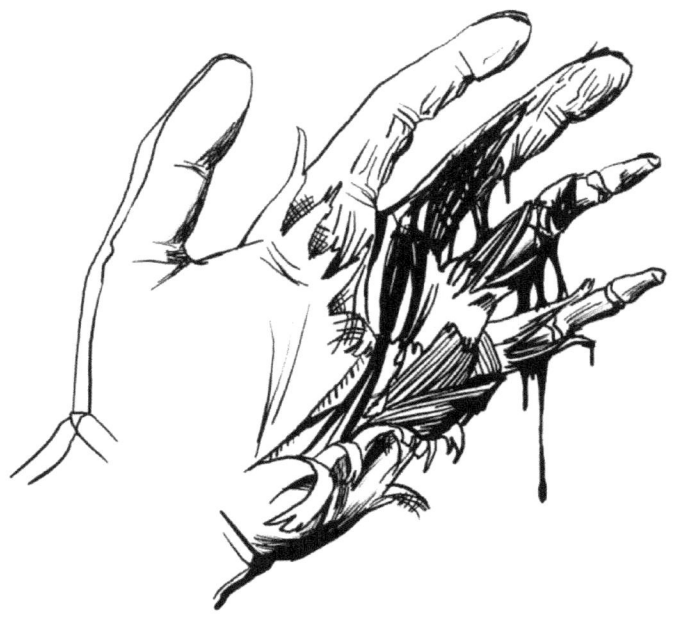

- CHAPTER FIFTEEN -
THE ONLY THING TO FEAR

Saber-Scorpion felt his stomach churn. His hands suddenly began to fade, growing pale and transparent. He could see the ground below through his own armor and skin, and as he watched, his nanomesh suit began to tear away. He looked down at his body and saw it full of ghastly wounds, his armor broken, his suit torn. His skin peeled away, revealing muscle and bone. He had just stumbled off a battlefield, shot full of holes. His skin was grey and smoky, like the mist... dead. Suddenly he felt his toe hit a rock, and he fell forward, only catching himself just in time to avoid landing headfirst in a pool of water. And then he saw his reflection. He was a wraith, a skull with hanging skin and empty eyes.

Fear's chill touch hardened into an icy grip. Saber-Scorpion's pulse began to race. What was happening to him? Had he really become a ghost? It was impossible. But how could it be impossible when it seemed so *real?* It was like a dream; something that would have been laughable to imagine in the daylight, but at night, as the mind wandered in sleep, it was absolute reality.

But this pure panic phase only lasted a few seconds, for Scorp knew what was really happening: the fear toxin was taking hold, amplifying the frightening aspects of his thoughts. Gritting his teeth, he splashed his face directly into the water. When he came back up, gasping from the ice-cold liquid, his senses felt clearer. His ghastly visage returned to normal in the reflection. As he retained control, he began to count the length of his breaths in seconds, using the breathing practice they had been taught in training.

The meditative technique worked, and Scorp began to move through the cave again, at a cautious pace, still listening and trying to see around him in the misty gloom. He walked with one hand touching the wall to his right at all times, taking careful steps forward, looking at the cavern floor more than anything else. He seemed to spend hours walking like this, and all the time a sense of dread grew greater and greater in his heart. Strange sounds began to reach his ears. In the distance he heard muffled voices talking. He slid into a crack in the wall to hide. Then he heard clanking metal, the click of a cocking gun. There was even a distant, muffled scream.

Scorp knew most of these sounds were figments of his imagination, but the question was: which ones? Were some of them real? As this doubt, this fear of the uncertain – the unknown – began to grip him, he paused to breathe. After a moment, he summoned up his courage and continued on, this time looking up from the floor. But this only made things worse. Now he could see great shadows rising in the mists, moving shapes of fearsome monsters... hulking, hideous Slashrim and great winged Draconians. Sometimes they seemed so real that he could reach out and touch them. Were these Slashrim still guarding this cave like a temple? No, that was impossible...

Again he switched back to concentrating on his feet and the earth beneath them, and he found he had to fight to convince himself that the floor was not shifting or falling away beneath his feet. At first he had tried to move silently so as to be unobserved, but now he found himself making louder and louder footsteps, just to supply a real sound to concentrate on instead of the imagined distant screams and muffled Slashrim roars.

And then, suddenly, a very real sound did ring out. It was a gunshot, its sound muffled by a suppressor, but there in that silent cave of fear it rang out in Scorp's mind like an atomic bomb. Scorp immediately threw himself to the ground and scurried between the wall and some nearby thick stalagmites. Dust flew into his face as another bullet struck the ground directly in front of him, and he froze as solid as the stone.

Now the fear was really gripping him. His instructors knew just what kind of situations he hated, and this was one of them: to be pinned down by gunfire from an unknown source. Some Enomegs, the stealthy sniper types, would have taken this situation any day over an outnumbered close-quarters encounter in a narrow hallway... but not Scorp, who was best with his blades, or even his hands and feet. Suddenly he felt something he had not felt for seemingly as long as he could remember: helplessness... and helplessness is the main avenue of fear. If only he could get closer to his foes... ascertain their location somehow. But they could be anywhere!

As he sat there, he thought he felt the stalagmite behind him move, and suddenly he realized that it was not a stalagmite at all – the rock was some kind of fabric... an enemy soldier!

Scorp whirled around and slammed his fist into... the stalagmite. He sucked in his breath and wrung his injured hand. This fear toxin was more potent than he had thought. How was he going to get out of this? Suddenly he felt the overpowering urge to simply run. It seemed to suddenly dawn upon him like the light of sanity in a stormy sky of confused thoughts: run, and get away from it all! If he ran fast enough, there's no way the snipers could shoot him down in all this fog. He could escape this death-trap and...

No. Dark-Dragon had said not to even consider turning back. He had to finish his mission. For twenty years he had trained for this, fought tooth and nail against far harder challenges than some dark foggy cave full of gas and a couple of snipers. He had to finish this; it was his goal in life, his only goal left. So again he tried a little reverse psychology to quell his fears: he told himself that he would be running away, only in the wrong direction.

Scorp jumped to his feet and ran. Sniper fire shattered the walls and floor, sending debris bouncing off his armor as he dropped into a forward roll, avoiding yet more bullets. And as he ran, he listened. Through the echoing din of gunfire, he managed to pinpoint the approximate direction from which the shots were originating and head toward that location.

Suddenly his feet slid off a pile of loose pebbles at the foot of what seemed to be a recent rockslide. The snipers were no doubt positioned at the top of it for protection, so Scorp dropped down low behind the largest boulder he could find. Another shot whizzed past him just as he did so, lighting up the dark cave with a spark as it ricocheted off the stone.

Scorp knew he would have to rush the snipers to beat them, but now his fear was almost palpable. He knew that the snipers could hit him at this range if he so much as showed his face. He had to think of some way to throw them off... to distract them or disrupt their aim. But it was so hard to think, with his heart pounding in his ears, and with the fear filling his mind and the area around him with phantoms and hobgoblins of every description. He felt the sudden urge to scream.

That was it. It was the only move that he could think of. Turning in the general direction he knew the snipers to be, he summoned up every ounce of courage left in his veins, took the deepest breath that he could, and let out a tremendous battle cry. The sound echoed off the walls, filling the small cave in an almost deafening reverberation. The sound frightened even him, but in that moment of excitement, he was able to use his original tactic to battle the fear: the tables were turned – now *he* was the monster, the terror, the night... and the enemy marksmen were his prey. In a matter of seconds, Scorp ascended the pile of loose stones with grace and dexterity that the snipers had never expected. Twin star-talon blades cut through the air, trailing fire, illuminating the cavern with sweeping red light.

Scorp bent down to inspect the bodies. Two snipers, working as a team... too close together for their own good. They looked like mercenaries, armed with a motley assortment of weaponry and gear, including gas masks to protect them from the cave's terrifying fumes. Had Xarkon hired mercs to be slaughtered in this exercise, or were these more criminals lured here with a promise of freedom? This time, Scorp did not reflect on the matter. He trusted to his commanders to have made the right decision. It helped that, in this instance, his enemies had at least been armed and stood a fighting chance.

He bent over to remove the gas mask from the nearest body, when suddenly its arm reached up and grabbed his wrist. Scorp gasped and gave the corpse a sharp kick to the side, jerking free... of the arm that had never really moved. He rolled his eyes and cursed himself, then bent back down to remove the mask. But what lay beneath? Staring eyes... the face of the dead. The face of the man he had killed, who had been trying to kill him for reasons he knew not. Could he face that, here in this room with this gas?

Scorp shook his head. Of course he could.

Redoubling his willpower, he jerked the gas mask free and, without pausing to look at the visage beneath, raised the device to his own head. For a moment, as the goggles surrounded his eyes and he took his first breath of fresh air through the filter, everything seemed to become clear. And then the fog returned, as he found it impossible to breathe. Gasping for breath and clawing at the black shroud covering his face, he jerked the mask off and threw it across the room. Why hadn't it worked?

Finally he summoned up the courage to look back at the body next to him... only to find it staring right back at him. He jumped and crawled backward until he nearly fell down the rockslide. After struggling to regain his balance, he looked back at the corpse to find it staring at the ceiling once again. Dark-Dragon was right; this fear gas was no laughing matter.

But he did see the answer to his problem with the gas mask: it had come apart, leaving the filtration part attached to the original wearer's pale, lifeless face, and the device torn apart and non-functional. Apparently they had been designed to break if removed. Scorp swore the foulest Slashrim oath he could think of. Clearly, he had to finish this on his own.

The Enomeg trainee continued on, moving deeper into the cavern. As he walked, the cave grew smaller and smaller, constricting itself, threatening to smother him, until it suddenly drew into a single, tiny crawlspace. Scorp felt the sides to make sure it was not an illusion. No such luck – this was an actual obstacle, and he had no choice but to pass straight through.

The dark hole seemed to him like a waiting mouth, ready to force him down its throat. It was barely big enough for a man to fit through, especially Saber-Scorpion in his Enomeg armor. He had trained to crawl through tight spaces like ventilation shafts, but this? This was a rocky, uneven little hole in a cave full of fear-inducing toxin. He felt certain he would panic and suffocate before reaching the end.

But he knew if he stood and thought about it longer, it would only grow more difficult. So, forcing these misgivings from his mind, he plunged in. As he crawled, the last thought he *did* have kept running through his head: *suffocate... suffocate...* Just how much air could there be this deep in a cave, anyway? Could there be a more deadly poison gas located deeper in the tunnels? Logic seemed to insist that Dark-Dragon and the instructors would not have sent him into a cave from which there was no possible escape.

Unfortunately, logic was outnumbered right now… overpowered by the multitude of fears that came washing over him as he shuffled along, listening to the scraping of his metal boots and bracers against the rock as he crawled. What about structural integrity? What if the place caved in? Was there water down here? The roof was dripping a lot. What if it flooded?

Scorp shook his head, as much as he could in the tight quarters. These were ridiculous fears. They were almost as ridiculous as the recurring sensation that he had been swallowed by some lurking monster, and its digestive fluid was now burning away at his armor as he crawled. He knew that if he looked down, he would see the liquid, even if it was not really there, so he kept his eyes facing forward… right into the other pair of eyes: the red ones, far down the tunnel. But they weren't real of course, so Scorp just closed his eyes and continued on. The terrifying sounds never ceased to assault him as he made his way ever more slowly onward. Finally, when he thought he could take it no more, when he was about to give up all hope and curl up in despair, his mind lost in madness… the floor fell out under his feet.

Scorp rolled out into the next room, coughing for breath. Despite his training in the importance of good breathing when in a tense situation, he had been breathing very little in the tunnel for various other reasons. He kept telling himself it was to avoid taking in too much of the gas, but it was probably because he was scared of running out of oxygen.

So now he leaned against a pillar of stone and tried to catch his breath, counting the seconds for each intake and exhalation. As he did so, he continued to hear the noises… the muffled footsteps, the talking, the screams, the loading rifles. But then, like a lightning flash in the dark, a single sound broke through all the others. It was the simple scuffle of a foot, but somehow, instinctively, Scorp knew this one was real.

He whirled, and his blades flashed online, lighting the pitch-black cave in their hellish red glow. His assailant was clad in solid black, form-fitting leather. Her head was covered by a full-face gas mask, and she wielded a long rifle with a blazer-shielded bayonet, which she swung in a wide arc, trying to keep her distance from the Enomeg. Saber-Scorpion fought defensively, blocking her blows and trying to ascertain her identity. Then, in a flash, he knew. For only then did he notice the wings.

"You!" he shouted. "Stop this! I tried to save you!"

Without responding, she attacked now with renewed vigor, and he continued to block in a panicked frenzy. She was surprisingly accurate with her spear-like weapon, and the blazer shield extended over the length of the barrel, preventing him from cutting it off without taking off her arm.

Scorp knew why Aeriella was here: Dark-Dragon meant for him to kill her. He was not to fail this task a second time, or he would never become an Enomeg. As he thought between slashes, he again felt fear's icy touch… but this time it was different. He felt afraid not that he would lose the test, or even that he might be killed… No, he felt afraid that he would actually do it.

And then, unexpectedly, the feelings of doubt and fear were replaced with pure rage. He was angry not at his attacker or even at himself, but at his instructors, even Dragon. They were pulling more dirty tricks, trying to break him, trying to turn him into one of them. They did not care for his personal ethics, for his own code of honor, for who *he* was. They only wanted him to fight for them as their tool, their weapon, to do what *they* said was right.

"Don't be a fool!" he shouted. "Don't you realize you're just doing what they want? You're giving in to them, following their plan!"

Still she was unheeding, perhaps unable to hear him. Her only response was to unsheathe and activate a blazer knife with her left hand. In a cunning move, she jabbed at Scorp with her gun in order to occupy his defenses, and then she tossed the knife straight at him. Scorp was a quicker dodge than she had thought possible, however, and the blade only grazed his arm, just cutting through the mesh there. To Scorp, this was enough to startle him. For the first time, he realized that if he continued on the defensive like this, Aeriella might actually kill him.

He had to fight back.

With that realization, brought onto him by the pain of the knife cut, he took a step forward and went on the offensive. The bayonet jabbed and sliced, keeping him at a distance, but the quarters were tight, and Aeriella found herself losing ground to Scorp's sudden flurry of quick but calculated slashes. Eventually her back hit the wall, and then everything happened in a flash. Scorp knocked her bayonet aside and ducked under it, grabbing the scope atop the rifle and jerking the weapon aside. A second knife had just appeared in Aeriella's free hand, but a quick slice from Scorp's blade sent it flying from her grasp, and then the blade snapped back around for the kill.

The starfire talon, unstoppable, burned right through her leather outfit and the defensive mesh beneath, and then singed flesh. It was only stopped by her scream... or so it seemed. Scorp had stopped himself just in time to avoid killing her, and now her scream caused him to pull back entirely. Suddenly he found himself seized by the fear again, but now the thing he feared... was himself. He really *was* the terror, the monster, the night. He could not even direct his own hands, could not control his mechanical killer instinct. This monster inside him had killed Daniel and almost killed Aeriella as well.

Suddenly a knife cut through his thoughts as he felt Aeriella's bayonet cut through his armor and into his side. He looked down to see the weapon jammed between his two chestplates. Then it slid back out, and Scorp saw flecks of pale foam dribbling to the ground – the wound-sealant nanocrystals automatically released by his nanomesh suit whenever it was breached. He fell to his knees.

As he fell, so did the illusion. The angelic wings faded from the back of his assailant, nothing more than a mirage conjured up by the effects of the toxin to amplify his deepest fears. The woman was a Human just like him, and soon he would die for his foolishness. A single thought arose in his mind:

Cat was right.

Location: Royal Arms Inn & Suites
Shardasha, Xarkon

"Come on, Erik. We don't have time for this right now."

Grimm III ignored Spectra's scolding and again tried to lean in for a kiss. She shoved him back, and he complied, pouting and grumbling about all work and no play. He felt in his pocket to give her the palm computer, but it was nowhere to be found. Then he saw that she had taken it from him and was already hooking it up.

"Sneaky little witch…" he muttered, looking around the room. "Nice place you got here."

Spectra's apartment was large and luxurious, its prominent feature being a wide desk on which she had spread her variety of electronic equipment. Her computer featured multiple high-definition holographic displays and uplink antennas… and a variety of other devices used for hacking and decoding that Three could not begin to understand.

"You know, I could get cozy in a crib like this. I even brought that wine I talked about. It was in that truck we used to get here. Who'd'a thought a truck driver would be packin' wine, huh? Take a look."

Spectra turned and gave the bottle a cursory glance. Her upper lip curled up in a sneer.

"Uh-huh. What kind is it?"

"The kind made from *grapes*, I reckon," Grimm replied. "You know, little round fruit, imported from Old Earth?"

"What kind of grapes?"

"There's *kinds* of grapes?"

Spectra blew out a sigh. "I should have expected this much from a man who drinks that pre-digested Slashrim slop."

"You mean *poj-poj*? It's an acquired taste… but hey, it's healthy."

"Of course it is, except for the alcohol. The Mahlok produce it in order to keep their Slashrim slaves fit and strong enough to work but too drunk to think of rebellion. That's why even Lashnar won't drink the crap."

Three shrugged. "Keeps me fit and healthy enough to kill folks, but too drunk to feel sorry for 'em."

Spectra rolled her eyes and turned back to her computer. Hacking into the private files of a Xarkon officer was not easy, but Spectra was an expert, and she knew all of the Xarkon army's standard security systems. It was not long before she smiled and leaned back in her chair. As Three watched, the holographic face of the Xarkon officer he had recently killed appeared on one of the displays. He was frowning, looking very displeased about something.

"That's the one I dusted off."

"Shh! It's playing."

The officer said, "This is Major Nido…"

"Codename," Spectra whispered.

"What?" Three grunted.

She paused the recording. "He's using a codename, in case the transmission is intercepted. Nido is Odin spelled backward."

"Pretty dumb codename if you can figure it out that easy. So you know this Major Odin?"

"No, the *officer* isn't Odin, you stupid ox! Odin is the ancient Norse god of the sky. Xarkonians are all mythology nuts, especially for Nordic myth. They're crazy about it – even have some neo-pagan cults. So I'm sure this is a codename, but I still have no idea who the officer is. So let's continue."

She pressed play, and the officer went on: "I am sick of this post and sick of being lied to. I'm in a very dangerous position here, and I want *out*."

There was no recording of the face that belonged to the gruff, static-filled voice that replied, "Negative. We can't put another officer on this; you're the only man for the job. You've had years of experience in intelligence and counter-intelligence. You know how to be invisible."

"Yes," said the Major, "I *have* had years of experience. That's why I don't understand why you aren't letting us move in. I'm invisible; my men have the whole *city* under lockdown. Nothing gets in, nothing gets out. But the longer I sit here idle, the more chance it is that Zegaldorph could still slip through our fingers!"

"How much security's he got in his tower?"

The Major gave an exasperated sigh and rubbed his forehead. "A lot. He's practically built another Mordark City Core fortress right here in Shardasha. He's got his entire tower under perfect lockdown."

"Then that's *exactly* why you can't move in. This is black ops, Major. You know we can't storm the place and leave a trail of bodies. I wish I could help you more, but I'm under pressure too. So is the rest of High Command."

Spectra paused the recording again and turned to Three with a smile. "So… our other mysterious officer is a member of the High Five…"

Three was just shaking his head, staring at the paused hologram with a look of disgust. "God, I wish Lashnar was here to see this. It's as bad as Mahlok brainwashin'. Even I can barely believe it! *Xarkon* was behind this 'terrorist incident' the whole damn time, just to knock off Zingledorph!"

"*Zegal*dorph," Spectra corrected. "But yes, you're right. I've suspected as much since the very beginning. I suppose the Emperor is hoping to end his dynasty on a high note by killing Zegaldorph and conquering Mordark. But let's see what else they have to say."

She resumed the hologram, and they heard the faceless High Command officer say, "But we can't take any risks. We have to make sure it gets done *right*. And we have just the men for that… just give 'em time."

"We don't *have* more time! There are rumors floating around among the civilians about Xarkon being behind this. If they see my men sit here and do nothing any longer, I'll have a riot to deal with as well. In short, General, the longer we wait, the more chance there is of this entire thing falling down around us."

"I don't give a damn about civilians!" the static-masked voice shot back. "If they start spreading rumors, have a few plain-clothes Spec-Ops shoot the bastards."

"My, my…" the Major chided, "getting awfully bloodthirsty, aren't we, General Black?"

"You aren't supposed to use my name, you moron! Make sure you destroy this tape once we're through, or you can expect a court martial."

"I didn't become a soldier to murder civilians! What if I *don't* delete this little conversation, Black?"

"Then you'll never leave Shardasha alive… Major Gi–"

In a sudden blink, the hologram disappeared.

Spectra blew out a sigh. "It looks like the good Major cut his own name off the recording, while leaving Black's."

Grimm III did not reply, but sat down in the most comfortable chair he could find, jerked the cork out of the wine bottle with his bare fingers, and took a series of noisy gulps. Then he smacked his lips and cleared his throat.

"Well, glad to see you're making yourself comfortable…"

Three nodded and inspected one of his shotgun shells. "Oh, yeah, yeah. Snug as a slug in a thug. Shotgun slug, that is."

Spectra just shook her head at this.

Three coughed again. "So anyway, why'd you say you cut off the Crownie transmission?"

Again she sighed. "Aren't you even paying attention? I didn't turn it off. The rest was deleted. Major *whatever* deleted his own name from the file and only left Black's."

"Who's Black? You know 'im?"

Spectra shot him a suspicious glance. One of her elegant eyebrows curved up.

Three gave a stupid grin. "You look so cute when you make faces."

"You don't know who General *Black* is? Next you'll tell me Mars was just a planet in the old solar system."

Three shrugged. "So I don't know the name of *every* stinkin' Crownie brass. So what?"

Spectra pulled up a holographic image of a tall, broad-shouldered man with close-clipped black hair and a beard. "You should know *this* officer, Erik. Jacob Black rose faster through the Xarkon ranks than any officer before him, even Lucas Mars. In fact, it's partially Mars's doing that he was promoted so quickly. The two of them trust each other implicitly and go almost everywhere together. They think alike, sound alike… they even *look* alike, except for Black being younger. Same height, same build…"

Three grunted out a laugh. "So maybe he's a fellow clone…"

Spectra shrugged. "Could be. Either way, we now have half of what we came for: we have the truth about what's going on here."

Grimm III nodded. "Great. Now we just need to get Zeeg."

"Yes, and we need to move quickly. I don't know who Black is sending in here, what 'men' he has prepared… but I don't like the sound of them. Call

Lashnar and get her to meet us here. I think it would be a very good idea for us to get to Zegaldorph before *they* do."

LOCATION: THE CAVE OF FEAR

The sniper rifle was an awkward weapon for close quarters combat, and its recoil was extreme, so the woman had been saving her shot for when she knew Scorp was down. Once she saw him fall to his knees, she stopped to level her rifle at his face. But as soon as Scorp's eyes gazed down that barrel, it awakened a final last-ditch instinct for survival. In a flash, both of his blades came online and slammed against the bayonet on her rifle at once, knocking the barrel aside just as she pulled the trigger.

The report of the weapon echoed so loudly through the room that it sounded like the cave was collapsing. This shocked the woman long enough for Scorp to deliver one well-aimed blow, the tip of his blade just slicing through the end of her gas mask filter. He then received a slice across the knee from her bayonet as he retreated. At first she pressed the attack, but Scorp gambled that he might have the advantage now – she seemed to have not even noticed the damage to her mask. Dropping into the most intimidating battle stance he could think of, he shouted, "Come on!"

Now she hesitated, the toxin just beginning to affect her, and he pressed the advantage. She backed up against the wall, so terrified that he was easily able to grasp the scope of her rifle again, and this time pull the gun right out of her hands. He tossed the weapon away and grabbed her by the arm. She cried out as he reached up and jerked the gas mask off of her face. As the full effects of the gas suddenly set in, she opened her mouth in silent screams like gasps, terror filling her features… features that Scorp recognized.

"It's okay," he said, "it's okay! Breathe… breathe…"

It took a few minutes before her breathing slowed and became more even, before her long-lashed eyelids began to droop and she stopped frantically struggling. Finally she blew out a long sigh and lowered her head, her long, raven hair falling over her face. Scorp put his hand on her forehead and looked into her wide hazel eyes as they blinked and looked around.

"You recognize me, don't you?" he asked.

"No…" she mumbled. "No, don't! I won't let you trap me again…"

"Did I trap you when I told you how to escape in the jungle? At least Dark-Dragon spared your life that time. He may not have been so kind to the *other* one I saved."

"They said… they said one can leave! They said one has to *die!*"

"But you can't kill me," Scorp said, and after a pause he finished, "and I won't kill you."

Again her breathing began to slow, and this time, as she stared into his cold but honest blue-grey eyes the way she had done in the jungle river months ago, it did not speed up again. "I would have killed you, you know."

He nodded. "Yes. I know."

"So why won't you do the same?"

Scorp looked away, saying nothing. He stood up and helped the woman to her feet. Then he picked up her sniper rifle, switched off the bayonet's blazer shield, and slung the weapon over his shoulder.

He turned back to her. "Were the other two snipers in the cave with you? Are there any more?"

She looked frightened again, clamping her hands over her ears as if to block out some sound that Scorp could not hear. He knew she was still feeling the effects of the fear toxin. Still, she was standing up to it surprisingly well. He touched her gently on the shoulder and repeated his question.

"Other two...?" she replied slowly. "I... I never saw any others."

He had no way of knowing if she was telling the truth, but it didn't matter. "If you say so. Are you claustrophobic?"

"No. I can take tight spaces, as long as I know I'll get back out."

He put an arm around her slender shoulders. Then, holding aloft his Starfire blade like a torch, he began to search the ceiling. Scorp had an idea – a vague hope, but it was all he could think of. He recalled the room that he had found after following the secret exit in his quarters – the room with the fans and the pipes leading away on all sides. That room, he thought, might have been made to vent the fear gas out of this very cave. Judging by the position of the entrance, these caverns did seem to be positioned right beneath the ETAB.

Beside him, he could feel the woman's breathing beginning to grow more rapid once again. He tried to think of a way to calm her...

"What's your name?" he asked.

"La... Larisa," she replied slowly.

"Larissa?"

"No, no – Lah-REE-Sa."

"Okay, Larisa. I'm looking for a hole in the ceiling, maybe with some kind of metal grate or vent covering it. See if you can help me."

She let go of him and looked around, suppressing the fear surprisingly well. He was glad to see that. After all, she would probably have to wait in the secret room with the gas until he could safely get her out after the test. The only problem with Scorp's plan was that the instructors would probably look for her body. He had to find some way to fake her death, but he could not think of one.

Why was he even bothering? The thought came unbidden into his mind. It was true that she had tried to kill him just now – *would* have killed him just now if he hadn't stopped her. But he could not shake the feeling that she was simply frightened, alone, desperate... and, after all, wasn't she really innocent? All she did was find out their *names*... right?

Did it really even matter to him? He wasn't sure.

"I need your help," he said. "I'm not going to harm you, but my instructors will search this place for your body to try and make sure I killed you. Do you know of a way I could fake your death?"

She looked at him wide-eyed, pushing her long black hair back behind her ears nervously. "I don't... Wait, I think... I might know a way. This gas in the air bubbles up from some kind of pit of boiling liquid. I passed it on my way inside, back the way we came."

Scorp nodded, though he was still looking at the ceiling. There was a large black hole far above, in one of the highest points, that the light from his saber could not seem to penetrate. It was too perfect a circle to be natural. At first he wondered how he could reach it, but then he remembered he was still wearing the prototype Enomeg armor, including its jetpack. He smiled.

"I think we can make this work," he said.

LOCATION: ENOMEG TRAINING ACADEMY BASE

Dark-Dragon paced back and forth anxiously. He stood at the far side of the Cave of Fear now, having left the other Enomeg trainees behind in order to await Saber-Scorpion at the exit. It was taking the boy too long, he thought. What was going on in there? Had he failed?

For the last few weeks, Dark-Dragon had been meticulously planning this final test for his Enomegs. He had studied each one of the potential graduates, learning all of their secrets, trying to discover what they truly feared, both the simple phobias and the deeper ones. Shadow-Cat was afraid of water. Not of being wet, but of great unknown depths, of tiring out and drowning. So her predetermined route through the cave would force her to swim the vast, dark lake. It was a long swim in any case, and even worse in the darkness, with the fear toxin acting on her.

Most of the Enomegs' fears were crystal clear. Barracuda preferred to fight with guns but was no stranger to fighting melee, where he usually prevailed via brute strength. For his test, Dragon had secured possession of two Stage Four Slashrim… a pair of "Trolls." Barracuda would have to fight them both at once, a pair of foes much larger than he, and far, far stronger. Seth relied too much on technology, so he would be allowed none, and must go in completely unarmed. Coyote would endure the same.

Blade-Mantis's fear was one of the hardest to determine. The young Enomeg seemed dauntless, capable of anything. In him, Dark-Dragon saw his true vision of an Enomeg soldier. Mantis was sure of the path he took, sure of his abilities… sure of everything. He was even sure of his faults, which he clearly showed in the Test of Supremacy when Raven beat him. Dragon had considered making him believe he was fighting a treacherous friend, but he had little doubt that if one of his friends did turn traitor, Mantis would not hesitate to declare him his enemy. So the only thing left for him to go with was generic fear. He would try to make Mantis's test as hard as possible, and constantly close off his retreat so he had nowhere to turn. Cobra would face a similar situation, since her fears were also difficult to determine.

Last were Blood-Raven and Saber-Scorpion. Dark-Dragon knew that he would have to make their tests the hardest. Despite his keen sense of satisfaction whenever he saw Mantis pass another test with flying colors and a spirit of joyous loyalty, Dragon still knew that Scorp and Raven were truly the best. Somehow, fate had gifted them with almost superhuman skill, and their training had honed that skill to a razor edge. Raven's only fear was a very simple one: he as afraid to lose. For his final battle, Dragon would face Raven himself. He would hold nothing back. Either he would introduce the boy to defeat or, hopefully, Raven would introduce it to *him*.

For Saber-Scorpion, he knew exactly what to do. In fact, Scorp might have the easiest fear of all to determine. First there was the preference for close-quarters fighting; that one was obvious. But even more than that, Scorp had another problem, one that was very rare these days... He had an acute case of *chivalry*. He always rushed to save the "damsel in distress," and it had made him fail where he might have succeeded in at least three tests against Raven. Twice he saved Shadow-Cat – even though she probably had only been in real trouble on the second occasion – and he had also helped *both* female prisoners escape in the Test of Loyalty.

That was not the very worst of it. Dragon still tried to convince himself that it was not Scorp who had killed Daniel, the trainee they had found burned and hanging from a tree. But it was also hard to believe that it was not. And what could he do about it? Scorp had only this one chance to redeem himself now... and judging by how long he was taking to finish his run through the cave, it was beginning to look like he had failed.

Dark-Dragon let out a long, disappointed sigh.

Finally, his waiting came to an end, as Saber-Scorpion emerged from the mouth of the cave. He looked haggard and terrified... He was soaking with perspiration, his hair was a mess, his face was bleeding in several places, and worst of all, his chest and leg were both covered in wound-sealant foam, meaning his armor had been punctured there. Apparently the gas had more effect on him than Dragon could have anticipated, for he looked completely out of sorts, glancing around as if lost and confused. When he spotted Dark-Dragon, he suddenly rushed at him, stumbling and clawing at the air. Dragon took a step back, and Scorp fell to his knees before him.

"Why?!" the trainee gasped. "Cat... You made me kill her! Made me kill Shadow-Cat! She fell... fell into that *pit*... Why?! Tell me *why!*"

Dark-Dragon quickly guessed what had happened. Apparently the gas had been much stronger than he anticipated, or else Scorp's willpower was weaker than he had been led to believe based on the young man's actions. Apparently, when Scorp faced the prisoner girl he had allowed to escape, the gas made him imagine her as Shadow-Cat.

Dragon reached down and put one hand on Scorp's shoulder. "Listen to me, Saber-Scorpion... Justin... It's going to be okay. You did *not* kill Shadow-Cat. She's fine. She is standing outside the cave entrance right now, waiting for her turn to go inside like you did."

Scorp tried to whisper a question, but he apparently could not even choke it out. He just lay there panting, trying to get his bearings as reality forced its way back in with all the fresh, untainted oxygen.

As if reading his mind, Dark-Dragon said, "Yes, you did kill a real woman in the cave. But it was not Cathryn. It was a prisoner, a convicted criminal – the very same prisoner that you helped to escape in the Trial of Loyalty: Raven's target. She told me what you did that day, how you helped her – a convicted assassin – to escape justice. And now you have rectified that error. You have redeemed yourself, accomplished what *had* to be done. Do you understand?"

When Scorp finally summoned up the strength to look up at his commander, Dark-Dragon almost took a step back in surprise. His face was not one of fear, sadness, or merely exhaustion; it was livid with rage. He was breathing deeply, his teeth bared, trying to struggle to his feet.

"Why… Why?! … Answer me! *WHY?!*"

"Because those were your *orders!* You can't pick and choose your missions, soldier. Bravery and supremacy mean respecting yourself, your own abilities, your own will… but loyalty and honor mean respecting the will of others! If you follow your own set of values above that of your country, then you are no better than the criminal you killed. You did it because that is what you were *ordered* to do. There is no shame in what you did – only honor."

"*Honor*," Scorp spat, as if it were a curse. "Don't hand me another speech about honor. I *know* what that girl did. She confessed her 'crimes' to me: She was used by her assassin father, forced to commit murders by her situation in life, not by any personal desires, and during the course of this she simply learned too much. She learned the names of the Enomegs! Every prisoner you sent us to kill no doubt had a similar story. You wanted them dead not to save Xarkon or keep the peace, but because *they knew too much!* They knew the *truth!*"

Dark-Dragon set his jaw and took a step toward his student, who suddenly leapt to a defensive fighting position. But Dragon remained utterly calm, as unmovable as a stone monument.

"The truth? Son, you can't *handle* the truth! That girl lied to you. She was the one who killed those men, who killed the Xarkonian officer and stole his secrets. There was no 'father,' not even a partner of any kind. She *used* you to spare her life! She played you for a fool!"

Scorp hesitated uncertainly for a second, but then his eyes narrowed. "And how am I to know whether she was lying… or you are?"

"Because *I* cannot lie. I'm not capable of it. Never have been. Ask me any question, and I will either tell you the truth, or refuse to answer."

"Was the ETAB originally designed to study Sarran prisoners?"

Dragon showed no surprise as he nodded in the affirmative. "Yes, it was. Though, as you can see, it has been repurposed."

"Is the Sarran prisoner I spared still alive?"

Dragon blinked. "Yes. Yes, she is."

"Why?"

His face turned to stone. "That, I cannot answer."

Scorp immediately looked away, his every muscle tensing… and then relaxing. Neither of them spoke for a very long time. They stood there for many minutes in silence, Scorp looking at the wall, and Dragon looking at Scorp. Finally, it was Dragon who broke the silence.

"It's over, son," he said, in a soothing voice. "You've completed your missions, all of them. You are now officially Saber-Scorpion…"

"The Enomeg warrior," Scorp whispered hoarsely. He said the name like it was a forlorn fate he was chained to, not something to be desired.

"No," Dragon said, "you are not a warrior; you are a soldier. You have proven that here today. There is a profound difference between warriors and soldiers. Warriors fight out of lust for blood, simply for the thrill of battle and competition, like animals out of control. Mercenaries are warriors; they fight for money, because fighting is simply their way of life – how they make a living. Warriors have no loyalty except to the battle itself. Like warriors, we too are born for fighting, and it's our way of life... but we are different, because we fight for a purpose. We fight with honor and with loyalty, serving a country and a greater cause. We fight to change the world, not simply because it's what we're good at, but because we know we can use our warrior gifts to make a difference... and we do only what *must* be done, *when* it must be done. No more, no less. We are *soldiers*. Do you understand me? That is the difference between a warrior and a soldier."

"I understand you, Sir..."

"*Dragon*," the old soldier said, tentatively placing a hand on the younger Enomeg's shoulder. "You can call me Dragon. We're both Enomegs now. You've survived the final trials; you've more than earned it."

Scorp responded with a limp nod. "Yes... Thank you... Dragon..."

Dragon punched him in the shoulder. "And *your* name... is Century-Sergeant Justin Saber-Scorpion, Enomeg super-soldier of Xarkon."

At these words, Scorp could not help but finally feel a slight glow of self-satisfaction. It was muffled by many conflicting thoughts and feelings, but it was there just the same. Dragon's scarred face wrinkled into a surprisingly kind smile, and he threw his arm around Scorp's shoulders. Then they walked together away from the Cave of Fear. The cave in which, Scorp knew, the young woman he had been sentenced to kill – be she innocent victim or clever assassin – was now hiding... still very much alive.

- CHAPTER SIXTEEN -
SNEAKY AS SUSPICION

Captain Jaleiko looked at the camp around him. He had never expected to be in the center of such a controversy as this. Here he was in a Xarkonian war camp where some of the most powerful people in the galaxy were meeting to discuss the fate of an entire city that was being held hostage by terrorists. It was only one city, yet the fate of all Humanity seemed to be hanging over his head.

On the hill ahead sat *Behemoth Bertha*, the huge mobile headquarters of Zygbar's armed forces. At the foot of that same hill, in a clearing just large enough to allow it, lay the shining *Silver Scepter* like an immense bird at rest. And there on a hill behind loomed the shadow of *Manegarm*, Mars's giant black walker.

And beside Jaleiko, the mere Captain of the Mordark Guard, strode Lucas Mars himself, High Commander of the Armed Forces of Xarkon.

And he was leaving.

"Will you at least tell me where you are going?" Jaleiko asked.

Mars nodded. "Of course. I hide no secrets. I merely have been called upon to attend an Imperial ceremony."

Jaleiko crossed his arms. "The battle may begin when we least expect it, Commander."

"My loyalty is first and foremost to the Emperor of Xarkon. When he calls, I answer. All else comes second."

Jaleiko could certainly understand that. He nodded, and Mars paused suddenly. He signaled for his escort to move on, and the soldiers did not hesitate to abandon him and continue to the transport. Mars's word was law, and they knew well that he could defend himself. To linger after being commanded to leave

213

would show disrespect to their leader, and disrespect, even for reasons of loyalty, was something Mars did not tolerate in the least.

"Jaleiko," Mars said when all the others were gone, "there is something I have been meaning to speak to you about… your Lord Zegaldorph. Do you really know him as well as you think you do?"

Jaleiko's eyes narrowed. "I know that he has always been a good leader, for a Mahlok, and you'd best not try to convince…"

"But do you know his history?" Mars interrupted.

Jaleiko shook his head. To his credit, he did not let his anger show, but right now he was feeling resentful toward Mars. The man was trying to test his loyalty, and that was something he could not abide. But he would accept this test, and he would pass it unwaveringly.

"Then allow me to enlighten you," Mars said. "Zegaldorph has led a life of treachery after treachery. To his people, the Mahlok, loyalty to blood is greater than loyalty to country, ideals, or anything else. And when I say 'blood,' I do not mean family, for the Mahlok will abandon even their direct family for their greater blood. By 'blood,' I mean their species. They believe their species to be superior to all, to be deserving of every glory, much as a Human patriot believes in his country. In most cases, a Mahlok will not leave his people for *anything*."

"But Zegaldorph did," Jaleiko said, undaunted. He already knew these facts.

Mars nodded. "Of course, this is not news to you, though I would advise you to think more deeply on what this… departure must have meant to him. Would you leave your own species, Humanity, to lead a small country on a world inhabited by, perhaps… Slashrim? Why would you even consider such a thing?"

"I wouldn't," Jaleiko responded, "but I'm not a Mahlok. And Humans are not Slashrim."

Mars shrugged. "Ah, but Zegaldorph *is* a Mahlok. And to most Mahlok minds, Humanity is perhaps even *lower* than the Slashrim. So tell me, do you know why he would do that? Why would he betray his own species to live in a Human nation?"

Jaleiko nodded. "Indeed I can. It was for freedom. The Mahlok are an oppressive species…"

"No," Mars said bluntly, "it was not for freedom. Mahlok are free to do anything they please within their empire. It was out of simple *greed*. The Mahlok care little for individual aspirations, preferring instead to see the big picture and think of their species above themselves. Zegaldorph, however, did not. He fled from his people and into Mordark, a place where he could be most safe from them, where he could hide… not be 'free.' And then he used his position to his advantage. Using the innate powers of his species and the mystique that surrounds them to create a cult of personality and fear, Zegaldorph rose through the ranks of your city's government… until he was on top. He gained power not for his people, but for *himself*."

Jaleiko could feel his facial muscles twitching now as the anger built up inside him, despite his best attempts to hide it. He did not try to suppress this righteous indignation, only to conceal it. Anger, after all, was his best defense against Mars's treasonous lies.

"And then," Mars went on, "he began to make the city even worse. Today Mordark takes in more taxes from its oppressed people than ever before. The enormous chasm between rich and poor continues to widen. Zegaldorph ignores the plight of the Humans under his care in favor of gaining riches, as he himself hides behind the great walls of the City Core. Do you know why he came here to Shardasha? To set up a trade deal, even as much as his country needed him back home."

Finally Jaleiko could take it no longer. "I will listen to no more of this, Mars. Your lies and propaganda will not work on me. My loyalty is too strong. If you truly think you understand me, then you should know that."

Mars nodded. "I do. And *that* is why I respect you. It is sad to see such loyalty, pride, and promise wasted on a leader who does not deserve it. Just consider what I've said, Jaleiko. Instead of pushing it aside, think about it. After all, if Zegaldorph's honor cannot stand up to the test of my mere words, then perhaps he truly isn't worthy of your devotion. Goodbye, Captain."

Jaleiko's expression was blank. After a moment he caught himself and responded, "Farewell, Sir."

Mars nodded, turned on his heel, and left. As he stepped into the transport that would carry him to the ETAB, he forced himself not to look back at Jaleiko and see if he could tell what the man was thinking. After all, he could not depend on Jaleiko siding with either him or Zegaldorph; he had to be prepared for either one. If he could convince Jaleiko to take his side before the death of Zegaldorph, then the battle afterward, with the pompous fools in CONON, would be so much easier. But as for the battle at hand, there was only one thing that would sway it: the Enomegs.

And he was going now to graduate them… and bring them at last to their first real mission.

Location: Shardasha, Xarkon

Grimm the Third surveyed the situation. Before him was the Mordark Embassy, one of the tallest towers in the city, no doubt filled with Zegaldorph's personal guards. All around it were slightly smaller buildings, no doubt filled with Xarkonian troops. And in the surrounding streets, a few small convoys of heavy tanks, hoverbikes, and light strike craft of Xarkonian, Zygbari, and various retired designs, were constantly on patrol… no doubt military soldiers pretending to be terrorists. Actually, Three thought, they *were* terrorists. Governments were often guilty of terrorizing their own people, he mused, but they seldom got the title that went along with it. Well, *he* wouldn't hesitate to give it to them.

"Ultraviolet," Three grunted into his commlink, "this place is locked down tighter than a…"

"Yeah, I know, a Mahlok's lips," came the response. "Honestly, Infrared, I'm surprised you have such a repertoire of sayings. One wouldn't think so from your relatively short history as a clone."

"Musta come with the programmin'," Three replied grumpily. "Look, just help me past this mess, will ya, woman?"

"You mean you can't get past them yourself? I thought this was your favorite part of the whole mission."

"If you told me I could start dishin' out random death and destruction, then yeah, I might be able to blow my way past 'em, along with maybe takin' out half the city. But you said we're tryin' to avoid detection."

"Correct. Despite your battle prowess, Infrared, it would not be wise to start a fight here. This is the most heavily-guarded region of Shardasha, and the results of a major battle here would not end well for you, no matter how powerful you think you are."

"Whatever. That's why I'm askin' you: *What. Do. I. Do?*"

Spectra blew out a sigh. "I do have a plan, but you won't like it. Maybe I should get our companion to explain it to you. Darkness, how are things on your end?"

"Smelly," Lashnar hissed back. "What do you expect in the sewers? More guards than I expected though… mostly Crownies still in uniform. But it's not as bad as above. I think we can make it,"

Three snorted. "The sewers? You *know* they're expectin' that. That's why there's so many guards down there. Probably plenty of traps too. Not to mention the filth."

"Oh, don't tell me you're scared of getting dirty, Red."

Three gave a low laugh. "No, I always thought that was *you.*"

"I don't *get* dirty. I'm too good for that. Now quit whining and come to my position. I'll see to it that my employers increase your payment by five percent for this little ordeal. Sound good?"

Grimm III shook his head, though he knew no one could see him. "Fine, fine. I'm on my way."

"I'll be waiting," Spectra replied. "See you in the sewer."

LOCATION: ENOMEG TRAINING ACADEMY BASE, LOWER TUNNELS

Saber-Scorpion, clad once again in his sleeveless black training outfit, quickly reached up and slid the tile of his bathroom floor back into position before descending the long, dark ladder. The girl whose life he had spared was most likely hungry, terrified, and exhausted. Scorp had already prepared a pack of rations for her. They were supposed to be for him, but he could go without. Besides, the longer he left her down there in that tunnel, the more likely she was to be found by someone. Perhaps even Shadow-Cat, who apparently frequented the tunnels more than anyone.

And Cat had killed her target in the Trial of Loyalty. She wouldn't hesitate to kill this one either.

Scorp found Larisa almost exactly as he had left her, but now she was sound asleep. He watched her for a few seconds, lying there on her side, her chest rising and falling. He noticed that she had unzipped her tight black leather jacket about half-way down, and apparently she was wearing nothing beneath it. An obvious attempt to secure his fascination, perhaps?

He had to admit there was something alluring about this young woman, but there was something... dark about her as well. Could what Dark-Dragon had said about her be true? Was she the real assassin?

"Larisa..." he said softly.

She looked up at him, her catlike eyes immediately alert.

"You didn't even stop to shave," she said amusedly.

He rubbed his face and frowned. Suddenly he decided that he was seriously at risk of falling in love with the first girl who didn't mind that fact.

"Come on," he said. "I have to get you out of here before someone comes down here and finds you."

She shook her head and got up. All sense of fear and helplessness seemed to have fled from her. In fact, she looked ready to fight... ready to kill. Only then, when she threw her long hair over her shoulder to straighten it, did he notice the red outline of a large hourglass shape on the back of her black leather jacket... like a black widow spider. Why was she dressed in attire like that anyway?

"So I suppose you have a plan for getting me out?" she asked, her head cocked to one side.

"We'll go back through my room, head for the hangar bay, pick up a pair of Hornets, and make our exit to the surface. Stay behind me, but keep hidden. If anyone spots us, this could get messy."

She grinned mischievously. "I'm sure you're very eager to take me back to your room, but doesn't one of these pipes probably lead somewhere closer to the hangar bay than just your bunk?"

Scorp raised an eyebrow. "Probably, but we don't have time to search them right now."

Larisa shrugged. "What do you think I was doing down here while I was waiting for you? Just sitting around? That one leads to a repair workshop, probably near some kind of hangar, if I'm guessing right."

He shook his head. "You weren't really asleep when I came in here, were you?"

She reached down to where she had been lying and picked up her sniper rifle. "Nope. Now come on, let's get out of here."

Scorp pointed to the weapon. "That's an unusual rifle."

Larisa's eyes widened, and she patted the barrel. "Yeah, I'm surprised your Crownie friends let me keep it."

"I don't recognize the type..."

"There is no *type*. It's heavily customized. The main body is Xarkonian, the barrel and stock Victorian, the scope Yavakarese... and this retractable blazer bayonet is Zygbari, developed for their Highlanders. My... father called it 'the Black Widowmaker.' Anyway, we should get moving."

With that, she turned and dove headfirst into the tunnel that she claimed led to the repair bay. Scorp followed behind her. He winced and hissed in pain as he tried to contort himself into the narrow tunnel.

"You alright?" Larisa asked.

"Not really," Scorp grunted. "I got stabbed, after all. Right here."

"Sorry about that. At least I didn't kill you though."

"Yeah," he muttered as they crawled on. "Nice outfit, by the way. I assume my 'Crownie friends' let you keep that as well?"

"Admiring the view?" she said slyly, glancing back at him.

"Actually, I mainly wanted to ask you about the red hourglass shape on the back of your jacket."

"Red is nature's danger color. Warns people to stay away."

"So I assume your name as a black-clad assassin was 'Black Widow' or something. Personally I would shed that mantle. Leave your old life of darkness behind..."

"Hmm-hmm," Larisa chuckled, "so you're already asking me to take off my clothes?"

Scorp shook his head. "Well, I see that your frightened attitude seems to have disappeared, along with the *innocent* one."

As Larisa put her hand on the bottom rung of the ladder leading up to the main floor, she looked back at him and said, "Well, it helps that a bunch of *black-clad assassins* are no longer trying to kill me."

Scorp gave no reply. Both of them knew that it would be safer to remain silent the rest of the way. When they reached the top, they found the room mercifully deserted. Scorp checked to make sure the way was clear, and then he led Larisa out into the hangar.

He saw her eyes go wide and her lips give a silent whistle as she scanned the rows of shining Hornet hoverbikes all around them. Hornets were originally racing bikes, some of the fastest in Human space, but Xarkon had converted them to military use, attaching machine guns and sleek armor plating. But Scorp led her past the Hornets to the corner of the hangar, where several hoverbikes were located that looked like they had just come out of a junkyard. He climbed atop one of these and told her to hold on behind him. She looked disappointed about the chosen vehicle, but hopped on anyway. It was a tight fit, and Scorp could feel Larisa's breath on his neck as she looked over his shoulder.

The vehicle's engine was almost entirely silent as Scorp drove to the quick vehicle exit ramp. The headlights reflected off the slick, dark metal walls as they went, the ramp spiraling upward to the larger of the two secret exits on the surface. The Enomegs went on private joyrides a lot, so there was little chance of anyone bothering them. Scorp opened the hangar doors, and they drove out into the open night.

As they came to a stop in the moonlit field, Larisa said, "I can see why no one would miss this bike, but can you be sure they aren't tracking it?"

Scorp looked slightly offended. "Actually, I built this bike myself, as a hobby. It's dependable. You heard how quiet the engine was."

She smiled. "Sorry. Didn't mean to offend you. It really rides quite well... for a piece of junk."

He shrugged. "Well, I was planning to paint it later, but I suppose you'll draw less attention this way. But no, there are no bugs. I scanned it right after I got back."

Larisa nodded. "Thanks."

She looked almost ready to take off into the night, but Scorp was not yet finished with her. He switched off the bike's engine and turned to the side to better face her. She saw the look on his face and slid back a bit.

"You don't get to go just yet. I have a few questions first. For starters, what's your full name? Your *real* full name?"

"Any chance I can get you to tell me *yours*?"

"If only I knew it… All I know is Justin Saber-Scorpion."

She looked thoughtful. "Justin… Justin… You know, I think your middle name was Randolph."

He knew he must have turned white as a sheet at this comment. "But you… don't remember my *last* name?"

Larisa shrugged. "Sorry. Really, I am."

Scorp blew out a sigh. "Don't worry about it."

"As for my name, well, I go by many. So many that I don't even quite know the 'real' one, if I even have one. Some in Xarkon know me as Larisa Sharapova. But most just call me Lisa Sharp."

Scorp nodded, not sure how to proceed. He was trying to get her to slip up and reveal the truth, or perhaps even reveal it on her own. That is, if what Dark-Dragon had said really was true. He hoped it was not.

"I see," he said. "So do you know where you'll go?"

"I… think I know a place. I've been avoiding it for years, but I guess now it's all I have left to turn to."

"Where?"

She looked up at him and cocked an eyebrow. "You think I'd say?"

"Fine, don't tell me then," he replied, and he pointed to a control panel on the bike. "This map should help you find it, wherever it is."

There was a moment of silence as they sat there on the bike together, under the light of Terra Nova's moons.

"So…" Scorp said at length, "do you have anything else to say?"

She put on an alluring expression, with her lashes half-closed and lips curled in a sly smile, and then slid closer and put an arm around him.

"And what do you *want* me to say?"

"Anything that you feel you should tell me…"

"Oh, quit playing obtuse!"

Suddenly she put a hand around the back of his head and gave him a long, slow kiss. Scorp tried to convince himself that he hadn't been looking forward to something like that… and that he wasn't being played for a fool.

After a moment, she drew back and ran her fingers through his hair. "I hope we meet again."

Scorp smiled wistfully. "You *should* be hoping the opposite."

With a sudden determination, Scorp slid off the bike. Perhaps she was still lying to him, perhaps not. He was not going to interrogate her. Perhaps it was because he really *couldn't* handle the truth, as Dragon had said. In any case, Lisa Sharp took immediate advantage of the situation, sliding forward to take the controls. Scorp took a step back as she revved the engine, looking disappointed at the low buzz that was her reward. Just as she looked about to take off, she glanced back at him.

"Okay, since you asked nicely…" she said. "I was an orphan. Never even knew my father. I grew up in the streets of Mordark, learning to take care of myself. Have you ever been to Mordark? And I don't mean Zegaldorph's *palaces* in the City Core. I mean the *slums*, outside the wall. Where the air is stale and the people staler. The only two emotions one finds there are sadness and satisfaction – one comes from not having enough money, the other from having more than enough. It's a cold place to grow up, but it taught me how to survive."

"And how to fight," Scorp said, dreading what was coming next.

"Yes. It was either that or become a plaything to be bought and sold like other girls. As an assassin, I was in control. So yes, it wasn't my father who killed the Xarkon officer and found that list of names… It was me."

"I knew it. You've just been using me… *seducing* me."

She let out a laugh. "Using you? Seducing you? Hardly. I didn't need to do a thing. You did it all yourself! With most men I'd at least have had to talk in a lower voice, show a bit more skin, that sort of thing… but with you, I just had to be female. In case you haven't noticed, it comes pretty naturally."

"You seemed to resort to the other in the end."

She smiled. "Maybe it's because I started to like you."

Scorp shook his head. "But you were still using me from the beginning. You knew the 'innocence' act would win me over the quickest."

"The quickest way to a man's heart," she said, patting her rifle, "is through his chest. Or back, if you prefer. I usually do. But no, I didn't seduce you, and I never even thought about killing you. Don't kill *yourself* over it either. We're both orphans, forced to kill or be killed, to fight for survival our whole life. Think about it. We're not so different, you and me."

"*No,*" Scorp said adamantly. "There's a difference. You're an assassin, a mercenary, just a warrior… I am a soldier."

"Are you?"

That was her last question, and then she was gone. The hoverbike's engines flared bright orange, leaving a short glowing trail behind as she sped off, before the glow died back down and disappeared completely. Scorp stood there for a long time, even after her hoverbike had disappeared over the distant hills of waving grass.

Throughout his training, it seemed that his feelings were constantly shifting between satisfaction and regret at the various actions he had taken. Apparently they had finally grown tired of it, and even the fact that she truly was an assassin could not sting him like he thought it should have. The satisfaction of saving her and following his own path mingled with the ache of his disloyalty and her revelation, and then they seemed to cancel each other out, leaving nothing but numbness… just a vague, hollow feeling.

Then a thought entered Scorp's mind that had never before reared its ugly head. He thought, only for a brief second, as he remembered her bike speeding off to wherever she willed it to go… that he envied her. He envied her freedom. Then years of training squelched these treacherous thoughts, and he turned back toward the base.

LOCATION: SHARDASHA SEWERS

There was a resounding splash as Grimm III landed feet-first in a deep basin of water. He came up spitting and looked around to find himself in a walled-off holding tank for the precipitation that ran through the storm drain above… the drain he had just crawled through. Coughing and sputtering, he swam toward the nearest tunnel opening he saw in the wall and pulled himself up. There was only a small trickle of water in the bottom of the main pipes, and Spectra was standing there waiting for him. She was as dry as the deserts of Zygbar, Three noted.

"Taking a swim?" she asked.

"I didn't know it was deep," Three replied, shaking himself off, deliberately showering her in drain-water. "Thought it was just a shallow pipe. Damn, it stinks down here. I wish I could turn off my olfactory sensors. Heh."

Three had shed his coat before entering the tunnels, so he was now wearing only his bright red mesh outfit and lightweight armor plating. It was made to resemble bones and muscle, he said, though Spectra was not quite sure how much it succeeded in that. Right now the nanomesh was set to black instead of red, to blend in with the darkness. Without his trench coat, the veritable arsenal that Three carried was fully visible… the wide array of shotgun shells in two bandoliers across his chest, with more shells strapped along one leg… the heavy pistol strapped to the other, and the sawed-off shotgun and blazer knife in sheaths on either side of his torso… and finally, the Scatterstar shotgun slung over one shoulder.

Spectra, on the other hand, was still in her black and violet "Spectral Glove," a custom-tailored, form-fitting nanomesh outfit that covered all of her body except a thin slit for her eyes and a hole on the back of her head for her long, shining black ponytail. She carried a small backpack and some gear on a belt, but was apparently unarmed except for a short, thin sword sheathed on the small of her back and her folded-up crossbow.

Then Lashnar joined them, carrying his – *her* – enormous Slashrim machine gun with its axe-head bayonet. Beyond a few belts of ammo and other weapons, she wore nothing. Her green eyes almost seemed to glow in the darkness, although in fact they were only reflecting the dim light filtering in from above. The spines along her back almost scraped the low ceiling.

"I can barely move around in here," she growled, her voice reverberating off the walls, "but I'm right behind you."

Spectra nodded. "Then let's move."

She took a pair of complex-looking goggles off her belt and slipped them over her head, tying her hair up in the strap. The tunnels became bathed in an eerie green light, and a map appeared on her HUD, hovering before her eyes. She then proceeded through the tunnels, with Grimm III and Lashnar following behind. It was quite a hike before they reached the area under the streets around Zegaldorph's tower.

"The traps will begin now," she said, "so switch your vision modes, Erik, to check for them. Lashnar, you just cover our rear and follow our lead. Ah, wait. I see some beams on infrared already."

Grimm III looked down. "What? On me?"

"Don't be silly. Watch."

With that, she reached into a pouch on her belt and drew out a single ball the size of a pinball. She tossed it into the tunnel, and out shot a cloud of thick smoke. One by one, the red laser-lights became visible… thin beams spanning the tunnel from one wall to the other. They crisscrossed the tunnel in a complex fashion, obviously placed in an attempt to be impassable.

"Huh," Spectra huffed, "how primitive. They might as well be using spike-filled pits or rolling logs. This is positively medieval!"

Grimm III gave a low laugh. "Sometimes when technology won't cut it, the best thing to do is get medieval."

"Well," Spectra said, "it's not *really* medieval. And in any case, it should be quite easy to cross. At least, *I* can make it. Can you?"

Three nodded. "Shouldn't be too hard. But there's no way Lashnar could fit."

"I'll stay behind and cover the entrance," the Slashrim growled. "I'm no good at sneaking anyway."

"Alright," Spectra replied, "you go back to the surface and keep an eye on the goings-on outside. Keep in touch and let us know if you see anything. As for you, Erik, just watch me and learn."

Spectra stepped easily over the first tripwire-positioned beam. Then she danced around the next two, which were crossed in an X-shape, and crawled under the next, proceeding in this way with surprising rapidity. The way she slithered beneath the lowest ones seemed like a feat only an octopus could accomplish. Grimm III watched all of her wriggling with keen interest.

Without even looking back, she said, "You can quit gawking and follow me now."

Three knew she was not in the mood for play at the moment, so he merely nodded and stepped over the first beam. Some may have thought the muscular mercenary unable to follow in the footsteps of his lithe female companion, but Three was not really all that large himself, and he was able to slink through the beams with impressive dexterity.

"And just think," Spectra said, sounding quite invigorated as she continued her gymnastics, "this is only a border crossing. We can expect it to get much worse as we go deeper into guarded territory."

"How much of this big-ass pipe is under here?"

"Oh, quite a bit. This is the drain system for the entire city, and storms on the eastern coast of Xarkon can get quite bad. The tunnels have to be big to prevent flooding."

"And to take care of the sewage, since the people of Xarkon are so full of –"

"Shhh! It's a guard."

They both paused, Three hanging quite awkwardly on one foot as he stepped over another beam. Behind them, they saw an armed Xarkonian soldier round the bend. He had his weapon drawn and was looking and listening intently. They were in quite a fix: one wrong movement and the beams would detect them, but if they stood still, the guard would surely spot them. Spectra carefully reached for her crossbow… and then a hiss echoed down the corridor, causing the Xarkonian to pause and look back. There was an echoing clink, and he walked off to investigate.

In their ears, the two infiltrators heard Lashnar's voice say, "I've drawn him off. Are you sure I can't just kill him?"

"I'd prefer you didn't," Spectra responded. "The Xarkonians will notice if one of their guards doesn't report in."

"Yeah, now get outta here, Lash," Three said. "If they spot you this whole place'll go on high alert."

There was no response. Perhaps the Slashrim had already reached the surface, and the signal wouldn't reach. As Grimm III and Spectra finally made it to the other side, they could only hope that was the case. The pipe split up ahead, and quiet footsteps could be heard echoing down one tunnel. Spectra held up three fingers – three guards in this patrol. They decided to do the simple thing and merely avoid them by going down the other tunnel. After a few minutes they had the guards well behind them.

"Stop," Three said, "I smell explosives."

"You *smell* them?"

Three nodded. "Yeah, I do. Plastic explosives. I can pick 'em out even in this stench."

"I see them now," Spectra said, and she moved toward a blob of something grey that almost blended in with the other gunk at the bottom and sides of the pipe. She pointed to the detonator stuck in one side of it.

"They must be remotely activated," she said. "I don't see a trigger mechanism. Maybe the guards meant to use them to seal the tunnel."

Three put a hand on her shoulder. "Speaking of guards…"

Spectra turned. She could hear them now as well. They were still only walking their patrol at a calm pace, but they were starting to catch up. Quickly, Spectra pulled a device from her belt and mashed it directly into the plastic explosives. Then they set off at a run. When they reached another bend in the pipe, Spectra turned to look back. She stood and waited until the guards were right on top of the explosives, then activated the device she had planted.

The explosion shook the whole tunnel and echoed away in both directions, probably for miles, Three thought. Without another word, the two of them took off at a run down the pipe.

They continued like this for quite a while, and Grimm III continued to marvel at the extensive size of the pipe network. By watching the map on her HUD, Spectra could tell that they were almost directly beneath Zegaldorph's tower. After the next bend, Grimm III spotted a bright light. Removing their night-vision, they looked ahead to see an especially large drain covering at the end of the next stretch.

"The light at the end of the tunnel," Three commented.

"Let's hope it's not an approaching train," Spectra added.

Still, they were assaulted by no traps or guards as they made their way toward the opening. When they were directly under it, they stopped and looked up. Through the grate above them, they saw a room… the interior of some kind of garage. Three looked at Spectra and shrugged.

And then the trap sprang.

Neither of them let out a scream of terror or even surprise – though Spectra did gasp – as the floor suddenly slid out from under their feet. They plummeted into a deep, square basin hidden under the piping, and even as they splashed into the water at the bottom, the trap door above them closed again, surrounding them with impenetrable darkness. Even their night vision was no use in such utter black.

A few choice swear-words from Grimm III echoed through the small room as he swam toward Spectra. He gripped her arm. "You alright?"

"I'm fine, thanks," she said. "I can swim, Erik."

"I hope you can swim good," he said, "'cause do you feel that?"

"The water level seems to be rising," she said, with an invisible nod.

Another tidbit of Three's limitless repertoire of vulgar language echoed off the walls as they rose slowly higher, treading water. They both felt along the sides of the walls the whole way, searching for a way out.

"Lashnar!" Three shouted into his commlink. "Lashnar, respond! We could use a bit o' help here!"

"Will you be quiet?" Spectra hissed. "There's no way the signal could get through all this piping."

"Then what am I *supposed* to do?"

"Explosives?" Spectra ventured.

"Too risky in these quarters. Wait, I can feel the roof now."

The room suddenly lit up as Spectra ignited the glowing blazer shield on her short sword. She held it against the metal above them, but it had little effect. Three grunted. Then he placed one hand against the trap door and pulled the other one back for a punch. When his knuckles struck the metal, a deep echo resounded throughout the room.

It was followed by yet another curse.

"Must you make such a fuss?" Spectra said.

"If you've got any other ideas," Three replied, preparing for another punch, "go ahead and try 'em."

She blew out a sigh and began feeling around on her belt, thinking hard. Then the pipe rang with another blow of Grimm's fist, and he smiled at the slight dent he made. His smile was cut off as the area suddenly went dark – Spectra's energy sword had been submerged. She switched it off and sheathed it, and out rang another blow, followed by another curse from Three.

"Is this medieval enough for ya?" he asked.

Spectra didn't reply; she just continued treading water, holding her head back to take a last gasping breath of air from the rapidly-shrinking pocket there.

Then the water reached the top.

- CHAPTER SEVENTEEN -
TWILIGHT RENDEZVOUS

"Today's the big day," said the Xarkonian Spec-Ops corporal, with slight but duly noted sarcasm.

Saber-Scorpion gave a short laugh. *The big day.* That was the understatement of the century. These Spec-Ops soldiers who had been lingering about in the ETAB in preparation for Mars's arrival seemed resentful of the Enomegs, whom they probably saw as their replacements. And the High Commander certainly had not come to personally graduate them when they had completed *their* training.

Of course, Special Operations training was rigorous, but nothing compared to the life of an Enomeg. It was speculated by the ETAB instructors that the Enomegs might actually never suffer from extreme battlefield trauma or post-traumatic stress disorder, since their entire *lives* had been a battlefield. From what Scorp had seen, this usually held true. Many Enomegs viewed war as one big game, one big test they had to pass.

Except, apparently, for him.

"They're waiting for you in the VR room," the corporal said, motioning down the hall.

Scorp stepped through the doors with the overwhelming feeling that he was stepping into a different world. The simulation was breathtaking. They were in what appeared to be an ancient temple made of shining black marble. Carved into recesses on all sides of the room were statues of the past Emperors of Xarkon. Empress Skye had the foremost position, a golden statue at the very opposite side of the room. Her arms were outspread, and her beautiful, lifelike face shone down on those assembled. Depicted in tiles on the floor was a golden Crown of Xarkon, with red gems embedded all around.

Eight stone pedestals were positioned in a circle near the middle of the room, on which lay six suits of shining crimson Enomeg armor... and two ebony ones. Scorp's heart skipped a beat. *Two* black exoskeletons? *Why?*

Once Scorp took his place, all of the graduating trainees were there, standing tall and proud, fists on their hearts, facing toward Dark-Dragon and Lucas Mars. Dragon was almost dwarfed by the towering High Commander, but his battle-worn face and shining onyx armor made up for it. At last, Mars spoke.

"You may be at ease," he said, his deep voice somehow reverberating off the onyx walls of the temple, holograms though they were. "I am, as you know, Lucas Augustus Mars, High Commander of the Armed Forces of Xarkon. I'm here to welcome you once and for all into the Xarkon military, where you will spend the rest of your careers as soldiers. You have already done much in the service of Xarkon, but all of that has been mere preparation for what lies ahead. For your every mission, you will be required to go above and beyond the call of duty. This is what makes you Enomeg soldiers."

Dark-Dragon now picked up his queue. "Remember that word: *soldiers*. For that is what you are, what you were born and trained to be. You are not mercenaries, not assassins, not warriors... all of these men are fighters, but they fight for money, reputation, the thrill of battle, or merely for their lives. You, as soldiers, serve a higher calling... an immortal cause, the cause of your country: Xarkon. The term 'super-soldiers' is nothing but an extension of what you truly are. You are soldiers. Remember it.

"The suits of Enomeg armor before you have been specifically designed for your own personal use. When connected with the nanofiber mesh body gloves you now wear, they form an almost living exoskeleton around you. They will augment your strength and speed and heighten your senses, all while still allowing for freedom of movement. But you are men, not machines, and you must never come to rely on these devices too heavily. For to do so, again, is to lose sight of what you truly are. These suits are mere tools. Give them to the average soldier and he would wear them with pride, perhaps accomplish great deeds... before being cut down due to his overconfidence and lack of training. As Enomegs, you will not succumb to this."

Dragon's own suit of ebony Enomeg armor shone in the light, its reflections even brighter than those on the walls of onyx behind him, as he turned to face the Enomeg graduates one by one. His expression was stern, but in his eyes was kindness and satisfaction, even joy. The Enomegs were his children, and today he was filled with pride.

"Tanya," Dark-Dragon said, "you are now Silent-Cobra. Step forward and don your armor."

Living up to her codename, Cobra nodded silently, took a few stiff steps forward, and picked up her first gauntlet. For a second, only a second, a smile flashed on her lips and in her keen eyes. It was more emotion than most had ever seen her show.

"Vincent, you are now Magnum-Coyote."

Coyote showed a much wider smile of satisfaction as he strutted forward and lifted the first piece of armor. He slammed his hand into the gauntlet with satisfaction, flexing his fingers, his eyes so lit up that they were almost aflame.

"Seth, you are now Electric-Eel."

Seth's face wore an expression of sheer awe as he took a few tentative steps toward the pedestal. As he moved, he glanced up at the towering golden statue of Empress Skye and looked as if he wanted to drop to one knee in reverence.

"Kade, you are now Gun-Barracuda."

Kade ran a hand over his slick head and took two long strides toward the table. Scorp was surprised that he seemed to be almost nervous. Taking a deep breath, he lifted the first piece of armor.

"Cathryn, you are now Shadow-Cat."

Scorp was glad to see the clear expression of joy in Cat's eyes as she stepped up to the pedestal, her footsteps utterly silent as always. She smiled, bit her lip, and reached gingerly for the first gauntlet.

"Lee, you are now Blade-Mantis."

Somehow, Lee showed even less emotion than Tanya had. It was amazing, Scorp thought, how he could be so casual in personal situations, even when on a mission, but whenever ceremony was called for, he showed only the most absolute discipline. Lee took a few measured steps forward as if marching, and then he lifted his helmet, gazing at it as if it were a holy relic.

"Justin, you are now Saber-Scorpion."

While watching the others, Scorp had wondered how his own reaction would appear. But now that the moment had come, he hardly thought about it. In truth, his expression was as emotionless as Lee's as he stepped up to the platform, though beneath the exterior waged a war of feelings. There was pride at his achievement, joy at finally accomplishing his goal… but there was also regret at what he had done to get here, and even a sense of unworthiness as a result. And finally, smallest of all, was a nagging feeling of doubt, as if this might not truly be what he wanted.

But when he picked up his black and blood-red Enomeg helmet, felt its weight, the weight of all the technology and power built inside… when he turned it over in his hands and stared into the intimidating, thin visor and shining faceplate… then all his regrets, fears, and doubts fled before it, as if too frightened to show themselves. Pride overrode them all, and he suddenly had the strange feeling that he was staring face to face with himself. This was his new face. Behind this helmet he could hide the mistakes of his past and become what he was truly meant to be.

Or at least, so it seemed at that moment.

"And finally… Luke, you are now Blood-Raven."

A thin smile of satisfaction spread over Luke's face as he took three carefully measured steps toward the pedestal. He stood straight, tall, and proud, as he fitted on each Star-talon emitter glove, one at a time. He took no care to conceal his pride and self-satisfaction.

While they were donning their suits, High Commander Mars said, "You may notice that two of the suits, both Blood-Raven's and Saber-Scorpion's, are black. After reviewing the results of the tests and other exercises, the rest of High Command and I have decided to overrule the decision made by the instructors. Raven and Scorpion have both given excellent performances throughout their training, and thus, instead of only one Enomeg Commander, there will be two."

Now Scorp could barely conceal his pride, and he looked across at Raven with what could only have been equally smug self-satisfaction. Raven squinted back at him, his jaw tight, trying – and failing – to conceal the outrage he now felt. Again Scorp was struck by how much similarity his face bore to that of High Commander Mars. With the two of them standing together in this room, the resemblance was almost uncanny. And then, in that very instant, Mars confirmed his suspicions.

He turned to Raven and said, "Congratulations... my son."

Normally a comment like this would not have caught their attention, since Dark-Dragon referred to them as his sons and daughters quite often, but Mars's tone, something in the way he said "my son" froze all of them solid. Even Raven merely stared, his mouth open slightly, his indignation at Scorp for having achieved the same rank as he suddenly forgotten.

"Yes, Raven," Mars said, "your real name is Lucas Augustus Mars II. Nearly two decades ago you were born to my wife, Gwyneth, only hours before she passed from this world. And as she died, I swore that I would give you the best care that Xarkon had to offer, as well as the best teaching and training. In short, I put you in the Enomeg program. There were times I almost regretted it, but seeing you here now, the best of the best... No father could be more proud of his son."

Everyone in the room save Dark-Dragon and Mars stood dumbfounded. Raven's chest rose and fell, and his eyes wandered. Scorp had never before seen him like this; he would have expected his pride to increase tenfold, but he seemed almost delirious. What could he be feeling now? Astonishment at discovering that the High Commander was his father? Or anger that Mars had subjected him to this life, had abandoned him to be raised by the military, away from any real family? Or simply that he had kept the secret from him? For the first time, Scorp felt the slightest bit of sympathy for the young man who had declared himself his rival.

Still unsure of how to react, Raven glanced at Dark-Dragon, whose expression was as stone. He only nodded once to the boy. After what seemed several minutes, Raven finally turned to Mars and nodded.

"Thank you... Father," he said, his voice slightly hoarse. He swallowed.

"Do not thank me," said High Commander Mars, "for I had little to do with it. You are the only one who deserves credit for this. Now... don your helmets and go get used to your new armor. Soon, *very* soon, you will get to test it out on the field. Your country needs you. Be prepared."

Saber-Scorpion looked around at the new, metallic faces of his comrades as they each donned their personalized Enomeg helmets. Then he twirled his own helmet over in his hands, and slid it over his head.

LOCATION: CAMP RAGNAR

Nick Wolf grabbed the edge of the table and hefted it into the air, tossing it over the Xarkonian soldier's head, so that it nearly tore a hole in the side of the tent. The soldier leapt to his feet and began to reach for his gun.

"You cheated!" Nick shouted, pointing an accusing finger at the soldier. "I thought you Crown-polishers never cheated!"

"I did not *cheat!*" retorted the soldier. "And would you keep your voice down? We're not *supposed* to be gambling at all!"

"Then hand over my sixty crowns and we'll call it a day…"

The Xarkonian threw his hands up in the air and stormed out of the tent. Nick Wolf rushed to follow the soldier… and ran directly into a dozen of them, all standing outside waiting for him. Nick merely laughed, his white teeth gleaming behind his thick yellow beard, and pushed up the sleeves of his stolen Xarkon uniform. Bolstered by the presence of his comrades, the Xarkonian gambler immediately socked Nick in the gut.

Nick hardly seemed to feel it. His return punch, however – a hard left at the Xarkonian's face – sent his opponent sprawling. Two of the other soldiers then jumped in, grabbing Nick's arms and trying to hold him while a third approached, holding a steel rod. Using the two men on either side of him for support, Nick leapt up and gave the one armed with the rod a two-legged kick, knocking him on top of the gambler, who was just trying to get up. Then Nick landed back on his feet and, giving a roar, swung both his arms together, sending the men holding them flying into each other.

It did not take long for a full-blown riot to ensue, with the disguised mercs emerging from their tents to help their commander, and more and more Xarkonians, already enraged that the mercenaries were allowed there at all, eagerly joining in to beat them back.

Then High General Jacob Black arrived. He drew his sidearm and fired once into the air, scattering the crowd. One drunken merc stumbled toward him, only to receive a sharp, impeccably aimed kick to the throat, sending him to the earth sputtering and wheezing. Black scowled through his beard at the congregation, inviting another to challenge him. Then he nodded in the direction of Rick Radcliff's *Silver Scepter*, which still sat idle a short distance off from the fight, behind one row of tents.

"I want you all to know," Black said, "that you're embarrassing all of Xarkon. Mars would be… disappointed."

No further threats were forthcoming, and none were needed. Their heads bowed in shame, the Xarkonian soldiers began to file back to their posts, as did the disguised mercenaries, until only Nick and Black remained.

The General approached the Warlord with a cold look on his face. "I want you and your men *out* of this camp by tomorrow, at the latest. Got it?"

Nick wiped a bit of blood off his lip and nodded. "Aye, Gen'ral."

There was no use in arguing his case. Especially since he could see that he was being watched. The young Victorian they called Ryan was standing between two tents not far away, staring at him intently. Nick coughed slightly and tried to look indifferent as he returned Ryan's stare and began drinking from his canteen. Ryan eventually looked away, but something in his eyes told Nick that the kid had spotted something. Then, after a few moments, his suspicions were confirmed when Ryan turned about on his heel and marched back into the *Silver Scepter*, shutting the door behind him.

Nick "the Werewolf" Wolf was a wanted man in Victory, since he had betrayed the nation to join first one and then another company of mercenaries. Luckily, he had been a clean-shaven and skinny young lad back then, and being as hairy and muscular as he was now, with his thick blond beard, he was virtually unrecognizable. Or at least, so he thought. Apparently Ryan was familiar with his history… familiar enough that he may have seen past the disguise of time. Either that, or he was just surprised to see any Xarkon soldier looking so unkempt.

Nick cursed under his breath as he stood up, threw back the last contents of the canteen, and exhaled with satisfaction after the fiery liquid had made its way down his throat. It was, after all, most certainly not water. Putting the cap back on the canteen and slinging it back over his shoulder, he marched off to find Jade.

LOCATION: SILVER SCEPTER CONTROL ROOM

"Ryan," Rick Radcliff said as the sergeant re-entered his ship, "I thought I said we were done discussing this. Your promotion was necessary. The other soldiers will respect it –"

"It's not that, sir," Ryan said. "I think I just saw someone…"

"Who?"

"Are you familiar with the name Niklas Wolff, sir?"

Rick swiveled his chair about to face him.

"The one they call Werewolf?" he said. "Yes. Former Lance-Corporal Nick Wolf left Victory at a *very* young age along with many members of his Special Forces unit to join up with the Highlander Guerillas in Zygbar. I hear they're now part of Zygbar's regular army, the traitors… They call them the 'High Desert Division.' After that, Wolf was rumored to have joined up with Grimm's Mercenary Army. I'm pretty sure this rumor is true, though our intel on Grimm's organization is surprisingly poor. I'm actually working on setting up a spy… one of your former colleagues in the Immortal Soldier project, as a matter of fact: Odysseus."

Ryan nodded. "Yes, Ethan. I remember him. But, sir… I think Nick Wolf is here, disguised as a soldier of Xarkon."

Rick frowned. "You mean that fellow with the ridiculous beard and hair? I actually asked Mars about him, and he said the soldier was just a rather alcoholic squad leader – said he's allowed some extra freedoms because of his effectiveness in battle. Personally, I had my doubts about that, since it doesn't sound like Mars to me… but what makes you think he's Wolf, of all people?"

Ryan shrugged. "Because he looks like him. I could see it in his eyes, and the shape of his brow and nose."

Rick's eyebrows went up. "Really? I must admit, if one of my other soldiers had said this I probably wouldn't believe them… but I have reason to trust your instincts. So you think Grimm's Army is involved here?"

Ryan shook his head. "I don't know, sir…"

Suddenly a voice blared out over the commlink, breaking into their conversation, "General Radcliff! Mars is arriving. His transport just returned."

Rick turned about in his chair and pressed the commlink button, "Aye, soldier. Thank you." He then stood up and turned to Ryan. "Looks like we won't have time to worry about it. We're moving out."

LOCATION: BAY OF SHARDS, SOUTH SIDE

It was quite a colorful team that stood assembled that day on the banks of Shardasha's bay, the Bay of Shards. First and foremost were Hans Thunder-Hawk and his team of Xarkonian Spec-Ops troopers, dressed in standard red and black, and behind them stood Ryan and Amazon, the first clad in mostly blue and the second in mostly silver armor, at the head of about twenty more men dressed in a combination thereof. Taking up the rear of the formation was Captain Jaleiko and the Mordark Royal Guard, clad in simple but effective grey urban camouflage. All were watching as the transport that would take them into the city began to rise from the waves. All in all, there were two dozen Victorians and twelve Mordark Guardsmen.

"I don't like it," Amazon said, while she and Ryan were standing out of earshot of the others.

Ryan blew out a sigh when he heard that familiar temper in her voice that was as fiery as her red hair. "Like what? Working in this international team, or my recent and unexpected promotion?"

She cocked an eyebrow. "Either one. But I don't resent you your promotion, Ryan. I know you didn't ask for it."

"Doesn't mean I didn't *want* it. I just didn't expect it."

She gave him an encouraging punch on the shoulder, her silver-armored gauntlet clanging against his blue-armored pauldron. "Hey, I always knew you'd be promoted before me, Ryan. All the students in the program knew it. Sometimes we get what we deserve faster than we expect. Anyone who stands in our way today is gonna learn that *very* fast."

Suddenly they heard Rick's voice beside them. "Yes, and you'd better get going just as quickly."

Amazon snapped a salute. "General!"

"At ease. I'm just here to shove you off. Now go on, Sergeant. Order your men to fall out."

Ryan did not hesitate to comply, though the loyal Victorian troops were already moving on Rick's word before Ryan even had to repeat it. All of the soldiers – Xarkonian, Victorian, and those from Mordark – left in the same transport: a large amphibious transport of Zygbari design. Zygbar had some of the best armored ground vehicles on the planet, so the submarine-hovercraft they loaned the insertion team served as their donation to CONON's efforts in

Shardasha. It was specifically designed for this sort of mission, with its heavy armor and effective camouflage. It was currently still a prototype, with no official name, so they nicknamed it the *Trojan Seahorse*.

After Mars and Rick gave their men a short pep talk, the *Seahorse* moved out, hovering out to sea before sinking into the waves. Rick left shortly thereafter, not wishing to remain in a Xarkon military camp with most of his soldiers gone, even if he was inside a flying fortress as secure as the *Silver Scepter*. Not too many hours after the *Scepter* had disappeared over the horizon, headed for a Victorian aircraft carrier that had recently arrived near the bay, Mars and Nick Wolf saw a lone, solid black Bergelmir transport come sliding over the hills on the opposite side of the camp. To Nick's surprise, he actually saw Mars smile.

And when the door to the Berg opened, Nick immediately saw why.

Out stepped nine soldiers, clad in some of the strangest armor the mercenary had ever seen. It was of a sleek, curved design, clearly as aesthetic as it was effective. But at the same time, it was highly intimidating, with a narrow, V-shaped black visor, and long, curved spikes extending from the elbows, knees, shoulders, and helmet. Each suit was slightly different, covered in a wide array of gadgets and bristling with customized weapons. Six of the nine soldiers wore their armor in shining crimson... but the last three were deep, reflective black, with dark burgundy highlights.

The shortest of the three black-clad soldiers left his men standing rigidly in a row as he approached High Commander Mars personally. At first Nick wondered why he did not salute, but then he saw that Mars's hand was extended. The soldier shook it like the hand of an old friend.

Nick could only stare and blink.

"Good to see you're here on time," Mars said.

"Even if we are, on the whole, a little late," replied Dark-Dragon.

"Don't worry, the soldiers that just left will take things quite slowly. First they have to find a way in, and we'll make sure that's not easy. Then they have to figure out what is going on, and we'll make sure that is impossible. And of course they have to find Zegaldorph, and *you* will make sure they only find his corpse."

Dragon nodded. "My Enomegs will see to that."

"Tell them they may be at ease here," Mars said, eyeing the row of supersoldiers on the horizon. "I need to speak to you in private about the mission plan. You should also send one of your team leaders to speak to Senior-Omega Archer."

Mars turned and extended a long arm toward a shadow sitting atop a distant hill. It was the silhouette of a folded-up machine: a Xarkonian Fox walker, built for recon missions.

"She's an expert scout who's been patrolling the perimeter of the city for quite some time now," Mars said. "She found several breaches in the 'terrorist defenses,' most of which we patched up, ensuring that we would determine the CONON team's only possible method of entry. But she may know more about where the true enemy is hiding out and the best place to move in. Whoever you intend to send into the Black Network hideout should ask her if she has any valuable intel."

Dragon turned and beckoned to his Enomegs. "Saber-Scorpion?"

Scorp marched forward until he stood beside Dark-Dragon.

"Head up to that hill," Dragon said, "and speak with the walker scout up there, Senior-Omega Archer. Ask her about the best way to get into the city, the whereabouts of the terrorist leaders, and…"

"And about what she thinks is going on," Mars interrupted. "She is very intuitive and may have figured something out that we have not. As I said, she's one of the best. Unfortunately, as is usually the case with the best, she is also quite… individual. She has a tendency to keep to herself, like right now, and she… takes breaks. I can't even raise her on the commlink."

"I'm on it, sir," Scorp said. "Anything else?"

"That's all, Scorp," Dragon replied. "She hasn't actually been in the city, so she'll likely not know much besides insertion."

Scorp nodded, turned, and walked off, without looking back. Behind him, Mars and Dark-Dragon watched him go.

"You told me you had some trouble with that one…" Mars said, furrowing his brow as he squinted into the horizon.

"I did," Dragon replied, nodding. "After all, the best are usually quite individual."

Saber-Scorpion ascended the hill without much interest, wondering why he had been given such a task when the scout's information could simply have been relayed to them and worked into the mission plan. Still, it felt good to get away from the others for a change, so he didn't mind much.

The sky was growing slightly dimmer now, as the sun prepared to set behind the horizon. He looked up and inspected the shape on the hill. It was clearly a Fox walker, with its sleek head, large transperium canopy, and huge, curved, dish-shaped "ears." One "ear" was a missile rack, and the other was what gave the Fox its name: the Fox-Ear Detector Dish. Capable of collecting a huge amount of sensory data, it made the walker one of the best tools in Nova Refuge for scouting out the terrain and gathering intelligence. The setting sun crowned the walker with a shining golden border.

Scorp knew what a Fox looked like, but he was unprepared for the sight of its pilot. She appeared very relaxed, lying on her side in the grass, staring away at the distant sea. The sun illuminated her golden hair, which was far longer than usual for the military. He had never heard of the Snake Legs pack and the things its unconventional pilots were able to get away with.

"Senior-Omega Archer, I presume?" Scorp said.

The pilot woman rolled over onto her back and turned her head to regard him. Then she looked up at him and smiled. He suddenly felt almost short of breath. Even Aeriella's beauty had not had this much of an effect on him. Perhaps it was the tranquil twilight setting… but he immediately thought she had to be the most beautiful woman he had ever seen.

Her features were regal, with high cheekbones and long, arched eyebrows, yet still they had a certain softness about them, leaving no shadow too sharp. They also possessed an exotic quality that immediately made her stand out from the many other pretty faces Scorp had seen. Some might even have said she looked strange, though they could only have meant it as a compliment. Though everything about her was stunning, her eyes were the most striking of all. Clear, deep, crystalline blue… like pools of glittering water in the twilight.

What in the *hell*, Scorp thought, was a woman like this doing in the Xarkon military?

"Ah, sorry about that," she said. She spoke with a North Xarkonian accent, which only served to accentuate the musical quality of her voice. "I didn't hear you coming."

"You would have to be especially perceptive," Scorp replied, "to detect the approach of an Enomeg. I'm Century-Sergeant Justin Saber-Scorpion, Enomeg Commander." It felt surprisingly good to say that.

She looked into his eyes. "Senior-Omega Amy Archer, of the Snake Legs walker pack, codename Falcon… and most people tell me that I *am* especially perceptive."

He instantly could understand why this was true. Her keen sapphire eyes seemed to be reading him like a book. This young woman was definitely strange, as they had told him. She did not salute or even stand up when she learned of his rank and identity. She just lay there, smiling. Most people in the Xarkon military would have taken offense at this, but Scorp couldn't even imagine being offended by her. He merely returned her smile.

"Commander Mars said you have intel about Shardasha," he said.

"There's not much to tell," she said, looking away. "I've been patrolling around the city for a while now, making stops like this one, scrutinizing the city from all angles. But all I've seen is… stillness. The city is tense, silent… waiting. Once I saw a civilian hovercar speeding away, but the perimeter defenses easily shot it down. I don't know how these terrorists have managed to take control of everything like this. It's… it's truly unbelievable."

She turned back to look at him, her eyes narrowing. He had a feeling that whatever she was about to say, it was important. So he simply assumed a relaxed position, resting his hands on his two holstered pistols, and waited.

"Don't you think it is?" she asked at length.

Scorp blinked. "Well… to be honest, I haven't thought about it much. Haven't had time. I only recently graduated, and then they dragged me off here. I suppose it is rather amazing though, yes."

"I didn't say amazing," Amy replied, shaking her head. "I said *unbelievable*. By which I mean, I truly don't believe that it could be possible. Something else is at work here besides these so-called 'terrorists.' I've been trying to figure out what, but so far, nothing…"

Again, most military officers would have scoffed at Amy's suspicions, saying that she did not know enough about the situation and was in no position to make wild, baseless guesses. But Scorp was fascinated. Something about her tone fully convinced him that she knew exactly what she was talking about.

He shrugged. "So… any hypotheses?"

"Well, so far, the terrorists have just been keeping people in. They haven't really tried to keep anyone *out*. They haven't had reason to, because… well, we haven't *sent* anyone in. Why is that?"

"I guess they were waiting to send *us* in. If anyone can slip in there undetected and take care of the situation, it's the Enomegs."

She looked at him curiously... not skeptically, he noticed, just curiously. Scorp returned her stare. In fact, he found he could hardly take his eyes off her.

Finally he said, "It almost sounds like you suspect Xarkon herself of being involved."

"Though it may seem treasonous," she replied evenly, "I certainly haven't discounted the possibility. Xarkon keeps many secrets, some of them dark. Like yourselves, for example."

Scorp knew all too well how true this was.

"You're right, of course. But either way, these dark secrets..." He pointed to himself, and then to the city. "...are going to try to find out those dark secrets. So any help you could provide would be most appreciated."

"Ah yes, facts; the only thing the military has time for. Very well. The most unguarded section of the city is the southeast corner. There's a small gap in the defense grid there because a turret was undergoing repairs when the city was captured, so it's still offline. That's where I would enter. And thank God I'm not going to. It's not very smart to enter a city no one ever leaves."

"So that's all you have to tell me?"

"If there was more I could say to help, I would."

"The point of insertion should be enough. Thanks. I'd better head back now. I'd hate to be late for my first mission."

As he turned to leave, he saw, out of the corner of his eye, Amy shaking her head behind him. For some reason, her air of disappointment made him pause. He turned again to regard her.

"What? What is it?"

"Oh, nothing," she said, turning to look back at the distant city and the ocean beyond.

Now Scorp knew he could not let it lie. So he walked back over to where she lay and looked down at her. She did not look up.

"I'd rather not lose sleep over what you might have said."

"Would you?"

Scorp thought of all the hours he had spent staring at the ceiling in his quarters at the ETAB. "Yes."

She blew out a sigh. "Stop looking at *me*, and look *around* you."

Scorp looked around. There was the war camp, down in the shadows at the foot of the hill behind him... the rows of tents, transports, and one or two Zygbari vehicles covered in camouflage netting. There was the folded-up Fox walker, intimidating at this close proximity even though it was the smallest of the mighty walking tanks that Xarkon had to offer. And there was the skyline of Shardasha, silhouetted against the setting sun, which glittered on the distant sea. The towers of the city reflected the red sunlight, looking as if they were lit aflame.

The far-off coastline on the opposite side of the Bay of Shards looked like a row of mountains on the other side of the world, rising out of the water, growing smaller until they disappeared halfway across the horizon. He could make out the battleships forming the blockade around the bay, their shapes mirrored in the waves, each of them almost a perfect silhouette of the Crown of Xarkon. It sent a shiver down his spine. It was really quite a picturesque sight, he thought… beautiful, certainly, but also almost… foreboding. It felt as if the world were holding its breath while a ticking bomb sat somewhere nearby, ready to go off when least expected.

"Now do you see?" Amy said. "I just couldn't understand how you could walk away from all this without really taking a look. What do you see when you look at all this?"

Scorp blinked. "I see… beauty, I suppose. And danger. It makes me think of a burning fuse, getting shorter…"

She nodded. "I'm glad to hear we see alike. This conflict, this 'Shardasha Incident,' will not end well. And I feel it will be nothing next to what could come afterward."

"World war," Scorp said gravely. "The *ultimate* war."

Amy blew out a long sigh. "It's very sad. When Humanity came here to Terra Nova, we were given a clean slate – a chance to really learn from the mistakes of the past and start all over again. And look… just *look* what we've done with it."

He nodded. "The same things we did with the last one."

He looked down at her and shook his head slowly. This time, she looked up at him expectantly, awaiting an answer. Suddenly Scorp felt all of his ambitions melt away. He no longer cared about besting Raven, about proving himself, about completing the mission. He suddenly felt that he could stay here forever, on the top of this hill, with this beautiful, unusual woman.

"They told me you were strange," Scorp said.

She smiled slightly, wistfully. "Yes, I am. Sorry if I go on. I don't mean to interrogate you. Guess it comes from a career in Intelligence. I just like to… get a feel for people."

Then she turned back to regard the sea. All thought of time left Scorp's mind, and he felt his legs give way beneath him as he settled into a cross-legged sitting position. Together they sat there, watching as the red disk of New Sol sank lower beneath the waves of the Infinite Ocean, igniting the sea and the clouds in burning shades of orange and magenta. For the first time he could seem to remember, the Enomeg super-soldier felt almost… at peace.

It was not until the stars showed themselves in the deep blue sky above that Saber-Scorpion finally gave in to that nagging part of his mind that was insisting he should return to camp. When he stood up to go, Amy rose up beside him. He was surprised at how tall she was; she was almost his height.

"I'll see if I can dig up some more intel," she said. "If I find anything at all, I'll let you know immediately."

Scorp blinked, as the thoughts of the present took hold in his mind again. "Yes… Thank you. I guess I'll go back to camp now. I… hope I'll see you around."

She nodded, looking thoughtful. "I think we'll see each other again. Good luck, Saber-Scorpion."

Scorp nodded and turned, with great reluctance, back to the camp.

"Wait," Amy said suddenly.

He regarded her over his shoulder. She was extending a hand, in which she held a small communicator. He took it and inspected it. It appeared to be a civilian model, not Xarkon military. Most Xarkon soldiers never carried their commlinks anyway; they kept them built into their helmets.

"What's this for?" he said.

"A way for us to keep in touch," she said. "I'll admit, I'm actually quite curious about what's really going on in Shardasha. So I'd like for you to tell me. And if I find anything, I'll tell you. Just, you know, keep in touch."

He blinked. "I can't keep information from –"

"Oh, no," she interrupted, "don't keep my information from anyone. Use it to your advantage, to finish the mission. Just don't keep any information from me either. I want to figure this out as much as you. And for some reason, I feel like I can trust you in this."

Scorp lifted the small, round communicator and inserted it into an empty pouch on his belt.

"Okay," he said, "I will. Although I must admit I'm curious as to what makes me seem so trustworthy."

She smiled and gestured to Shardasha. "You can see the city. Most people look out there… and they can't see it for all the buildings."

Scorp gave a short laugh and shook his head. Here he was again, he thought… being pretty much used by a woman. She was probably a spy for the Victorians, Yavakaro, or someone else. That would pretty much follow the usual line of events in his life. And as usual, he felt no urge to fight it.

They nodded to each other once more, and then Scorp turned toward the dark camp in the distance. He left the hilltop in a daze, suddenly realizing what Amy had meant about *facts*. There was something utterly mundane about them, something simple, blunt, and ugly. That was how he now perceived the world as he walked back into it… back into the reality of the cold metal vehicles and canvas tents that made up Camp Ragnar. It felt as if he had just awoken from a dream, and now the cold, hard world was being thrust back upon him, unwelcome but unavoidable.

He suddenly felt that he wanted to go back to sleep.

- CHAPTER EIGHTEEN -
INTO SHARDASHA

To the south of Shardasha, west of Camp Ragnar, lay a smaller camp set up by one of Xarkon's walker packs. Walker squads were referred to as "packs" for the same reason that their officers all used ranks derived from wolfpack hierarchy, like "Alpha-Wolf," "Beta-Wolf," and "Omega." The reason was that all Xarkon walkers were named after canines, from the humble Fox to the mighty Dire Wolf.

Infantry were a formidable fighting force, especially the Enomegs, but they were still only Humans, and could only be lightly armed. Tanks could back them up, but these crawling vehicles could be obstructed by anti-tank barriers and certain types of terrain. Hover vehicles, one of the newest innovations on the battlefield, could traverse land and sea with ease, but they were restricted in that they could not carry as much weight.

But walkers, the kings of the earthly battlefield, suffered none of these defects. They could cross any type of terrain with ease, carry immensely heavy loads, be equipped with any type of weapon, and could hold their own against almost any foe. For combat on land, they were the ultimate weapon.

Most Xarkonian walkers were supported by a pair of reverse-joint legs, like the hind legs of a quadruped animal or those of a dinosaur, rather than the straight legs of a Human. The Xarkonians claimed they were less top-heavy and harder to knock off-balance than Humanoid legs, though there were advantages and disadvantages to both builds.

Of the walkers that now stood deactivated and silent around the camp, only one did so upon humanoid legs. It was a Dingo, the walker of Harry "Viper" Dalton. He would have no other kind. After "dropping out" of the Enomeg program, Viper had been transferred to the regular Xarkon military academy in Xarkopolis, the capital city. His instructors immediately noticed his aptitude with computer technology and wanted him to work as a hacker for Intelligence. Viper, however, loved walkers, and was able to convince his instructors that he should be put in the walker division. He had even begun engineering new walker designs for the military, but so far none of them had caught on… It seemed Xarkon just loved their reverse-joints too much, though Viper could hardly understand why.

He was currently sitting on the foot of his Dingo, in front of the campfire he and the other members of the Snake Legs had built for their enjoyment. He was staring at his helmet, on which was painted the image of a viper's head, with its fangs extending down over the visor.

All of the walker pilots in the Snake Legs had custom-painted helmets and codenames, but these were not chosen by High Command like those of the Enomegs. They were self-chosen, and each expressed the walker pilot's own individuality. Viper, after all, was a snake in the grass. The other pilots in his crew were named assorted things like Rhino, Atlas, Legs, Jackpot, and Cronic. Some applied better than others.

And Falcon…

Viper looked up to see her walker deactivating in front of him. The tall, slender legs of the Fox folded up under its heavy head, and it settled down into the grass. The canopy opened with a hiss, and Amy climbed out. The Fox was one of the few walkers that allowed for such a quick and easy exit. Many required ladders, which were usually provided by the support vehicles, to reach the hatch from the ground.

"You look starry-eyed," Viper said frankly, as usual. He paused for a moment before adding, "But then, you always do, since your eyes look like stars anyway."

She smiled and shook her head. "Not this again…"

"So tell me, has anyone ever mistaken you for Empress Skye? I mean, with your beauty and brains, and wearing Xarkon's colors…"

She cleared her throat. "So, have you talked with any of the Enomegs yet, Viper?"

"Oh, so they've arrived, huh? Mars said they would. No, none of 'em cared to pay us walker pilots a visit. I guess they're still at the main camp."

"I talked to one of them, the one they call Saber-Scorpion. He definitely carried himself with confidence in his abilities..."

"Who wouldn't in those exoskeletons? I feel confident of my abilities when I'm in my Dingo too. If there's one thing I would have liked to get out of my days as an Enomeg, it would be that armor…"

"It was more than that though. But the strangest thing was that under it all he seemed very emotionally confused and *un*confident."

Viper gave her a sly smile. "How can anyone help feeling that way when they're around you?"

Amy rolled her eyes. "Viper, can't you ever take me seriously?"

Viper coughed. "What? I take you more seriously than anything!"

"Well, then stop joking around. I'm trying to have a meaningful conversation with you about your past. Do you ever wish you had finished your Enomeg training?"

"Never," he replied easily, twirling his helmet in his hands. "You know me, so you know why. It's the same reason *you* didn't stay where they stuck you, in Intelligence. We're individuals. We pick our own road. That's why we're in the Snake Legs!"

"Yes, exactly… but this Enomeg, this Scorpion… he seemed to be an individual too, despite the training. I could tell he had conflicting feelings about his role, that his life hadn't taken it all out of him."

Viper snorted. "Nah, you must've been mistaken. He was probably just anxious to get to the fighting and annoyed at having to wait around."

One of Amy's eyebrows went up. "But isn't that exactly how *you* feel, Viper?"

He laughed. "Amy, if you wanna know how I feel so bad, why don't you come over here and sit down beside me. Then we can get to seriously knowing how each other… you know, feels."

She rolled her eyes. "*Seriously*, Viper. I thought you said you were taking me *seriously*…"

He wagged his eyebrows. "Oh, I'm serious alright."

Amy took a deep breath and let it out in a sigh. Finally she gave in and sat down on the other "toe" of the Dingo's massive foot.

"Now," Viper said, "what were we talking about again?"

Amy slapped her forehead.

LOCATION: CAMP RAGNAR

"Welcome back, my friend," said Lee Blade-Mantis.

Saber-Scorpion looked up. It had been a few hours since his chat with Amy Archer on the hill, but he could not seem to get his mind off her. He had not even noticed Mantis standing there, as silent as he was. Ever since the end of their training, Scorp had noticed a certain coldness about many of the Enomegs. Even Seth's constantly carefree personality, which had been such an encouragement to Scorp in the past, now seemed to have faded to stern silence. He got the same feeling from Cat. And, he realized suddenly, he felt the same way himself.

But Mantis never changed. When times were serious, he was deadly serious. In times of leisure, he was the most fun-loving Enomeg of them all. And throughout it all, nothing shook or even jostled his steadfast loyalty to Xarkon. His philosophy remained as immovable as a mountainside.

"You look starry-eyed," Mantis said frankly, as usual.

"I've just been… thinking," Scorp replied.

"So have we all. There's something about this whole terrorist incident. Everyone seems strangely tense. I overheard Raven talking with High Commander Mars. Mars may be his father, but he still speaks to Raven as if he were merely a favored soldier. Everything hinges on us, was what the High Commander said. They've all been waiting for us. It's like this is just one huge training exercise, all made for the Enomegs."

Scorp shook his head. "*Huh.* And I guess Lord Zegaldorph of Mordark is just pretending to be a hostage to play along and help?"

A grin enveloped Mantis's face. "No, I suppose he's not. And I doubt even Mars would go so far as to kidnap the leader of another country just for a training exercise. Still, it all seems a bit strange, don't you think?"

Scorp thought back to what Amy had told him. "Yes... it is. I never really thought about it before, until... By the way, Mantis, I want to ask you something: What do you know about this walker pilot, Amy Archer? She's a Senior-Omega in the walker division. Mars said she was strange, and he was right. She's more than strange – she's... extraordinary, really."

Mantis's eyebrows shot up. "Hmm... sparked your interest, has she?"

"She's very perceptive..." Scorp said slowly. "I think she may know more than she's telling me. About Shardasha, and possibly more."

"Interesting," Mantis said, and he opened up the canvas entrance to a nearby tent. "Let's see what we can dig up about her."

Scorp followed him into the tent, where a soldier sat asleep at a computer terminal, surrounded by an array of equipment. He was apparently a communications officer, though he could just be a techie. Mantis tapped the man on the shoulder, and he woke with a start.

"At ease," Mantis said. "I'm Blade-Mantis, Enomeg. If you're going to sleep on the job, do it over there in the corner so I can use this computer."

The soldier nodded, looking almost terrified. He quickly scampered out of the chair and sat down in another one in the corner. After a few seconds, he thought better of this as well and asked permission to leave. Mantis told him to return in an hour or so, and then he sat down at the computer terminal as the soldier slipped away.

While Mantis manipulated the holographic interface, bypassing some lewd images the previous user had been breaking regulations by viewing, Scorp kept talking. "You probably think I'm crazy, don't you?"

"My friend," Mantis said amusedly, "I know you are crazy. We have trained together long enough for me to know that you are crazy, as they say, like a fox. In fact, I sometimes think you should have been given *that* codename instead of Scorpion!"

Scorp snorted. Mantis knew he would never have accepted any name but Saber-Scorpion. "Actually, I think that would have suited *you* more. Well, partially anyway. I can't think of any animal that would suit you completely. What's an animal that's deadly in battle, loyal to the core, steadfast, and resolute, yet still finds it in himself to goof off and act like a nut at any opportunity?"

Mantis laughed. "That's the most ridiculous thing I ever heard."

"I don't know how you do it, but that's you."

"Well, that's enough about me then," Mantis said, with slight embarrassment. "I've dug up some info on your Archer friend. Quite a looker, isn't she? And quite a record too. She joined the Armed Forces at almost the minimum age… Surprising, but then, her parents were both military too. She was put in Intelligence, her father's career, where she gained an excellent reputation as an interrogator. They say she was a natural."

"I believe that part," Scorp put in. "Go on."

"After two years of working with them, she requested a job as a scout. Claimed she was sick of sitting behind a desk. They delayed her transfer for a year, but finally her request was granted. At first it looks like she got really low-level assignments… but then she did recon for a walker team in a particularly important off-world mission. After that, she was often given assignments as a walker pilot. A more experienced pilot, Harry 'Viper' Dalton, personally requested her for his squad, Walker Squad 212, also known as the uh… 'Snake Legs.' He says she seemed to take naturally to the walker."

"So now she's Walker Division, not Army Scout Corps?"

"Yes, but she still does mostly scout work, it says. A Fox is her favored machine, since it's a scout walker. Quite a career-jumper, no?"

Scorp nodded. He was not sure what he had been expecting, but he felt disappointed somehow. For some reason, he had expected Amy to have more of a history, to be more important.

Mantis was looking at him thoughtfully. "My friend, you are not telling me something…"

Scorp paused before replying, "Lee… what is your philosophy? You heard the speech Dragon gave at the graduation about soldiers and warriors… so which are you? A soldier or a warrior?"

For a while, Mantis was silent. He stared at the hovering holographic computer screen in thought.

"My friend," he said at last, "have you ever had one of those special moments when suddenly reality stands out… becomes pure clarity against the background of foggy confusion that usually governs our lives? When all the questions you've ever asked suddenly stand explained? When the world, instead of seeming like a confusing mess of alternate paths, suddenly lays itself flat before you like a map?"

Scorp stared at Mantis, thinking back. He remembered when he had first saved the assassin girl, Larisa, during the Trial of Loyalty. He had felt so sure of himself afterward, so sure that he was doing the right thing, because he was doing what he felt in his own heart to be right. But after that, further events and revelations had raised so many other questions…

"No," Scorp said at last. "No, I never have."

Mantis grinned and threw out his hands. "Me neither!"

Despite feeling a little angry that Mantis was not taking him seriously enough, Scorp did crack a smile. "So you have *no* philosophy then?"

Mantis shook his head. "Ah, but I do. And it closely resembles Dark-Dragon's. You see, we as individuals are infinitely small, infinitely unimportant beings. Our entire lives are mere blips in time, hardly even enough to record, and in the realm of size, we are but tiny organisms crawling upon rocks hurtling through the vastness of space. We are merely droplets of water, hardly even noticeable on our own. But when we devote ourselves to a principle, to a cause…

then we become much more. A single drop of rain can do almost nothing, but the ocean waves can *reshape the world*. One drop of water is gone in an instant, but the sea itself… is *eternal*."

Scorp was still smiling. "Not quite."

Mantis shrugged. "Excuse my metaphor. Few things, if any, are truly eternal. But perhaps *something* out there is, even if we have no idea what. The impression our efforts leave on the world behind us may be eternal enough. And nothing is quite so good an effort as fighting for the ideals you believe in… like honor, bravery, and loyalty. But it is a hard fight. We must never falter, never give in to the temptations of the moment that will cause us to stray from the cause. The *cause*, my friend, is everything."

Scorp was serious now. He looked into Lee's dark eyes and saw only staunch determination there… strong resolve and discipline. He seemed so certain he was right. And that, Scorp realized, was what he himself lacked most. No matter what situation he was in and what decisions he made as a result, he never seemed to feel sure about them… about anything.

"For one who claims to have never had that strike of clarity," Scorp said, "you seem awfully sure of yourself."

"No, not quite. I am sure of myself, but not *positive*. To pretend to know everything with absolute certainty is pure Human foolishness. And Humans, as I said, are infinitely small and unimportant creatures. But I tell you what, my friend: when I have that moment of clarity, I will let you know."

Scorp smiled. It was good to have someone like Mantis to talk to… to fall back on. Steadfast as a mountain…

"Is that a promise?" Scorp asked.

"It is a pledge, my friend," Lee said with another grin that nearly engulfed his face. "I give you my word of honor."

Scorp nodded. "Then I promise you the same."

Suddenly they heard a voice from the door behind them. "Ah, you guys take everything too seriously."

Seth Electric-Eel strutted in and handed Scorp and Mantis each a canteen filled with some strange-smelling liquid. He grinned and sat down in the corner chair that had recently been deserted by the communications officer, and took a long swig from his own canteen.

Scorp frowned at this sudden interruption from a serious conversation. "Seth, what is this stuff? What are you getting into now?"

Seth scratched his red hair, speaking in a slightly slurred voice. "Oh, I got to thinkin' about how everyone is acting all stern now that we're real Enomegs and stuff. Then I noticed this bunch of regulars loungin' around with this yellow-bearded guy, drinkin' from these canteens here. I swiped a few, and now I know why they were so happy."

Mantis's nose wrinkled. "It smells like –"

"Oh, come on, Lee," Seth chided, "try and *relax* every now and then. That's *my* philosophy in life: make the most of it, 'cause you never know when it might end. Now, I propose a toast, in celebration of our graduation…"

"I don't drink…" Mantis said, in a voice that clearly indicated he knew he would be ignored.

"To the Enomegs!" Seth shouted. "To our fellow graduates, to friends who didn't make the cut, to Xarkon… and the mission ahead."

"Amen to that," Scorp said, raising his canteen and taking a small swallow. He nearly gagged.

Seth laughed. "Drink, comrades! For soon… it's into Shardasha."

LOCATION: JUST OUTSIDE CAMP RAGNAR

As Scorp and Mantis were beginning their conversation, Luke Blood-Raven stopped his hoverbike beside a tree not far outside the fringes of the camp. The twisted black tree looked like a fitting location for any melancholy raven. He dismounted from his bike, drew out his pistol, switched off the blazer shielding system, and fired the bare metal bullets at the branches of the tree, each shot striking its target, sending splinters of wood flying. When he reached the foot of the tree, he activated his star-talons and began cutting, unleashing a flurry of furious slashes, lopping off limbs and leaving a network of burn marks all over the surface of the trunk, screaming into the darkening night as he slashed. Then he lashed out with his feet, kicking away, kicking, kicking… but he had not cut deep enough for the tree to fall. It merely stood there, as if ignorant of his efforts.

As he stood catching his breath and swearing silently, he heard a voice behind him say, "What was *that* all about?"

Raven whirled to face Shadow-Cat, who had managed to follow him, silently as usual, all the way from the base. She was looking at him in a quizzical manner, shaking her head in disapproval.

"I can't believe him!" Raven shouted. "I *don't* believe him!"

She threw her arms out wide. "Who?"

"Mars! He thinks he can just walk in and… Oh, forget it. It's not worth talking about."

"Wait, wait," Cat said, holding up her hands. "You're actually *mad* because the High Commander is your father?"

"I said forget it!" he shouted, heading back to his hoverbike.

She quickly intercepted him. "But I think it *is* worth talking about. What's wrong, Luke? Lee and I overheard your conversation with Mars about how it was all up to us, bla, bla, bla… but what got you so riled up? Is it because of his whole 'proud father' attitude or what?"

Raven clenched and unclenched his fists in front of his face, as if clawing for the right words. "I… I don't know what to say. He's just so arrogant, and… What makes him think he can just step in and take credit for everything I've done? It's like you said – I should be *proud* to be the son of High Commander Mars… that's what they'll *all* say!"

Clearly, Raven was not very good at expressing himself, but Cat was finally beginning to get the gist of it. As he stood there fuming, his features contorted into an amazingly Mars-like portrait, she finally understood.

"What you're saying is… people will talk about 'the deeds of Mars's son,' not 'the deeds of Luke Blood-Raven.'"

He closed his eyes and sat down on the bike, slicking back his hair, which had become somewhat longer now. Cat herself had told him a few weeks ago that he would look better with a little more hair, and, she thought, he really did. However… it made him appear even more like his father.

"Something like that," he said at length. "I don't know… there's more to it than that, but…"

"Well, maybe we could talk about it," Cat replied, "find a workaround. It's better than attacking that tree. It didn't do anything."

Luke gave a reluctant smile and slid onto the hoverbike, Cat taking a seat behind him. A short joyride wouldn't be so bad, he decided, before they had to rendezvous and move out. As he revved the bike's engine and glided off over the hills, with Cat gripping onto his waist, he tried to forget his anger… but that, he thought, was one of the few things in life that he had never been very good at.

LOCATION: SHARDASHA OUTSKIRTS

At the location Amy Archer had described, where the defenses of Shardasha were weakest, the camouflaged Bergelmir transport now entered, hovering into the outskirts of the city. The small buildings surrounding them were as dark and ghostly-silent as the shadows of the skyscrapers not far behind. None seemed to notice the nearly quiet and invisible passage of the armored troop transport as it slid along the streets, a small moving grey box among so many larger, immobile ones.

Inside the Berg sat the Enomegs: Blood-Raven, Magnum-Coyote, Electric-Eel, and Shadow-Cat sat on one side… and Saber-Scorpion, Blade-Mantis, Gun-Barracuda, and Silent-Cobra sat on the other. Between them hovered a long, holographic map of the Xarkon coastline. And at the far end of this map, standing with his back against the door to the Berg's main cabin, was Dark-Dragon, his armor reflecting the hologram's red glow.

Dragon began his briefing without introduction, jumping right to the information. He pointed to a city on the map, which was now growing in size as the view zoomed in.

"Shardasha," Dragon said, "as you know, is one of Xarkon's most important port cities. Currently, it is under complete lockdown. According to what they're saying in CONON, this is an extremely high-scale terrorist incident. This dot indicates the Zygbari amphibious troop transport vehicle called the *Trojan Seahorse*, which is headed toward the Xarkon coastline. Inside are soldiers from Victory, Xarkon, and Mordark. Their insertion location is here on the docks, and from that point they will move into the city, with orders to neutralize the terrorists, secure any hostages, and retake control of Shardasha's defense systems."

"Are those our orders, too?" Seth asked.

"No, they are not. In fact, the Xarkonians in the *Trojan Seahorse* will exit the ship here, before ever entering the city, as was secretly planned. If we fail, they will be our backup. But our own mission is completely Black Ops, off the record. No glory, no medals. If we fail, Xarkon will disavow all knowledge of our existence. Is this clear?"

The Enomegs nodded their understanding.

"Then I'll fill you in on the situation. Obviously, nothing I'm about to say can leave this room. First of all, no force of terrorists has truly taken possession of Shardasha. Xarkon still retains complete control of the city and its defense grid. *We* were the ones to put this city under lockdown."

Scorp could not shake the feeling that he had known this all along, and so had Amy Archer. But to hear it spoken so bluntly did give him a bit of a shock. With Xarkon resorting to such methods, what now separated them from the dishonorable terrorists they claimed to fight? Was Dark-Dragon going to try to justify this?

"This was done in order to give us – to give *you* – a clear shot at your mission objectives. These objectives include the elimination of two major thorns in Xarkon's side: Zegaldorph, the corrupt Mahlok Lord of Mordark… and the leaders of the criminal organizations that he protects within the boundaries of his filthy excuse for a country."

"Wait," Coyote interrupted, "are you talking about the one they call the Big Boss? The leader of the Black Network? We're going to kill *him?*"

"Of course not, soldier. Xarkon doesn't waste her time shooting at phantoms. All evidence points to the conclusion that the Big Boss does not even exist. It's likely that he's an imaginary figurehead conjured up by various mob bosses working together in order to distract potential assassins."

Barracuda nodded. "True. I've heard that assassin woman, Lisa Sharp? She's killed *three* Big Bosses, and each time a new one just pops right back up. Assassins like her never could bag Zegaldorph either."

Scorp froze solid the moment the name 'Lisa Sharp' left Barracuda's lips. Was she really such a well-known assassin that *he* knew about her? How could Scorp not have known? She had probably expected him to jump at the name when she first revealed it to him. *'Larisa,'* indeed… As he thought of that midnight conversation with the hitwoman, he suddenly realized the high irony of this moment: they were going in to assassinate targets that she herself had previously gone after. She had been right: they were not so different after all. The irony was so bitter, Scorp could almost taste it.

"But *we* will," Dragon said, in reply to Barracuda's earlier comment. He then pressed a button on his wrist.

Suddenly the hologram in the middle of the room changed. The map disappeared, giving way to a three-dimensional hovering bust of Lord Zegaldorph, his bald head outlined with its intricate black designs. The image rotated to give all of the Enomegs a good view of every angle.

"Blood-Raven, you will lead Team Onyx. It will be up to you, Coyote, Eel, and Cat to infiltrate Zegaldorph's embassy here in Shardasha and eliminate him as discreetly as possible. Be sure to avoid using anything Xarkonian to kill him. I have here some civilian knives you may use, or steal a knife from the building's dining area and kill him with that, if you can. Make it look like a treacherous royal guard did the job. They don't carry solid blades, only energy ones, but maybe you can plant evidence on them. Handle it the way you see fit."

Again the hologram shifted, but this time three busts appeared. The first depicted a dark-haired man with a pockmarked face but a winning smile. It was easy enough to guess that he was the Black Network leader. The other two could immediately be identified as Sarrans: one male and one female, both with angular, perfectly chiseled features, as usual. The male had entirely black hair – rare among the Sarran – while the female's was entirely white – a fact that was said to indicate exceptional psionic ability. Scorp could hardly believe that they were going to send him after a Sarran target once again.

"Saber-Scorpion," Dragon went on, "you, Mantis, Cobra, and Barracuda will be Team Obsidian. It will be your job to eliminate the other... wild cards. Foremost is the man suspected of leading the Black Network's operations within all of Xarkon. They call him 'Lucky' Jim Crow. The other two targets are Idelma'ik – the male Sarran – and Folirayoth – the female. Both are leaders of the legendary Sarran terrorist organization known as the Blackwings. All of these leaders were set to secretly meet with Zegaldorph in Shardasha. *That* is the reason we closed off the city. We simply couldn't let a golden opportunity like this pass us by.

"The meeting was supposed to take place in a casino owned by Jim Crow himself. Your targets should still be inside. But be warned: they have the place locked down almost as tightly as Zegaldorph's tower. Luckily, you don't have the same restrictions as Team Onyx. You are, in fact, under orders to cause maximum destruction. Make sure all computers in the building are wiped clean and destroyed, along with any paperwork. These criminals will be taking the blame for the Shardasha incident, so we don't want any evidence revealing that they were not involved. And of course, leave no one alive."

Barracuda grinned. "Break in, kill everything that moves, and blow up everything that doesn't? Now *this* is my kinda mission."

Scorp swallowed. "What kind of dirt do we have on them? What are they accused of?"

Dragon shrugged. "High treason, grand larceny, wholesale murder, blackmail... you name it, and the Black Network has been involved in it. As for the Blackwings, they were infamous during the Xenocide War for assassinating dozens of high-profile military and political leaders. The fact that they may now be active in Xarkon once again is enough cause for concern. And of course, both groups are accused of organizing the Shardasha Incident. You and your team will make sure of that."

Scorp could barely contain his righteous indignation. "If these people are truly guilty of all those crimes, then why do we have to–"

"Because those are your *orders*, soldier." Dragon interrupted firmly.

"*Soldier?* This isn't war!"

Dragon took a step forward, the blood red hologram flickering from view as he walked directly through it. "No, this *isn't* war! This isn't war because right now there *is* no war. There is only peace, peace among men. And *this* is how we keep it."

After a moment of silence, he added, "Scorp, it was a battle for me to convince High Command to award you the leadership position you have. If you fail this mission, you can be sure they won't let you keep it. And now, if there are no further questions, prepare to disembark. If you need to contact me, call me Igneous, not Dark-Dragon. That name is too well-known. Good luck, Enomegs."

LOCATION: BAY OF SHARDS

"We can't afford to sit and plan any longer. We have to move in!"

Ryan watched as Captain Jaleiko stormed back and forth across the deck of the Xarkonian battleship with which they had docked, shouting angrily at the Xarkonian Spec-Ops commander, Hans Thunder-Hawk. Ryan already did not trust Thunder-Hawk, whose blank stare of disdain as he looked down from his towering height clearly hid other feelings. But Jaleiko was being irrational.

"That is not going to happen," Hans said. "My men and I are under orders to sit tight until things settle down a little. The terrorists have likely noticed the recent activity around here and might be getting nervous. If they get *too* nervous, then they might get trigger-happy with the city defenses they've taken control of. We don't know if they can really fire on the city itself or how much of it they can destroy, but we don't think they're bluffing. And if they can't get what they want, they'll settle for making an example."

"Just as Xarkon will settle for making an example of Zegaldorph?" Jaleiko shot back.

Thunder-Hawk shook his head again. "Politics is not my concern, Commander Jaleiko. I just follow orders. However, I do know enough about politics to realize I can't order *you* around. If you wish to move in, then you're free to take your royal guardsmen, or whatever they're called, and proceed. But don't come running back to me when the city begins to explode around your ears… along with your Lord Zegaldorph, *if* he's not the one behind it."

Captain Jaleiko hefted his rifle and motioned to his contingent of guardsmen. "Very well. Men, follow me! I hope you Xarkonians can arrange your own transport with one of your submersible ships, because my men and I are moving in with the *Trojan*. Ryan, are you coming?"

Ryan had been wondering vaguely where Victory was supposed to fit in with this whole conflict. Personally, he cared little for both Mordark *and* Xarkon. All he knew was that Victory had to discover the truth about what was going on here. So he nodded to Jaleiko and turned to his troops. They all stood there, awaiting his orders. He looked back at Amazon and shrugged. She grinned, cocking her rifle.

Of all the Immortal Soldier codenames that had been issued, Ryan thought, Evelyn's was the most fitting. Her warlike spirit was as fiery as her red hair. Sometimes she was almost frighteningly violent, but her joyful bloodlust always managed to bolster his spirits as well as that of the rest of his troops. Sometimes that was what it took.

And his spirits needed boosting right now as he turned and gave the orders to the rest of his men. "Alright, everyone, listen up! We're moving into

Shardasha! We'll approach the city by sub as close as we can while still avoiding detection. From there on, you'll have to swim. The first objective is to rescue Zegaldorph, Lord of Mordark, who is being held hostage somewhere in this city. The second is to ascertain whether or not the terrorists have the ability to destroy the entire metropolis… and stop them if they do!"

He paused a moment and took a deep breath, then turned back to them. "Are we clear?"

"Yes, sir!"

"Alright, let's move!"

With that, the soldiers of Victory and Mordark quickly descended the ladders leading back down to the amphibious Zygbari vehicle where it lay floating on the sea below.

Thunder-Hawk called to them, "Good luck! My men and I will keep in touch and join you when our commander gives the word."

The special operations sergeant watched as the Victorian soldiers descended the ladder to the transport submerged beneath the frothing waves.

It was not until after the last bit of the *Trojan* had disappeared that Hans reached for his communicator and said, "They're on their way."

"Yes, sir," replied the Xarkonian soldier on the other side. "The ambush is prepared."

Hans switched off. He doubted the poor soldiers, Xarkonians though they were, could deal with all the highly-trained troops that Victory and Mordark had sent… but if they failed, their deaths would at least convince the Victorians that this was truly a terrorist incident. He would see to that.

But oh, how he envied them. He wanted nothing more than to test his own Enomeg training against those two Victorian "Immortal Soldiers." He only hoped that his former comrades, the other Enomegs, would get the chance that he would not.

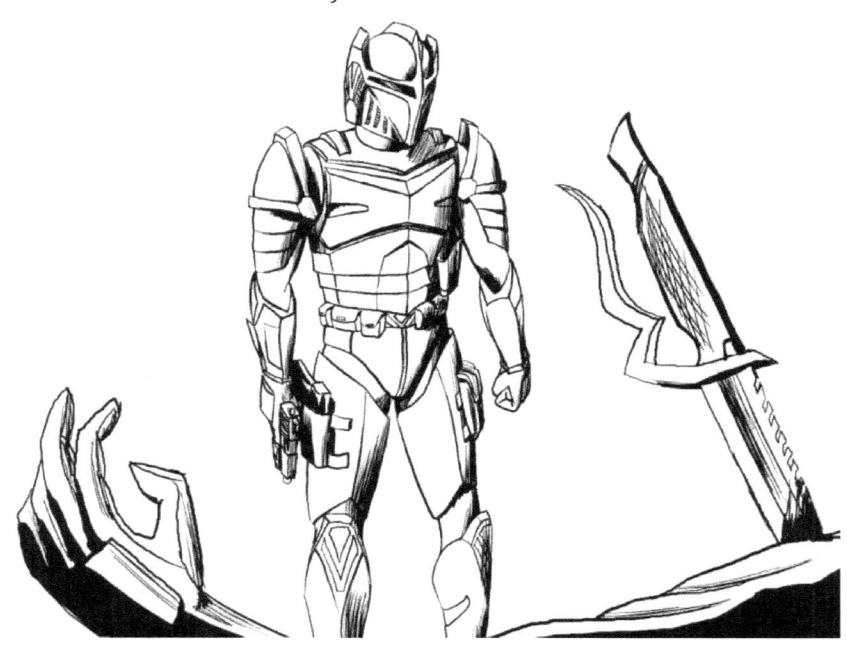

- CHAPTER NINETEEN -
WITH ONE STONE

The dark streets were silent and empty, the lights powered down so that the moons provided the only source of illumination. The citizens of Shardasha, the city under siege from both within and without, were locked safely away in their homes in the residential districts, probably asleep, though almost certainly not soundly. Here in the commercial areas, the shop windows were silent, and not a single hovercar was to be found, either on ground level or on the higher landing platforms that cast shadows down on the Enomegs as they walked.

Gun-Barracuda was grumbling. "I don't like it here. Too quiet. This is a ghost town, not a battlefield."

"We do not choose our battlefields, my large friend," Mantis said, fiddling with the controls to his helmet's HUD map. "But worry not; we will arrive at ours soon enough. The casino containing our enemies is not far now. ETA… about five minutes. Just keep walking."

"Whatever," grunted the giant Enomeg as he finished attaching a device to his left gauntlet.

Scorp frowned. "Is that what I think it is, Barracuda?"

"The way I figure," Barracuda replied slowly, "Sarran wings gotta be real flammable, right? You know what they say: better to light a flamethrower than curse the darkness. Or somethin'."

"Somehow I doubt the Sarran are 'real flammable,' as you say," Mantis said. "They have been fighting the Mahlok for years… creatures with powers over fire that make that weapon you have there look like a toy. So perhaps you should rethink this flamethrower tactic."

"They're not expectin' a Mahlok attack, Mantis," Barracuda growled. "I think this baby'll catch 'em by surprise."

Mantis opened and closed his mouth. Finally he said, "Hm. Very well. Either that or *they* will surprise *you*."

Saber-Scorpion looked at his soldiers, all of whom were walking ahead of him. They were all equals in his eyes. He did not deserve to command them. In fact, it should have been the other way around. Gun-Barracuda, Silent-Cobra, and Blade-Mantis were each loyal to the core.

Saber-Scorpion was not.

"I'll take point," he said, in his best commander voice. "You three hold position here until I give the word. I want to scout out the casino alone."

"If you need a scout," Mantis offered, "I should be the one to go. I was the best student in the psionics exercises."

Scorp knew he was right. Precious little was known about the psychic powers exhibited by most Sarrans, but they did know that their powers allowed them to "feel" the thoughts and emotions of another being, letting them sense the presence of an approaching enemy. In the Enomeg class on psionics, they had been taught to discipline their mind and clear it of all unnecessary thought, to move like a machine, driving toward one goal alone and acting only on instinct.

How the instructors measured the results of these tests, none of the trainees knew… but Mantis had been the indisputable best, followed closely by Cobra. This was one field in which Saber-Scorpion had *not* excelled, and he knew why. Even now, he found it hard to concentrate on a single goal, his mind swimming with thoughts and doubts. If emotions and thoughts were likened to points of light visible only to Sarran eyes, his were probably burning with the light of a thousand suns.

But still he answered, "No, I'll go. If I need you, I'll contact you."

"No offense, Scorp," Barracuda growled, "but maybe you should listen to Mantis before you blow this whole mission–"

"Dark-Dragon put me in charge," Scorp interrupted. "I don't need you to question my orders, just follow them. You are to hold position here until I contact you again. Understood?"

They all nodded, but Barracuda clearly showed his anger at being forced to do so. Still, Scorp was less concerned about him than his other two companions, both of whom fixed him with the piercing gazes of good friends who knew he was not acting like himself. Barracuda might dismiss his attitude as brash eagerness to prove himself as the best, but Mantis and Cobra would either think he had changed a lot since the end of their training… or, far more likely, they would suspect he had ulterior motives. Still, they agreed to it. So, wasting no time, Scorp turned and headed in the direction of the casino.

"He's gonna kill this mission," Barracuda said when he had gone, "even if he doesn't kill himself."

Cobra looked worried, staring off at the alley into which Scorp had disappeared. As usual, she said nothing.

Mantis did the same for a few seconds, and then merely shrugged. "I'm sure Scorp will be fine. In the meantime, I suppose we can... just relax."

Barracuda growled. "I don't wanna *relax*; I want a piece of the damn action! Our first real mission, and we get ordered to stand around..."

"Are those snack machines?" Mantis ventured.

Barracuda looked quickly in the direction he indicated and snorted. "Not bad. It's been eons since I had any real junk food."

As the larger Enomeg moved in the direction of the vending machines, Mantis fished around in the pouch on his belt. "I think I brought some extra crowns with me..."

He was interrupted by a loud crash, and looked up to see Barracuda drawing his leg back out of the broken machine, as snack packages spilled out all over the pavement.

"Or," Mantis said, "if you don't mind destroying and stealing the property of Xarkonian citizens, that will also work."

"A penny saved..." said Silent-Cobra.

LOCATION: MORDARK EMBASSY, SHARDASHA

Shadow-Cat took a deep breath, leaned forward, took off at a run, and then leapt right out the window. Blood-Raven ran forward to watch as she cleared the gap between their building and the nearby tower of Lord Zegaldorph. Cat's acrobatics, as usual, worked perfectly. She cleanly grabbed the flagpole extending from the side of Zegaldorph's building and stopped herself from plummeting to her doom on the streets below.

Raven watched her swing in a complete loop over the flagpole and blew out a sigh. "Showoff."

"You know, this isn't a holo-game, Cat," Seth put in.

Magnum-Coyote just laughed.

Using both observation and guesswork, the Enomegs had already ascertained that only a few floors of Zegaldorph's tower would be constantly well-guarded. Certainly the bottom floors were among these, and perhaps the very top floors were as well. So they had to take the middle road. The feat of acrobatics had been Cat's idea, as was the method of entry, which she was now attempting to pull off.

Cat tied her grapple around the flagpole and, after testing her weight on the cable, let go with her hands. Dangling now only from the cord extending from the back of her armor, she drew a small device from her pocket and pressed it against the glass of the window in front of her.

Beside him, Raven heard Seth muttering to himself. Though Shadow-Cat was a skilled security hacker, as they all were, Seth was actually the best. So to make sure that no security system detected their entrance, Raven had ordered Shadow-Cat to let Seth do all of the hacking himself by remote. It was all done via the computers built into their Enomeg armor. Seth entered the appropriate commands on the control panel on his wrist, and then he nodded to Raven, who turned back to Shadow-Cat.

Cat saw the light on the device glow green. Security bypassed. She reached out and pressed a second button on the machine, which began to beep. Cat then calmly grasped the flagpole above her again, untied the cable, and began to swing. Once she had gathered enough momentum, she swung her legs up into the air, did a loop around the pole, and landed in a cat-like position on top of it. Then, almost the instant she landed, there was a crash below her, followed by the tinkle of shards of broken glass.

Cat swung back down and flew feet-first through the broken window, landing softly inside the building. She stood, turned, and nodded to Raven. The others did not perform her pole-vaulting tricks, instead choosing to simply fly over one by one using their jetpacks. Magnum-Coyote was the last to cross, and once inside, he immediately dropped a strange object he'd been holding. The large, dead bird-like creature landed with a thud on the floor.

"Good thing we found that beast on the roof," Eel commented.

"Yeah, good thing..." Coyote replied sarcastically, wringing out his bloody gloves, "but I still think it would have been better to cut a nice neat *hole* in the window."

"Do you really think that was big enough to have broken through the glass?" Cat asked. "Do you think anyone will believe it?"

"Doesn't matter if they believe it or not," Raven said. "At least there's an excuse here, so hopefully they won't put the place into immediate red alert. Now let's get a move on before they come to investigate that crash. Everyone go radio-silent. Use HUD-com and hand signals. Understood?"

The four dots on Raven's helmet HUD that represented the Enomegs immediately flashed green – confirmation of orders received and status ready. Raven nodded and pointed down the hall. As swift and silent as shadows, they disappeared. The guards were not far behind them, but they never saw a trace... besides the broken window and the dead bird, of course. After many tense days of duty during the city lockdown, the two guards that first arrived were quite terrified by the sight of the large, mangled, bloody corpse lying in the pool of shattered glass.

The first guard cursed under his breath.

"What the hell..." muttered the second.

"Looks like a kegric," said the first.

"I know what it is, but..." He switched on his commlink. "Chief, we've got a broken window here, and a bloody big dead bird. Kegric buzzard. Orders?"

In his own office seven stories up, the Chief of Security for the Mordark Embassy building leaned forward over his desk. "This is Security Chief Dawson. All floors on Orange Alert; there's been a possible break-in. I'm not taking any chances..."

Location: Black Network Casino, Shardasha

There was only one building overlooking the casino, and Saber-Scorpion was now making his way toward its roof – ascending one staircase at a time, since the elevator was out. As he rounded the fifth bend in the stairwell, he encountered a reflective surface on the wall… and almost caught himself saluting his own image.

It was a startling sight, to see himself clad in armor of the same color and nearly the same design as that of his commander and mentor, Dark-Dragon. He only reluctantly tore himself away from the sight, and as he continued, he realized how much it had bolstered his spirits. He would carry out this mission, he told himself, for Dark-Dragon's sake. Perhaps later, an Emperor would come along more deserving of his loyalty.

But if not… then what? Perhaps, a part of him said, the Enomegs would have to again don the mantle of assassins and defend their country from its own corrupt Emperor. He tried to imagine sneaking into Emperor Orrick's palace and doing the deed himself, but nearly every part of him revolted at the very idea. What was he doing even thinking such things? He shook his head and tried to focus on the task at hand.

Finally, he reached the roof, the light of Terra Nova's twin moons washing over him. He approached the edge cautiously, peering down at the casino below, his eyes alert for sentries. The entire building was decorated in lights of various shapes and sizes, most of them powered down to a dim glow merely for illumination, or not lit at all. The great arching sign on the front read "Orrick's Palace." Scorp almost laughed out loud at the irony. The décor was even complete with a giant rotating bust of the Emperor – though with a generic, featureless face – wearing the Crown of Xarkon.

Through with admiring the advertising, Scorp switched on his helmet's optical zoom and turned his mind to more serious matters: the guards. The many floors of the casino-hotel were lined with balconies and large windows, and quite a few of these featured a standing guard, weapon in hand. Some of them had heavy sniper rifles mounted to the balcony railings, and they periodically used their scopes to scan the neighborhood. Scorp was glad he had on his exoskeleton's automatic camouflage before exiting to the roof… the Black Network was taking no chances.

Then he finally spotted what he had been looking for: a Sarran. Upon zooming in on him, Scorp saw, much to his surprise, that this specimen had both his hands and his dark wings tied together, and he was being led down the hallway at gunpoint by one of the Network thugs. Scorp crouched down and breathed a sigh of relief. Apparently he would be a lucky player at this casino, for fate had finally dealt him a decent hand.

"Scorp to Team Quickstrike," he said into his commlink. "I've scoped out the casino. Move in to my position. It's time to start our attack."

"On our way," Cobra replied.

He heard Barracuda give an eager growl. "It's about time! I bet my share of all the money we can raid from the gambling machines that I get the most kills."

Mantis laughed. "I'll take that bet, and raise you my last candy bar from that vending machine."

"Deal."

LOCATION: SHARDASHA DOCKS

At the docks of Shardasha, not far from the very same spot where Grimm III and Lashnar had come ashore only a few nights ago, a shape now rose from the waves that looked from a distance like a long-dead crusading knight rising from a watery grave. It was Ryan, his highly-advanced armor now resembling a medieval warrior more than ever in its dull grey urban camouflage mode. As he pulled himself up onto the pier, he was followed by Amazon and the other Victorians, their armor a matching shade of grey.

The team moved out in exact formation, marching along the pier as if out on parade, each step full of Victorian pride. Behind them, following in a very similar manner, came Captain Jaleiko and the Mordark Royal Guard, who tossed down their swimming gear as soon as they were on dry land, since their regular armor did not have it built in like the Victorians'.

Suddenly the commanders' communicators blared to life: "Orion, Jaleiko, this is Thunder-Hawk. I'm picking up Xarkon soldiers headed your way. A group of defectors working with the rebels, probably. You might want to take up ambush positions before they're right on top of you."

Ryan halted and looked around. They had reached the city streets now, the moonlight reflecting off the windows of the buildings around them. There was certainly plenty of cover.

"How many?" asked the Victorian. "Any armor?"

"Certainly some light armor, or I wouldn't have detected them. Looks like two Jotun hovertanks. Can't say how many infantry…"

"How do you know they're defectors?"

"They've taken some pains to hide their signals, which Xarkon soldiers wouldn't. There are some other things too. Look, if you want, I can hail them and try asking, but that'll tip them off pretty quick."

"Forget it; I believe you. Orion out."

Ryan was certainly not opposed to taking out some Xarkonians.

He turned to face Jaleiko. "Captain, you should position your men to that side of the street, in those alleyways. I'll take this side. Get ready; they have light armor, two hovertanks."

Jaleiko nodded and waved his men into the alleyways on one side of the street. Ryan nodded to Amazon, and the Victorians took up positions on the opposite side.

Ryan opened up a channel to all soldiers, including both his and Jaleiko's. "They should be coming from the north any minute now. Remember, hit them from a distance. If we let them get between us then our cover's no good and we'll end up shooting each other from across the street."

"Sergeant Arkanian," Jaleiko answered, "please do not presume to give orders to my men."

"We have to work together, Captain," Ryan answered, "or we will die together. Now, do you have antitank weapons? Half my men are armed with shoulder-mounted missile tubes."

"None."

Ryan swore under his breath. "Fine. Just give supporting fire then."

"We will be a sufficient distraction for you, Sergeant. My men are good at that. Just wait and watch."

Ryan was watching, but for the tanks, not for any tricks from Jaleiko. He did not even have to switch on his night vision under the bright light of Terra Nova's moons. Finally he saw them turn the street corner far ahead. There were at least twenty soldiers, which meant that, between his forces and Jaleiko's, the enemy was outnumbered by about a dozen.

The trouble lay in the two Jotun hovertanks… the least of Xarkon's armored vehicles, but still a threat. They were relatively small vehicles about the size of a hovertruck, armed with a pair of starfire cannon on top and a pair of anti-personnel blazer machine guns on the front. All of this was controlled by a single pilot seated behind a thick sheet of transperium, driving the vehicle with a complex set of controls that made use of both the hands and feet for maximum precision. These features all added up to a tough but agile, well-armed vehicle – the perfect anti-infantry unit.

They would have to take the Jotuns down fast.

"Jaleiko," Ryan said calmly into his commlink, "would you like to give some orders now?"

"We're ready when you are," was the Captain's only response.

Ryan blew out a sigh. So it was all up to him to do the planning.

He opened up a channel to all the soldiers and said, "Amazon, I'm putting you in charge of the antitank soldiers. Station yourselves in the alleyways and fire one missile at a time, then retreat to the next alley. Don't stay in the same one. When you run out of alleys on this side of the street, fall back to that hovercar parking garage at the end of the road there. Corporal Swiften, I want you to hold that garage until they arrive and provide covering fire for their entry. That's our point of last stand. Take your men to the very top, and wait for my next command."

Greg Swiften was one of Ryan's better soldiers – a real wizard with grenades. He heard him give a reply in the affirmative, and then Amazon followed. They ran off to fulfill their orders.

"Captain Jaleiko," Ryan went on, "I want you to give covering fire, but your men shouldn't stay in the same alleys either. That makes them a target for those tank cannons, and none of these buildings will stand in the way of those. When you run out of cover, fall back to the parking garage too."

Ryan saw the moonlight glint off the reflective black hull of the second Jotun as it rounded the corner. The two tanks were in single file, preventing them from taking out both armored vehicles at once. The patrol was moving slowly, but now that they were on the main street they started to pick up speed. The helmeted heads of the soldiers turned this way and that, the light reflecting off their black visors as they did so. Ryan was surprised they were so attentive. It was like they expected something. He noticed some of them had non-standard weapons or coats that didn't match their uniform. Definitely rebels, he thought. Or else they're trying to *look* like rebels…

"Time to draw first blood," Ryan said. "Before they see us… Five rockets, at that first tank. Once you get a clear shot, confirm. Amazon will paint the target and give the word."

Amazon pressed a button on the side of her helmet, and a beam shot out and lit on the tank – visible only in the Victorians' heads-up displays. In Ryan's own HUD, he saw her light go blue, followed by the other soldiers'.

Amazon slid her finger into the trigger guard of her assault rifle's grenade launcher. "On my mark… fire!"

One after another, five streaks of smoke trailed across the sky, illuminating the buildings in flashes of red-orange light. An anti-missile laser, something Ryan had not expected on such a small vehicle as this hovertank, automatically cut down the first projectile, exploding it in midair, but it was not fast enough to get the others. The tank's wide turret was blown to scrap by a fireball… but the rest of the vehicle did not stop moving. Armed now with only its anti-personnel guns, the Jotun kept coming.

"Supporting fire!" Ryan shouted.

The Xarkon soldiers were moving out now, but both the Victorians and Jaleiko's troops popped out from every alley and opened fire on them as they scrambled for cover, some hiding behind the wide armor panels of the Jotun tanks, others behind anything they could find on the street. At least three went down immediately, and then the second Jotun fired its main guns. The loud THOOM of the cannons split the air, and half of one of the buildings across from Ryan came crashing down in a shower of glass and debris. An unlucky Mordark soldier was blown away with it, as his comrades moved around behind the structure to the next alley.

"Swiften, finish off that first Jotun," Amazon ordered calmly.

The grenadier did not hesitate to comply, drawing out one of his specialized adhesive grenades and activating it. As he looked down from atop the parking garage, his helmet's HUD perfectly calculated the trajectory of his projectile as he drew his arm back for the toss. The throw was perfect, the explosive landing right on top of the tank and sticking there. The Xarkonians barely had time to turn, look, and then throw themselves to the ground before the vehicle exploded. As the hoverpads lost power, the Jotun's charred hull hit the ground with a thud.

Ryan carried two pistols: a standard Victorian blazer sidearm… and a heavily-customized Harpy Eagle magnum, loaded with explosive bullets. He now drew out the latter and took careful aim at one of the Xarkonians fleeing back down the street. One shot sent the enemy packing, landing face-first on the pavement. After a few more parting shots, Ryan turned and ran back in the alley. Several of his soldiers joined him.

"Don't go in that parking garage until the second tank is down," Ryan ordered. "Amazon, how's it coming?"

Again they heard the streaking rockets and another explosion. Finally, Ryan thought.

Jaleiko's voice broke in over the commlink, "Second tank has lost main guns. Wait… it looks like it's bugging out."

"Affirmative, Captain. Now you and your men fall back to the parking garage on the double. We'll engage the infantry from in there. Amazon, fall back!"

By this time, Ryan and his men had arrived at the parking garage, which loomed a full six stories over them. He saw the squad leader Swiften above signal that the coast was clear. Upon running up the ramp inside, they discovered it was full of parked hovercars of every shape and size. Ryan was surprised; he had expected it to be as empty as the city streets mostly were.

"Plenty of cover here," Ryan said, "but I'd prefer the battle didn't make it this far. Amazon, head up there and take over from Swiften. My men and I will hold down the fort here."

"And we'll join you," came the voice of Captain Jaleiko.

Ryan saw Jaleiko and his men approaching from the other side of the parking lot. They each unclipped a T-shaped metal device from their belt and held it up. There was a flash of light, almost blinding, and the row of royal guards flourished their red energy blades in a salute. Jaleiko drew his own sword, a blazer model with a solid blade, and advanced to the front of his men. They dropped their salute, deactivated their weapons again, and assumed battle positions, taking cover behind hovercars and support pillars. Jaleiko took position beside Ryan.

"Impressive display," Ryan said.

He, on the other hand, was much more practical. He merely drew out one of his long blazer daggers and the smaller of his two pistols, and then crouched behind a hovercar and waited. Jaleiko noted the hand-guard on the dagger curved over the first finger and then back down over the rest, forming a shape somewhat like the letter R. The knife was quite an intricate weapon; certainly not a standard Victorian Bowie-II or the like. It looked custom-made.

Ryan saw the Mordark guard captain watching him and said, "Better keep your eyes on the street out there. Someone's coming."

Right on queue, the first of the enemy soldiers arrived. If Ryan had found the display of Jaleiko's guards impressive, Jaleiko found Ryan's brutal show far more so. It left him speechless. With a mere glance to check his enemies' positions, the Victorian rolled out from behind cover and, while lying prone, shot down the first two of the Xarkonians just as they set foot on the ramp. The next two opened fire, but the Victorian Immortal presented too low a profile, and all their poorly-aimed shots went wide.

Then Ryan curled up and rolled straight down the ramp, right toward the soldiers. They hardly had time to react as his dagger plunged into the first soldier, between his armor plating, then drew back out and flew through the air into the neck of another. He drew out his pistol now, even as the shots of the next few enemies struck the back of the dead body he still held in front of him like a shield.

Ryan took a few steps forward and then threw the body onto his next enemy, knocking the man off his feet. He then drew his second dagger, slicing at the neck of the last soldier visible. His first swipe missed, but the enemy did not.

Ryan felt the burst of bullets strike his duranium armor plating. Only one shot made it past the armor, lodging in his shoulder, but by then it was too late for his foe, who had a dagger lodged in a far more vital position. Meanwhile, the soldier on which Ryan had thrown the body was struggling to aim his heavy Xarkonian assault rifle while lying on his back. Ryan merely turned, stepped on the barrel of the man's gun, and fired a shot into his head, the magnum bullets blasting right through his transperium visor. He went limp.

The young Victorian surveyed his work, planting another bullet into a soldier who twitched, and then he turned and regarded Jaleiko, who stood staring speechlessly at the top of the ramp. The whole fight had been so quick and deadly that he hadn't even found a chance to fire a shot. Without wasting time, Ryan quickly gathered both of his daggers, jerking them out of the bodies of his foes, deactivated the still-sizzling energy shields, and sheathed them. Then he switched on his night-vision, ran up the ramp, and entered the parking lot, where the fight was now going strong.

"How did they make it in?" he asked.

"They must have used the lift on the other side," Jaleiko answered. "I didn't even know it was there."

Ryan swore. That elevator should have been disabled before the fight began. Did he have to tell his troops how to do everything? Swiften should have thought of it… but it was no use dwelling on that now.

Ryan ran up the stairs to the second level. As soon as he stuck his head out, a bullet whizzed right past it, the projectile's blazer shield flashing in his night-vision. Ryan drew his smaller pistol and fired randomly toward the shot's source. As the Xarkon helmets ahead withdrew behind cover, Ryan took note of their positions. Then he slipped behind the nearest hovercar and hid himself as well as possible.

"I need a sit-rep!" Ryan barked. "I've got hostiles on floor two; where are the others?"

"All of my men are up top," Amazon responded, her voice followed by the sound of gunshots. "Looks like most of the other Crownies are too."

Ryan unhooked a grenade from his belt. "Good," he said.

He activated the explosive and cocked back his arm, estimating the distance to the cars just ahead of where he had spotted the enemy soldiers. He would have rolled the grenade under the cars… but many hovercars sat flush with the ground when deactivated, with no gap beneath them. So he was forced to toss it into the air. His aim was true, and after the echoing explosion he was rewarded with a few screams. Jaleiko and the royal guards moved up to flank Ryan, and within a few seconds they had cleared the room.

"We're coming to reinforce you, Amazon. What's the best way up?"

"We're on the south side, at the top of the main ramp. If you head up the lift, you'll come up behind the Xarkonians… unless they see you coming."

"Doesn't sound like a good idea. We'll come up your way."

It did not take long for Ryan and his men to clear the next few floors and emerge on the roof, where the moonlight was again sufficient to see by. The top of the building was covered in broken glass from shattered car windows, as both sides continued firing at one another from across the lot. Several of the vehicles had been reduced to smoking metal frameworks by rockets and grenades.

Ryan ducked behind a car beside Amazon just as another spray of bullets whizzed over his head. "How many hostiles left?"

"Maybe ten?" she ventured.

He looked up at his HUD and saw the Victorians had only two men down, leaving them with a total of thirty-three troops, counting Jaleiko's guards. Only a few were mildly injured.

"Let's drive them back," he said. "Swiften, you and your squad come with me. Amazon, Jaleiko, you and the rest give suppressing fire. Now!"

As the soldiers stood and let fly a barrage of bullets, prompting the Xarkonians on the other side to take cover, Ryan and Swiften's team stood up and set off at a run, heading around the right side of the lot. Once a Xarkonian's head appeared, and Ryan took a few shots at it, but missed. Then, as he neared the far side of the building, all of the Xarkonians set off at a run toward the elevator. As the doors of the large, car-sized lift closed, Ryan and Swiften ran forward to watch the platform descend.

"It's going down," Ryan said.

"It sure is," Swiften replied, drawing out two grenades.

Ryan put a hand on his arm. "Put those up. Let them go. If we keep fighting them, they'll keep fighting back. I don't want to lose any more men. Amazon, go see to the wounded! We move out as soon as we can."

Location: Sewers under Mordark Embassy

The sound of bending, tearing metal screeched and echoed through the sewer tunnels like the scream of a raging bull elephant. Had there been any observers, they would have seen four hands emerge from the rending steel. The two mercenaries pulled themselves up to the surface, slick with dripping water. One was clad in shining violet-black... the other in blood red.

- CHAPTER TWENTY -
FIRE AND BLOOD

"I told you… we thrive on information. It's our lifeblood, babe."

"Lucky" Jim Crow prodded the Sarran female's cheek with the barrel of his rifle. Despite having her hands, legs, *and* wings tied up with steel cords, Folirayoth did not even flinch, and her pale eyes seemed to bore into him. He cocked a half-hearted grin and moved his gun barrel to push back a strand of her hair, which was stark white, even though her features were youthful. He thought this would have made her husband, Idelma'ik, shoot him a hostile glare if nothing else, but his face remained utterly emotionless.

"I hate Sarran," said Lucky Jim Crow.

Idelma'ik, the male with black hair and wings, continued his calm stare, his chiseled features unmoving. "So do many of your kind. You envy us for our appearance, our grace, our long life, our abilities of flight, and our powers of mind and spirit. You envy everything about us, and so you hate. Perhaps it will comfort you to know that the feeling is mutual. I hate you for buying Sarran prisoners of war and selling them like lab animals to scientific facilities all over Human space. Yes, I have *my* information too."

Jim Crow grinned. "So you thought you'd just come down here in the middle of our meeting with Zegaldorph, steal our information and find out our sources, and then assassinate me?"

"Assassinate?" Idel said evenly. "Amusing. You actually think yourself important enough for the use of that word. No, we were not here to assassinate you. We were simply going to kill you. I doubt your organization would even have cared."

"Well, you screwed up." Jim taunted with a laugh. "You both screwed up bigtime, and now look at you: held hostage and soon headed to some lab just like your kin. Tell 'em I said 'hi.'"

There was a moment of silence, interrupted only by the distant sound of music coming from farther inside the casino. Crow walked over to the window and signaled to one of the guards outside, who responded with a shrug. The coast was still clear.

Then the female, Folirayoth, pierced him with her gaze. "You're afraid. Your fear is almost palpable. You know that Xarkon has this city under lockdown, and you know they are not going to accept responsibility for it. No, they will pin it on someone… a criminal, perhaps. Someone like you. Any moment now, they could be arriving, and from any direction…"

Crow turned and brandished his assault rifle, again to no visible effect on his prisoners. He was about to make another threat, but thought twice about it and simply turned away from them, trying to appear entirely indifferent. He looked back out the window at his pacing guard… when suddenly the man's forehead spat out a burst of blood. Crow watched as the sentry's body fell against the balcony railing, flipped over the top of it, and plummeted down to the street below.

Crow dove for cover and activated his commlink. "What the hell is going on out there?! Some sniper just dusted off my window guard!"

"All's clear here, boss, but I'll –"

Jim Crow heard the reason the guard had been cut off… the sounds of gunshots were now echoing from farther in the casino. They were rapid, repetitive, and extremely loud. It sounded almost like a light machine gun. Who would carry around a weapon like that? Soon it was followed by a tremendous crash, and then the reports of many more weapons. He only hoped they were those of his guards. Desperately, Jim Crow looked around for a way to escape… and caught the yellow eyes of the female Sarran again.

"They're here," she said.

LOCATION: MORDARK EMBASSY, SHARDASHA

All was quiet in the Royal Guard Armory of the Mordark Embassy in Shardasha, Xarkon. Half of the full Guard force had accompanied Lord Zegaldorph on his business trip to Shardasha, and they had never left his side. Half of *this* number was currently awake and guarding Zegaldorph in his private quarters on the highest floor of the building, while the other half was asleep in the armory. They had no quarters, preferring to sleep where they were surrounded by weapons and soldiers, well-guarded and safe. Nothing could sneak its way into their armory. Nothing was there except shadows.

But one of the shadows was moving.

She approached a guard sleeping soundly on a bench and carefully removed the small silenced pistol from its holster on his belt. The Mordark Royal Guard were not allowed to carry bladed weapons to avoid the possibility of treachery, since such weapons were one of the few things capable of piercing the skin of their Mahlok master. Energy blades had almost no effect upon his kind, so they served as the main armament for the royal guards… besides their blazer rifles and pistols.

This pistol, along with the few others she had stolen from the armory, would serve as evidence against the man that Shadow-Cat had now chosen to play the role of their traitor. Of course, the pistol would have little effect upon Zegaldorph, but it could help against the other guards. For the Lord of Mordark himself, the Enomegs had brought plenty of bladed weapons that would have been available to the guards, mostly civilian knives. Armed with her new acquisition, Cat slipped out of the armory as silently as she had come. The room now contained one less shadow.

She reemerged into the hallway, shoving the pistol into her belt and handing the other three to her companions: Eel, Raven, and Coyote. Magnum-Coyote weighed the weapon in his hand a bit, checked to make sure it was loaded, and then twirled it on his finger.

"Good quality pistols," he said. "Very quiet, no doubt. But this is almost ridiculously low-caliber, even for an HPG weapon. Didn't they have anything bigger in that armory? This would hardly kill that bird we left in the hall back there."

"Cut the whining, Coyote," Raven snapped.

"Yes, *sir*," Coyote muttered, shoving the weapon into his extra holster. "Back to robot mode. Transform and roll out."

Zegaldorph's quarters were located on the floor above them, which was smaller than the one below. So far the Enomegs had taken the emergency stairs, disabling the alarms as they went. But the stairs did not reach top floor, and even if they were crazy enough to try them, the elevators were all locked down by the security alert they had triggered.

"I can't believe we have to go out the window again," Seth Electric-Eel commented gloomily.

Raven shook his head. "Last time I checked, you were supposed to be super-soldiers. So why… are you *all*… *whining*?"

"Sorry, sir," Seth replied.

Shadow-Cat, meanwhile, was finishing her removal of the window. She set the glass down gently on the floor and then leaned out, looking straight up. Behind her, the Enomegs could see the city, with the sides of the skyscrapers dark and oppressive against the night sky.

"Time to be spiders," Cat said, and then she disappeared.

Seth swallowed. "It's not that I'm afraid of heights; it's just falling from them that scares me."

"It's not the fall that gets you…," Coyote put in.

"*Coyote*…" Raven said threateningly.

"Oh, I forgot. Robot mode."

Blood-Raven walked closer to the window and looked up. The landing platforms, tiny from a distance but huge in person, that encircled the peak of Zegaldorph's tower, now loomed above them like a ceiling to the sky. They were supported by a spider web of crisscrossing beams and scaffolding, including several support beams that extended down to the side of the building next to their window exit. These beams extended out to the edge of the platform above at a sharp upward angle. They could see Cat already climbing upside-down along one of these now, headed steadily upward. Below her lay the dark city, only a few sparse windows alight in the silent buildings.

Raven glanced back at Seth and Coyote, the moonlight from outside glinting off his onyx armor as he did so. "You two first. I'll take up the rear."

Seth, clearly trying not to think about this predicament, immediately swung out onto the scaffolding. Hand over hand, foot over foot, without pause, he climbed. Coyote gazed at the city below before stepping out, and he gave a long whistle, quickly looking up to see if he had enticed Seth into looking down. The other Enomeg ignored him, however, so Coyote merely shrugged and began to follow. The steel beams had plenty of good handholds in the form of crisscrossing bars for added strength. It was like they had provided the Enomegs with a convenient, if awkward, ladder.

Raven replaced the window behind them before beginning to climb. Upon feeling the weight of his body hanging over thin air, even Raven had to admit to himself that the feeling was unsettling. Every time he took his hand out to reach for the next handhold, his heart seemed to skip a beat… but with the thrill of the event, not with fear. He was enjoying every moment of it.

Ahead of him, Coyote said into the commlink, "Tradition dictates that at this point someone has to say: 'The trick is not to look down.'"

"Well, let's certainly not break with tradition…" Raven replied exasperatedly, as he continued to ascend, hand over hand, "but I'd *prefer* if you kept radio-silent."

"Ah, come on, Raven," Coyote laughed, "you saw the guards in there. They've been on yellow alert since this incident started… so they've gotten pretty relaxed about it by now."

He was silenced by a sudden gust of wind… not because it was that loud, but because it nearly swept them off their handholds. One of Seth's feet came loose, but he quickly replaced it and held on tight. They all clung for their lives, hugging the slanted metal beams close. After a few seconds, the wind passed. Seth breathed a sigh of relief and cursed over the commlink.

"I said com-*silent*," Raven hissed. "Honestly, the next one of you that chatters at all will get a personal beating from me when we get to the top."

There was no reply, which meant the affirmative, Raven assumed. They continued on. Soon, Cat reached the top. She clambered up to the rim of the support structure and reached up over the edge of the landing platform. Her hand touched a metal railing, which she grasped and used to pull herself up. Hanging from only her hands, with her feet dangling over thousands of feet of emptiness, she peered through the bars.

Into the commlink, she said, "I spy, with my little eye…"

"*Cat*," Raven snapped, "what did I just say about com chatter?"

"Do be quiet, Raven," Cat replied calmly. "I'm holding on up here by just two hands and trying to tell you about the guards I see on patrol. I don't know if I have a good grip…"

"Kind of like my grip on the command of this unit, obviously," Raven replied.

"*Each of us* is a unit, dear," Cat said priggishly. "Ah, the guard's gone now. It's safe to move."

Raven only grunted in response and continued to follow.

"Sir?" came Coyote's voice teasingly. "Did she just call you dear?"

"I swear… by every power… that might exist," Raven said through clenched teeth, now laboring for breath from all the climbing and talking, "that when we get… to the top of this… I'm going to beat that sense of… *humor…* right out of you… Coyote."

One by one, the Enomegs swung up over the edge of the landing pad. As soon as their feet hit solid metal, they rushed for cover behind a stack of shipping crates. When they had all joined Cat, she pointed in the direction of the three sentries on patrol. Raven peered out and looked at them. Then he looked back at Coyote, raising three fingers. Nodding, Magnum-Coyote slowly and deliberately rose to his feet, took a peek over the top of the crates, then swung out, holding his gun with both hands… and fired three shots.

"Clear," Coyote said, not feeling the need to waste words anymore.

Raven nodded. "Move."

The Enomegs leapt from their hiding places and began a sprint across the open platform. Far ahead of them was the great wall of glass that was the only thing separating them from the inside… from Lord Zegaldorph, wherever he was on this floor. Thankfully, there was a door this time too.

"Guard!" Seth hissed.

They did not halt, but they all spotted him soon enough. A guard inside just rounded the corner in the hall, coming into view of the landing platform. If he so much as turned his head, their entire mission could be over. Magnum-Coyote slowed to a halt.

"Slow down or you'll give us away," he said.

"No time!" Raven snapped back, drawing his pistol as he ran.

Cocking the weapon, Raven ran straight to the door and punched in the security code that Seth had hacked out of the building computers earlier. Even as the door slid open, he leaned inside and fired.

"Clear," Raven said.

The others joined him. Together they moved through the hall, taking down one more guard before reaching the last corner. Raven took a peek around and saw the door that undoubtedly led to Zegaldorph's makeshift "throne away from the throne." The door was surrounded by a flame motif made of solid gold. On either side of the door were windows looking out at the city, so the Enomegs could only guess that Zegaldorph's throne room was in a small section protruding from the outside of the building, almost hanging in midair. As far as they knew, there was no landing platform on this side of the skyscraper, so it must have been built this way for the view.

"Just one guard," Raven told the others. "I'll take him. Eel, go find a computer terminal and see what you can do to handle security, and maybe even give us a clear path in and out. Hurry before they figure out the guards are no longer reporting in!"

Seth nodded and slid away, running back down the hall.

"Can't just gun down this guard," Coyote said. "He's one of the Royals... too heavily armored, and I can't find a weakness with that red cloak he's wearing in the way."

"But there's another weapon they all carry..." Raven said, and he clenched his fists, "energy blades. I'll go first. Cat, follow me. Coyote, you wait here and provide cover fire if things get hot. Go!"

Cat and Raven took off at a silent, shuffling run. The guard, wearing a red cloak with some kind of tall collar that concealed the back of his head, was still facing away from them when Raven came up behind him. In the blink of an eye, Raven's handblades flashed online and sliced in two arcs, cutting a cross into the guard's back.

The sliced-off lower half of the crimson cloak floated down to the floor, but Raven's eyes were fixed on his enemy's back, which was now revealed to him. It was orange and radiant, with a glowing white-hot X marking where his blades had sliced. As he watched, the white turned to yellow, then orange, then red as it dissipated completely away into the now-cooling skin. But by then, Raven was backing quickly away.

The man now turned to regard them, bringing his bald, red-skinned head into view, covered in ornate black patterns like tattoos. There was no mouth or nose, only two thin yellow slits for eyes, glowing with inner fire. It was the face of a Mahlok.

"Get your knife out, Cat!" Raven shouted. "It's Zegaldorph himself!"

LOCATION: ORRICK'S PALACE CASINO, SHARDASHA

Saber-Scorpion signaled to Barracuda and Mantis to fall in behind him as they approached one of the side-doors of the Black Network's casino.

"Mantis," he said, "you get us in. Cobra, you provide sniper cover from the outside and make sure no one escapes while we do the butcher's work. But remember, if you see any hostages, you are to leave them alive."

"Dragon said no evidence —" Barracuda began to protest.

"You let me worry about that!" Scorp snapped, pointing a thumb at his ebony breastplate. "Or have you forgotten my rank? Now just get that monster of a gun ready."

Barracuda hefted his Buzzsaw machine gun. "Aye, sir."

Ahead of them, Mantis had just finished working the door. He gave the signal, and he and Scorp fell into position on either side as it slid open. After a few seconds, a guard walked up to check... and Mantis quickly and expertly slid the edge of his blazer katana across the man's throat. Then he and Scorp slipped inside, heading in opposite directions, while Barracuda simply headed straight forward.

The Enomegs found themselves in the main gambling hall; a vast open space with a raised walkway around the perimeter for spectators to watch the action on the floor below from a high vantage point. In the center were rows upon rows of gambling tables of various shapes and sizes, for all sorts of games… and hanging high overhead was another huge faceless bust of a Xarkonian Emperor, covered in glittering lights.

There were thugs everywhere, all armed and clad in black body armor, but they hardly noticed Mantis and Scorp entering… for all of their attention was distracted by the hulking form of Gun-Barracuda, his armor now shifting back to its default crimson red. Even as the guards reached for their weapons, Barracuda lifted his machine gun, pointed it up, and pulled the trigger. His entire body shook as the weapon sent a non-stop stream of blazer bullets into the sparkling decorations on the ceiling. Sparks flew from the myriad lights on the giant Emperor bust as it came crashing to the floor, crushing many of the guards and gambling tables beneath it. Even as the room exploded around him, Barracuda did not stop shooting. Many of the guards who had hidden behind the gambling machines and tables found their cover exploding from an onslaught of high-powered blazer fire.

"New player!" Barracuda shouted with a laugh, "Warm up the dice!"

By this point, the guards on the balconies above had their guns drawn and leveled… but Scorp and Mantis were already there, and not a single guard got off a shot at Barracuda before their focus was drawn to a more immediate threat. Scorp and Mantis both took out their first two targets in the same way, sending a blade in the first man's back while firing a few well-aimed shots at the second with their pistol. They then fell back to the shadows before the other thugs could even get a clear look at what was attacking them. Below, Barracuda continued his killing spree unobstructed.

"Four… five…" the enormous Enomeg said to himself as he fired away while heading for the nearest cover.

He laughed as the thugs' bullets tore apart the slot machine behind which he had crouched, spilling heaps of Xarkonian crowns onto the floor. Barracuda waited for the gunfire to slow down, and then he went prone and let off another spray of ammunition with his Buzzsaw. The sparks that showered from the exploding lights all around set the carpeted floor ablaze, and if there had ever been any order in the ranks of the Black Network guards, it was entirely lost now as they ran for cover from both bullets and licking flames. Barracuda fed these flames with his flamethrower, lighting up every spot he saw that wasn't already ablaze.

"Six, seven… eight…"

Each Enomeg now had one floor to himself: Barracuda was on the main level while Scorp and Mantis took care of the balconies to either side. Any guards who tried to flee the building soon discovered that the Enomegs had that base covered as well… when Silent-Cobra invariably picked them off with her sniper rifle, littering the street outside with bodies.

Mantis made sure that no more gunners on his side of the balcony would be bothering Barracuda from above, and then he made his way toward a recessed side door marked "employees only." A guard was hiding in the alcoves to either side, but the door itself was wide open. Not wasting time, Mantis stepped directly out in front of the guards and slashed the first one across the chest with his blazer katana. The man's body armor was unable to stop the combined might of heat and steel, and he went down without a struggle, but the Enomeg felt a few of the bullets from the other soldier strike his force shield, which flared up with the impacts. The man was backing up as he fired, but not far enough to be out of reach of Mantis's second slice, the very tip of the well-aimed blade catching his throat. Mantis stepped through the spray of blood and into the room the two men had been guarding.

He spoke into the commlink. "Scorp, I've found some kind of computer room."

"Destroy everything you see," Saber-Scorpion replied, "and make sure *nothing* is recoverable. I'm heading up to the next floor."

Scorp ran up the first flight of stairs he encountered with his guns blazing. His bullets shredded into the feet of the men who had been running down to meet him, causing them to stumble down over each other in a great mass of limbs and firing guns. Without pausing to ensure they had been neutralized, Scorp fired his jetpack and flew right over them, landing on the next bend in the staircase above. He then continued on, headed to the floor where Cobra had reported spotting the two prisoners.

"Any word, Cobra?"

"Eight kills," she responded. "None I've seen have escaped. The two Sarrans are still tied up on the sixth floor, south side."

"Anyone else in the room?"

"Affirmative, at least one guard, but I can't get a shot at him. He knows I'm here."

"I'll take care of it. Just keep covering the streets."

"On it."

This last transmission was followed by the crack of Cobra's rifle as she cut down another would-be survivor. When he reached the sixth floor, Scorp stuck his star-talon right between the two doors and pried them open. He was met immediately by gunfire, but ducked back quickly enough to avoid being hit. The sound of guards approaching up the stairs behind him made him pause. He pulled a frag grenade off his belt and armed it. When he heard the first guard below take a shot at him, he tossed the grenade and dove through the door he had just opened, bullets whizzing past as he rolled.

As the explosion of his grenade echoed through the building, followed by screams, Scorp looked around to find himself in a luxurious hotel hallway, lined with doors. Poking out of every other door in the hallway… was the barrel of a rifle, all pointed straight at him. The strange thing was, he did not see anyone holding them. Wasting no time, he pressed his body tightly against the nearest door as the bullets whizzed past. Then he stabbed the controls and sliced the door open, ducking quickly inside.

Scorp took in the layout of the hotel room at a glance, and one feature caught his eye; it was connected to the adjacent room by a locked wooden door. He removed this obstacle with his star-talon blade the same way he had done the others and came up behind the two men who had been waiting for him to reemerge into the hall. They barely had time to turn a startled glance in his direction before he riddled them with bullets.

Reloading his SMG quickly, Scorp looked for a door leading to the next room. There was none; the room was only connected to the one he had just left. Undaunted, he approached the door back to the main hall, picking up the dead guards and tossing one of them over each shoulder as he passed. Just after throwing their bodies out into the hall in plain view of their comrades, Scorp paused. They appeared to be wearing some kind of advanced HUD visors that were wired directly to an attachment on their rifles.

Cursing, Scorp spoke into his commlink. "Barracuda, Mantis, be advised: the guards on the upper floors are equipped with gun-cams, so they won't be exposing themselves when firing. They just poke out their guns, aim using their heads-up display, and shoot."

"Affirmative, Scorp," he heard Mantis respond. "I'm heading to the upper floors now."

"Still cleaning up the bottom here," Barracuda said. "Cobra, a couple of 'em bugged out and headed for the garage. Can you confirm…"

Suddenly an explosion rocked the building, and Scorp saw the area outside the windows behind him briefly glow orange.

"Confirmed," Cobra said. "Your explosives did their job. The getaway car is toast."

Barracuda laughed. "Great. Can you confirm how many kills they got? I'd say at least three."

Another gunshot rang out into the night. "Two. I just had to finish off one of them."

"Okay, cut the chatter," Scorp ordered. "You can keep a kill count without talking about it."

"Yes, sir," Mantis replied. "However, I have just reached the backup power generator. Area clear. Should I cut the lights?"

Scorp picked up the gun-cam rifle and inspected the device on the barrel. It appeared to have built-in light-amplification. The dark wouldn't really bother these soldiers… but it could still give Scorp an advantage.

"Do it."

Suddenly the hum of machinery throughout the building died away, and all of the myriad lights of the casino went dim. By this time, Scorp was already moving as quickly as he could. Even as the first pair of guards in the next room were still looking around in confusion, reaching to activate their night vision, the Enomeg was upon them, stepping right through the door and cutting them down with his blades. He then shoved their bodies out into the corridor with the others. This time a few wild shots slammed into the corpses, and he heard a loud swear from the man who had fired. The sight of the bodies was having its desired effect: the guards were starting to get panicky.

Scorp again proceeded to the next room. Just before entering the main hall again, however, he raised a hand to the controls on the side of his helmet. On either side of his visor were installed a pair of powerful lights capable of emitting twice as much illumination as his even his Starfire hand-blades. When he stepped out into the hallway and activated these, the guards using their night vision cameras hardly knew what hit them. The half-blinded men almost thought the shafts of light waving before their eyes were merely figments of their imaginations... right before they stabbed into their chests. Done with his dirty-work, Scorp deactivated the star-talon blades.

With a surprising note of satisfaction, he muttered, "Twelve."

LOCATION: MORDARK EMBASSY, SHARDASHA

Blood-Raven and Shadow-Cat activated their personal energy shields and drew out their cold steel knives... just before the wave of fire from Zegaldorph's outstretched hands washed over them, throwing them off their feet. Only their fireproof armor and shielding saved them from being reduced to ashes on the spot.

Even as the flames engulfed him, eating away at his shielding, Raven shouted, "Coyote, shoot any guards you see! Leave no witnesses!"

"That won't be a prob–" Coyote began, but he was abruptly cut off as an arm grabbed him around the throat.

His attacker lifted him easily, far too easily, off his feet and slammed him bodily into the wall so hard that the surface splintered and broke. Coyote quickly raised his pistol, but his assailant's free hand caught his wrist and crushed it in an iron grip. Coyote cried out in pain and dropped his weapon... then quickly kneed his attacker between the legs. There was an intake of breath, and the Enomeg felt the iron grip over his throat loosen.

Coyote quickly scooped up his Dirge. "That move always works."

His assailant was wearing a solid red suit of some kind of armor mesh, covered in a few places by silvery armor. His black hair was a mess, and one of the green eyes under his pair of bushy white eyebrows was apparently missing, the cavity covered by an eyepatch. Coyote took all of this in over the span of less than a second, and then he fired two shots into the man's stomach, right into a crack in his armor.

Then the Enomeg paused, and his attacker sprang again. To Coyote's utter astonishment, the man actually slapped the gun right out of his hand, kneed him in the chest, and, clamping a red-gloved hand over the front of his helmet, slammed his head into the wall – two, three, four times. Coyote slid to the ground, apparently knocked out cold.

Grimm III stepped over the body and into the hall.

Two royal guards had exited Zegaldorph's throne room and were now aiding their master in the hallway. It was a strange sight, the two Enomegs each armed with one activated hand-blade and one large machete-like butcher knife, battling it out with Zegaldorph's red-caped guards, while behind them the Mahlok watched with his two glowing yellow eyes.

270

"Zegaldorph!" Three shouted. "I'm here to get you outta this city!"

The Mahlok looked up past the fighting to regard the mercenary for the first time. Just then, Raven successfully knocked aside the blade of the guard he was battling and planted his butcher knife in his throat. Then he drew it back out and advanced on Zegaldorph.

But Grimm III was faster. He barreled into the Enomeg's back, knocking him to the floor with his shoulder. Unfortunately, quarters were tight, and this knocked Raven right into the leg of the second royal guard. The man was knocked off balance just long enough for Shadow-Cat to finish him. Not about to lose the opportunity, she leaped over the two bodies and, ducking under Zegaldorph's spray of fire, moved to stab the Mahlok in the gut.

Her blade only got to graze his skin, releasing a thin line of hot yellow blood, before Grimm III grabbed her by the arm and wrenched her away, lifting her off her feet and slamming her into the nearest wall. To Cat's surprise, the blow completely knocked the wind out of her, and she felt her body go limp as a rag doll.

Behind them, Raven crawled to his feet and saw Three clamping his hand over Shadow-Cat's throat. With a roar of rage, he launched himself at the mercenary, bearing down with all his weight and the strength of his legs. It was just enough to knock the practical walking tank off his feet, though only for a second. But as soon as he let go of Cat's throat, Three's other hand slammed into Raven. Even through his armor, Raven felt the sheer force of the blow as it struck his shoulder. He thought he felt his collarbone break.

"What *are* you?!" he had a chance to cry out, before Grimm III kicked him in the chest.

Raven managed to grab onto the mercenary's foot, but it was no use, for Three simply used this to push the Enomeg even farther, and Raven was sent stumbling backwards. Finally he felt his back hit a window, heard glass shatter, and down he fell. At the last second he managed to grab onto the sharp edge of the broken glass and grip it tightly. He tried to fire his jetpack, but apparently it had been damaged in the fight, for it did not respond. As his legs dangled over certain death, the wind blowing around him, Raven felt an uncontrollable rage now burning inside of him, as strong as the rage he'd felt after his battle with Saber-Scorpion in the Test of Supremacy. Channeling this rage into his arms, he started to pull himself up.

When Cat had collected enough strength to stand, she saw Grimm III and Zegaldorph exchanging heated words, and then she noticed Raven's bleeding fingers – the glass having cut even through his nanomesh gloves – gripping the broken window. She quickly moved to the window and grabbed his wrists, as Three and Zegaldorph ran off down the hall. She thought she saw the mercenary give her a parting wink… though since he had only one eye, he may have just been blinking.

Cat helped Raven up and found him full of life and sputtering curses. Though hurt, neither of them was ready to quit, and they could tell merely by looking at one another that they were both itching to go after Grimm III and Zegaldorph. Raven's chest was heaving less because he was out of breath and

Justin R. Stebbins

more because he was full of rage. How had that mercenary managed to beat him so easily? He had never expected such a man to exist. If he could face him again, and this time knowing what to expect…

"Eel!" Raven shouted over his commlink. "Eel, Zegaldorph is getting away! See if you can do something to stop him, slow him down, anything!"

Instead of Electric-Eel, it was a soft feminine voice that answered: "Oh, I won't stop *him*, but I will stop *you*."

The floor shook as two heavy duranium doors suddenly dropped down from the ceiling, closing off the hallway on either side of the Enomegs. Similar doors began sealing off each of the windows, one by one. Then a strange, shimmering gas could be seen hissing from jets on either side of the hallway. Cat and Raven were looking around desperately for an escape route when they heard a voice on the commlink. It was Dark-Dragon.

"Jump, Raven! Out the window, now! Just do it!"

It only took until the "now" before Raven grabbed Cat's arm and, dragging her behind him, ran and leaped through the broken window. They fell a couple of feet, and then landed with a clang on top of the Bergelmir transport, which was apparently flying at skyscraper height over the surface of the city streets. And almost as soon as they had left the building, the entire hallway they'd been standing in was engulfed in flames, which roared now out of the broken windows. Apparently Zegaldorph liked his security systems to fit his personal tastes…

Opening the upper hatch of the Berg, Cat climbed down inside, with Raven following behind her. Dark-Dragon was sitting there waiting for them, stony silent, his hands clenched together as he stared at the opposite wall in thought.

"Get us out of here, G," he said to the pilot. He had no idea why they called her G; probably something to do with G-forces.

"Yes, sir," she replied.

Dragon turned to Raven. "Tell me what it is you saw, Luke. Tell me everything."

"It was a man…" Cat began, but Raven cut her off.

"It wasn't a man!" he shouted. "No man could fight like that! He was faster, stronger, tougher than any man I've ever encountered! He tossed me around like a sack of –"

"He was a cyborg," Dragon interrupted. "I've faced one before, as you know."

They felt the craft lurch under them as it landed back on solid ground. The Berg was only a hover vehicle, normally incapable of rising much more than a meter off the ground, but here in the city it could fly considerable heights thanks to the booster devices under the streets.

They heard Coyote's voice coming from the vehicle's speakers: "Igneous, this is Coyote. Onyx team is split up. I've lost contact with Raven and Cat. Currently moving in on Eel's position to save his sorry hide…"

"I'm relieved to hear from you, Coyote," Dragon replied, and his tone backed up the statement. "Raven and Cat are with me. Keep me updated when you find Eel and I'll prepare an extraction."

"Roger. Coyote out."

Raven took a seat. "A cyborg... just like Arnold Beiderman... the one you killed. But how did you do it? We need to know!"

"Did you short him out?" Cat asked. "Using EMP maybe?"

Dragon shook his head. "Won't work. He's fully shielded from the stuff, and even if you manage to get past the shielding, the internal circuitry's mostly immune to it. Barely even makes him sputter."

Raven nodded. "So what was it then? There must have been something more to it than what they say."

"I'm sorry to disappoint you, but there isn't. I simply used my hand-blades... and I cut him apart, bit by bit. It was a long fight, and perhaps the hardest one-on-one battle of my life. Well, until I faced *you* at the end of the Trial of Bravery, Luke," he finished with a smile.

Raven blinked. "That's it? You just... cut him up, like they say?"

Dragon nodded. "That's all there is to it. I took him out with my star-talons. Nothing else would work."

Raven gave a loud laugh and clapped Dark-Dragon on the shoulder pauldron. "All right! This should be no problem then."

But Dark-Dragon did not share in his former student's enthusiasm. "Not exactly. You see, the cyborg soldier plan that Dr. Beiderman was working on also called for *training* these proposed cyborg soldiers in how to fight. Arnold was an old man who had been in poor health before the operation, and he was still a challenge, even for me. Now, if someone were to take *soldiers* and combine them with cyborg endoskeletons..."

Cat shook her head slowly. "That man we saw... the cyborg who attacked us... he looked like..."

Now Raven was grave as well. "Grimm. He looked like Eric Grimm ... leader of Grimm's Mercenary Army."

"But it wasn't him," Dragon said with certainty.

Cat squinted. "How can you be so sure?"

Dragon gave her a mirthless smile. "Because Grimm is on our side."

LOCATION: SHARDASHA STREETS, WEST SIDE

"You sure you'll be okay?"

As they made their way down the street, Amazon looked over at Ryan's shoulder. The bullet of the one lucky Xarkonian soldier who had managed to hit him with enough direct fire to pierce his armor had lodged in his shoulder, rupturing his nanomesh suit. The suit had automatically released nanocrystal wound-sealant foam, so now Ryan had a puffy white mass sticking out of the crack between his pauldron and chestplate.

He shrugged, apparently feeling no pain in doing so. "I'm fine, Eve. I'm more concerned about our Xarkonian 'backup,' to be honest..."

He fell silent. Amazon cocked her head, inviting him to go on.

He shrugged. "It's just a feeling. Those Xarkonian 'traitors' just didn't seem... I don't know; something about them just wasn't right."

"I know what you mean," said Captain Jaleiko, jogging to catch up with them. "If a bunch of Crownies decided to join up with terrorists, which seems unlikely in the first place, you'd think they'd at least refuse to do all the fighting themselves. I didn't see *one* man who wasn't wearing Xarkonian armor in that group. It'll take more than a few trench coats to convince me those were mercs."

Ryan nodded. "That's what I was thinking. It just doesn't add up."

Again they lapsed into silence. All that could be heard in the city streets was the marching of the soldiers' boots, as they made their way toward Zegaldorph's tower in the center of town. Ryan looked up at the stars reflecting off the windows of the skyscraper... and paused.

"Is that a Bergel–"

His words were cut short by the sight that followed. They all noticed it; the glint of light that appeared near the top of the tower as fire shot from the windows... and a pair of dark bodies could just be seen tumbling onto the transport Ryan had spotted not far below. Someone had jumped out of the skyscraper window onto a Xarkonian troop transport. The three allies quickly exchanged glances.

"We'd better hurry," Amazon said.

Ryan nodded. "Jaleiko, what's the best way into the embassy?"

The Mordark commander shook his head, his features contorted with rage. "Dammit, I wish I knew! I've never even *been* to Shardasha before!"

They all jumped when a hissing, gravelly voice suddenly came from a nearby alleyway: "*I* know a way."

The soldiers of Victory and Mordark stood amazed. Stepping from the shadows of the narrow alley was a massive, heavily-armed Slashrim with deep red skin, striped with black. He held his clawed hands out wide in a gesture of peace, though his green eyes glowed with clear resentment at having to do so... and the machine gun hanging from his shoulder, which looked too big for a Human to even lift, did not look peaceful at all.

Ryan casually put a hand on the Harpy Eagle magnum pistol at his side. "Identify yourself."

The Slashrim's red lips curled back from his sharp white teeth. "I am Lashnar, former soldier of Helexith, former slave, and current soldier of fortune... I am a mercenary."

Jaleiko looked impressed. "I've come into contact with many of your kind in Mordark. You speak very well for a Slashrim."

The beast shrugged his spiked shoulders. "Why do you think I left Helexith? The Mahlok prefer their soldiers loyal and *stupid*. I'm neither."

Jaleiko made the connection to his own Mahlok lord, Zegaldorph, and his eyes narrowed. Ryan put a hand on the commander's shoulder and shook his head.

"So why are you offering to help us?" he asked.

"I work for a certain individual who prefers to remain anonymous," Lashnar replied. "My employer wishes for me to tell you that Zegaldorph is not behind this terrorist incident, and has asked me to help you in arranging for the Mahlok's safe escape."

Jaleiko's eyes widened. "You *know* who's behind the lockdown? Tell us immediately!"

A low growl issued from deep in the Slashrim's throat. "Don't be dense, Captain. Who do you *think?*"

"Seriously?" Amazon exclaimed in astonishment. "They locked down one of their own cities?"

Ryan glanced at the street behind them, but there was thankfully no sign of their "reinforcements" from Sgt. Thunder-Hawk. "Xarkon. So we were right all along."

"Yes," Lashnar growled, "but you were too slow to do anything about it. Typical Humans. Here, take this communicator. It will link you in with my employer, and she will connect you with Zegaldorph's head of security. Hopefully Commander Jaleiko here can say something that will convince them to just let us in… after I get you past the patrols around the building, that is."

Jaleiko caught the commlink as it was tossed to him, and then he wiped off the sweat that had been beading up on his forehead. Apparently these revelations had been getting to him. He kept glancing back over his shoulder nervously.

"There must be a better way to live…" he muttered, "without all this fire and blood."

- CHAPTER TWENTY-ONE -
THE BEST LAID SCHEMES

It was a long, hard fight down the hall before Saber-Scorpion reached his goal. He could tell immediately from the enhanced security on the large, double doors that this was the room. He examined the security systems on the door to see if he could hack his way in, but whoever was in there probably already knew by now that he was coming anyway. So he simply took a deep breath and stabbed his blade into the crack between the two doors. As soon as it was through, they slid open.

Surprised, Scorp took a step back. The room beyond the opening was a luxurious office with a wide, probably bullet-proof desk and a large window with a balcony. In the center were two chairs, each with a Sarran bound tightly to it – a male with pitch-black wings and hair, and a female with snow-white ones. Behind the desk stood another thug with an assault rifle... a pockmarked man with slicked-back hair wearing black body armor. The barrel of his rifle was trained on the female Sarran.

Scorp kept his own weapon pointed directly at the mob boss. "Lucky Jim Crow, I presume?"

"Here to finish what your Sarran assassins couldn't accomplish?" Jim Crow taunted, steadying his rifle, with the desperate look of a man who was about to gamble everything he had. "How'd you get them to work for the Crown anyway? I didn't know Sarrans were open to *brainwashing*."

Scorp glanced at the captives. "Poor choice of hostages, Crow. These Sarran mean nothing to the Crown. Time to die."

He took a few steps forward and raised his SMG, hoping Crow would give up on the hostages, but apparently he was determined to take them out anyway. The crime boss raised his rifle and sighted toward Folirayoth's head. Scorp paused in mid-stride.

"Ah!" Crow hissed triumphantly. "I caught that! You *do* care about these featherdusters! Well then, put down that gun... nice and easy..."

Scorp decided to risk it. Slowly, very slowly, he began to lower his SMG to the ground. All the while, he kept his eyes on Crow, looking for some kind of opening. The Black Network mob boss merely smiled, seeing what seemed like imminent success. But then, for some reason, Crow suddenly looked down at his weapon as if in shock... and met Idelma'ik's eyes.

The Sarran returned his stare. "Goodbye, Crow."

Scorp's spray of bullets sent him flying backward until he tumbled right over his chair. After walking around the desk to be absolutely sure his target was dead, Scorp turned to the two bound Sarrans.

"Why did he look down like that?" Scorp asked.

The Sarran cringed at the mechanical quality of his voice, filtered as it was through his helmet's mask. This, combined with his soulless black visor in place of eyes, unnerved them considerably. They sat there silently, staring intently at him, their faces expressionless.

"Did he drug you?" Scorp asked. "Can you answer me?"

Idelma'ik lifted his head. "We are fine, Xarkonian. We are simply considering what to make of you."

He spoke with a much stronger Sarran accent than had Aeriella. It gave his voice a slightly effeminate, almost sing-song quality. Sarran males cared little about appearing a bit "effeminate," however, since their society was female-dominant. Hence, it was the female who made the decision.

"But we will answer your question," said Folirayoth. "Weak minds, you see, are very open to suggestion. It's not mind control, not really. We can't influence a person's thoughts, not without giving away our presence in their minds and inviting them to fight back, but we can give them subtle feelings. For instance, what would you do if you suddenly felt that you forgot to insert a power cell into your weapon, or to switch the safety off?"

"I'd keep a level head and at least bluff it instead of looking down like he did. Still, that was a sharp move... whichever of you did it."

"Actually," Idel replied, "we both did. Sarran mates share a close personal bond. We are of two bodies, but one mind... in a way. It is difficult to fully explain in your clumsy Human speech. We do not require words to communicate."

"So what will you do now, Human?" asked Folira. "Free our earthly forms from these bonds, or free our spirits from these earthly forms?"

Scorp paused. "Do either of you know a Sarran named Aeriella?"

For a moment, the faintest hint of actual surprise showed on their features, and Folira asked, "Human, will you show us your face? We find it uncomfortable to hold a conversation with a face of metal."

Scorp reached up and pressed a button on the side of his helmet. His visor slid up, and his faceplates slid back, leaving a T-shaped opening that revealed most of his features.

"Yes, he is the one…" Idel said slowly. "He could only be the young Human she showed us in her memories… her savior."

Scorp looked back and forth between the ivory and ebony winged Sarran mates. "You *spoke* with Aeriella? Is she here?"

"Yes," Idel replied. "She slipped into the city a few weeks ago, apparently in an effort to save us. She was, however, only able to contact us briefly before our captors returned. She is presently at large in the city."

"I believe," Folira put in, "that she was going to return to us when she found another way out of the city, since her own place of entrance was blocked off. But she did have time to tell us of how you helped her escape from Xarkon's clutches. We thank you very deeply for that."

There was only just enough emotion in her voice to make Scorp feel that she was sincere in her thanks. Sarran minds were so sensitive to the feelings of others that their own emotions seemed extremely subdued to other species, making them seem almost cold and indifferent. But Scorp knew it was not meant in this way. After all, if you were a creature who could hear the slightest sound, the slightest rustle or breath, with extreme clarity and volume, why would you ever care to scream, or even raise your voice above a whisper? So it was with the Sarran and emotions. To them, Human passions were almost overwhelming.

"So what now, Human?" asked the male Sarran, Idelma'ik. "Will you give us the same chance you gave to our sister in need? Will you give this chance to the other Sarran captives in this building as well, our fellow 'Blackwings' as your people call them?"

"You're both hostages during this terrorist incident, which either Crow or his employers likely caused," Scorp lied, "and he said you were here to kill him, so yes, I am letting you go. Do you have a way out of the city?"

"No," Idel replied. "As we said, the entrance Aeriella used was blocked off after her arrival. We were hoping you could help us with that."

Scorp nodded and switched on his commlink. "Scorp to Team Obsidian: the target has been eliminated. Time to cash in the chips. I'm releasing some hostages, so make sure they get out safely."

"Dammit…" he heard Barracuda pointedly mutter.

"Keep it together, Enomegs. Mantis, Barracuda, start setting up those explosives. We'll rendezvous on the roof on my mark. Understood?"

Scorp saw the confirmation lights appear on his HUD. Satisfied, he began cutting the bonds on the Sarrans' arms, legs, and wings with his star-talon blade. The legendary wings of the Sarran would not help in their escape from the city, since the skies were more closely watched than any other route. The way the Enomegs had entered would no doubt be under close scrutiny now, and it was the only way Amy Archer had mentioned…

Archer. Suddenly remembering the commlink she had given him, he jerked it off his belt and hit the button.

"Saber-Scorpion to Falcon. If you can hear me, respond."

278

After only a second's pause, her voice answered. "Is that you, Scorp? Sorry, I ah, had it turned down…"

"It's me."

"Find out anything about what's going on?"

Scorp quickly dismissed the idea of telling her about Xarkon's involvement. "Actually, I was wondering if you could help me out again. I need another way out of the city… one you haven't told anyone else about."

"Now, Scorp, I thought we were going to *exchange* confidential information here. I know you know something…"

Scorp laughed. "What are you, some kind of undercover journalist?"

"Or a spy, perhaps? No, but I used to work in Intelligence, remember? Maybe you could just say I hate not knowing what's going on."

Scorp licked his lips. "What if I told you that the alleged terrorist in charge of this whole incident is lying at my feet with a bullet in his head? My bullet, of course."

"I'd ask what you mean by 'alleged'?"

"Perceptive. But I asked you for another way out of Shardasha…"

"Alright, alright. I might know a place. There's an old tunnel leading under the hills nearby that was closed for repairs right before this whole mess started. I had a look inside earlier but didn't report it since most of it seems to be collapsed anyway. You couldn't get a vehicle through, but infantry might be able to squeeze past the rubble."

Scorp looked at the Sarran hesitantly. He knew how much their kind instinctively hated tight spaces. Their starship cockpits were the most spacious in the Refuge, and it was not only to accommodate their wings. But Folirayoth and Idelma'ik looked undaunted.

"The Blackwings are soldiers," said Folira. "We can make it."

"Are you sure?" Idel asked. "Our men are not *all* soldiers, if you remember."

"Then now is the time for them to learn to be."

Scorp raised his eyebrows at this. He knew that Sarran regarded females as wiser, more perceptive, and calmer under pressure, so they almost always were the leaders by default… yet still it surprised him. Even in modern Human society, the male and female roles in this kind of exchange would usually have been reversed.

"Alright, Falcon, just tell me where to go."

"I'll transfer the coordinates to you via the regular channels. But if you have any more information for me…"

"I'll let you know."

Amy blew out a sigh. "Fine. Falcon out."

Scorp pressed a button on his helmet's controls, and the visor of his helmet slid back down over his eyes, displaying a wireframe map of the city on his HUD. Amy's coordinates showed up as a yellow dot.

He turned back to the Sarran. "Can you get your people out of here?"

Idel nodded. "Yes. As I understand it, they are being held somewhere on the lower levels."

"Then gather them up. I've found you a way out."

The two Sarrans glanced toward each other for a brief second. Their expressions did not change, but Scorp could guess that, had they been Human, they would have been looking suspicious. They did not trust him. And when they looked back up and met his eyes, he felt certain they knew that he knew this as well. It was as if an entire conversation had just passed without a word.

"There is a way, Human," Folira said, "that we can put aside our mutual mistrust born of misunderstanding, and, at the same time, we can learn of your escape route without you having to say a word."

"I know what you're suggesting," Scorp replied, "but I can't allow you to read my mind."

"Because it holds so many of Xarkon's dark secrets?" Idel prompted. "Such as the fact that you were not truly sent here to save us, but to kill us and attempt to put the blame for this incident on our heads, as you are doing with that mob boss there? Do not take us for fools. Like all Humans, you think so loud we cannot help but hear you."

"You're at least half right," Scorp calmly replied. "I was sent here to kill you. So since I'm not, maybe you should show a little trust."

"Or maybe this is all some scheme," Idel went on. "Maybe you can't even trust the informant you just contacted. She could be setting up a trap."

"Like you were setting up a trap for Jim Crow and Zegaldorph?"

"Zegaldorph was *helping* us set up this trap for Crow. With his help, we were about to take down the most powerful mob boss in your country. And you wish to kill us both for it?"

Scorp shook his head. "Why would Zegaldorph want to take down the Black Network? I know for a fact he gets most of his money from crime."

"You misunderstand Zegaldorph's position in this. The gangs exert great power over him. He despises their corrupting influence, but he cannot attack them directly for fear of reprisal, so he helps *us* do it for him."

"And you trust him? A Mahlok? You're *Sarran*. Your species warred with the Mahlok for millennia!"

"He has earned our trust more than you have, Human!"

"*Enough*," Folira broke in, in a commanding tone. "This pointless bickering is only breeding greater and greater misunderstanding!"

Idel immediately backed down, even lowering his head in shame.

"Of course, you are right, my love. I... am sorry. My apologies, Human. I was raised in the Blackwings, and before Folira and I reformed the group, we were taught to despise your kind. Sometimes those old emotions can still become ignited. One would think the example of Zegaldorph, our helpful Mahlok ally, would have taught me a lesson."

"Sarrans and Mahlok fighting together..." Scorp muttered. "What's next? The Slashrim joining in?"

Folirayoth smiled. "You see now why we perform the psychic linking during any kind of negotiations? Most disputes are born of misunderstanding, and this can be alleviated once each side is allowed to fully grasp not only the facts behind the other side's stance, but also their *feelings* on the matter. All beings think and feel differently…"

Scorp nodded. "Yes, very idealistic. But it doesn't change the fact that I can't let you read my mind. I can't trust you not to probe around for hidden secrets. If that means you don't trust me in return, so be it."

"No," Folira interrupted. "There is no need for that. We will take the information you offer, and thank you for your help. You have done much for us, and risked much. We are grateful."

Scorp nodded. "Thank you. Now, we've wasted too much time already. Go get your friends, and I'll order my men to let you go. I'll set up a computer for you with the escape route location. Just be ready to move."

The two Sarrans headed for the door, but Folira looked back once more. "I will tell Aeriella what you did for us. She did seem concerned before, about just *why* you helped her…"

Scorp paused. "Tell her… that I guess I'm *not* a soldier, after all."

LOCATION: MORDARK EMBASSY ROOF

They swept out onto the roof, walking at a brisk pace. Grimm III and Zegaldorph walked together, flanked by four Mordark royal guards. Three hoped Spectra was able to get out of the building safely. For some reason, she seemed very intent on staying well out of sight, especially of Zegaldorph.

Of all the Native species he had met first-hand, Grimm III always felt most at home with Slashrim, like Lashnar. They were coarse, vulgar, and best of all, utterly honest. They never beat around the bush and never dressed things up to pretend they were better than they really were, as Humans did constantly. Grimm III could understand them almost better than his own species. And one other thing he understood… was why they had come to worship the Mahlok. Because even though he liked the Slashrim best of all the Natives, he could not deny that the Mahlok were the most impressive.

Zegaldorph's translucent skin, like that of all his kind, was red, glowing slightly orange with the heat of his fiery core, and it was covered in a complex pattern of black lines, artistically curving over his muscles like natural tattoos. But, as with all creatures, Mahlok eyes were windows to their fiery souls, and consequently they glowed with an intense yellow-white heat. They had no pupils. How they had evolved on their volcanic planet was, like every other facet of Mahlok biology, a complete mystery to Human science.

When Zegaldorph spoke, it was with a deep voice that one could imagine echoing from the heart of a volcano. It seemed like the kind of voice one would expect from a creature whose rubbery skin was as tough as stone and who possessed no mouth or nose. Exactly how they spoke through that skin, no one was quite sure – the sound of their voice just seemed to emanate from their very being. It was easy to see why the Slashrim worshipped these beings as gods. With their imposing appearance, near invulnerability, and their amazing power to emit flame from their very skin… they practically *were*.

"Tell me again who you are," said the Lord of Mordark.

"I've gone by lotsa names," Three answered. "Some folks know me as Erik the Red. Those who know me and like me call me Erik. Those that know me and *don't* like me – a much bigger group – just call me Three. I'm Grimm the Third, second clone of the leader of Grimm's Mercenary Army."

"You fight well for a Human," Zegaldorph commented. "Too well, in fact. Not like a Human at all. Most of your kind are far weaker."

Three nodded. "That's because o' this."

The mercenary stopped, reached up to the metal patch covering one of his eyes, and flipped it up. Underneath was revealed a gaping cavity… but not an empty one. Where the skin stopped, metal took its place, and out of the hole where there should have been an eye protruded an array of three cylindrical lenses, turning this way and that in coordination with his other, biological eye. One of the lenses glowed red.

"A cyborg…" Zegaldorph said, his pupilless eyes narrowing.

"You got it," Three replied, flipping the patch back over his mechanical eye. "My entire skeleton and lots o' my guts and just about everything else you can think of was replaced with robotics. Faster, stronger, and tougher than normal Human parts. And best of all, they don't get old. Sometimes they take a little fixin' up, but they don't rot away like organics."

Zegaldorph nodded and gave a low chuckle. "I can see why you would want to do that, considering how long you Humans live. Only the Achmer have a shorter average lifespan."

Three nodded. "Yeah, and in my case it was even shorter. I'm a clone, right? Well, the old man made us age real fast, and it was supposed to slow down when we hit about thirty or somethin'. Only it didn't stop. I probably won't ever live to see a real thirty years. I just look it. And the only way I can slow it down is by fixin' myself up like this."

"Fascinating," Zegaldorph said, nodding. "So just how old are you?"

Three shrugged. "Can't say for sure. Closest guess I have is about… nineteen. All my fighting skill is 'inherited.' That is to say, it was transferred from the deepest memories of dear old dad. He'd honed his skills to a razor edge, until they were practically instinct. And then he gave that instinct to me. Don't even try askin' me how. I don't know how the hell that machine works. Don't wanna know. Only Grimm's scientist, Hal Flyphe, knows what makes it tick. Unfortunately the thing that makes *him* tick, his brain, don't always work right. He's got a mind like a clock, that one… but it's a cuckoo clock."

Zegaldorph gave another chuckle. "Quite an interesting Human, you are. So why have you come to rescue me? But no, we had best save that question for later. Yes, now it is time to escape, I think. You've done your job well, my good Human-cyborg-mercenary-clone."

They were standing in front of Zegaldorph's ship now, in the very center of the landing platform atop his skyscraper. The personal starship of the Lord of Mordark hardly looked like it befit someone with such a title. Painted a gaudy combination of red, orange, and yellow, it was sleek as a racing hovercraft, with the largest engines Three had ever seen on a vehicle its size.

"What the heck is this thing?" Three asked.

"The *Afterburner*," Zegaldorph answered, "my personal starship; perhaps the fastest, toughest, and probably the most expensive aerospace vehicle of its size. I have occasionally entered starship racing competitions in the craft, and frequently won, and I have burned whole sections of Mordark from its controls. It's armed with a firestorm cannon and thermite bombs."

"Well, now it's an escape ship for four. You, me, and two guards?"

As he had done throughout the conversation, Zegaldorph did not really turn to regard him as he replied, "Hmm… I am not sure if I trust you enough to let you ride in my ship."

"I ain't sure you're understandin' me," Grimm said with a laugh. "I'm bein' paid to haul your char-grilled ass outta this city in one piece. And I'm gonna see to it that I don't fail, even if it means tearin' apart all your guards here, tyin' you up, and tossin' you in the back o' your own ship. 'Cause when I'm paid, I *always* see the job through. We clear?"

Zegaldorph nodded. "Hmm… Quite. Such conviction is admirable, and I suppose even my flames would have trouble stopping you. Very well, climb aboard. Take one of the back seats."

As Three walked up the boarding ramp, he said, "I know just where to go. Head for –"

Zegaldorph interrupted him with a flat, "No."

Grimm III clamped his jaw shut as he sat down and strapped in. "So… just where do you plan to go then?"

"I'm going to help out another group of beings who are trapped here in this wretched city… who share a mutual hatred of mine."

"Zegaldorph, I told you: I'm here to save *you*, not –"

The Mahlok interrupted him again with a burning stare. "And now you're here to save *them*. You will help me, mercenary. If the only thing you obey is money, I have that horrid stuff in abundance. I will gladly pay you all the blood-stained guildars, crowns, or Victorian credits that you require. I will even pay you in gold if you wish. It matters not to me."

Three blew out a low whistle, but looked back over his shoulder as if unsure of something. Licking his lips, he reached deep into a pocket on his belt. Zegaldorph turned to look as the mercenary drew out a small red cube and tossed it in the air. Then he opened his hand out flat. It was a translucent red gambling die. It had landed on the number six.

Three shrugged. "Let's do it."

LOCATION: ORRICK'S PALACE HOTEL & CASINO

The Enomegs of Team Obsidian made their rendezvous on the roof of the casino. Mantis and Barracuda came by the stairs, double-checking their explosives along the way, while Cobra rocketed from the opposite building with her jetpack, and Scorp flew up from the lower balconies the same way after seeing off the two Sarran. Once they were all together again, Scorp gave the standard hand-signal for mission objective complete.

"Good job, Enomegs," he said. "We're done here. I assume you wiped all the computer databases, Mantis?"

Removing his helmet and grinning, Mantis nodded. "There is no remaining evidence to indicate that the Black Network was *not* behind the Shardasha incident."

Scorp returned the nod. "And all the explosives are in place if we have to blow the joint?"

"Hopefully we will," Barracuda responded. "Yeah, they're in place."

Scorp glanced at Silent-Cobra. "And no escapees?"

Cobra shook her head. She said nothing of the Sarran that Scorp had ordered them to let go, and the others failed to mention it as well. He was grateful. Despite this, even with the mission accomplished and the area clear, the Enomegs did not simply relax. They reloaded their weapons and made sure everything was in prime working order, all while tensely awaiting word from Raven about the results of the second half of their mission... the elimination of Zegaldorph. Only Mantis, as always, tried to lighten the mood.

"So..." he said, "final count? I got twenty-one."

Barracuda gave a hideous grin. "Twenty-two. My highest count for a single battle so far."

Cobra shrugged. "Twenty-three."

"Twenty-nine," said Saber-Scorpion, and they all turned to look at him. "The last two rooms before Jim Crow's had about six people each."

Barracuda shook his head. "And you aren't even wounded."

"They didn't seem very highly trained. Little more than street thugs, really. Not quite professional-grade Victorian soldiers. Also, they were tense, probably near panic from spending all these weeks trapped in the city."

"Still, that means they had nearly a hundred men," Mantis said thoughtfully. "This was no small operation. A powerful man has fallen today."

They fell silent after that, and neither Mantis nor Barracuda mentioned the previous bet they had made. Scorp wondered how Team Onyx was faring. He cared little for Raven's fate, but the others... Cat, Seth, Coyote... He knew they had been given the more difficult mission. Still, Scorp waited for Cobra to report that all of the Sarran hostages, who were still making their way out on the streets below, were completely out of sight before he contacted Dark-Dragon.

Finally she turned and said, "They're gone, Scorp."

Saber-Scorpion breathed a sigh of relief and activated his commlink. "Igneous, this is Obsidian. The mission is a success. We are now –"

He was interrupted by the roar of an engine high overhead, and Barracuda's shout of, "Contact! Eyes to the sky!"

The Enomegs simultaneously rushed for cover as a bright red and yellow aerospace craft swooped down over their heads, blasting them with its heat. By the time the craft landed on the opposite rooftop, Barracuda was already reaching for his shoulder-mounted rocket launcher... only to find that it wasn't there. He had left it behind for this mission in order to take the flamethrower. He cursed and dove back behind cover.

"Igneous, Onyx," Scorp shouted, "you won't believe who just crashed the party over here!"

"We know," Dark-Dragon replied. "It's Zegaldorph, along with an unknown cyborg, and possibly a few royal guards. We're on our way now, Obsidian. Keep him occupied until we get there."

"A *cyborg*?" Scorp echoed, sliding his Ironslinger out of its sheath and cocking it.

"Alright!" Barracuda shouted, unfolding the stand on his machine gun and mounting it against the edge of the roof. "Looks like we get to bag ourselves *both* objectives! I just wish I had a rocket launcher…"

They watched as the boarding ramp of the fire-colored starship lowered and four passengers quickly rolled out, one after another. Barracuda let off a few wild shots in their direction, but they moved too fast, crouching down behind the edge of the roof. Scorp sighted down the barrel of his Ironslinger, eyeing the roof for movement, but all he saw were a few hands appearing at intervals, apparently giving signals.

Cobra, who had been watching this exchange through the scope of her high-caliber sniper rifle, said, "They must realize we've already cleared out this building. I could try shooting through the barrier…"

"Do it," Scorp ordered. "Mantis, Barracuda, come with me!"

All at once, the three Enomegs ran toward the edge of the roof and fired their jetpacks. One of Zegaldorph's guards looked up to fire at them, but a bullet from Cobra's rifle whizzed past his head, causing him to withdraw just as quickly. By the time the Enomegs landed, their four targets were already heading back for the ship. Zegaldorph was in the lead, flanked by his two guards, while a mysterious mercenary who looked stunningly like Warlord Eric Grimm of Grimm's Army took up the rear, firing at the Enomegs with a full-auto shotgun.

"That merc must be the cyborg!" Scorp said to his teammates. "I'll take him! You two head around and cut off Zegaldorph!"

As Scorp ignited his blades and charged the Grimm-clone, Barracuda shouted, "Frag out!"

The grenade landed right between Zegaldorph and his ship, but before it could go off, the Mahlok extended a hand and blasted it with a wave of fire, blowing it back away from them. Then it exploded, but the force of Zegaldorph's continuous flames deflected much of the shrapnel, and the ship took the brunt of the blast. The *Afterburner* lurched from the explosion, toppling off its landing gear and onto one side. By this time, Barracuda and Mantis had arrived, and they quickly engaged the two royal guards.

Meanwhile, Scorp was left to deal with the Grimm-spawn. The sight of an Enomeg super-soldier charging forward with Starfire blades activated and swinging would have terrified many, and at least intimidated the majority of the rest. Grimm III, however, only smiled. With lightning reflexes, he braced himself, raised his shotgun, and let fly. The round of shot sailed right over Scorp's head as the Enomeg rolled under it, coming up right beneath the mercenary's chin and slamming an energy blade into his gut.

Scorp heard his weapon fizzle against the merc's energy-absorbent mesh, burning away at it and penetrating the skin beneath. Then he felt a cold steel blade slash him across the arm, and he stumbled back. Three was brandishing a long blazer combat knife now, with blood along the rim. Scorp flexed his arm; the blade had only just made it through – it was little more than a scratch. Still, it had startled him. Grimm III smiled again, just before one of Cobra's bullets nearly took off his ear.

"Call off your sniper!" Three shouted. "Let's do this like men!"

Scorp paused. "Cobra, let me handle this one. If you see anyone else come within sight, shoot them, but this one's mine."

"Your funeral," came the typical Silent-Cobra reply.

"That grenade didn't even faze Zegaldorph, you know," said Grimm III. "A bit o' shrapnel ain't enough to get under Mahlok skin."

"All your talking is getting under mine," Scorp said.

Three laughed. "I applaud your attitude! Let's go!"

Dropping into an attack stance, the Enomeg charged. Grimm III activated the blazer shield on his combat knife and deflected the first of Scorp's blows, and then the battle began in earnest. Blade met blade as the mercenary blocked and dodged all of Scorp's strikes with amazing speed and dexterity. Every time his long, glowing knife blade descended, Scorp could feel the strength of the cyborg's mechanical arms behind the blow, and it was all he could do to deflect it.

But Scorp had studied Dark-Dragon's defeat of the cyborg Dr. Beiderman all those years ago. Keeping his distance, he never let the mercenary get too close, always dancing around his slashes, as his own flashing star-talons spun and struck, landing little nicks and cuts on his enemy whenever possible. It was a tedious and frustrating tactic, and it had its desired effect. Three clenched his teeth and flew into a rage.

With a half-mechanical roar, he leapt straight at Scorp, his arms out wide. The Enomeg knew the edge of the roof was right behind him; Three had been pushing him backwards through most of the fight, pressing his advantage. Scorp tried to dodge, but he was becoming exhausted and his reflexes were just too slow to avoid the raging cyborg. Three slammed into him like a duranium wall, and Scorp was thrown onto his rear, the back of his head slamming against the roof edge.

Without pause, Three charged again. Now Scorp saw his chance. He brought both feet up and, using the mercenary's own momentum against him, lifted him right over his head and then over the edge of the wall behind him. With a scream of rage, Grimm III went careening down toward the street below. The crash when he hit the bottom was an unimpressive thud. Without even turning to look down at the results of his move, Scorp jumped up and ran to rejoin Mantis and Barracuda. Unfortunately, they were nowhere to be seen. The only things in sight were the overturned *Afterburner* and a door leading to a flight of stairs that descended into the building below.

Scorp shouted into his commlink, "Cobra, get up here as soon as you can! Mantis, Barracuda, status report!"

But it was Dark-Dragon who answered. "Scorp! We're right behind you! Step out of the way!"

Scorp turned around and looked up to see the black Bergelmir behind him, with the armored side panels lifted up and Enomegs hanging off the edges. Then, on top of it all, Scorp heard the civilian commlink Amy Archer had given him buzz loudly. He jerked it from his belt.

"What is it?" he prompted.

Amy must have heard the urgency in his voice, since she cut straight to the point. "Things are heating up out here. Incoming fighters have been spotted to the south. Most of the walkers and armor are headed there now, including Viper and General Black."

As Blood-Raven, Shadow-Cat, and Magnum-Coyote jumped down onto the roof beside him, Scorp asked, "Any idea whose fighters they are?"

"Looks like Yavakaro," Amy replied, "and maybe some Victorians too. No way to be sure, but definitely from across the pond."

"This just keeps getting better," Scorp said.

As he put the communicator away, Raven turned and taunted him, "Having trouble, Scorp?"

"Yeah, I'm having trouble… yours! You're the idiot who let his target escape!"

Finally he got a response on the commlink from Mantis, who was obviously winded. "Scorp… Zegaldorph is headed to the bottom floor… He's alone. Barracuda and I… we took out the guards, but my suit's damaged, and they nearly cut Barracuda's leg off…"

Scorp was about to respond when the voice of Dark-Dragon cut him off. "Get back up here, Mantis, and bring Barracuda with you. The rest of you, get to the bottom floor and take out that Mahlok!"

They did not require a second urging. All at once, Scorp, Raven, Cat, and Coyote leaped right over the edge of the roof and plummeted toward the street below, firing their jetpacks to break their fall. Cobra descended from the opposite roof in the same manner. They met at the bottom and immediately set off at a run toward the nearest entrance to the building behind them. Oddly enough, the nearest entrance was actually a hole smashed directly through the steel and concrete wall… a hole, Scorp noticed, in the vague shape of a man. Had he taken the time to glance over his shoulder, he would have seen a deep indention in the asphalt in the place where the cyborg Grimm-spawn's body had landed, but nothing else.

Hardly a ray of light penetrated the interior of this level of the building, so the Enomegs were forced to switch to light-amplifying night vision. Coyote and Raven were in the lead when they burst into the building's main parking garage. There were a slew of hovercars and bikes there, and seated in one sleek black convertible model – a Helios Zoom2, by the look of it – were Zegaldorph and Grimm III. Three was apparently hotwiring the vehicle with one of his cyborg implants. Upon seeing the Enomegs, he looked up, gave a wink, and switched on the hovercar's headlights.

The Enomegs, however, had been smart enough to think of this and had already switched off their night vision. Still, the brightness of the headlights was enough to disorient them, and Three sped toward the garage door. He was about to climb out of the car in order to smash the door down or hack it open when Zegaldorph put a red-skinned hand on his shoulder. Standing up in his seat, the Mahlok placed both his hands together, building up the heat within them until they glowed yellow-white, and let fly an enormous fireball. The door was blown completely off and landed bent and blackened in the street outside… at the same instant that a bullet landed in Zegaldorph's shoulder. Seeing the spurt of glowing blood, Grimm III jerked Zegaldorph back down into his seat and sped off. Saber-Scorpion cocked his smoking Ironslinger for another shot, but by then they were gone.

"I got him in the shoulder," the Enomeg said.

"Just hop on!" Cat shouted back.

Scorp looked around to see his comrades all mounted on hoverbikes, hacking into them as quickly as possible with their suits' built-in computers. Shadow-Cat had already started hers and was signaling to Scorp to mount up behind her. He quickly complied, and they sped off behind Cobra and Coyote. Raven, Scorp noted, was already ahead of them all.

LOCATION: BERGELMIR TRANSPORT, ABOVE SHARDASHA

"This is entirely unacceptable!" was the response Dark-Dragon had expected from High Commander Mars when he contacted him and told him about the trouble they were having… about the escape of Lord Zegaldorph. Mars's actual response was perhaps even more unsettling.

"You did well, Dragon," Mars said. "No one could have anticipated the arrival of the cyborg. He was a wild card, unexpected and unplanned for."

"But what do we do now, sir?" Dragon asked.

"See if you can cut off Zegaldorph. At least find out where he runs."

Dragon nodded to the pilot of the Bergelmir. "I'm on my way back to Zegaldorph's tower now. I think he may head back there, where it's safest."

"Good. Stay there and wait for him. I will need you later, Dragon."

"Thank you, sir. Dragon out."

When the communicator was switched off, Dragon blew out a sigh. The three Enomegs in the Berg with him – Seth, Mantis, and Barracuda – looked up at him expectantly. Dragon returned their gaze with the air of a father looking down at his kids who were about to lose their first team screamerball game. His expression was disappointed, but still proud that they were giving it their best, doing well… and best of all, still alive. Because even though screamerball could get pretty rough, this was no game – it was real.

"How are we doing?" he asked.

Barracuda looked down at the hardened wound-sealant foam on his leg. "I won't be dancing any, but I can still walk and shoot, sir. If nothing else, I can provide cover fire from the Berg here."

Mantis nodded. "One-hundred percent here, sir. Seth was able to repair my shield system."

Seth gave one of his kid grins. "Ah, I didn't 'repair' anything. It just needed resetting 'cause of the overload. It must've taken a lot of hits from those royal guards' energy swords. As for me, I'm fine, sir. My vision seems to be clearing up from whatever was in that stun dart that hit me."

Barracuda picked up the projectile, which Seth had brought on board, and inspected it. "Looks like a bolt for a Yavakarese XB8 compactable crossbow. Who'd actually use one of these in the field?"

"No time to worry about that," Dragon said. "Just be ready, Enomegs, because this battle's not over yet. In fact… I think we're just getting started. Oh, and Barracuda… blow the Casino."

Grinning, Barracuda scooted to a seat where he could look back out of one of the vehicle's gun-holes. He then pulled the detonator out of a pouch at his side… and pressed the trigger.

LOCATION: CAMP RAGNAR

High Commander Lucas Mars was pleased. Everything was going precisely according to his plan. All he had to do now was play his own part, and he would savor every moment of it. In fact, he had just been on his way from the communications tent to his personal walker, *Manegarm*, when a familiar horde of hoverbike riders had interrupted his walk.

"You're not even supposed to be here, Grimm," said the High Commander with outward calm.

Grimm I switched off his bike, and the beat-up old machine lowered gently to the Earth. It was customized beyond recognition. To the front was attached a shield-like piece of metal in the shape of the Grimm's Army skull emblem, the "Not-so-Jolly Roger." Its long, pointed, viper-like teeth extended forward like spears, and below them could be seen two half-concealed machine guns. Extendable blades ran along the sides, and all of it was painted black and green, except for the skull, which was a light metallic grey.

"Nick told me what's goin' on, Mars," said the mercenary warlord. "This is gonna get tough. And you know what I like to say: When the goin' gets tough…"

Mars nodded. "The tough get going."

"Actually, I was gonna say: When the goin' gets tough, the tough get paid double." He gave a crooked-toothed grin.

Mars frowned. "This is not according to our plan."

"Yeah, but neither are those Yavakaro fighters takin' their sweet time approachin' your coastline. And neither was that cyborg your Enomegs told you about, who, by the way, is of particular interest to me. Your plan's fallin' apart, ain't it?"

Insulting Mars's plans usually made him go into a stone cold silence, far more threatening than anger. But this time he actually visibly calmed, and even smiled ever so slightly. Grimm's bushy white eyebrows went up.

"It *isn't?*" the warlord asked incredulously.

The High Commander shook his head. "No. The *Emperor*'s plan may be, and the plans of the Victorians and CONON… but as the plans of my enemies fall apart, all of their pieces fall perfectly into place… in *mine*. Even your arrival was anticipated."

Grimm frowned. He hated being predictable. Still, it was hard to slip anything past a man like Lucas Mars. Nothing ever seemed to truly enrage the stoic High Commander. Grimm wondered just how much it would take, just what kind of person it would take, to truly get under the man's skin.

"So you know why I'm here?"

Mars nodded. "You're going into Shardasha to hunt down your escaped clone and destroy him. I wish you luck, but it's none of my business."

Grimm shrugged. "Well, fine then, I'm glad you don't object, 'cause I'm goin in. I'll see if I can take care o' what your Enomegs couldn't handle while I'm in there too. Then maybe we can apply my version of 'when the goin' gets tough.' Alright! Riders, to your positions!"

Nick Wolf, who had now changed back into his usual battered battle armor, climbed onto his hoverbike, and Jade immediately fell into place on the seat behind him, now once again clad in her full suit of armor as well. The other lead riders were there beside him, including Grimm VII or "Seven," the only Grimm-clone still loyal to his army; Hurk, the hulking orange Slashrim brute; and someone Nick didn't recognize. Seated on a sleek black hoverbike far too advanced for the usual new recruit was a similarly sleek black-clad woman, who lifted up her bike helmet's visor and winked at him.

Nick grinned. "Hey, who's the new blood, boss?"

"Oh, her?" Grimm replied with a laugh. "We picked her up just this mornin'. Been tryin' to convince her to join up for years now. Apparently somethin' finally set her straight. Nick, you ever heard o' the Black Widow?"

Nick whistled. "Have I ever! They say she's offed three Big Bosses, and the Black Network had to name a new one each time, pretendin' like nothin' ever 'appened."

"Well," said Lisa Sharp, her voice enough to turn the head of every merc nearby who wasn't already staring at her. "I may have killed a few. But I really prefer Xarkonian officers. It's always nice to knock a Crownie off his self-important little throne."

After this, all heads immediately turned toward Mars, but the High Commander did not dignify the remark with any kind of response whatsoever. He merely looked back at Grimm and asked, "Are you done now? Neither of us can afford to waste time."

Grimm cleared his throat. "Start your engines, boys! Let's *ride!*"

The roar of the hundreds of hoverbikes, many with engines customized as much for noise as for speed, was enough to echo off the distant hills and nearly deafen anyone standing next to them without protection. Mars was already walking off before the dust started to rise from their departure. When he reached the foot of his walker, he climbed straight up to the cockpit in mighty *Manegarm*'s armored head. Once he sat down inside, the holographic control panels all around him flashed online, illuminating the area in deep red. His communication console, however, was flashing the most.

"This had better be important," Mars said.

The communications officer on the other end replied, "Sir, it's the one you've been waiting for: the Yavakaro squadron leader."

"Put him on."

"Yes, sir. Setting up the link. You may speak to him… now."

The High Commander still paused a moment for effect before simply saying, "This is Mars."

An energetic voice came back at him, "This is Wing Commander Carter of the Yavakaro Aerospace Force! My squadrons are closing in on your position, accompanied by Victorian fighters under Star Captain Harrier Radcliff! We have orders to open fire on your camp, your forces, and the city of Shardasha, unless you agree to withdraw your forces and peacefully release all those trapped within!"

"And who might that be, exactly?"

"You know who, Commander! Lord Zegaldorph of Mordark, Commander Ryan Arkanian and his soldiers from Victory, and Captain Jaleiko of the Mordark Royal Guard!"

Mars's finger hovered over the commlink button for a few seconds. He did this not because of indecision, but for dramatic impact… and because he was savoring the moment. His answer, he knew, could determine the future of Humanity in the Refuge… a future he had already decided. Finally his gloved finger fell upon the button with all the gravity of an iron gavel striking the block on the judgment day of mankind.

And Mars said: "No."

- CHAPTER TWENTY-TWO -
THE BATTLE OF SHARDASHA

The Helios Zoom2 hovercar raced around another corner in the street, tilting as it slid through the air. It was followed immediately by the hoverbikes, which slid even farther due to their faster speed and lighter weight, nearly crashing into the side of a skyscraper. Grimm III used this to his advantage, taking as many turns as possible, as close to the buildings as he could get, hoping to send some of his enemies into them. But the Enomegs never fell for it. Three knew he could not keep it up; the Zoom2 was one of the fastest legal hovercars, but eventually the lighter, speedier hoverbikes would overtake him.

"Which way?" he shouted to his Mahlok passenger, "Which way?!"

Zegaldorph pointed right around the next turn, but protested loudly, "This leads out of the city, yes, but we will never make it! The whole place is still under lockdown!"

"Just shut up and let me take care of it!"

He didn't bother going into details, but Spectra had informed him of a weak spot in the defenses, where the turrets were either shut down or distracted, leaving it clear for a target as small as a hovercar to escape. Unfortunately, Three would still have to deal with the hoverbikes behind him, but he hoped…

Zegaldorph's hissing exclamation interrupted his thoughts. "Can you take care of *that?*"

"Holy…"

Up ahead was the highway that Three had planned to take. It was raised on tall pillars, leading out to a distant moonlit hill and then riding up over it. But standing on that rise and the hills all around it, scattered about like an army of giants, loomed nearly a dozen Xarkonian walkers, led by a towering humanoid

Dingo perched right on top like a silent and watchful colossus, with the highway running right between its feet. Among the walkers sat several support craft and armored vehicles, including tanks armed with surface-to-air missile racks. All of them were pointed in the same direction, though Grimm could see nothing beyond them except the starry night sky.

Then, as the tiny hovercar drew rapidly closer, a deafening roar shook the earth all around. The walking machines of war were beginning to unload their arsenal. Smoke wafted from the exhaust ports behind their missile racks as shafts of flame erupted from the front, propelling warheads toward the distant aerospace craft, which were even now launching their own missiles in return. Interceptor lasers cut through the sky and explosions lit the earth below. The thunderous roar seemed to consume all other sound, reverberating deep in the riders' chests, rattling the buildings all around.

The Battle of Shardasha had begun.

"Want to turn around now?" Three asked.

Zegaldorph's reply was entirely calm and collected. "No, you were right; this is the only way. Now, while the walkers are distracted. At the very least, the Enomegs should think twice about following us. This is the time!"

The Mahlok turned to regard his mercenary partner in time to see Three's single eye go wide with shock. His mouth dropped open, and out came a Human curse, for once.

"Oh, shit."

Zegaldorph quickly spotted the cause of his concern. Racing across the terrain under the highway they were about to enter was an enormous horde of hoverbikes of all shapes, sizes, and armaments. In the light of a walker's laser beam, Three clearly saw the long-toothed skull emblem on the front of one of the bikes, and the black cape that flapped behind its rider. Gunning the engine, Three aimed for the highway on-ramp, hoping to reach it first... but it was too late. Even now, the Grim Riders were closing in around it, cutting off his exit like water flowing around a stone. That left only one alternative.

"Hang on, Zeeg!" the mercenary shouted.

As they passed a tall holographic road sign – offline, of course – Three caught onto the pole with an outstretched hand and swung the hovercar around. They did a complete one-eighty in under a second, rocketing off in the opposite direction with hardly any loss of momentum, and it was all Three could do to hold the hovercar steady as it righted itself. It would have made most Human passengers sick, but luckily this particular hovercar contained no Human passengers... not entirely Human, at least.

This turned them right into the path of the oncoming Enomeg soldiers. Midair explosions peppered the sky above Shardasha as the Xarkonian walkers and tanks fought the Yavakarese fighters, but the Enomegs paid no heed. They were engaged in a game of chicken with two fugitives who were being chased by a whole army of hoverbike-riding mercenaries just turning into town. The roar of their collective engines somehow even drowned out the battle beyond.

The first in the line of Enomeg bike riders was Blood-Raven, followed by Cobra and Coyote, with Cat and Scorp taking up the rear, sharing the same bike. Seeing their enemy abruptly change direction and start speeding toward them, they quickly veered aside… except for Scorp, who caught Cat's arm and stopped her.

"Get beside him!" he shouted.

"Are you nuts?" Cat replied, but she obeyed anyway.

The hovercar went careening past like a jet, but Scorp managed to latch on with an extended arm. The extendable climbing spikes on his bracers dug into the driver's shoulder, ripping out a chunk of flesh before flying back into one of the back seats and sticking there instead. Dangling by one arm as the cyborg's blood splattered onto his visor, Scorp soon slammed in the spikes on his other arm, pulling himself into the hovercar's back seat. He ducked down just in time to avoid a blast of flame from Zegaldorph, who had just noticed their unwanted passenger.

Meanwhile, behind the hovercar, the Enomegs veered their bikes about in time to avoid crashing into Grimm's oncoming horde. A few of the mercenaries were firing off shots at the hovercar now, trying to catch either Grimm III or Zegaldorph with a bullet. Scorp stuck his head up and received a low caliber pistol round into the back of it, which bounced off his helmet but left him disoriented. Seeing this, Grimm III calmly reached back, grabbed the Enomeg by the horns of his helmet, and jerked him out of his seat.

Scorp went flying and landed on his back on the pavement, bouncing once before skidding to a stop. Remembering the pursuing cavalry, the Enomeg did the only thing he could think of to avoid being run over: he lay down as flat to the road as his armored exoskeleton would allow.

A blast of blazing hot air wafted over his body as the hundreds of hoverbikes zoomed overhead, and Scorp's HUD began to flash a heat warning, as his nanomesh suit compensated as much as it could. The screaming roar of the souped-up motors of the Grim Riders was nearly deafening. Some of the mercs had even attached blades to their hovercraft, and Scorp felt a few of them graze his force shield, which he thankfully had activated just before jumping onto Grimm III's hovercar.

Finally, the roaring stopped, and Scorp could hear the howling and jeering of the mercs as they left his prostrate form behind. He stood up slowly, looking around for any oncoming stragglers, but there were none. But now there was something else, perhaps even more intimidating, standing in his way: the huge, metal-clawed foot of a walker.

Scorp ripped out his handheld communicator as he looked up at the towering Fox. "Amy?!"

"Climb up!" she replied. "I know you can!"

LOCATION: MORDARK EMBASSY ROOF

Ryan Arkanian looked around him at the landing pad atop Zegaldorph's tower. This was one of the highest points in the city, and he could see most of Shardasha from here, including the Rhaen River that ran through it into the Bay of Shards and the Infinite Ocean beyond, all bathed in the bluish light of Terra Nova's double moons. Standing there with him were all that remained of his men and Jaleiko's, plus some of the Mordark guards that had still been in the building when they arrived… and the great red Slashrim who had led them there, Lashnar. Thankfully, Jaleiko had convinced Security Chief Dawson to let them in without much argument. But when Dawson filled them in on the situation, he had grim news indeed.

"So Zegaldorph is gone?" Ryan asked.

"Yes," said the overweight security chief, scratching the back of his balding head. "A mercenary, some guy with an eyepatch, sneaked into the building through the sewer system and ran right through my security, no problem, all the way to Zegaldorph's room."

"My partner," Lashnar clarified, "Grimm III. He's one of Grimm's clones. We were hired by an anonymous third party to infiltrate Shardasha and extract your cuddly little Mahlok lord."

Dawson nodded. "Yes, and he did that. After fighting off some Xarkonian assassins clad in armor like I've never seen before, he grabbed Zegaldorph and split – headed for the roof. Then the security system kicked in, sealing off the hall behind him, but the Xarkonians still managed to escape through the windows. They were extracted by a black Bergelmir transport. We took a few shots at it, but no good…"

Jaleiko impatiently interrupted him, saying, "So Zegaldorph left in the *Afterburner*, which was right here. Well then, which way did he go? Come, man, tell us what you saw!"

"He said he was headed to Orrick's Palace, Captain, to help some Sarran rebels there and –"

Jaleiko's eyes went wide. "The Emperor's palace!"

Lashnar gave a monstrous laugh. "No, you *gekbo*; it's a casino! It's on the south side of town."

"Show us," Ryan said.

Lashnar turned and walked to the edge of the platform, then gestured out toward the southern shore. That was when Ryan saw them: a small army of walkers and tanks visible between the buildings and on the hills beyond, firing at a squadron of oncoming fighters. Bursts of grey smoke hung in the sky where rockets had been intercepted by enemy warheads, and laser anti-missile systems split the air like silent lightning. Then, even as they watched, a great explosion blossomed up from one of the smaller towers in the southern part of the city. Beside Ryan, Amazon let out a low whistle.

"Today's forecast…" she said, with a note of eagerness in her voice and a smile on her lips as she squinted into the night, "war."

"That…" Lashnar said grimly, "I believe, was the casino."

"What?!" Jaleiko exclaimed. "Dawson, is that true?"

The security chief's mouth was hanging agape. "I, uh… that is, I'm not a gambling man. I can't be certain. But yes… yes, I think it could be."

Jaleiko cursed. "What is going *on* down there?"

"Just stay calm," Ryan said. "I'm trying to find out."

Ryan had been trying to contact General Rick Radcliff for hours now, but the jamming field around the city was extremely secure. Still, this situation called for another try. To his surprise, his transmission got through this time. Rick responded with a clear note of relief in his voice.

"My God, it's good to hear from you, Sergeant. I'm sure you've been having your fair share of trouble in there, but out here, everything's gone straight to hell."

"I noticed, General. One of the buildings in the city just exploded. What happened?"

"Everything at once. I was contacted by a Yavakarese aircraft carrier stationed not far off the coast of Xarkon. They said they'd been waiting there to keep an eye on things and had just been contacted by a trusted informant they had inside the city, who told them that Xarkon had turned out to be behind the entire incident and was planning to kill the hostages. The carrier launched a few wings to attempt an extraction, so I followed in the *Scepter*, at a distance, with Harrier and his fighters in escort. When we got there, the Yavakaro squadron leader contacted Mars, asked him to surrender the hostages… and he said…"

At this point Rick dropped off. Ryan waited a few seconds, looking around at his men. All of them were either staring at him or at the explosions in the distance. They looked anxious. Amazon and Lashnar, however, looked positively itching with eagerness, gripping their weapons in anticipation of the possible coming fight. Jaleiko, to Ryan's surprise, looked almost horrorstruck, his mouth slightly agape. When he saw Ryan's blue eyes facing toward him, however, he tried to regain his composure. Ryan assumed he was worried about Zegaldorph. He'd never seen a man so loyal to his leader.

"Said what, General?" Ryan finally prompted. "What did he say?"

"No."

"What?"

"*No.*" Rick repeated. "That's what Mars said. Just… no. It seems so much like him, you think I would have expected it, and yet… it was chilling, the way he said it. Something about it was just chilling."

The way Rick was speaking, it was clear that it had been. Ryan thought he even detected a small hint of admiration in Rick's voice for his most despised enemy, Lucas Mars.

The Grand General cleared his throat. "Anyway, we're coming in to get you. We can't just drop in from space, because the city's defensive turrets have plenty of anti-starship weapons on them, and we'd be even more exposed to their fire up there. Luckily, we know a place where one of the turrets is offline. Mars has reinforced the spot with walkers and tanks of every kind, but breaking through there is still our best bet to –"

Suddenly Ryan heard another voice cut in over the commlink. It was Jenkins, who was probably still in the *Silver Scepter*'s control room with Rick.

"General Radcliff," he said, "you might want to take a look at this."

"What… is that?" he heard Rick ask.

"Looks like… hoverbikes," Jenkins answered.

"Ryan," Rick said, "something big might be headed your way. We just saw possibly more than a hundred *hoverbikes* headed into the city, behind the Xarkon defense lines. Only one person I know is crazy enough for 'tactics' like that: Grimm. Looks like you were right about Nick Wolf being back there in that war camp. You'd better get ready."

Ryan turned to face his men. "This just keeps getting better. Listen up, everyone! Set the table, because we're about to have company!"

"It's about time!" Amazon exclaimed. "The bikes should be able to use the city's hoverboosters to fly up to at least landing platform D. We should set up a defensive perimeter there."

Ryan nodded. "Dawson, get your men on it! We'll join them as soon as we're able."

"Uh… right," said the security chief, swallowing. "I mean, yes, sir."

"Do you think any of them will be able to get up here to the roof?" Jaleiko asked.

Dawson shook his head. "Oh, no way. Only a vehicle capable of actual flight could make it up here."

Lashnar, who had been scanning the perimeter of the city with a monocular device since the positioning of her species' eyes did not allow them to use Human binoculars, suddenly gave a low growl. "You mean like that Nidhogg dropship headed in from the east? It looks like the black Bergelmir you saw is on course to meet it."

Ryan slid on his helmet and turned to Amazon and the rest of his men. "Better get ready, Victorians! We're stuck in a frying pan… and surrounded by the fire."

LOCATION: RIVERSIDE AVENUE, SHARDASHA

Grimm III, who had long ago switched off his cyborg body's pain receptors, glanced sideways at the glinting metal showing up through the enormous wound that the Enomeg had inflicted in his shoulder. His nanomesh suit had already emitted a spray of nanocrystal sealant over the gash, but there was still a trickle of blood getting through. Three ignored it and returned all of his concentration to the task at hand: piloting his battered hovercar away from the army of hoverbikes at his back.

"How can we lose 'em?" Three shouted into the wind.

Over the roar of engines, the wind in his ears, and the gunshots still sounding off behind them, Three barely heard Zegaldorph's booming voice shout in reply, "Go that way! Into the Gardens!"

Three knew what he was referring to. There was a complex series of archways in Shardasha called the Arcing Gardens. It was a resort that catered to the especially rich, and very few could afford to live in one of its terraces. Each room in the twenty or so tall, thin towers there took up an entire floor, and was connected to every other tower by an archway lined with plants that hung from the edges like the Hanging Gardens of Babylon, one of the wonders of ancient Earth. The arches varied in structural formation and shape, and the towers varied in height and design, so the whole place took on the look of an ancient ruin combined with a sort of random artistic style.

It was there that Grimm III was now headed, rising higher into the sky as he pulled his hovercar up, aided by the hover-booster devices built into the city streets. The Helios Zoom2 flew over the prestigious resort, then suddenly swooped down low, followed closely by the Enomegs and the Grim Riders, many of whom had to swing back around after passing in order to right their course. A few of them even ran into each other and went crashing to the streets below.

"Keep formation, dammit!" Grimm shouted into his commlink.

The flock of hoverbikes, dark against the bright sky, was a strange sight as it whirled down toward Arcing Gardens, like a murder of crows chasing a fleeing bird, with the four Enomegs in the lead. But one black hoverbike was now breaking off from the horde.

"Grimm, this is Widow," said the calm voice of Lisa Sharp in the warlord's ear. "I'm gonna go find a sniping position to cover you when you get to Zegaldorph's tower. That's got to be where he's headed."

"Right," Grimm replied. "Take a few of the boys with you; see if you can set up an ambush."

"I work alone, Grimm."

Grimm cursed, but he had no time to argue about it. He was rapidly approaching the first of the garden terraces now, and it was going to be a tight fit for him and his army. Meanwhile, on the street below, a single Fox walker looked up at the wheeling hoverbikes overhead.

Saber-Scorpion, although he was now stuffed into the small, rarely-used copilot space behind Amy Archer, felt strangely relaxed. He had been instructed, of course, on how to pilot just about every vehicle of war that Xarkon had to offer, but never before had he actually ridden a walker out onto the battlefield. Even though Amy was the one piloting, merely sitting inside of this smallest of Xarkonian walkers gave him a feeling of power. He could feel the vehicle lurching under him as the war machine traveled, its powerful legs taking long strides with all the surety and grace of an animal's. It was also rather peaceful under the Fox's armored canopy, cramped as it was. The din of battle was distant and muffled, and the ride was surprisingly smooth. And of course, he had Amy with him. Somehow she seemed to emit an almost palpable aura of calm, even in battle situations.

"Are you looking at this?" she said suddenly, breaking into his thoughts. "There's a viewscreen above you."

"I see it," Scorp replied, staring at the image of hoverbikes whirling overhead. "Can't you launch a missile at any of them?"

"I doubt it. They're too small and moving too erratically."

"Moving where?"

"I think I know. Look ahead."

Scorp did as instructed, and he saw the hanging gardens arcing above them in great, graceful formations. The nearest bridge was barely low enough for them to walk under. An idea burst into Scorp's mind, and he grabbed his copilot controls. Amy did not protest as he pointed the head of her walker toward the uppermost arches, the machinery beneath them groaning as it moved, leaning the riders backwards.

Scorp felt the slightest tinge of the sort of thrill Barracuda must have felt every time he blew something up… as he pulled the trigger to the Fox's main guns. A pair of loud, sizzling blasts could be heard on either side of the cockpit, and two great beams of white light, tinged with red, flashed into the sky, slamming into the bridge that spanned the tops of the two towers far above. The Fox blasted again and again, and the bridge began to fall...

Grimm III gritted his teeth and gunned the Zoom2's engine as he saw the arch beginning to collapse ahead of him, shot down by that unexpected little walker. Through the opening they raced, even feeling a few pebbles of debris bounce off them as they passed. The Enomegs were next, making it just in time, while behind them, Grimm I had to dodge a falling slab of steel-reinforced stone as he tried to pass.

Several of his mercenaries were not so lucky. Parts of the bridge slammed down on top of them, or they slammed into the pieces, or dislodged earth and vegetation entangled them and pulled the hapless riders to the ground below. Grimm cursed into his commlink and pulled his bike to a halt, with Nick and Jade hovering to a stop beside him and Grimm VII nearly slamming into him from behind. He heard Hurk growl angrily.

"Watch it, you idiots!" he screamed into the commlink. "Go around or go over!"

He then followed his own advice and soared over the falling debris, but he could not stay high for long. Three and Zeeg were taking to the low ground, through the middle of the tangled gardens, and he would soon lose sight of them. He could still see the Enomeg hoverbikes hot on their tail, having slipped in before the interference of that Fox walker…

That Fox. He'd have to do something about that.

"Mars," Grimm shouted into his commlink, "what the hell do you think you're doing? Some dumbass walker o' yours came trottin' in here and shot a building down on top of my troops! Call it off, or I'll blow it to Hades!"

Mars's voice was like ice. "Are my ears malfunctioning, or are you presuming to give me orders, Grimm? I thought we had this discussion."

Grimm cursed. "What?! I'm not – I'm *askin'* you, Mars!"

"I know you're asking," Mars replied frostily, "but I expect you to show me *respect*, Grimm. Are we clear? You have to ask me *nicely*."

Grimm punched the side of his bike in frustration, his armored glove leaving a dent. "Fine, fine. Commander Mars, I *humbly request* you call off that Fox walker and tell 'em we're on the same damn side here!"

Even though he was many kilometers away by now, probably just joining Viper's walker pack at the battle on the city border, Grimm could almost see the cool smile creeping over Mars's features.

"No problem," said the High Commander.

LOCATION: SHARDASHA OUTSKIRTS

Viper yanked back on his walker's controls until his computer locked onto the next incoming fighter. He heard the loud, roaring hiss of the missiles leaving the silo not far above his head. A few of the warheads were shot down by auto-target missile interceptor lasers, but the others struck true. The silvery aerospace craft erupted in flame and twirled toward the ground, trailing smoke. He saw a parachute come rippling out and fired a laser beam into it out of spite. He could not help but smile as it caught fire and burned, then disappeared into a pillar of smoke.

The rest of the wave was leaving now. Good, a lull in the battle. He quickly flipped up his helmet's HUD visor and turned back to another control panel, one that shouldn't even have been present on a standard Dingo. It was his personal tablet computer, which he had hotwired into the walker himself. He punched a few buttons on the screen and continued trying to hack his way into the nearby city defense turret. That Heimdall turret could make all the difference in this battle, and he wanted it back online. Unfortunately, it appeared to be damaged. Viper was an expert with computers, but this one simply wouldn't respond.

Viper dismissed that thought and turned to check his roster. Rhino, possibly his best pilot, was still going strong, along with two other pilots, Atlas and Legs. Jackpot, Cronic, and Travesty were damaged but still in fighting condition. Unfortunately, Canada had been on the front lines, and her walker was crippled. Viper quickly ordered her back to base for repairs. Only Burney was completely destroyed, his signal lost. One of the heavy rockets from the enemy bombers had blown his little medium walker apart.

"I'm gonna get a piece of that gunship out there if it's the last thing I do," he heard Rhino growl over the comm.

"Easy, Rhino," Viper said. "Your orders are to hold position."

His entire pack stood stock still, the dull dread of mid-battle calm stealing over them. So everyone was accounted for... except for one: Falcon. Where in the Refuge had Amy run off to now?

As if reading his mind, the tremendously deep voice of High Commander Mars roared out of his commlink, demanding, "Viper, I need a sit-rep. Now. One of your walkers has been spotted in the city and is mucking up operations there."

Viper turned down the bass volume, wishing that he hadn't installed a custom sound system inside his walker and left it connected to the communicator. "I'd like to know where she went too, sir, but I haven't the slightest clue. She never even told me she was leaving!"

"I assume you're talking about S.O. Archer?"

"That's right, sir." He wondered vaguely how Mars could remember the names of not only his subordinates, but also the subordinates who were *subordinate* to his subordinates.

"Well then find out what's wrong and let me know. I'm *en route* to your location in *Manegarm* to take over. Mars out."

In addition to the anger he felt at being so abruptly relieved of his command while on the field, Viper also felt the cool relief that he always felt once he ended a conversation with Lucas Mars. The two feelings cancelled each other out, and he blew out a sigh. He switched the commlink to a personal channel with Amy and scanned his map display. There was her falcon-shaped indicator. She was in the city all right.

"Falcon, this is Viper. Where…?"

She cut him off. "I'm currently in the middle of the city, near the Arcing Gardens. Just following orders, sir."

"Don't give me that 'sir' stuff, Falcon, and don't try to dance around the truth. What's really going on in there?"

"I'll let you speak to the one *giving* the orders…"

Another voice came over the line, one Viper hadn't heard before. "This is Enomeg Century-Sergeant Saber-Scorpion. I've ordered Falcon to help me, Beta-Wolf. You'll have to do without her."

Viper felt his temper flare up. "I'll have to do without one of my best walker pilots? My scout, part of *my* hand-picked wolfpack? What on Terra do you need a walker for, '*super*'-soldier?"

"Best thing for a chase, Commander," the Enomeg replied. "Now, if you don't mind, I'm rather busy. Exactly what I'm doing is currently classified information. Scorp out."

Viper cursed, and he made sure to do so just before he switched off the commlink. He opened the channel to Mars and was answered immediately.

"This is Mars."

"Sir, she's AWOL. Not my fault. Said one of your Enomeg guys ordered her into the city for some reason. He wanted a walker. I talked to him. Name's Saber-Scorpion."

"Ah yes," Mars said, his tone changing entirely. "Well then, I understand. It's out of your hands. I will speak with the Enomegs about it later. You can…"

Viper looked up. The fighters were coming back around again, and this time the Victorians were coming in with them. Their silver and blue hulls gleamed in the moonlight, the V-shape of their wings giving them the look of shining arrowheads, fired by archers too far away to see. As Viper watched, however, they engaged their reactive camouflage, enshrouding their hulls in a dull, deep blue-black that blended perfectly with the night sky.

"The fighters are back!" he exclaimed.

"But I can tell you are busy," Mars concluded. "I'll be there as soon as possible, Beta-Wolf. Mars out."

Viper swore, and then he flipped down his HUD visor. He was beginning to dislike these Enomegs almost as much as he disliked everyone *else* who gave him orders.

LOCATION: ARCING GARDENS RESORT, SHARDASHA

Grimm III and Zegaldorph zigzagged between the arches and towers, trying to lose the black-armored Enomeg who was hottest on their tail, Blood-Raven, but with no luck so far. As they went deeper into the complex, it became harder to maneuver, but no matter how close they cut it through the hanging vines, under the arches, through tiny holes in webs of support beams... the Enomeg stayed right behind them, mimicking their every move.

Finally he got even braver and took one hand off his controls long enough to fire at them. Raven knew the bullets of his blazer pistol would have almost no effect on either a Mahlok or a cyborg, but it was worth a try.

Three cursed. *Back to basics*, he thought. He then drew his short, double-barreled shotgun from the sheath at his side. Taking careful aim, he fired. The first blast of shot grazed the Enomeg, mostly bouncing off his personal shielding, which flared up as it was hit. The second shot went wide as the Enomeg dodged around another tower.

"To Hell with this place!" Three heard Zegaldorph shout beside him, and suddenly the area was lit up with red flame.

Reaching out with one glowing hand, the Mahlok torched the vegetation hanging from each arch they passed under, as well as the ones they crossed over. When they saw Raven again, bursting through one of the walls of fire the Mahlok had created, Zegaldorph turned and aimed a blast of licking flame straight at the oncoming soldier. His bike was engulfed and instantly exploded, but Raven himself came flying right out of the ball of fire, his jetpack trailing two tails of blue-white Starlight heat.

The black-armored super-soldier landed right on the back of the Helios Zoom2 hovercar, his hands gripping the back seat as he tried to pull himself inside. Three signaled to Zegaldorph to take the controls, as he climbed over the seats toward the rear of the vehicle. Raven pulled himself into a crouch just above the back seat and lunged out with a sharp kick, knocking Three sideways. The Enomeg did not miss the chance to spring on his off-balance opponent, bringing his arm around as his star-talon blade flashed online.

Grimm III's world turned bright red as his cyborg endoskeleton's warning system erupted, blaring out that his armor and skin had been breached, and his internal hull was taking heat damage. Reaching down and grabbing Raven's wrist, he jerked the blade back out of his stomach and wrenched the Enomeg's arm up toward the air. Meanwhile, Zegaldorph was forced to pull up abruptly to avoid the hoverbike that was now rushing toward him with the added speed of its Enomeg rider's jetpack. Only after pulling up did he notice he may have gone too far.

Raven heard Coyote's voice in his ears, saying, "Raven, duck!"

The Enomeg barely crouched in time, as the side of the bridge under which they passed struck Grimm III in the back, knocking him right out of the hovercar. Unfortunately, his hand still held Raven's wrist in its iron grip, so the Enomeg was taken along with him. Down they fell, and Raven felt the wind knocked out of him as he landed on a lower bridge, his fall mercifully broken by the garden foliage left unscorched by Zegaldorph. Then he felt his arm jerked down by a great weight that might have pulled it out of its socket had his suit not compensated, enhancing his strength. Looking down, he saw the problem: dangling from his arm, which was hanging over the edge of the archway, was Grimm III, looking beaten all to hell and with many of his internal metal parts now showing, but otherwise very much alive.

Raven was about to lash out at the cyborg with his free blade when he was saved by the oncoming Grim Riders. The bike that struck Grimm III was piloted by Hurk, whose slow Slashrim wits did not enable him to dodge in time. The impact of the vehicle, however, was enough to make the cyborg's vision black out, and down he fell, collapsing along with the rubble of one of the bridges below him. Raven looked down to see if he was still moving, but nothing could be seen except clouds of dust and rushing hoverbikes, which were now speeding past him both above and below.

"Coyote…" Raven groaned, his entire body racked with pain, "I'm out… of the race… wounded, but I'll live. What's the situation?"

"Zeeg's still headed for his tower!" the other Enomeg responded. "Cobra and I caught up with him, but he keeps flaming us!"

Suddenly the commanding voice of Dark-Dragon cut in on their conversation. "Raven, we're coming to pick you up. Coyote, you and the others break off pursuit and rendezvous with me at Raven's location. Scorp should already be on the way. Let's finish this!"

LOCATION: MORDARK EMBASSY

"This is a huge mess we're in the middle of," Ryan said to Jaleiko as they stalked the outer hallways of Zegaldorph's tower, "but the only thing to do is sit it out."

Jaleiko was staring out the windows to their right, looking at the smoke that still hung, barely visible, over the battlefield at the edge of town.

"Meaning?" he prompted.

"Meaning that we hold the fort here, and we stay alive. The safest way out of this city was the coast, but now Xarkon is sure to be watching that closely, waiting for us. Every other exit is either blocked by Heimdall turrets, armor units, or those walkers out there. But if General Radcliff can get in to save us, he will. And if your Lord Zegaldorph is still alive, he'll probably come back here too, once he realizes there's no other way out."

Ryan turned to Security Chief Dawson. "Any word?"

The man anxiously tugged at his ear. "Well, uh… yes. We were contacted by that mercenary a moment ago, the Grimm clone."

Jaleiko's face turned to stone. "And why were we not informed of this sooner?"

The guard swallowed. "That is exactly what I'm trying to find out, Captain. I would love to know. My men seemed to have ignored the message for a while because it came in on the wrong line, and…"

"You know, Dawson," Jaleiko replied with icy coldness in his voice, "I am embarrassed to even stand in the face of such a colossal failure as you. In better days, men like you would at least have had the honor to end their own shameful life."

Beside the Mordark royal guard, Ryan Arkanian's eyes narrowed. "With all due respect, Captain, that comment was positively... *Xarkonian*."

Jaleiko shook his head. "Forget it. Just tell us the message."

Dawson wiped his forehead. "It... it was nothing all that important anyway. Nothing we didn't already know, that is. The mercenary was just trying to tell us that the path was blocked and that he and Lord Zegaldorph had to come back around. He said they're headed back here now."

Jaleiko turned away and spoke quickly into his communicator: "This is Jaleiko. I want eyes on all sides of the tower searching the city for..."

"I already found them," replied the gruff voice of Lashnar, who had linked into their commlink channel earlier. "East side; they're swinging this way now."

Ryan and Jaleiko ran down the hall toward the east side of the building, followed by the overweight head of security, puffing as he ran. They joined Lashnar just in time to see the last of the horde of flying hoverbikes dipping down below the horizon into the hanging gardens.

"Those are the ones Radcliff warned me about," Ryan said.

Lashnar growled. "Where are they going?"

"They must be after Zegaldorph."

"Do we have eyes out there?" Jaleiko shouted into his commlink. "Get me some eyes out there! I need a sit-rep!"

They were running now, around the perimeter of Zegaldorph's tower. Ryan was following Jaleiko, who seemed to have no particular destination in mind, just a lot of nervous energy and a need to vent some of it. Eventually Ryan put a hand on his shoulder and spun him around.

"Jaleiko! We're going nowhere!"

"*I* am. Once I find a vehicle, I'm heading out there."

"But he's coming to *us!*"

"It might be too late by then!"

They were interrupted by Security Chief Dawson on the commlink. "Captain Jaleiko, a group of Sarran are requesting entry into the building. They claim to have had contact with Zegaldorph."

"Let them in," Jaleiko said without hesitation. "They must be the ones Zegaldorph went to help."

Ryan shot him a questioning glance and was about to make a comment when Amazon's voice blared in his ear through the commlink, shouting, "North side! North side!"

They immediately fell back to running. Jaleiko reached the north side of the building first and burst through a pair of doors that led out to one of the smaller landing platforms about halfway up the tower. They could see several hoverbikes in the distance, lit by the glow of the moons. It was a horde not quite the size of the one they'd seen earlier, but still enormous, chasing a lone black hovercar, which looked damaged and was trailing smoke.

Jaleiko ran to the very edge of the platform and said, "If that's the Grimm-clone mercenary and not Lord Zegaldorph, then I'm going to shoot him down right here."

"Then you'll have to kill me too," Lashnar put in, looking down at the Human standing beside her, who was at least a head shorter.

Jaleiko stood taller and rested a hand on the hilt of his energy sword. "You want me to do it now?"

Lashnar gave one of her low, gurgling laughs. "I want you to *try*."

"It's definitely Zegaldorph," Ryan put in as the car drew closer, and then he spoke into his commlink. "Amazon, make sure the platform below this one is covered. He could be losing altitude…"

"Negative," came the reply. "He's headed right for you!"

Ryan drew his pistol and stared into the oncoming hoverbike horde. They were coming within small arms range now, and a few of the mercenaries' bullets began to strike the platform at their feet. A bright green glow could be seen at the forefront of the riders, and though many of the bikes had glowing engines that trailed white fire behind them, this one in particular caught Ryan's eye. It looked almost like a miniature green star, and it was getting brighter, lighting up the nearby bikes in green.

Ryan knew what it was. "Is that a starfire cannon? All men, aim for the glow! Take it down!"

Even as Lashnar, the Mordark guards, and the Victorian soldiers all leveled their rifles at her, Jade continued to charge her arm-cannons. Standing half-crouched on the back of Nick's hoverbike, her knees on either side of him, the streets of Shardasha far below, she had locked her two guns together, combining their power. The field stabilizer forks around the barrels had split apart and then combined, forming an emitter four times as large at the end of the connected barrels, which now glowed with the light of a tiny green sun. Once the starfire blast was fully charged, she raised her eyes and locked onto the black hovercar just ahead, aiming for its Mahlok pilot…

And just when Zegaldorph was almost on top of the landing pad, she fired. The comet of green-white light split the air and struck Zegaldorph directly in the back. For a split second, he could be seen like a Human-shaped form composed entirely of white light, before finally he exploded in a veritable supernova of flame.

"Noooo!" Jaleiko shouted, threatening to throw himself into the blast until Ryan jerked him back.

From out of the explosion came two objects: the charred remains of the Helios Zoom2 hovercar fell from the bottom… and from the top flew what remained of Zegaldorph, his body blackened and trailing fire. Jaleiko immediately ran forward and caught the limp form, the impact of which knocked him to the ground and sent him skidding backward. Ryan inspected Zegaldorph briefly; he had never seen a Mahlok with skin so dark. It was not a good sign – it meant his inner fire was fading, or already extinguished.

Now bullets split the air all around them, coming from both the Victorians and security guards in the skyscraper and from the mercenaries on their hoverbikes. Ducking under the shower of ballistics, Ryan grabbed Zegaldorph under one armpit as Jaleiko tried to raise himself to his feet.

"Help me with him!" Ryan shouted.

Suddenly Lashnar lumbered up, pushed Ryan aside, and grabbed both Jaleiko and Zegaldorph with one great, clawed hand each. The Slashrim easily carried the two charred forms inside, and bullets pinged off Ryan's armor as he ran to cover her back. Once the doors were shut behind them, they heard the whoosh of the hoverbikes turning just outside the window, moving to circle around the tower, firing at the windows as they went.

"Zegaldorph?" he heard Jaleiko shouting, between coughs. "My Lord, can you hear me?"

Ryan turned to see the royal guard captain, who was burned black in several places from the Mahlok's fire, propping the Lord of Mordark up against the wall. Lashnar, meanwhile, had moved to one of the windows and had broken a crack to stick her machine gun through, eager to rejoin the fight. Ryan moved to help Jaleiko with Zegaldorph. The Mahlok's skin was dark, almost black, and his lidless yellow eyes, usually bright yellow or even white, glowed a dim, deep reddish-orange.

"I am… alive, Jaleiko," Zegaldorph moaned, all of the awesome power seeming to have fled from his voice, which was now weak and muffled, a distant echo of its former self.

"What happened?" Ryan asked.

Jaleiko shot him a dark-eyed glance that said "not now," but Zegaldorph still answered.

"I had to vent the energy," said the Mahlok. "I felt the blast… strike me from behind, and I… knew it would overload my core. So to avoid… blowing up from the inside out, I… expended… as much of it as I could… in a burst of flame. It was enough to push me toward… the landing platform. But I am weak now… cannot feel… anything…"

"Save your strength," Jaleiko said. "When we find Grimm, we'll make sure he pays for this."

They were about to help him up, but Zegaldorph put a hand on Jaleiko's shoulder. "The mercenary… he is not an enemy. *Mars* is the true enemy. Mars… did this… *all* of this…"

"Jaleiko's right," Ryan interrupted. "Let's get you out of here. You can tell us everything later."

Ryan and Jaleiko helped the Mahlok to his feet and carried him down the hall toward the center of the building, where it was safest. A short ride in the lift took them to a small infirmary, where they lay Zegaldorph on one of the beds. Jaleiko quickly began preparing some kind of medical device meant for re-energizing expended Mahlok, even as he called in several more royal guards to help him protect his lord. Ryan was about to leave the room when he felt Zegaldorph feebly grab him by the wrist.

"I want to know… what is happening… as well," he said.

Ryan turned to the Mahlok and answered him as quickly as possible, telling him of the CONON meetings and their results, how he had been labeled a terrorist. Zegaldorph in turn told them of his reasons for going to help the Sarran, since he had worked with them in a plan to take down the Black Network crime boss Jim Crow, and he did not want to see them taken down with him as scapegoats by Xarkon. Jaleiko then informed him of the two Sarran who had requested entry.

"I'm glad you let them in," Zegaldorph said. "Tell Idelma'ik I will meet him at the roof."

Jaleiko shook his head. "Amazing that Xarkon could plan something so twisted…"

"General Radcliff must hate them even more now," Ryan said. "They've broken the international laws set up by CONON. It's not just war, it's a criminal war."

"All war is criminal," Zegaldorph said gloomily. "Who is the more criminal, the murderer who kills a handful of individuals, or the politician who sends entire armies to their doom? But what does it matter anyway? How I despise politics, wars… and laws. Crimes…"

"I agree, my Lord," said the loyal Captain with a nod.

"When we get back to Mordark," Zegaldorph concluded, "the first thing we do… let's burn all the lawyers."

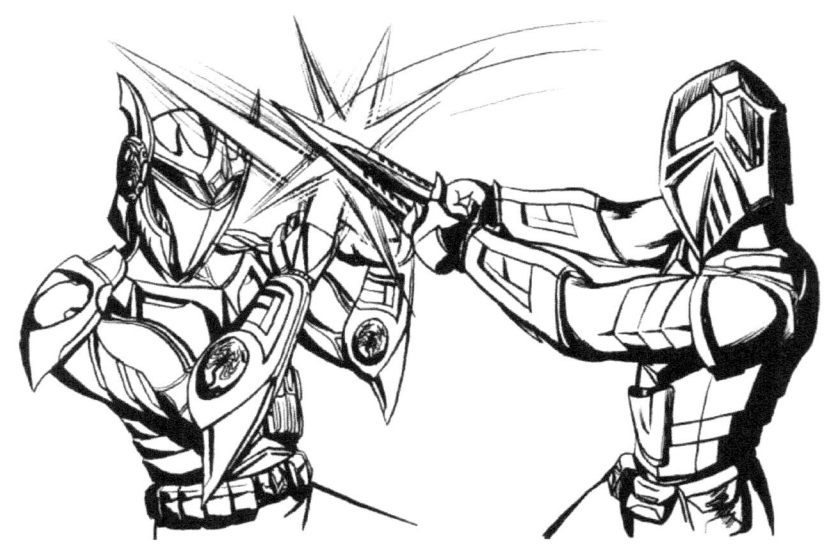

- CHAPTER TWENTY-THREE -
LIVE BY THE SWORD

The light-footed Fox stepped nimbly – almost daintily – over the fallen debris, making its way through the vine-covered ruins of its garden hunting ground. The flock it had been pursuing had long since passed, but a few stragglers remained, injured and unable to move. As it passed a fallen arch, covered in vines and leaves, it paused, one foot still held in the air. Perfectly poised, it turned its head to inspect its prey…

Having half-fallen, half-climbed the rest of the way down to the streets again, Blood-Raven groaned as he pulled himself out of the wreckage and gazed up at the scout walker looming over his head, with its pair of radar dish "ears" silhouetted against the sky. He watched as the machine lowered itself to the ground, crouching down on its haunches. The back half of the canopy slid open, and Saber-Scorpion climbed out.

The two ebon-armored Enomeg commanders stared at each other. Scorp's exoskeleton had received a few light scratches on the chestplate from the blades of the Grim Riders' hoverbikes, but the nanomachine layer had coated over them so they were nearly invisible. Raven's armor, on the other hand, was dented on the chest plate, which meant he had struck something very, very hard. His leg had received a cut from something apparently sharp enough and hard enough to slice through the nanofiber mesh, releasing a line of wound-sealant foam.

"Status?" Scorp asked as he approached, searching the burning debris for sign of movement.

"Green," Raven responded, without looking up. "Just a scrape and a sore arm. Where the hell is Dragon?"

"Is that disrespect I hear in your voice?"

"Oh, shut up, Scorp. You *got* your victory. Now I'm gonna go get mine. I can't just sit here and wait!"

"*My* victory? *Your* victory? You think this is still some kind of competition? Some kind of game, where all that matters is winning? Do you think this is the VR room, and the men we killed were just holograms, or volunteer soldiers we shot with stun guns? You think they're going to get back up and congratulate you on a job well done if you win?"

Raven shrugged. "Who gives a damn? Just get out of my way unless you want to join them."

During Scorp's tirade, Raven had been putting on his helmet and checking his gear and physical condition. Satisfied, he now stepped up and pushed past Scorp. Saber-Scorpion watched him walk up to the foot of the crouched Fox walker, in which Amy Archer sat with her arms crossed over the edge of the cockpit, her head resting in her hand, listening intently to the two Enomegs.

"You there, pilot!" Raven shouted up at her. "I am Century-Sergeant Luke Blood-Raven, Enomeg Commander, and I'm commandeering this Fox! Climb out quickly or I'll throw you out!"

Scorp stormed up behind him angrily. "Forget it, Raven! Get your own ride!"

"That's exactly what I'm doing," Raven replied coolly, without turning to face him. "Now you can either come *with* me or play it smart and stay out of my way."

Scorp grabbed him by the shoulder, jerking him around. Raven immediately swung a punch at the other Enomeg, but Scorp caught it and twisted his arm. Raven danced around the attempted throw, wrenching his arm back out of Scorp's grip. Both of them cocked their fists back...

Then the outraged voice of Dark-Dragon blared out in both of their helmets. "Enomegs! Cease this foolishness immediately or both of you can just leave that black armor you're wearing *behind* when we exit this city! Am I understood?"

They both looked up to see the blazing light of a Nidhogg dropship's twin thrusters burning in the night sky above. The vessel kicked up a great cloud of dust as it landed amidst the debris, so that Amy was forced to shut her walker's canopy. From the open troop compartment of the vehicle, Dark-Dragon glared down at them with an air of absolute indignation. All around him sat or stood the other Enomegs, looking down at their commanders with more worried expressions.

"Get in," Dragon said. "*Now.*"

Scorp and Raven fired their jetpacks, landing gracefully in the open door of the Nidhogg. Before taking his seat, Scorp paused and looked back over his shoulder, staring down at the Fox walker below, which was now rising again to its feet.

Scorp quickly spoke into the communicator Amy had given him: "Falcon, stay on patrol around Zegaldorph's tower and report if you see anything approaching."

"I should probably return to Viper," Archer replied.

"I'd rather have you on patrol. A recon walker isn't much use on a battlefield like that one anyway."

Scorp took his seat in the Nidhogg.

"I get the feeling you're trying to protect me, Saber-Scorpion."

Scorp was glad she could not see his face. Then again, it didn't seem to matter. Apparently he was either very easy to read, or Amy was just very good at it.

"Just help me out, Falcon. I'll take it up with Viper later."

Dragon shut the hatch and ordered the pilot to take off. Into the air they rose, the ship's boosters roaring beneath them. Dragon stood in the center of the troop compartment, his hands locked together behind his back, just staring. Scorp and Raven sat on opposite ends of the compartment in the direction he was staring, and both of them felt unnerved by the metallic gaze of the helmet he had replaced on his head.

"This is it," said the veteran Enomeg, his voice grim. "It's now or never, Enomegs. Zegaldorph and all his guards, including the Victorians sent in by General Radcliff, led by two of their 'Immortal Soldiers,' are all holed up in the Mordark Embassy tower, along with an unknown number of mercenaries. Now, with Zegaldorph's ship gone and enemies closing in from all sides, they have nowhere to go. Nowhere to run, nowhere to hide. Our grip, the grip of Xarkon and her allies, is tightening around them."

"I won't let them slip through my fingers again," Raven said with determination.

Dragon shook his head. "You certainly will if you keep fighting with your own allies! That goes for both of you! I need everyone on the same side for this, like soldiers of the Crown are supposed to be! This isn't going to be easy. General Radcliff and his boys, along with their Yavakarese allies, are trying to break through our walkers and tanks to the south. Once the way is clear, they'll bring in the transports and try to extract their people from the city. Meanwhile, Camp Ragnar has broken up, half of it moving to reinforce the walkers, the other half headed straight into the city, right for Zegaldorph's tower, which is currently surrounded by the Grim Riders."

"Sounds like they have no way out," Seth commented.

"Oh, they do. If the Victorians can break through the city defenses, it will be clear sailing for the *Silver Scepter* to get their men out. There's really nothing *inside* the city to stop it, except us and Grimm's hoverbikes, and we're like gnats next to that flying fortress. Shardasha's defensive turrets can swat down anything short of a capital ship with ease, but they have trouble firing into the city itself. Because of this, the Vics'll try to keep the *Scepter* back until they can clear a safe path along the ground for the Grand General. But we have to move fast. We'll take the tower from the top and head down, and Mars's forces will enter the tower from the bottom and head up."

Raven looked up. "Mars's forces? The High Commander is here?"

"Yes," Dragon said gravely, "*everyone* is here. This day will be remembered as the first battle of the New World War, the first war between all great Human nations since the Exodus..."

He paused for effect, scanning over the faces of each of his Enomegs. Though most other men and women would have been worn and tired from all of the action they had already seen, his super-soldiers were keen-eyed and itching for battle, even the ones nursing injuries. Barracuda had reattached his shoulder-mounted missile launcher. He and Raven seemed to have forgotten about their injuries – they were running diagnostics on their armor, checking their weapons, and flexing their muscles, just like the other Enomegs. They were all focused on the task ahead, on the target that would soon be in their sights. All except Saber-Scorpion, who sat at the back, lost in thought.

"This is the first battle of the Ultimate War," Dark-Dragon said. "Now let's win it."

LOCATION: ARCING GARDENS RESORT

Grimm III fell onto his back, and for a moment silence overwhelmed him... at least until he heard the rest of the Grim Riders rushing by overhead, though he could barely see them through all the dust stirred up by the fallen debris. All around him lay the rubble of the bridge he'd dislodged, and according to the diagnostics reading on his HUD, he'd suffered a few internal damages. He flexed his fingers and legs, his joints popping and whirring with every movement. Slowly, and not without difficulty, he pulled himself to his feet and looked around.

He was on the roof of a short, squat building next to one of the resort towers of the Arcing Gardens, and he could hear voices on the street below. Three had never heard Xarkonian soldiers argue on the battlefield. Indeed, they seldom exchanged words, and were well known for their stoic loyalty. Not so with the two Enomeg commanders he now heard. Considering taking advantage of the scrap, Three scrambled toward the edge of the roof and looked down. He immediately dismissed all thought of attack. One Enomeg he felt he could take, but two Enomegs and a walker? He decided to just sit it out.

Again he found himself quietly waiting, cursing his ill luck. For the first time, he noticed that the sensation of touch was not present over much of the left side of his face. He reached up to discover that his eyepatch was gone, and so was half the skin on his cheek, all the way down to his chin. He could feel the raw metal of his cyborg skull beneath. The mercenary snorted. At least now he was following the standards of cyborg tradition. He knew he would be able to repair it – it was amazing what they could do with cloning and artificial tissue these days – but it would cost him dearly. And he just hoped his hair would still grow properly.

Then he heard the roar of engines in the sky above and looked up to see the descending Nidhogg transport. Soon the two Enomegs had flown inside, and the Fox walker stood up and stalked off. Now was his chance. With all the strength left in him, Three stood, clambered atop the pile of rubble under which he'd been hiding, and just as he saw the sheen of the black metal dropship overhead, launched himself up and grabbed it.

At first he found himself clinging to an armored "tooth" that helped form the ship's Crown of Xarkon shape, but he knew he could not hold onto that for long, and the ground below was getting farther away all the time. Looking up – and trying hard to resist looking the *other* way – Three saw a few bits of piping on the dropship's belly above him. Swinging his legs, he managed to slide his foot around one. Then he followed it with his hands, clambering up until he was snug against the underside of the massive Xarkonian vessel. He felt the wind whip at his hair and the exposed skin where his suit had been torn in his fall, as the Nidhogg set off at its fastest speed toward the uppermost point of Zegaldorph's tower.

Between clenched teeth, Three muttered, "There's gotta be a better way to make a living."

LOCATION: SHARDASHA OUTSKIRTS

Viper was never sure if he loved or hated being a leader in a battle like this. He hated leaders in general, because he typically disliked following orders and preferred to do his own thing. But on the other hand, the feeling of power and importance that leading an army gave him always bolstered his spirits. He hated the responsibility of defending his country, but the glory... now *that* he could live with.

But now Mars had taken both.

Viper sneered resentfully at the intimidating silhouette of *Manegarm*, shadowed against the night sky. He had to admit it was an impressive walker, although it would have been even more impressive in the shape of a man instead of a beast. As it was, his humanoid-shaped Dingo was nearly just as tall anyway. What was the big fuss about?

"General Black," Viper heard Mars say over the commlink, "order your lighter tanks ahead of the AA guns. Better that the enemy fighters shoot them first instead of the ones that can shoot back. Viper, bring your walker unit back into proper anti-air defense formation around my position."

Viper was surprised Mars was letting him give the orders himself, so he jumped to obey. It turned out to be just in time, for once their vehicles were in position, the next wave of Yavakaro bombers appeared on their sensors. Viper knew they were just softening up the enemy for the main wave of Victorians, who were reputed to have the best aerospace forces on all of Terra Nova. Rick's son "Harrier" had yet to show himself. All the fighters were preparing for the moment when the *Silver Scepter* would arrive.

"Commander," Viper said tentatively, "I suggest firing in volleys."

"Don't just suggest, Beta-Wolf," Mars replied. "Go ahead and give the order. I'll take charge if I need to."

Viper wasn't sure if that was a good thing or a bad thing, but he gave the order anyway. "All units, pick a target and fire on my mark!"

He waited. The more missiles that were fired at once, the better chance that more would make it through without being dodged or intercepted by automatic laser countermeasures, with which many advanced aircraft were now fitted. Also, he was waiting to see if the enemy would fire first. It was not long before they were close enough, the glint of the moonlight on their hulls barely visible above the distant mountain range. Viper's computer locked onto the nearest craft.

"Fire!" he shouted, and the missiles loosed.

Both sides fired at once, with warheads raining down into the ranks of the walkers as more flew up into the swarms of advancing fighters. Many were intercepted on both sides, exploding in midair. Some were dodged, and others managed to hit their targets, riddling the ground with burning slag. Some of the missiles even ran headlong into each other, creating even more massive fireballs for the impressive fireworks display. From the windows of the nearby buildings, those citizens who had not yet evacuated the premises watched in terror and awe.

The fighters burst through the wall of hanging smoke, swinging around for another pass. The air was so thick with dust that Viper was relying entirely on instruments for the moment. He saw on his HUD that several of his allies were turning about to fire at the retreating fighters.

"Resume firing positions!" Mars bellowed.

"Forget the buggers!" Viper shouted. "Watch for the Vic's!"

As if on queue, they came. This next wave of Victorian fighters was composed entirely of Black Knight stealth craft, invisible to the walkers' detection systems until they were directly upon them and firing. General Black cursed as his front row of tanks took heavy losses, although Mars's order to keep the anti-air units in the back saved most of those. Unfortunately, as they tried desperately to get a lock on the slippery stealth craft, in came the heavier Victorian ships: Star-Captain Harrier Radcliff and his squadron of Paladin fighter-bombers.

The Captain's personal fighter cut through the cloud of smoke like a knife blade, trailing blue fire. Harrier was far ahead of his squadron, so he was the first to be fired upon. The walkers' missiles locked on and launched just as he passed overhead, and behind him they trailed. Up into the air he went, spinning off to one side and then flying between two skyscrapers, which were soon riddled with explosions as the pursuing missiles struck them. Waterfalls of broken glass showered down from the points of impact.

"Ignore him!" Mars thundered. "Watch the horizon!"

It took less than a breath for Harrier's squadron to arrive behind him, safe now from some of the fire thanks to their leader's brave distraction. The Paladins came in recklessly low, firing at the walkers with both missiles and direct-fire blazer weapons. Viper heard pilots screaming over his earpiece as their vehicles were blown to scrap. Many of them never even saw it coming. But the walkers got their fair share too, especially Mars, who let loose with every gun that *Manegarm* had, ignoring the heat and power warnings blaring in his ears as he did so.

Viper had been expecting the arrival of the cavalry too, but he had found it harder to pull his eyes away from Harrier's breathtaking piloting skills than had

Mars. One of the enemy fighters was bearing straight down on him, firing his blazer machine guns, which breached Viper's hull in several places. But the Dingo was tough, and before it could take significant damage, Viper let fly the heavy Starfire cannon blast he'd been charging all along. The projectile raced above the blackened battlefield like a shooting star, lighting up the hanging smoke as it passed, striking the fighter square in the cockpit and destroying it in a supernova of light…

But Viper wasn't even looking anymore; he was scanning his HUD. His forces were at half strength. In fact, there were more of General Black's tanks still intact than there were of his walkers. The Victorians had hit them hard, and now they were coming back around in coordination with their allies from Yavakaro. Each group had swung around to an opposite side.

They would hit them all at once, from every direction.

As Viper considered this, Mars was issuing orders without an ounce of fear in his ever-commanding voice: "Units east of the highway, look east! Units west of the highway, look west! Keep your eyes peeled and *fire at will!*"

Then, once again, the air burst into flame.

LOCATION: MORDARK EMBASSY, SHARDASHA

It was a strange sight: a towering skyscraper, one of the tallest in Shardasha, surrounded by a swarm of mercenary hoverbikes buzzing around it like angry bees. The walls of the building were spitting fire as the defenders, consisting of security guards, Mordark soldiers, and the remaining Victorian soldiers of Ryan's team, fired from the windows with everything they had. They were not entirely unsuccessful; occasionally one of the bikes would fall from the sky, a lone black dot, and go plummeting to the earth. Usually it was because the rider had been shot, but sometimes it was the vehicle… and the pilot had no choice but to ride it all the way down.

But not all of the mercenaries were in the air. Grimm I, Grimm VII, Nick Wolf, Jade, Hurk, and a handful of other elite mercs had dismounted their bikes and now stood on one of the landing platforms jutting from the side of the building… the same platform, in fact, that the wounded Zegaldorph had landed on earlier. Grimm was standing near the edge, looking around at the city below. He could see a few Xarkonian units moving about, including that pesky Fox walker, and there was the unmistakable shape of a Nidhogg on approach in the distance.

"Let's see who gets the prize first," Grimm said loudly to the warlords standing on either side of him, Nick Wolf and Grimm VII. Then he activated his commlink. "Black Widow, report!"

"I'm in position," Lisa Sharp responded coolly. "I just reached the top of the Stormflier Corporation building and should be able to cover most of Zeeg's tower from here. In fact…"

There was a crack over the commlink, followed by a tiny 'plink' from a window above Grimm and a scream.

"Good, good, just keep covering us," Grimm growled.

Then he turned back toward the building. Most of the mercs on the platform, including Jade, were now crouched behind their hoverbikes, firing up at the defenders who were fortified in the windows above and around them. It was not the best position in which to be; the Victorians had the high ground, the low ground, and everything in between. Grimm watched as one of his elites took a bullet in the shoulder and was knocked right off the edge of the platform, falling toward the street below with a high-pitched cry of terror.

"I'm goin' in!" Grimm shouted. "Nick, Jade, Hurk, Drakk, you're with me! Seven, you stay out here and keep things in order!"

"Yes, sir!" shouted Grimm VII, just as a bullet ricocheted right past his face, coming so close as to rustle his hair.

"Hurk, get the door!"

The hulking burnt-orange Slashrim let out a ferocious snarl and, even as several bullets struck him, ran toward the glass, covered on either side by Grimm, Nick Wolf, Jade, and the smaller Slashrim named Drakk. The material of the windows, though tough, shattered as soon as it felt the impact of the heavy Slashrim's horned shoulder. Down it went in a shower of shards, but Hurk immediately came rushing back out, followed by six Mordark security guards, flanked by Victorian soldiers who were now breaking more windows in order to fire at Grimm and his men and keep them from entering.

"Turn around, ye stupid troll!" Nick Wolf shouted at Hurk, as he gave him a shove back toward the door. "Everyone rush 'em!"

With a war cry almost as blood-curdling as that of the Slashrim before him, Nick Wolf tossed his rifle into the air and grabbed it by the center, activating its axe-like blazer-shielded bayonet. In he ran, swinging his weapon at the windows the Victorians were breaking, slicing one Vic across the chest. Then he jumped through the window and unslung his hatchet, now fighting with both weapons and hacking through the stumbling Victorians as they tried to reassemble. Hurk and Drakk joined him immediately.

More of the defenders were blown away by Jade's Starfire rifles as Grimm took up the rear with a few of his elites, rolling through the window and firing with his submachine gun. Then one of the Victorians, a woman in some kind of strange, silvery armor, drew a blazer sword and managed to battle her way past Nick, taking several of her comrades with her as she led them on a retreat. She finished by taking a heavy swipe at the mercenary and disarming him of his smaller axe. He stumbled backward and let her go.

"Fall back! Head up toward the roof!" Amazon shouted as she ran. "We're breached! Fall back!"

Nick looked impressed. "Not bad fer a girl."

"Shut up," Jade said. "You wounded?"

"Got a few nicks, but I'll live."

"Good," Grimm said, turning in the opposite direction of the hallway from where the Victorians had headed. "Let the Vic's go. Probably just a distraction anyway. We'll find our own way up. Come on, boys! We've got us a Mahlok candle to snuff."

Stepping over the shattered glass, dead bodies, and discarded weapons and ammunition, Grand High Warlord Eric Grimm led what remained of his ragtag team deeper into the building. Behind them, one of the guards who had been playing dead crawled to his feet and reached for his gun… right before a pair of bullets from Lisa Sharp sent him back onto the ground. Grimm did not even glance over his shoulder to look.

LOCATION: MORDARK EMBASSY ROOF

Ryan strode out onto the roof of the building, followed by Jaleiko, Lashnar, and Zegaldorph. The Mahlok Lord was still naked, his lean but muscular form artistically accentuated in lines of black. As the Victorian watched, he saw a tendril of flame leap from the Mahlok's eyes and lick at his forehead, evidencing the return of his powers. Jaleiko was decked out in his ceremonial garb now, his red cape proudly flowing behind him. Lashnar looked ready to kill, as always. And there stood the two Sarran, clad in metallic black battle armor, an unusual color for Sarran garb to be sure… the color of the "Blackwings." Both were male, one with pitch-black wings and hair, and the other with greyish-brown.

"So you're the infamous Sarran 'terrorists' I've heard so much about," Ryan said, extending a hand. "I'm Sergeant Ryan Arkanian of the Victorian Army. It's a good thing they sent *us* instead of Yavakaro soldiers, or a fight would have broken out already. Your group knocked off a lot of important people there during the Xenocide War."

It took Idel a moment to recall the practice of shaking hands, and he seemed displeased as he did it. "Yes, I suppose 'we' did. I was not there, however, and we are composed of different individuals now. I am Idelma'ik, leader, along with my mate Folirayoth, of those you call the Blackwings. This with me is Doriad, one of my finest warriors and brethren. We have news for you, and we must speak quickly: we were released from our captivity by a Xarkonian soldier, though he wishes to keep his identity a secret."

"A Xarkonian?" Jaleiko exclaimed in surprise.

"Yes," Idel went on, "and he granted us with a route out of the city. Most of my people are leaving there now, led by Folirayoth, but I felt some debt was owed to the one Mahlok who had ever aided us in time of need."

Lord Zegaldorph nodded. "I… am honored."

"And a Slashrim too, I see…" Idel said, with a rare show of expression in the form of a raised eyebrow. "What brings him here?"

Lashnar ignored the incorrect gender pronoun and snorted. "I'm not interested in politics, if that's what you're getting at. I'm just here 'cause I'm getting paid. I'm starting to think I'm not getting paid *enough* though…"

Ryan was about to speak when he was interrupted by Amazon's voice coming in over his commlink: "Grimm's Army has breached the building! My team fell back, but the mercs don't seem to be following us…"

"Good," Ryan responded. "Head up to the roof right away, and bring as many men as you can with you. We'll make our last stand here."

"On our way!"

After waiting a moment, Idelma'ik went on. "But that is not all... We also bring dire news of your enemy. Those who chased you were the same as the one who released us: super-soldiers, far beyond the abilities of most of your kind. They call themselves the Enomegs."

Ryan nodded. "So... Xarkon's secret super-soldiers... I doubt they've given up yet. They're probably headed up here in that Nidhogg Lashnar spotted."

Zegaldorph shrugged. "I escaped them once already, and so did these Sarran. They don't sound that threatening."

Amazon arrived on the roof then, and Ryan greeted her, telling her to give her men some rest and prepare for the battle ahead. Then the blue-armored knight walked to the edge of the roof and donned his helmet again to look out across the city through its built-in binoculars. The battle below still appeared to be going strong. Smoke hung thick in the air, but he thought he could see a silver streak that looked like Harrier's fighter. He knew they wouldn't send in the *Scepter* until the coast was absolutely clear.

"I could destroy this tower," Zegaldorph said behind him, in a distracted sort of tone.

Ryan turned to face him. "What?"

"Explosives," said the Mahlok, looking around wistfully. "Oghr-Pyron explosives are set up all throughout the building."

"Oghr-Pyron?" Amazon said. "Never heard of it."

Ryan shrugged. His knowledge of explosives was extensive, and he knew about Pyron – the same flammable material that was used by the Firestorm Cannons often found on heavy walkers, but...

"*Oghr*..." Lashnar growled, "a Slashrim word for a Slashrim chemical: brutal and deadly."

Zegaldorph nodded. "Indeed. Your kind were using Oghr as an explosive long before we, the Mahlok, even came to your planet. I enjoy... shall we say... *pyrotechnics*, so I experiment with them at times. When Oghr is mixed with Pyron it has the most splendid effect of not only being extremely destructive and incendiary, but also undetectable to most explosives scanners."

Security Chief Dawson, who had climbed to the roof along with Amazon's group and was still out of breath, was taken aback. "What? W-where is this stuff stored, um, my Lord?"

Zegaldorph shook his head. "Suffice it to say that you would never find it, Human. But if I were to ignite it, it could take out quite a bit of this accursed city."

Behind his helmet, Ryan's lips tightened, "No, I don't think that will be necessary. I'm not exactly what you would call a big *fan* of Xarkon, but I wouldn't want to blow up that many civilians needlessly. It's bad enough that their country has put them in so much danger, but we would look like – would *be* – the villains ourselves if we –"

"Ryan!" Amazon shouted suddenly. "Nidhogg, incoming!"

They whirled to see the massive Xarkonian air transport flying up toward the roof, paying no heed to the bullets pinging off its hull from the few remaining defenders inside the building. The vehicle was solid black, moving like a shadow, ominous and threatening.

"They're here," Ryan said, drawing his pistol, "the Enomegs."

The Nidhogg roared up above the very top of the skyscraper, its spiked, Crown-shaped form rising like the teeth of some ebony demon whose jaws were about to close upon the defenders below. Ryan thought he could make out a Human shape moving on its belly, but he did not have time to consider it as the dropship doors opened, and out came the Enomeg Soldiers. They flew down on their jetpacks, two at a time, cool and confident, their deep crimson and onyx armor glistening in the slowly-brightening night sky.

The Victorian soldiers who had followed Amazon raised their rifles to fire, but Ryan held up a hand to stop them. The Enomegs did not fire either; they simply settled down on the roof and formed a long line. Though the battle raged below them on all sides, the landing platform remained eerily silent.

Dark-Dragon stepped forward and pressed a button on the side of his helmet. His visor withdrew, and his faceplates opened partially, revealing a Y-shaped portion of his face, surrounded by menacing black metal. Ryan looked into the experienced blue-grey eyes of that old war veteran and saw nothing but determination. No doubt, no fear, not even any active thought or planning, just pure determination. Dark-Dragon knew his goal, and he was taking the only course now available to him: straight through. He nodded once in the direction of Lord Zegaldorph and then turned back to the Victorian sergeant.

"I will give you one single chance," he said. "Surrender the tyrant you protect, and I will make sure your life, and the lives of your men, are spared. You have my word, as a soldier."

"And as a soldier," Ryan replied with matching calm, "you know that is not possible."

Dragon nodded. "All too true. In that case, it will be an honor to fight you. Blades only?"

Ryan nodded. "I have no argument against honorable combat."

The Enomeg commander smiled… a surprisingly honest smile.

"You have no idea how refreshing it is," Dark-Dragon said, "after fighting nothing but Zygbari rebels for years, to finally hear someone say that. Very well, blades it is. May the best man win. *Enomegs!*"

Suddenly the entire landing pad was lit by the glow of starfire and blazer swords. On one side stood Dark-Dragon, Saber-Scorpion, Raven, Seth, Cat, and Coyote with their two star-talon blades apiece, and Mantis with his blazer sword. On the other side stood Ryan with his long blazer daggers; Jaleiko and Zegaldorph with their starfire blades; Amazon, Idelma'ik, and Doriad with their blazer swords; and Lashnar with her bayonet-tipped machine gun and a long, wicked knife she had drawn from a sheath on her leg. Barracuda and Cobra had remained in the dropship to provide covering fire if necessary, and the Victorian soldiers on the roof stood by for exactly the same purpose. But neither side pulled their triggers.

"My Lord," Jaleiko said, keeping his eyes fixed on the Enomegs as he spoke, "you should fall back and let the Victorians protect you."

"Nonsense, Captain," Zegaldorph replied, with renewed fire in his voice. "It has been far too long since I last killed with my own two hands. This is as much my fight as it is yours, and if I die, so be it."

Dark-Dragon looked doubly satisfied at this comment as his visor and faceplates snapped shut, covering his face in cold duranium once again. Raising his star-talon, he shouted, "Charge!"

The medieval melee that ensued was something one would never have expected to find on a modern battlefield, but perhaps that was why it existed. Some historians speculated that the return of the sword as a weapon of war was heralded by the advent of such high-tech protections as force shields and nanofiber mesh, which were best breached by personal contact. But it was more than this. For so many centuries had man fought his fellow man at a distance – waging war with increasingly powerful rifles and artillery that could hit targets the Human eye could not even see – that the very nature of the warrior had rebelled against it.

By the time Humanity reached the Refuge and especially in the years afterward, something of a new mentality had developed in the wealthiest Human nations about the nature of war. And now, as the first major war of man against man began in earnest – despite the involvement of the Mahlok, Sarran, and Slashrim on Zegaldorph's tower roof – the mentalities of honor that had been growing in Victory and Xarkon culminated in this: the first battle of the Ultimate War, the Battle of Shardasha, and this round would be fought as a duel of muscle and blades. Or so some historians would say, debating the fight endlessly in the years to come.

But for those there on the landing pad that day, such an academic argument would have seemed petty and pointless in comparison with the battle itself. The chaos of flying shafts of light and duranium was nearly incomprehensible to the onlookers, and it was all the combatants could do to discern which blade was whose, who was fighting which enemy. Before long, they began to break away into personal duels and groups, as combatants endlessly lost and gained ground, circled and dodged.

As the only Enomeg who had drawn a solid blade, Mantis posed the greatest threat to the heat-absorbing Mahlok skin of Lord Zegaldorph, so he was the first enemy Captain Jaleiko had targeted. This left Zegaldorph himself to deal with Dark-Dragon, who quickly drew a blazer knife with his off-hand. Magnum-Coyote found himself tangling with the surprisingly skillful Slashrim, Lashnar; and Raven and Cat had their hands full with the two Sarran blade-masters, Idelma'ik and Doriad. Meanwhile, the two Victorian Immortals, Ryan and Amazon, were engaged with Saber-Scorpion and Electric-Eel. To any onlookers on the ground below, it now appeared that a pulsating star sat atop Zegaldorph's tower, so bright was the flash of blades.

"Looks like it's gonna be a good, long fight," said Grimm III.

The mercenary was glad that Nidhogg dropships stood so high off the ground when they landed. On any normal transport, he would have been nearly crushed while hanging on the ship's belly. As it was, he crawled to one side and reached up to the boarding hatch above with one hand, feeling about until he got a good grip. Then he swung out and pulled himself up, peering over the bottom of the opening and into the interior of the Nidhogg.

It was occupied by two Enomegs. One giant bald one was sitting in the corner, fingering a machine gun with the familiar look of bloodlust burning in his eyes. The second, a slim female, was watching the melee below through the scope of her sniper rifle, clearly waiting for a chance to pitch in. Three briefly considered pulling himself up and engaging both targets, but he knew that would be ridiculously foolhardy. So, instead, he merely let go of the ship and dropped down to the platform below.

The mercenary crouched down low to avoid being spotted by any of the combatants in front of him. Luckily, they were much too preoccupied to glance at the slightest movement, so Three was able to slip away unnoticed, dropping off the back of the roof onto the slightly lower perimeter platform behind him. Hiding against the wall, he activated his commlink. Unfortunately, he could not quite remember what their current codenames were supposed to be, so he just switched to an older set.

"Ultraviolet, this is Infrared," he said. "You copy?"

Spectra's reply sounded both frustrated and relieved. "Erik, where have you been? I've been trying to raise you forever now! Listen, this is getting much too hot for us – we need to go."

"What? But what about Zegaldorph?"

"Forget him. I'll see to it that you get paid whether he lives or dies, but this mission's scrubbed, as of *now*. Rendezvous at…"

"I don't think so," Three interrupted. "Lashnar's still up there, and I've got a score to settle. I *don't* leave jobs half-done."

She blew out a sigh. "I was afraid you would say that. Look, just… just stay there. I'm on my way."

Three scowled. He hated waiting, and furthermore, he found himself a bit worried about Lashnar. Turning back to the wall, he jumped up, grabbed the edge, and did a chin-up until he could see onto the main level again. The grand melee was still going strong. Well, at least he had a show to watch.

At the start of the battle, Shadow-Cat had followed Blood-Raven as he desperately tried to reach one of his primary targets: Zegaldorph, Ryan, or Amazon. He was eager to prove himself either by completing his mission or defeating a rival Victorian super-soldier. But his plans were thwarted by the two Sarran, Idelma'ik and Doriad, who suddenly dropped in between the Enomegs and their goals, unfurling their wings so that the Xarkonians could not even see their targets.

They drew their weapons – long swords, straight and double-edged, made of a bluish-tinted metal alloy developed by the Achmer to be nearly as light, and thus nearly as fast, as an insubstantial energy blade. On their other arms, the Sarran bore round suspended-energy shields glowing like twin suns. Raven danced around, trying to move past the Sarran, but they mirrored his movements, their wings remaining outspread, the tips of them dangling just over the Enomegs' heads. Cat noticed these obvious weak spots in their defense and took a swipe at one of Idelma'ik's feathered limbs.

"Wait!" Raven called to her, but it was too late.

The Sarran withdrew his wingtip in the blink of an eye, avoiding Cat's strike, and at the same time, aimed a slash at her exposed side while she was distracted. Cat dodged just in time to avoid being cut in half, but the blade did cut right through her personal force shield and left a gash on her nanomesh suit, which spat foam.

Raven swore. While all the Enomegs had been trained in a wide array of fighting styles, this was an obscure Sarran style that only the sword-obsessed trainees – like Raven, Scorp, and Mantis – had bothered to learn. Humans called it the Sword of the Temple style, since it was traditionally passed down through the ranks of the elite guards of the Temple of Harmony. Idel had apparently been trained at some point by a Sarran Templar. The wingtips were used as lures, inviting non-Sarran foes to see them as a weakness and attack, thus leaving them open for a strike. It seemed an obvious trick when one thought about it, but in the heat of battle, it was easy to find oneself striking at anything that looked like an undefended body part.

Raven immediately moved to intercept Idel from continuing his attack on Cat. It was a tight fit between the two of them, however, and Idel was a skilled foe. The Sarran Templar were some of the greatest swordfighters in the Refuge, easily a match for any skilled Human, even a "super-soldier." Raven quickly found himself on the defensive, barely deflecting the strong swings of the Sarran's blade and energy shield. Further enhancing the fury of the battle was the occasional appearance of one of Idel's wingtips, providing just enough of a distraction to keep Raven on the very edge.

The Sword of the Temple style was said to employ strength and precision more than speed, but either Idel had changed the style, or Raven was unprepared for the reality of facing a Sarran using it. Idelma'ik was far more agile than he had expected, and the absolute precision of his attacks made them hard to dodge. But the most surprising thing was the shield, which was not a simple force field like Raven's personal shielding system, but a hot suspended energy field of the same type used for some swords. Thus, it was both a defense system and a weapon, since it could cut on impact.

"A shield," taunted Raven, panting as he finally was able to back off and circle his enemy, "is the refuge of a coward."

"Two blades," replied the Sarran, his precisely-chiseled features set like stone, "are the sign of a madman."

"The madman and the coward," Raven said with a laugh, brandishing his weapons. "Who will tri–"

Raven's words were cut off as he felt a blast of air from the Sarran's flapping wings strike him, almost knocking him off balance. Up Idel flew, descending again to make a great downward slash at Raven's head from above. The Enomeg dropped down and rolled, but the sword still grazed his side, breaching his personal shield. Raven heard his suit blare a warning in his ears, and suddenly he felt as naked as if he were wearing his old training outfit of black cloth and padding. Suddenly, the painful truth became clear to him...

He was losing.

Meanwhile, Cat was faring even worse. With his sword, shield, and wings, Doriad was a tough foe to match, and his continued rain of blows seemed to be guiding her in the direction of Idel, hoping to corner her or allow the other Sarran to attack her from the rear. Cat realized how close she was coming to the other duel when one of Idel's wings flashed right past her face. Then it struck her in the back, knocking her sideways. Doriad's blade soon followed, knocking out her force shields. She was helpless.

Then Raven was there. Throwing one arm around her, he fired his jetpack, flying away from the Sarran warriors. His control was limited, however, and they both skidded along the rooftop to a halt, lying on their sides. The Sarran soon swooped down in pursuit, just as the Enomegs were getting back to their feet. Raven attempted to resume his fight with Idel, knowing that Cat would be no match for him, but Doriad moved to intercept. Surprisingly, he seemed nearly just as skilled as his leader, pushing Raven back even as Idel engaged Shadow-Cat.

Suddenly the cold touch of fear Raven had felt when his shields fell was replaced by the blinding heat of fury. With a yell, he charged, forcing Doriad into the defensive. The Sarran suddenly found his foe's strikes too quick to follow, and even with his shield, he had a hard time blocking them all. Doriad tried to distract the unrelenting flurry of blows with a wing-lure, but this proved to be a mistake, since Raven had been waiting for it.

The strike happened so fast that the Sarran did not have time to react. Doriad stifled a scream of pain as his severed wingtip landed on the roof amidst a shower of feathers. Raven had just managed to cut far enough in to hit the limb itself, and the horror of this unexpected injury seemed to shake his opponent's resolve just as much as its pain did. Smiling at his apparent triumph, Raven moved in with all he had... just as Idel dropped down behind him from above. Raven twirled, barely ducking under the swing of his sword.

"Retreat, Doriad!" Idel shouted.

Raven snarled. "Damn backstabber!"

"Two can play at that game," he heard Cat put in.

Idel soon discovered what a grave mistake he had made by abandoning his fight with Cat in order to attack Raven. Doriad shuddered as her twin starfire blades punctured his back, between the armor plating, and then his entire form went limp, tumbling to the ground with outspread wings. Cat paused to look down on the tragic sight, seemingly almost regretting what she had just done.

But Idelma'ik showed no emotion. Indeed, his face seemed to grow even colder, and he redoubled his concentration, his attacks growing faster and faster. And Raven, already tired from his furious battle with Doriad, suddenly found that it was all he could do to keep up.

When he had left the ETAB for the final time, Seth Electric-Eel knew that he would never again witness as perfect a duel as that between Saber-Scorpion and Blood-Raven. But the battle now taking place before his eyes between Scorp and Ryan Arkanian seemed almost to mirror it. It looked like an elaborate dance that moved too fast for the eye to follow, the flash of Scorp's star-talons upon Ryan's long blazer daggers appearing like a swarm of flickering stars that hovered between the two soldiers almost playfully. Amazon and Electric-Eel still stood on opposite sides of the fight, staring in awe at the duel before them, too mesmerized to move to engage one another.

Scorp and Ryan had similar feelings. Even as they tried their best to improvise, invent moves, cut corners, and take risks… their foe seemed to predict all of it, even mirror the very same moves. Ryan had been highly trained in swordsmanship in case just such a fight as this should ever take place, but he had not been versed in all of the same styles as the Enomeg soldiers. Yet somehow, the very movements of his foe seemed familiar; the times he chose to strike or feint, to dodge or parry, seemed almost… predictable. And to his utter astonishment, Scorp felt exactly the same. Neither of them could gain an edge.

Then Seth saw an opening and decided to take it. Ryan had moved around in his direction, and the Enomeg charged at what seemed to be an exposed spot in the Immortal Soldier's defenses. But the blue knight saw him and ducked under the blow, taking a stab at Seth as he did so. The Enomeg dodged to the side… where Amazon was waiting. She took a swing at his exposed back with her blazer sword. He was caught off-balance when the heavy blade struck him, sending him stumbling. His shields flared, protecting him from harm, but down he fell, right off the edge of the landing pad.

Scorp paused, dropping into a defensive stance to prepare for Ryan's next attack. He tried not to think about Seth, hoping he could handle himself. Scorp knew he would need all of his concentration to battle both Victorians.

Then Ryan too jumped over the edge. Scorp and Amazon both ran to see the results of this unexpected move. Not two meters below them was another, smaller platform jutting out of the side of the building. Electric-Eel had fallen on it and was trying to get to his feet when Ryan landed on top of him. Their blades clashed as the Victorian attempted to finish off his prone opponent. Scorp quickly leapt down to join them, and Amazon followed.

Electric-Eel was fighting desperately now. His training flashed before his eyes, his opponents from the Test of Supremacy flickering in to replace Ryan at intervals. He saw Raven and Saber-Scorpion, the blade-masters who had defeated him almost with ease. He remembered how Raven had knocked him prone, just like he was at that very moment, before finishing him off brutally and painfully…

Scorp hurried to aid his comrade, but Amazon came up right beside him and lashed out with her sword, forcing him to dodge. Scorp dropped into a defensive stance and deflected her next blow, quickly observing that she had now drawn out a second blade – a pure-energy one slightly shorter in length – to back up her main blazer sword. The Victorian wielded this unusual combination to surprising effect, using the energy blade to deflect some of Scorp's strikes while making her offensive slashes with the heavier sword, the weight of which made it harder for Scorp to deflect.

Amazon felt the thrill of triumph as she saw her foe block her heavy sword with both of his star-talons, leaving him open for an attack by her energy blade. But in the blink of an eye, Scorp twirled, making a parry that Amazon had thought impossible. Her shock at seeing her surprise attack so easily deflected lasted only for a fraction of a second, but that was all it took.

The Victorian's shields flared and burned out as the Enomeg's starfire blade slashed her side. She made a desperate swing with her long sword, and again Scorp deflected it with both blades, but this time he gave them a scissor-like twist, wrenching the weapon right out of her grasp. Scorp caught the handle of the sword in midair and held it high above his head, while Amazon raised her remaining blade in a feeble attempt to block this final, no doubt deadly blow.

But it never landed. Instead, she only received a kick to the side, sending her slamming against the wall and knocking the wind right out of her. Then Saber-Scorpion tossed her blazer sword like a javelin straight toward her comrade's back. Scorp's aim was true, and the weapon glanced Ryan on the shoulder, causing his personal shields to flare before bouncing off and falling over the edge of the roof, toward the streets of Shardasha far below. Scorp then pointed his star-talon back toward Amazon, who immediately froze.

Ryan turned. Scorp glanced around for Seth, but he was nowhere to be seen. Then he noticed a pair of hands clinging to the edge of the platform, and Seth pulled himself up. He waved. Scorp nodded.

"I don't like stabbing people in the back," Scorp said, "but you'd better leave Seth alone unless you want me to change my mind. This is between you and me."

Ryan nodded. "Then you do the same with Amazon."

"I never planned to do otherwise," Scorp replied, withdrawing the blade he had been pointing at her, so that she finally started breathing again.

Ryan was not sure if he could trust this Xarkonian, so he began moving between him and Amazon as slowly as he could, while Scorp circled around between Ryan and Seth. Neither of them broke eye contact with the other as they moved to defend their companions. Ryan knew he did not have time to battle this foe; his mission was to protect Zegaldorph and his other allies on the roof, and these Enomegs were distracting him from that goal. Still, that meant he was distracting the Enomegs as well. If only he could eliminate at least one of them...

Then Saber-Scorpion struck, rushing in with his left blade held up defensively as his right came in for a low jab. Ryan dodged the strike and made a low stab of his own, which Scorp parried, following it with a downward slash that Ryan blocked. Again the dance resumed, the two warriors moving like mirror images. The floor of the platform was littered with debris, but they stepped around it as if it were not even there, their feet apparently guided by some sixth sense... for their eyes were concentrated entirely on one another.

Yet somehow Ryan realized when he had successfully moved between the Enomegs and Amazon, for he stopped and shouted, "Amazon, go back and help the others! Now!"

"You sure you can hold them off?" she replied.

"Yes, now go! Go, go!"

Reluctantly, the other Victorian obeyed, jumping up to the top of the wall and pulling herself back onto the main platform. Scorp was waiting for his foe to glance back and make sure she was safely gone, but Ryan gave no such opening, the thin black visor of his helmet locked firmly onto Scorp's. Again the battle resumed. Ryan made a feint toward Scorp's left at exactly the same time that the Enomeg made a slash at his leg. Both attacks were easily dodged by their target, and they were followed by sideways slices from the right that intercepted each other in mid-flight.

The two blades sizzled and popped, screaming with the release of energy against one another's shields, as the warriors held them against each other, glaring over the top of them. Then they pushed away, and Ryan made a double-bladed attack straight down at Scorp's face, which he blocked with a cross-blade parry. Again they found themselves staring at each other as their blades crackled between them, threatening to explode from the heat.

Suddenly Scorp realized what his enemy was doing: Ryan was trying to make him lose his blades, either by overloading them or making them waste their gas. If they went out, he would be disarmed, but even if Ryan's daggers lost power for their energy shields, the solid blades would still remain intact. So Scorp withdrew from the shoving match and dropped into a defensive stance. He surveyed the field: Electric-Eel was behind Ryan now, on his feet again and looking ready to backstab the Victorian, withholding his attack only because Scorp had told him to do so.

"Eel, get back to the roof!" Scorp shouted, echoing Ryan's earlier orders to Amazon. "Help the others! I can handle this one!"

Seth nodded and took off at a run toward the wall, but Ryan suddenly made a flamboyant spinning kick, which struck Eel in the chest and sent him onto his back. Scorp took the opportunity to make a scissor-like double-slash at his opponent, and Ryan felt the blades strike him on the back as his shields overloaded... but he did not let it slow down his retreat. He ran toward the wall and, in one graceful motion, jumped to the top and pulled himself up. Saber-Scorpion and Electric-Eel exchanged glances, and Eel quickly fired his jetpack to follow.

When he landed, he found Ryan waiting for him. Seth blocked the first two dagger strikes, but they kept coming, fast and hard. He heard Scorp fire his jetpack behind him, and he glanced sideways to see his comrade land on the edge of the upper platform.

That glance was the last mistake the Enomeg ever made. When he looked back, Ryan had already moved – ducking down low and charging under Seth's defenses. Ryan's blade slid in between the cracks of Eel's chestplate, burning and piercing through his nanomesh armor.

It was all over then. Saber-Scorpion took a jab at Ryan, but the Victorian maneuvered Seth's impaled form like a shield. In slid his second dagger, and Seth let out a stifled gasp of pain. As he fended Scorp off, Ryan backed away toward the battle. Finally he slid out both of his weapons, tossed away his human shield, and rushed back to help protect Lord Zegaldorph.

As Electric-Eel stumbled onto his kees, his last few labored breaths coming slower and slower, Scorp felt time slide to a crawl. He could not see Seth's familiar red-orange hair, or his blue eyes staring up at him, but he could almost picture them there behind that black slit of a visor. Scorp ran forward, and down the Enomeg fell into his arms. Before he could even reach to check Seth's wounds, the heads-up display in his helmet registered it for him...

UNIT: ELECTRIC-EEL – DOWN

That did not mean simple incapacitation; it meant a complete loss of vital signs, despite the best efforts of the suit to resuscitate its wearer. Even his Enomeg exoskeleton's automatic first-aid features could not save him. The truth hit Saber-Scorpion like the weight of his falling companion: Seth, Electric-Eel, one of the first fully-trained Enomegs, the invincible super-soldiers of Xarkon... and one of his closest friends... was dead.

- CHAPTER TWENTY-FOUR -
OUT WITH A BANG

Shardasha, the city under siege, looked like Hell. The once-grassy hills on the outskirts of the city were reduced to ash, fires burning where clumps of brush and trees had once stood. Downed fighters dotted the landscape, their tailfins sticking up like devilish forks protruding from the earth. Ruined tanks blended with the low-lying buildings, smoking and devastated, while the high-rising skyscrapers were riddled with craters caused by stray missiles and ballistic fire. Walkers that had toppled to the ground lay scattered about like fallen monuments, while others, destroyed on their feet, stood decapitated, with holes blown through their chests, like giants blasted into oblivion by some vengeful god. And above it all, the entire hellish field was marked by pillars of smoke rising away into the sky to blot the heavens.

Viper's humanoid Dingo was one of the few walkers still moving, accompanied by what was left of his pack, the Snake Legs, and Mars's seemingly invincible *Manegarm*. General Black had retreated most of his tanks into the streets of the city, to keep them as concealed as possible from the whirling fighters, whose constant rain of fire had only now ceased… for how long, none of them could tell. Harrier's squad had been devastated by their near-suicidal attack runs, but it was undeniable that they had succeeded in their mission: there was no longer sufficient anti-air artillery in place to prevent the flying fortress of the *Silver Scepter* from entering the city.

"Jake, Viper," Mars said, "report."

"Triple-A all but neutralized," replied Jacob Black. "What's left is pulled back into the streets for cover. Together with the walkers, it *might* still be enough to at least damage the *Scepter*..."

Viper checked his squad screen. Burney, Atlas, and Legs were all down – possibly dead, since they hadn't reported back even after their ejection pods had fired. Rhino, Jackpot, Travesty, and Cronic were all that was left of his team, and none of them had made it through the fighting without sustaining damage. Even Viper's own walker had lost an arm. Falcon was still nowhere to be found.

"This is crazy," Viper said. "We're on our last legs, literally. I'm not risking what's left of my pack on a *suicide* mission that'll barely slow Radcliff down! The Snake Legs are going to walk away from this, not crawl!"

"And the Lord said unto the serpent," Mars recited musingly, "'Upon thy belly shalt thou go, and thou shalt eat dust all the days of thy life.'"

"That's not funny," Viper snapped.

General Black gave a gruff chuckle. "Well, Radcliff *does* always brag about being a Christian."

Viper snorted. "Well, until he summons lightning, thunder, and earthquakes, I'll remain a bit skep–"

He was cut off by a deep, tremendous thud that shook the entire field, causing a few more showers of glass to tumble from the broken windows of the nearby structures, vibrating the Xarkonians' cockpits and causing their holographic control panels to blur with static. Viper cursed.

It was the first volley of fire from the *Silver Scepter*. Soon the ground around them was being blown apart by ballistics and energy blasts, sending chunks of dirt and ash clouding the air. Viper could barely make out the sound of Mars ordering all units to open fire, followed closely by someone letting out a scream through the commlink right before they were blown apart. He *hated* it when they did that.

Travesty's voice came next. "Missiles locked on – interceptors are out! Ejec–"

Her words were cut off as the rockets struck her walker, which was standing right next to Viper. The shockwave of the explosion nearly knocked Viper's Dingo off balance, and a chunk of slag that had once been part of the nose of Travesty's Wolverine walker ricocheted off Viper's transperium viewport. Looking out the back, he saw her escape pod trailing smoke. He would have to find out later if she made it out of the blast alive. For the moment, he just spun his walker about for the quickest way out of the city and pushed it to full speed.

"Retreat!" he shouted into the commlink. "Rhino, Jackpot, Cronic – *retreat!*"

"What about Mars?" came Rhino's reply.

Viper looked at his rear viewscreen to see *Manegarm* slowly but surely ascending the tallest hill, staying just high enough to keep the rise itself between him and his target but still allow his main guns to fire.

In his cockpit, Mars was casually fine-tuning his weapons' aim after allowing his computer to calculate the trajectory of the main rail gun and match it with the velocity of his distant Victorian target. He heard the machinery both above and below him clicking and whirring as the immense cannon made its minute adjustments, and as his walker's legs settled down into a crouched position to brace it for the weapon's intense recoil. Then he instructed his missiles to begin locking on as he grabbed his controls and pulled the trigger for the rail gun.

There was a thunderous roar as the slug left the cannon, and the *Silver Scepter* was knocked off course, tilting to one side.

In his command center, Rick grabbed the backs of the gunners' chairs as his vessel rocked and groaned. He quickly righted himself and leaned over one of the gunner's shoulders, inspecting the readouts on his control panels. The shields of his vessel had endured the hit, though just barely. They would not withstand another. The General then spoke into his commlink.

"Gunners, lock onto that walker and begin charging the main starfire cannons. Pilot, take us as close behind that skyscraper as possible for cover. Once we pass by it, open fire with the Gauss guns *and* the starfire."

"A risky move, firing all main guns at once…" Jenkins put in.

Rick held up a hand for silence. He suddenly remembered exactly who he was fighting and had an idea. It would be a risk, but it might be their only chance against that monster of a walker Mars had created.

"Wait…" he said. "Pilots, once we get behind the skyscraper, fire all lower thrusters and bring us up as high as possible, as fast as possible, before we fly back within the walker's line of sight."

"Rick…" Jenkins said cautiously, "that will strain our energy flow to the limit. We'll probably lose shields and–"

"Just do it!"

Mars watched as the *Scepter* dipped lower behind the skyline, dropping out of sight behind the tallest tower. The High Commander shook his head. Surely the Grand General knew that *Manegarm*'s rail gun would fire right through that building. It was foolish of Radcliff to assume Mars would hesitate to fire on a civilian structure. *Any residents*, he thought, *who have not yet evacuated are fools in any case, and this is war. Wars have casualties.*

With his targeting computer still tracking the *Scepter*'s last visible trajectory, Mars waited until the rail gun was again ready to fire and pulled the trigger. The thunderclap split the air again, and a vertical geyser of dust and glass burst from the side of the skyscraper behind which the *Scepter* had disappeared. Mars waited for the ship to show itself, eager to see how much damage he had caused… when suddenly he saw its angular nose emerge into view much higher than he had anticipated… above the spot where his rail gun had penetrated. Rick had dodged the shot while out of sight.

"Clever…" Mars muttered.

He jerked his walker into reverse, and it rose to its feet again and began backing down the hillside for cover just as the earth in front of it exploded into flame. The *Scepter*'s starfire blast had hit the ground, but its two Gauss slugs had reached their intended target. Mars felt *Manegarm* shudder and lean backwards. The legs automatically compensated and began to stagger back, even as the walker's force shield overloaded from the impact.

But the High Commander would not be defeated so easily. Jamming his walker's throttle to full, he began to reascend the hillside.

Viper shook his head as he saw *Manegarm* lumber back up the hill. "I don't believe it. The man's completely insane."

"I'm going to help him," he heard Cronic say with conviction.

"I'm with you," Jackpot chimed in. "Turning about now..."

Viper stammered. "W-what? You're *all* insane?"

Mars looked about to see his fellow wolves rejoining him. He said nothing, but tapped his commlink button, causing his status indicator on their Heads Up Displays to blink. Together the giants ascended the hill with a lumbering stride. Once they rose to its apex, they leveled their guns toward the horizon... just as the Scepter disappeared from sight, followed by the remaining fighters as they swung around to escort.

The walkers fired off a few more missiles at the fighters, most of which were intercepted by various countermeasures, but they knew there was little they could do now. Despite their best efforts, the Victorians had slipped through their net and made it into the city.

"Lucky bastard..." Jackpot muttered.

"It was more than luck," Mars said. "He beat us today. We'll have another chance though, wolves. But later – I doubt Rick will be exiting this way. So follow your pack leader and let's head back to Camp Ragnar."

Meanwhile, above Shardasha, the Victorians inside the *Silver Scepter* were celebrating, Colonel Jenkins grinning from ear to ear while Rick let out a sigh of relief. Harrier was shouting triumphant cries over the commlink as he ordered his remaining fighters into escort formation around the *Scepter*.

The Grand General had taken a huge risk. If Mars had decided *not* to fire upon the civilian building – to instead wait for the *Scepter* to reemerge – his slug would have torn right through the unshielded gunship for certain. But luckily, Rick's assessment of the High Commander's personality had proven true, and they had made it with hardly a scratch. Even now their shields were beginning to recharge. Not far off on the horizon, Rick could see the Mordark embassy skyscraper, with the Grim Riders still buzzing around it like insects.

"Head straight for Zegaldorph's tower," Rick ordered calmly. "Be cautious, but go as quickly as you can. It looks like Ryan will need our help."

LOCATION: MORDARK EMBASSY ROOF, OUTER PERIMETER PLATFORM

Grimm III had been afraid of dying many times in his life. When he had first decided to leave the Grim Isles, he'd feared his mercenary "father" would find out and execute him for his treachery. When he'd discovered his body was still aging more rapidly than normal, he had feared it would spiral out of control and he would wither into a corpse. When he'd first begun to undergo wild, revolutionary treatments and purchase experimental cyborg implants, he'd feared there would be terrible side-effects. But since then, he had seldom felt afraid of anything, so invincible had his mechanical endoskeleton made him.

But suddenly, one glance over his shoulder reminded him of how it felt to be afraid… though he refused to let it show.

The green-armored girl that had just stepped out onto the platform behind him was armed with a strange, arm-mounted starfire canon, its stabilizer fins whirling around the fully-charged capsule of explosive energy hovering at the end of the barrel, lighting up the platform with its green-white glow. She was soon joined by a pair of mercenaries that Three immediately recognized: Nick Wolf and Three's own dear old man, Grimm the *First*, who gave a hearty laugh upon seeing his clone dangling from the edge of the main landing pad, not daring to jump down for fear of being blown to bits.

"Well, well, well," said the Grand High Warlord, "if it ain't good ol' Number Three. Fancy seein' *you* here. I see you've been makin' 'upgrades' to my poor ol' body."

Three bared his teeth, turning his head so that Grimm could see his glowing mechanical eye, and the strip of metal skull beneath it. "Why don't you come over here an' let me show 'em to ya…"

"I wouldn't move, if I were you," said Nick Wolf. "Jade's starfire cannon could blow the legs off a small armored *walker* – there's no tellin' what it could do to *you*."

"Ah, let's find out anyway," Grimm I said, and he raised his hand to give the order.

But then Nick Wolf suddenly grabbed the warlord and threw him to the ground as a flying crossbow bolt whizzed past his head. Spectra's projectile exploded in midair, knocking off Jade's aim just slightly as she released her charged-up blast. Grimm III let go of the wall just in time to keep the projectile from hitting his torso, but not fast enough to avoid it entirely. His internal warning system blared in his ears as his hand was blown off at the wrist and the explosion washed over him.

A second explosive bolt from Spectra's crossbow filled the area with fire-retardant mist, putting out the flames on Grimm III's skin. She then rushed in and pulled the mercenary to his feet, pushing him toward the wall.

"*Now* can we get out of here?!" she shouted.

Three ducked as Nick Wolf's handaxe went spiraling just over his head. "Not bloody *yet*," he growled.

Standing up with determination, he drew out his long blazer combat knife and advanced, signaling for Spectra to distract Jade. Spectra was about to protest, but she just blew out an exasperated sigh and drew her thin blazer sword, advancing on the young mercenary girl, who had now activated her own energy blade, with one of those glowing cannons still mounted to her other arm.

Grimm I was still getting back to his feet, so Nick moved to defend him against Grimm III. Three intercepted the mercenary's axe with the stub of his burnt-off arm, causing it to stick there, and then jabbed his knife at Nick's gut. Nick dodged, baring his teeth and growling as he grabbed Three's wrist with his free hand. The cyborg tried to use his superior strength to toss Nick aside, but, growling like an animal, Nick somehow resisted. For a second, Three was caught off-guard by this feat of inhuman strength.

Then he headbutted Nick in the face. Luckily for the Werewolf, his helmet caught the brunt of the blow, but the cyborg skull dented in his metal-framed visor, which was shaped to resemble the eye-guard of an ancient Viking helmet, causing it to obscure his vision. As Nick struggled to pull the helmet off, Three pushed past him. In one smooth movement, he sheathed his knife, jerked Nick's axe out of the stub of his arm, and hefted the weapon high, its blazer shield glowing… aiming for the prone Grand High Warlord.

"Now," Grimm I said slowly, with a sarcastic smile, "you wouldn't do that to me – to your *'father'* – would ya, boy?"

"Are you my father, or am I your brother?" Grimm III said. "Either way, we're both just scum. The less of us, the better."

The axe descended just as Grimm I brought his arm up to deflect, activating the energy shield mounted on his armored bracer. But he underestimated Grimm III's speed, and the shield did not come on in time… before the blazer axe cleaved directly through his wrist, leaving a burnt stub. Grimm screamed in pain through bared teeth.

"An eye for an eye," Three said, pointing to his cyborg ocular array, "and a hand for a hand. Looks like we're still even."

"Not a chance!" Grimm growled, drawing out a blazer magnum and firing two explosive rounds into Grimm III's chest. "Try all you want, but you'll always be in Third!"

Three recoiled from the impact of the blasts, the second of which blew right through his armor mesh and revealed more of the cyborg metal beneath his skin. Suddenly the thought of his own mortality rushed back to Grimm III as he considered how many times he should have died that night. Just as Nick finally freed himself from his bent helmet, Three rushed back toward Spectra.

"Alright," he said, "*now* let's get out of here."

Spectra, who was being pushed very rapidly backwards by Jade's swordsmanship and rapidly-charging rifle, shouted, "It's about time!"

With that, the two freelancers made a hasty getaway over the wall above as the Grimm's Army mercs behind them once again opened fire.

LOCATION: MORDARK EMBASSY ROOF, MAIN LANDING PLATFORM

Captain Jaleiko let out a sharp cry of pain as Blade-Mantis's star-talon cut into his leg, and then the Enomeg's katana sliced directly across his chest. The Captain of the Mordark Guard had fought well, but he was no match for the master swordsman. Wasting no time to make sure he was dead, Mantis jumped over Jaleiko's curled-up form and ran to help his comrades.

Lord Zegaldorph fared a little better. Dark-Dragon had fought nearly every type of being in the galaxy before, but never a Mahlok Infernal such as Zegaldorph, trained from his earliest years in how to make full use of his fire abilities. Whenever the blade of Dragon's combat knife got too close, a burst of flame would shoot out of the Mahlok's body at that exact spot, pushing Dragon back or at least disrupting his aim. Zegaldorph was an absolute expert with the natural powers of his species, and Dragon had to keep on his feet to avoid the bursts of fire of various shapes and sizes that the Mahlok would occasionally throw at him, not to mention his twirling energy blade.

But when the Lord of Mordark saw his guard, Jaleiko, fall to Blade-Mantis, and when he noticed Idelma'ik attempting to avenge his fallen comrade, Doriad, fire suddenly burst from the Mahlok's legs, sending him soaring into the air. He tried to head for Idel, but Mantis fired his own jetpack and flew up beside him as he passed, slicing at him with his sword. Zegaldorph attempted to use his defensive fire-shield technique, but it was not enough to stop the katana's long, razor edge.

The Mahlok plummeted down beside the Sarran, his hot yellow blood splattering the ground. Ignoring the wound, he rose to his feet and raised his white-hot starfire sword again, carelessly allowing the tip of it to graze him as only a Mahlok could. He was now clothed again... by a shield of pure flame, which circled and whirled around him as he pushed his way past both Raven and Cat, whose energy blades could not even harm him. Then, together, he and the Sarran tried to hold their ground against the Enomegs, who were now closing in on all sides.

It was a pairing the like of which had never before been seen by Human eyes... or perhaps ever before in the history of Nova Refuge: a Mahlok and a Sarran, fighting together as one. And then, as if to complete the strangeness of this alliance, a Human and a Slashrim – Amazon and Lashnar – arrived to complete the defensive circle. Magnum-Coyote had sliced Lashnar's machine gun in half, and she was now wielding only the barrel, with its attached bayonet, like a battleaxe. Amazon had lost her sword and now had only her standard Victorian Bowie-II energy blade. Together, however, the five of them were able to hold off the Enomegs, at least for a while. But the circle was growing ever tighter, ever more desperate...

Meanwhile, Gun-Barracuda, eager for a piece of the action, had secretly exited the Nidhogg dropship and started sneaking around to the other side of the building on the lower platform, limping as he walked. Now one of the Victorian soldiers spotted him and raised his rifle. Barracuda knew he would get in trouble for breaking up the honorable duel that Dragon had set in motion, but at this point he no longer cared. The Enomeg glanced over his enemies – only 15 of Ryan's original 24 troops remained – and decided to act. He hefted his A12-GLS assault rifle – smaller than his usual Buzzsaw LMG, though just barely – and took aim.

Luckily for him, his were not the first shots fired. At that exact moment, everything seemed to happen at once. Not only did Ryan reappear, rushing back from his fight with Scorp and Electric-Eel, but the explosion of Jade's starfire cannon echoed across the rooftop, and Grimm III and Spectra soon appeared as well, followed by gunfire from Grimm and Nick Wolf. The Victorian soldiers glanced to see the cause of this chaos, giving Barracuda the perfect opportunity to begin hosing them with bullets.

Silent-Cobra took the deep stuttering bangs of Barracuda's rifle as a signal for her to open fire as well. She immediately planted a sniper rifle round into the forehead of a Victorian on whose face she had been patiently training her crosshairs since the fight began. The crack of her rifle was soon followed by another shot from far in the distance – Lisa Sharp had finally reached a point high enough on the opposite building to cover the rooftop of the embassy. Suddenly that rooftop found itself being torn apart by gunfire, the fighters still engaged in the melee pausing to consider the situation.

But that was nothing compared to the firepower that came next.

Ryan got the earliest warning when he heard Rick's voice in his ear, shouting, "Get down, Ryan! We're firing! Gunners, target the Nidhogg first!"

Dark-Dragon noticed the rapidly approaching *Silver Scepter* at nearly the same instant and shouted into his commlink, "Abandon the dropship, Enomegs! Get out *now!*"

Saber-Scorpion had just left the body of Seth behind and was headed toward the fray when Cobra made her desperate leap out of the Nidhogg, which was just taking off to escape. Then the *Silver Scepter* arrived, its multiple guns trained on the dropship. The bolts of white-hot energy from Rick's gunship tore through the transport's shields, followed immediately by several ballistic rounds that split the hull apart. Debris rained down over the landing pad as the crippled Nidhogg went sailing into the edge of the roof, shaking the entire structure, knocking them all off their feet. The doomed vessel then continued careening down toward the city streets below.

Scorp had already scrambled back up to his feet before they even heard the echo of its crash. He frantically ran toward the edge of the pad, searching for some sign of Cobra. She had landed on the lower platform along the perimeter, where she still sat crouched, apparently injured. Now the *Silver Scepter* was opening fire on the infantry with its smaller, pinpoint guns, and the entire landing pad was riddled with the spattering of blazer rounds.

Scorp heard the voice of Dark-Dragon in his ears: "Take cover! All Enomegs, take cover!"

But Saber-Scorpion had already lost one comrade; he was not leaving without Cobra. Into the rain of bullets he ran, his shields rapidly losing power as he felt several rounds strike him, almost sending him off balance. He grabbed Cobra under the arm and hefted her to her feet, half-dragging her with him behind a large slab of armor that had fallen off the destroyed Nidhogg.

Scorp looked her over for any sign of injury. "Status, Cobra?"

"I'm fine," she replied, but he quickly saw that it was a lie; her armor was dented, and a few rounds had apparently gotten through to her side, for it was covered in flecks of nanocrystal foam.

Meanwhile, on the main platform above, Lord Zegaldorph was grabbing Ryan and gesturing toward Grimm III and Spectra, who both appeared to be wounded. "Sergeant! Tell your General not to harm the mercenaries! Now!"

The Victorian nodded quickly. "Rick, mark the Grimm-clone and the woman with him as friendlies! Repeat, the Grimm-spawn and his partner are our allies! Do *not* shoot them!"

Rick's predictable response was an incredulous, "*What?*"

"They saved Zegaldorph!" Amazon shouted.

"Fine, fine," Rick relented. "Just sit tight. Extraction is on the way!"

Grand General Radcliff's great Victorian gunship now hovered just beyond the edge of the platform, its lower thrusters blazing as its great, arching wing overshadowed most of the landing pad. Fire sprouted from the side as, manually controlled by gunners on the inside, the starboard turrets fired with extreme precision, striking the Enomegs on their shields as they maneuvered for better cover.

As the Enomegs watched Amazon and Zegaldorph attempt to drag the injured Captain Jaleiko toward the ship, Raven shouted into his commlink, "We can't let them get away! Fire on Zegaldorph! Fire! Fire!"

The Enomegs burst from their cover, shooting with whatever ranged weapons they had. Ryan and Lashnar returned fire, and Idel drew his energy pistol and joined them, backed up by the ship's turrets and the soldiers inside that now defended the open boarding hatch. Grimm III and Spectra also helped as they moved slowly, back to back, in the direction of the *Scepter*. The Enomegs immediately found themselves forced back behind cover. Mantis's shields flickered and dissipated, and he was thrown to the ground as a heavy machine gun round cut into his shoulder. Raven, who was closest, immediately grabbed him and pulled him behind cover again.

The roar of Coyote's Dirge split the air, and a bullet slammed into Zegaldorph's leg, punching through the Lord of Mordark's skin and causing him to stumble and drop Jaleiko. Unfortunately this also caused Dark-Dragon's shot, which was aimed at the Mahlok's head, to miss, thus saving him long enough for Amazon to pull him inside. Grimm III and Spectra soon joined them, followed by Lashnar.

"Get Jaleiko!" Zegaldorph shouted.

"No time!" Ryan replied, hopping aboard, followed by Idelma'ik. "He probably won't make it anyway. Rick, get us out of here!"

Then Gun-Barracuda leapt from his cover. He'd been hiding surprisingly close to the gunship, right next to where he had taken out the last of Ryan's Victorian soldiers, only two of whom had escaped into the *Scepter* with their lives. The massive Enomeg stood tall and lobbed an activated frag grenade right into the closing hatch of the gunship. Then he threw himself back behind cover as blazer fire poured down around him. There was no great explosion, not even a muffled boom, but Barracuda did not wait for one. He was already preparing his shoulder-mounted rocket launcher, which he had retrieved from the Bergelmir during their ride up.

"Doesn't anyone else around here have any damn firepower besides me?" he shouted.

That was when Jade flew up with her jetpack and let fly another charged-up blast from her starfire cannon. The green-white comet of light was followed shortly by Barracuda's rocket, and both projectiles struck the *Scepter* at once, rocking it slightly and blowing a pair of craters in the armored hull. But before they could get off another shot, they heard Harrier's fighter squadron on approach.

"Don't fire on the roof!" Rick commanded his son over the commlink. "Friendlies might still be down there!"

"Don't worry," Harrier replied. "I'm just gonna buzz the tower."

The silver aerospace fighter came soaring right overhead, followed by the Paladins, one by one, so low that the soldiers on the roof thought they could feel the draft from the thrusters. The sound of their engines was blasted into the Enomegs' ears, but that did not stop them from standing and running toward the stairs. They soon realized, however, that the fighters were not attacking, but were merely turning to follow Rick. If they had decided to bomb the roof, the Enomegs would have been dead already.

Over the Victorians' commlinks, Harrier could be heard shouting, "Woohoo! Look at 'em scatter!"

Back on the roof, Dark-Dragon stood up and watched the Victorians turn about, headed the same way they had come. Then the Enomeg turned to regard his men, shouting, "All units, report!"

All of the Enomegs checked in on his HUD, giving their status as OK... except for a few.

"Took a hit to the shoulder," Mantis said, "but I'll live."

"I grabbed a few bullets with my *other* thigh," Barracuda grunted, "and one in the arm, but it'll take more than that to put me down."

Coyote snarled, "My helmet took a hit, and I think the computer's busted. The HUD keeps fizzling out. But otherwise I'm green."

"Cat got scratched a bit," Raven said, "but she and I are fine."

Saber-Scorpion was the last to answer. "This is Scorp. I'm fine. Cobra is injured, but stable. Seth... Electric-Eel is dead."

Somehow, the silence that followed that comment was louder than anything the Victorian fighter engines could have managed.

LOCATION: MORDARK EMBASSY, UPPER FLOORS

After retreating from the edge of the city, Lucas Mars led a group of ground forces, those which had been the least damaged in the battle, toward the center of Shardasha. He arrived at the foot of the Mordark Embassy tower not long after the *Silver Scepter* arrived at the top. Gathering every soldier he could muster, the High Commander ordered his men to clear each floor of the building, while he ascended alone through the center, headed for the roof. As he left another elevator and headed up the last few flights of stairs, however, he suddenly ran into a bit of an obstacle.

"Well, well... Captain Jaleiko," Mars said with a thin-lipped smile.

The Captain of the Mordark Guard stood only three steps above the High Commander, looking down at the taller man over the barrel of his blazer pistol. Jaleiko leaned heavily against the wall, his breathing ragged, with deep, bloody gashes visible across his chest and leg. Yet his gun arm did not waver.

"I've got you at my mercy now, you villain," he said, his expression stern and unforgiving. "Your twisted schemes will die with you. The world will never suffer under your rule. What you have tried to start here will never see completion. Your war will never begin. I'll prevent years, *decades* of bloodshed here and now."

Mars did not stir a muscle. He stood calmly with his hands at his sides, ignoring the barrel of the weapon pointed at his face, looking Jaleiko directly in the eyes. His deep voice echoed in the staircase as he responded, "Actually, Jaleiko, I think it's *you* who are the villain."

"Oh, really? How so?" Jaleiko said with a laugh, lifting his gun a little higher. "I have remained loyal to my Lord, while you dance around the orders of your own Emperor and ignore CONON at your whim! I am going to protect my country and save the entire world from your pointless war! So tell me, Mars... how, precisely, am *I* the villain here?"

Mars's steel-grey eyes narrowed. "Villains talk too much."

In the blink of an eye, his long arm shot out, grabbed the Guard Captain's wrist, and twisted it sideways so that the shots he had been waiting to fire went wide, striking the wall. Mars then jerked him down the stairs and snapped his knee up into Jaleiko's stomach. Wrenching the pistol from Jaleiko's grip, the High Commander twirled it over in his hands and fired three quick shots into the Captain. Giving only a little grunt, Jaleiko slumped over and slid down the stairs, leaving a trail of blood behind. After giving him one more shot for good measure, Mars ejected the gun's magazine and dropped the weapon onto his opponent's lifeless form. He then continued his steady ascension as if nothing had ever happened.

The High Commander burst out onto the roof and immediately started giving orders.

"Grimm," he said, "I want you and your troops to forget this building and leave the city. Rendezvous with Roscoe at the *Bertha*. I'll contact you when you get there."

Grimm nodded. "Hope you don't mind if my men loot the place on the way out."

Mars waved at him dismissively. "Fine, just be quick. We have things to take care of. Raven, I have three more Nidhoggs headed up to the roof right now. Gather the Enomegs and come with me; we'll be heading back to the camp with Grimm."

Raven nodded briskly, but said nothing. Then he looked back at his comrades, most of whom were standing around Seth's lifeless body. The newly rising sun cast the entire scene in a dim red light as Dark-Dragon removed the young man's helmet and closed his blankly-staring blue eyes. Most of the other Enomegs had removed their helmets as well, and stood with them held against their chests, watching Dark-Dragon. Saber-Scorpion, however, stood near the edge of the roof, staring away at the first rays of the morning sunrise reflecting on the windows of the city.

"Dragon," Mars said in a slightly quieter voice, "your work here is done. You may stay, and leave with the dead."

Dragon nodded. "Raven," he said, his voice dry, "take Mantis, Barracuda, and Cat on the first Nidhogg. Scorp, you take the rest on the second. I'll follow on the third once I'm finished here."

"Of course," Raven replied. "You three, come with me."

As Grimm gathered his mercenaries and exited back down into the building, Raven's team gathered with Mars, preparing to board the first transport that was just now rising into view. As the Enomegs climbed into the Nidhogg, several Xarkon medics stepped out, moving to help Cobra, who was the most injured, and see to Seth's body. Dragon spoke with a few of the Enomegs before they left, but Saber-Scorpion could not hear what he said, nor did he particularly care to.

Life is strange, he thought as he looked down at the city of Shardasha, a few of its residents now visible in the windows and on the balconies below, watching the show above. They seemed like ants to him, ants he was sworn to protect, but whose lives seemed small, distant, and hard to understand. He had never lived among them; he sometimes found it hard to even truly think of them as Human.

It seemed like only yesterday that he had been just a student in the brotherhood of Enomeg super-soldiers in training. A hard life, he thought, but one he was used to. What would seem to any of the civilians in this city to be a life in hell had been home to him. Then, suddenly, he'd actually been thrust into the real world for the first time, on his first real, important mission. Or so they'd told him. He had fought, sweated, bled, and died a little on this mission… and for what? Scorp couldn't say. They had failed, and he wasn't even sure that was a bad thing. All of it seemed pointless to him now.

A familiar gruff but surprisingly gentle voice beside him said, "You know who tipped them all off, don't you?"

Scorp shook his head, trying to clear it. "Who? Tipped off who?"

Dark-Dragon nodded toward the smoke that still hung in the air over the battlefield on the edge of the city. "The Yavakarese, the Victorians, all of them. You know who tipped them off."

Scorp shrugged. "One of the mercenaries, I guess. That woman in the black outfit with the Grimm-clone cyborg looked Yavakarese…"

Dragon looked thoughtful. "Maybe. But there's another possibility. A certain Sarran woman who entered this city not long before we arrived. You know her name…"

Saber-Scorpion looked up. "Aeriella?"

Dragon nodded. "Yes, I thought you'd know. She was the Sarran you spared in the Test of Loyalty. A test you failed… and so did I."

All Scorp's emotions gave way to confusion. "What do you mean?"

"I let her go too," he said in a near whisper, staring off into the distance. "This is all my fault, just as much as it is yours. I let weakness stay my hand, just as you did. I let the Sarran woman go. I could not kill her, Saber-Scorpion. I was… I was too weak. And this is my punishment. The Enomegs have failed. I have failed… utterly. There may not even be a Third Phase of Enomegs now…"

Scorp, astonished, turned to look at his trainer… but the older man's battle-scarred face was blank.

"And what about Raven's target?" he asked. "You put her in the Test of Bravery so I would kill her."

Dragon nodded. "Yes, another sign of my weakness. I should have killed her myself. Instead I pushed my problems onto you, trying to make you what I was not. Trying to make you better than me. Stronger. I can only hope it worked."

Scorp shook his head, finally giving way to his emotions. "Mercy isn't a *weakness*, Dragon. It is what makes us *Human*. Years ago, you fought the cyborg soldier project to keep the super-soldiers Humans instead of robots. But when we resist our emotions, live only to carry out orders, then what is left that *separates* us from robots? Xarkon would use us merely as tools, as weapons. Where do you draw the line between loyalty and the *true* honor found in doing what is *right*? Between being loyal to country or merely following blindly and mindlessly? Our emotions are what make us *men*, instead of machines."

Dragon did not respond. He kept his eyes closed... Scorp hoped he was lost in thought.

After a moment, he whispered, "By the Crown... what have I done?"

Scorp did not know what he meant, but he had more to say. "I never became a machine. I never let my training change who I was born to be..."

Dragon suddenly whirled, pointed to Scorp's chest, and shouted, "You were born to be a *soldier!*"

Scorp shook his head. "A *soldier?* A soldier, Dragon? Soldiers fight for a cause, to defend a family. I *have* no family. I fight only because it is what I was born to do; because it is all I know how to do. I am no soldier... I am a warrior."

Dragon did not reply. For a moment, both of them were silent, neither one bothering to look back at the shocked expressions of Cobra and Coyote as they caught fragments of the argument, or at the curious faces of the Xarkon medics. Then Scorp decided to come fully clean.

"I still let her go, Dragon," he said. "Raven's target, Lisa Sharp. I didn't kill her in the Test of Bravery either. I helped her escape *again*."

Little did Scorp know that Lisa Sharp was currently in the nearby skyscraper toward which he was gesturing, headed back to her hoverbike to rejoin the Grim Riders.

Slowly, Dark-Dragon opened his eyes. "Then we are both still weak... and the Enomeg project is even more of a failure than I ever imagined. Emotions are merely the animal side of Human nature..."

Scorp resisted the urge to grab his commander by the shoulders and shake him. "And would you rather be an animal or a *machine*?"

The look of disappointment on Dragon's features was suddenly compounded with disgust. "Justin, stop trying to justify your actions and look around you! What good has come of what we have done? By our failure, we've just helped to bring about the beginning of what could be the greatest and most terrible war ever fought, and we've already lost the first battle! Think about *that*, Saber-Scorpion."

"But we should never even have *been* here!"

"Not now, Scorp. I will hear no more of this. Here comes the other Nidhogg. Get ready to move out."

With that, the commander brushed past him and walked back to join the others. Scorp stared after him, and then turned back to the city.

Location: *Silver Scepter* Troop Compartment

Jenkins got up and brushed himself off. He had been expecting something like Gun-Barracuda's grenade attack and already had a bomb disposal device at the ready. As soon as the grenade landed inside, he threw the bowl-like device atop it, and it clamped instantly to the floor, buckling only slightly as the grenade inside exploded. When he picked it back up, all that remained underneath was a blackened dent in the floor paneling. Ryan breathed a sigh of relief.

"Quick thinking," he said.

"Thanks," Jenkins said. "This sure is a handy device to keep around. Keep one inside everything that has a boarding hatch, I say. Better than using your helmet…"

General Radcliff stepped in then from the cockpit, massaging his temples, as he often did.

"What about that hit we took?" Ryan asked.

"Took out one of the gunners, but otherwise we're okay."

Zegaldorph had been placed on a fold-out medical bed in the troop compartment, and a medic had just finished inspecting him. The Mahlok had a number of wounds… a gunshot on the shoulder, a slash across the back, and a bullet in the leg, among others. Each one was now sealed with what looked like slick black stone, the result of Mahlok blood clotting. Actually, Ryan thought, he looked remarkably well for someone who'd had a pack of super-soldiers trying to kill him all day long. He was certainly a tough one.

"He'll be fine, sir," one of the medics said. Ryan wondered vaguely how much they knew about Mahlok biology, but he did not question their analysis. Zegaldorph was sitting up and looking around; that was good enough for him.

Rick smiled. "Good." Then his smile faded as he turned to Grimm III, Lashnar, and Spectra. "And what about you three?"

Though all eyes were on the three strangers, they remained entirely calm. Three and Lashnar were slouched against the wall, with Spectra crouched behind them. The Grimm-clone cyborg, who looked more cyborg than anything else at the moment, was toying with a cigar they had told him he was not allowed to light while he was in the ship, and Spectra appeared to be adjusting her watch… although there was a high likelihood it was not a watch at all. Lashnar was chugging a disgusting, greenish-brown liquid, much of which ran down her face as she drank.

"We're all fine over here, Chief," Grimm said with a half-metallic grin, waving his stub of a wrist. "A-okay."

Rick frowned. Even the way the clone grinned reminded him so much of his former subordinate officer, Grimm I, that he could not help but sneer. Every time Grimm smiled, no matter what the reason, it always looked to Rick like a half-sarcastic, half-menacing sort of smirk. It was no different with his clone.

Grimm III turned his head and whispered to Spectra, "He hates me."

"It doesn't matter," she said dismissively.

"So you're a cyborg," said Rick Radcliff. "I was under the impression that no fully-functional cyborg endoskeletons actually existed. So how did a clone of my old *lackey* manage to get an operation like that?"

Three blew out a sigh. "Listen, Radcliff – Can I call you Rick? – Rick… I hate Grimm as much as you do. Maybe more. See, he carelessly slopped together that cloning machine with the help of his pet mad scientist, 'Doctor' Flyphe, and then started makin' us Grimm-spawn before he even knew what he was doin'. The machine was supposed to make us age up to a certain point and then stop, only… it didn't always stop. The first clone, Grimm II, came out as a freak and went nuts. Me, I looked okay… but I wasn't. I'm rapidly degenerating. *That's* why I'm a cyborg. *That's* why I have to spend every crown, vic, and guildar I earn on surgeries to replace dyin' organs. And *that's* why I hate Grimm."

Rick looked intrigued, and perhaps ever so slightly more sympathetic, but it was hard to be sure behind his chrome visor. "Where did you get the parts from? The black market?"

Three nodded. "I guess you could call it that. My 'old man,' Grimm, has connections. Tons of connections. When I was slippin' outta his base, I took a lotta things, includin' some information on his contacts, and one of 'em had quite an offer… a cyborg endoskeleton prototype, one of the ones made by Doc Beiderman before he went crazy. Don't know who the seller was, or how he got 'em, but he asked quite a price. When I contacted him, he could tell I was determined, so he set aside one of the prototypes for me. I've been buyin' it, bit by bit, performin' the surgeries at hospitals whose doctors he was able to bribe…"

"I believe he was part of the crime syndicate known as the Black Network," Spectra put in.

Rick shot her a hostile glance. "I'm not on *you* yet."

She nodded. "Very well, General."

"Well, that's about all there is to say anyway," Grimm III concluded. "I've got just about all of the parts in me now, though I still owe quite a bit."

"And you?" Rick asked, turning to the giant red Slashrim.

Lashnar gave a low growl. "I was born into the Helexith army. When I tried to escape, the Mahlok sold me into slavery. When I tried to escape slavery, this mercenary helped me out. End of story."

"Well, I thank you for the explanation," Rick said, nodding, "but you'll have to excuse me for saying that I'd still like to hear at least one good reason to allow you three to remain here on my gunship. I'm hoping your female partner has it."

"*I'm* fem–" Lashnar began to protest, but Spectra cut her off, standing up and raising a hand.

"Here you go," she said, handing Rick a small data card.

The Victorian gave her a quizzical look, then inserted the end of the card directly into a port built into the side of his HUD visor. His mouth fell open almost immediately. After only a few seconds of glancing over the file, he removed the card and handed it back. Then he nodded to Ryan, Amazon, and the other Victorians.

"They are clear to stay aboard the vessel; do not interfere with them. The woman can do as she likes, but still keep an eye on the other two."

Ryan nodded. "Yes, sir."

"Jenkins, Ryan, Amazon, I'd like you to come with me into the cockpit. There are some things we need to discuss in private."

The soldiers nodded and followed their commander through the door. Once they were gone, Grimm III breathed a relieved sigh and crouched down on the floor not far from Zegaldorph to relax.

"Spectra," he said, "you mind tellin' me what kinda card gets us that sorta treatment by the Grand General of Victory?"

"Yes," she replied, "I do mind."

Three shut his mouth. There was no use arguing the point when she took up that tone.

"Thank you again for your help, mercenary," they heard Zegaldorph say in a low voice beside them. "I know you were only doing it for the money, but you went far beyond what most would have done."

"Eric likes to rush headlong into deadly situations," Spectra put in. "A trait of fools... and perhaps the occasional hero."

Three shrugged. "It's what I do. How else is a man supposed to get a reputation? 'Course, bein' more than half machine helps too."

"We lost today," said Zegaldorph, his eyes brightening slightly as he stared up at the ceiling of the ship's troop compartment, "but this was only one battle in the war to come. Tell me, cyborg... do you know what the Mahlok do when they lose a battle? When they discover that they will be unable to take a planet on which they have set their sights?"

"What?"

"*I* do..." Lashnar said, her eyes narrowing.

Zegaldorph's eyes went thin as well, like a pair of fiery fissures in which burned all the heat of a planetary core. "When the Mahlok see that they cannot take a certain world, cannot conquer it, cannot keep it... then they utterly destroy it. Burn the land and boil the sea. Well, here's to tradition."

Spectra stood up and moved closer to the medical table, looking down at the Mahlok. "The explosives," she said. "You mean to detonate the explosives in your tower?"

"Your friend is knowledgeable," Zegaldorph said. "How did you know about my Oghr-Pyron?"

"I have my information."

Grimm grunted. "She's secretive too."

The Mahlok nodded. "And she is also correct. I only hope I have not waited too long to take some of the Xarkonians with it. Mercenary, will you aid me? Can you help me send the detonation signal?"

Spectra tapped the device on her wrist. "I can, if that is your wish. Just tell me how."

"You'll just be provin' 'em right, you know," Grimm III said, "provin' you really are the terrorist they say you are."

"Also won't send a good message about your people," Lashnar put in. "Conquest, hatred, fire and destruction. That's what the Mahlok mind consists of, they say. You won't be doing anything to change that. The Humans–"

"I don't care what the Humans think or what they do. If this results in a war being avoided, so be it. If this results in a war being *ignited*, so be it. Who can know what the results of an action will be? All I know is that I have the power to perhaps kill a few of those 'super-soldiers' who tried to kill me, to give my loyal guard Jaleiko a soldier's funeral, to destroy a portion of Xarkon's precious little city, and what I *want*... is to watch it *burn*."

"It might not be a bad move," Spectra said to Three. "If we could take out even a few of those Enomegs..."

"Thank you," said the Mahlok. "Just send this signal..."

LOCATION: MORDARK EMBASSY ROOF

As he sat there on that war-torn rooftop, watching his comrades and waiting for the second Nidhogg dropship to arrive, it suddenly struck Saber-Scorpion just how tired he now felt. Every muscle in his body ached, as did his mind and spirit. He was physically, mentally, and emotionally exhausted. The long day had finally taken its toll, on both him and the others. Dark-Dragon sat on the far northern corner of the platform now, his head bowed, while the medics behind him finished checking out Cobra and placing Seth's body on a stretcher.

Finally, the transport arrived. Scorp could hear its engines roaring as it ascended toward the southern side of the platform. But then came another roar – much louder – a thunderous, reverberating blast that seemed to shake the entire world. It was followed by the screech of rending metal and the crash of breaking glass, and the entire platform on which the Xarkonians stood began to shift. It leaned sideways, toward the east, giving all upon it an excellent view of the next-door skyscraper as they began tilting toward it...

Scorp was already on his feet by then, running and jumping to avoid the scattered debris and bodies while trying to keep his balance on the rapidly angling rooftop. Ahead of him, he saw Magnum-Coyote sprinting at top speed toward the dropship, whose door was just now rising into view. Behind him, Silent-Cobra struggled to catch up, but her injuries caused her to stumble. She tried to fire her jetpack, but it sputtered and quit, apparently having been damaged by the bullets from Rick's gunship earlier.

Saber-Scorpion, his fatigue entirely forgotten, suddenly came up behind her and grabbed her arm, throwing it over his shoulder. Carrying her beside him, he made a desperate final push toward the dropship door. He could see Coyote inside, screaming at the pilot, trying to tell him which way to fly in order to best line up with the rapidly-falling landing pad. The slant of the crashing tower roof was getting steeper now, and Scorp felt his body sliding sideways...

In a last, desperate attempt, Saber-Scorpion fired his jetpack, while still holding onto Cobra. The blue-white flames licked the surface of the platform behind him as he flew up toward the dropship just above. Cobra reached out, Coyote grabbed her arm with both hands, and then Scorp heard his jetpack sputter, his starlight gas tanks finally run dry. Coyote let out a cry of pain as he suddenly felt the weight of both fully-armored Enomegs at the end of his arms. His nanomesh suit hurried to compensate, enhancing the strength of his muscles, keeping him from dropping them... but it was still not enough to pull them up.

So Scorp let go.

The fall was surprisingly short, before he felt his back strike the landing pad, knocking the air right out of his lungs. Flames erupted past him from the Oghr-Pyron explosives going off below, but luckily the platform itself was still intact. He immediately began to slide, headed toward the edge of the now nearly vertical rooftop, which itself was headed into the side of the nearby building as it fell. As Scorp looked down, he saw it hit, smashing windows and bending metal beams, the sound of it all nearly deafening.

Scorp knew he could not ride the tower roof all the way down, especially as it began to split apart from the stress of the fall and the side of the building it had just struck. So, planting his feet against the floor behind him as well as he could while still sliding, Saber-Scorpion used every ounce of his strength to jump, propelling himself toward the windows of the neighboring building into which the rooftop had just crashed.

He felt hard metal strike his lower abdomen; he had landed right at the bottom of one of the skyscraper windows, his arms and head smashing through what was left of the broken glass. Reaching out quickly, he grabbed the edges of the window and hauled himself inside, standing up just as the dust of the destroyed building behind him wafted through the windows, filling the room with an impenetrable grey-brown haze.

Scorp's helmet tried to compensate, enhancing his vision with light amplification, allowing him to see just enough to make his way toward the exit door. But then he felt the floor begin to move again... This tower was falling too! Too out of breath to even curse his ill luck, Saber-Scorpion made a mad dash toward the far side of the building, breaking through one of the windows there just as the floor began to tilt. He grabbed the edges of the window and pulled himself through, looking around quickly.

The city outside offered no hope of escape; all of the buildings might as well have been miles away. Then his vision turned downward, toward what was separating them from him: it was a river. A deep, dark, wide river – the Rhaen, which flowed down from the Backbone Mountains to feed the Bay of Shards. Without stopping to think about it, Scorp heaved himself through the opening, planted his feet upon the edge, and catapulted out...

For a moment, he seemed to hang suspended in midair, the building behind him crumbling as the level that Zegaldorph's tower had struck fell upon the floors below in a cataclysmic chain reaction, which the Mahlok himself had perfectly engineered for maximum destruction. Stretching himself out, Scorp formed the most perfect diving position he could, hoping it would be enough to cut through the water below rather than be smashed upon it. Looking down, he saw the river rising rapidly up to meet him... just before it was obscured by a cloud of smoke and dust.

Then all went black.

- CHAPTER TWENTY-FIVE -
SOJOURN

Grimm III felt positive that he was in way over his head. After all his years of skirting around Grimm's Army and their bounty hunters by taking low-profile jobs to make a living, he had somehow let himself get talked into a highly political mission regarding a world leader like Zegaldorph… and now, as a result, he was damaged almost beyond recognition, much of his skin gone, completely missing his left hand, and was smack in the middle of what could be the greatest war humanity had ever known… as well as smack in the middle of a top-secret Victorian military installation.

It was the last place in the Refuge that he wanted to be.

"How the hell do I let myself get talked into these things, Lash?"

Beside him, Lashnar replied, "Because you're getting stupider. Must be something in the cigars."

"I think I need a new hobby, 'sides killin' folks. What else do I like? Hmm… food, I guess. You know anything about cookin', Lash?"

"A male Slashrim looking for a mate once asked me that," she replied flatly. "I roasted him alive."

"Nevermind. Guess I'll just stick to dice poker."

"By the way, you still owe me eighty vics from our last game."

"Shut up, Lash. I'm tryin' to listen to Rick."

After leaving Shardasha, the Victorians and their allies had headed straight for their home country, making record time across the Infinite Ocean before finally landing in… some kind of military base. Only the Victorian leaders knew where. They insisted that their "guests" leave in a Victorian dropship to ensure that they remained clueless as to their true location. Currently, Grimm III and Lashnar were cooling their heels in that very dropship, waiting for Spectra and Zegaldorph to finish arguing with Rick Radcliff on the other side of the hangar. With his cybernetically-enhanced auditory sensors, Three could easily hear what they were saying.

"It was a bad move," said the Grand General to the Lord of Mordark.

"It was *my* move," answered the Mahlok. "I will take full responsibility for it."

"Good," Rick replied, jabbing a gloved finger at the still-naked Mahlok's chest. "You will have ample chance to do that. Because of your foolish action and your involvement of mercenaries and Sarran terrorists, CONON has called for *another* pointless meeting to debate what happened in Shardasha. The Ordinator *knows* that Xarkon was behind the entire incident, yet he wants to be able to publicly denounce *your* actions and give the Emperor a chance to defend himself. It's ludicrous! He'll delay the war for weeks and invite the enemy to our very doorstep... and after last night, who knows what Orrick – or Mars – will be planning this time."

Spectra, still hooded and masked, commented, "So turn the wheels of representative government, General. Would you throw the proverbial monkey wrench into the very system your people support?"

Rick set his jaw, then blew out a long sigh. "Nevermind. We can debate this later. I must ask that the two of you leave with your mercenary friends in the Hospitaller transport we've provided. God speed to you all."

The two immediately took their leave and went to join Grimm III and Lashnar on the other side of the hangar floor. Once they were inside, the great Victorian vessel, which was dwarfed by the massive *Silver Scepter* sitting beside it, lifted off and flew directly toward the far wall. What seemed to be a wall of sheer metal there flickered and buzzed, turning slightly off-focus as the dropship passed directly through it like water. Then the hologram closed in again behind them, restoring the appearance of metal on the inside and a rocky cliff face on the outside.

Cliffside Base was Victory's most top-secret military installation. Built into a cutaway carved directly into a seaside cliff face, its positioning blocked it from satellite view, while a holographic projection protected its hangar opening from visual detection. The base had been constructed after the research station around which the entire country was founded – which also served as its capitol building – was destroyed during the Xenocide War by orbital bombardment courtesy of Harmony. Many anti-starship rocket silos were built deep underground around Cliffside, and the entire area could be protected by a massive shield if necessary. All of this was constructed in case another galactic war started... just like what was happening right now.

Rick blew out yet another sigh as he stalked off toward an exit door from the hangar. "This is going to get much worse before it gets better..."

Beside him, Ryan Arkanian, who had been listening to the whole conversation silently, licked his lips as he followed. "General... may I ask who that masked woman was? What exactly was on that card that she showed you in the *Scepter*?"

The Grand General stopped and turned to face him. "It was a pass from the Six themselves – Yavakaro's ruling council. Each member of the council has two Hands, elite personal bodyguards and agents who do their every bidding. She could have been one of those. On the other hand, she could have merely been hired by the Six. Or maybe… she could be one of the council members herself."

"It's possible… but why would one of them be out there sneaking around Shardasha with mercenaries like that Grimm-clone and his pet Slashrim? It's pretty hard to believe…"

"A tip, Ryan: never find anything hard to believe when deep down you *know* it to be true. That is what keeps my faith strong. In light of this recent information, there is no doubt that all humanity is in this now. And I know this to be true, as much as John Exsyl doesn't want to believe it: the Ultimate War is about to begin."

LOCATION: SHARDASHA, XARKON
RUINS OF THE MORDARK EMBASSY

Shadow-Cat lifted the slab, held it for a moment, and then faltered. She slipped and fell… into Raven's waiting arms. Cat immediately wriggled free and brushed herself off, looking back up at the spot where she'd been standing. But she could not even tell where that was; the heap of wreckage and debris was too huge, far too huge…

"Cat," Raven said, "you're not doing anyone any good out here. None of us are. We're just too tired. Leave the job to Hans; he's one of us, a former Enomeg, remember?"

Cat looked around. The entire world was grey… the street was grey, the wreckage was grey, the sky was grey, and all of the Enomegs had their armor set to grey camo mode. Grey smoke still lingered in the air, coating everything in a thin layer of ashen dust. A few fires still burned here and there where the residue from the Oghr-Pyron remained stuck, and no amount of fire retardant sprayed by the Xarkonian rescue teams could seem to put it out. The soldiers still searching for their comrades' bodies were led by Hans Thunder-Hawk, the former Enomeg trainee turned Army Spec-Ops officer. The full Enomegs were also there, but most were too tired to help.

"Coyote…" Cat said, "tell me what…"

"I saw again?" Magnum-Coyote finished for her, blowing out a sigh. "I told you, Cat… I saw Dragon slip and fall, and then Scorp jetted up holding Cobra. I pulled her in, and Scorp fell back onto the platform. He ran toward the next-door building when the landing pad smashed into it, and he jumped into one of the windows, right before the whole building…"

"Fell," Silent-Cobra concluded, sitting on the edge of the deactivated Bergelmir nearby, her face even more like stone than usual.

"You never saw him come out," Cat said, more as a statement than a question.

Coyote shook his head. "Sorry, Cat. I had the pilot swing around and look, but he was nowhere to be seen."

Raven half-dragged Cat back toward the door of the Berg and laid her down inside. She tried to get up, but found that she could barely lift her exoskeleton-clad body back up to a sitting position. Leaning heavily against the wall, she looked up at Raven and nodded.

"Okay… I'll take a quick rest, but then…"

Raven immediately took a seat beside her, and once the other Enomegs had joined them inside, he knocked on the door to the cockpit twice. The pilot took off, the vehicle lifted into the air, and it disappeared into the dust. Cat took one look back, but the grey cloud had closed in behind them. There was nothing left but ashes and dust.

LOCATION: UNKNOWN

Saber-Scorpion awoke as if from a nightmare… and into a dream. He could barely recall last night's events; they were blurry even as they came rushing back to him. The chase, the battle on the roof, the death of Electric-Eel, the explosion, and the fall… into water. That seemed to be the last thing he could recall… the feeling of the river swallowing him in one sudden burst.

So how had he gotten here?

He was lying in a soft bed, his armor gone, his wounds clean and neatly bandaged, his body aching but undeniably comfortable. All around him hung curtains looking like white mist hanging from golden bedposts, which were styled as if they had come from a time before this world. Despite this dreamlike environment, Scorp's first reaction was to seek escape, and his warrior instincts were further heightened by the detection of a shadow moving beyond the veil. It was a great shape, much taller than a man… rounded, as if it were a pair of wings…

Scorp pushed the curtain back and saw exactly what he expected: the Sarran Aeriella, standing there holding a tray of food and drinks. She was utterly beautiful, with her soft auburn hair and wings contrasting with the pristine white gown she wore, which matched the rest of the room… if it could even be called a room. It was actually more of a garden, surrounded by a low wall and Greek style pillars that held up nothing but a ring of stone opening up to the sky above, in which rays of sunlight pierced through the cloud cover like heavenly spears.

"I don't…." Scorp coughed, trying to speak. "I don't know who gathers the souls of the dead, but someone had better call him… I think he sent me to the wrong place. Shouldn't there be… fire and brimstone?"

Unlike many Sarran, Aeriella had apparently been around Humans long enough to smile at this comment. "Well, I suppose that depends on the Earth religion to which you adhere. I know not how an angel of your monotheistic religions may have acted, but according to the early Nordic myths that Xarkon so admires, I'm sure the valkyrie who brought you here knew exactly what she was doing."

Scorp lay back down in the bed and looked up at the gently swaying leaves of the exotic plants that arced overhead. "So which one are you? The angel or the valkyrie?"

"I know not," Aeriella replied as she set her tray on a table nearby. "According to the beliefs of my people, I am but a humble soul in the service of Afaelya, the Great Spirit through which all beings are connected."

"Good enough for me."

She smiled again as she sat down on the bed beside him and inspected his bandages. "So do you not believe in anything then?"

He shrugged. "I've never really thought of religion as anything more than a subject to learn in class. Most people just follow the religion of their parents. My only parent was Xarkon, and she isn't exactly religious... unless you count worship of the Crown."

She reached down and placed her hand upon his. "I did not ask whether you believed in a religion. I was asking if you believed in *anything*."

Scorp's expression clearly indicated that he wished to speak of more serious matters, though Aeriella would have insisted there was nothing in the universe more serious than belief in the powers that created and govern it.

"Aeriella," he said, "what happened? How did I get here? Where are the other Enomegs? Where's Dark-Dragon?"

The Sarran did not look away, but a shadow seemed to fall over her face as she answered, "He fell, Saber-Scorpion. I saw him. The man you knew as Dark-Dragon... is no more. I am sorry."

Scorp closed his eyes and said nothing. Somehow, he had already known it to be true, so the confirmation that he was correct did not shock or surprise him. It only deepened the hollow feeling inside.

"As for your other questions," Aeriella went on, "I found you unconscious on the bank of the river in the city below us, and I brought you here. As far as I know, all of your other companions are alive and well in the Xarkon camp outside this city."

This time, Scorp did look surprised. "We're still in Shardasha?"

"What is left of it," Aeriella replied solemnly. "But be still, my heroic warrior... We are in the uppermost part of one of the towers of the Arcing Gardens, and all of your countrymen are far below, scouring the rubble of the Mordark Embassy. We are safe for the moment."

She leaned in and kissed him again, this time on the cheek, but he reluctantly pushed her away.

"Aeriella..." he said.

She put a finger over his lips. "Shh... we can speak of such matters later. For now, we are safe. Be still a while and relax... you deserve it."

"You want me to *relax*?"

She smiled, and he felt her strange, golden eyes piercing into him. Leaning forward, she kissed him again, this time on the lips. He sat up and moved to put an arm around her back, but there he felt her wings. She laughed lightly when she felt his fingers touch them, and the wings unfurled, enveloping both man and Sarran in their embrace, casting them in shadow. Scorp felt her soft feathers rub against his back.

"Relax," she said, her voice seeming to come from all around him. "Open your mind…"

His own voice sounded harsh and terrible when it replied, "Are you trying to learn my secrets?"

He felt her lips against his, even as her voice replied inside of his consciousness, "I am giving you the opportunity to experience the harmony of thoughts and emotions that only a Sarran mind-link can bring. It is a like a concert of sensations at once mental, emotional, and spiritual. Let down your defenses, Saber-Scorpion. Let someone love you…"

"Why would someone like you," Scorp thought, knowing she would hear the words as if he were speaking them, "want to love a rough, violent, born killer… a trained weapon… like me?"

"You think Humans have nothing to offer the Sarran? You think our heavenly allure does not have its balancing opposite? You are rough, yes, and as you might put it, as earthly as we are heavenly… but you are full of passion and emotions that you feel with an amazing strength that can hardly be found among my people. Your emotions are a symphony, Saber-Scorpion. A chaotic symphony, yes, but a dramatic one. All you need do is open your mind to let your symphony be in harmony with mine. Release your emotions…"

He felt her kiss him again, and now he felt her presence in his mind as well. Scorp resisted, as if by reflex, for only a moment… but he was too weak, her voice too alluring. He felt the mental fortress he had erected long ago crumble beneath her gentle onslaught, and give way to the bright, soft light of the peace that she offered. He felt himself being carried away to other worlds. He saw into her mind… catching glimpses of her captivity in a cold grey cell in Xarkon, mingled with beautiful vistas of Sarran cities, golden towers protruding from mountains of snow and ice. He left Earth and his own troubles far behind, and it seemed he would never wish to come back.

LOCATION: XARKON UNDERGROUND HEADQUARTERS

"Where… where am I?"

Blade-Mantis's thin eyes grew thinner as he gave Shadow-Cat a caring smile and placed a hand on her shoulder. "You are in the legendary Xarkon naval base known as the Seadragon's Maw, remember? I guess you were more tired than you thought…"

Cat sat up and looked around. A cave ceiling lined with metal support struts arced overhead, glistening in the rippling light that was reflected off the water below, where sat a single Xarkon warship in the immense docking bay. The Nidhogg that had brought them there sat on a narrow platform nearby, along with most of its former occupants.

"Has there been any news?" Cat asked at length.

Mantis sighed. "I'm afraid not. No sign of Dragon or Scorp has been found. No body, not one piece of armor… nothing."

Cat narrowed her eyes as she stared out at the sunlit sea. "Then there's still hope…"

"There is always hope, yes. But you should be ready for any possibility, Cat."

She turned to him and gave a reluctant smile. "I know. I'm sorry, Lee. I guess I just have a hard time accepting that three Enomegs are just… *gone*… A harder time than some of the others, anyway."

They looked toward the dropship again. Silent-Cobra sat alone and silent as ever on the farthest edge of the pier, with her legs crossed in a meditative position and her back turned to the sea. Magnum-Coyote and Gun-Barracuda were together for once, standing on the edge of the platform and staring down at the waves below. Occasionally they would fire a random shot into the water, causing the report of their weapon to echo through the entire complex. They ignored the annoyed glances that the other soldiers would shoot their way; none of the navy men dared ask the Enomegs to stop.

"I wouldn't say they have an easy time dealing with it," Mantis replied, "just that they have *ways* of dealing with it. We all have our own ways. What's yours?"

Cat gave him an almost hostile glare. "You first, Mantis. What's your 'way'? You just remember that this is *war*, that they were *soldiers*, and that makes everything okay?"

He blew out a sigh. "Yes, I suppose that *is* what I do, Cat. The three men we lost from our team gave their lives for the mission and its cause, and I plan to honor their memories by continuing to fight for it, even if it means I share their fates… an end I would accept willingly, even gladly, as they might have done. That is all I can do, and all that I would ask anyone to do for me. It's what they would have wanted."

Cat looked away. Mantis tried to think of something else to say to comfort her, but decided she just needed some time. He slipped away quietly and headed off to join Cobra in meditation. Once he was gone, Cat looked at the sparkling waves beyond the mouth of the cave and shook her head.

"Perhaps it's what two of them would have wanted… but I'm not so sure about the third."

She tried not to think of the time she had spent with Scorp… with Justin. Her days as a trainee in the ETAB already seemed like a lifetime ago, in light of recent events. They were supposed to be Enomeg soldiers, trained to deal out death and also to deal *with* it, as they had done since childhood. Many of the students had died during training, pushed too hard by the harsh regimens that the instructors inflicted upon them. But as a result, those who made it through seemed all the more invincible, too tough to ever die.

So now, it was pretty hard to accept the fact that three of them had died on their very first mission.

She was startled from these thoughts when she noticed another of the Enomegs had seated himself beside her. She turned angrily, expecting to see Mantis interrupting her thoughts again with his too-perfect attitude, but instead her eyes fell upon Raven. He was wearing only a pair of shorts, with a bandage wrapped around his leg and a few more in other places that had sustained wounds. The dim, flickering half-light of the watery cave accentuated his perfect physique with dark shadows.

"What do you want?" she asked, though less harshly than she had first intended.

He seemed to want to avoid looking her directly in the eyes as he answered, "I just didn't want to be alone right now. Most everyone else seems to be avoiding me."

"Well, I *do* want to be alone, if you don't mind."

"Come on, Cat! How do you think I feel? You seemed to know it even better than I did back at the camp that night."

"I don't know how you feel. I can't think about it right now. All I know is, with Scorp and Dragon… gone…" She found she could make it no farther than that.

"I'm the leader of the Enomegs," Raven finished for her.

Cat muttered, "It *is* what you've always wanted…"

"Not you too!" Raven exclaimed angrily. "Why does everyone think I should be happy about this? Dragon was my mentor, Cat, more like a father to me than… than *Mars* will ever be! And without Scorp, now everything falls on me. Everyone looks to me to be solid as a rock, unbending, without any feelings of my own. They're acting like *I'm* Dark-Dragon now!"

Still she did not turn to look at him.

"Come on," he went on, much more softly. "Why don't you come for a walk with me? We can talk."

"Give me a break, Luke."

He seemed about to respond, but stopped himself and just went on staring into the water. There were a few moments of tense silence, broken only by the distant clanging of a repairman working on a ship component elsewhere in the cave. Finally Raven stood up to leave.

Cat immediately blew out a loud sigh. "Fine… okay."

Raven helped her up, and then he put his arm around her. It didn't make her feel as bad as she thought it would.

"I'm sorry for what I said, Luke. About you and Scorp and Dragon."

"Don't worry about it," he said. "I've forgotten about it already."

LOCATION: ARCING GARDENS RESORT, SHARDASHA

The wind blew with a cool, moist breeze that both awakened Saber-Scorpion and made him feel naked. Then he realized that he *was* almost naked, so he moved to put on some clothes. Aeriella had left Scorp's Enomeg exoskeleton piled beside his bed. He immediately slid into the pants of the nanomesh under-armor, which tightened to adjust to his body as he put it on. It was amazing how natural this uncomfortable suit felt to him now… like a second skin. As he looked at the helmet in his hands, he thought: this is the face of Saber-Scorpion. He had never thought of the suit as a disguise, but somehow, as he put it back on, it felt like he was assuming another identity, becoming someone else again. It was someone he knew far better than he knew the identity he was leaving behind… whoever that was.

Then he heard Aeriella approaching behind him.

"Leaving so soon?" she asked.

"I'd hardly call this soon," Scorp replied, turning to regard her. "I've spent too much time here already. I have to go, for your sake even more than mine. The longer I remain, the more danger you're in. Xarkon will come searching for both of us. I can't risk that, and besides… Xarkon is my home."

It somehow felt strange for him to say that. Though logically it was quite true, the words felt wrong on his tongue, and only then did he realize he had probably never spoken them before. He had no home… not really. Xarkon was always moving him from place to place, sometimes to secret installments in other countries or on other planets…

"You are arguing with yourself, Saber-Scorpion," Aeriella put in. "I can hear it as easily as if you were screaming to yourself in the mirror."

Scorp gave a short laugh. "Call me Justin."

She returned his smile. "Justin… I think you're discounting one possibility. You don't have to run from Xarkon. You don't have to give them your back. They stole you from your family, trained you to be their weapon… now, you could turn that *against* them. Turn and *fight* them."

Scorp's face went blank. Never before in his most rebellious or insubordinate moments had he actually gone so far as to consider *fighting* Xarkon. It was all he had ever known, all he had ever been taught to care about, to love… and to turn and try to *destroy* it…

"No," Scorp replied adamantly. "No, that's not possible."

Aeriella took a step toward him and gave him a pleading look. "But… I'm not asking you to go to *war* with Xarkon, Justin, just… help us take the little steps that we can to free our people from Xarkonian control."

Scorp shot her a suspicious glance. Was she trying now to use him as *her* weapon instead, to turn one of Xarkon's tools against it?

"Xarkon," Scorp replied, "has done no more to your people than any other Human country. Yavakaro fought your kind more than Xarkon did during the Xenocide War. Do you want me to go to war with them too – with all Humanity? My entire species?"

"Of course not! I could not ask you to fight against your own kind any more than I could be convinced to fight the entire High Council of Harmony. But you *know* what Xarkon has done. You saw it with your own eyes! Remember the picture on the wall?"

Scorp's eyes narrowed. "The Sarran anatomical drawing I found? How do you know about that? How…" He sat down on the bed and put a hand over his eyes, massaging his forehead. "How could you…"

She moved to sit down next to him, placing a hand on his back. "I… I could not help but see, Justin. When two minds join…"

The Enomeg looked up at the vine-entangled pillars all around them and the sky shining through above… then suddenly got up and began putting on the rest of his armor. "You should go, Aeriella. You don't have much time left to escape anyway. You may take whatever information you gleaned back to your leaders, Idelma'ik and Folirayoth, the Blackwings. Take it and go."

"I… I thought you had entered into the mind-link willingly. I would never have tried to *force* my way into your thoughts, I swear it…"

Aeriella looked up at him with her long, thin Sarran eyes slightly wider than normal. Scorp got the feeling that if Sarran were not taught from birth to control their emotions, Aeriella might have been in tears. He felt the urge to put his arm around her. Instead, he picked up one of his star-talon gauntlets and tossed it to her. She caught it reflexively.

"Hopefully," he said, in a low voice, "for your sake, we'll never see each other again… so take this. It's all I really have to give… Besides, you might find it useful. Take it to remember me."

She took a deep breath and nodded. Standing slowly, she removed a long golden necklace from a hidden pocket in her robe and handed it to him, placing it in his palm and closing his fingers around it. He did not get a good look at it, but it appeared to be shaped like a four-pointed star, the symbol of Harmony. Aeriella then kissed him on the forehead and took a step back.

"And you take this," she said, "to remember *us*. Do what you must, Justin Saber-Scorpion, to live with your curse… the curse of having been a soldier born and bred."

Scorp carefully slid the heirloom she had given him into a pouch on his belt. "No. A soldier bred, perhaps… but a warrior born."

"A warrior is merely a soldier without a cause," she replied.

"A warrior is one who follows his own cause. A soldier can only follow his orders, while a warrior follows his heart. I have always followed my heart. Call it weakness… But I believe there is still good in Xarkon, Aeriella. There are good people here. If I can do anything to change it for the better, I promise…"

Suddenly the Enomeg started, his head turning toward the pillars at their right, between which lay a staircase leading down. Scorp could practically hear Aeriella asking him what he saw or heard, but he indicated to her to remain silent and find a place to hide. He did not need to speak for her to comprehend his meaning, and she did not need to nod to indicate she understood. It was almost as if they were now linked… sharing thoughts…

Before Scorp could think more on the subject, however, he saw someone approaching up the stairs. It was a woman in a red Xarkon pilot uniform, but wearing the specialized helmet of an infantry scout. She was looking directly at him, walking calmly forward. With a casual twist of her head and body, a long braid of golden blond hair appeared over her shoulder. She then removed her helmet…

"Amy?" Scorp said in surprise.

She nodded to him, but said nothing. He noticed her keen blue eyes were glancing around the room, as if she knew someone else was there, although Aeriella had hidden herself quite well behind one of the pillars. Suddenly Amy lifted the blazer pistol she was carrying and sighted down the barrel directly toward the Sarran's hiding place.

"Hold fire!" Scorp shouted, shoving her weapon upward.

He was too late to stop her from pulling the trigger, but luckily he caused her shot to go wide, and apparently Aeriella had already sensed the danger and ducked. The Sarran came slowly out from the shadows, extending her wings and arms upward in a show of peace. Amy shot Scorp a suspicious glance, and he felt those crystalline orbs bore into him almost as deeply as did the Sarran's.

"What's going on here?" she asked, in a calmer tone than Scorp would have expected.

Somehow Scorp felt the truth would serve him best, so he replied, "She saved my life."

"Why?"

Aeriella answered, "Because he saved mine… a long time ago."

Amy holstered her pistol and nodded. "In that case, I'm glad you repay your debts. I'm Senior-Omega Archer of the Xarkon Walker Division. I've been looking for Saber-Scorpion all day. It's good to find more than just a dead body waiting for me. The others will appreciate the good news too."

"How'd you know to look here?" Scorp asked.

Amy removed a small handheld communicator from her belt and waved it in front of Scorp's face. "I was able to track the signal of the communicator I gave you. Apparently you left it on, although you haven't seen fit to *answer* it…"

"I didn't know it acted as a *tracking* device…"

"It doesn't normally," the scout replied, "but Viper taught me how to trace it. So do you want me to report your whereabouts to base camp, or…" She glanced between him and the Sarran pointedly.

Scorp let out a sigh of relief and shook his head. "No, thank you, Senior-Omega. I'll just come with you. Aeriella…"

"I take my leave," said the Sarran, and giving a bow, she headed toward the edge of the room.

In a few great sweeps of her reddish brown wings, Aeriella ascended toward the clouds above, then swooped down like a hawk to sail through the streets below, following the path the other Blackwings had taken. Scorp watched her go, his eyes following her until he remembered he was not alone. Then, picking up his helmet, he turned to follow Amy back out of the building. As they headed down the dark staircase into the resort tower's interior, the walker pilot inspected Scorp's pensive expression.

The Enomeg looked back at her. "Why did you let her go?"

"Why did you?"

He found he had no answer for this; none that he could say, at any rate. If Amy had just tried to dodge the question, it worked.

"You look a bit rough," Amy said.

Scorp rubbed his chin. "Yeah, let me guess: I need a shave. I look more like a bum than an Enomeg soldier, right?"

She laughed. "What? I didn't say that. Actually, it looks fine. Makes you look less like every other Xarkon soldier I see."

Scorp just stared.

She looked confused and laughed again. "What? What did I say?"

He blinked and shook his head. "Oh, nothing… So who else is looking for me? The other Enomegs?"

"No," she replied, "they all left with Mars. So did Viper and the Snake Legs. All that's left are some soldiers sorting through the debris of Zegaldorph's tower, under the command of someone they call Thunder-Hawk. And me, of course. I told Viper I was staying, since I thought I might know how to find you."

Amy's voice was casual as she said this, but Scorp realized what it meant. She had left her group and disobeyed her commander, fought against how tired she had to feel after the Battle of Shardasha, and spent perhaps all day scouting the city for him, trying to lock onto the signal of the commlink she had given him. It was more than any of the Enomegs had done. She had looked very hard to find him…

"There are good people left in Xarkon…" he muttered, echoing his earlier words to Aeriella.

"Yes," Amy said with a smile, "there are. If you're willing to look hard to find them."

- CHAPTER TWENTY-SIX -
THE WILL TO POWER

The light poured into the vast hangar like water bursting through opening floodgates as the overhead hangar doors slowly slid back to reveal the sky above. The main hangar of the Xarkon Underground Headquarters was an enormous pit covered by duranium doors that were made to look like part of the natural terrain overhead, which was dry and flat, covered in rough grass and scrub. The Enomegs gathered in the hangar could see the artificial shrubbery atop the doors as they slid into their dark alcoves.

Meanwhile, in the harsh blue-white sky above, the Xarkon Fafnir aerospace gunship descended like the mythical dragon after which it was named, spreading the shadow of its wingspan over the soldiers congregated below. Among these soldiers was Shadow-Cat, who had come as soon as she heard that part of the search party was returning from Shardasha. Raven had followed her there and put one arm around her shoulders. She had not protested, so thus they stood when the boarding hatch of the Fafnir lowered, and the occupants began to file out.

Cat could hardly believe her eyes. They had not received word that any survivors had been found, or at least if they had, no one had informed the Enomegs… yet there he stood, as if nothing had ever happened. Saber-Scorpion had his helmet under one arm, and besides the care-worn expression he now wore, he looked the same as ever. Beside him strode the scout walker pilot, Amy Archer, the two of them walking in step, looking down at their feet and speaking to each other as they descended the ramp.

Only when he reached the bottom did Scorp seem to notice Cat standing there, and only then did Cat seem to remember that Raven had his arm over her

357

shoulder. Yet Scorp merely looked at her and waved, as if he did not notice either. Then, before either of them could speak, a chorus of shouts echoed through the room, and Mantis and Coyote came rushing forward to greet him, looking him over for any sign of injury before punching him on the arm and slapping him on the back.

Across the room, Barracuda was staring with mouth agape. Then he seemed to catch himself and merely waved a hand dismissively. "Ah, I knew he'd make it."

"Saber-Scorpion!" Mantis shouted with a laugh. "My friend, I thought to never see you again! It's hard to believe you are truly walking back from death like this, and looking as good as ever, I see."

"Apparently," Coyote said, still grinning, "it takes more than bullets, blades, falls, explosions, and a couple of burning, crumbling skyscrapers to keep Saber-Scorpion down."

Scorp met their enthusiastic greetings with a smile as he replied, "It would seem so. I think Dark-Dragon might not have been so lucky though."

Coyote nodded solemnly, and Mantis gave the Heartbeat salute in honor of their fallen commander.

Raven approached at this point and said, in a perfectly even tone, "Welcome back, comrade. So how did you manage to make it out of there?"

Scorp looked back at Amy, who was still standing by the foot of the Fafnir's boarding ramp. The walker pilot gave him a knowing look, but it disappeared quickly.

"I found him," she said, "on the bank of the Rhaen River that runs through the city. Apparently he dove into it and lost consciousness, and had been floating downstream ever since."

"Good thing you were wearing an Enomeg nanoduranium exoskeleton then," said Shadow-Cat, somewhat sheepishly, as if she could think of nothing else to say. "I doubt many other suits of armor would have let you float like that."

Scorp shrugged. "Or maybe I just swam to the bank before I tired myself out. I almost can't believe I made it either."

"I can," said Silent-Cobra, whom no one seemed to have noticed approaching. She nodded to Scorp and said, "Scorp. I knew you'd be back."

Scorp returned her nod, though he somehow detected that behind her stoic demeanor, she was happier to see him than she let on. He doubted she liked the idea of him having sacrificed himself to save her.

"I think it's time to celebrate," Coyote said, "and drink to fallen comrades. I smuggled a few cans of old Steinburg into the base, and…"

"Maybe we should save them for later," Scorp replied. "S.O. Archer said she would show me around the base a bit first, and I think I might have some injuries that could use a look."

Shadow-Cat looked like she was about to speak, but Raven interrupted her, saying, "You're right; you'll need to be in top shape. You got back just in time for an important mission Mars has lined up. We're supposed to ship out in less than two days, so be ready."

Scorp blew out a sigh. "No rest for the wicked…"

Raven watched as Scorp walked off with Amy, headed for the far end of the hangar. He then turned to address Shadow-Cat, but she was nowhere to be seen. So he too walked off. Mantis watched as each of them departed alone, and then shook his head sadly. Clearly, the Enomegs were already growing farther and farther apart.

LOCATION: NUTOPIA, VICTORY
TWO DAYS LATER
YEAR: 333 PA

High Commander Lucas Mars looked over his men as they sat before him in the dark, cramped Nidhogg troop compartment. All of the remaining Enomegs were there – Scorp, Raven, Cat, Mantis, Coyote, Barracuda, and Cobra – but they were no longer clad in their usual exoskeletons. Instead, each wore the highly decorative crimson and gold uniform of a Xarkon Royal "Bloodguard," complete with cloth tabards and modern stylized versions of what looked like ancient Greek or Roman open-faced helmets. Fittingly, they were armed with nothing but swords and ceremonial pikes – the only weapons allowed inside of the CONON space station besides those carried by the CONON guards. Outside the dropship, they could see the surface of Terra Nova far below, a sea of stars overhead, and the great, saucer-shaped space station floating off in the distance, its hull gleaming in the light of New Sol.

"War," said Lucas Mars, his bass voice seeming to vibrate the very hull of the dropship. "War is eternal, ingrained in Human nature. So long as men are free, there will always be war. This is not something to be feared or hated. It is as natural to us as breathing, eating, dying. It is part of what makes us men. War is constant, hardly ever changing, and always changing back when it does. The weapons vary, but the goals remain the same, and so does the essential method of achieving one's goals: to *kill* one's enemy.

"War is unavoidable. The only way to make it seem otherwise is to hide it, to kill behind the scenes and in the shadows, without honor or valor. For years now, this has been the state of war here in Human Space, in this galaxy we call Nova Refuge, thanks to scheming politicians like Chancellor O'Donnell, the Council of Six, Victory's ever-changing impotent political figurehead, and yes… even our own Emperor, Marius Orrick. They fear another war between men here in this modern age, here in this new world, and so they continue to plot, steal, and murder instead.

"For decades I have lived with this, even helped it along, following the orders of my Emperor and hoping that what I was doing was right. My life, my calling, is to serve. But was it truly Xarkon I was serving? Was it truly the nation of honor, bravery, loyalty, and supremacy that I so loved? No. The answer is no. It was, it *is*, merely a leech, eating up more and more of the galaxy without any true power over its own hunger, hoping merely to remain unnoticed, so that it may grow *fatter* instead of stronger.

"I first realized this when I met your commander and mentor, Dark-Dragon. He was the physical embodiment of all Xarkon strives for: a true man of honor, bravery, supremacy, and loyalty to the very end. He and I saw eye to eye on many things, but there was one step he was unwilling to take – one line he was unwilling to cross – and that was to disobey the man to whom he had sworn loyalty: the Emperor of Xarkon. Dark-Dragon was loyal to the very end, until his death in Shardasha, still following the commands of his Lord.

"And now that very Lord heads toward CONON to tell the rest of the world that we had nothing to do with this incident. He will tell them that we were not even there. He would deny Dark-Dragon's very existence, along with the existence of the other young Enomeg who died in the city that fateful day: Seth Electric-Eel. The Emperor wishes to lie, to keep up the veil of shadows and secrecy that he has sustained for so long. Well *I* say: no longer."

Mars continued looking at each of them in turn as he towered above them, his steel grey eyes gleaming like a drawn blade. "What I ask of you today is to take the step that Dark-Dragon would not dare to take, to cross that fateful line. I ask you to fight for the glory of the Crown and the ideals it represents… by turning against the man who undeservingly wears it. I ask you to turn against our Lord, the Emperor of Xarkon.

"I have spoken of this plan with the rest of High Command – with High Admiral Ignatius, General Black, and many other military leaders, and even members of the Emperor's own guard. They are all behind me. The only people left are you: the Enomegs. If you disagree with me, if you believe that we should continue to maintain the Emperor's façade as Dark-Dragon did, even if it dishonors his name, then so be it: my plans end here. But if you stand with me, then together we can fight for a better Xarkon; one of which Dark-Dragon and our nation's founders would have been proud."

Suddenly Mars stopped looking down at them and fixed his eyes directly forward, his already rigid form stiffening even further. "Enomegs, children of Dark-Dragon… I plan to *execute* Marius Orrick."

Saber-Scorpion hardly knew how to react. Looking around at his comrades, he saw that they felt the same. Their expressions each showed astonishment, even fear at this prospect, then became largely blank. It was as if some vital bit of programming in their minds had been contradicted. Kill the Emperor, bearer of the Crown? Such a thing was hardly even imaginable.

Seeing their reactions, or lack thereof, Mars went on: "Yes, I plan to execute him for his crimes, for staining the honor of the Crown he wears and the nation it represents. This will be done out in the open, not behind a curtain of lies as the Emperor would have done with Lord Zegaldorph in Shardasha. The eyes of the entire world will see the Emperor die by *my* hand, and I will make his crimes clear for all to understand. If this is unacceptable to you, simply speak. Speak freely, as you would have done with Dark-Dragon."

Still there was hardly a reaction. The Enomegs exchanged glances now, but every face into which they looked mirrored their own expression of indecision.

All but one.

Saber-Scorpion rose from his seat and looked Mars directly in the eyes, his mind for once completely resolute. "I stand with you, Commander. Just tell me what must be done."

Raven gave Scorp a quick glance and, not to be outdone, stood up and gave the heartbeat salute. "I am with you, Father. Not just for Dark-Dragon, but for all of Xarkon."

The air in the room grew distinctly chill, as the Enomegs realized the step they were taking. The next to stand was Shadow-Cat, though she clearly looked reluctant. She was followed by Magnum-Coyote, and then Gun-Barracuda. Silent-Cobra still looked unsure, and glanced at Blade-Mantis, who was staring at the ground. Then she stood as well. All eyes were suddenly on Mantis, and the small man's own dark orbs soon returned the stare. His face was as determined as any of theirs... yet he remained seated.

In a quiet but even voice, he said, "It's not right."

"Mantis..." Cat began.

"It is not *right*," he repeated, more emphatically. "When we became Enomegs, we took an oath to protect the bearer of the Crown, whoever that man or woman might be. As you once said yourself, Saber-Scorpion: governments change. Governments change, emperors change, people change, times change... but an oath, my friends, does not. Dark-Dragon was loyal to the end, and so am I. I will *not* raise a hand against the Emperor of Xarkon."

There was a long moment of silence then. Even Mars did not speak, but merely watched the Enomegs, as they in turn watched their devoted comrade. Gun-Barracuda's gruff voice was the first to break the silence.

"So you'll stand against us then?"

Mantis looked away. "I will not stand against you... but I will not stand with you either. I ask you to consider this: the Emperor is an old man. You may only be cutting a few years off his life. He could die tomorrow, of natural causes, and he has no heir. Of course, I am sure the High Commander has considered this, yes?"

"Indeed I have," Mars replied. "I have been considering that for nearly the last decade. During that time, the Emperor has hardly appeared to age a day. He has remained just as old and feeble, but just as alive."

"Yeah, just look at him," Coyote put in. "He has all the qualities of a corpse except the essential one."

Scorp nodded. "A lot can happen between now and his death, Lee."

Still Mantis did not budge. "This is not what Dark-Dragon would have wanted."

"Are you sure?"

Now Mantis looked up, his face like stone. "Yes, I am sure. But if this is the will of all the Enomegs and all of Xarkon High Command, then I will not stand in the way. I will not stand against you, but I will not stand with you either. Do as you will, as you believe is right. I will do the same."

Raven shook his head. "And what are you going to do then?"

"Just tell me where to be," Mantis said, looking away. "I will stand anywhere... anywhere but in that room when it happens."

"You can stand guard beside the dropship then," Mars said, "and make sure no one tries to sabotage it to cut off our extraction. I'll make sure the other soldiers follow your commands. As for the rest of you, you will be with me in the

Emperor's booth, along with two other guardsmen, the other members of High Command, a few political figureheads, and of course Marius Orrick. You need do nothing but stand and watch, and then when the Victorians send their 'neutral' CONON guards to cut off our escape, you and I will cut a path directly through them."

"With these?" Coyote grumbled, shaking his shining black ceremonial spear.

Mars nodded. "Indeed. You have been trained in their use, as well as the use of those swords at your sides. Your armor and weapons may seem primitive and ceremonial, but the blades are energy-shielded and the armor nanoduranium, just as sturdy as your own Enomeg exoskeletons, though perhaps not as flexible. Still, I think you can manage. I myself will use my own blazer claymore, *Angurvadel*."

Barracuda snorted. "Your sword has a *name*?"

"Watch your tone, Kade!" Raven snapped.

Suddenly Mars drew out his blade – a long, thick, double-edged broadsword, far different from the ceremonial sabers that most of them carried. The crosspiece of the hilt was shaped like the Crown itself, made of crimson metal and imbedded with a single blood red gem. He held the tip of this weapon up toward Barracuda's throat, looking directly down its razor edge like a runway, for the two men were of nearly equal height. Scorp was astonished at the speed with which Mars unsheathed the weapon; it did not look light, yet Barracuda had not even had time to react.

"Yes, it has a name," the High Commander said, his eyes suddenly gleaming with inner fire, "the same name as the flagship of Xarkon's space fleet, the name of a legendary sword of ancient myth with the power to fell giants. I have heard its name means 'stream of anguish,' and its rune-engraved blade would light aflame in times of war. Today it shall blaze like Nova Core itself, and its edge shall taste royal blood! But enough talk. Prepare yourselves, soldiers of Xarkon, for the coming hour of reckoning!"

LOCATION: THE CONON GREAT HALL

Tension filled the air around Victory. The news waves were abuzz with talk of the Shardasha Incident, and although few details had been leaked to the press, they were running wild with speculations, as always. Already the news had been sent through the interstellar relay system – a network of space buoys that helped to transmit signals between planets at speeds faster than light. Within days, other systems in Human Space and beyond would get the news, and citizens from Outlook to the Hub would be talking about what was happening... or at least, what they *thought* was happening.

Now it was up to the leaders of humanity on Terra Nova to set the record straight.

But would they? Ryan thought. *Probably not.*

Sergeant Arkanian was on the uppermost platform of the multi-layered stadium that was the CONON Great Hall. He was currently situated directly behind the entrance to the Victorian "tower," waiting for the others to arrive. From here, he could see all of the Big Four's enormous obelisks and the smaller towers of the other countries around them, each one a monument to its nation's pride. Below lay the window looking down to the surface of the planet, as if the whole satellite was a great eye watching over Terra Nova, and that window was its lens. But above was another lens, looking up, far and away into space, into a galaxy dominated by so many other forms of life. Sometimes, Ryan thought, Humanity forgot to look through this second lens.

Now the Yavakaro council members were arriving. Two of them headed for their own booth, while the other four came toward the Victorian one. For masked, nameless beings, it was remarkable how different they each were. The first was a short and rather rotund, older man. He was followed by a young man and a young woman, both with very keen, dark eyes. And an unmistakable Sarran male with great grey wings took up the rear. All four were dressed in dark, silky purple robes. Ryan could hear the fat man and the Sarran arguing under their breath, but the young man and woman were speaking clearly and calmly to one another. Ryan noted that, oddly, the guards of every male councilman were male, and the females' were female.

"We told you," said the woman's voice, deep yet smooth, "that we will not be held back, Brother."

If the woman's voice was deep, the man's voice was yet deeper, though slightly raspy and menacing. "We worry for your safety, Sister."

"We worry for all our safety, even here in this great space station, a symbol of peace. The Hands," she gestured to the Hands of the Six, their *naginata*-wielding bodyguards in ceremonial armor, "can only do so much with their spears and their namesake weapons."

The man ignored this comment and went on. "We simply find it odd that you yourself are so active, yet you support Yavakaro taking a *passive* role in world affairs. Should we not stand up for what is right?"

"Can we truly *say* what is right, Brother?" replied the woman, evenly. "We are but Humans, just like those we are declaring wrong."

"Do not cloud the issue at hand, Sister. Stay focused. Lord Zegaldorph needed to be deposed. We are but Humans, as you say, but he is not. He is a Mahlok, a dictator, and a poor and unpredictable leader. His country is a blight on the planet."

"And I suppose all other world leaders and countries are perfect?"

Ryan watched as the council members began to enter the Victorian tower through the doors, one by one, each one flanked by one of the Hands. The other four guards took up positions outside. The last two council members to enter were the man and woman, and the man suddenly stopped to whirl around and face her. He looked almost ready to grab her.

"You do not want us as your enemy, *Sister*," he said, in a voice so low that Ryan could barely make it out. "If we are to improve the world, we must start by relieving the apathy of our –"

Suddenly one of the Hands stepped forward as if to break up the fight. He whispered a few words to the male Councilman, who straightened his robes and stepped back. The guard nodded to the woman, whose female guard was also conversing with her. All four of them then nodded and entered the Victorian tower.

Ryan was still considering this exchange and its meaning as he followed them. He found the Victorian booth crammed full that day, with all the representatives in their usual spots, along with their guests, the Yavakarese and their guards. As usual, Rick Radcliff sat up front, nearest the view of the Great Hall, along with Ordinator John Exsyl. This time, Amazon was there with them. Ryan quickly joined her.

"This is such a joke," she commented as soon as he sat down.

"I don't think the meeting will be all for show," Ryan replied. "Exsyl knows what he's doing, even if Rick doesn't think so."

"What, has he told you something he hasn't told us?"

"No… It's just that I think he has something up his sleeve."

"Well, I wish he'd at least let us carry weapons up *ours*," she replied. "I feel naked without my gun."

Ryan laughed. "You get used to it."

Finally John Exsyl stood and gestured to their Yavakarese guests. "Welcome, councilors of Yavakaro! I believe that you have something for us."

"Yes," said the older male council member, who seemed perfectly willing to get right down to business, "we do. As you know, all information uncovered thus far from the Battle of Shardasha only tentatively links Lucas Mars with the incident..."

"And I suppose you have something better," Rick said.

This time the Sarran council member spoke up. "We do. We have a recording that was recovered by one of our agents from the personal effects of a military officer inside the city. In it, the officer directly identifies members of Xarkon's High Command giving him orders to lock down the city and pretend to be terrorists. He even refuses an order they gave him to kill civilians in order to hide the information."

"I don't guess–" Rick began, but he was cut off by Exsyl.

"Here comes the Emperor," the Ordinator said, looking across the vast coliseum toward the metallic burgundy pillar of Xarkon on the other side.

Emperor Orrick looked as old and frail as ever, but there was a peculiar energy about him, a keenness in his drooping eyes. He looked almost desperate, licking his lips nervously as he tried to build up his confidence and composure. Finally he straightened up as much as his back would allow and took a step forward.

"I see no reason to waste time," he said into the microphone, his amplified voice croaking out of every speaker in the building. "Cohen, is everyone accounted for?"

Far be it from Howard Cohen to be anything but cheerful, even on as foul a day as this. He smiled with nothing but kindness across at the Emperor, as if to say that it would all be okay in the end. He knew it would. All of the others only hoped he was right.

"Aye, my Lord," he said, bobbing a slight bow. "All the representatives are present, even every member of the Six, though some are in the Victorian booth. The world is all ears."

The Emperor nodded, and after what seemed a long pause, he spoke. "I will lie to none of you, my fellow Humans and allies... There has been a terrible tragedy. The events in Shardasha escalated into battle, just before ending in disaster. The terrorists who had control of the city were more deeply entrenched than we could ever have thought, and far more well prepared. They hired mercenaries from Grimm's Army, soldiers of fortune to fight the defenders of peace, and used them to try to frame Xarkon for this horrible crime. And then, when their plot looked bleakest, they pulled their secret weapon... Do you know what that was?"

Rick shook his head in disgust. "We should put a stop to this, John. No one here needs to listen to this old corpse spewing his lies."

Exsyl shot the General a very disapproving glance. "Stand down, Rick. Let him speak, for now. Let him work himself into a hole. Let him weave a bigger web of lies, until he gets caught in it himself."

The Emperor looked positively vehement now, though his scrawny frame looked exhausted by the mere act of giving this speech. "Zegaldorph's entire tower detonated, as soon as the Lord of Mordark was clear of the blast! More than that, it collapsed upon the other towers of the city, causing massive destruction! Many of Xarkon's soldiers, sent in to rescue the Mahlok, were killed. There is only one explanation for this turn of events: The tower was detonated by none other than Lord Zegaldorph himself!"

Zegaldorph's powerful and alien voice blew from the speakers like a blast of fire. "I object! Look upon me now, Terra Nova, and judge me as you wish. I bare myself before you; I hide behind nothing."

Ryan looked down at the smaller tower of Mordark nestled between Zygbar's great golden-orange dragon head and Xarkon's dark blood-red pillar. The Mahlok truly had bared himself. As was the tradition of his people in their early days, he wore no clothing whatsoever. His shining red-orange skin, covered in its artistically flowing black markings, was plain for all to see.

He spread his arms wide. "I am a Mahlok," he said. "Some of you may hate me for it. Others may look upon me in awe, as did my close friend and bodyguard, Captain Jaleiko, who tragically lost his life in this disaster. He accepted me for what I am, and now I ask you to do that as well. Yes, I *did* destroy my tower. The way of my people when we are losing a battle is to leave nothing behind to lose, to leave as little as possible in the hands of the enemy. That is simply our way. And though you may not believe me after what I have done, though you may be blinded by prejudice and propaganda, it is *Xarkon* who is the enemy. They held me prisoner in my own tower in that accursed city before the Victorian strike team came to rescue me."

Now Ordinator John Exsyl stood. "Lord Zegaldorph is correct. Grand General Radcliff and representatives from Yavakaro have already confirmed Zegaldorph's words."

"Ordinator Exsyl," Emperor Orrick interrupted, "are you sure you wish to make such an accusation so early in this diplomatic process? Have you considered the possibility that Zegaldorph may be lying to you?"

"The only person lying here is you," Zegaldorph replied calmly, his voice echoing across the chasm of the stadium as the speakers amplified it, "constructing a fortress of falsehoods to hide behind…"

"Lies?" the Emperor shouted, as much as his weak voice could muster. "You destroyed half a city! You admitted it yourself!"

Ryan watched the proceedings with rapt attention. He had never seen the CONON council in such a state of disarray. Usually, the good-humored voice of Howard Cohen was able to calm the representatives and convince them to solve their issues peacefully. This time, however, his interruptions were completely ignored, drowned in a torrent of accusations of lies and subterfuge. It was then that Ryan noticed the only podium that remained silent was that of Zygbar. Roscoe O'Donnell was sitting thoughtfully, drumming his fingers, occasionally shooting a furtive glance toward the Xarkon tower, as if he were waiting for something.

And then it came.

Suddenly a very familiar voice boomed throughout the complex, echoing off the walls. It was so deep and powerful that the listeners could feel the impact of it in their chests, as if they had been struck in the chest and had the wind knocked out of them. It spoke one single word, the very word they all most dreaded to hear, and immediately all were silenced.

"War."

All eyes turned to the speaker, and there they beheld the towering form of Lucas Augustus Mars, High Commander of the Armed Forces of the Xarkon Empire. His keen, nearly colorless eyes swept the world below and the national leaders opposite him with the cool, calculating gaze of a man who, in an almost detached way and without a single shred of doubt, felt he stood above and beyond all that he surveyed. Normally such an attitude would inspire outrage or offense, but Mars seemed so certain of it, and something about him seemed to make it feel so *right*, that all who looked upon him felt themselves almost agreeing. It was chilling, Ryan thought, the effect this man had on people.

"Today you have heard too many lies," he said, standing in his usual position, with his arms behind his back. "No more."

Behind him, Emperor Orrick started to speak, but Mars turned and shot him a glance that cowed him immediately. In the perimeter of the booth, the Bloodguard, both the disguised Enomegs and the actual guards themselves, did not move. Neither did the other members of High Command, nor the Emperor's political advisors. They did nothing.

"Xarkon is with me," Mars said coldly, without a shred of pity or even self-satisfaction, "and the rest of the world should listen. It is time you knew the truth."

Though it seemed to take all his willpower to pull his eyes from the High Commander, Ryan shot a glance toward Rick. "He's up to something. We should stop him… somehow."

Rick held up a hand half absentmindedly, demanding silence. Even he, the greatest enemy of Lucas Mars, now sat spellbound by the man's powerful performance. Ordinator Exsyl seemed not to have even heard Ryan. He stared at Mars as if there was not another living being in the world. Ryan glanced back at the Yavakaro representatives, but it was hard to read their expressions behind their masks.

"The truth," Mars went on, "is that Xarkon *was* behind this attack. At the behest of our leader, the Emperor, we held our own city under siege, used our own people as hostages, all to trap and kill a single man... a single Mahlok. Our tactics were cowardly, cruel, unnecessarily destructive, and lacking in honor. This is not the way of Xarkon. And now, before you all, even you, Lord Zegaldorph of Mordark, I apologize for the behavior of my nation. The man who now wears our Crown has stained it with his dishonor. He has shamed our entire nation and marred our history. Instead of honorable, brave, loyal, and strong... he has revealed himself to be weak, corrupt, dishonest, and perhaps worst of all... a coward."

Across the theater of CONON, jaws hung open. It was as if the whole planet had fallen speechless. Ryan looked around urgently, hoping to see someone making a move to stop whatever was going down, but all stood mesmerized. He thought about making some quick commands himself, but he was only a Sergeant in the infantry, seated next to the Grand General... who did not budge.

Meanwhile, behind Mars, Emperor Orrick was sputtering, his mouth opening and closing as his entire body shook. "Mars... What... What treachery is this?"

"And I assure you," Mars concluded with an air of finality, "that it will not happen again."

With that, he drew his sword. The great duranium claymore that functioned as his ceremonial officer saber was more than half as long as the Emperor was tall, but Mars hefted it as if it were made of plastic. The blazer shield shimmered and glowed white-hot as it spread over the surface of the shining blade. The High Commander turned to face the Emperor, presenting his back to his audience.

"If you are not a coward," he said slowly, "then draw your sword. It is your decision whether you use it against me... or upon yourself."

The old man's jaw twitched. "G-Guards..."

The red-robed Bloodguards did not move, though one female twitched slightly. Cobra's hand inched toward her sword... then fell back to her side. None would make a move against the High Commander.

Loudly but evenly, Mars repeated: "If you would die as a man of honor, draw... your... *sword*."

The Emperor stiffened. "No. No, I will not."

"In that case, stand and be executed."

In the flash of an eye, the intake of a breath, it was done. The few in that station who dared to blink actually missed it. The sound of hot energy slicing through flesh could be heard over all the speakers, and there was a collective gasp as the onlookers realized what had happened. The Emperor's head landed on the carpeted ground, followed by his body, both making hardly a sound. Many of the representatives fainted on the spot. The world leaders leapt to their feet.

But the soldiers of Xarkon, both the Enomegs and the Emperor's own Bloodguard, still would not budge. When Mars looked at them, they stiffened and gave the heartbeat salute. He had their full support. All of Xarkon was behind him… and all the world was before him.

Mars turned about now, his sword held aloft over his head. "Xarkon deserves better than this! Ours is the greatest of all nations, as can be seen at this gathering here today. The troubles of other countries attract little attention from this hall, as they are full of whining, petty squabbles and pretentious melodrama. But when Xarkon speaks, the world watches and listens! We alone have the courage to do what is necessary, the will to do what is right."

At this point, one of the two members of the Council of Six still in the Yavakaro booth tried to make an objection, but Mars spoke on, his powerful voice overriding the interrupter with almost no effort.

"The political squabbles of weak leaders like those present here today, like the withered husk whose head now lies at my feet, will only result in more needless bloodshed, cowardly killing of defenseless civilians, and covering of the facts with pretty lies and bedtime stories. War is a constant, ever-present fact. Even as a nation claims to be at peace, it is fighting internal and silent battles, and constantly preparing for a *real* battle when the time comes. Peace is nothing more than an illusion – an improperly defined stage of the constant state of war that dominates all life. What you call peace… I call reloading. So it is time we stopped this reign of fear and murder, fighting our petty skirmishes in the shadows, and brought our conflict into the light of day, like men! The current peace is a lie! Peace must be won by *war!*"

At this point, the other leaders were veritably screaming into their own microphones to drown out the overwhelming power of the man that towered over them. In the top of his gargantuan podium, Mars stood like a colossus. The light illuminated his face from below, outlining his severe features and the arch of his heavy brow. His near-colorless grey eyes shone like twin points of polished steel. The voices of the other world leaders – the Councilors of Yavakaro, the Senators of Victory, the Archons of Apollo – all of them were like the distant and meaningless clamor of the crowd before the might of Lucas Mars. His voice, like the voice of a god, cut through theirs as the bow of a ship parts the sea.

"Hear me, men of Xarkon!" he shouted. "My kinsmen! The Ultimate War is upon us. I know this war I ask you to fight is a great one, but I do not ask you to fight it *for* me, as *he* would have. I ask you to fight it *with* me! A great leader is not one who commands others to fight for him from afar. A truly great leader, and a truly great man, fights his own battles. And then, out of loyalty and respect, even love... his men follow him."

Mars looked down. He saw the Crown of Xarkon lying on the ground, and he picked it up with his sword. Removing the burgundy ornament from the tip of the weapon, Mars then held it aloft for all to see. Many expected him to place it on his head right then and there, but Mars was sensible enough not to show that much audacity. He moved slowly, with calm precision, even as the other world leaders clamored to action, arguing and making calls to their subordinates, some getting up to leave.

"And now," the High Commander said, still holding the crown before him with reverence, "let us wait no longer. No more does the curtain of lies hide our eyes from the truth. The time to act has come. *'Cry havoc, and let slip the dogs of war!'*"

He turned and began to march out of the booth, headed toward the rear exit, with the High Commanders, advisors, and guards falling into step behind him. The Emperor's body remained untouched – a pile of fine clothing containing somewhere within it the shell of a man who had once ruled a nation. Mars hefted his blade, still stained with royal blood, and nodded to his men. Behind him, the Enomegs, military officers, and Bloodguards drew their swords. Before them, the back doors of the Xarkon tower burst open, leading out to the perimeter walkway of the CONON stadium building.

Meanwhile, in the Victorian booth, the Senators were panicking and scrambling for the door, shouting to the grey-armored CONON guards to defend them. The Hands of the Six had formed a defensive wall in front of the four Yavakarese councilors and were leading them toward the exit. But General Rick Radcliff shoved through them all, followed shortly by Ryan, Amazon, and Ordinator John Exsyl.

Once he was out on the perimeter walkway, Rick turned to see the Xarkonian representatives headed around on the opposite side of the stadium. No doubt they were moving toward the exit located just between both towers. Even now, many of the Victorian senators and Yavakaro councilmen were headed there as well.

"Guards," Rick commanded loudly, "escort the representatives! Get ahead of them and cut off the Xarkonians! On the double – move, move!"

"Doesn't this place have multiple exits?" Ryan shouted back.

"It does, but no one seems to be heading for them! We just have to follow the crowd!"

Amazon cursed. "Politicians… Should have made 'em do fire drills."

Ryan and Amazon led the charge, followed by Rick and the CONON guards. Together they pushed right past the fleeing representatives and took up the front. Running at a frenetic pace, they managed to reach the exit ramp just before the Xarkonians, who were marching along with cool confidence.

Rick turned. "Ryan, take this."

Ryan caught Rick's officer sword as the General tossed it to him. There was hardly ten feet between the two opposing groups, and Rick suddenly turned and ordered one of the CONON guards to give him his weapon. The man – who was sworn to be a neutral guard of the CONON Great Hall but could not deny his ultimate loyalty to his country, Victory – immediately handed Rick his assault rifle.

Rick swung the weapon toward the oncoming Xarkonians. "Halt!"

He barely had time to get the barrel leveled when the foremost Bloodguard leapt straight at him.

369

In the blink of an eye, Saber-Scorpion – for it was he who was the first to attack – grabbed the barrel of Rick's rifle, shoving it aside as he both disarmed the General and knocked him off his feet. Ryan was more prepared for the assault, and had already drawn Rick's sword and dropped the scabbard when he saw Scorp raising his new rifle… and aiming directly for Ryan's head. The Victorian, trained not to be a bodyguard but a survivor, ducked reflexively aside just as the shot was fired. The bullet whizzed right past Ryan's head… and into that of John Exsyl, the Ordinator of Victory.

None of the politician's loyal defenders even noticed as he fell, so great was the chaos at the time. Already the other representatives were panicking, and this threw them into a greater frenzy. Now the Xarkon Bloodguard were engaged in a heated swordfight with the Yavakarese Hands of the Six, as well as Ryan and Amazon. Meanwhile, behind them, Mars and his cohorts marched calmly down the exit ramp leading to the hangar. Their guards allowed themselves to lose ground to the Victorians and Yavakarese, until all were within the bounds of the ramp.

As the combatants proceeded down the ramp, Rick Radcliff looked around for a gun… until his eyes fell upon his leader and close friend, John Exsyl. The Grand General rushed to the Ordinator's side, but he could tell immediately that there was no hope – the bullet had hit Exsyl directly in the forehead, and he stared at the ceiling with wide, lifeless eyes. Without wasting another second, Rick grabbed another assault rifle from a CONON guard who had been cut down by one of the disguised Enomegs, and checked to make sure it was loaded. He then moved to join his comrades, flanked by several more guards who were just now arriving.

"If you can get a clean shot, men," the General shouted, "don't hesitate to take it! I don't care *who* it is! I want that hall painted Xarkon's color with Xarkon's *blood!*"

His men rallied behind him, eager to partake in the battle. Soon the entire tunnel between the exit ramp and the landing pad outside rang with echoing gunfire from both the Victorians inside and the Xarkonians outside the compound, who still carried weapons. It was the battle all had feared, taking place right in the headquarters of the very establishment that had been created to prevent it from happening. As he confidently strode out onto the landing platform outside, Mars reveled in the irony of it all. Had he been a less composed man, he might have even thrown back his head and laughed.

It was finally here.

The Ultimate War had begun.

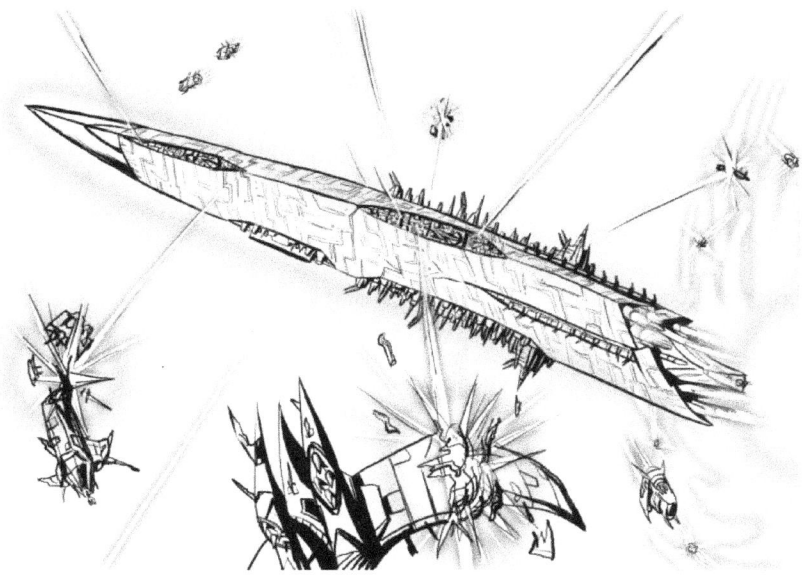

- EPILOGUE -
A STORM IN WAITING

Against a canvas of black, dotted with stars and painted by the swirling magenta brush-strokes of a nearby nebula, floated a motley fleet of grey metal ships, looking more like space debris than vessels of war. Each one appeared to be barely holding together, salvaged from battlefields and refitted as well as possible, decorated with bright streaks of red and green paint and blade-like pieces of scrap sticking out at odd angles.

In the center of this field of floating slag lay a great jump ring – an octagon of thin energy beams created by a circle of small satellites. Normally such installations were found near highly populated planets, creating "highways" through the Breach, the alternate dimension through which starships had to travel to reach speeds faster than light. But this particular one lay alone in the void, with no sign of civilization visible for billions of miles.

It was a Breach Well, as they were known – a trap created by pirates to pull convoys out of trade lanes a little too early, bringing them right into a waiting ambush. This particular one was installed along a main thoroughfare through Helexith space, the section of the galaxy ruled over by the Mahlok and their Slashrim armies. And the Slashrim rebels who had built it were waiting to capture another convoy belonging to their former overlords.

Finally, their patience paid off. In the center of the enormous octagon, a spark of illumination appeared, creating ripples in the light around it – distortions in the very fabric of reality. The Slashrim ship captains watched as the satellites

371

drew outward, expanding the ring to a greater and greater diameter… and did not stop.

The rebel captains felt a chill as they watched the ring continue to swell. Why was it growing so large? What kind of convoy had they just captured? Meanwhile, the light in the center gradually increased, and suddenly there was a flash like a supernova as a hole was torn through space and time. Out came the travelers of the Breach, into the waiting claws of the Slashrim pirates… but it was no supply convoy that they had caught.

In some ancient Slashrim tales, the universe was actually an unimaginably immense cave of onyx, surrounded by stalactites and stalagmites as large as planets that glistened like stars, sparkling in the night sky. Those Slashrim who still believed these legends suddenly wondered if one of those very same stellar stalactites had broken loose and fallen into their trap. Like the arrowhead of a god, made of glittering obsidian, it pierced through the wavering portal, its upper and lower halves – if it could have been said to have any – adorned with many smaller spikes, covered in lights… vast cities of ebony skyscrapers.

The Slashrim warships all fired at once, peppering the sides of the great black dagger with explosions of every imaginable size and type, caused by weapons of every design, from Starfire cannons to nuclear warheads. The enormous spike of shadow began to crack and split, long patterns of lines like ancient runes glowing red-orange upon its surface.

But the Slashrim knew that this was no sign of damage. These lines of fire upon the enemy's hull meant one thing: this blade of shadow that had thrust itself into their side was a Mahlok warship. More than that, it was the very flagship of their fleet: the flying city of fire that Humans knew – only from stories – as *Pyropolis*. And it was charging its weapons.

As the snakes of light slithered their way over the huge blackened blade, they began to gather at certain spots and glow white-hot, creating points of light atop tall, pointed towers. The motley pirate ships immediately began to turn and flee, but it was too late. The air was split with shafts of fiery light from the guns of *Pyropolis*, like spears of the sun, each one tearing through the shields of a rebel vessel.

It was not a battle. It was a slaughter.

Inside one of the loftiest towers that jutted from the top of the enormous black vessel, a tall Mahlok Lord sat clothed in nothing but a flowing, silken black cape that spread out over his tall captain's throne as he watched the chaos from the viewports all around him. His thin, yellow slits of eyes revealed no emotion as they scanned the ship's command crew of Mahlok and only the most loyal and intelligent stage-three Slashrim below.

His voice rolled like thunder from the depths of a volcano, echoing throughout the room: "*Enxith Zuithra, ka zuok ogref.*"

Or as a Human might put it: "Admiral Zuithra, status report."

Below, a female Mahlok – her body ensnared in grasping claws of black metal that passed for her uniform – looked up. "My Lord, damage to our hull is negligible, and we have destroyed three of the enemy ships already. They do not stand a chance."

"Good," replied Zuhaxellod X, ruler of the Dominion of Helexith. "Let the cannons of *Pyropolis* burn these heathens like the bolts of vengeful fire cast forth by the gods themselves. For we are their harbingers, this ship is their holy sword... and I am their avatar. I am Zuhaxellod, voice of Helexith. I am a living god."

All around him, the Slashrim quaked in fear, nearly falling to their knees in reverence as he gave this speech. The only thing that kept them from throwing themselves into obeisance was the knowledge that he would destroy them with a mere glance if they took a single moment away from their appointed tasks of managing their Lord's sacred vessel.

"All ye who hear me," Zuhaxellod continued, knowing that his voice would be transmitted throughout the stars of Helexith space, "know that this is what comes of heresy against the Lord Helexith, of rebellion against his galactic empire that has stood for countless millennia. The Mahlok are the incarnations of Helexith himself, and the Slashrim are his chosen people... but if either one should turn away from him, they will then taste the full measure of his divine fury."

Suddenly, Admiral Zuithra looked up from her control station and signaled to the Mahlok overlord, who rose immediately from his throne and descended to the deck.

"I must have a word with the Admiral in private now," he said as he strode past his crew, Zuithra and a great black Slashrim joining him as he walked. "When I return, I expect to see nothing left of the heretics but dust and debris no larger than a fighter's wing."

The three commanders exited the bridge to a small, dark side-room, the onyx walls of which immediately lit up with bright orange patterns of light as they entered. When the X-shaped duranium doors were shut behind them, Zuithra and the Slashrim chieftain bowed to their leader.

"My Lord," said the Mahlok Admiral, "Valgerogk has received–"

Zuhaxellod waved her into silence. "What is this about, Vasha Valgerogk? Speak quickly."

The Slashrim Zrillak opened his bright red eyes and bared his glistening white fangs, both of which contrasted strikingly with his deep black skin covered in shining onyx scales. The Mahlok often performed experiments on their Slashrim subjects to make them more fit for battle, mutating their unique genetics with such modifications as extra arms, the ability to shift hues and camouflage their skin, and natural armor scales like Valgerogk's.

A reply gurgled up from deep inside the Slashrim's throat: "The Prophecy of the Millennium Trigger has finally come to pass. I have received a transmission from our agents in Human Space that a war has just erupted on their precious jewel of a homeworld, Terra Nova. The leaders of their largest factions, Victory and Xarkon, were beheaded in a single stroke, inside the very bastion of their alliance, the space station headquarters of their so-called 'Council of Nations of Nova Refuge.'"

The Mahlok always referred to operations undertaken by the military of Helexith as Prophecies, proclaiming that the events they had planned would soon come to pass, for such was the will of Helexith. If any of their followers should fail at any stage of an operation, it was deemed a result of a lack of faith in Helexith, and they were punished severely. Operation Millennium Trigger was one of their longest-running Prophecies, and only now after nearly two hundred years had stage one finally been achieved.

There was no visible reaction from the Mahlok overlord, except for the slightest brightening of the yellow-white glow deep behind his eyes. "It has begun, as was inevitable. All shall come to pass as Helexith foresaw."

Vasha Valgerogk fell to one knee, bringing his enormous height down to one more equal with the two Mahlok who stood near him. "Your will is my command, Lord Zuhaxellod. Our warships wait in deep space near Human territory now as always. Speak, and it shall be done."

Admiral Zuithra shook her head. "Do not be foolish, Valgerogk. The war has only just begun. The point is to let the Humans weaken themselves–"

The voice of Zuhaxellod reverberated through the room as he commanded: "Silence! I have not given you permission to speak, Admiral Zuithra. *I* will tell the Vasha and all others who follow Helexith of what is to be done… *and no other.*"

The female Mahlok immediately fell to her knees and leaned forward until the flat of her mouthless face touched the floor at Zuhaxellod's feet. "Yes, my Lord. I beg your forgiveness."

"We will speak a while in private, Zuithra. As for you, Valgerogk, return to your post, but make no further moves. Indeed, speak not of this to any other until I give the word. Zuithra, however insolent, is correct: we must wait for the Humans to cripple themselves with their internal strife before we can take advantage of it."

The Vasha – a Slashrim word meaning "chieftain" – smiled as hideous a smile as ever to cross a Slashrim face. "At last, we can finish what our ancestors began so many centuries ago!"

Zuhaxellod raised a single red-skinned hand. "Have patience, Valgerogk. All things come, as even the Humans say, to those who wait. For now, return to your post and see about quelling what remains of this rebellion among your people."

Once the Slashrim had left, Admiral Zuithra stood and brushed herself off. "That humiliation was unnecessary."

"On the contrary," replied Zuhaxellod, "it was *absolutely* necessary. You, I, and the rest of our people must never show any feeling other than absolute devotion to Helexith – to *me*. Faith is a powerful thing, but surprisingly fragile. The minute we reveal ourselves not to have it, the brutes that follow us may start to doubt their religion. All it takes is a whisper…"

Zuithra nodded. "It shall not happen again, my Lord."

"See that it doesn't," Zuhaxellod said as he stepped out onto the bridge, followed by the Admiral. "We would not want the eras of progress we have made to go to waste. We have waited *millennia* to finish the task we began against the Humans. To them, it is hardly more than a myth. They have all but forgotten it…"

Zuhaxellod X gazed through the great viewports all around them at the immense city that lined the vessel called *Pyropolis*, and at the bolts of energy flying from the towers that were still blasting the last of the rebel ships outside into space dust.

"But gods," he said, "have long memories."

INFORMATION CODEX

A brief summary of the characters, factions, species, and locations of Nova Refuge. For more extensive information, visit www.novarefuge.com

CHARACTERS

XARKON LEADERS

Marius Orrick – The current Emperor of Xarkon. Now rarely seen in public, his power and health are both waning in his old age.

Lucas Mars – High Commander of the Armed Forces of Xarkon. Tall and imposing, he is respected by nearly everyone. He currently serves as the public face for Xarkon and is rumored to be the country's *de facto* ruler.

Jacob Black – High General of the Xarkon Ground Forces. Black wears a false beard, which he exchanges with Lucas Mars when Mars requires a disguise and a decoy, since both men have a similar height and build.

XARKON ENOMEG SUPER-SOLDIERS

Dark-Dragon (John) – The last of the original Enomegs and current leader of the Enomeg project. He considers his trainees to be like his children even as he teaches them to be super-soldiers.

Saber-Scorpion (Justin) – One of the brightest Enomeg pupils. Though his loyalty to Xarkon often wavers, his skill in battle does not.

Blood-Raven (Luke) – The brash, headstrong, and handsome star student of the Enomeg project. Raven's battle prowess is only matched by his drive to best his main competitor, Saber-Scorpion.

Blade-Mantis (Lee) –One of the most skilled Enomegs, Mantis is known for his stoic loyalty when on the battlefield, but fun-loving playfulness when off.

Shadow-Cat (Cathryn) – An attractive female trainee who is a natural expert at the art of stealth and infiltration.

Electric-Eel (Seth) – Red-haired and energetic, Seth is a wizard with computers and mechanical devices. Very skilled, he seems to glide through training without letting it affect him emotionally.

Gun-Barracuda (Kade) – Tall, bald, scarred, and muscular, Kade is the most imposing of the Enomegs physically, but is more intelligent than he may seem. He greatly enjoys his job, and keeps a count of every successful kill.

Magnum-Coyote (Vincent) – A handsome and headstrong Enomeg known for his disrespectful attitude and joking around even when on the battlefield.

Silent-Cobra (Tanya) The most skilled female Enomeg in battle. Her short-cropped black hair and stoic attitude speak of her discipline and loyalty.

XARKON WALKER PILOTS

Harry Dalton (Viper) – Formerly a trainee in the Enomeg program but kicked out early due to lack of discipline, as evidenced by the length of his dark hair.

Currently a Beta-Wolf in the Xarkon Walker Force, leader of an equally rebellious but skilled walker pack called the Snake Legs.

Amy Archer (Falcon) – A Senior-Omega walker pilot and the scout for the Snake Legs. With clear blue eyes and long blonde hair, Falcon is best known for her looks, but she is also a highly intelligent introvert who remains distant even from the rest of Viper's squad.

VICTORY LEADERS

John Exsyl – Current Ordinator (political leader) of Victory. A kind-hearted old man known for his wisdom and understanding.

Rick Radcliff – Grand General of the Victorian Defense Forces, obsessed with keeping peace on Terra Nova under CONON. Lost his sight due to a rare alien disease contracted while off-world, requiring him to wear a specially-designed reflective HUD visor at all times in order to see.

Joshua Jenkins – A Colonel in the Victorian Army and right-hand man to General Rick Radcliff. Extremely loyal to Victory.

Harry "Harrier" Radcliff – The headstrong and handsome son of Rick Radcliff. Harry is one of Victory's greatest fighter pilots.

VICTORY IMMORTAL SUPER-SOLDIERS

Ryan Arkanian (Orion) – The most highly-skilled soldier in Victory's super-soldier project, chosen as a protégé by Rick Radcliff. His family was destroyed by Xarkon, and now he searches for information about their fate while fighting to avenge them. Currently a Sergeant in the Victorian Army.

Evelyn (Amazon) – Ryan's friend during their training as Immortal Soldiers, Amazon loves the thrill of battle even more than she loves her country.

GRIMM'S ARMY LEADERS

Eric Grimm I – "Grand High Warlord" of his namesake army of mercenaries, currently allied with Lucas Mars. Notable by his eyepatch (wound caused by Rick Radcliff), white eyebrows, and rough speech and appearance.

Douglas Boyle – Famed bounty hunter turned mercenary who enjoys killing his opponents in honorable duels. Currently Grimm's right-hand Warlord.

Nick Wolf – A yellow-bearded Victorian soldier who left his country to work as a Highlander mercenary in Zygbar, but was offered a better deal by Grimm. He is known as the "Werewolf" for his fearless ferocity in battle.

GRIMM'S ARMY MERCENARIES

Jade – Leader of Grimm's highly-trained warrior-children, raised by his army to be soldiers after the death of their mercenary parents. Jade seldom speaks or shows her face, and is an expert with her arm-mounted starfire cannons.

Grimm VII – Engineered to be loyal at the price of reducing his intelligence, "Seven" is the only Grimm-clone still in the Grim Army. Grimm trusts him but also despises him for his stupidity, denying him the rank of Warlord.

Hurk – A hulking fourth-stage Slashrim "Troll" with rusty-orange skin and muscles as large as his brain is small. Often serves as Grimm's enforcer.

ZYGBAR LEADERS

Roscoe O'Donnell – Current High Chancellor of Zygbar, but really more of a dictator. Fat, talkative, and mustached, he earned his position through guile and retains it through propaganda and an extensive cult of personality.
Azar Khan – Roscoe's chief General in charge of Zygbar's grand army. Known for his ruthless "any means necessary" approach to battle.

OTHER WORLD LEADERS

Howard Cohen – A fat and jovial ambassador from the pacifist country of Apollo who also serves as the coordinator for the meetings of CONON, the Council of Nations of Nova Refuge.
The Six – The mysterious secret council in charge of Yavakaro, who keep their identities hidden behind long robes and masks when in public.
Zegaldorph – Lord of the small country known as Mordark, which lies on a peninsula jutting from northern Xarkon, Zegaldorph is one of the tiny handful of Mahlok ever to have betrayed his own people to live with Humans.
Borad Jaleiko – A strong and imposing soldier, Captain of the Mordark Guard. Almost fanatically loyal to his Lord, Zegaldorph.

NATIVES

The High Council of Harmony – The Native alliance that has ruled more than one third of the Nova Refuge galaxy for many centuries. Composed entirely of angelic Sarran and mysterious, aquatic Achmer.
Idelma'ik and Folirayoth – Sarran mates who lead the infamous Sarran rebel organization known to Humans as the Blackwings, fighting for Sarran rights without the approval of the Council of Harmony. Idel has black wings and Folira, white. Folira is an expert psionic and Idel a master swordsman.
Aeriella – A Sarran and agent of the Blackwings, captured by Xarkon for her attempts to free that country's Sarran prisoners.
Lashnar – An intelligent, red-skinned, female third-stage Slashrim currently on the run for escaping slavery twice. Works as a freelance mercenary with Grimm III, who freed her from her second set of captors while on a job.
Zuhaxellod X – Leader of the Helexith Coalition, the other Native faction equally as powerful as Harmony. His people, the Mahlok, enslaved the Slashrim to be their soldiers by corrupting their religion so that they would worship the Mahlok as gods. Zuhaxellod claims to be the avatar of this god.
Zuithra – A female Mahlok admiral of the Helexith starship fleet.
Valgerogk – A high-ranking Slashrim Vasha loyal to the banner of Helexith.

OTHER CHARACTERS

Eric Grimm III – Grimm I's most successful clone, "Three" is almost completely identical to his creator, right down to his independent streak. He now works as a "lone wolf" mercenary, doing odd jobs while hiding from Grimm I, who hunts him.

Spectra –A mysterious and shadowy agent who is rumored, but never confirmed, to have been the catalyst in many important events. She frequently works with Grimm III, but does not trust him with her many secrets.

Lisa Sharp – A beautiful dark-haired woman captured by Xarkon under the accusation of attempting to assassinate military officers in High Command. Also goes by the names Larisa Sharapova and "Black Widow."

SPECIES

When Humanity arrived in the Refuge, they quickly discovered they were not alone. At first, they collectively referred to the many new species that they discovered as "aliens," but many Humans realized the irony of this term given their present situation, and thus they began to refer to their newfound competition by a new moniker: the Natives.

MAHLOK
(pronounced "MĂL-lock")

Originating from the planet Omolgeth in what Humans call the Hell's Eye system, the Mahlok are approximately the same size and build as Humans, but with slightly more elongated heads. Their faces are featureless, with no mouth, nose, or ears – only a pair of long, luminous yellow eyes without pupils. How they speak is a mystery, their voices seeming to emanate from within. Their skin is rubbery and translucent, but covered in strange, artistic black lines that typically outline their musculature, like natural tattoos, which differentiate between individuals. This skin appears deep red most of the time, but glows brighter and turns orange or yellow when the Mahlok make use of their inner flame. It is this mysterious "inner flame" – the functionality of which continues to baffle Human xenobiologists – that gives the Mahlok the intimidating abilities that have, in addition to their cunning, enabled them to become one of the most powerful species in the Refuge. Using their inner heat, the Mahlok can project gusts of flame from their skin, using it for a variety of purposes, including attack, flight, and even shielding in some cases, although the more complicated uses of the inner flame require years of training and practice to master. Nonetheless, it is no great surprise that some other species, most notably the Slashrim, worship the Mahlok as living gods. The Mahlok almost seem to believe this themselves, for they typically look down on all other creatures in the galaxy as lesser beings. As a result, they very seldom mingle with other civilizations, except for monetary gain or conquest. Their empire of Helexith spans one third of the galaxy.

SLASHRIM

Hailing from the same star system as the Mahlok, which Humans call Hell's Eye, the Slashrim originated on the planet now known as Slasheth. While possibly the strongest, fastest, and toughest Native species physically, the Slashrim are culturally and intellectually primitive as a whole. They have a somewhat dinosaur-like appearance, with rough, leathery skin, sharp teeth, slit pupils, and multiple horns protruding from their body. This can cause some Humans to mistake them for slow-moving, cold-blooded reptiles, but they are in fact endothermic and quite fast in nearly any temperature. Slashrim never stop growing, and their growth is typically separated into individual stages that determine their caste in Slashrim society. In their earliest years, the one-meter-tall Yillik or "Goblins" serve as menial workers, most becoming soldiers when they reach the two-meter-tall Grommuk or "Orc" stage. They reach their peak of intelligence during the Zrillak or "Lizardman" stage, when they are most dinosaur-like in appearance, with elongated snouts and tails. This is also when they most often reproduce, although it is noteworthy that only a Slashrim can truly tell the difference between a male and female of the species (by use of pheromones), since like reptiles their reproductive organs are not externally visible. Further stages of growth, like the Buyok or "Troll" stage, show increased size with decreased intelligence. Due to the typically short and violent life of a Slashrim, few reach the truly immense Wogrok or "Ogre" stage, and *very* few to the final Sovalok or "Pseudodragon" stage, at which point they begin walking on all fours and behaving like a non-sapient animal. The Slashrim are one of the most numerous species in the Refuge, and have little sense of cohesiveness, forming many warring tribes and freely intermingling with other cultures. Many now perform menial labor in Human societies. The vast majority of Slashrim, however, serve (and worship) the Mahlok under the banner of Helexith.

SARRAN
(pronounced "SAR-run")

The most Human-like of all the Native species are the Sarran, who appear at first glance to be little more than Humans with large, feathered wings sprouting from their backs, and smaller ones on their ankles. Other physical differences include slightly pointed ears, high-arching brows, and thin, elongated eyes. With their sharp, angular features and nearly always well-toned physique (due in part to their high metabolism), Humans typically find them quite attractive. This, combined with the fact that they are the only Native species with which cross-breeding is possible, has resulted in a few half-Sarran, half-Human children, although these are rare because of the typically aloof and reclusive nature of the Sarran as a whole. Perhaps the most intriguing aspect of the Sarran, however, is their mysterious psionic extrasensory perception. The Sarran can sense the presence and feel the emotions of another being whenever they are nearby, and if they are touching the individual, they can even read their actual thoughts. Because of their ability to detect a change in emotion without any outward physical sign, the Sarran seldom show their own emotions physically, thus leading Humans to see them as cold and severe. The Sarran accredit their powers to a "great spirit" they call Afaelya, through which they claim all beings are connected. Human scientists scoff at this idea, but what little research into Sarran psionics has been allowed so far has been unable to provide a better explanation.

ACHMER
(pronounced "OCK-mer")

Perhaps the most mysterious of all the Native species, the Achmer are an aquatic people known for their vast, almost unrivaled intellect. Physically, however, they are quite weak, especially when taken out of their native element, water. Their heads are long and bony, with a shield-like carapace protecting their large brain. The face, small in comparison to the rest of the head, consists of three eyes above a writhing mass of tentacles that serves as a mouth, with a four-pronged beak hidden inside. The Achmer have long, serpentine bodies lined with eel-like fins, with a pair of long tentacles that split into three "fingers" on the end that serve for their arms, and smaller tentacles behind those that can provide limited locomotion on dry land. They cannot breathe out of the water, however, and so must travel about in special suits that provide them with respiration, mechanical legs, and a vocal apparatus for speaking in the air. Coldly rational, their culture has no known religion and very little in the way of artwork. However, they are said to possess the most advanced technology in all the Refuge, most of which they keep a closely-guarded secret. A largely peaceful and very reclusive species, Humanity typically considers them mostly harmless.

SKRAKKI

These insect-like Natives are not what some might consider "sapient" beings. Individually, they are little more than animals, following primitive, single-minded instincts unique to the role they were born to serve in their hive. Together, however, they form a network of collective consciousness that can sometimes outwit even the cleverest Human. Physically, the Skrakki come in such a wide variety of forms that they are impossible to truly classify. Each time a colony spore lands on a new planet, its offspring may evolve to be drastically different than the Skrakki living on other worlds. Still, nearly all types have hard, armored exoskeletons, claw-like arms, and some type of venom. Years ago, they were a great scourge in Helexith space, spreading from planet to planet in strange hibernating egg pods, but now they have mostly been brought under control. Their place of origin remains a mystery.

FACTIONS

By the time Humanity made its Exodus to Nova Refuge, at least four major Human cities had already been established on Terra Nova, based around the four original research colonies of the major Earth powers. Years of separation from their founding nations had caused these cities to grow independent, with their own leaders, systems of government, and military forces for defense against the Natives. When the world leaders of Old Earth arrived on Terra Nova, they were forced to cooperate with (or bow to) the existing city-states instead of recreating their old countries. Thus, these four city-states became the major factions of Human Space. Together, these "Big Four" had enough power to fight off the Natives during the Xenocide War. But if any one of them were to try to face Helexith or Harmony alone, they would find themselves sorely outmatched.

This is why they are now united under the Council of Nations of Nova Refuge, or CONON.

XARKON
(pronounced "ZAR-con")

The Old Earth faction known as the Alliance of the Sword first established two research outposts on Terra Nova: the Extraterrestrial Advanced Research and Colonization Outposts North and South, or XARCON (north) and XARCOS (south). When XARCOS was overrun by hostile Native forces (mostly Slashrim), XARCON was turned into a veritable fortress with a strong military force. After the Exodus, the old acronym meaning was lost, and it became known simply as Xarkon. During and after the Xenocide War, Xarkon established itself as one of the leading Human factions, perhaps the most militarily powerful one of all. In the year 232 PA, Lady Kristal Skye – the head of state at that time – declared herself Empress and designed the crimson Crown of Xarkon, turning the country into an absolute monarchy with the Crown as its emblem. This was the peak of Xarkon's power, known as the Age of the Golden Skye. Since the last member of the short-lived Skye Dynasty stepped down, however, the power of Xarkon with its reign spread over many different planets, has waned under the rule of lesser sovereigns. But the proud citizens and soldiers of Xarkon still remain true to their warrior history and their tenets of honor, bravery, loyalty, and supremacy. Xarkon's national colors are red, black, and gold, and their military units are typically named after elements of ancient Norse mythology (examples: Jotun, Nidhogg, etc.).

VICTORY

Established almost immediately after XARCON by the UTS (United Terran States), Victory Station was even larger and more technologically complex than its competitors. After the Exodus, it became the founding point for the nation of Victory. Since their city-state was established on the Terra Nova continent mostly inhabited by the peaceful Sarran, however, the Victorians were never forced to concentrate on their military development as much as Xarkon. This was why, when the Sarran finally took retribution against Human conquest of their land, the original Victory Station was unable to defend itself against orbital bombardment by a Sarran capital ship, and it was destroyed. This spurred the Victorians into action, and the Victorian Defense Force soon became nearly as strong as the Armed Forces of Xarkon. Had it not been for Victory's efforts at establishing an alliance between all four major nations, Humanity might have lost the Xenocide War. This was why they created the Council of Nations of Nova Refuge, or CONON, originally building its chief council building upon the very site of the destroyed Victory Station in the city of Nutopia, though it was later moved to an orbital space station for the sake of neutrality. Their dream is to spread democratic and republican forms of government throughout Human Space, using CONON to unite all of Humanity. Victory's national colors are blue, white, and silver, and their military units are typically named after warrior classes from Ancient Earth history (examples: Hoplite, Legionnaire, Hussar, Paladin, etc.).

YAVAKARO

(pronounced "Ya-VOCK-are-oh")

Although it was the last research station of the initial "Big Four" to be constructed, Yavakaro (its name derived from the Sarran words for life, peace, and wisdom) was built by the Pan Asian Coalition (PAC) with intentions to be the first city of a new colony from the very start, making it the largest settlement on the planet at that time. Because of this, they have become the leading nation in terms of economy and technological advancement. Perhaps close contact with a native Achmer settlement rubbed off on the Yavakarese people, for they tend to keep many secrets, surrounding themselves in mystery. Their system of government is an oligarchy, controlled by a secret council of six men and women whose identities remain unknown, their faces obscured by masks when in public. The ornate nature of the deep purple robes and cloth masks worn by the Council of Six speaks of the strange combination found within Yavakaro of modern technology and ancient culture and tradition. One of the most peaceful of the Big Four, Yavakaro looked to its northern neighbor, Victory, for help during the Xenocide War, thus cementing the two nations' places as allies. Yavakaro's national colors are purple, white, and yellow.

ZYGBAR

(pronounced "ZIG-bar")

During the Xenocide War, the outpost hardest hit by the warlike Slashrim was the desert nation of Zygbar (named after a Mahlo-Slashrim word thought to mean "blessed land" but which actually meant quite the opposite). For Zygbar, the Xenocide War lasted nearly a hundred years longer than for the other nations in the Big Four, as many Slashrim tribes continued to fight long after the Treaty of Womloc had been signed. During the Age of the Golden Skye in Xarkon, Empress Skye sent her armies to conquer their southern neighbors, the Zygbari. For years afterward, Zygbar was officially part of the Empire of Xarkon, but the Crown's grip over the region was never very tight, and rebellions raged constantly. Finally, after the Skye Dynasty had stepped down in Xarkon and the Orrick Dynasty took the throne, a Zygbari insurgent group known as the Sun Dragon Rebellion managed to overthrow the Xarkonians and retake control of Zygbar. Just as the new government was attempting to tighten its control over the still-chaotic nation, however, their chief weapons supplier, Roscoe O'Donnell, overthrew the leader and set himself up as "Chancellor." Since then, his campaign of propaganda and restructuring has been surprisingly effective in bringing the poorest of the Big Four up to par with its competitors, even earning it a seat in CONON. Zygbar's national colors are desert camouflage tones highlighted in orange and gold (the colors of the fabled Sun Dragon).

GRIMM'S ARMY

When a powerful band of pirates and raiders based out of some islands near Xarkon continued to plague Victorian waters and skies, Victory sent a pair of their best military leaders, Rick Radcliff and Eric Grimm, to bring the situation under control. They were successful in destroying the pirates' operations, and together they returned to Victory as war heroes. But relations between the two commanders were strained, and after Grimm was accused of stealing money from the wealthy Rick Radcliff and even assaulting his wife, Radcliff challenged him to a duel and won, leaving Grimm alive but minus an eye. The frustrated war leader then returned, along with several Victorians still loyal to him, to the islands he had previously conquered. In the years afterward, Grimm forged the remaining pirates and criminals into a band of mercenaries feared by even the greatest Human nations. Through cunning tactics and military knowhow gained from a hard life of constant war, Grimm has taken control of much of the underworld of Human Space, turning his personal army into a galactic superpower, their guns up for hire to the highest bidder. Grimm's Army vehicles and uniforms come in a variety of shapes and sizes, but are usually highlighted with areas of green and emblazoned with Grimm's emblem, the long-toothed, runny white skull he took and modified from the local pirates... now known as the "Not-so-Jolly Roger."

HELEXITH
(pronounced "Hell-LECK-sith")

Centuries before Humanity ever took to the skies of Earth, the Mahlok were already leaving their homeworld and setting out to conquer others. Their first victory was on the nearby planet now known as Slasheth, the homeworld of the Slashrim. But the Slashrim, though scattered, divided, and culturally and technologically primitive, were tougher, stronger, and more numerous than the Mahlok, so the latter species had to use cunning to gain control. They did so by corrupting the religion of the largest Slashrim tribe, who worshipped a sun god called Helexith. The Mahlok claimed to be the prophets of Helexith, telling the Slashrim that their leader, Zuhaxellod, was his very avatar.

Through military might and cunning use of propaganda and fear tactics, the Mahlok slowly gained complete control over the Slashrim species, thus forming the Empire of Helexith. As their technology advanced and they were able to travel between stars, the Mahlok and their Slashrim armies began to forge a galactic empire that spread over nearly a third of Nova Refuge. Their constant expansion was stopped only when they met the Achmer, the first people to defeat them in battle, and later the Sarran, who had then allied with the Achmer in the High Council of Harmony. When Humanity arrived in the Refuge, Helexith was already weakened from a long war with Harmony, and thus the Humans were able to defeat them during the Xenocide War on Terra Nova, to which the Mahlok never gave their full attention. Since then, the Mahlok have bided their time, keeping to themselves in their own vast section of the Refuge, building up their immeasurably vast fleets and armies.

Harmony

The Achmer were the first to encounter both the Sarran and the Mahlok. The Mahlok immediately met them with war, while the Sarran came to them seeking peace. When Helexith continued to assault both the Achmer and the Sarran with their seemingly endless fleets, the two species joined together to form the High Council of Harmony, a representative parliament in which each planet had an equal say in the government of their section of space. Together they were able to push back the Helexith fleets, but their armies were stretched too thin to aid their own people on the planet Terra Nova when the Humans began fighting the Xenocide War. After their losses there, Harmony was the first to suggest the treaty of Womloc to end the fighting between all three peoples. Since then, they have kept to themselves, building up their defenses in case of another attack by any group. The number of stars controlled by the Achmer and Sarran together actually outnumbers even the Empire of Helexith, each world operating independently but working together in the Council. Thus, in many ways, the High Council of Harmony can be said to be the most powerful faction in all of Nova Refuge.

Glossary

A quick reference guide to some of the terms used in this novel.

AAA – Anti-Air Artillery, or "Triple-A."

Aerospace – Used to describe aerial vehicles that can fly both in a planet's atmosphere and in outer space. Most modern planes are aerospace vehicles.

Afaelya – The religion and chief goddess of the Sarran people.

Behemoth Bertha – The immense mobile artillery vehicle and command center of the Zygbar army, used as a base of operations in the field.

Bergelmir – Small Xarkonian hover transport, nicknamed "the Berg."

The Black Network – A huge crime syndicate whose influence reaches throughout Human space. Its leader is known only as "the Big Boss," who might very well be one man or many men, or perhaps not a man at all.

Blazer – A combination of the words "bullet" and "laser," referring to the laser-shielded bullets commonly used by modern military forces. The term is also used for knives and other weapons that have a similar hot laser "shield."

The Breach – The common nickname for the alternate dimension of reality through which starships travel in order to achieve faster-than-light speed and thus fly between planets and stars.

Buzzsaw – The type of blazer light machine gun used by Gun-Barracuda.

CONON – The Council of Nations of Nova Refuge, the alliance forged by the major Human nations of Nova Refuge in order to keep peace and unity throughout their species and their third of the galaxy.
Crown – Besides referring to the emblem of Xarkon and the Emperor's crown itself, the Crown is also the name of Xarkon's standard unit of currency.

Duranium – A light-weight but incredibly strong alloy that is now the most commonly used metal by all galactic militaries.

Ecirron – The ice-covered homeworld of the Sarran people.

EMP – Electromagnetic Pulse, disables most electronic equipment.

Energite – A mineral used to contain the fusion reactions that power most advanced technology. The crystals can eventually decay with continued use.

Enomegs – The super-soldiers of Xarkon.

ETAB – The Enomeg Training Academy Base.

Fafnir – A class of heavy Xarkonian aerospace transport/gunship.

Force Shield – A suspended energy barrier that can deflect projectiles and disperse heat attacks. Used by most modern vehicles as an extra layer of armor, and by starfire blades to contain and shape their heat.

Grommuk – The second stage of Slashrim development, at which point they are about the same size as a Human.

Guildar – A type of currency originally invented by the Independent Commerce Guild of Nova (ICGN), the guildar is now commonly used throughout the galaxy, particularly by smaller nations that are part of the guild and those wishing to take advantage of the guild's privacy laws to conduct less reputable forms of business. Many larger factions, such as Xarkon and Victory, disallow use of the guildar in favor of their own national currencies.

Hoverpad – The common name for the devices used to generate the lift that keeps hover vehicles floating above the ground. In most major cities, the hover capabilities of hoverpads are augmented by underground devices beneath the streets that allow them to fly to a height of many stories.

HPG – Hoverpad Gauss. The technology that propels the caseless ammunition now used by nearly all modern government-issue firearms. Hover technology is used to propel a projectile at extreme velocity through a row of Gauss-rifle style coils without the need for chemical explosives or bulletshells.

Immortal Soldiers – The super-soldiers of Victory.

Ironslinger – The lever-action high-caliber rifle used by Saber-Scorpion.

Katana – A type of sword used by the Japanese Samurai of ancient Earth.

Klagk – An ancient Slashrim curse word, the original meaning of which has been lost to time. Like most curse words, it is now used to refer to just about any person, thing, or situation that has earned the speaker's ire.

Manegarm – The immense black personal command walker designed specifically for High Commander Lucas Mars.

Nanocrystal – Some types of nanomesh armor have the ability to release a "foam" of nanocrystals when breached that helps to seal wounds.

Nanomesh – Nanofiber Mesh, a type of body armor material containing nanomachines that give it a wide variety of special abilities, including reactive hardening and automatic camouflage.

New Sol – The name for the star and the star system in which Terra Nova, the new homeworld of Humanity, is located.

Nidhogg – A relatively small Xarkonian aerospace transport craft.

Nova Core – An immense red giant – the largest ever recorded – located near the center of the Nova Refuge galaxy.

Nova Refuge – The Human name for the galaxy in which the events of this novel take place. Sometimes called "the Refuge" for short.

Omolgeth – The volcanic homeworld of the Mahlok people.

Ordinator – The top elected official in the Victorian government.

Pax Nova – The treaty signed by all member nations of CONON making it illegal for any Human nation to go to war with another.

Poj-poj – A Slashrim drink made from the plants of their homeworld. Thick, greenish-brown, and smelly, it is quite nutritional, but also quite alcoholic, designed to keep workers healthy but too drunk to consider rebellion.

Queen Skye's Revenge – Flagship of the Grimm's Army sea armada.

Rail Gun – A gun that propels a projectile along electromagnetic rails that accelerate it to a faster and faster velocity as it continues down the barrel.

RPG – Rocket-Propelled Grenade. A cheaper alternative to missiles.

Scatterstar – The fully-automatic blazer shotgun used by Grimm III.

Seadragon's Maw – The immense Xarkonian sea-cave docking bay attached to the Xarkon Underground Headquarters.

Silver Scepter – The personal command gunship of General Rick Radcliff.

Slasheth – The homeworld of the Slashrim people.

SMG – Sub-Machine Gun, a small close-range fully automatic firearm.

Sovalok – The last and largest of the Slashrim growth stages, at which point they become immense quadrupeds known to Humans as "pseudodragons."

Spec-Ops – Special Operations. Xarkon has a corps of highly-trained soldiers who concentrate on Special Operations and are second only to the Enomegs.

Starfire – The colored heat/light energy created by burning Starlight Gas.

Starlight Gas – A mixture of fumes harvested from gas planets. The most common type of fuel in the Refuge, it is burned by everything from aerospace fighter engines to cannons and energy blades.

Star-talons – The unique starfire blades used by the Enomegs. The blade emitters are attached to the top of the Enomeg's gloves.

Terra Nova – The new homeworld of Humanity, its name meaning "New Earth." Located in the New Sol system in Nova Refuge.

TSC – Terran Standard Cycle, or Earth-year. The length of one year on the original planet Earth.

Vasha – The Slashrim word for "chieftain," the leaders of their tribes.

Vicks or **Vic's** – Slang terms for Victorians, or for Victorian Credits, their standard unit of currency.

VTOL – Vertical Take-Off and Landing

Womloc – The dark, inhospitable southern continent to which the Native inhabitants of Terra Nova were exiled by Humanity after the Xenocide War.

The Xenocide War – The war in which the united forces of Humanity defeated the Natives present on Terra Nova and then exiled those who did not evacuate the planet to the dark continent of Womloc.

XUH – The Xarkon Underground Headquarters.

Zek Skorpyn – The small machine pistols favored by Saber-Scorpion.

Zrillak – The third stage of Slashrim development, also known as the "Lizardman" stage, since at this point they develop elongated snouts and tails. This is the "adult" stage, at which they are the most intelligent.

Zuhaxellod – The leader of the Helexith faction, who claims to be the very earthly avatar of the god after whom the group is named. Each time the current leader dies and a new Mahlok is appointed to his place, he loses his old name and takes up the name Zuhaxellod. The current leader is the Tenth Zuhaxellod, or Zuhaxellod X.

Visit Us Online!

 ™

WWW.NOVAREFUGE.COM

Official website of Nova Refuge, featuring news, stories, artwork, comics, and extensive information about the characters, creatures, locations, and technology of the NR universe!

 ™

WWW.SABER-SCORPION.COM

"Saber-Scorpion's Lair" is my personal website. Visit to check out all of my other projects and creations, and join the discussion forums to talk about Nova Refuge and almost anything else!

www.ingramcontent.com/pod-product-compliance
Lightning Source LLC
Chambersburg PA
CBHW071150020726
47502CB00002B/354